Praise for *The Mammoth Book of Steampunk*

"Of the dozens of newly minted steampunk anthologies out there, I cannot imagine any one of them being better than this gorgeous anthology. Editor Wallace has collected stories that show both the range and the depth of imaginary worlds that today's authors can create, each one seeming to redefine not only what steampunk is, but what it can do, ranging across the globe and involving politics, religion, and sexuality. These stories go the extra mile and I cannot recommend this collection too highly. It's one of the best books of the year." *Galaxy's Edge*

"*The Mammoth Book of Steampunk*, edited by Sean Wallace, focuses on newer elements of steampunk and proudly includes work by Mary Robinette Kowal, Jay Lake, Cat Rambo, Ekaterina Sedia, Catherynne M. Valente, Genevieve Valentine and more." *Kirkus Reviews*

"*The Mammoth Book of Steampunk*, edited by Sean Wallace, includes five original stories (and a large selection of good recent work). All the originals are worthy of attention." *Locus*

"World Fantasy Award-winning editor Wallace has compiled an outstanding anthology of thirty stories (including four originals) sure to satisfy even the most jaded steampunk fans, and engage newcomers and skeptics. Each story exemplifies steampunk's knack for critiquing both the past and the present, in a superb anthology that demands rereading." *Publishers Weekly*, starred review

"What I liked best about the majority of these short stories was that they're true to steampunk; no real unusual deviations for those of you looking for goggles and corsets . . ." *Wired*

The Mammoth Book of Steampunk Adventures

Sean Wallace

ROBINSON

RUNNING PRESS
PHILADELPHIA · LONDON

ROBINSON

First published in Great Britain in 2014 by Robinson

A CIP catalogue record for this book
is available from the British Library.

UK ISBN: 978-1-47211-061-9 (paperback)
UK ISBN: 978-1-47211-075-6 (ebook)

Typeset in Plantin by Hewer Text UK Ltd, Edinburgh
Printed and bound by CPI Group (UK) Ltd, Croydon, CR0 YY

Robinson
is an imprint of
Constable & Robinson Ltd
100 Victoria Embankment
London EC4Y 0DY

An Hachette UK Company
www.hachette.co.uk

www.constablerobinson.com

First published in the United States in 2014 by Running Press Book Publishers,
A Member of the Perseus Books Group

Books published by Running Press are available at special discounts for bulk purchases in
the United States by corporations, institutions and other organizations. For more
information, please contact the Special Markets Department at the Perseus Books Group,
2300 Chestnut Street, Suite 200, Philadelphia, PA 19103, or call (800) 810-4145, ext. 5000,
or email special.markets@perseusbooks.com.

US ISBN: 978-0-7624-5464-8
US Library of Congress Control Number: 2014934590

9 8 7 6 5 4 3 2 1

Digit on the right indicates the number of this printing

Running Press Book Publishers
2300 Chestnut Street
Philadelphia, PA 19103-4371

Visit us on the web!

www.runningpress.com

Contents

Introduction

Steampunk is Alive and Well, Thank You Very Much

What more can one say about steampunk that hasn't already been said? Apparently, quite a lot. Just when you thought this subgenre was past its sell-by date, this anthology provides compelling evidence that authors can take now-familiar steampunk ideas and concepts and breathe new life into them.

Writers and and readers *love* steampunk – it allows us to play with and think about history in new and wondrous ways. It lets us trample on old tired beliefs and consider what could be, ponder alternative possibilities. Not only do these tales reimagine history – and therefore our futures – they show you just how wide and broad the theme truly is; simply slapping some clock parts and gears onto a story doesn't make it steampunk.

E. Catherine Tobler's "Green-eyed Monsters in the Valley of the Sky, An Opera" (original to this volume) is a perfect example of mixing familiar tropes and creating something marvellously exciting. Who would think you could combine dinosaurs with opera and come up with a steampunk story that takes place largely in an island in the sky and make it work? And let's throw in some Shakespeare, too, while we're at it. In addition to the story's mystery and adventure, there is an underlying theme of love we may not understand until it completely unfolds. As Serafina says: "He has made you into something you were not prepared to be."

Chris Roberson's inventive take on the Frankenstein story demonstrates one of the core appeals of a Steampunk tale. As Chabane, laments in "Edison's Frankenstein", you can't escape tradition. However, he also realizes: "Maybe it wasn't all of the tomorrows that mattered . . . Maybe what was truly important was preserving the past, and working for a better *today*. Perhaps *that* was the only real way to choose what kind of future we will inhabit."

As we mull over how best to choose our future, we are faced with an ongoing, senseless war in Jonathan Wood's "Anna in the Moonlight". (Another original to this volume.) This irrational war is brought about because two old friends – both in positions of power – have a disagreement over religion and technology. Aren't we facing similar challenges today in science vs religion debates? And yet the individual is all but forgotten. "In creating their myth of our times, Lords Simon and Percy, the newspapermen, my fellow historians, have all forgotten something. They have forgotten you and me, the common men and women forced to live in the world they are forging."

Many great pieces of fiction deal with social issues of the day. And steampunk is a perfect vehicle for this. C. S. E Cooney creates Candletown and explores the difficult circumstances of the mining industry in "The Canary of Candletown". The mine workers are offered mecha-limbs when they lose theirs or otherwise fall ill, making them even more dependent on the Company. And speaking of better living through technology, Gord Sellar's story, "The Clockworks of Hanyang", explores themes of creator/maker and machine. He examines the results of humankind's arrogance in creation, ". . . their human makers had built them into something worse than slavery: incompletion was the lot of the great mass of mechanika, an incompleteness of development, an utter desolation of each mechanika's secret potential." We see more evidence of how the machines we build can turn on us in Cherie Priest's "Tanglefoot", when Madeline cautions young Edwin about his mechanical creation and friend Ted: "Keep him close, unless you want him stolen from you – unless you want his clockwork heart replaced with something stranger."

Nor can steampunk be contained only to the milieu of Victorian England. Indeed, the cables of steampunk stretch far. We discover an Aztec narrative in "Memories in Bronze, Feathers and Blood" from Aliette de Bodard. Ken Liu surprises us with Chinese demon hunters who don't behave the way one expects in "Good Hunting", and Nisi Shawl takes us to the Congo with "The Return of Chérie".

Not all the stories here are cautionary tales. There is no lack of entertaining adventure stories. After all, it is often the sense of adventure, of invention, and even mystery and intrigue that first draws us to steampunk. This anthology rewards even the most well-read steampunk reader with a wealth of satisfying stories. We find adventurers running off to capture ancient, perhaps extraterrestrial, artefacts in Carrie Vaughn's "Harry and Marlowe and the Talisman of the Cult of Egil". We hold our breath in anticipation when two old flames reunite in Samantha Henderson's "Beside Calais". And we are charmed and delighted by the mechanical crustacean in Margaret Ronald's "The Governess and the Lobster".

Steampunk over? Not by a long shot. And this anthology will show you why.

Ann VanderMeer

Love Comes to Abyssal City

Tobias S. Buckell

To be an ambassador meant to face outsiders, and Tia was well prepared for it. There was the overpowered, heavy, high-caliber pistol ever strapped to her right thigh. Sure, it was filigreed with brass and polished wood inlay, a gunsmith's masterpiece, but it was still able to stop many threats in their tracks. A similarly crafted-but-functional blade swung from her hip. And then there was the flamethrower strapped to her back.

This was not so much for threats, but for contraband and outside material forbidden in the Abyssal City.

Today she'd taken the elevators up the edges of the ravine that split the ground all the way down to the hot, steamy streets a mile below. Overhead, tall, wrought iron arches and glass ceilings spanned the top of the ravine, keeping life-giving air capped in. Up here, near the great airlocks, the air bit at her skin: cold and low enough on oxygen that you sometimes had to stop and pant to catch your breath.

"Ambassador?" the Port Specialist asked, his long red robes swirling around the pair of emergency air tanks he wore on his back, his eyes hidden behind the silvered orbs of his rubber facemask. His voice was muffled and distant. "Are you ready?"

"Proceed," Tia ordered.

Today they examined the long, segmented iron parts of a train that hissed inside the outer bays. The skin of the mechanical transporter cracked and shifted, readjusting itself to pressurized air. From the platform she stood on, she surveyed the entire length of the quarantined contraption.

It had thundered in, unannounced, on one of the many rails that criss-crossed the rocky, airless void of the planetary crust.

It was a possible threat.

"Time of arrival," the Port Specialist intoned, and turned his back to her to grab the long levered handles of an Interface set into the wall. He pulled the right handles, pushed in the right pins, and created a card containing that data.

"Length," Tia called out. She bent her eyes to a small device mounted on the rim of a greening railing. "One quarter of a mile. One main motor unit. Three cabs. No markings. Black outer paint."

Behind her the Port Specialist clicked and clacked the information into more cards.

A photograph was taken, and the plate shaved down to the same size as the cards and added.

A phonograph was etched into wax of the sound of the idling motor that filled the cavernous bay.

All this information was then put into a canister, which was put into a vacuum tube, which was then sucked into the city's pipes. "The profile of the visiting machine has been submitted," intoned the Port Specialist.

"We wait for Society's judgement," replied Tia, and pulled up a chair. She sat and looked at the train, wondering what was inside.

The reply came back up the tube fifteen minutes later. The Port Specialist retrieved the card.

"What does Society say?" Tia asked.

"There is a seventy per cent threat level," the Port Specialist said.

"Time to send them on their way," Tia said. "I will help you vent the bay."

But the Port Specialist was shaking his head. "The threat level is high, but the command on the card is to allow the visitors into the sandbox. Full containment protocol."

Tia groaned. "This is the worst possible timing. I had a party I was supposed to attend."

The Port Specialist shrugged and checked the straps on his air mask. He tightened them, as if imagining the possible danger of the train to be in the air around him, right this moment. "And I have a family to attend," he said. "But we have a higher duty right now."

"I was going to be introduced to my cardmate," Tia said. The first step in a young woman's life outside her family home. The great machine had found the person best suited for her to spend the rest of her life with.

It would disappoint her family and her friends that she would be stuck in lockdown in the sandbox with some foreign people waiting to make sure they cleared quarantine.

The Port Specialist handed her the orders. "Verify the orders," he said.

Tia looked down at the markings, familiar with the patterns and colors after a lifetime of reading in Society Code.

A large chance of danger.

But they were to welcome in this threat.

"Hand me an air mask and a spare bottle," Tia sighed.

The Port Specialist did so, and Tia buckled them on. She checked the silvered glasses on the eyeholes and patted down her body armor. She put in earplugs, pulled on leather gloves, and then connected a long hose to the base of her special gas mask.

"Hello?" she said. "This is Tia."

The sounds and sights of what she saw would be communicated back through, and monitored by Port Control, with the aid of a significant part of Society's processing power. Crankshafts and machinery deep in the lower levels of the city, powered by the steam created from pipes below even that, would apply the city's hundreds of years of algorithms and calculations to her situation and determine what she would do next.

And Port Control, really someone sitting in a darkened room in front of a series of flashing lights, would relay that to her.

"This is Port Control, you are clear to engage," came the somewhat muffled reply from the speaking hose.

Tia walked up to the train, stopping occasionally to yank the bulk of the hose along with her, and rapped on the side of the steel door.

Pneumatics hissed and the door scraped open. Tia's hand was on the butt of her gun as a man, clad in full rubber outer gear and wearing a mask much like hers, stepped forward, a piece of parchment held out before him.

He had a gun on his waist, and his hand on it as well. They approached each other like crabs, cautiously scuttling forward.

Tia snatched the parchment, and they retreated away from

each other. She read the parchment by holding it up where she could both read it, one handed, and keep an eye on the other man.

Manifest: three passengers.

Passenger one and two, loyal and vetted citizens of a chasm town two stops up along the track. Affiliation: Chasm Confederation.

Passenger three was an unknown who had ridden down the track from places unknown. Affiliation: unknown.

Tia reported this all back to Port Control.

"Go ahead and let them in," Port Control said.

Tia nervously waved her assent at the man in rubber, and he turned around and waved the passengers out of the car.

The first two, a husband and wife team with matching gold-plated lifemate cards dangling from their necks, were diplomats. They carried briefcases full of paper network protocols, and rode up and down the rail to pass on packets of information between the cities and towns. They stepped down, the tips of the tails of their bright-red diplomat suits dragging on the ground slightly as they walked past.

Tia bowed to them, somewhat clumsily in her gear.

"What is the threat level?" the male diplomat asked.

"Sandbox," Tia told him.

With a sigh they walked around her toward the airlock leading out.

The third passenger stepped down.

He had long hair cut to just above his ears and dark eyes partially hidden by wire-rimmed glasses. He pulled a giant trunk with wheels mounted on the corners. A leather-bound notebook dangled from a gold chain looped around his neck, as did a mechanical pen.

With a cautious step forward, he bowed, and then straightened. "My name is Riun," he announced.

He went to walk around her and follow the diplomats, but then realized he'd let go of his wheeled trunk. He awkwardly turned back for it.

Tia smiled beneath the heavy mask.

The sandbox was a hall that could seat two hundred. The center was dominated by several long tables, while the periphery had cots that folded out from the wall.

By the far end, clear one-way mirrors allowed observers to view the sandbox.

Overhead, large metal balconies allowed Society's Reporters to look down on the sandbox and constantly file new cards with the machinery of Society, updating the computing machine that ruled them all with all the moves the quarantined made.

Every fifteen minutes the reporters would change shifts, to prevent contamination.

As the diplomats huddled together in the far side of the room, not interested in company, Tia removed her cumbersome protective gear and joined Riun at the table.

"Your city is strict about outside influence," Riun observed, looking around the sandbox.

"There are murals on the lower alleyways," Tia said. "Some of the cityfolk believe that during the Ascendance Wars the city's programs, during the great Downshifting, became somewhat paranoid of outside infection."

"The Ascendance Wars?" Riun asked, looking puzzled.

Tia stared at him. How much of an outsider was he? Suddenly she thought about the warning, and wondered if maybe Riun was something far more dangerous than she realized.

Should she even be talking to him?

But the machine hadn't flagged Riun to be separately sandboxed. Nor had Tia been handed any warnings to shun him.

"Were you schooled in your city's history?" she asked.

He smiled. "Of course. But I am not schooled in yours."

"The great thinking cities of the world tried to reach for the stars, but fought among each other to reach them first and over control of the skies. The fighting grew so perilous and killed so many people that the machines that ran the cities decided to Downshift. They would only use mechanical technology, slow thought, to run the systems of their cities. The city used to use 'quantum chips' but now only uses steam and gears and cards."

Riun chuckled. "Always different stories."

"What?"

"I find, from city to city, there are different stories and variations on the stories," Riun said.

"And what is the story *your* city tells?" Tia asked loudly, while thinking to herself that surely this was auditory contamination, and why wasn't the city flagging this conversation yet? Hearing that the city's histories were false was dangerous.

Wasn't it?

Then again, Tia realized, she'd only seen the murals or heard tales. She'd never heard the city give an official history.

Riun cleared his throat. "According to the histories of my city, the Downshift came when the great Minds of this world created a shield to save us from a war with the other minds out in the Great Beyond. In order to save us, they banned all methods of information that could be transmitted through the air."

"And which one do you believe?" Tia asked.

Riun smiled again, large and welcoming. "I think they're all shards of some older truth we've forgotten," he said. "That's why I travel the world, listening, gathering, and meeting the citizens of the cities."

He opened a case of notes and showed her hand-drawn sketches of other cities, other night skies. Handwritten notes of tales, and descriptions of systems.

"Why?" Tia asked. "Why leave your city?"

"Why not?" He shrugged.

The hours dragged on. Food was delivered by chutes, and they ate on the large, empty tables in silence.

Afterward Tia sat and watched Riun read a leather-bound book he pulled out of his large trunk until she couldn't stand the boredom. "Do you play Gorithms?" she finally asked.

"Of course."

"There're several playing stands near the far walls," she said. "Care to join me?"

They set up on the small playing table, connected the pneumatic tubes, and a few seconds later the dual packs of cards appeared.

Tia unwrapped hers and laid them down with a thwack as Riun delicately laid his out behind the dark glass of his privacy shield.

They looked at each other over the rim of the shields.

"You play?" he asked. She couldn't see his smile, but the eyes twinkled.

"Always."

Today's game was five flowchart sequences with equations, solvable by sub games with the cards. Tia quickly solved her sequences, passed on the marker cards, and looked up.

"You're quick."

"Five points," Riun said. "If my results agree."

Which they didn't. One of the sequences tied.

Tia cross-checked with his cards and he rechecked hers. No tie; they came to the same conclusion by playing out the math. Tia was right.

Riun placed the markers in the tube and watched them get sucked away. "You're quick," he said. "And accurate."

"Ninety per cent accuracy rate on simple sub games like that."

Down in the belly of the beast their results would be tabulated, the result of a low-priority calculation request. Maybe they'd just helped calculate which lights should be left on above some city street. Or regulated the pressure of a valve somewhere. You never really knew. All you knew was that the thousands of games constantly being played helped comprise the total computational capacity of the entire city.

Streets released traffic along paths that helped simulate equations, games were tied into the city's calculations, and some suspected that even lives had some sort of calculating function, in the cities.

Some Gorithim games were checkerboards, or mazes, or just patterns. You never knew what the tubes would hand you. But playing them was usually fun, if not sometimes puzzling, and it gave you something to do.

Particularly when stuck in the sandbox.

"Another game?" Tia asked.

"I don't know if I should." Riun's eyes crinkled. Was he smiling? "I think your mind is far quicker than mine."

Tia looked around pointedly. "I'll be gentle. Besides, do you see anything else you could be doing with your time?"

Riun conceded the point and tapped the delivery button. "Since you promised," he muttered.

As they waited for the next game to arrive, Tia craned over the shield to get a better look at his whole face. He did have the remains of a smile still. "Tell me about the places you've visited," she suggested.

And Riun began to spin tales of cities perched near cliffs with pipes dug far into the crust of the world to deliver steam, or dug into giant pits, and even one at the top of a tame volcano.

$$\star \qquad \star \qquad \star$$

Quarantine broke. Three days of playing Gorithims, eating, and putting up with the diplomats pointedly ignoring them. All the while, the fifteen-minute shift changes of observers continued in the gantries overhead, shuffling in and out to observe them all.

It wasn't all that unusual for Tia, who enjoyed the gentle rhythm. She'd done several quarantines already. And, to be honest, there were worse people than Riun to get stuck with. He was easy on the eyes, and he could chatter on about the rails he'd traveled, the citypeople he'd met, and the places he'd been. But in a neutral manner, not a boasting one.

She liked that.

When the doors cracked open, Riun excitedly packed his things. "Thank you for the company," he said, and gave her a half-bow.

"My pleasure."

And they parted ways, Tia headed for the south switchbacks, threading her way down through the houses clustered on the ravine's steep walls. Riun would be headed for the guest houses, from where he'd launch a campaign of interviews and his explorations of the new city.

It felt, Tia thought, vaguely treasonous to wonder whether she could submit herself as Riun's minder to the city while she was getting ready to meet her family and her new cardmate.

At the card ceremony, Tia arrived stripped out of her ambassador's garb. She now wore her red leathers, with a bustle designed to shove and prod and push her into what her mother called a more pleasing shape, though Tia preferred the comfortable fit of her work clothes. Her hair had been carefully brushed down, and adorned with brass clips.

Here she was, an ambassador, an elite trainee tasked with the city's defense, and her parents had spent money to have her mate-card bronzed; they were not powerful or rich enough to afford gold. Tia carried it in her gloved hands up the street toward the sub-routines check palace and Gorithims parlor that dominated the nearest intersection.

There, in black leathers and a tie, was her cardmate.

According to the lifelong database kept by the city, her life in punched out rows and marks, this was the unmarried city man with the best statistical chance of making her happy.

Actually, that wasn't technically true, was it?

No, this *pairing* was the most statistically valid and most likely to work. There might be someone else better for her, but who wouldn't be interested in her.

Could she fall in love with this man? He cut a fine figure. Dashing dark hair and large eyes. A certain precision to his movements that spoke of self-control and quickness. Those were qualities she loved in a person.

It was long a tradition to know nothing about your cardmate. Getting to know each other was half the excitement. Who was this person you were matched to by the great city?

That was something to discover.

But did it make her another switch or lever? Was this truly the person she would love, if left alone? Or was this another calculated move by a greater calculation, testing some subroutine?

The two families moved together, their center of focus the two cardmates.

Tia held out her bronzed card. "It says we are most compatible."

Her cardmate held out his silvered card. "Then let us verify it."

They put the two cards into a machine, and it whirred and clicked, and then a green light glowed.

Compatible.

"My name is Owyn," the man said.

"I'm Tia."

She hung his silvered card around her neck, and he her bronzed card.

It was done.

On the first night, she was expected only to eat a dinner with Owyn. A celebration of a new life that was to slowly bloom. She'd done that, sitting politely in place, and asking after his family. They were a family of silk merchants, and Owyn occasionally rode the rails to other towns and even some cities in order to trade for the city. And normally . . . that would have been fascinating and exotic to her.

Tomorrow there would be a banquet, with dancing and instruments. And on the third day . . .

Well, on the third day, her parents and friends and extended family would walk in a procession down the road, and Owyn's parents and friends and extended family would do so as well, all carrying possessions to the new couple's home, where there would be yet another celebration.

And after that, everyone would withdraw, leaving them alone.

It should have been all she was focused on. So why was she wondering how Riun was doing, his first night alone in the city?

Her stomach full of rich food and tea, Tia climbed up on her roof and looked up at the atrium lights far overhead. Somewhere else Riun might be looking back at the same lights, she thought.

And then she swore at herself and climbed down the wrought iron ladder along the side of her parents' house and sneaked off into the night.

Riun answered the door to the guest houses with a frown. "Tia?"

She slid right past him.

He was puzzled, but offered her tea from a side table and lit some lights. His hair was disheveled, and he wore his nightrobe tied tight around his waist.

They sat in the large foyer near the coolant fans. At night, this close to the city's lower depths, it grew hot.

"What's wrong?" Riun asked.

"What makes you think anything's wrong?" she asked.

"You're an ambassador, here in the middle of the night." He looked guarded, and tired. "Should I begin repacking?"

"You've done nothing wrong." She curled up on a small couch and hugged her knees.

"Then why are you here?"

Tia sighed. Typical of men, to miss the obvious and wallow in their own confusion. It was no wonder the great City Minds took to giving out cards that told you who your best match was. "To see you," she said, a bit more angrily than she'd meant.

And why hadn't he picked up on that? Or did city women who'd just met him show up at his door at odd hours of the night all the time?

Riun downed the last of his tea and stood. He walked over and sat next to her, and Tia felt a thrill of excitement run through her as the couch shifted from the added weight.

But Riun didn't look happy. A weary look had replaced what she had hoped was intrigue. He reached over to her neck and held up the silvered card. "That isn't wise," he murmured. "I am here at the courtesy of your city, and I will be expelled if I violate that hospitality. Your city has computed the best possible match already for you. I will not endanger that."

He let go of the card suddenly and pulled his hand back.

For that, she found herself even more interested in him. "You're right," she said.

He relaxed, slightly.

But Tia grabbed his hand. "You're right: you're an outsider. The city never had a chance to run your profile. Maybe we would have been a good match. But we'll never know. We could never know. And maybe the city made a mistake. There are mistakes made, that's why there are error checks." That's why every game of Gorithms involved cross-checks for secondary points.

Riun pulled his hand gently away and stood up. "Tia, I'm something new and exciting. An outsider. Maybe even a little scary. Many are attracted. I will not destroy your life on a fancy. I can't." He walked to the door.

It was time for her to leave.

At the door she paused, and then looked up at him. "Don't you get lonely, out there? Traveling those lines by yourself? Don't you wish you could share those adventures?"

He looked pained. "It is lonely out there, Tia. But few have the courage to truly abandon all they've ever known. It sounds exciting, but when it really comes down to it . . . they can't make that jump."

He'd been let down in the past.

Tia imagined him watching someone realize what they were doing and rush out of a train at the last second, leaving him alone inside, pulling away.

What would it be like to rip yourself out of the guts of a city for good?

Her father sat in the chair by the entryway playing soligorithm at the family games table. It was odd to see him up this late. He worked an early morning shift at the calculating farms, running numbers on slide rules along with thousands of others.

He set his playing cards aside and held up a red letter. "This woke us up. It came through mail chute. Priority. For you."

Tia read it. A simple warning, generated somewhere deep inside the city's bowels, just for her.

It forbade her from seeing Riun for the duration of his stay. Any violation would result in his expulsion.

"Is there a problem?" her father asked.

Tia folded the letter up. "Did you read it?"

"I did." He looked back down at his cards. "Some of us have had friendships or . . . more, before our cardmates were revealed. People we knew and thought we liked. Over time, you realize you were mistaken. The city is wise."

"Did *you* want someone else?" Tia asked.

Her dad turned back to the cards. "Tomorrow is the banquet, Tia. You should focus on that."

Tia walked up the stairs to her room. In bed she lay down and reread the warning.

It wouldn't be fair to Riun to get him expelled because of her own confusion. He was a traveler, an explorer of new cities. She wouldn't rip this one from him, she decided.

Her cardmate sat across from her, partially hidden behind a staggering assortment of elaborate cakes, pots of loose teas, coffees, and fancy aerated drinks.

It seemed like half her street had boiled out of their multi-storied tenements bolted to the sides of the beginning of the ravine's steep climb to celebrate.

And Tia found herself forcing her smile.

One of her aunts patted her shoulder sympathetically. "It gets better," she whispered. "Give it time. All of us are in shock at first. It's okay."

So apparently her smile was not very believable.

Later into the night Owyn found her, trying to hide behind a flower display.

"Are you feeling well?" he asked hesitantly.

"Everything is fine," Tia insisted.

Owyn stood awkwardly by her, then finally nodded and walked away. Tia sighed. He looked crushed and frustrated. And none of this was really his fault, was it?

Neither of them left the banquet happy. When Tia got home she just sat in the middle of her room, frustrated and getting angrier.

Her dad knocked and entered the room. "We have a problem," he said.

"I'm sorry," Tia said, looking down at the carpet on her floor. "The city provides. It calculates the best outcomes for us. We have jobs we are engaged with. Lives that are often fulfilling. And I know that Owyn is a good choice. I'm struggling, but I think I'll get through."

"Your aunt just sent a runner, he's at the door. She says a quarantine order has been issued for you." Her dad squatted down in front of her. "What have you been doing, Tia?"

His face was so full of concern it hurt to see. Tia flinched. "I haven't done anything since I came home."

"There must be probabilities or some new calculations the city has made," her father muttered. He sat down on another chair and rubbed his forehead. No doubt he was wondering where he had gone wrong in raising her. Or trying to figure out what he could do.

Which was nothing.

"Or," Tia said, "the city is right." It was strange to think of *the city* itself bringing its attention on her. It was more than strange: it was scary.

"What do you mean?" her father asked, looking up.

"I'm an ambassador. I'm exposed to things that come into the city. It's my job to stop them. It does mean there is a risk. And I know who I need to talk to."

"You can't leave, there are ambassadors on the way," her father protested, but Tia was already out of her chair.

She used a long black cloak with a hood to help her slip around the shadows of the streets and flit her way to the guest houses.

When Riun opened the door again, she pushed him back inside and closed the door behind her.

"What did you do to me?" she demanded.

"What are you talking about? What are you doing here?"

"There's a quarantine command on me. You've infected me with *something*; I want to know what."

"It's just me," Riun protested. "I'm not an agent. I'm not anything. I don't *have* anything."

"Then you must have gotten something from someone else,"

Tia insisted. "Do you have anti-city propaganda you've been exposed to or thoughts?"

"What? No!"

"What city sent you?" Tia poked his chest.

"It was my own idea. I wanted to see the world. That's all."

Tia threw herself down on the couch. "Then why am I suddenly a threat to peace and order? Why is the city going to quarantine me?"

"I don't know," Riun said. He looked just as upset as she did. "There's always a risk, being a traveler. That you picked something up somewhere. Some mannerism that a host city will get upset by. But I swear to you, Tia, I haven't set out to do anything to you. I would never forgive myself if I did."

She looked at him sharply. "You seemed quick enough to push me out of the guest house earlier."

"For both our sakes, Tia. You and I both know you have a cardmate. You have a place in this city. I won't jeopardize your life here."

But he already had. Just be revealing his existence, she realized.

She opened her mouth to try and explain this, and a loud rap came from the door.

"Open up!" shouted an authoritative voice. "Traveler Riun, in the name of the city open up!"

Tia stood. "I've ruined it all for both of us, haven't I?" The city had figured out she came here. Now Riun would be expelled.

"What will they do to you?" Riun asked, eyes narrowed. He didn't seem to be worried about expulsion. "Answer me quickly, for I've been to many cities, and the punishments for disorder vary wildly, Tia."

"Long-term quarantine," Tia said. "Maybe a year. A recomputing of my personality profile based on an interview, pending release. Re-education during the quarantine."

Riun grimaced. Tia stood up and walked over to him. "It's not your fault, Riun," she said. "It's mine for wanting something that isn't mine to have."

She touched his lips with her fingers. To her frustration, he didn't seem to be sharing the moment with her. His brow was creased with thought, as if he were struggling with something.

Then he gently held her shoulders. "And what is it you really want, Tia? Is it me or the traveling? Or to escape the city? Some want to leave it, but there are always more cities, more places you'll have to navigate carefully. More places you'll be considered an outside threat by the city's Mind."

Tia looked into his eyes. He looked quite earnest at this moment. So she returned that with honesty. "I know I'm attracted to the outside. I think that's a part of it. And I think a part of it is you as well. I hope that's the greater part. But how am I to know? You are not my cardmate."

The hammering on the door stopped. They would be breaking it down shortly.

"If you truly are in love with both, and not just one of those things, then come with me," Riun said, and held out a hand.

Riun led her to his room and pulled on a coat, then swept his books and notes into his trunk.

"Lock my door," he said.

Tia did, hearing the ambassadors crashing against the outside door. It creaked, seconds away from breaking open.

"It's not uncommon for travelers to have to run for it when a city changes its mind," Riun said. "So we always have a way out that we note for each other."

He kicked at a panel, and a small section of the wall swung aside. They walked into the empty room next door and closed the false wall behind them. Outside, ambassadors trooped down the hallway and started banging on Riun's door.

Riun took them through two more rooms until they stopped at one with a window onto an alley.

They squeezed through, yanking his trunk along with them, and clattered out into the alleyway. Riun pulled his collar up, making to run for the street, but Tia stopped him.

"This way," she said, pointing at their feet. Wisps of steam leaked out from the edges of a manhole. "There'll be watchers on the streets. I know the steam tunnels."

Inside the dark tunnels they ran for the edge of the city, and emerged near the ravine elevators. Again, Tia directed them away from the street. "I know a faster way; my dad works around here," she huffed.

They broke through the doors and ran down the long halls of a calculating factory instead. Clean white, brightly lit, and filled with thousands of sober-faced men and women, leaning over abacus trays, flicking beads in response to equations being offered up to them by blinking lights near their control boards.

Their presence caused a rippling effect of commotion as they passed through, with calculators in clean white robes standing up to shout at them.

Tia threw open the rear doors, and they pushed past the handfuls of people waiting to board the city elevators. Curses and complaints followed them, but Riun shut the cage to the elevator and Tia hit the switches.

The elevator climbed up the side of the ravine, hissing and spitting as it passed street after street level, and the roofs of houses at the lower levels, and clinging to the sides slowly slid past them.

There was a balcony on the High Road near one of the bridges that ran along under the glass roof that capped the city. Riun grabbed Tia's arm, and pulled her over to the railing. "Look," he said.

Tia did, and gasped. The city below was changing. People were spilling out onto the streets. Lights were turning on. It wasn't orderly, or staggered in shifts as normal. Instead, the focus of the disturbance was the calculating building they'd run through. People were wandering the streets randomly, not using the flowchart sidewalks and lights.

There was chaos in the Abyssal City and it was spreading.

Lights flickered randomly, and gouts of steam burst from below the streets.

"Did we cause that?" Tia asked, looking at the masses of pedestrians wandering aimlessly about, shouting and arguing. They could hear the grinding shudder of machines coming to a halt over the bubbling hum of discussions and arguments drifting upward from the entire city. "Did *you*?"

She glanced at him, and realized from the look on his face that he was just as horrified as she was. "I'm just a traveler," he whispered. "Just a traveler."

They looked at the spreading chaos, rapt. "Do you think it'll bring the entire city to a stop?" she asked.

Riun shook his head. "No. No, I've seen this before. It's a temporary fault. A system failure." Warning klaxons fired to life throughout the city. "Soon they'll order a return to homes, empty the streets. Stop all the machines then restart them. Order will return."

"I've never seen anything like it," Tia said. Not in all her life. It unnerved her. She'd always thought of society, the system around her, as stable and everlasting and solid.

Yet here she was, with Riun. And there chaos was. In the distance, she heard the rumble of an intercity train.

They had to move through the sandbox and get to it.

"Listen," Riun told her, hearing the train and turning to face her. They were so close, their lips could almost touch. "If you leave with me, I can't promise you anything. I can't promise you a home or a city that you fit into. I can't promise you my love, I've only known you a week. All I can promise is a travel partner, and the fact that I do find you beautiful and interesting, and I want to escape with you. Can that be enough?"

Tia pulled the silvered card off her neck and looked down at it. "Yes," she said. "I'm willing to take chance and uncertainty."

And then she threw the card out into the space over the ravine and watched it flutter away, down toward the steaming, chaotic streets of the city.

A Mouse Ran Up the Clock

A. C. Wise

Simon watched the mouse scale the clock's side, whiskers thrumming. The clock struck, and the mouse quivered in time. Its paws lost their hold, and the mouse fell, its legs beating the air as Simon bent to retrieve it.

Carefully, he turned the creature on its back. He could feel the flutter-beat of a heart through the skin, and above it the gentle ticking of a different kind of mechanism. He soaked the corner of a cloth in chloroform and held it near the mouse's mouth and nose until the shivering stopped. Then he picked up a scalpel and tweezers, peering through his glasses, and opened the creature up.

The mouse's insides whirred, and the same honey-colored light that had lit its ascent winked off golden gears. Simon made a few minute adjustments; tightening here, and resetting a balance there, and then he righted the mouse. Waking, the mouse blinked and ran its paws over its whiskers before running for a hole in the baseboard.

The bell hanging over the shop door chimed and Simon looked up. Hastily he pulled the watch, which he should have finished that morning, towards him and feigned absorption in his work. Hard boots clicked over the wooden floor, and the man's shadow filled Simon's peripheral vision, blocking the light. The man cleared his throat and Simon looked up. His heart went into his throat.

"Herr Shulewitz? Simon Shulewitz?"

"Yes?"

Simon could barely swallow. He fought to keep his hands from trembling as he set the watch down and straightened his shoulders, trying to meet the *Staatspolizei* man in the eye. The officer held his peaked cap under one arm, and the rest of his uniform was in perfect order – pressed and clean with sharp lines and not a speck of dust. The row of medals across his breast would have been blinding if the sun hadn't been behind him.

"Herr Shulewitz," here the man attempted something like a smile, but it pulled the deep scars around his mouth into ghastly lines and Simon fought the urge to shudder. "Are you aware that you have a vermin problem?"

"Sir?"

Simon gripped the counter until his knuckles were white to keep himself from visibly shaking.

"Vermin, Herr Shulewitz. Mice."

The officer drew a plain white handkerchief, folded over to hide what was inside, out of his pocket and lay it on the counter between them. Simon's heart beat high in his throat as the officer reached out one gloved hand and nudged the folds of cloth aside.

One of his mice, looking as though it had been crushed flat by a boot, so gears mingled with blood and fur, lay within. Simon could not help his hand flying to his mouth. The *Staatspolizei* officer smiled.

"A very curious creature, don't you think, Herr Shulewitz?"

"I . . ." Simon faltered. Tears burned behind his eyes, threatening to fall and make his fear visible. He tried not to think of shattered shop windows and cries in the night; neighbors who disappeared never to be seen or heard from again. It was easy to deny as long as darkness covered it, but now it was broad daylight and the officer was standing right in front of him. Simon darted a quick glance behind the officer. Were his neighbors drawing their curtains, bringing false night and pretending they didn't see?

"A very curious creature indeed, one with a great many uses, don't you think?"

It took Simon a moment to register that the officer was still speaking, still studying him with strange bright eyes, and still smiling his terrible slashed smile.

"I believe, Herr Shulewitz, that the Emperor would be very interested in such a creature, and the man who created it. And if the Emperor is interested, then *I* am interested."

The officer reached out then, and his leather-clad grip was surprisingly strong on Simon's upper arm.

"Pack what clothing you need. You are in the service of the Empire now."

It was not a question.

Unfamiliar landscape slid by outside the train window – a blur of green and brown. Simon had never been farther than a few miles outside his hometown before. Across from him in the private compartment, Herr Kaltenbrunner, as the officer had eventually introduced himself, was still looking at the clockwork mouse. When Simon had asked where he was being taken, Kaltenbrunner had smiled his terrible smile and replied, "Lodz, Herr *Tinker*."

Simon had heard of Lodz, a shadowy city far distant, which he pictured as grey and full of rain.

"Truly remarkable!" Kaltenbrunner exclaimed, turning the mouse over again to examine the gears within.

"Machinery melded with living flesh. Truly you are a visionary. Think, just think, of how such a thing might be employed – scoop out the eyes and put in eyes of glass instead and there you have it, the perfect spy! It goes tiny and unnoticed through every house at night, seeing who has been naughty, and who has been very, very bad."

"It won't work," Simon answered distractedly.

He was still gazing out the window. For the moment he had forgotten to be afraid, and he continued to forget as he divided his mind between the outside world and the thing Kaltenbrunner was proposing.

"A mouse needs a brain to live. You can augment what is there, but you can't take too much out. A device to watch behind glass eyes is simply unfeasible."

"Ah, but it *is* feasible, Herr Tinker, if you know the right methods to employ."

Simon dragged his gaze away from the glass and blinked. Kaltenbrunner had once more tucked the mouse carefully away. There was something in the officer's eyes, in his smile, that made it seem as though all the heat had suddenly drained out of the car.

"The Emperor has many interests. Clockwork is only one of them."

Simon opened his mouth, but Kaltenbrunner lay a finger across his lips, his eyes shining.

"You will see soon enough, Herr Tinker."

The train seemed to pick up speed then, as though through Simon's alarm, hurrying them across the countryside towards the city full of rain.

When they arrived in Lodz, Simon saw little besides the platform and the plain brick walls of the station. Almost immediately upon disembarking Kaltenbrunner slipped a black cloth over Simon's eyes and tied it tight, binding his hands as well before bundling him into the back of a cart. He smelled the sharp scent of animal flesh, and heard a whip crack, and then they were rumbling forward.

The road was poorly paved, and the cart jounced painfully over broken stones, leaving Simon bruised. His flesh was tender when they stopped again, and Kaltenbrunner took his arm. Simon was half dragged from the cart and led blind through the streets of the city. He stumbled once, but Kaltenbrunner hauled him up.

Around him, the city was full of noise. Simon could hear footsteps, shuffling over the broken stones. Did nobody notice him being led away? Or did they simply not care? Simon pictured the men and women of the rain-filled city, heads bowed, hats pulled low, eyes downcast and perpetually shadowed.

"Almost there now." The officer spoke close to Simon's ear, so Simon could feel hot breath, scented with brandy.

All around them rose the stench of the city. It smelled of bodies, too closely packed, and waste, both animal and human. It stank of tallow, and oil, garbage and blood. Even blind Simon could feel the closeness as they pushed through narrow streets until they stepped through what seemed to be a gateway, and they were suddenly alone.

The air felt damp on his face, and he longed to pull the blindfold away. The rope binding his wrists cut into his skin. Beyond the cloth the light lessened, and the surface underfoot changed, and Simon knew they had stepped inside. Echoes of their footfalls bounced back to them, and Simon lost count as they twisted through corridors until at last he heard a door being opened.

Kaltenbrunner half-pushed him through, and all at once the blindfold was pulled roughly away and Simon blinked. They were in a vast space with a high ceiling of corrugated metal. Workbenches spread with objects Simon couldn't even begin to name were scattered across the floor among other debris, so it looked like a scrap yard brought inside. Dim grey light filtered through glass panels and lit the floor in strange pale patches, broken by beams and pillars, which kept the structure upright and cast long shadows on the floor.

At first Simon thought they were alone, but a sound among the scattered chaos made him turn. A man who had been seated at a workbench rose and came towards them. Like Simon he was young, but with darker hair, an added brightness to his eyes and a kind of fierceness in his smile.

"Hello, you must be Simon. Our good friend Ernst here told me he was going to fetch you."

Simon stared. He could clearly see the yellow star sewed to the man's sleeve. His face was too thin by far, and there was no question he was a prisoner, yet he stood here shaking Simon's hand and calling the *Staatspolizei* captain by his first name.

"Who . . ." Simon managed, but he could get no further.

"Your partner, Herr Tinker, Itzak Chaim Bielski."

Even when the door had clanged shut, and Kaltenbrunner had left them alone, Simon continued to stare.

"Let's have a look at your little toy, shall we?"

Itzak crossed to one of the many work tables, kicking clutter out of the way as he went. Still feeling as though he was blind, Simon stumbled after him. Only at the table did Simon see that Itzak now held the white handkerchief. He had not even seen Kaltenbrunner give it to him. Itzak spread the cloth and his expression wrinkled into one of faint disgust.

"He didn't leave us much to work with, did he? Still, I'm sure in all this mess we'll be able trap ourselves a replacement. What did you use?"

"What? Oh, crumbs, whatever I had, in a box lined with rags soaked in chloroform. I rigged the box to spring closed once they were inside."

Simon couldn't help grinning a little, coming out of his distraction. He had been staring around at the wondrous room and the first spark of curiosity was beginning to grow into something like excitement. There were tools and parts here he would never have been able to get back home – a veritable treasure trove of riches.

"Crumbs. I think I can manage that."

Itzak lifted a sheet of metal to show a half-eaten crust of bread underneath.

"Here." He tossed the bread to Simon. "You start on building that box, and I'll see if I can't find us some chloroform."

Simon allowed himself to become lost in the work – forgetting everything but the delicate movements of his hands as he spring-loaded the trap and lined it with the rags Itzak had found.

"I think I've seen some coming in over there." Itzak pointed, and Simon carried the loaded trap over and set it down where the other had indicated.

"And now we wait."

Itzak crossed his arms over his chest and leaned back. "So where did they bring you in from?"

"Near Tuchola."

As the words passed his lips, it was as though Simon had been struck. Work had been a good substitute for shock, but now that one had worn off and he was still, the full weight of this situation came crashing down around him. Everything he knew, everything he loved, had been left behind. He was simply gone, plucked out of his life as if he had never been.

"You're shaking. You look like you could use a smoke."

"Don't smoke," Simon murmured.

"Then I'll do for both of us."

Simon looked down at his hands, pinned in the pale light from overhead and trembling like moths. A million questions tripped on his tongue and pressed behind his teeth. He could scarcely find the breath to ask the first of them, but somehow he managed.

"What am I doing here?"

There was a faint snapping sound from the corner where they had set the trap; the spring releasing and the door falling into place. Simon couldn't help jumping at the sound. Suddenly it was hard to breathe.

"That."

Itzak pointed, and then brushed past Simon as he went to retrieve the trap. He grinned around his cigarette when he straightened, trailing smoke back to the workbench to hang like ghosts in his wake. Simon watched as Itzak released the door and tipped the sleeping mouse onto the table.

"There you are. Go to it."

"I don't understand."

"Work your magic." Itzak waved his hands. "Though I'm afraid you're going to have to go a little farther than usual and take the brain and eyes out as well."

"Kill it?"

Simon started back.

"Only temporarily."

Itzak grinned, and there was something in it – in his teeth and his eyes – that reminded Simon of Kaltenbrunner. Not cruelty, exactly, not joy in pain, but a kind of wildness; something dangerous.

As if in a dream, he moved to the workbench and sat down.

Simon found his hands were surprisingly steady when he set to work. A kind of numbness had taken hold. It was as though he was looking out through someone else's eyes, watching someone else's hands as they worked. Itzak peered over Simon's shoulder with curiosity.

"You're in my light," Simon murmured, not looking up.

"Sorry."

He heard Itzak chuckle and then shift to lean against one of the other benches. Smoke drifted around them as Simon picked up the blade and began to cut.

"Why me? Or why just me?"

He spoke quickly, and what he hoped was casually, forcing himself to concentrate on the mouse. His heart was beating as fast as the creature's should have been.

"It wasn't just you. I guess Ernst didn't tell you? They raided the whole city, really smashed it up. Or at least that was the plan. It wasn't just your town either."

"What?"

Simon whirled around and immediately sucked in a sharp breath of pain. The scalpel slipped and cut his palm, and a bright red line of blood appeared.

"Easy, there."

Itzak handed Simon a cloth, and Simon pressed it to the wound.

"I suggest you hurry up. We're losing light, and besides you don't want that thing to stiffen up." Itzak pointed to the mouse. "Herr Kaltenbrunner is a great man for results."

For the first time Simon heard a note of bitterness creep into Itzak's voice. A smile that was not quite a smile twisted the edges of the other's lips, but before Simon could meet his eyes, Itzak turned away. Reluctantly, Simon turned back to his work.

"There."

Simon breathed out at last. He had the mouse almost hollowed out, lying on its back with the gears in place. The creature was utterly still.

"But I don't see what good it will do."

"Ah." Itzak's eyes shone. "Just you watch. Now it's my turn."

Simon stood back, and it was his turn to move cautiously behind Itzak and peer over his shoulder. The light was almost gone and shadows pooled around them. Simon leaned forward to see better, and he could hear a grin in Itzak's tone.

"You're in my light."

Simon withdrew further into the shadows, and watched as Itzak spread pale long-fingered hands. For the first time he noticed how delicate they were, and for the first time he noticed the scars crossing the knuckles and running up to disappear beneath Itzak's loose sleeves. He shivered. Kaltenbrunner was a man for results indeed.

Itzak hunched over the mouse on the table, and Simon heard him muttering something unintelligible. At first he thought the other was talking to him, and he made to step forward. But it was as though something was pushing him back, some intangible force that made the air heavy so it seemed to thicken around Itzak – thicken and grow darker.

Beneath the untidy mop of Itzak's hair, his brow grew paler and broke out in little beads of sweat. His eyes rolled back, flickering in his head, and for a moment Simon was afraid the other was having a seizure. All at once Itzak's head snapped back, and he opened eyes of pure white that made Simon start back. Then Itzak's head lolled forward, drained, and he grinned.

"There."

He stood shakily, and stepped aside as Simon drew closer. At first nothing had changed except that the creature had been turned right side up again. Then the mouse on the table twitched. There was a click and a whir, and its eyes flew open. Simon gasped. The eyes were blood red, and it took Simon a moment to realize they were colored glass or some kind of translucent stone.

Simon watched in amazement as the mouse scurried forward and leapt nimbly off the edge of the table.

"Look here."

Itzak drew something out of his pocket, and held it out for Simon to see. It was a plain round of glass, mirrored and reflecting the ceiling. As Simon watched, the glass clouded and changed, and then the warehouse jittered into view. The angle was all wrong though, and Simon felt dizzy and sick. It was as though he was scurrying along the floor, seeing through the mouse's eyes.

He glanced up. Itzak was still pale, and there were new shadows around his eyes showing a clear strain.

"How?"

"As I'm sure our good friend Ernst told you, the Emperor has many interests – the occult among them."

"I never thought it would work, not something this large."

Simon grinned as he wiped blood from his hands with a rag

"And now we're producing one a week!"

Itzak laid his hand on the horse's quivering flank, and nodded distractedly. Itzak's hair hung in a sweaty tangle, hiding his eyes, but behind it Simon sensed strain. He had never fully realized the toll their work took on his partner. He had been too wrapped up in his own excitement – their successes together, a fusion of metal and magic beyond his wildest dreams.

"Are you all right?"

Simon slid a cigarette from its carton and passed it to Itzak, who took it in trembling fingers. It took Itzak three tries to light it.

"You need some fresh air. Do you think Kaltenbrunner might let us out for just a little while?"

Simon glanced around the workspace that had essentially been his home since he had arrived in Lodz. It struck him that he had lost track of time, and he had no idea how long he had been here. The quality of light falling through the windows above wasn't enough to show the change in seasons, just enough to light their work and dazzle off the crystals and gears and scrying mirrors that littered every surface.

"Sure, why not?"

Itzak's lips peeled back from his teeth in a smile that left Simon thinking of a skull.

"Isn't he afraid we'd try to escape?"

"Would you?" Itzak raised an eyebrow. "Besides, where would we go? Lodz is a closed city, or didn't you know that?"

Simon shook his head.

"Sounds like *you* need some fresh air."

Itzak took his arm and pulled Simon towards the door, banging on the metal with the flat of his hand.

"Hey! This one is finished, and my friend and I need a walk."

After a moment the door slid open, and the guard on the other side regarded them with a look of disdain. Without a word, he jerked his head, indicating the blank corridor beyond him, which Simon had never actually seen.

"Just like that? It's that easy?"

He stared in wonder as Itzak led him to an outer door where another guard let them out. Burnt-white sunlight greeted them as they stepped out into an enclosed yard of stone. Simon blinked and held his hand up to shade his eyes.

Itzak led him towards a high wall topped with razor wire where a third guard looked them over once, and then undid a heavy lock and opened the gate. On the other side Simon turned and gawked back at the building they had come from. It was a sprawl of featureless stone and metal, squatting ugly over a courtyard of flat grey. The first thing that struck him was that there wasn't a tree in sight.

"They're really just going to let us walk around?"

"Oh, they'll set someone to tail us, I'm sure. And they'll use our own little toys against us too, I'd imagine."

Itzak pointed upwards as a bird shot overhead, twittering. Simon shivered. Was it just his imagination or had the bird's eyes been mirrors, and had its wings clicked and whirred? He pushed the thought from his mind as they made their way into the narrow streets. The ground sloped downwards, and because of the slight hill Simon could see what Itzak had meant before – the city was surrounded by a massive wall.

The smells that had greeted him on his first day assaulted him again now, but somehow worse. Piles of garbage filled the sidewalks, and men and women with hollow eyes moved around them. Simon caught his breath. Some were wearing no more than rags, and beneath the rags they were bone thin – and each one among them wore a yellow star sewn to their clothing.

A sound made Simon turn. They had come to a crossroads where four of the narrow streets spilled into a kind of town square. In the middle was a dry fountain, stained brown where water had once run. In front of the fountain stood one of his and Itzak's creations.

The horse let out a terrible scream – no natural sound – and its metallic hooves glinted cruelly in the light as it reared and struck the air. In spots, the creature's glossy black flanks had been peeled back to show silver gears and pistons, which lent the horse an unnatural strength. Astride the creature, and gripping its mane, was a black-clad *Staatspolizei* officer, brandishing a riding crop.

The officer was shouting something incoherent above the terrified crowd. Simon was jostled forward and then he saw the source of the panic. A woman with a shawl pulled close around her thin shoulders cowered back against the dry fountain, clutching a bundle against her chest. Only when the bundle let out a plaintive wail did Simon realize it was a child.

"Stop!"

He heard someone yell, and a man darted forward, pulling the terrified woman back. The horse's hooves landed, and sparks struck from the stone. The officer wheeled around.

"You!"

The man who had rescued the woman froze, and then slowly turned. The officer nudged the horse forward, staring down with burning eyes. Then without another word he brought the crop down hard across the man's face. The man crumpled and screamed. The crowd had fallen silent and, like Simon, they huddled in mute horror as the officer jumped down from his mount and went to the fallen man. The officer's boots clicked on the stone, the same bright metal as his horse's hooves, and there was a sick sound as his foot connected with the man's ribs.

The fallen man jerked, and he coughed blood on to the stone. The officer struck him once more, and then turned swiftly and remounted, riding away. For a moment longer the crowd remained frozen, and then a woman dashed forward and knelt at the man's side.

"Somebody, help him!"

"Annah?"

Simon blinked and stepped forward. The woman looked up,

and their eyes met over the body of the man. Her family had run a shop near his and lived above it as he had lived above his, but her face seemed so incongruous here that Simon merely stood gaping. She regarded him with wide eyes out of a face far thinner than he remembered. Her cheeks were hollow and smudged with dirt. His gaze flickered down to the hurt man.

"My uncle."

There was a bitter edge to her voice, and she did not take her eyes off Simon as she tried to get her hands under the fallen man's shoulders and lift him. Simon crouched and reached to help her, but she jerked back, glaring at him.

"Don't touch him."

"I'm sorry, I just wanted to help."

"You've done enough already." Her lips curled in a sneer, which did nothing to hide the core of hurt behind her words. Simon blinked again. Was she afraid of him?

"Annah, please."

He reached out a hand towards her, trying to put kindness and reassurance in his eyes. He saw himself reflected in her dark gaze, and all he saw was a traitor. He tried to conjure words of comfort to assure her he was just like her, but the words stuck in his throat, tasting a lie. He had enough to eat; he had a roof over his head. Simon let his hand fall.

As if she read all this in his eyes, she pulled back her sleeve so Simon could see the scars lining her arms. Her eyes remained locked on his as she let the fabric fall. Her voice was very soft when she spoke again.

"In case you're wondering, they're all over my body."

"Why?" Simon swallowed hard, and his voice trembled. He was afraid of the answer. A vague memory drifted to the surface of his mind, a memory of Annah's father giving him a hard candy and waving Simon's payment away when he and Annah had both been young and it was Simon's father who ran the watch shop.

"Because I stole an extra ration of bread to feed a sick man who was dying, and your toy spies caught me."

"I didn't know . . ."

"Of course you didn't!"

The anger had returned to her voice, and it struck him like a physical blow, stealing his breath and all the words he might have spoken in return. He felt dizzy and sick all over again. A hand touched his elbow, and Simon turned. Itzak stood behind him, looking grim.

"We'd better go."

Slowly, Simon straightened. Annah's gaze followed him, still crouched over her uncle who lay broken on the stone. Her dark shadow-haunted eyes stayed with him even as he let Itzak lead him away.

"I didn't know."

Simon's head rested in his hands. He sat at one of the workbenches, and Itzak leaned against another, watching him.

"What did you think we were doing here?"

Itzak's voice was very soft. Smoke curled around him, trapped in the light, and Simon thought of Annah's face, tortured and thin.

"I didn't think. I just got so caught up in everything . . . things I never thought were possible. I never stopped to *think*!" Simon's hands shook as he ran them through his hair. "What do we do?"

He glanced up, eyes wild. Itzak's expression was hard to read behind the veil of smoke.

Before either of them could speak again, the door of their workspace was hauled open with a sound of tortured metal, and both men flinched. Kaltenbrunner stood framed in the doorway, grinning at them. If anything the scars on his face seemed to have deepened, forming a patchwork of stitched skin that made Simon think of a mask; utterly inhuman. The *Staatspolizei* captain's eyes shone, and Simon felt cold settle in the pit of his stomach like a ball of ice.

Kaltenbrunner's steps echoed hollowly as he crossed towards Itzak and Simon. He held a roll of papers under one arm, and he laid them on the table, but he did not smooth them flat.

"I hear there was an altercation in town earlier today." He spoke casually, but his eyes continued to gleam. "I was relieved to hear that neither of you were *involved*. The Emperor would hate to lose two such valuable minds."

He smirked visibly now, scars tightening across his skin, and Simon felt his fists close into balls at his side. For one mad moment, he wanted to launch himself at the *Staatspolizei* man, but Itzak caught his eye and the other shook his head. Then, just as easily as if he was slipping on a mask of his own, Itzak grinned and stepped forward, touching Kaltenbrunner's shoulder as if they were old friends.

"What have you got there, Ernst?" He gestured to the papers still rolled on the table.

Kaltenbrunner's eyes narrowed for a moment, and then he smiled. "New orders from the Emperor. Plans."

Unceremoniously, he swept a number of Simon's tools aside and spread the papers, smoothing them down. Both Itzak and Simon stepped forward to look over Kaltenbrunner's shoulder.

The diagram showed a roughly spherical shape, which seemed to contain other smaller spheres within – a construction of interlocking metal and gears, delicately wrought. Simon frowned slightly, pulling the diagram closer. Kaltenbrunner was watching them and there was something both amused and almost hungry in his gaze.

"I shall leave you to it, then."

For a moment Simon thought the captain was about the sketch a mocking bow. Instead he turned sharply on his heels and moved for the door. The smile did not leave his lips, and it lingered in Simon's mind, chilling him, even when the door was closed and they were alone.

There had been something in Kaltenbrunner's eyes, in his smile, something that nagged at Simon like a persistent itch on the wrong side of his skin. He turned to Itzak, his mouth open to ask the other's opinion, but Itzak's expression stopped Simon's words in his throat.

Shadows carved Itzak's features and his shoulders were slumped as though in defeat. Something in his haunted eyes reminded Simon of Annah, crouched over her uncle's fallen form. It was an expression he had never seen in Itzak's eyes before, and it left him more than cold.

"What's wrong?"

Simon found his voice at last, and glanced back at the plans Kaltenbrunner had left. He studied the diagram again, frowning, and again the nagging sensation came to haunt him. Then at last it clicked in his mind.

"It's all copper and wire. There's no heart, no substance, it's just an empty shell. There's nothing inside."

"Not yet."

Itzak's voice was a raw whisper, and Simon turned to him, alarmed. There was a strange look in Itzak's eyes, at once bright and full of shadows.

"I don't understand."

Itzak shook his head, and then smiled a humorless smile. "Then consider yourself lucky."

Simon stared at him, uncomprehending, but his partner said no more.

Something tugged at the edges of Simon's consciousness, pulling him up from dreams where wheels with bright sharp teeth spun ceaselessly and crushed faceless people beneath them. Shadows transformed the scrap metal and junk into blurred and unfamiliar shapes of darkness. The scrying mirrors and crystals were blind eyes, watching him.

Slowly Simon sat up, looking around for the thing that had woken him. A fire-shaded point of light burned in the darkness. There was a slow intake of breath, and for a moment the light illuminated a face. Smoke curled away from Itzak's cigarette, and Simon moved towards him.

Itzak's lips were moving, but Simon could hear no sound. The other seemed unaware, or uncaring, of Simon's presence. Now that he was right beside the other, Simon could hear the murmured words and he jumped. Itzak seemed to address him, but without once glancing his way.

"I could do it. I could make the thing work. Kaltenbrunner knows it, and he knows that I know. He knows I'll be tempted to try, just to show it can be done."

"What?"

Simon strained forward, trying to catch the words. Itzak's head snapped up, startling him. The other's eyes burned as bright as the cigarette in his hand. After a moment, Itzak smiled, showing the shadows and the strain.

"We're very alike, you and I." His voice was soft again, and he took another deep breath. Smoke curled around them. "We're fascinated not only by the working of things, but by the possibility of them. If we suspect something can be done, we want to try, to push ourselves just a little bit farther to see if it really will work. And we will push to the exclusion of all else."

"What are you talking about, Itzak?"

Simon realized his voice was trembling. He was frightened, but he was no longer sure whether it was for, or of, the man in front of him. Suddenly the other seemed just that, *other*, alien and strange. Itzak's features were pale, almost translucent, and that same wildness, that same danger Simon had seen the first time they had met, shone brightly in his eyes.

"I have an idea."

Itzak's voice was barely audible and something in it made Simon want to shiver.

"Do you trust me?"

Itzak's eyes found Simon's in the dark and pinned him. Simon forced himself to look at the myriad things he saw there – hurt, fear, and yes, madness too. But it was all part of what made Itzak what he was, and slowly Simon found himself nodding.

"Good, because I can't do this alone."

The night was cloudless and moonlight spilled through the glass to touch Simon as he crouched over Itzak on the floor. Above them, the golem loomed, wrapped in shadow and watching over them with unseeing eyes. Simon held a knife, but his hand was shaking so hard he couldn't keep it still.

"I can't do this." He spoke through clenched teeth.

Itzak moved his head to either side, checking the bonds on his wrists, and then turned back to face Simon.

"Yes, you can. You have to."

The moonlight showed Itzak's skin, and it was terribly white. His chest was bared, showing the scars that ran over his ribcage and legs and arms, disappearing around to his back, which was pressed against the cold floor.

"What if it doesn't work?"

"It will!"

Itzak's voice was fierce, and it startled Simon so he almost dropped the blade. Itzak's eyes pinned him, burning mad and frightened all at once. Simon's heart was in his throat and he swallowed hard around the lump it made. Suddenly he realized that, of the two of them, he had no right to be afraid.

"I'm sorry," Simon murmured.

Itzak nodded, his lips pressed into a thin line. "It's okay. You have to hurry though. Just do it, quickly. Don't even think about it."

Something like a grin twisted Itzak's lips, and Simon shook his head, feeling tears coming to his eyes.

"I never have."

He took a deep steadying breath, and plunged the knife in.

There was more blood than Simon could have imagined. Despite what he knew intellectually, it still surprised him – the red spilling over his hands and leaving them slick.

Simon gagged and was nearly sick as he reached into the cavity he had made, lifting Itzak's heart in his hands. He was sharply aware of his own heart, its beat twin to the one he held. Through it all Itzak's eyes remained on him, bright and wild, and the other continued to breathe in shallow panting breaths. Simon could almost see the net of will with which Itzak held himself together.

Simon felt a moment of panic that froze him where he was. He was holding Itzak's heart in his hands and it was still beating. He knew what he was meant to do, but he couldn't get his limbs to obey his command. He was a man of parts and gears, not flesh and blood. Mice and horses were one thing, but a man, his friend . . .

Simon shook himself and, trembling, he walked over to the golem and opened the plate covering its chest. Everything was laid out as he and Itzak had planned and built it, gleaming coldly in the light. Simon took a deep breath and forced doubt away. He let his hands take over, and did what Itzak had advised – he didn't even think about it.

As though from a great distance Simon watched his hands moving in a red-white blur. Metal was joined to flesh as if it was the most natural thing in the world. Moonlight caught the characters on the golem's forehead, and they winked back at Simon. Beneath them, the creature's face was lifeless and still.

He stepped back. His hands were still red, but they were no longer shaking. A strange calm filled him as he regarded the golem. He took one last steadying breath, then he raised his bloodstained hand and brushed it gently across the golem's brow.

Itzak gasped behind him. Simon turned in time to see his friend's body go rigid, and then strain terribly upwards as if he was trying to pull free of his bonds. There was still a gaping hole where his chest had been, and red ran in ribbons over the white of Itzak's skin. Then, as though a string had been cut, Itzak slumped back and was still.

The golem opened its eyes.

They were not Itzak's eyes. They were strange things of mirror and glass, and though blind, they saw. The golem trembled, and then took a lurching step forward. There was a scream of tortured metal – a scream that might also have been a cry of pain.

Simon felt a pang of fear, strangely mixed with guilt. Now the wildness of Itzak's shape matched the wildness Simon had seen so often in his eyes; there was nothing left to hold the pain and darkness at bay. And the shape Itzak wore now had been built for only one thing. But it had been Itzak's choice. It was the only way.

For a long time, Simon merely cowered in the shadows, listening. The first cry cut through him like a knife and he felt it in his very bones. He was sure he would never move again, and they would find him one day – bones amongst the twisted metal and gears. A terrible crashing sound followed the first cry, and then a dull roar.

All at once Simon was on his feet and running. He pelted through the corridors, pushing past shouting officers. Panic was a tangible thing, thickly filling the air. The golem was tearing the *Staatspolizei* headquarters apart piece by piece. Simon heard another scream, and he felt heat rush towards him as something caught aflame.

A door leading off to the side of the corridor opened, and something made Simon stop and turn. Flames framed a man, making him a shape of blackness, torn from the light. Simon stared and the man turned slightly, just enough so that the light was no longer behind him, and fell on his face instead.

Firelight played in the deep lines on Kaltenbrunner's face. His eyes shone. Simon had expected rage, but there was none. The hunger and the amusement were gone as well. What Simon saw in that gaze was far more terrible still. All around them, *Staatspolizei* officers, dragged up from their sleep, screamed and died and burned, and Kaltenbrunner's eyes locked on Simon's. In silence they seemed to say, *In this moment, Herr Tinker, you and I are not so different after all.*

The faintest of smiles touched the mask of Kaltenbrunner's face – a smile that was not a smile at all. Then as others were turning to run away from the chaos and the flames, Kaltenbrunner turned back to the burning room. His eyes finally left Simon's, and he closed the door.

There was no guard at the door leading into the courtyard, and none by the gate, but the lock was still in place. Simon tore his shirt off and began to climb. At the top he wrapped the torn fabric around the razor wire, leaving it behind as he dropped down safely on the other side.

Then he was running again. Breath burned in his lungs, and he legs ached as he pounded into the narrow streets. Someone was shouting, and it took Simon a moment to realize it was him. He was laughing too, and there were tears in his eyes. He could smell smoke, heavy with ash, drifting down from the direction he had come.

"Out! Out! Everybody out! We have to leave, now!"

He banged on doors, on windows and walls, any surface he could get his hands on. A wild, uncontrolled panic boiled through him as he moved through the streets. Doors behind him began to open, and frightened thin faces peered out. He could see it in their eyes, like Annah, they didn't trust him; at best they thought him mad.

People were starting to step out onto the street though, barefoot on the stone. Some had noticed the fire up on the hill, and their distrust was immediately forgotten. There were more shouts, and they began to move.

"Leave your things. Take a little food, only what you can easily carry. Come on!"

Simon rushed forward; exhilaration, shot through with panic, carried him. His eyes lit on a woman standing in a doorway, watching him. Annah's eyes were frightened, but her expression was hard. Her arms were still crossed over her chest, and she was watching him with suspicion.

"Annah!"

Simon rushed forward and caught her hands. This time she did not pull away. She glanced past him to the flames, and they reflected in her eyes.

"Hurry, we have to leave, now!"

He was fully aware of the metallic sound that had been on the edge of his hearing for some time now – it was coming closer. Annah darted another glance over his shoulder, and her eyes widened, then she nodded silently. All around them bodies pressed, wild in their panic. People were already making for the walls.

"We have to go, now!"

Simon gripped her hands hard, and at last he felt her fingers soften beneath his.

Annah turned and called into the small room behind her. Her uncle and two small children emerged, looking fragile and frightened. Without thinking, Simon lifted one of the children into his arms and began to run, glancing back over his shoulder just long enough to see that Annah was following him.

Simon's heart was in his throat as he ran. People were scrambling up the walls, some of the *Staatspolizei* officers among them. Those too weak to climb were being left behind, stepped on in the panic of others to escape. Someone above him, whose face he couldn't see, reached down thin arms and Simon handed the child up into them. Then he too began to climb.

At the top of the wall he paused, one leg hung down inside the ghetto and the other out. The headquarters and the warehouse burned with angry red flames that clawed at the black sky. What moon there had been was now obscured by smoke and backlit against the flames on the hill were small figures running. Among them was one large figure, a blot of shadow against the night. Even from this distance Simon thought he heard a tortured metallic scream, and he thought of the heart that beat within the metal chest of the golem.

"What *is* that thing?" Annah whispered.

Simon turned, and Annah's eyes met his. She was straddling the wall too, breathing hard. A hot wind full of ash lifted her hair around her face, and once more he saw the thinness, the bruises, and the unmoving shadows. Simon turned back to the chaos, his eyes locked on the golem. Firelight reflected on Simon's cheeks and showed tears running like blood. His voice was very soft.

"A friend."

Tanglefoot

Cherie Priest

The Clockwork Century

Stonewall Jackson survived Chancellorsville. England broke the Union's naval blockade, and formally recognized the Confederate States of America. Atlanta never burned.

It is 1880. The American Civil War has raged for nearly two decades, driving technology in strange and terrible directions. Combat dirigibles skulk across the sky and armored vehicles crawl along the land. Military scientists twist the laws of man and nature, and barter their souls for weapons powered by light, fire and steam.

But life struggles forward for soldiers and ordinary citizens. The fractured nation is dotted with stricken towns and epic scenes of devastation – some manmade, and some more mysterious. In the western territories cities are swallowed by gas and walled away to rot while the frontiers are strip-mined for resources. On the borders between North and South, spies scour and scheme, and smugglers build economies more stable than their governments.

This is the Clockwork Century.

It is dark here, and different.

Part One

Hunkered shoulders and skinny, bent knees cast a crooked shadow from the back corner of the laboratory, where the old man tried to remember the next step in his formula, or possibly – as Edwin was forced to consider – the scientist simply struggled to recall his own name. On the table against the wall, the once estimable Dr Archibald Smeeks muttered, spackling his test tubes with spittle and becoming increasingly agitated until Edwin called out, "Doctor?"

The doctor settled himself, steadying his hands and closing his mouth. He crouched on his stool, cringing away from the boy's voice, and crumpled his overlong work apron with his feet. "Who's there?" he asked.

"Only me, sir."

"Who?"

"Me. It's only . . . me."

With a startled shudder of recognition he asked, "The orphan?"

"Yes, sir. Just the orphan."

Dr Smeeks turned around, the bottom of his pants twisting in a circle on the smooth wooden seat. He reached to his forehead, where a prodigious set of multi-lensed goggles was perched. From the left side, he tugged a monocle to extend it on a hinged metal arm, and he used it to peer across the room, down onto the floor, where Edwin was sitting cross-legged in a pile of discarded machinery parts.

"Ah," the old doctor said. "There you are, yes. I didn't hear you tinkering, and I only wondered where you might be hiding. Of course, I remember you."

"I believe you do, sir," Edwin said politely. In fact, he very strongly doubted it today, but Dr Smeeks was trying to appear quite fully aware of his surroundings and it would've been rude to contradict him. "I didn't mean to interrupt your work. You sounded upset. I wanted to ask if everything was all right."

"All right?" Dr Smeeks returned his monocle to its original position, so that it no longer shrank his fluffy white eyebrow down to a tame and reasonable arch. His wiry goatee quivered as he wondered about his own state. "Oh yes. Everything's quite all right. I think for a moment that I was distracted."

He scooted around on the stool so that he once again faced the cluttered table with its vials, coils and tiny grey crucibles. His right hand selected a test tube with a hand-lettered label and runny green contents. His left hand reached for a set of tongs, though he set them aside almost immediately in favor of a half-rolled piece of paper that bore the stains and streaks of a hundred unidentifiable splatters.

"Edwin," he said, and Edwin was just short of stunned to hear his name. "Boy, could you join me a moment? I'm afraid I've gone and confused myself."

"Yes, sir."

Edwin lived in the basement by the grace of Dr Smeeks, who had asked the sanitarium for an assistant. These days, the old fellow could not remember requesting such an arrangement and could scarcely confirm or deny it any more, no matter how often Edwin reminded him.

Therefore Edwin made a point to keep himself useful.

The basement laboratory was a quieter home than the crowded group ward on the top floor, where the children of the patients were kept and raised; and the boy didn't mind the doctor's failing mental state, since what was left of him was kind and often friendly. And sometimes, in a glimmering flash between moments of pitiful bewilderment, Edwin saw the doctor for who he once had been – a brilliant man with a mind that was honored and admired for its flexibility and prowess.

In its way, the Waverly Hills Sanitarium was a testament to his outstanding imagination.

The hospital had incorporated many of the physicians' favorites into the daily routine of the patients, including a kerosene-powered bladed machine that whipped fresh air down the halls to offset the oppressive summer heat. The physicians had also integrated his Moving Mechanical Doors that opened with the push of a switch; and Dr Smeeks's wonderful Steam-Powered Dish-Cleaning Device was a huge hit in the kitchen. His Sheet-Sorting Slings made him a celebrity in the laundry rooms, and the Sanitary Rotating Manure Chutes had made him a demi-god to the stable hands.

But half-finished and barely finished inventions littered every corner and covered every table in the basement, where the famed and elderly genius lived out the last of his years.

So long as he did not remember how much he'd forgotten, he appeared content.

Edwin approached the doctor's side and peered dutifully at the stained schematics on the discolored piece of linen paper. "It's coming along nicely, sir," he said.

For a moment Dr Smeeks did not reply. He was staring down

hard at the sheet, trying to make it tell him something, and accusing it of secrets. Then he said, "I'm forced to agree with you, lad. Could you tell me, what is it I was working on? Suddenly . . . suddenly the numbers aren't speaking to me. Which project was I addressing, do you know?"

"These are the notes for your Therapeutic Bath Appliance. Those numbers to the right are your guesses for the most healthful solution of water, salt and lavender. You were collecting lemon grass."

"Lemon grass? I was going to put that in the water? Whatever would've possessed me to do such a thing?" he asked, baffled by his own processes. He'd only drawn the notes a day or two before.

Edwin was a good student, even when Dr Smeeks was a feeble teacher. He prompted the old fellow as gently as he could. "You'd been reading about Dr Kellog's hydrotherapy treatments in Battle Creek, and you felt you could improve on them."

"Battle Creek, yes. The sanitarium there. Good Christian folks. They keep a strict diet; it seems to work well for the patients, or so the literature on the subject tells me. But yes," he said more strongly. "Yes, I remember. There must be a more efficient way to warm the water, and make it more pleasing to the senses. The soothing qualities of lavender have been documented for thousands of years, and its antiseptic properties should help keep the water fresh." He turned to Edwin and asked, with the lamplight flickering in his lenses, "Doesn't it sound nice?"

"I don't really like to take baths," the boy confessed. "But if the water was warm and it smelled real nice, I think I'd like it better."

Dr Smeeks made a little shrug and said, "It'd be less for the purposes of cleanliness and more for the therapy of the inmates here. Some of the more restless or violent ones, you understand."

"Yes, sir."

"And how's your mother?" the doctor asked. "Has she responded well to treatment? I heard her coughing last night, and I was wondering if I couldn't concoct a syrup that might give her comfort."

Edwin said, "She wasn't coughing last night. You must've heard someone else."

"Perhaps you're right. Perhaps it was Mrs . . . What's her name? The heavy nurse with the northern accent?"

"Mrs Criddle."

"That's her, yes. That's the one. I hope she isn't contracting the consumption she works so very hard to treat." He returned his attention to the notes and lines on the brittle sheet before him.

Edwin did not tell Dr Smeeks, for the fifth or sixth time, that his mother had been dead for months; and he did not mention that Mrs Criddle's accent had come with her from New Orleans. He'd learned that it was easier to agree, and probably kinder as well.

It became apparent that the old man's attention had been reabsorbed by his paperwork and test tubes, so Edwin returned to his stack of mechanical refuse. He was almost eleven years old, and he'd lived in the basement with the doctor for nearly a year. In that time, he'd learned quite a lot about how a carefully fitted gear can turn, and how a pinpoint-sharp mind can rust; and he took what scraps he wanted to build his own toys, trinkets and machines. After all, it was half the pleasure and privilege of living away from the other children – he could help himself to anything the doctor did not immediately require.

He didn't like the other children much, and the feeling was mutual.

The other offspring of the unfortunate residents were loud and frantic. They believed Edwin was aloof when he was only thoughtful, and they treated him badly when he wished to be left alone.

All things considered, a cot beside a boiler in a room full of metal and chemicals was a significant step up in the world. And the fractured mind of the gentle old man was more companionable by far than the boys and girls who baked themselves daily on the roof, playing ball and beating one another while the orderlies weren't looking.

Even so, Edwin had long suspected he could do better. Maybe he couldn't *find* better, but he was increasingly confident that he could *make* better.

He turned a pair of old bolts over in his palm and concluded that they were solid enough beneath their grime that a bit of sandpaper would restore their luster and usefulness. All the gears and coils he needed were already stashed and assembled, but some details yet eluded him, and his new friend was not quite finished.

Not until it boasted the finer angles of a human face.

Already Edwin had bartered a bit of the doctor's throat remedy to a taxidermist, an act that gained him two brown eyes meant for a badger. Instead, these eyes were fitted in a pounded brass mask with a cut strip of tin that made a sloping nose.

The face was coming together. But the bottom jaw was not connected, so the facsimile was not yet whole.

Edwin held the bolts up to his eye to inspect their threadings, and he decided that they would suffice. "These will work," he said to himself.

Back at the table the doctor asked, "Hmm?"

"Nothing, sir. I'm going to go back to my cot and tinker."

"Very good then. Enjoy yourself, Parker. Summon me if you need an extra hand," he said, because that's what he always said when Edwin announced that he intended to try his own small hands at inventing.

Parker was the youngest son of Dr and Mrs Smeeks. Edwin had seen him once, when he'd come to visit a year before at Christmas. The thin man with a fretful face had brought a box of clean, new vials and a large pad of lined paper, plus a gas-powered burner that had been made in Germany. But his father's confusion was too much for him. He'd left, and he hadn't returned.

So if Dr Smeeks wanted to call Edwin "Parker" once in a while, that was fine. Like Parker himself, Edwin was also thin, with a face marked by worry beyond his years; and Edwin was also handy with pencils, screwdrivers and wrenches. The boy figured that the misunderstanding was understandable, if unfortunate, and he learned to answer to the other name when it was used to call him.

He took his old bolts back to his cot and picked up a tiny triangle of sandpaper.

Beside him, at the foot of his cot underneath the wool blanket, lay a lump in the shape of a boy perhaps half Edwin's size. The lump was not a doll but an automaton, ready to wind, but not wound yet – not until it had a proper face, with a proper jaw.

When the bolts were as clean as the day they were cast, Edwin placed them gently on his pillow and reached inside the hatbox Mrs Williams had given him. He withdrew the steel jawbone and examined it, comparing it against the bolts and deciding that the fit was satisfactory; and then he uncovered the boy-shaped lump.

"Good heavens, Edwin. What have you got there?"

Edwin jumped. The old scientist could be uncannily quiet, and he could not always be trusted to stick to his own business. Nervously, as if the automaton were something to be ashamed of, the boy said, "Sir, it's . . . a machine. I made a machine, I think. It's not a doll," he clarified.

And Dr Smeeks said, "I can see that it's not a doll. You made this?"

"Yes, sir. Just with odds and ends – things you weren't using. I hope you don't mind."

"Mind? No. I don't mind. Dear boy, it's exceptional!" he said with what sounded like honest wonder and appreciation. It also sounded lucid, and focused, and Edwin was charmed to hear it.

The boy asked, "You think it's good?"

"I think it must be. How does it work? Do you crank it, or—"

"It winds up." He rolled the automaton over onto its back and pointed at a hole that was barely large enough to hold a pencil. "One of your old hex wrenches will do it."

Dr Smeeks turned the small machine over again, looking into the tangle of gears and loosely fixed coils where the brains would be. He touched its oiled joints and the clever little pistons that must surely work for muscles. He asked, "When you wind it, what does it do?"

Edwin faltered. "Sir, I . . . I don't know. I haven't wound him yet."

"Haven't wound him – well, I suppose that's excuse enough. I see that you've taken my jar lids for kneecaps, and that's well and good. It's a good fit. He's made to walk a bit, isn't he?"

"He ought to be able to walk, but I don't think he can climb stairs. I haven't tested him. I was waiting until I finished his face." He held up the metal jawbone in one hand and the two shiny bolts in the other. "I'm almost done."

"Do it then!" Dr Smeeks exclaimed. He clapped his hands together and said, "How exciting! It's your first invention, isn't it?"

"Yes, sir," Edwin fibbed. He neglected to remind the doctor of his work on the Picky Boy Plate with a secret chamber to hide unwanted and uneaten food until it was safe to discreetly dispose of it. He did not mention his tireless pursuit and eventual production of the Automatic Expanding Shoe, for use by quickly growing children whose parents were too poor to routinely purchase more footwear.

"Go on," the doctor urged. "Do you mind if I observe? I'm always happy to watch the success of a fellow colleague."

Edwin blushed warmly across the back of his neck. He said, "No, sir, and thank you. Here, if you could hold him for me – like that, on your legs, yes. I'll take the bolts and . . ." With trembling fingers, he fastened the final hardware and dabbed the creases with oil from a half-empty can.

And he was finished.

Edwin took the automaton from Dr Smeeks and stood it upright on the floor, where the machine did not wobble or topple, but stood fast and gazed blankly wherever its face was pointed.

The doctor said, "It's a handsome machine you've made. What does it do again? I think you said, but I don't recall."

"I still need to wind it," Edwin told him. "I need an L-shaped key. Do you have one?"

Dr Smeeks jammed his hands into the baggy depths of his pockets and a great jangling noise declared the assorted contents. After a few seconds of fishing he withdrew a hex, but seeing that it was too large, he tossed it aside and dug for another one. "Will this work?"

"It ought to. Let me see."

Edwin inserted the newer, smaller stick into the hole and gave it a twist. Within, the automaton springs tightened, coils contracted, and gears clicked together. Encouraged, the boy gave the wrench another turn, and then another. It felt as if he'd spent forever winding, when finally he could twist no further. The automaton's internal workings resisted, and could not be persuaded to wind another inch.

The boy removed the hex key and stood up straight. On the automaton's back, behind the place where its left shoulder blade ought to be, there was a sliding switch. Edwin put his finger to it and gave the switch a tiny shove.

Down in the machine's belly, something small began to whir.

Edwin and the doctor watched with delight as the clockwork boy's arms lifted and went back down to its sides. One leg rose at a time, and each was returned to the floor in a charming parody of marching-in-place. Its bolt-work neck turned from left to right, causing its tinted glass eyes to sweep the room.

"It works!" The doctor slapped Edwin on the back. "Parker, I swear – you've done a good thing. It's a most excellent job, and with what? My leftovers, is that what you said?"

"Yes, sir, that's what I said. You remembered!"

"Of course I remembered. I remember you," Dr Smeeks said. "What will you call your new toy?"

"He's my new friend. And I'm going to call him . . . Ted."

"Ted?"

"Ted." He did not explain that he'd once had a baby brother named Theodore, or that Theodore had died before his first birthday. This was something different, and anyway it didn't matter what he told Dr Smeeks, who wouldn't long recall it.

"Well he's very fine. Very fine indeed," said the doctor. "You should take him upstairs and show him to Mrs Criddle and Mrs Williams. Oh – you should absolutely show him to your mother. I think she'll be pleased."

"Yes, sir. I will, sir."

"Your mother will be proud, and I will be proud. You're learning so much, so fast. One day, I think, you should go to school. A bright boy like you shouldn't hide in basements with old men like me. A head like yours is a commodity, son. It's not a thing to be lightly wasted."

To emphasize his point, he ruffled Edwin's hair as he walked away.

Edwin sat on the edge of his cot, which brought him to eye level with his creation. He said, "Ted?"

Ted's jaw opened and closed with a metallic clack, but the mechanical child had no lungs, or lips, and it did not speak.

The flesh-and-blood boy picked up Ted and carried him carefully under his arm, up the stairs and into the main body of the Waverly Hills Sanitarium. The first-floor offices and corridors were mostly safe, and mostly empty – or populated by the bustling, concentrating men with clipboards and glasses, and very bland smiles that recognized Edwin without caring that he was present.

The sanitarium was very new. Some of its halls were freshly built and still stinking of mortar and the dust of construction. Its top-floor rooms reeked faintly of paint and lead, as well as the medicines and bandages of the ill and the mad.

Edwin avoided the top floors where the other children lived, and he avoided the wards of the men who were kept in jackets and chains. He also avoided the sick wards, where the mad men and women were tended to.

Mrs Criddle and Mrs Williams worked in the kitchen and laundry, respectively; and they looked like sisters though they were not, in fact, related. Both were women of a stout and purposeful build, with great tangles of greying hair tied up in buns and covered in sanitary hair caps; and both women were the mothering sort who were stern with patients, but kind to the hapless orphans who milled from floor to floor when they weren't organized and contained on the roof.

Edwin found Mrs Criddle first, working a paddle through a metal vat of mashed potatoes that was large enough to hold the boy, Ted, and a third friend of comparable size. Her wide bottom rocked from side to side in time with the sweep of her elbows as she stirred the vat, humming to herself.

"Mrs Criddle?"

She ceased her stirring. "Mm. Yes, dear?"

"It's Edwin, ma'am."

"Of course it is!" She leaned the paddle against the side of the vat and flipped a lever to lower the fire. "Hello there, boy. It's not time for supper, but what have you got there?"

He held Ted forward so she could inspect his new invention. "His name is Ted. I made him."

"Ted, ah yes. Ted. That's a good name for . . . for . . . a new friend."

"That's right!" Edwin brightened. "He's my new friend. Watch, he can walk. Look at what he can do."

He pressed the switch and the clockwork boy marched-in-place, and then staggered forward, catching itself with every step and clattering with every bend of its knees. Ted moved forward until it knocked its forehead on the leg of a counter, then stopped, and turned to the left to continue soldiering onward.

"Would you look at that?" Mrs Criddle said with the awe of a woman who had no notion of how her own stove worked, much less anything else. "That's amazing, is what it is. He just turned around like that, just like he knew!"

"He's automatic," Edwin said, as if this explained everything.

"Automatic indeed. Very nice, love. But Mr Bird and Miss Emmie will be here in a few minutes, and the kitchen will be a busy place for a boy and his new friend. You'd best take him back downstairs."

"First I want to go show Mrs Williams."

Mrs Criddle shook her head. "Oh no, dear. I think you'd better not. She's upstairs, with the other boys and girls, and well, I suppose you know. I think you're better off down with Dr Smeeks."

Edwin sighed. "If I take him upstairs, they'll only break him, won't they?"

"I think they're likely to try."

"All right," he agreed, and gathered Ted up under his arm.

"Come back in another hour, will you? You can get your own supper and carry the doctor's while you're at it."

"Yes, ma'am. I will."

He retreated back down the pristine corridors and dodged between two empty gurneys, back down the stairs that would return him to the safety of the doctor, the laboratory, and his own cot. He made his descent quietly, so as not to disturb the doctor in case he was still working.

When Edwin peeked around the bottom corner, he saw the old scientist sitting on his stool once more, a wadded piece of linen paper crushed in his fist. A spilled test tube leaked runny grey liquid across the counter's top, and made a dark stain across the doctor's pants.

Over and over to himself he mumbled, "Wasn't the lavender. Wasn't the . . . it was only the . . . I saw the . . . I don't . . . I can't . . . where was the paper? Where were the plans? What was the plan? What?"

The shadow of Edwin's head crept across the wall and when the doctor spotted it, he stopped himself and sat up straighter. "Parker, I've had a little bit of an accident. I've made a little bit of a mess."

"Do you need any help, sir?"

"Help? I suppose I don't. If I only knew . . . if I could only remember." The doctor slid down off the stool, stumbling as his foot clipped the seat's bottom rung. "Parker? Where's the window? Didn't we have a window?"

"Sir," Edwin said, taking the old man's arm and guiding him over to his bed, in a nook at the far end of the laboratory. "Sir, I think you should lie down. Mrs Criddle says supper comes in an hour. You just lie down, and I'll bring it to you when it's ready."

"Supper?" The many-lensed goggles he wore atop his head slid, and their strap came down over his left eye.

He sat Dr Smeeks on the edge of his bed and removed the man's shoes, then his eyewear. He placed everything neatly beside the feather mattress and pulled the doctor's pillow to meet his downward-drooping head.

Edwin repeated, "I'll bring you supper when it's ready," but Dr Smeeks was already asleep.

And in the laboratory, over by the stairs, the whirring and clicking of a clockwork boy was clattering itself in circles, or so Edwin assumed. He couldn't remember, had he left Ted on the stairs? He could've sworn he'd pressed the switch to deactivate his friend. But perhaps he hadn't.

Regardless, he didn't want the machine bounding clumsily around in the laboratory – not in that cluttered place piled with glass and gadgets.

Over his shoulder Edwin glanced, and saw the doctor snoozing lightly in his nook; and out in the laboratory, knocking its jar-lid knees against the bottom step, Ted had gone nowhere, and harmed nothing. Edwin picked Ted up and held the creation to his face, gazing into the glass badger eyes as if they might blink back at him.

He said, "You're my friend, aren't you? Everybody makes friends. I just made you for *real*."

Ted's jaw creaked down, opening its mouth so that Edwin could stare straight inside, at the springs and levers that made the toy boy move. Then its jaw retracted, and without a word, Ted had said its piece.

After supper, which Dr Smeeks scarcely touched, and after an hour spent in the laundry room sharing Ted with Mrs Williams, Edwin retreated to his cot and blew out the candle beside it. The cot wasn't wide enough for Edwin and Ted to rest side by side, but Ted fit snugly between the wall and the bedding and Edwin left the machine there, to pass the night.

But the night did not pass fitfully.

First Edwin awakened to hear the doctor snuffling in his sleep, muttering about the peril of inadequate testing; and when the old man finally sank back into a fuller sleep, Edwin nearly followed him. Down in the basement there were no lights except for the dim, bioluminescent glow of living solutions in blown-glass beakers – and the simmering wick of a hurricane lamp turned down low, but left alight enough for the boy to see his way to the privy if the urge struck him before dawn.

Here and there the bubble of an abandoned mixture seeped fizzily through a tube, and when Dr Smeeks slept deeply enough to cease his ramblings, there was little noise to disturb anyone.

Even upstairs, when the wee hours came, most of the inmates and patients of the sanitarium were quiet – if not by their own cycles, then by the laudanum spooned down their throats before the shades were drawn.

Edwin lay on his back, his eyes closed against the faint, blue and green glows from the laboratory, and he waited for slumber to call him again. He reached to his left, to the spot between his cot and the wall. He patted the small slip of space there, feeling for a manufactured arm or leg, and finding Ted's cool, unmoving form. And although there was scarcely any room, he pulled Ted out of the slot and tugged the clockwork boy into the cot after all, because doll or not, Ted was a comforting thing to hold.

Part Two

Morning came, and the doctor was already awake when Edwin rose.

"Good morning, sir."

"Good morning, Edwin," the doctor replied without looking over his shoulder. On their first exchange of the day, he'd remembered the right name. Edwin tried to take it as a sign that today would be a good day, and Dr Smeeks would mostly remain Dr Smeeks – without toppling into the befuddled tangle of fractured thoughts and faulty recollections.

He was standing by the hurricane lamp, with its wick trimmed higher so that he could read. An envelope was opened and discarded beside him.

"Is it a letter?" Edwin asked.

The doctor didn't sound happy when he replied, "It's a letter indeed."

"Is something wrong?"

"It depends." Dr Smeeks folded the letter. "It's a man who wants me to work for him."

"That might be good," Edwin said.

"No. Not from this man."

The boy asked, "You know him?"

"I do. And I do not care for his aims. I will not help him," he said firmly. "Not with his terrible quests for terrible weapons. I don't do those things any more. I haven't done them for years."

"You used to make weapons? Like guns, and cannons?"

Dr Smeeks said, "Once upon a time." And he said it sadly. "But no more. And if Ossian thinks he can bribe or bully me, he has another thing coming. Worst comes to worst, I suppose, I can plead a failing mind."

Edwin felt like he ought to object as a matter of politeness, but when he said, "Sir," the doctor waved his hand to stop whatever else the boy might add.

"Don't, Parker. I know why I'm here. I know things, even when I can't always quite remember them. But my old colleague says he intends to pay me a visit, and he can pay me all the visits he likes. He can offer to pay me all the Union money he likes, too – or Confederate money, or any other kind. I won't make such terrible things, not any more."

He folded the letter in half and struck a match to light a candle. He held one corner of the letter over the candle and let it burn, until there was nothing left but the scrap between his fingertips, and then he released it, letting the smoldering flame turn even the last of the paper to ash.

"Perhaps he'll catch me on a bad day, do you think? As likely as not, there will be no need for subterfuge."

Edwin wanted to contribute, and he felt the drive to communicate with the doctor while communicating seemed possible. He said, "You should tell him to come in the afternoon. I hope you don't mind me saying so, sir, but you seem much clearer in the mornings."

"Is that a fact?" he asked, an eyebrow lifted aloft by genuine interest. "I'll take your word for it, I suppose. Lord knows I'm in no position to argue. Is that . . . that noise . . . what's that noise? It's coming from your cot. Oh dear, I hope we haven't got a rat."

Edwin declared, "Oh no!" as a protest, not as an exclamation of worry. "No, sir. That's just Ted. I must've switched him on when I got up."

"Ted? What's a Ted?"

"It's my . . ." Edwin almost regretted what he'd said before, about mornings and clarity. "It's my new friend. I made him."

"There's a friend in your bunk? That doesn't seem too proper."

"No, he's . . . I'll show you."

And once again they played the scene of discovery together – the doctor clapping Edwin on the back and ruffling his hair, and announcing that the automaton was a fine invention indeed. Edwin worked very hard to disguise his disappointment.

Finally, Dr Smeeks suggested that Edwin run to the washrooms upstairs and freshen himself to begin the day, and Edwin agreed.

The boy took his spring-and-gear companion along as he navigated the corridors while the doctors and nurses made their morning rounds. Dr Havisham paused to examine Ted and declare the creation "outstanding". Dr Martin did likewise, and Nurse Evelyn offered him a peppermint sweet for being such an innovative youngster who never made any trouble.

Edwin cleaned his hands and face in one of the cold white basins in the washroom, where staff members and some of the more stable patients were allowed to refresh themselves. He set Ted on the countertop and pressed the automaton's switch. While Edwin cleaned the night off his skin, Ted's legs kicked a friendly time against the counter and its jaw bobbed like it was singing or chatting, or imagining splashing its feet in the basin.

When he was clean, Edwin set Ted on the floor and decided that, rather than carrying the automaton, he would simply let it walk the corridor until they reached the stairs to the basement.

The peculiar pair drew more than a few exclamations and stares, but Edwin was proud of Ted and he enjoyed the extended opportunity to show off.

Before the stairs and at the edge of the corridor where Edwin wasn't supposed to go, for fear of the violent inmates, a red-haired woman blocked his way. If her plain cotton gown hadn't marked her as a resident, the wildness around the corners of her eyes would've declared it well enough. There were red stripes on her skin where restraints were sometimes placed, and her feet were bare, leaving moist, sweaty prints on the black and white tiles.

"Madeline," Dr Simmons warned. "Madeline, it's time to return to your room."

But Madeline's eyes were locked on the humming, marching automaton. She asked with a voice too girlish for her height, "What's that?" and she did not budge, even when the doctor took her arm and signaled quietly for an orderly.

Edwin didn't mind answering. He said, "His name is Ted. I made him."

"Ted." She chewed on the name and said, "Ted for *now*."

Edwin frowned and asked, "What?"

He did not notice that Ted had stopped marching, or that Ted's metal face was gazing up at Madeline. The clockwork boy had wound itself down, or maybe it was only listening.

Madeline did not blink at all, and perhaps she never did. She said, "He's your Ted for now, but you must watch him." She held out a pointing, directing, accusing finger and aimed it at Edwin, then at Ted. "Such empty children are vulnerable."

Edwin was forced to confess, or simply make a point of saying, "Miss, he's only a machine."

She nodded. "Yes, but he's your boy, and he has no soul. There are things who would change that, and change it badly."

"I know I shouldn't take him upstairs," Edwin said carefully. "I know I ought to keep him away from the other boys."

Madeline shook her head, and the matted crimson curls swayed around her face. "Not what I mean, boy. *Invisible* things. Bad little souls that need bodies."

An orderly arrived. He was a big, square man with shoulders like an ox's yoke. His uniform was white, except for a streak of blood that was drying to brown. He took Madeline by one arm, more roughly than he needed to.

As Madeline was pulled away, back to her room or back to her restraints, she kept her eyes on Edwin and Ted, and she warned him still, waving her finger like a wand, "Keep him close, unless you want him stolen from you – unless you want his clockwork heart replaced with something stranger."

Before she was removed from the corridor altogether, she

lashed out one last time with her free hand to seize the wall's corner. It bought her another few seconds of eye contact – just enough to add, "Watch him close!"

Then she was gone.

Edwin reached for Ted and pulled the automaton to his chest, where its gear-driven heart clicked quietly against the real boy's shirt. Ted's mechanical jaw opened and closed, not biting but mumbling in the crook of Edwin's neck.

"I will," he promised. "I'll watch him close."

Several days passed quietly, except for the occasional frustrated rages of the senile doctor, and Ted's company was a welcome diversion – if a somewhat unusual one. Though Edwin had designed Ted's insides and stuffed the gears and coils himself, the automaton's behavior was not altogether predictable.

Mostly, Ted remained a quiet little toy with the marching feet that tripped at stairs, at shoes, or any other obstacle left on the floor.

And if the clockwork character fell, it fell like a turtle and laid where it collapsed, arms and legs twitching impotently at the air until Edwin would come and set his friend upright. Several times Edwin unhooked Ted's back panel, wondering precisely why the shut-off switch failed so often. But he never found any stretched spring or faulty coil to account for it. If he asked Ted, purely to speculate aloud, Ted's shiny jaw would lower and lift, answering with the routine and rhythmic clicks of its agreeable guts.

But sometimes, if Edwin listened very hard, he could almost convince himself he heard words rattling around inside Ted's chest. Even if it was only the echoing pings and chimes of metal moving metal, the boy's eager ears would concentrate, and listen for whispers.

Once, he was nearly certain – practically *positive* – that Ted had said its own name. And that was silly, wasn't it? No matter how much Edwin wanted to believe, he knew better . . . which did not stop him from wondering.

It was always Edwin's job to bring meals down from the kitchen, and every time he climbed the stairs he made a point to secure Ted by turning it off and leaving it lying on its back, on Edwin's cot. The doctor was doddering, and even unobstructed he sometimes stumbled on his own two feet, or the laces of his shoes.

So when the boy went for breakfast and returned to the laboratory with a pair of steaming meals on a covered tray, he was surprised to hear the whirring of gears and springs.

"Ted?" he called out, and then felt strange for it. "Doctor?" he tried instead, and he heard the old man muttering.

"Doctor, are you looking at Ted? You remember him, don't you? Please don't break him."

At the bottom of the stairs, Dr Smeeks was crouched over the prone and kicking Ted. The doctor said, "Underfoot, this thing is. Did it on purpose. I saw it. Turned itself on, sat itself up, and here it comes."

But Edwin didn't think the doctor was speaking to him. He was only speaking, and poking at Ted with a pencil like a boy prods an anthill.

"Sir? I turned him off, and I'm sorry if he turned himself on again. I'm not sure why it happens."

"Because it wants to be *on*," the doctor said firmly, and finally made eye contact. "It wants to make me fall, it practically told me so."

"Ted never says anything," Edwin said weakly. "He can't talk."

"He can talk. You can't hear him. But *I* can hear him. I've heard him before, and he used to say pleasant things. He used to hum his name. Now he fusses and mutters like a demented old man. Yes," he insisted, his eyes bugged and his eyebrows bushily hiked up his forehead. "Yes, this thing, when it mutters, it sounds like *me*."

Edwin had another theory about the voices Dr Smeeks occasionally heard, but he kept it to himself. "Sir, he cannot talk. He hasn't got any lungs, or a tongue. Sir, I promise, he cannot speak."

The doctor stood, and gazed down warily as Ted floundered. "He cannot flip his own switches either, yet he *does*."

Edwin retrieved his friend and set it back on its little marching feet. "I must've done something wrong when I built him. I'll try and fix it, sir. I'll make him stop it."

"Dear boy, I don't believe you *can*."

The doctor straightened himself and adjusted his lenses – a different pair, a set that Edwin had never seen before. He turned away from the boy and the automaton and reached for his paperwork again, saying, "Something smells good. Did you get breakfast?"

"Yes sir. Eggs and grits, with sausage."

He was suddenly cheerful. "Wonderful! Won't you join me here? I'll clear you a spot."

As he did so, Edwin moved the tray to the open space on the main laboratory table and removed the tray's lid, revealing two sets of silverware and two plates loaded with food. He set one in front of the doctor, and took one for himself, and they ate with the kind of chatter that told Edwin Dr Smeeks had already forgotten about his complaint with Ted.

As for Ted, the automaton stood still at the foot of the stairs, its face cocked at an angle that suggested it might be listening, or watching, or paying attention to something that no one else could see.

Edwin wouldn't have liked to admit it, but when he glanced back at his friend, he felt a pang of unease. Nothing had changed and everything was fine; he was letting the doctor's rattled mood unsettle him, that was all. Nothing had changed and everything was fine; but Ted was not marching and its arms were not swaying, and the switch behind the machine's small shoulder was still set in the "on" position.

When the meal was finished and Edwin had gathered the empty plates to return them upstairs, he stopped by Ted and flipped the switch to the state of "off". "You must've run down your winding," he said. "That must be why you stopped moving."

Then he called, "Doctor? I'm running upstairs to give these to Mrs Criddle. I've turned Ted off, so he shouldn't bother you, but keep an eye out, just in case. Maybe," he said, balancing the tray on his crooked arm, "if you wanted to, you could open him up yourself and see if you can't fix him."

Dr Smeeks didn't answer, and Edwin left him alone – only for a few minutes, only long enough to return the tray with its plates and cutlery.

It was long enough to return to strangeness.

Back in the laboratory Edwin found the doctor backed into a corner, holding a screwdriver and a large pair of scissors. Ted was seated on the edge of the laboratory table, its legs dangling over the side, unmoving, unmarching. The doctor looked alert and lucid – more so than usual – and he did not quite look afraid. Shadows from the burners and beakers with their tiny glowing creatures made Dr Smeeks look sinister and defensive, for the flickering bits of flame winked reflections off the edge of his scissors.

"Doctor?"

"I was only going to fix him, like you said."

"Doctor, it's all right."

The doctor said, "No, I don't believe it's all right, not at all. That nasty little thing, Parker, I don't like it." He shook his head, and the lenses across his eyes rattled in their frames.

"But he's my friend."

"He's no friend of *mine*."

Edwin held his hands up, like he was trying to calm a startled horse. "Dr Smeeks, I'll take him. I'll fix him, you don't have to do it. He's only a machine, you know. Just an invention. He can't hurt you."

"He tried."

"Sir, I really don't think—"

"He tried to bite me. Could've taken my fingers off, if I'd caught them in that bear-trap of a face. You keep it away from me, Edwin. Keep it away or I'll pull it apart, and turn it into a can opener."

Before Edwin's very own eyes, Ted's head turned with a series of clicks, until the machine fully faced the doctor. And if its eyes had been more than glass bits that were once assigned to a badger, then they might have narrowed or gleamed; but they were only glass bits, and they only cast back the fragments of light from the bright things in the laboratory.

"Ted, come here. Ted, come with me," Edwin said, gently pulling the automaton down from the table. "Ted, no one's going to turn you into a can opener. Maybe you got wound funny, or wound too tight," he added, mostly for the doctor's benefit. "I'll open you up and tinker, and you'll be just fine."

Back in the corner the doctor relaxed, and dropped the scissors. He set the screwdriver down beside a row of test tubes and placed both hands on the table's corner. "Edwin?" he said, so softly that Edwin almost didn't hear him. "Edwin, did we finish breakfast? I don't see my plate."

"Yes, sir," the boy swore. He clutched Ted closely, and held the automaton away from the doctor, out of the man's line of sight should he turn around.

"Oh. I suppose that's right," he said, and again Ted had been spared by the doctor's dementia.

Edwin stuck Ted down firmly between the wall and his cot, and for one daft moment he considered binding the machine's feet with twine or wire to keep it from wandering. But the thought drifted out of his head, chased away by the unresponsive lump against the wall. He whispered, "I don't know how you're doing it, but you need to stop. I don't want the doctor to turn you into a can opener."

Then, as a compromise to his thoughts about hobbling the automaton, he dropped his blanket over the thing's head.

Bedtime was awkward that night.

When he reached for the clockwork boy he remembered the slow, calculated turn of the machine's head, and he recalled the blinking bright flashes of firelight in the glass badger eyes.

The doctor had settled in his nook and was sleeping, and Edwin was still awake. He reclaimed his blanket and settled down on his side, facing the wall and facing Ted until he dozed, or he must have dozed. He assumed it was only sleep that made the steel jaw lower and clack; and it was only a dream that made the gears twist and lock into syllables.

"Ted?" Edwin breathed, hearing himself but not recognizing the sound of his own word.

And the clockwork face breathed back, not its own name but something else – something that even in the sleepy state of midnight and calm, Edwin could not understand.

The boy asked in the tiniest whisper he could muster, "Ted?"

Ted's steel jaw worked, and the air in its mouth made the shape of a "no". It said, more distinctly this time, and with greater volume, "Tan . . . gle . . . foot."

Edwin closed his eyes, and was surprised to learn that they had not been closed already. He tugged his blanket up under his chin and could not understand why the rustle of the fabric seemed so loud, but not so loud as the clockwork voice.

I must be asleep, he believed.

And then, eventually, he was.

Though not for long.

His sleep was not good. He was too warm, and then too cold, and then something was missing. Through the halls of his nightmares mechanical feet marched to their own tune; in the confined and cluttered space of the laboratory there was movement too large to come from rats, and too deliberate to be the random flipping of a switch.

Edwin awakened and sat upright in the same moment, with the same fluid fear propelling both events.

There was no reason for it, or so he told himself; and this was ridiculous, it was only the old Dr Smeeks and his slipping mind, infecting the boy with strange stories, turning the child against his only true friend. Edwin shot his fingers over to the wall where Ted ought to be jammed, waiting for its winding and for the sliding of the button on its back.

And he felt only the smooth, faintly damp texture of the painted stone.

His hands flapped and flailed, slapping at the emptiness and the flat, blank wall. "Ted?" he said, too loudly. "Ted?" he cried with even more volume, and he was answered by the short, swift footsteps that couldn't have belonged to the doctor.

From his bed in the nook at the other end of the laboratory, the doctor answered with a groggy groan. "Parker?"

"Yes, sir!" Edwin said, because it was close enough. "Sir, there's . . ." and what could he say? That he feared his friend had become unhinged, and that Ted was fully wound, and roaming?

"What is it, son?"

The doctor's voice came from miles away, at the bottom of a well – or that's how it sounded to Edwin, who untangled himself from the sheets and toppled to the floor. He stopped his fall with his hands, and stood, but then could scarcely walk.

As a matter of necessity he dropped his bottom on the edge of the cot and felt for his feet, where something tight was cinched around his ankles.

There, he found a length of wire bent into a loop and secured.

It hobbled his legs together, cutting his stride in half.

"Parker?" the doctor asked, awakening further but confused. "Boy?"

Edwin forced his voice to project a calm he wasn't feeling. "Sir, stay where you are, unless you have a light. My friend, Ted. He's gotten loose again. I don't want ... I don't want you to hurt yourself."

"I can't find my candle."

"I can't find mine either," Edwin admitted. "You stay there. I'll come to you."

But across the floor the marching feet were treading steadily, and the boy had no idea where his automaton had gone. Every sound bounced off glass or wood, or banged around the room from wall to wall; and even the blue-gold shadows cast by the shimmering solutions could not reveal the clockwork boy.

Edwin struggled with the bizarre bind on his legs and stumbled forward regardless of it. No matter how hard his fingers twisted and pulled the wires only dug into his skin and cut it when he yanked too sharply. He gave up and stepped as wide as he could and found that, if he was careful, he could still walk and even, in half-hops and uneven staggers, he could run.

His light was nowhere to be found, and he gave up on that, too.

"Sir, I'm coming!" he cried out again, since the doctor was awake already and he wanted Ted to think he was aware, and acting. But what could Ted think? Ted was only a collection of cogs and springs.

Edwin remembered the red-haired Madeline with the strap marks on her wrists. She'd said Ted had no soul, but she'd implied that one might come along.

The darkness baffled him, even in the laboratory he knew by heart. Hobbled as he was, and terrified by the pattering of unnatural feet, the basement's windowless night worked against him and he panicked.

He needed help, but where could it come from?

The orderlies upstairs frightened him in a vague way, as harbingers of physical authority; and the doctors and nurses might think he was as crazy as the other children, wild and loud – or as mad as his mother.

Like Madeline.

Her name tinkled at the edge of his ears, or through the nightmare confusion that moved him in jilting circles. Maybe Madeline knew something he didn't, maybe she could help. She wouldn't make fun of him, at any rate. She wouldn't tell him he was frightened for nothing, and to go back to sleep.

He knew where her room was located; at least he knew of its wing, and he could gather its direction.

The stairs jabbed up sharp and hard against his exploring fingers, and his hands were more free than his feet so he used them to climb – knocking his knees against each angle and bruising his shins with every yard. Along the wall above him there was a handrail someplace, but he couldn't find it so he made do without it.

He crawled so fast that his ascent might have been called a scramble.

He hated to leave the doctor alone down there with Ted, but then again, the doctor had taken up the screwdriver and the scissors once before. Perhaps he could be trusted to defend himself again.

At the top of the stairs, Edwin found more light and his eyes were relieved. He stood up, seized the handrail, and fell forward because he'd already forgotten about the wire wrapped around his ankles. His hands stung from the landing, slapping hard against the tile floor, but he picked himself up and began a shuffling run, in tiny skips and dragging leaps down the corridor.

A gurney loomed skeletal and shining in the ambient light from the windows and the moon outside. Edwin fell past it and clipped it with his shoulder. The rattling of its wheels haunted him down the hallway, past the nurse's station where an elderly woman was asleep with the most recent issue of *Harper's New Monthly Magazine* lying across her breasts.

She didn't budge, not even when the gurney rolled creakily into the center of the hallway, following in Edwin's wake.

When he reached the right wing, he whispered, "Madeline? Madeline, can you hear me?"

All the windows in the doors to the inmate rooms were well off the ground and Edwin wasn't tall enough to reach, so he couldn't see inside. He hissed her name from door to door, and eventually she came forward. Her hands wrapped around the bars at the top, coiling around them like small white snakes. She held her face up to the small window and said, "Boy?"

He dashed to the door and pushed himself against it. "Madeline? It's me."

"The boy." Her mouth was held up to the window; she must have been standing on her tiptoes to reach it.

Edwin stood on his tiptoes also, but he couldn't touch the window, high above his head. He said, "I need your help. Something's wrong with Ted."

For a moment he heard only her breathing, rushed and hot above him. Then she said, "Not your Ted any longer. I warned you."

"I know you did!" he said, almost crying. "I need your help! He tied my feet together, all tangled up – and I think he's trying to hurt Dr Smeeks!"

"Tangled, did he? Oh, that vicious little changeling," she said, almost wheezing with exertion. She let go of whatever was holding her up, and Edwin heard her feet land back on the floor with a thump. She said through the door's frame, beside its hinges, "You must let me out, little boy. If you let me out, I'll come and help your doctor. I know what to do with changelings."

It was a bad thought, and a bad plan. It was a bad thing to consider and Edwin knew it all too well; but when he looked back over his shoulder at the nurse's station with the old lady snoring within, and when he thought of the clattering automaton roaming the laboratory darkness with his dear Dr Smeeks, he leaped at the prospect of aid.

He reached for the lever to open the door and hung from it, letting it hold his full weight while he reached up to undo the lock.

Edwin no sooner heard the click of the fastener unlatching then the door burst open in a quick swing that knocked him off his hobbled feet. With a smarting head and bruised elbow, he fought to stand again but Madeline grabbed him by the shoulder. She lifted him up as if he were as light as a doll, and she lugged him down the hallway. Her cotton shift billowed dirtily behind her, and her hair slapped Edwin in the eyes as she ran.

Edwin squeezed at her arm, trying to hold himself out of the way of the displaced gurneys and medical trays that clogged the hall, but his airborne feet smacked the window of the nurse's station as Madeline swiftly hauled him past it, awakening the nurse and startling her into motion.

If Madeline noticed, she did not stop to comment.

She reached the top of the stairs and flung herself down them, her feet battering an alternating time so fast that her descent sounded like firecrackers. Edwin banged along behind her, twisted in her grip and unable to move quickly even if she were to set him down.

He wondered if he hadn't made an awful mistake when she all but cast him aside. His body flopped gracelessly against a wall. But he was back on his feet in a moment and there was light in the laboratory – a flickering, uncertain light that was moving like mad.

Dr Smeeks was holding it; he'd found his light after all, and he'd raised the wick on the hurricane lamp. The glass-jarred lantern gleamed and flashed as he swung it back and forth, sweeping the floor for something Edwin couldn't see.

The doctor cried out, "Parker? Parker? Something's here, something's in the laboratory!"

And Edwin answered, "I know, sir! But I've brought help!"

The light shifted, the hurricane lamp swung, and Madeline was standing in front of the doctor – a blazing figure doused in gold and red, and black-edged shadows. She said nothing, but held out her hand and took the doctor's wrist; she shoved his wrist up, forcing the lamp higher. The illumination increased accordingly and Edwin started to cry.

The laboratory was in a disarray so complete that it might never be restored to order. Glass glimmered in piles of dust, shattered tubes and broken beakers were smeared with the shining residue of the blue-green substance that lived and glowed in the dark. It spilled and died, losing its luminescence with every passing second – and there was the doctor, his hand held aloft and his lamp bathing the chaos with revelation.

Madeline turned away from him, standing close enough beneath the lamp so that her shadow did not temper its light. Her feet twisted on the glass-littered floor, cutting her toes and leaving smears of blood.

She demanded, "Where are you?"

She was answered by the tapping of marching feet, but it was a sound that came from all directions at once. And with it came a whisper, accompanied by the grinding discourse of a metal jaw.

"Tan . . . gles. Tan . . . gles . . . feet. Tanglefoot."

"That's your name then? Little changeling – little Tanglefoot? Come out here!" she fired the command into the corners of the room and let it echo there. "Come out here, and I'll send you back to where you came from! Shame on you, taking a boy's friend. Shame on you, binding his feet and tormenting his master!"

Tanglefoot replied, "Can . . . op . . . en . . . er," as if it explained everything, and Edwin thought that it *might*, but that it was no excuse.

"Ted, where *are* you?" he pleaded, tearing his eyes away from Madeline and scanning the room. Upstairs he could hear the thunder of footsteps – of orderlies and doctors, no doubt, freshly roused by the night nurse in her chamber. Edwin said with a sob, "Madeline, they're coming for you."

She growled, "And I'm coming for *him*."

She spied the automaton in the same second that Edwin saw it – not on the ground, marching its little legs in bumping patterns, but overhead, on a ledge where the doctor kept books. Tanglefoot was marching, yes, but it was marching towards them both with the doctor's enormous scissors clutched between its clamping fingers.

"Ted!" Edwin screamed, and the machine hesitated. The boy did not know why, but there was much he did not know and there were many things he'd never understand . . . including how Madeline, fierce and barefoot, could move so quickly through the glass.

The madwoman seized the doctor's hurricane lamp by its scalding cover, and Edwin could hear the sizzle of her skin as her fingers touched, and held, and then flung the oil-filled lamp at the oncoming machine with the glittering badger eyes.

The lamp shattered and the room was flooded with brilliance and burning.

Dr Smeeks shrieked as splatters of flame sprinkled his hair and his nightshirt, but Edwin was there, shuffling fast into the doctor's sleeping nook. The boy grabbed the top blanket and threw it at the doctor, then he joined the blanket and covered the old man, patting him down. When the last spark had been extinguished he left the doctor covered and held him in the corner, hugging the frail, quivering shape against himself while Madeline went to war.

Flames were licking along the books and Madeline's hair was singed. Her shift was pocked with black-edged holes, and she had grabbed the gloves Dr Smeeks used when he held his crucibles. They were made of asbestos, and they would help her hands.

Tanglefoot was spinning in place, howling above their heads from his fiery perch on the book ledge. It was the loudest sound Edwin had ever heard his improvised friend create, and it horrified him down to his bones.

Someone in a uniform reached the bottom of the stairs and was repulsed, repelled by the blast of fire. He shouted about it, hollering for water. He demanded it as he retreated, and Madeline didn't pay him a fragment of attention.

Tanglefoot's scissors fell to the ground, flung from its distracted hands. The smoldering handles were melting on the floor, making a black, sticky puddle where they settled.

With her gloved hands she scooped them up and stabbed, shoving the blades down into the body of the mobile inferno once named Ted. She withdrew the blades and shoved them down again because the clockwork boy still kicked, and the third time she jammed the scissors into the little body she jerked Ted down off the ledge and flung it to the floor.

The sound of breaking gears and splitting seams joined the popping gasp of the fire as it ate the books and gnawed at the ends of the tables.

"A blanket!" Madeline yelled. "Bring me a blanket!"

Reluctantly, Edwin uncovered the shrouded doctor and wadded the blanket between his hands. He threw the blanket to Madeline.

She caught it, and unwrapped it enough to flap it down atop the hissing machine, and she beat it again and again, smothering the fire as she struck the mechanical boy. Something broke beneath the sheet, and the chewing tongues of flame devoured the cloth that covered Tanglefoot's joints, leaving only a tragic frame beneath the smoldering covers.

Suddenly and harshly, a bucket of water doused Madeline from behind.

Seconds later she was seized.

Edwin tried to intervene. He divided his attention between the doctor, who cowered against the wall, and the madwoman with the bleeding feet and hair that reeked like cooking trash.

He held up his hands and said, "Don't! No, you can't! No, she was only trying to help!" And he tripped over his own feet, and the pile of steaming clockwork parts on the floor. "No," he cried, because he couldn't speak without choking. "No, you can't take her away. Don't hurt her, please. It's my fault."

Dr Williams was there, and Edwin didn't know when he'd arrived. The smoke was stinging his eyes and the whimpers of Dr Smeeks were distracting his ears, but there was Dr Williams, preparing to administer a washcloth soaked in ether to Madeline's face.

Dr Williams said to his colleague, a burly man who held Madeline's arms behind her back, "I don't know how she escaped this time."

Edwin insisted, "I did it!"

But Madeline gave him a glare and said, "The boy's as daft as his mother. The clockwork boy, it called me, and I destroyed it. I let myself out, like the witch I am and the fiend you think I must be—"

And she might've said more, but the drug slipped up her nostrils and down her chest, and she sagged as she was dragged away.

"No," Edwin gulped. "It isn't fair. Don't hurt her."

No one was listening to him. Not Dr Smeeks, huddled in a corner. Not Madeline, unconscious and leaving. And not the bundle of burned and smashed parts in a pile beneath the book ledge, under a woolen covering. Edwin tried to lift the burned-up blanket but pieces of Ted came with it, fused to the charred fabric.

Nothing moved, and nothing grumbled with malice in the disassembled stack of ash-smeared plates, gears and screws.

Edwin returned to the doctor and climbed up against him, shuddering and moaning until Dr Smeeks wrapped his arms around the boy to say, "There, there. Parker, it's only a little fire. I must've let the crucible heat too long, but look. They're putting it out now. We'll be fine."

The boy's chest seized up tight, and he bit his lips, and he sobbed.

Benedice Te

Jay Lake

Galvezton, Texian Republic, 10 May 1961

Algernon Black-Smith glanced back at the hissing scream of a pressure relief valve to see a great steam ram out of control. Eighteen feet high, twelve feet wide, with burnished copper eagles in relief across the steel airstreamed prow, the vehicle smashed across the electro-guide barrier in the center of the street and rolled toward him with the inevitability of Manifest Destiny.

Scattering wogs like ninepins, Algernon dashed for an open door. He looked behind him as he ran to see the steering bogies of the steam ram twist toward him – someone was trying to kill him! – but the mechanism's momentum was too great. Spewing sparks off the cobbles of Mechanic Street, the ram toppled onto its right side as it swung in his direction, accompanied by the screams of terrified pedestrians and the stench of burning brakes. Algernon stopped in the doorway, horrified yet fascinated, as the huge machine surrendered to Sir Isaac's immutable laws and rolled over the Galvezton foot traffic. Two Papist nuns were caught for a moment, their red faces shrieking within their white wimples, before the careening ram ground them to sludge between the cobbles.

The ram continued to roll, its back end describing an arc with a radius equivalent to the engine's forty or so feet. Horses, mules, men and women: all fell before the mighty wall of metal. White gas lamps lining the electro-way exploded as the sliding ram snapped their poles and gutted their plumbing. It came to rest, frame out, against the block of buildings in which Algernon sheltered. A cloud of damp, heavy dust settled over the entire scene.

Appalled at the carnage, and what was intended to be his starring role therein, Algernon reached up to touch the fresnel lens of the steam ram's vast headlamp, a cyclopean orb vacant of reason.

The warm glass stung his fingertips, bringing Algernon back to himself. Simple prudence and good tradecraft alike dictated a swift retreat from a damaged boiler of that size. As Algernon pushed his way through screaming wogs toward the back of a ragged, stinking little chop house, he wondered which of his friends or enemies wanted to kill him in such a messy, public way. Behind him, escaping steam screeched in a steadily rising wail.

"Mr Black-Smith, the Consul-General will see you now." The butler, an Iberian almost as well comported as an honest Englishman, bowed. The fellow smelled of barley water.

Algernon followed him along marble-tiled halls to a large set of doors, gilded with an inlaid hagiography of precious gems. Her Imperial Majesty's Consulate-General in Galvezton was located in the Bishop's Palace, that worthy having been summarily invited some years earlier by the Royal Marines to remove himself to other quarters. The business was a continuing minor scandal in Mexico City and Rome, but the dignity of the British Empire had been at stake, Galvezton being the largest port in the eastern Americas. It apparently pleased the current Consul-General to retain much of the Papist decor of the place. The hushed quiet and elaborate artwork were a startling contrast to the chaos of yesterday's events.

The butler swung open one door and announced Algernon. "Mr Algernon Black-Smith, British subject, gentleman, bachelor of arts of Balliol College, Oxford, master of laws of the Sorbonne, in Her Imperial Majesty's service without portfolio, paying a courtesy call."

"Eh," grunted the Consul-General. "Come in."

Algernon stepped into the office. The sun glowed through tall stained glass windows in all the colors Spanish art could produce. The thick walls of the Bishop's Palace showed in the depth of the window wells. The room had that strangely gentle scent of paper rot that one found in old mansions.

The Consul-General, Lord Quinnipiac, was a rough-featured man with blue marbled eyes set in a classically aristocratic horsey face. The man possessed every advantage of breeding and position

Algernon so painfully lacked, and so Algernon regarded him with an automatic resentment.

Quinnipiac sat at a scarred worktable, a small mechanism spread before him in pieces. "Ironman," the Consul-General said, renewing his examination of the pieces on the tabletop. Algernon hated that nickname with a passion, but it had followed him from Public School through university and into the Queen's service.

"Sir, the world is broad and wide." It was the opening line of the most ordinary secret recognition phrase used by his branch of Her Imperial Majesty's service.

"One should have stout men by one's side," replied Lord Quinnipiac. That was the most common response. He looked back up from his mechanology project with a toothy smile. "Welcome to my humble abode here in the cloaca of the Texian Republic."

"Sir." Algernon stood at respectful attention. He was newly assigned to Galvezton as Facilitator-in-place for the Confidential Office. The Consul-General was not within Algernon's chain of command, but in every other way that counted, the man stood above Algernon in Her Imperial Majesty's service, and probably always would. If nothing else, he had a claim on Algernon's time and attention by virtue of his office.

Lord Quinnipiac waved the valve cap of a hydraulic pressure line at a copy of the *Galvezton Daily News* resting on one end of his worktable. "Some damned fool has destroyed a valuable steam ram downtown yesterday. Fenian scum, I'll wager, stirring up trouble for the old sod once again. No respect for property. Fecking white wogs, those Irish."

"What sort of ram?" asked Algernon, avoiding the Irish question. What was Lord Quinnipiac telling him, summoning him to the Bishop's Palace just to bring this up? In Algernon's imagination burnished copper eagles screamed with the sound of escaping steam.

Lord Quinnipiac put down the pressure line and picked up the newspaper, shaking it out to study the article. "Ah. No great loss. Colonial make. Olds-Edison Carg-O-Master VI, it would seem." He laughed. "Our Texian friends never seem to tire of buying inferior mechanology for political reasons. If I ruled only three hundred sea miles from the homeport of the French Caribbean Fleet, I would damned well ensure *I* had the best British manufacture in every essential application."

Algernon wanted to leave the subject of the steam ram, but his attempted murder had the fascination of an old bruise. Why the deuce was Quinnipiac going on about it? "How was the engine destroyed? Surely not by happenstance."

Without referring to the paper, Quinnipiac looked Algernon in the eye. "The ram jumped the electro-guide, rolled over and slid across Mechanic Street. Shoved up against a building, then the main boiler blew."

He does know, thought Algernon. *He had something to do with it, somehow. But why?* "Anyone hurt?"

"No sign of the engineer. Some wogs died, but no one of significance."

So we are pretending it wasn't about me. "I presume the newspaper gives a cause for this accident."

The Consul-General's marbled blue eyes peered out of his long, wind-reddened face as he studied Algernon. "No, Mr Black-Smith, it offers no explanation. Do *you* have a theory?"

"No, sir." He didn't dare express his personal interest in the problem. *Let Quinnipiac think him a fool.*

"Very well then." Lord Quinnipiac shrugged, tossing the paper to the floor. "As it happens, I would have you travel to San Antonio de Bexar."

San Antonio de Bexar was the capital of the Texian Republic and seat of the Roman Catholic Church in the Americas. An uneasy relationship at best, Algernon knew. And perfectly well staffed with his colleagues from the Confidential Office. "Sir?"

"The Archbishop and the Mexican throne have conspired to steal certain of Her Imperial Majesty's privy secrets. They have concealed their ill-gotten booty in Texian territory in hopes of throwing us off the scent. This is being handled through my office for reasons of, ah . . . confidentiality." Quinnipiac actually winked at him.

Algernon nodded slowly. The Consul-General was playing an odd game, verbal orders outside the chain of command, no briefing books, no *bona fides* from Algernon's own superiors in the Confidential Office. This stank of high politics.

Quinnipiac continued. "The problems in Boston and London have been dealt with, and we are looking into diplomatic leaks in Her Imperial Majesty's High Commission in San Antonio de

Bexar, but I need someone trustworthy to recover what he can of the documentation."

"I see," said Algernon, who didn't. The steam ram's "accident" had to be connected with this affair. The Consul-General didn't have the right to order Algernon on this wild goose chase, but the other man certainly had the right to *ask* him to pursue it. And it would give Algernon a chance to find out why he'd been so publicly attacked. "I shall depart forthwith, sir."

"Very well. I will send a pneumat-o-graph informing your superiors that you have graciously taken the assignment at my request. You may draw whatever funds you require from my bursar."

The Consul-General returned his attention to the project on the table. Algernon watched him slide cylinders and valves together for a few moments before speaking again. "Sir?"

Lord Quinnipiac looked up, annoyance flashing in his marbled eyes. "You have your orders."

"What have they stolen? For what am I looking?"

"That's an Official Secret, my boy. Afraid I can't tell you. But you'll know it when you see it. There can't be too many of Her Imperial Majesty's Crown Privy Report binders laying about in San Antonio de Bexar."

"Thank you, sir." Algernon bowed, turned to leave. As he approached the double doors, there was a sharp crackle from behind him, then a whoosh as something whined past his shoulder to shatter against the upper panel of the left-hand door. Chips of wood and shards of gem inlay burst into the air. Algernon momentarily shielded his eyes with a forearm, then turned back to the Consul-General.

Lord Quinnipiac held the smallest pistol Algernon had ever seen, the hydraulic pressure line clipped to the butt of its grip. The room reeked of machine oil. "Watch yourself, boy." The Consul-General's expression was flat, devoid of the humor in his voice. "Texas is a dangerous place."

The express train from Galvezton to San Antonio de Bexar passed without stopping through a few small towns, some Anglo-Texian, some Mexican wog, some native wog. Mostly it passed through countless miles of Texas coastal swamp that eventually transitioned to blackland prairie. To Algernon's eye, the landscape had merely exchanged one sullen, grassy aspect for another.

The Texians had not yet constructed the latest generation of ordinator-controlled pneumatic-vacuum underground railroads now common in Europe, so the express only went about eighty miles per hour on surface rails. A zeppelin would have been far more comfortable, but the schedule was inconvenient. Algernon used the hours in his private compartment to wonder who had tried to kill him, and what role Quinnipiac might have held in the affair. *By God*, thought Algernon, *nobody would play him the patsy.*

The crime must be connected with the missing Crown Privy Report binder in San Antonio de Bexar. Even if Quinnipiac wasn't playing him straight, it was unlikely the Consul-General would have directly arranged such a public death for one of Her Imperial Majesty's civil servants. Algernon wondered how accidental Quinnipiac's hydraulic pistol discharge had been. A warning, certainly, not an attempt on his life.

He would never be free of high-born idiots like Quinnipiac interfering with his career. Algernon had been born to a bourgeois family in Baltimore, that self-contradictory capital-in-exile of British Papism. His parents' aspirations had sent him to Public School in New England and on to Oxford, while sending them – eventually – to the poorhouse, much to his great disgrace. Algernon would never live down his middle birth no matter how far he moved up along the fringes of power.

And move up he had. His first mission as one of Her Imperial Majesty's Confidential Office Facilitators had been a virtual death sentence, but Algernon had succeeded against long odds. On his own in the protectorate Buddhist Kingdom of Mongolia he had recovered the Crown of the Bogd Khan from Chinese-backed Kazakh insurgents and single-handedly negotiated the capitulation of Urga to the besieging Royal Marines.

That early and spectacular success had only led him to equally daunting assignments, first in Russian Aleskaya, then in German East Africa, until some higher-up in the Confidential Office realized he was doing too well too soon in his career for one of his undistinguished birth. Since the fall of '59, Algernon had been shunted aside from serious work, relegated to messaging diplomatic bags via steam packet or zeppelin to obscure ports such as Windhoek, Goa and Vancouver. Being sent to Galvezton as Facilitator-in-place had, relatively speaking, seemed a plum job.

However shaky its legitimacy, this new assignment to San Antonio de Bexar would enable Algernon to create a success that could not be ignored. He could put paid to his anonymous enemy and count coup against the nobly titled twits who ran his life.

Smiling, Algernon leaned his head against the window glass to feel the vibration of the train in the bones of his skull. The endless South Texas prairie outside his window offered no further counsel.

San Antonio de Bexar, Texian Republic, 13 May 1961

The Texian capital straddled the San Antonio River. On the north bank stretched the vast complex of the Alamo, old ramified adobe parapets surrounded by soaring glass edifices. The Alamo complex held both the seat of Papist authority in the Western Hemisphere as well as the government of the secular Republic, an uneasy mixed use. The south bank was the secular city, great merchant banks and insurance companies, their twenty-storey granite skytowers connected by a Swiss funicular, the very latest in transportation mechanology. The Mexican High Commission dominated the south bank, facing off the Alamo with a frighteningly misplaced gothic architecture in an echo of old conflicts, complete with an heroic statue of Santa Anna cast from the bronze of captured Texian cannons. Connecting pneumatic and funicular lines raveled all the buildings, as they did in many frontier cities. London at least had the grace to conceal hers beneath the street.

Passing through the city center, the Galvezton Express rolled into the enclosed Estación de Alamo with a scream of brakes and shrieking steam. Algernon disembarked into the close, musky air of the platform, amid wogs shouting at one another in Spanish, French, Indio tongues and some few in English. Texian, Mexican and Church couriers stood by the sealed cars at the back of the train, dashing away one after another with their black-and-red confidential bags. Nowhere amid the chaos did Algernon see anyone from Her Imperial Majesty's government. Unsurprising, if Lord Quinnipiac truly feared leaks in the High Commission here. The Consul-General would scarcely have notified anyone of Algernon's arrival. The implication was clear: Algernon should not try to contact the local facilitator from the Confidential Office, not until he had learned more.

Which was fine. Algernon had always preferred to work on his own, without close supervision. Furthermore, in this case, he had a personal concern – finding his would-be murderer – that was better kept to himself.

He stood on the platform, considering his next move. Algernon had never been to San Antonio de Bexar. After a moment's thought Algernon tipped a waiting wog to take his steamer trunk to the Menger Hotel, just east of the Alamo complex. Valise in hand, he set out to find his counterparts in the Texian government.

"I need to speak to Mr Browning, please."

Algernon faced a female secretary seated at a large desk beneath a Texian seal with the added motto "*Cave Custodem*". The otherwise-empty antechamber smelled of dust and furniture oil. The outer door had proclaimed this the "Bureau of Antiquities". "Antiquities" was the not-very-secret code name the Texians used for their external intelligence service. Every Texian High Commission in the world had an antiquities attaché. Doors to each side of the desk were labeled "Exports" and "Imports".

"*¿Como?*"

God help me, thought Algernon, *it was a white wog*. He could have sworn the woman was European.

"Señor Browning, *por favor.*" His Spanish didn't go very far.

The woman shook her head.

"Really?" Algernon set his valise on her desk, opened the snaps. The female wog watched with interest.

There were good reasons women were generally not considered employable within the Empire, Algernon fumed. With the exception of Her Imperial Majesty, of course. Asking for Mr Browning was supposed to gain admittance to the offices of friendly intelligence services, assuming one knew how to find them. Leaving again was another matter entirely.

Algernon removed a miniature daguerreograph from his bag. It was of the latest mechanology from the Lucas Works in England, quite small at perhaps six inches long with a narrow barrel. Holding the pistol grip, he sighted the daguerreograph at the secretary.

"*¡No!*" she yelled, diving under the desk.

The daguerreograph clicked as it impressed a daguerreotype of her empty chair. Algernon pulled out the plate and quickly inserted another. He aimed it at the seal this time, centering on the star in the middle.

A door hidden in the paneled wall behind the desk opened. "Come in, Mr Black-Smith," said a tall, dapper man with broad shoulders. Algernon was quite startled to see Istvan Szagy. Szagy was from a cadet branch of an important Austro-Hungarian noble family. He had been a year ahead of Algernon at Choate, and prefect in his house, as well as a role model for Algernon, at least between canings, buggeries and other assorted Public School torments. Algernon vaguely recalled that Szagy had planned to go into the import-export business. Szagy's English was, as always, flawless. "Mr Browning will see you now."

Algernon impressed a daguerreotype of Istvan Szagy in the doorway before he lowered the miniature daguerreograph and followed him through.

"Was it necessary to threaten to shoot Carmella?"

"Was it necessary to have a wog at the front door who can't speak a Christian tongue?"

Istvan sat at a small desk topped with files, binders and a film reader. "Spanish *is* a Christian tongue, Algernon. I should make an effort not to forget that if I were spending time here."

Algernon studied Istvan Szagy. Ten years out of Choate, Szagy still had his upperclassman's body, slim-waisted and pale. The familiar shock of blond hair showed no gray yet, but there were lines around the man's verdigris eyes. "What are you doing in Texian service, Istvan?"

"Roughly the same thing you are doing in Her Imperial Majesty's, I imagine." Istvan's smile was tight-lipped. "And what brings you to the lovely San Antonio de Bexar?"

They were deep within the bowels of the Alamo, in a windowless office chilly from the thick inner walls of the fortress. Algernon was acutely aware that if he never walked out of the Bureau of Antiquities the world would be no wiser. "I've an errand to run for Lord Quinnipiac."

There. He had established his high-level sponsorship. A flimsy form of insurance, but stronger than none.

"One of Mr Browning's errands?"

"Yes." Algernon paused, then added, "as well as a little business of my own."

"Interesting. Well, you'd hardly start roaching on the Republic by walking in here first. And I cannot imagine you stirring up trouble for us on your own account."

"No. Assuming it wasn't you that stirred up trouble for me in the first place."

In the strained silence that followed, Algernon scanned Istvan's desk. It was the desk of a man tasked with too many objectives: overflowing with maps, messages and files, rings of tea stains stretching across entire archaeologies of paper. The initials "I.S." appeared on so many of them that this obviously wasn't an office borrowed just to interview him. Furthermore, a bottle of Istvan's favorite brandy, well remembered by Algernon from their Public School days, rested on a sideboy.

"The Texian Republic has had no interest in you . . . up to now," Szagy finally said. "In the meantime, kindly stop reading my correspondence or I shall be forced to have you shot."

"Why don't you use an ordinator?" Algernon looked up to meet his host's eyes with a small smile. It was like being back at Choate all over again – the camaraderie, the threats. "All this filing, all this reading."

"Don't like having the damned things around. Besides, something that costly is beyond the scope of our legislative appropriation. Her Imperial Majesty may have all the money in the Bank of England, but us Texians live and die by cotton, cattle and crude oil. Most of which we sell to you."

"Perhaps I can help." Algernon knew that two Mark VII Lovelace units were gathering dust in the cellars of the Bishop's Palace in Galvezton, having been replaced by newer devices straight out of the boffin works at Bletchley Park.

"And why would you do that?"

"The Mexican Throne has something belonging to Her Imperial Majesty. Lord Quinnipiac believes it to be concealed here in San Antonio de Bexar. *Quid pro quo.*"

"And what would that 'something' be?"

"A Privy Report binder."

"Lord Quinnipiac wouldn't tell you what was in it, eh?" Istvan laughed. He pulled a sheet of type-impressed foolscap from under a smashed Krupp machine pistol cast in bronze. "Got a pneu directly from H.I.M.'s Consulate-General in Galvezton a few hours before you came. I decided to hold it back from my superiors to see what might turn up. You, in this case."

Istvan handed the pneumat-o-graph to Algernon, who read the hand transcription from a presumably cryptogrammed original.

::: HIM-CG-GALVZ TO REPTEX-ANTIQ-SADBXR ::: STOP : ALGERNON BLACK-SMITH A-K-A IRONMAN IN TRANS TO SADBXR : STOP : ARMED-DANGEROUS : STOP : APPREHEND IN STRICTEST SECRECY HOLD FOR H-I-M GOVT : STOP : ALL REQUIRED FORCE AUTHIZED : STOP : REPLY ONLY THIS OFC : STOP ::: LORD QUINN : HIM-CG-GALVZ :::

"Ridiculous," said Algernon. "I am not armed." His chest felt cold and tight. Clearly, it was Quinnipiac who had tried to have him killed. *Why?* Was the binder real, or some other plot afoot? "I see," he muttered.

"No, you don't, unless you're a damn sight smarter than I am, which I know from Choate that you are not." Istvan smiled more broadly and a produced a derringer from his desk drawer. "Oh, and, by the way, I place you under arrest in the name of the Republic of Texas."

Algernon carefully laid both hands flat on the front edge of Istvan's desk. "Very well. Now what?"

"Now we go for a short walk."

Algernon had taken more than a few people for "short walks" in his career. He knew what that usually meant. He could smell the sudden, sharp odor of his own fear.

The Swiss-built funicular car lurched away from the Dillardo's building, home to the largest group of shops in the Republic. Algernon sat gripping his valise, staring out at the skytowers. The car was roughly the shape of a bullet, windowed all around with glass except for the automated mechanology enclosed within the roof-spine. It hung from cables strung in tandem with the pneumatic lines that drove the car. Despite the modernity of the design, the interior had the familiar public transit smell of old shoes and hydraulic fluid.

Istvan had cleared the car by the simple expedient of showing a fare inspector's badge. Now they were alone high above the ground, lurching from tower to tower on the long haul from Dillardo's to the Zoological Gardens east of the city. The derringer was no longer in evidence, but Algernon wondered if Istvan planned to drop him onto the railroad tracks as they crossed.

"Even our best recorders do not work well up here," said Istvan. "That was a treasonous statement I just made, by the way."

This is it, then. Algernon imagined the plunge from the funicular car, the scream he would be unable to bottle in, the wind whipping across his ears like the slaps of his childhood governess. "So what are we doing here?"

"Speaking in the most secrecy I can manage on the spur of the moment." Istvan grinned, his natural bully's smile Algernon remembered so well from Choate. "Far away from unfriendly ears both Texian and Papist in that damned Alamo rat palace. There's a question I want to ask in privacy. Consider this, Ironman: why would Lord Quinnipiac send a pneu directly to the Bureau of Antiquities and not go through H.I.M.'s High Commission here in San Antonio de Bexar? Especially a pneu as sensitive as a termination order for one of Her Imperial's more successful field agents?"

"Because the bastard wants to kill me!" Algernon shouted, pounding his fist against the glass wall of the car. This would be a stupid way to die, at Istvan's hands. He whirled, stalking down the length of the car, his frustration having finally gotten the better of him. "And I don't even know why. Quinnipiac told me he suspects corruption here, complicity in the matter of the missing Privy Report. But someone tried to kill me in Galvezton two days ago. Quinnipiac made it clear he knew all about it before sending me on this snipe hunt. A steam ram jumped the electro-guides and nearly ran me down."

"No harm done, eh?" asked Istvan. "Maybe a few wogs got squashed?"

Leaning against two of the iron ribs of the car, Algernon stared down at a landscape of cottonwoods and pecans as the funicular lurched closer to the zoological gardens. It could have been him ground to paste between the cobbles, like screaming nuns. But it hadn't been. "No, no harm, I suppose."

"No harm. They're just wogs," said Istvan. "*That's* why I work here. Wogs are people too. Texas is a far cry from Budapest, London or Boston, but wogs *are* people here. Her Imperial Majesty has them snuffed out like candles at the first inconvenience. Suddenly, you're Quinnipiac's candle. How does it feel to be a white wog, Ironman?"

The car lurched past another cable tower. Algernon began whispering to the glass. "I've used a Thompson gun to force askaris forward against German armor in Tanganyika. In 1955, I threw Kazakh women over the walls of Urga. I once drove an entire Inupiat village to overrun Russian artillery. We do what we must, Istvan, to maintain order in the world, and the supremacy of the British Crown. You may be right about the wogs, but regardless of that I have my sworn duty." He stopped, gathering his words. *Duty*, thought Algernon. Duty, even in the face of attack by his superiors. Was this what he continued to struggle for? An early death for someone else's political convenience?

Algernon turned away from the window to face Istvan again. "I don't understand something. Lord Quinnipiac could have had me killed in Galvezton without difficulty. Why send me to you?"

Istvan nodded, as if he had following the same line of thought. "I have reason to believe the stolen Privy Report is real, not a cover story. Perhaps he wants your death to contribute to whatever is momentous about that document. You would make excellent cover for a plot – a man of proven ability and ambition, resentfully believing he'd been denied advancement due to his station of birth."

"I *have* been denied advancement. I will overcome that handicap in time. That's the price I pay for being an Englishman." He smiled toothsomely at Istvan. "There is no finer fate on God's earth. Now, let me ask you a treasonous question of my own. Do you know what is in the report?"

"With luck, we both will soon." Istvan stood to open the door of the funicular car to the ringing of a safety bell. "We exit here."

They were still high above the ground.

Algernon was not afraid of falling, in the usual sense. He swam for sport, and had jumped from some stern cliffs while on seaside holidays. Istvan, though, had grabbed Algernon's arms and simply shoved him from the car, valise and all. As Algernon fell, he was pleased to realize he was not screaming. He was surprised to see Istvan leave the car to fall above him, pacing Algernon in his descent.

Istvan called out to Algernon, but his words were lost in the wind. Somehow, Istvan looked less alarmed than Algernon felt. Algernon twisted his body to see a quarry lake approaching very rapidly. He released his valise and tucked into a dive just before impact.

It was like being beaten with hammers. The flat slap of the water tore at every joint in his body even as he cleaved the surface. Algernon twisted, arcing out of his sharp drop to avoid what was doubtless a rocky bottom. His lungs felt collapsed by the impact, and all he could see was a murky green. Algernon had no idea where the surface was. His head ached from the impact with the water and he could not find his balance. His nose stung with the itch of water forced into his sinuses.

Algernon began to kick, just to establish direction and get himself out of the cloud of bubbles that had followed him into the water. He still couldn't tell where the surface was. His lungs stung while his mouth threatened to swell open and breathe in the entire lake. Red flashes of panic overwhelmed his murky vision of the world.

Something grabbed his ankle. Algernon tried to scream, caught himself in time, and kicked with his free foot. He was being pulled down, pulled under. His red flashes were going to black. Algernon knew he was about to drown as a hand caught his collar and pulled him to the surface.

"Good God, man!" Treading water, Istvan shook his collar. "You lettered in aquatics at Choate. Keep your head next time!"

Algernon coughed, then spat, choking on lake water and gratitude. Following Istvan's lead, he swam toward one of the bounding cliffs.

They shook off the worst of the lake water inside a pocket cave at the waterline of one of the quarry walls. Somehow Istvan had also saved Algernon's valise, though it was soaked. His papers were certainly ruined. Perhaps the daguerreograph could be salvaged.

"What was the purpose of that?" Algernon asked. The plunge and his subsequent soaking had driven the temper right out of him, restoring his rightful analytical perspective.

Istvan took off one shoe, dumping water and sludge. "I don't do it very often, for reasons that should be clear. Not to mention it would eventually be noticed. But you have disappeared."

"From whom? Certainly not you."

"Mexicans. Papists. British. Perhaps even elements of my own government." Istvan took off his other shoe. "Whoever wants you dead. I fear what may happen if the Republic is implicated in this growing British scandal."

"You're going to a lot of trouble for me."

"I'm going to a lot of trouble for Texas. That it benefits a fellow Choate alum and a British gentleman is mere lagniappe."

"Thank you, nonetheless."

"Think nothing of it."

They rose, Algernon now holding his dripping valise. Istvan led him to the back of the cave where he opened a hidden door. A narrow corridor lit by a few white gas lamps trailed into a dim distance.

The Bureau of Antiquities had a large complex in the cave system just east of San Antonio de Bexar. Algernon was impressed at the effort to which the colonials had gone, although it was more understandable with European nobility such as Istvan on their staff.

As they walked along, Istvan explained that the cave complex had its own electrical dynamos and hydraulic pumps. Water was drawn from the quarry lake, while fuel and hydraulic pressure were brought in from city mains. What surprised Algernon was the degree and sophistication of the miniaturized mechanology all around him.

"Look," said Istvan, leading them to an equipment room. He handed Algernon a sealed wooden box about the size of a loaf of bread. "This is a self-contained Stirling engine. It drives an electromagnetic emitter. A man could carry this inside a common valise or dispatch case and report his whereabouts and activities by wireless, from a distance of perhaps several hundred yards. This will bring our tradecraft into the twentieth century!"

"I've never see the like," said Algernon.

"Of course not." Istvan's smile was tight again. "It was designed and built by wog boffins on staff here."

"Wog boffins." Algernon shook his head. *What was the world coming to?*

"And here . . ." Istvan picked up a pistol about the size of the one Lord Quinnipiac had fired at Algernon, but lacking a hose clipped to the butt of the grip. "We've been working on miniature high-pressure vessels for steam efficiency. That's produced some side benefits." He chambered a round. "Super-compressed air. Not as efficient as ordinary gunpowder, but portable, unlike hydraulics, and much quieter. Perfectly fine for short work and doesn't tip off gunpowder-sniffing dogs."

Istvan fired the gun into the wooden cladding at the far wall of the underground room. Splinters flew with a sharp thump, but there was no echoing report whatsoever.

"I suppose you've got ordinators down here too," said Algernon.

Istvan smiled big again. "L'Argent Internationale, the best Paris will export. Two metric tons of fine-tuned Continental mechanology."

Algernon thought again of the Lovelaces stored down in Galvezton. They were a fraction of the capability of the Texians' froggie L.A.I., but at a fraction of the size and cost as well. Her Imperial Majesty's ordinator boffins, whom the yobs called "stackers", were combining small, cheap units to do the work of a bigloom like Istvan's L.A.I. "I thought you didn't have the budget for ordinators."

"In the office, on the congressional budget, no. Down here, on the President's privy budget, it's a different tale entirely. Furthermore, no prying eyes and ears here except our own." Istvan laid the gas pistol back down on the table. "Enough. I believe I've made my point."

"The Texian Bureau of Antiquities is the equal of anything I've seen outside of England," admitted Algernon, though it pained him to say it. *And I am safe here,* he thought.

Coward.

They left the equipment room.

In the briefing room where their walk ended, Algernon found his steamer trunk atop a conference table. The gaslights were wicked up to a brightness that rendered the brasswork on his luggage difficult to look at. The room was hot and close despite being enclosed in damp stone. A small, dark wog in a passable imitation of a Savile Row suit stood behind the trunk.

"Mr Black-Smith," said Istvan, "allow me to present Señor Browning of the Imperial Mexican Security Directorate."

"Call me Oswaldo," said Señor Browning in a perfect Boston accent. He nodded his head slightly at Algernon. "Harvard, sir. Forgive me if I do not mention the year."

Istvan had gone on to Harvard as well. The old-boy network would explain this unlikely cooperation between rivals. Almost as unlikely as Istvan's cooperation with him.

"My trunk," said Algernon. "How did it get here?"

"Señor Browning and I often cooperate on matters of mutual interest," replied Istvan. "He received a tip about your property and had it diverted by his agents in the railway baggage service."

Thus keeping Istvan's hands clean, Algernon thought. Istvan really was keeping a low profile on this affair.

"Would you care to open it?" asked Oswaldo. "Slowly, please."

Algernon found the keys inside his soaked valise. He inspected the trunk carefully. His hand-signs were missing – the small hairs he routinely trapped in the hinges missing, the aligning scratches on the brightwork where the locking tongue folded up. Algernon checked along the bottom edge for a small nick the trunk had acquired from shrapnel in Russian Aleskaya. The scars on his thigh twinged in sympathy at the thought, while the trunk's brass binding was smooth.

"This is not my trunk, gentlemen," he said. "An excellent copy, but not mine."

Istvan folded his arms and leaned against the doorway. "Are you sure? It appears to have your tag on it, and the appropriate shipping labels."

"Wouldn't you know *your* own?" Algernon asked. "However, I will open it." He inserted the key and turned it slowly. The lock clicked open, then the locking tongue popped out. Algernon flipped up the clasps. "Ready?"

Istvan and Oswaldo nodded.

He raised the lid. Inside was the small tray he used, with his shaving kit, shoe kit, and various personal possessions. Algernon inspected the tray with care. It appeared to be the tray from his original trunk. He lifted it out to reveal folded clothes.

After fully unpacking the trunk and laying the contents out on the conference table, Algernon did a quick inventory. "Curious. I am missing a pair of wool suit pants, two shirts and a pair of shoes."

"The trunk," said Oswaldo. "May I?"

Algernon looked at Istvan, who shrugged.

Oswaldo began to examine the trunk with painstaking care. He patted the lid, the sides, the bottom, then shifted the trunk in place so it rested on its back. "Do you routinely have a false bottom on your trunk, Mister Black-Smith?"

"No."

"You do now. Perhaps that is why some of your clothing is missing." Oswaldo produced a bowie knife, at which Istvan seemed startled. "¿Con su permiso?" he asked, then immediately began to cut at the lining.

A Crown Privy Report binder tumbled out of the bottom of Algernon's trunk, the gold-tooled 'E.R.' plainly visible on the red leather cover.

Oswaldo smiled. "Someone is quite the humorist. Your Lord Quinnipiac, I assume."

As Algernon stared horrified at this evidence of his apparent treason, Istvan picked up the binder and opened it.

"It's blank," the Texian agent said. He riffed through. "All the pages are blank."

The three of them sat for hours in the same briefing room, having long since exhausted small talk as their tea cooled. The trunk and all its contents had been removed for forensic analysis, while another Texian team worked on the Crown Privy Report binder itself. Istvan had refused to leave until they verified more details about the book. Oswaldo Browning remained as well, for the same reasons. The scent of the quarry lake intensified as Algernon's legs chafed in his damp trousers. *Answers*, he thought, *we are approaching some answers*.

Gröning, the lead forensic analyst, finally came in with a set of onionskin charts rolled up beneath his arms. The analyst was a classic Junker Prussian – riding boots, tight uniform jacket, arrogant. His rumpled white lab coat did little to soften his demeanor.

"Here is what we have found," Gröning said, a Mitteleuropan accent harsh on his voice. He set the charts on the table. "Nothing in the trunk, nothing on the trunk, nothing in or on the clothes. The book, however, his pages are odd."

"How?" asked Algernon as all eyes in the room turned toward him.

"He consists of two hundred and fifty-six pages of high-rag paper. This is a very fine grade of handmade paper, as one might expect for use by the Queen. However, the grain of the pages varies. Some are cut and bound long grain, some cross grain, and a few at odd angles. This is very unusual, largely for esthetic reasons, but also printing and manufacturing inefficiencies. Further, each page has differing and somewhat random watermarks covering an unusually large area of the paper."

"What does that mean?" asked Istvan.

"We have no idea." Gröning patted the charts. "Here is a detail showing the grain orientation on each page. I have also included diagrams of the watermarks on the first ten pages."

After Gröning left, the three of them pored over the analyst's diagrams. "Could the differing grain be a cryptogram?" asked Algernon. He was a field man, this was boffin work, but his life had been placed at stake against this mystery.

Oswaldo shook his head. "No. There are only two hundred and fifty-six examples of perhaps six distinct paper types – long grain, short grain and several angled grain variations. It would be dramatically inefficient to have produced this entire book for such small a cryptogrammatic base. Not enough information could be embedded."

The chart copies of the binder page watermarks were no more revealing. They were a collection of erratic squiggles that wandered across the pages. On any given page they had an apparent baseline, but the baselines varied their angle on each of the first ten pages.

"Look," said Algernon. "Some of them have distinct boundaries. Page seven, for example. You could lay a straight edge across here and none of the squiggles would extend past it."

The copies of the watermarks were on the same onionskin as

the charts of the book layout. Oswaldo tore page seven off, about the size of a calling card, and held it up to the light. "Here," he said handing it to Algernon, "see what you make of it."

Algernon held it up to the light, turned it back and forth. The squiggles looked familiar. He picked up the chart with the other pages, and laid the squiggles over each page one by one, holding the combined papers up to the bright gaslights.

"Aha . . ." Algernon tore page one, a long grain page, out, and held it up to the light against page four, the next long grain page. He twisted them together. "If you take two succeeding pages with the same grain and align the watermarks along *their* respective baselines instead of the page's baseline, you get . . . Greek. There is a message, written in the Greek alphabet, broken up in the watermarks." He peered at the words. "I can't make sense of it, but this is a hasty hand copy. If we did this same thing to the original pages, we'd get the Greek letters copied down correctly."

"Thank you, Algernon," said Istvan. "I have a perfectly competent cryptogrammatics section. I'll pull them onto this."

Once the Greek letters were deciphered, they turned out to be in cryptogrammatic groups that corresponded to a standard Imperial British series. Algernon spent his time in the Texian caverns bothering the cryptogrammarians at their work and playing with what toys his keepers would allow him to touch in the equipment rooms, always shadowed by one of several large, sulking minders. Those minders were wogs of various sorts, a none-too-subtle message from Istvan that Algernon couldn't quite bring himself to resent. He disliked the forced inaction, but consoled himself with the thought that they were making progress in the mystery of the binder, and therefore, the attempt on his life.

Istvan came back three days later, finding Algernon at lunch in the refectory. He dismissed Algernon's current minder. Algernon knew something had happened with the binders – there was excitement in the caves that morning, whispered conversations that broke off at his approach – but he had no idea what it meant yet.

"They've cracked it," said Istvan, sitting down across the table.

Algernon picked at some stewed beef tips that smelled much better than they looked. That the Texians could crack an Imperial code was not actually good news, but he was still glad to learn something. "What have the boffins found?"

"Engineering data, apparently."

"Engineering data?"

Istvan had a lab report in his hand. He offered it to Algernon. "Here, what do you make of this?"

Algernon looked at the report, flipping through the pages. "It appears to be an abstract describing the theory and practice of finely wrought mechanology, smaller than the eye can see. Miniature steam engines, other machines using fluidic and mechanic principles, that might perform work in microscale. My God . . ." He put the report down. This *was* the sort of thing people were killed for, without a second thought. "How did this ever leave London?"

"And wind up in a colonial town like San Antonio de Bexar?" Istvan had his tight smile again. "We were hoping you might know."

"*I* didn't bring it!"

"One of our theories is that you and Lord Quinnipiac set us up to crack the secret of the book for you, along with the codes, so you could exploit the information to your own mutual ends. As traitors to the Crown, presumably. I don't happen to believe that, but the President favors the idea."

"The President?"

"We could go to war with the British Empire over your little red book, Algernon. This microscale mechanology is the greatest invention since the steam engine, perhaps since gunpowder. Why would Lord Quinnipiac have set you up with it?"

"He couldn't have wanted me to break the cryptogram," said Algernon. "Especially not with your help, begging your pardon. That doesn't make sense. My guess is that he had previously misappropriated the Crown Privy Report binder and wanted it to come back in his hands legitimately."

"If we had picked you up as asked and returned you, he could have 'discovered' it in your trunk," Istvan pointed out.

Algernon's chest felt cold and tight again. "What have you said to him about me?"

"That we're holding you pending an internal investigation."

"True enough." Algernon shook his head. "Miniaturized mechanology. Think of the implications for our tradecraft."

"Medicine," replied Istvan promptly. "Ordinational science. Communications. All of it. The betterment of the human condition."

"Whoever owns this will own the world," whispered Algernon. Right now, that was Istvan.

"Who do you suppose it was that did the original research?"

Algernon considered that. "Last year there was a firebombing at a research consortium in Geneva. They were said to be building long-range rockets. It's no great secret that the Confidential Office has committed attacks like that before – preventative scientific intelligence."

"So some of your lads may have destroyed the lab where this miniature mechanology was being developed."

Algernon nodded, drumming his fingers on the lab binder. "Otherwise, why wouldn't they already be out with this? If it already exists, it couldn't be hidden for long. These notes are only a summary of a well-researched mechanology. Enough to reproduce the basic work, but the supporting detail is certainly not all here. Good God, the patents alone would fill shelves."

"So you believe Lord Quinnipiac wants this for his own?"

Algernon thought back to the small hydraulic pistol in the Consul-General's hand, and the fascination with mechanology that hobby bespoke. "Yes. It has to be him. No one else could have arranged everything that has happened. He set up the steam ram accident in Galvezton – had it been successful, he could have 'discovered' the binder in my personal effects, and returned it with no one the wiser as to whether he had previously copied the research.

"Two accidents in succession would have been too obvious, so he sent me off to you on a wild goose chase. If I had somehow succeeded in recovering the book on my own, he would have gotten it back from me. If I failed, he would have gotten the book from you, simply from your efforts to avoid an international incident. My arrest as a traitor, or even my death, would have caused little comment in Boston or London. Then, set up his own boffin works and . . ." Algernon trailed off. *What if Quinnipiac had already set up his works?* "It must have seemed failure-proofed to him."

What if I set up my own works?

"I will try to convince our President of your version of the story. In the meantime, think of a way you and I can deal with Lord Quinnipiac without creating a *casus belli* between our nations."

San Luis Pass, Texian Republic, 17 May 1961

The zeppelin *RTS Mirabeau Lamar* cruised eastward from San Antonio de Bexar toward Galvezton. Algernon looked down at the scrubby South Texas landscape, an echo of his train trip the previous week.

They were using the Presidential zeppelin, a top-of-the-line luxury cruiser from Zeppelin Werk GmbH in Greater Germany, and it was appointed accordingly. Texian cedar paneled the walls, giving the cabins inside the gondola a frontier look, along with a gentle odor dissonant with the high-mechanology transport. Puma and wolf-skin rugs dominated the lounge, at the feet of huge chairs made from cattle and deer horns. The galley seemed capable of producing only inedible fried foods or a terrifying chili. The entire airship stank of refried beans, a food for which Algernon had never cared. He longed for a good boiled English dinner.

Istvan was dressed as a papist cleric, allegedly on the staff of the Papal Nuncio to the Texian Republic. Lord Quinnipiac expected to meet them at San Luis Pass, the channel on the south-western end of Galvezton Island. A lighthouse sat on the lonely windswept point, marking this distant south-western entrance to Galvezton Bay. Istvan had sent pneus explaining the Nuncio's alleged offer to broker the handoff of the English traitor.

Algernon smiled. He would have vengeance on Quinnipiac for his assaults, and put paid to the problem of the stolen Privy Report at the same time.

As the open water of Galvezton Bay slid past below the belly of the zeppelin, Istvan patted Algernon on the shoulder. "We are almost here."

"And you believe that Lord Quinnipiac will allow himself to be separated from his Royal Marines?"

"We must try," said Istvan. "His greed will work for us."

Algernon watched the red-brick lighthouse come into view. San Luis Pass was a narrow neck of water between two sand spits. The lighthouse stood on the Galvezton Island side of the pass, presiding over little more than chopping waves and wheeling gulls. Algernon spotted a roseate spoonbill following the surf line, pink plumage visible against the greenish white roil of the Gulf of Mexico.

At the base of the lighthouse a sand-wheeled steam ram was parked, puffing desultory smoke from its stacks. It had two sand-wheeled cars hitched behind it, and a squad of Royal Marines deployed around it in their green battledress. *Lord Quinnipiac has come expecting a fight*, thought Algernon. *We shall give it to him, but not what he planned for.*

The zeppelin came about to beat against the sea breeze toward the lighthouse. Algernon heard the great engines straining. Shouted commands accompanied the release of the field mooring line from its nose cowling. The marines on the ground below scrambled to retrieve the cable, then worked to secure it to the bulk of the steam ram. The zeppelin's captain kept the engines running at open throttle to fight the wind and keep strain off the mooring line.

"There's Quinnipiac," said Istvan, pointing to a figure in black tails who climbed out of the second car. "I'll go wave him up."

The captain drove the zeppelin, shuddering in the wind, down toward the lighthouse until their altitude was perhaps a hundred feet. Algernon could hear Istvan at the hatch, shouting. He could no longer see the Royal Marines or Lord Quinnipiac directly below him. The zeppelin bobbed in the wind. The chuffing click of a winch below decks was surely the crew winding Lord Quinnipiac up in a bosun's chair.

"So . . ." Lord Quinnipiac paced the deck, heedless of the animal skins beneath his feet. "Mr Black-Smith, you are being returned to us."

Istvan kept his head down, hands folded. Algernon noticed his old friend worked his rosary. Keeping his own hands behind his back as if bound, Algernon said nothing.

Lord Quinnipiac addressed Istvan. "I understand Her Imperial Majesty's, ah, item, is being returned with the traitor?"

Istvan nodded, opening the door behind him and stepping backward. Algernon shifted his hands behind his back, making sure his finger was on the trigger.

Istvan walked back in the room with the Crown Privy Report binder. Handing it to Lord Quinnipiac, Istvan slipped and dropped the binder on the floor between them.

"Gods, man, have a care," said Quinnipiac as he knelt to pick up the red leather book. Istvan bent from the waist to reach down and grabbed the book at the same time. Algernon brought the miniature daguerreograph up from behind his back and pressed a daguerreotype of Lord Quinnipiac, kneeling in front of a Papist official in full regalia, transferring control of a Crown Privy Report binder.

At the sound of the daguerreograph's click, Quinnipiac looked up at Algernon. "Damn your eyes!" The Consul-General swore, and dropped the book again to lunge for Algernon. Istvan tackled him from behind in best Choate rugby fashion.

Algernon kicked Quinnipiac in the side of the head, to accelerate their discussion. He got down on the floor and stared into Quinnipiac's marbled blue eyes. "Listen, sir. We've got a daguerreotype of you kneeling to a Papist with Crown secrets in your hand. I'll make sure that image is never released if you'll drop this business about me stealing the Crown Privy Report binder. I'll courier the binder to the Viceroy in Boston, give you the credit for recovery, and we'll all look good. Or you can try to ruin me while I succeed in ruining you." He and Istvan were banking on Quinnipiac's self-interest.

Quinnipiac strained against Istvan's hold on him. "And let you have what's in that thing? Are you mad?"

"The damned thing is a blank book and you know it," snapped Algernon, hoping the Consul-General would take that bait in the distraction of the moment. "I'll never know why you made such a fuss, but by God, sir, you shan't murder me for empty pages."

Quinnipiac suddenly relaxed, a small smile stealing across his face before he began to chuckle. "Well, lad, you know just looking at one of those books is treason, to which you've now admitted."

With an immense sense of relief, Algernon removed the plate from the daguerreograph. He placed it in the inside pocket of his morning coat. "You have admitted the same, sir. We can both fall or prosper on your word here."

"The game is done, then." Quinnipiac glared up at Istvan. "Let me up, man. You're no more a Papist than I am."

"*Benedice te*," said Istvan, pulling Quinnipiac to his feet with an armlock.

Algernon retreated to the galley to avoid further tempting the Consul-General as Istvan continued to whisper quiet threats. Honor had been satisfied, and the problem of the binder solved, with his skin still whole. Algernon knew he should be pleased.

"Naturally you have a copy of everything," said Algernon later.

Istvan smiled his broad smile. "Naturally I can't tell you that."

"They'll know the book's been tampered with."

Istvan shrugged. "You recovered it, you're a hero. We've sent official commendations for you via pneu to the High Commissioner in San Antonio de Bexar and to your Viceroy in Boston. That should cause some confusion if Quinnipiac gets snarky clever in his reporting."

What if Quinnipiac has a secret boffin works already set up, Algernon wanted to ask, *working on this miniature mechanology?* He didn't dare say that – he knew Istvan had the same thought, Istvan knew Algernon did, but if they kept silent about it, they could part friends.

Algernon watched the Texas countryside fall away. The zeppelin headed for Nouveau Orleans, capital of French America. He would report to the Consulate-General there, fairly safe from Quinnipiac's interference, and be sent on to Boston, and maybe even London, as a hero.

"Or we could keep it all for ourselves," he whispered. *Set up our own works.*

"No," said Istvan. "Duty to the Crown, old friend. If you ran off empire-building with that stuff, you'd just be another white wog."

Algernon patted the red leather book. "Then it's a damned good thing God made me an Englishman."

Istvan made the sign of the cross. "*Benedice te*," he said.

I will be back, Algernon thought, *hunting Quinnipiac's secrets, and maybe Istvan's as well. I will be back.* "Thank you, Istvan. I may need your blessings."

Five Hundred and Ninety-Nine

Benjanun Sriduangkaew

In the morning they burned the last farang corpses.

Some of the children made a game of this, lobbing Molotov cocktails in amber and green, making bets. Who would catch fire first, that slavering pervert from Angrit, that wife-beater from Australia, that pedophile from Canada who bought boys in Soi Pratuchai?

They all burned equally well, fat sizzling in the air, hair crisping with foul odors, cologne and grooming products. Nathamol watched, and was not sorry.

A pick-up came to collect soon-to-be carrion; with mask and gloves on, Nathamol supervised the loading. Beyond the boundaries they would be deposited for the glass storms and murdering clouds, and turn to nothing very much, their prestigious citizenship going to dust with them. Only Thai ID chips mattered these days. She had seen women turning hard-worn first-world passports in their hands before dropping them into garbage compactors or pyres. Useless now; useless forever.

Before the war Muangthai and America were excellent friends; the latter proved this by putting its soldiers in Krungthep's streets, spy-chips in Krungthep's skyscrapers, and data-mining trojan on websites Thai citizens frequented. Certain parts of Muangthai after all were so very Chinese in blood if not in name, not least of them Krungthep itself, and America must protect everyone against Chinese interests. The government smiled collectively, quietly migrated to Russian administrative software known for being proof against snooping, and life went on. China and Muangthai remained on amicable grounds.

The situation was growing fraught by then. Zodiacally it was a tiger year, and everyone knew tigers gobbled up everything. Earthquakes, flash floods, hurricanes, a presidential election that went badly in America: some were blamed on Chinese sabotage. Nathamol could not conceive how an entire government decided such a conclusion was reasonable. Perhaps the Hollywood blockbusters were right – she had always gotten the impression that America was ruled by uninterrupted lines of war-mongering psychopaths.

"War's what they froth at the mouth for," her room-mate Rinnapha said over little Japanese cakes and orange tea, in a Siam Square café. "It's how they went deep into debt. All that money thrown at military research while their people go hungry and homeless in the streets."

"We're deep in debt too," Kwankaew pointed out dryly, "and if we weren't up to the nostrils in farang spies we'd be throwing trillions into weapons development, same as anyone else."

Under the chill of air conditioners at full blast and unable to imagine a day where electricity wouldn't be abundant, Nathamol tried to keep pace with the conversation. She was – knew herself to be – dreadfully apolitical, with no real opinion on anything. Usually this made her a fine listener, but in the company of her vocal friends she always felt lacking, like she should be contributing insight or at least passion.

Nathamol set down her forkful of cheesecake and edged her way into conversation. "Have you heard from your cousin in Los Angeles, Som?"

Rinnapha's forehead creased. "It's been weeks since the last email. Funny, Pim used to call every day. Didn't want us getting worried. I hope she gets back soon." Two soldiers sat down at the next table, blond and splotchy from Krungthep heat. Without missing a beat Rinnapha switched to beautiful, pitch-perfect Angrit: "But America's a country of murderous lunatics, I've *no* idea why she wanted to visit."

The soldiers scowled. Nathamol hissed, "Som, in Thai, please."

Rinnapha laughed.

A month after that they found out Pimnapha had been murdered, one of the casualties at her campus. An attack that left students and personnel looking even faintly East Asian dead; an attack that repeated elsewhere, in hotels and hospitals, in so many cities and airports throughout that glittering land where Hollywood stars and post-modern cathedrals lived.

The work of a fringe supremacist group, a green-eyed CNN newscaster said, looking mournful and serious. They watched this announcement together in their dorm room; Rinnapha's mouth became thinner and thinner, her knuckles whiter and whiter. Nathamol could not, quite, make herself put her arms around her room-mate. She wanted to. But she told herself it wasn't that she was a coward; this simply wasn't her place, so she stayed quiet as the next news item unreeled, a mass arrest of Yemeni visitors on terrorism charges.

A secret budded at their university after that. Thammasat had always been political to a fault. Nathamol, a law student, knew little of it beyond that Rinnapha and Kwankaew, neurologist and engineer, were part of it. Neither told her anything, but she knew the secret would flower into something dangerous, something frightening.

Over textbooks they'd sometimes joke what they would do if conflict erupted between superpowers. "Learn Chinese." This, glib, from the only boy in their group.

Kwankaew, who had spoken fluent Taechew since age five, chortled. "I knew that'd come in handy someday other than asking for red envelopes. And to think Ahma was preparing me for enlistment in the world-domination army!"

Elbow-jabs and arm-pinches were traded. The following summer, as if their little chat had been oraculous, the People's Republic of China and the United States of America went to war.

As global wars went its beginning was subdued. Nathamol heard of blackouts in New York, Chicago, other interchangeable names that didn't signify much to her. She was mostly just glad the farang soldiers vacated their premises in Krungthep and her aunt, a MICT sysadmin, told her that it was much easier to obfuscate American data-miners. "Most of it is automated," her aunt explained, diluting down to layman's language, "but when there isn't anyone on the other end working it's down to just scripts, and those are easy to stop. You see what I mean?"

She nodded, though she didn't see. Absurdly, she was more anxious about her finals than this development. Later she'd find it astounding she could worry over something so trivial, but at the time it'd seemed important. A degree. A finishing.

More than the graduation, Nathamol fretted over how to ask Rinnapha out. If Rinnapha even liked girls – she hadn't dated anyone, had mentioned no crush either on boy or tom. Would rejection break Nathamol's secret; would their friends call her a disgusting pervert? Would her mother hear about it?

And Rinnapha was intelligent, outspoken, determined: Nathamol knew she was none of those. She suspected Rinnapha only let her tag along to exercise calming influences when they got a little too loud, a little too controversial, in public. "A good thing you are around too," Professor Vipannee, who oversaw their dorm, liked to say, "or we'd have had to kick Kwankaew and Rinnapha out a long time ago, and them being so bright."

Nathamol had the feeling this was her only real academic worth, since her performance was – at best – average. She couldn't imagine practicing law. Unlike some in her classes, she couldn't even blame her mother, who had let her freely pick a faculty. She'd pursued law because it'd seemed the thing to do.

Still. Still. Rinnapha had a way of biting her lip when she concentrated that made Nathamol, unreasonably, flush; she had a way of smiling that made Nathamol immediately smile back, however she felt at the time. In the middle of debate Rinnapha exuded fierceness difficult to ignore, and sharing a not-large room with their beds close gave Nathamol acute insomnia on occasion.

It was after lunch, one day, that Rinnapha pulled her out of the cafeteria – "There's something you *have* to see – it's still a secret now, but I wanted *you* to see."

Nathamol's cheeks pinked. They rarely went anywhere on their own. It was always the entire posse. She'd miss afternoon classes, but it didn't even occur to her to protest.

They went by bus, rushing through a crush of bodies into a car full of tourists chattering in Gwangtung, Malay, Vietnamese. The ASEAN still wasn't the power it aspired to be, but it'd come a long way to ease traveling and business. Nathamol had always wanted to see Singapore. A master's there, perhaps. It might be the turning point she needed, to become less like herself and more like Rinnapha. Refinement, worldliness.

To her mortification they disembarked near the Grand Hyatt.

Nathamol gesticulated wildly at her white shirt, pencil skirt and yellow Thammasat pin. "We *aren't* going in there. They're going to kick us out."

"I'll tell the receptionists we're on a field trip. Seriously, nobody cares. Thammasat students are plenty respectable." Rinnapha took her elbow, linking arms. "Look casual. Don't hyperventilate."

Rinnapha led her through the lobby, which was furnished equal parts in upholstery and suited businesspeople, then downstairs while singing the praise of the half-price hotel bakery after seven thirty. Nathamol kept her mouth shut about not being able to afford chocolate and preserves this expensive, half price or not. Their sensible student heels clicked on marble. She felt grubby, out of place, and avoided eye contact. Rinnapha came from a well-off family, but it was a difference they could usually bury.

They made their way into the bar. It was closed, but nobody stopped them or informed them of the opening hours. Past immaculately varnished tables and seats tucked neatly in, Rinnapha stopped at a patch of the wall. She took out her phone and did something with it.

Where there had been stylish, shiny wood panels there was now a door. "How did you do *that*?"

"Magic," Rinnapha said.

"You're making fun of me."

"Not a bit. Identification by dream, Ying. Much better than retinal or fingerprint. More secure, too."

Bewildered, she followed Rinnapha into a narrow passage, whitewashed cement, then a service lift that smelled of rust. Mostly though she inhaled Rinnapha's scent, sweat and faint tamarind, just on this side of edible. Did Rinnapha know how soft her hair looked?

The lift stopped, hissing open. Rinnapha thumbed her phone and, with metallic clicks, a dozen naked bulbs glassed in pale blue and green snapped to attention. Light like unforecast monsoon drenched the steel ceiling and parquet floor. Incense smells clustered cloud-thick. Among all this, dead center, sat Chaomae Guanim on a dais: blacked brass for hair, lab-grown ivory for robes. Her chest rose and fell, and her skin glistened mother-of-pearl. Eyelashes finer than northern silk. For all the brass she looked alive.

"She seemed like the logical choice," Rinnapha said. "All of them will be Chaomae Guanim. She has a *lot* of manifestations."

"I don't understand."

Rinnapha smiled wide, that expression which always jolted Nathamol's pulse to a mad race toward—*what* she couldn't even name, couldn't even realize. "Protection. When America and the rest are done it's going to be rough. But this, the chaomae network, will keep us safe from anything short of a tectonic shift."

"Chaomae network," Nathamol repeated and couldn't keep from giggling. "It sounds like a union for lady gang leaders."

"*Ying*. Don't be awful. Listen, it's a focus for *intent*. You can distill that, turn it into energy more efficient than electricity, solar power, anything. Prayers and mantras are ideal, but there's not enough of either to go around, so I started looking into dreams. Tough stuff, that, but we found a way. A little like using sleeping brains for processing power? Only there aren't circuits, there's no need for a connective infrastructure so it can keep going no matter what. It's elegant. I'm so proud of it. I won't ever do anything this fine again, this perfect or this powerful."

Rinnapha's face, in blue-green light as though underwater and she a mermaid, effulgent and alive. Nathamol had never wanted— to touch, to do more than look – she'd never wanted Rinnapha so desperately. Her hand lifted, slow, and she knew this would be the moment, the opening. *Please*. "Som—"

Her friend turned to her, eyes glittering. "There's something else, Ying. I wanted you to be the first to know."

Nathamol could not, quite, breathe. Her skull pounded. *Please*. "What is it?"

"This will sound strange, but you do like girls?"

Her palms sweated. "Who told you that?"

"Fai did. Wait, don't get angry yet." Rinnapha tugged at the silver chain around her neck. It was long, and only now could Nathamol see what its length hid: a silver ring that must've rested against Rinnapha's breast. An embedded ruby sliver glinted. "She only told after I'd, well—this ring. Kwan has a matching one. As soon as the finals are done, we're going to marry."

Something in Nathamol quivered. Nerves pulled too taut, on the verge of *snap*. "Oh. When did you . . . ? If I'm the first to know." She sounded so calm, as though from the bottom of a pond.

"We've been really careful, it looks weird to people since neither of us is tom or dee and—you don't need me to tell you about it.

We're going to try and have a wedding. You'll come?" Rinnapha took her hand, squeezed it tight. "When you find your special someone we'll help, every step of the way. Promise."

"Oh," Nathamol said, faint and distant. "Thank you."

Rinnapha and Kwankaew kept their word; they flew into the wild territory of being wife and wife just after the finals, which took place two months before those of law students. Friends gently teased Kwankaew for needing to have her dress tailored larger than the wasp-waisted ones off the rack.

No monk married them and the too-new phiksunee order did not want to risk the status they'd won with tooth, nail and forbearance beyond human ken. The wedding was still technically legal. Kwankaew's family disapproved. Rinnapha's disowned and severed her from a considerable inheritance, the family connections that'd have guaranteed her a fine position wherever she went. She didn't appear to care; her work with the chaomae project had earned her respect and extravagant pay. Her superiors mightn't like her marriage, but she was too valuable. Besides, the Minister of Public Health lived with a woman openly.

Nathamol returned from the wedding – quiet, attended by less than twenty – to stare at the empty bed opposite hers in the dorm room, at the wardrobe that no longer held Rinnapha's uniforms, at the bathroom cabinet that no longer contained the cat mug, the pink toothbrush and haphazard rarely used make-up.

She plunged into revisions and graduated with much better results than previously anticipated. She interned at court, and on the first day sat through an abuse case. The defendant was a Mr Mors, the prosecutor a woman who represented girls from rural Chiang Rai, and the trial was conducted in Angrit with westerners making up more than half the jury. Mors had been accused of molesting and abusing girls he'd been supposed to educate and convert into good Christians. So many farangs sat in attendance, Mors's friends and family, teeth gritted and quietly scowling. Even Nathamol had felt intimidated, wrestling with the irrational thought that these people could not possibly do wrong; that she should be deferring to them, appease them because they spoke Angrit in a certain way, because they looked expensive and secure.

Because their western brand-name clothes, their foreign smells, made them celestial. Beings she should worship.

Mors walked free. *Not guilty. Not guilty.* A second trial almost happened. But while Thai rapists and pedophiles had no embassies to flee to, farang ones did, and that was that. Mors was, after all, American.

Then, almost incidentally, the world broke and the chaomae network went into operation, five hundred and ninety-nine brass-and-ivory Guanim flaring to life, puissant with mantras Rinnapha and her team had been storing up like coins in a piggy bank.

Nathamol couldn't remember what sunlight looked like. All natural light had attained a wan lunar quality, and in her one-room apartment she only had lamps and candle stubs. The chaomae infrastructure demanded all the dreams and chants and wishes, leaving no energy to spare on anything else. Power plants had been flooded or destroyed by American saboteurs, and most streets were gas-lit.

She held two jobs: immigration officer and pyre supervisor. Regulating the burning was important. Bodies couldn't be piled up and torched just anywhere, or the smoke would clog up what remained of the clean air. Neither career was as prestigious as practicing law, but the new struggling Krungthep had little need for solicitors, and prestige had gotten Rinnapha nowhere but dead.

Four years on and it still hurt. Assassination by American sniper. Kwankaew had devoted all she had, all she was, to countermeasure projects, arms and espionage. "The war isn't over," Kwankaew would often say when they met. It scared Nathamol. It reminded her that there might, would, be repercussions for the deaths, the corpses she had personally helped incinerate by the dozen.

Nathamol began her day in the Immigration Bureau, eight sharp, behind reinforced glass that separated her from a waiting hall too small for so many. Thai faces mostly, stained and haggard from their treks through the national subway tunnels, six–seven hundred kilometers' worth of walking and scavenging what she could not imagine. Their ID cards were given priority; Chinese ones followed. It was wise to stay on good terms with the country that fought America and won. Stranded Chinese needed only to wait for shielded aircrafts at Suvarnabhumi; Beijing remained standing with much of its infrastructure intact. Nathamol tried to imagine that. Computers that worked, cell phones that functioned, hospitals with medical technology from this century. All she had was candlelight.

Toward the end of her shift she was down to thirty-five applicants, her fingers numb from wielding stamps. Red for *no* and condemnation back to the subway, blue for *yes* and clawing out some semblance of a life in the streets. The state couldn't provide housing any more. BTS trains had become makeshift residences, crammed end to end. Nathamol could scarcely remember their rumbling purr, the serpentine sleekness of the steel carriages at rush hours.

A couple, Thai woman and a western man some twenty years her senior. Without even thinking Nathamol stamped his papers red. "I'm sorry," she said in Angrit. Years past she'd have been flustered, worrying over her pronunciation, her accent, whether it'd impress whites or embarrass her. "You aren't a Thai citizen."

The man thrust his face at the pane. His complexion was raw chicken frozen for too long, and he reeked of tobacco, human waste. She tried not to gag. "I've been living in Maehongson for five years! Married to her for three!"

"That doesn't make you Thai. I'm going to have to ask you to leave. We can give you some water and food, but that's all."

Vorapol wasn't physically intimidating, but he had a good stare and the westerner wilted under the policeman's regard. The wife stayed and received Nathamol's blue approval. Most Thai–farang couples separated here. The westerner would have died in any case, another carcass for the pyres. Already just from breathing Krungthep he might have caught the plague.

The waiting room emptied gradually, the air lightening to a breathable point. Her last one before she signed off. "Khun Maneerat Puangjit," she said and eyed the logs left by her colleagues. Blue, then. This one had had a German husband, unpronounceable name, recently deceased. "Welcome to Krungthep Mahanakhon. My condolences for your loss."

"No need, officer. Congratulate me instead."

Nathamol looked up, startled. "That's the first time I've heard it put that way."

The curve of Maneerat's mouth was more riddle than smile. "Could you point me to orientation officers?"

"There aren't any." She eyed the clock. It'd have to be wound up soon. Everything was made of scraps, and always on the verge of breaking down. "But I'm coming off my shift. Can you wait?"

Maneerat was from Yala, which meant exquisite eyes and a hint of khamtai in her low thrumming voice. They exchanged nicknames: Maneerat was Bua, which Nathamol thought fitting. A flower that doesn't easily fade.

Nathamol hailed a pedicab and told the driver, a girl in hijab and school uniform, "Siam Paragon."

They went up rusted, dead escalators and stained marble walkways. Many of the windows and walls had been knocked out for ventilation, but it reassured Nathamol that the mall retained its essential nature: a collection of meticulous storefronts, gravitas and class. In place of light bulbs, paper lanterns hung Loy Krathong-bright, dappling floor tiles in puddles of turquoise and tangerine, magenta and maroon. Nathamol picked an eatery purveying naan and curries.

They slotted into a corner table. A little boy started pedaling a fan; his older sister took their order. "The meat's lab-grown," Nathamol explained while Maneerat scrutinized the menu. "It's all safe to eat, or at least I haven't died to it. So what did you study?"

"There must be respectable jobs you can get without a degree *now*, surely?"

"Chulalongkorn, Thammasat, Mahidol and most of the rest are still around and operating." Nathamol's neck warmed and she knew she was being defensive. "Maybe you did something vocational? That's in high demand."

Maneerat shifted her battered suitcase under the table, holding it between her knees. "For the last six years I've been a farang's wife, officer. You would call it prostitution."

The flush marched to Nathamol's cheeks. She occupied herself with her masala. Agriculture had moved underground; it was fortunate that spices and rice both thrived there. Between mouthfuls she could feel Maneerat studying her. Her last attempts at small talk petered out. She had never been subjected to anyone's scrutiny so intensely. So many years of invisibility and she'd settled into that, comfortable with it, wanting nothing more.

A couple took an adjacent table. Nathamol glanced at the tom surreptitiously, wondering how anyone could live with breast-binding for that many hours a day. The dee was pretty even by dee standards, immaculate and long-haired with not a wisp out of place. They held hands and looked into each other's eyes, girlishly delighted. They seemed so young.

"You can stay with me until you find somewhere better," she offered as she paid the bill with ministry-watermarked notes; those had slightly more value, and civil servants' custom was courted anywhere. "I've got a sofa."

Maneerat looked at her. "Do you," she said slowly, "offer this to everybody?"

"Of course not. I live on my own."

"Your family?"

"My mother and sister live too far to commute." She did not say that her brother had been out of town when *it* happened. In her dreams he would stand alone on an empty highway, head uptilted and smiling, as the sky deepened to ochre and the air sharpened to glass.

"Ah." Maneerat finished her food and wiped her mouth. Her trimmed nails glinted blue. "I'll repay you. As soon as I can."

Nathamol's apartment was a nest where memories laid eggs that hatched into dreams, into nightmares. Photos of Rinnapha, photos of her brother, college yearbooks leaning against faded wallpaper *kinnarees*. She thought of rushing in and covering them all up under bedsheets, but it was too late – Maneerat's foot was over the threshold – and there was no hiding things she had never meant to put on display. This was only the third time she'd invited anyone in, and the other two occasions had been premeditated; she'd had time to put everything away, leaving just a set of threadbare furniture, an empty room that'd absorbed nothing of her but smell and sweat. "It's not much to look at," she said and stared at a spot on the carpet.

"I've been living in a dank Pattaya basement smelling of fish sauce. Subways full of roaches and rats and sick people. This? This is the last word in luxury. And you have running water?"

"Yes. It's weak, but clean."

"My," Maneerat breathed. "You're living almost like it was normal."

She wasn't, but did not say so. Listening to the gurgling, she worried that Maneerat might find fault with the toiletry. The wrong color of shampoo.

Maneerat emerged towel-wrapped and glitter-slick. Deprivation had thinned her collarbones to knife blades, adding years to her she didn't have; even then Nathamol had to avert her eyes from shadows that collected at the base of her throat, that pooled between her breasts. Mysteries half glimpsed, doors just ajar.

Nathamol fixed her attention elsewhere. They'd only just met.

She introduced Maneerat to the apartment, what little there was of it – "There's a power generator downstairs, but mostly it doesn't work so don't try the sockets. Communal washing machine's at the end of the hall, you pedal to get it going. The phone and radio run on batteries."

Maneerat unlatched her suitcase, dug through sets of underwear and jeans, and exhumed a plastic box. Wordlessly, she handed it to Nathamol.

Inside, tightly packed, sat unbranded cubes. Rechargeable sodium batteries. "You could," Nathamol said, dazed, "buy out this block and have everyone evicted. Get years' worth of food."

"I started stockpiling when things went downhill. Think of them as my contribution to the rent." Maneerat shrugged. Wet hair slid off her shoulders, seaweed fronds. She twisted a handful between her fingers and pursed her lips. "Is it true that all the farangs are dead? From being sick."

"Yes. It happened after the shielding went up." After Rinnapha's assassination. Farang men had been rounded up during the initial outbreak and put under quarantine. Embassies had railed shrilly, but since they'd been staffed by farang men that soon quieted. "Some farang women survived, but it doesn't seem to touch anyone else. No one understands what happened or how."

Maneerat's expression clouded. She straightened and opened the window, inhaling deep. "The air's become so clean. I used to hate Krungthep, but the last four years it was all I could dream about. I dreamed it ugly, I dreamed it beautiful, but I never dreamed it'd be safe to breathe. All the way to the lungs, until you can feel it in your stomach."

The next morning, Kwankaew rang. Meet at Chatuchak Park, at so-and-so o'clock. Less a social call and more a command vested with the authority of guilt. Nathamol left Maneerat with a list of addresses where she might find work.

Waiting for a cab, she watched other tenants leave the *soi*, which they shared with a hardware store and a book rental. She toyed with the ten-baht coins in her pocket, thinking of picking up something light, a period novel. Currency wasn't useless yet, but if food production didn't improve it would soon be.

"I heard you got a new room-mate."

"People are nosy," Nathamol said in Angrit.

Samantha leaned against a lamppost. It didn't keep her from looming. "If you keep doing that how'll I learn Thai?"

She smiled non-committally. Samantha was a new tenant who intimidated her more than a little, and not just because she was one of the few remaining farang. The clipped speech perhaps, which made her think of soldiers, or the way every crease in Samantha's face looked as though it'd been carved onto her rather than accumulated with years, as though she'd been born looking exactly this old. "I'm heading out. Maybe I can introduce my room-mate to you later."

"That'd be good. A boy?"

"That wouldn't be proper," Nathamol murmured. Living several floors down Samantha probably hadn't noticed the rare few times she'd brought someone home. Then again, sometimes she'd catch the woman watching her in a peculiar, lingering way she didn't like.

Samantha chuckled, a sound like landslides.

At the park, Kwankaew was waiting for her by the lake, one leg tucked under a long skirt hem-flecked with grass, a small laminated book and a bottle of chilled coffee in her lap. "I just came from a meeting with Ambassador Wong Mianying." She poured the coffee into two plastic cups, offering one to Nathamol.

"You've become very important." Nathamol never asked exactly how much, or what office Kwankaew held. Whatever it was, it wasn't public.

"I've become underpaid and overworked, more like. Which is why I want to ask you, again, to come work with me."

Nathamol stopped sipping. "I'm not a scientist, or engineer, or anything useful. I've already told you that."

"You undersell yourself. I want someone who can think but who's not drowned in theorems and numbers. A fresh head. I know you can keep secrets." A sharp inhalation, a crack in composure. "I know you'll do this for Som."

The coffee, sweet-milky and cold, clogged in Nathamol's mouth. She clenched the perspiring plastic cup. It crackled. "That's not fair."

"It's not dangerous, and I need people I can trust." Kwankaew's fingers tangled, wringing as though she meant to crush damp green air to pieces. "What I'm doing will keep us all safe. Your family, Som's memory."

She was still wearing that ring. Both rings, ruby chip glinting in each, around one finger. Perfectly matched pair.

"What about my job?" Prevaricating.

"I'll get you transferred. Today. You're free?"

Of course she was. Kwankaew must have chosen this day for a reason.

Kwankaew signaled for a covered pedicab, whose driver wore no uniform but had such a bearing that Nathamol could not mistake him for anything but military or police. Inside, hidden from the world by black glass and tarp, Kwankaew opened her little book, full of secrets, and unfolded contracts for Nathamol to sign. Unbelievable that a few years ago everything had been digital – signatures and legal documents, ID cards and books.

They entered an unassuming clinic, the back of which was stocked with mortar, pestle, jars of pastes and herbs like a traditional Chinese pharmacy. Down, and down, to a railcar that hissed and chugged on brown Chao Phraya water. Nathamol folded herself small and tried not to think. Now and again strobe lights stabbed into the car, jarring her. She saw rivets, pipes, maintenance doors: old MRT infrastructure. Under them wheels screeched against tracks built for vehicles several centuries more advanced. She smelled rust, age, sulphur.

They disembarked at Queen Sirikit station. Boarded-shut convenience stores and bakeries, defunct turnstiles and ticket dispensers. Muck and rust, and a low keen of wind tunnel somewhere above. Kwankaew stood still for a time, and the graffiti-sprayed wall between two vending machines became a sliding door.

Magic, Rinnapha had said, and because the Americans hadn't understood it they killed her.

*   *   *

What Kwankaew had assigned her – jokingly calling it homework – was exactly that: a list of minutiae to prioritize. Anyone who walked through the fresh market regularly or peered at restaurant menus with their crossed-out items marking shortage would have been able to do this work. Nathamol recognized that Kwankaew herself didn't have the time, that ticking off agricultural projects required the evaluator be impartial, but she felt faintly disappointed. She knew she shouldn't be; this was safe, good and meaningful. There were even plans for an eventual revival of the power grid, water supply, waste disposal. Kwankaew had coded them in geometric shapes and pastel colors, rather than words or numbers. Paranoia, though perhaps justified. "There are spies," Kwankaew had told her. "They blend in. You don't have to be white to belong to America."

Nathamol had started. They'd sat among dozens of researchers grinding away at computers joined by cables thick as wrists to a small Guanim. This one had her own wall shrine, seated over everyone's head, proper veneration with little dishes of fruit offerings. Everyone ate those at the end of the day, for luck and because no one wasted fruit. "What do they want with us?"

"None of their countermeasures work as well as our dream-engines. Even *I* don't understand their core functions – only Som really did. If they ever fail . . ." Kwankaew's brows deepened. She turned away. "I need access to her initial experiments, but those happened before I joined. She was brilliant but insanely disorganized. All her notes probably got flushed or ruined in a washing machine or stuck in a corrupted drive somewhere and she never backed any of them up. She was absolute about the system being perfect. The Americans think it's some kind of weapon."

"But it's—"

"Ninety per cent of their expatriates died here. They were preoccupied at the time, but they've had years to wonder: was it us, or China? An aircraft Wong Mianying was meant to board exploded last month. Some of my people felt threatened. I've moved them, their families, into secure housing. Good thing most scientists don't marry or we'd have been overcrowded."

In the here and now Nathamol tilted back against the water tank, which was empty – rain a phenomenon of the past – and drew the blankets closer around herself. Few came up to the roof except to hang up or retrieve laundry; lines of them stretched out, dripping and sometimes fluttering in the rare breeze. The height and solitude cleared her head, and she'd thought it an ideal spot to finish Kwankaew's assignment. But maybe she shouldn't be alone. She tried to think as Kwankaew might. Was she in the open up here, was she exposed, what could happen?

Her mind stumbled and she couldn't think like that. She'd been a law student. Who in Krungthep could be more ordinary than she, more removed from clandestine plots and politics shaping a nation?

Footsteps, a creak of hinge. "There you are," Maneerat said. "The farang woman told me you'd be up here. Can I join you?"

Nathamol put aside her papers, closing the binder. "Sure."

She didn't quite expect Maneerat to burrow into the blankets, rearranging the topmost duvet so it would drape over them both. It took enormous self-control not to leap out of her skin when Maneerat slipped an arm around her.

"Much better." Maneerat sighed.

"Fifteen degrees," Nathamol said and hoped she didn't sound as stunned as she felt. The warmth from Maneerat communicated despite the layers of clothing. A denim-clad hip against her own, a line of thigh and knee and shin. "It's gotten very cold outside Krungthep, I heard."

"I felt it, in the tunnels. But I never came out, though they said the storms stopped sometimes, and you could breathe without dying." Maneerat's eyelids fluttered. "I wasn't that brave."

"You walked all the way here from Pattaya."

"That wasn't brave. That was a gun I have."

"A gun."

Maneerat snorted. "I didn't shoot anyone. But it told people to leave me be."

They stayed to watch the expressway light up below them, vendors taking up positions by lampposts to hawk flashlights and drinks to bikers and cabbies. Nathamol pointed out the monitor balloons as they rose, gondolas festooned in epileptic disco colors. The Chang Building stood just visible, bas-relief outline wreathed in the writhing lights that'd replaced the stars.

Maneerat told her of the village-stations that'd sprung up underground, the camps that filled the tunnels and dead cars. Some were run by gangs, others by committee, and economy balanced on the bartering of liquor, firearms and scavengings. Maneerat met people who went above during storm-calms and ranged through countryside gone to brown, touching rice stalks black as coal and bits of roof on asphalt like seashells on sand. They'd come down with tales of ghosts, canned food, and electronics that by chance continued functioning. Not long, but they were hoarded and coveted all the same.

"That man died two years in," Maneerat said with utter indifference. The German had mistaken a gangster for a prostitute; the woman's answer had been to knife him in the face and shoot him in the knee. No medical attention had been found in time, and that had been that.

"He and his friends liked to talk how backward we were, how hopeless, like I couldn't understand Angrit – like their wives or Thai step-children couldn't. They hated Muangthai. I always wondered why they stayed here, why they even came."

"Did it . . . disgust you?" She didn't say, *Weren't you disgusted with yourself, didn't you find it degrading?*

Maneerat heard those regardless. She stiffened and drew away, dislodging the shared duvet. "Did you ever have to help your mother pay farmer loans?"

"No, but—"

"Did it ever occur to you that looking at dirty old farangs sideways and knowing they were absolutely beneath you was a luxury?"

"I didn't think of it like . . . that."

"Ah," Maneerat said and with perfect precision slapped Nathamol in the face.

The ringing lingered after Maneerat was gone. Nathamol touched her cheek. It was fever-hot. She sat unmoving for a long time, breathing slowly, and put her papers in order: wrote down a few more ideas occurring to her in cold duty.

Nathamol was in the shower when Maneerat returned, unlocking the door with a spare key, and stepped into the bathroom. No shower curtain hung from the empty rusted rings – there had never been any need for it – and there was nothing for Nathamol to cover herself with. So she did not.

"I'm back," Maneerat said quietly, not averting her eyes, not even pretending to.

"What if I asked you to pack your things and go?"

The other woman looked down. She removed her hairband, busy work, and twisted it between her fingers. "I'm not apologizing because I got angry at what you said. But I know I shouldn't have done more than get angry." When Maneerat's eyes returned to Nathamol's face they were wide. Her lower lip caught between her teeth, sawed back and forth. "Are you asking me to pack my things and go?"

Maneerat didn't need her, didn't need this dinky apartment. Nathamol knew that. "You could afford a nicer place than this."

"That's not what I want. I like the sofa. The roof."

The pressure, between fury and relief and nerves, eased slightly from Nathamol's chest. She turned back to the wall. "Then I guess you can stay."

She thought Maneerat would leave. Instead she heard a rustle of clothes, and when she looked again Maneerat's brassiere had fallen to join jeans and blouse. Then she was bare, and there next to Nathamol. Without a word she took the soap and lathered Nathamol's back. Under the recalcitrant showerhead, they did more than scrubbing each other's shoulder blades; paused just long enough to towel off so they wouldn't drench everything in the room.

They sought each other's soft places and tasted each other's salt, writing their impatience in nail-marks and teeth-prints. A glass storm brewed inside Nathamol's ribcage. It poured out of her into Maneerat's mouth, a thousand shards of windows, a hundred fragments of skies.

"I think I've found my problem. They're all dead."

"Who are?" Nathamol asked automatically, not really listening to what she heard. In the lab much of what she did was routine paperwork, routine check-ups of machines, measuring voltages to keep them from shorting out or overheating. Power supplied by the miniature Guanim was not efficient, prone to fluctuations, and had to be recalibrated constantly. She was no electrician, but the tools were intuitive. She felt useful and competent, and more alive than she'd been with her job at Immigration.

Kwankaew shook papers so wrinkled and stained it was obvious she'd had to straighten them out from crumpled wads. "Som's test subjects. The ones she tried her prototype on, to see if it could work. I get the impression they were individuals with unusually vivid inner lives. Who had focused dreams." Kwankaew made a face. "This sounds like hogwash. It's not even a little bit scientific. She might as well have written notes about cursing people with buffalo hides."

A slow chill spidered up her vertebrae. "Her tests killed them?"

"What? No! She scanned brainwaves, put them through mild stimuli, that sort of thing. It's just that most of them didn't live in Krungthep and probably didn't survive. Som didn't even keep their names, so it's all moot anyway." Kwankaew nodded at her assistant Thanakit, a neurologist from Isaan. "He's been drawing up concepts for artificial dreams. If it was possible to get back to where Som started, I could maybe reverse-engineer some things, optimize others."

Nathamol made another circuit, deep in thought, jotted down corrections to be made for several power sockets. When she got back to Kwankaew's desk she sat down. "Do you have the results from Som's first subjects?"

"Some." A pen jab at the tattered papers.

"Could you match them with people? There are a lot of refugees, and if the—the neural signature's unique . . ." Heat warmed the back of her ears. "I'm probably talking nonsense."

"You aren't. Thanakit!" The assistant sauntered over and snapped a mock salute. She held up one of Rinnapha's notes. "How soon can you come up with a recognition protocol?"

"Easy, boss. A couple days or three."

"I want it by tomorrow," Kwankaew said and raised an eyebrow when he started protesting. "Be glad I'm not asking for it by the end of the day. Earn your keep. And, Ying, that was simple but— let's just say most of us would have come up with some stupid convoluted thing involving lots of numbers. Just to calculate the statistical likelihood of whether those subjects might still be alive, or trying to replicate their brains. But ID-matching sensors I can get installed everywhere. Simple. Efficient. I told you, you undersell yourself."

Nathamol grinned, giddy. "Are you offering me a raise . . . boss?"

"Oh for—not you too. Don't call me that. I heard you sneezing by the way, so get some pills from the cabinet. Wouldn't want you to give us all the flu. Us academic types are delicate."

She nodded, but her smile dried and crumbled. She wasn't contributing anywhere near enough to earn this privilege. Kwankaew's facility enjoyed a luxury found nowhere outside of the king's household: the best medical care that could still be had. It hadn't gotten to the point where a cold could be fatal, but she heard giving birth these days was a challenge. With more and more entering Krungthep, it was all the hospitals could do to keep up, and was the next generation of doctors and nurses to be trained in archaic medicine and acupuncture? How much more aid was China willing to give, and how much more could they accept?

She came home to Maneerat propping a mirror on law textbooks and applying eyeshadow. "Oh," Maneerat said, looking faintly embarrassed. She'd put on a shimmery purple dress, black bolero, and silver choker. "I was just leaving – I'd have left a note. I found a job. I don't suppose you'd . . . walk me there?"

"I would," Nathamol said, shrugging on the jacket she'd just taken off. She tried not to sound too eager. "What kind of work is it?"

"It's something. You might like it."

On the way out Nathamol hesitated; should they hold hands? Would Maneerat want to? They walked side by side, centimeters apart, and sometimes their fingers would brush, would collide.

Maneerat's workplace was just a few *soi* away, and when they stopped it dawned on Nathamol what this place was. The club was warm inside, neon lit, a hum of conversation, utensils, clinking glasses and a diesel power generator. There were more tom–dee couples than Nathamol had ever seen in any one place.

"I've never been to—one of these," Nathamol whispered after Maneerat had spoken to the owner, a tall, muscled woman guarding the bar. "What do you do here?"

"Be presentable. Khun Vee says she gets too many toms, not enough—well, you know. And she wants someone to take care of first-timers, break the ice. So they wouldn't be scared and lonely." Maneerat ushered her to one of the divans. "Maybe I could practice on you."

"Won't people mind? We look like two dee."

"I think Khun Vee's past caring about that." Maneerat nodded toward a table on the far end, where two women sat almost in each other's lap, one in hijab, the other in lacy blouse and wide skirt. "This isn't some sort of sex club. It's just a place to be, to chat. What do you think of it?"

A place to not hide, she thought. Maneerat was right. Nobody cared; nobody glanced at them sidelong. "It's nice," Nathamol said and realized that wasn't enough. "It's *wonderful.*"

Maneerat first smiled a little, then widely. "I'm glad. I thought you'd find it . . . indecorous. Sleazy."

"I wouldn't. I'd have liked to find somewhere like this when I was younger, but I was too shy." And she still was. She fiddled with the cuff of her jacket.

"I'm glad. I really am." Maneerat's painted nails drew paths in Nathamol's palm, gentle-sharp. "Can I kiss you?"

A look up before she lowered her eyes, gazing at shiny fabric through a filter of lashes and pleased embarrassment. The purple dress clung. It became Maneerat, but then she imagined anything Maneerat put on was flattering. "Here?"

"Here."

It was brief, but as her eyelashes beat against Maneerat's skin she was *happy* and she had forgotten what that felt like. A smear of transferred lipstick later she murmured, "You've got to teach me how to use make-up."

"You look fine. I'll get us—do you drink?"

Nathamol laughed. They were getting to know each other all backward. "Sorry, no. Get me something cheerful?"

By the end of the evening, Maneerat had made a round of the tables, getting acquainted with regulars, speaking to a group of girls who'd come for the first time; offered a sip here and a sip there, when she came back to Nathamol she was red and tipsy. Vee asked them if they needed escort getting home; Nathamol demurred – they lived close by enough, and she didn't want to impose any more than she already had.

Maneerat was giggling and teetering on her feet by the time they reached the apartment. Nathamol fished for her keys, but having to support Maneerat's weight made even that a challenge. So when Samantha opened the front gate from the inside and asked if she needed a hand she was all too glad. The farang's arms corded as she lifted and carried Maneerat upstairs, but she made it look effortless. "You're strong," Nathamol said, pressed to say *something.*

"In my line of work I'd have to be."

"You've never said what you do."

"The kind of career with a lot of men in it, though you fixed that."

Nathamol didn't know what to make of that; Angrit was so imprecise – *you* could be individual or collective. Did Samantha believe the disease had been a Thai plot? She didn't push; she wasn't that tactless. Instead she thanked the farang politely and maneuvered Maneerat into the bed. She wet a clean towel and wiped Maneerat's arms and face down, wrinkling her nose at the alcohol smell. Come morning, Maneerat was going to have a splitting headache; she amused herself with the prospect of teasing Maneerat just a little.

She didn't wake up in her own room. It took a full minute to process that – gray ceiling, funereal decor, an icon of bleeding Yesu in his undignified loincloth and starveling's ribs. Nathamol always thought it inappropriate Christians dressed up their prophet like that, exposed and ugly.

Hard wood dug into her back. She pushed herself up using shoulders and elbows – her wrists were bound behind her, her ankles duct-taped into numbness. Fear pricked her throat, acidic.

Maneerat crouched by the altar. Over her, Samantha sat on a stool, a gun carelessly pointed in her direction. There were bruises on her face. By the side, a slim brunette stood, face closed like a fist. She too was armed.

Samantha turned to look at Nathamol. "Good, you're awake," she said and walked over, heavy booted footsteps, and settled on the pew.

Nathamol's breath hissed through her teeth.

"Tell me about your work. We've never talked about that, have we? And us being neighbors."

"Why are you doing this?" She swallowed, loud.

"Seventy-thousand dead Americans. Farang to you, people to us."

She choked back brown-bile laughter. People! Farangs were almost little gods, shrines springing up for them wherever they went. "That just—just *happened*. And I'm not important enough to know anything."

Samantha did not blink those huge blue eyes as she backhanded Nathamol. Salt and blood flooded her mouth. "You started working for the Ministry of Defense two weeks ago, directly under Kwankaew Srithongkul."

"But I don't know *anything*."

"I know," Maneerat said, voice slurred and Nathamol thought *Please, don't talk*, "why those farangs died: they deserved it."

A little gesture from Samantha and the brunette administered the butt of her gun to Maneerat's head. Nathamol heard a crack and strangled back a little cry as Maneerat crumpled, chin on chest and blood on bodice.

They were blindfolded, gagged, and hoisted up shoulders. Nathamol breathed shallowly and kept her ears open. The farang women spoke infrequently, but she caught a few scraps of conversation: they had to keep moving.

When they stopped next time, Samantha bent one of Nathamol's fingers so far backward it almost touched her wrist. Then it did, and she screamed and told them – which was not much, and they didn't believe that she knew so little. They brought a sloshing bucket, and shoved Nathamol's head into it. They kept her there until her lungs burned, jerked her out by the hair, and did it all over again. She vomited on their shoes.

There came a day when there were no questions, no water, no bone breaking. Nathamol waited until the minutes stretched into a certainty that nothing would be done to her for the next hour, or the next few hours, and she wept relief.

A hand touched hers, groping its way from wrist to forearm, to face: encountered either tears or drool or both and paused. "Ying?"

"Bua," she whispered back even though there was no telling if they were on their own, if either American was listening.

Maneerat's feet and hands must be as bound as her own; they could not do anything more than press close, press tight, against each other. Warmth to warmth. "I kept meaning to ask," Maneerat murmured. There was still wrongness in her enunciation, her mouth not having healed or having been hit over and over. "You don't live on your own because your family's too far from the immigration bureau. I kept thinking about it and it made no sense."

Nathamol felt no pain, only a distance from her own body. It was this freedom that let her laugh. "That's all you wanted to talk about?"

"Yes. No." Spoken straight into her ear, with breath gone stale but real and Maneerat's. "It's because your mother and sister don't know about—well—isn't it?"

"I never knew how to tell them." Khunmae, I like girls? Nong Ping, if older sister marries it'll be a woman? "They'd have been disappointed."

"Mine, too."

Their captors were so much on the move that they seemed to have no time for further interviews. It occurred to them, gradually, that she could be of no further use: when this did they spoke – three distinguishable voices, Nathamol counted – in rapid-fire Angrit. Samantha decided that the next time they had to move they'd kill their captives.

This was said in such a concise way, as she might have said that she meant to weed a vegetable patch.

The next time they were alone they talked about going to school in Yala, about family. One of Maneerat's sisters had the habit of playing the same song over and over, and that'd drive her a little mad or out of the house shared between too many – grandparents, an uncle, several aunts and in-laws. Growing up, she'd had to share everything, including her mother's affection. School for her had ended at sixteen; the state took care of tuition fees, but she couldn't attend classes and work at the same time.

They did not talk about the weight or texture of a gun. They did not talk about the sound it would make, fireworks-clap, that would fill their ears and be the last thing they heard instead of each other's voice.

When the blindfold was ripped off she could not tell if it was day, night or some nebulous moment between. She blinked up at a strange woman, Indian and muscular, who knelt limned in slatted light, pale yellow bars across her face and Velcro vest as she cut through the bindings. "Khun Kwankaew sent me," she said softly. Next she freed Maneerat, and Nathamol's throat tightened when she saw how much caked blood there was, how many bruises. The Indian woman pressed a black bead into Nathamol's ear; immediately her skull filled with a buzz of chatter and pounding footfalls.

The woman led them to the fire exit, pointed up, and shut the heavy door between them. She had, Nathamol registered belatedly, a gun.

The stairs stretched on interminably. First they ran, taking two steps at a time, until they couldn't. Nathamol's lungs threshed and her legs trembled, but she kept on. Bearing some of Maneerat's weight, she kept on.

On the roof the sun was rising. Up so high Guanim's shield was just a gloss between eye and sky; Nathamol saw jagged blades of light, clouds, and a distance she'd forgotten existed. The world had become so narrow, the horizon so small.

They found a shade and eased each other down onto cool concrete. Maneerat cradled her broken hand, soft. "I'm sorry I didn't speak up. Because I knew."

"About what?" Her voice rasped paper dry. There were tears in her, but she felt curiously serene, deep in a still well.

"Four years ago I was paid to join an experiment. Did some tests, answered questions, had my head monitored. Funny, I thought at the time, everyone else was a bargirl, a rent boy, that sort of thing ... The girl in charge, a student really, said it was easier to synchronize frequencies under a common intent."

"Som," she breathed. "You were one of her subjects." Was that how Kwankaew had found them and sent help – had the Americans passed checkpoints where Thanakit's protocol had been installed? She hadn't thought that possible; she hadn't thought of anything at all.

"When I heard farangs started dropping dead, like their brains just shorted out, I thought, *Am I going to hell, will I be reborn a pig or a roach?* Then I stopped caring. I figured they'd be in an even worse place."

Nathamol slit her eyes against the light. It was bright here, and she imagined she could see more than the jaundice yellow of fallout, that there were rose and lotus tinting the clouds. "If you'd said that," she said softly, "I think she'd have killed us both. But this way she kept me alive. In case I would give her something more, something useful."

Maneerat sighed into her neck. "Ying. You're too forgiving."

"Because I want to be. When we're safe ... do you want to meet my family? I'll tell them you're a co-worker. You'll like my sister."

A hand with torn fingernails cupped her cheek carefully. "Will there be a ring at the end of it?"

"As many rings as you like."

They lapsed into silence, watching the dawn. Nathamol listened to the bead in her ear, bursts of gunfire and stretches of silence.

The fire door opened, almost soundlessly, creaking just once. Samantha stepped through, bloodied and panting. Her left hand clenched around the grip of a pistol.

There was no hiding. The two of them sat in plain sight, and the farang did not waste time; she leveled the pistol, took aim.

A gunshot was just as shattering as Nathamol had imagined, louder than movies had made them out to be, the sound solidifying and settling by her eardrums.

The bead crackled. Kwankaew's voice, muted by the ringing in her skull: "I'm glad you are safe."

She'd never been in a helicopter. There'd been plane rides, but this was different. The motion of flight vibrated through seat and window, making her teeth chatter: a thin shell separating her from emptiness and terminal velocity. She thought of calm days in riverside temples. She thought of making *krathong* in art-and-craft classes. Things that weren't like now, things that lay distant and separate from what her life had become; from what had happened. In her lap, Maneerat slept, having curled small and fetal, her breath a warmth feathering Nathamol's skin.

Between Kwankaew's hands the gun lay quiescent, bearing no traces of killing, no echo of its desperate noise. "I'd been looking for that woman," she said, ragged as though she'd been running. "Almost as good at hiding as she was with a sniper rifle."

"She killed Som."

"Yes." The gun returned to its holster and she wanted to ask, *When did you learn to shoot?* "Let me look at you."

A first-aid box. Alcohol-blued swabs scraped away the grime; her fingers were splinted, wrapped in gauze. Kwankaew put the supplies back with astonishing tidiness. They didn't speak again until they had touched down on the Grand Hyatt, until they were kneeling before the first Chaomae Guanim under halogen bulbs green and blue. Each lit an incense stick, an offering of light and prayer trickling into the goddess-engine, into the network that drank it in synaptic pulses.

Kwankaew got up last, and when she stood she was clutching the engagement rings, which glittered crimson. "I had no right to pressure you into working with me, Ying. You shouldn't have gotten involved; you shouldn't have been marked. None of this is right."

Standing in Maneerat's arm, all Nathamol could think of was this: this fitting together, like puzzle pieces fallen out of different boxes but which by chance had met, interlocked. "No, but we talked about this. You wanted Som's subjects."

Maneerat inclined her head. "Working with you seems the safest, and Ying thinks with my data you might be able to extend the shielding. Do other useful things."

"I could. Understand, Khun Maneerat, you'll be risking your life."

Nathamol smiled painfully. Her other hurts had receded to a distance. "Bua and I know that. But the Americans will be coming back, and if we don't do anything, we'll probably be dead anyway."

Kwankaew loosened her hands, looking down at the welts her own nails had raised in her palms. "What if I ask you to help turn Som's machines into weapons?"

They shared a glance, a nod. "Yes," Nathamol said.

"Then let me show you something." She opened the same small book Nathamol had seen before, and from it extracted three grainy stills. Aerial shots of armored vehicles nosing at wrecked power plants. "These are recent, taken outside Kuala Lumpur."

"They're coming, then." Maneerat's voice was calm, but her hold had tightened around Nathamol.

"A question of whom, Beijing or us, and they're by far better defended." The photographs were slipped back into the book. "When the Americans come this time, we'll be ready."

Nathamol did not know if they would be; she didn't see, even, how they could be. They left the first Chaomae Guanim, walking close, hand in hand. Around them the goddesses hummed, a grid five hundred and ninety-nine strong. A divinity brought first to protect, and now perhaps to fight, for Krungthep. A divinity Rinnapha had given her life to invoke.

And now it was their turn.

Smoke City

Christopher Barzak

One night, I woke to the sound of my mother's voice, as I did when I was a child. The words were familiar to my ear, they matched the voice that formed them, but it was not until I had opened my eyes to the dark of my room and my husband's snoring that I remembered the words were calling me away from my warm bed and the steady breathing of my children, both asleep in their own rooms across the hall. "Because I could not stop for death," my mother used to tell me, "he kindly stopped for me." They were Dickinson's words, of course, not my mother's, but she said them as if they were hers, and because of that, they were hers, and because of that, they are now mine, passed down with every other object my mother gave me before I left for what I hoped would be a better world. "Here, take this candy dish." Her hands pushing the red knobbed glass into my hands. "Here, take this sweater." Her hands folding it, a made thing, pulled together by her hands, so that I could lift it and lay it on the seat as my car pulled me away. Her hand lifted into the air above her cloud of white hair behind me. The smoke of that other city enveloping her, putting it behind me, trying to put it behind me, until I had the words in my mouth again, like a bit, and then the way opened up beneath me, a fissure through which I slipped, down through the bed sheets, no matter how I grasped at them, down through the mattress, down through the floorboards, down, down, down, through the mud and earth and gravel, leaving my snoring husband and my steadily breathing children above, in that better place, until I was floating, once more, along the swiftly flowing current of the Fourth River.

When I rose up, gasping for air, and blinked the water from my

eyes, I saw the familiar cavern lit by lanterns that lined the walls,
orange fires burning behind smoked glass. And, not far
downstream, his shadow stood along the water's edge, a lantern
held out over the slug and tow of the current, waiting, as he was
always waiting for me, there, in that place beneath the three rivers,
there in the Fourth River's tunnel that leads to Smoke City.

It was time again, I understood, to attend to my obligations.

History always exacts a price from those who have climbed out to
live in the world above. There is never a way to fully outrun our
beginnings. And here was mine, and he was mine here. I smiled,
happy to see him again, the sharp bones of his face gold-leafed by
the light of his lantern.

He put out his hand to fish me from the river, and pulled me up
to stand beside him. "It is good to see you again, wife," he said,
and I wrapped my arms around him.

"It is good to smell you again, husband," I said, my face pressed
against his thick chest. They are large down here, the men of
Smoke City. Their labor makes them into giants.

We walked along the Fourth River's edge, our hands linked
between us, until we came to the mouth of the tunnel, where the
city tipped into sight below, cupped as it is within the hands of a
valley, strung together by the many bridges crossing the rivers
that wind round its perimeter. The smoke obscured all but the
dark mirrored glass of city towers, which gleamed by the light of
the mill-fired skies down in the financial district, where the
captains sit around long, polished tables throughout the hours
and commit their business.

It did not take the fumes long to find me, the scent of the mills
and the sweaty, grease-faced laborers, so that when my husband
pulled me toward the carriage at the top of the Incline Passage, a
moment passed in which my heart flickered like the flame
climbing the wick of his lantern. I inhaled sharply, trying to catch
my breath. Already what nostalgia for home I possessed had
begun to evaporate as I began to remember, to piece together
what I had worked so hard to obscure.

I hesitated at the door of the Incline carriage, looking back at
the cavern opening, where the Fourth River spilled over the edge,
down into the valley, but my husband placed two fingers on my

chin and turned my face back up to his. "We must go now," he said, and I nodded at his eyes like chips of coal, his mustached upper lip, the sweat on his brow, as if he were working, even now, as in the mill, among the glowing rolls of steel.

The Incline rattled into gear, and soon we were creaking down the valley wall, rickety-click, the chains lowering us to the bottom, slowly, slowly. I watched out the window as the city grew close and the smoke began to thicken, holding a hand over my mouth and nose. An Incline car on the track opposite passed us, taking a man and a woman up to the Fourth River overlook. She, like me, peered out her window, a hand covering her mouth and nose as they ascended the tracks. We stared at each other, but it was she who first broke our gaze to look up at the opening to the cavern with great expectations, almost a panicked smile on her face, teeth gritted, willing herself upward. She was on her return journey, I could tell. I had worn that face myself. She had spent a long year here, and was glad to be leaving.

They are long here, the years in Smoke City, even though they are finished within the passing of a night.

At the bottom, my husband handed me down from the Incline car, then up again into our carriage, which was waiting by the curb, the horses nickering and snorting in the dark. Then off he sent us, jostling down the cobbled lane, with one flick of his wrist and a strong word.

Down many wide and narrow streets we rode, some mud, some brick, some stone, passing through the long rows of narrow workers' houses, all lined up and lean like soldiers, until we arrived at our own, in the Lost Neighborhood, down in Junction Hollow, where Eliza, the furnace, blocks the view of the river with her black bulk and her belching smoke. They are all female, always. They have unassuming names like Jeanette, Edith, Carrie. All night long, every night, they fill the sky with their fires.

Outside, on the front stoop of our narrow house, my children from the last time were waiting, arms folded over their skinny chests or hanging limply at their sides. When I stepped down from the carriage onto the street, they ran down the stairs, their arms thrown wide, the word "Mother!" spilling from their eager mouths.

They had grown since I'd last seen them. They had grown so

much that none of them had retained the names I'd given them at birth. Shauna, the youngest, had become Anis. Alexander was Shoeshine. Paul, the oldest, said to simply call him Ayu. "Quite lovely," I said to Anis. "Very good then," I told Shoeshine. And to Ayu, I said nothing, only nodded, showing the respect due an imagination that had turned so particularly into itself during my absence. He had a glint in his eyes. He reminded me of myself a little, willing to cast off anything we'd been told.

When we went through the door, the scent of boiled cabbage and potatoes filled the front room. They had cooked dinner for me, and quite proudly Anis and Shoeshine took hold of either elbow and led me to the scratched and corner-worn table, where we sat and shared their offering, not saying anything when our eyes met one another's. It was not from shame, our silence, but from an understanding that to express too much joy at my homecoming would be absurd. We knew that soon they would have no names at all, and I would never again see them.

We sipped our potato soup and finely chewed our noodles and cabbage.

Later, after the children had gone to bed, my husband led me up the creaking stairs to our own room, where we made love, fitting into one another on the gritty, soot-stained sheets. Old friends, always. Afterward, his arms wrapped around my sweaty stomach, holding me to him from behind, he said, "I die a little more each time you are away."

I did not reply immediately, but stared out the grimy window at the rooftops across the street. A crow had perched on the sill of the window opposite, casting about for the glint of something, anything, in the dark streets below. It cawed at me, as if it had noticed me staring, and ruffled its feathers. Finally, without turning to my husband, I said, "We all die," and closed my eyes to the night.

The days in the city of my birth are differentiated from the nights by small degrees of shade and color. The street lamps continue burning during the day, since the sun cannot reach beyond the smoke that moves through the valley like a storm that will never abate. So it always appears to be night, and you can only tell it is day by the sound of shift whistles and church bells ringing the hours, announcing when it is time to return to work or to kneel and pray.

No growing things grew in Smoke City, due to the lack of sunlight. On no stoops or windowsills did a fern or a flower add their shapes and colors to the square and rectangular stone backdrops of the workers' houses. Only fine dusty coatings of soot, in which children drew pictures with the tips of their fingers, and upon which adults would occasionally scrawl strange messages:

Do Not Believe Anything They Tell You.

Your Rewards Await You In Heaven.

It Is Better That Others Possess What I Need But Do Not Understand.

I walked my children down the road, past these cryptic depictions of stick men and women on the sides of houses and words whose meanings I could not fathom, until we came to the gates of the furnace Eliza, whose stacks sent thick plumes of smoke into the air. There, holding the hands of my two youngest, I knelt down in the street to meet their faces. "You must do what you are told," I instructed them, my heart squeezing even as I said the words. "You must work very hard, and never be of trouble to anyone, understand?"

The little ones, Anis and Shoeshine, nodded. They had all been prepared for this day over the short years of their lives. But Ayu, my oldest, narrowed his eyes to a squint and folded his arms over his chest, as if he understood more than I was saying. Those eyes were mine looking back at me, calling me a liar. "Do you understand, Ayu?" I asked him directly, to stop him from making that look. When he refused to answer, I asked, "Paul, do you understand me?" and he looked down at his feet, the head of a flower wilting.

I stood again, took up their small hands again, and led them to Eliza's gates, the top of which was decorated with a flourish of coiled barbed wire. A small, square window in the door opened as we stood waiting, and a man's eye looked out at us. "Are they ready?" he said.

I nodded.

The window snapped shut, then the gate doors began to separate, widening as they opened. Inside, we could see many people working, sparks flying, carts of coal going back and forth, the rumble of the mill distorting the voices of the workers. The man who had opened the gate window came from around the corner to greet us. He was small, stocky, with oily skin and a round face. He smiled, but I could not manage to be anything but straight-faced and stoic. He held his hands out to the little ones, who went to him, giving him their hands as they'd been instructed, and my heart filled my mouth, suffocating me, so that I fell to my knees and buried my face in my hands.

"Stupid cow," the gateman said, and as soon as I took my hands away to look up, I saw Ayu running away, his feet kicking up dust behind him. "See what you've done?" *Do not look back*, I told Ayu with my mind, hoping he could somehow hear me. *Do not look back or you will be detained here forever.*

Then the gates shut with a metallic bang, and my small ones were gone from me, gone to Eliza.

The first month of my year in the city of my birth passed slowly, painfully, like the after-effects of a night of drunkenness. For a while I had wondered if Ayu would return to the house at some point, to gather what few possessions he had made or acquired over his short lifetime, but he stayed away, smartly. My husband would have only taken him back to Eliza if he found him. That is the way, what is proper, and my husband here was nothing if not proper.

We made love every night, after he returned from the mill, his arms heavy around my waist, around my shoulders. But something had occurred on the day I'd given up the last ones: my womb had withered, and now refused to take our love and make something from its materials.

Still, we tried. Or I should say, my husband tried. Perhaps that was the reason for my body's reluctance. Whenever his breath fell against my neck, or his mouth on my breasts, I would look out the window and see Eliza's fires scouring the sky across the mountaintops, and what children we may have made, the idea of them, would burn to cinders.

"You do not love me any more," my husband said one night, in my second month in the city; and though I wanted to, badly, I could not deny this.

I tried to explain. "It is not you, it is not me, it is this place," I told him. "Why don't you come with me, why don't we leave here together?"

"You forget so easily," my husband said, looking down into his mug of cold coffee.

"What?" I said. "What do I forget?"

"You have people there, in the place you would take me."

I looked down into my own mug and did not nod.

"It is what allows you to forget me, to forget our children, our life," said my husband.

"What is?" I asked, looking up again. Rarely did my husband tell me things about myself.

"Your bad memory," said my husband. "It is your blessing."

If my memory were truly as bad as my husband thought, I would not have been returned to the city of my birth. He was incorrect in his judgement. What he should have said was, *Your memory is too strong to accomplish what you desire,* for I would not have been able to dismiss that. It is true, I wanted nothing more than to eradicate, to be born into a new world without the shackles of longing, and the guilt that embitters longing fulfilled.

But he had said his truth, flawed as it was, and because he had spoken this truth we could no longer look at each other without it hovering between us, a ghost of every child we had ever had together, every child I had taken, as a proper wife and mother, to the gates. They stared at me for him, and I would turn away to cook, clean, mend, to keep the walls of the house together.

Another month passed in this way, and then another. I washed my husband's clothes each day in a tub of scalding water. The skin on my hands began to redden, then to peel away. I began to avoid mirrors. My hair had gone lank and hung about my face like coils of old rope, no matter how I tried to arrange it. I could no longer see my own pupils, for there was no white left in the corners. My eyes had turned dark with coal dust and smoke.

One day a knock at the front door pulled me away from the dinner I was making for my husband's return from another sixteen-hour shift. When I opened the door, a man from the mill, a manager I vaguely recognized, was standing on my stoop. He held a hat against his protruding stomach, as if he had taken it off to recite a pledge or a piece of poetry. "Excuse me," he said, "for interrupting your day. But I come with sad news."

Before he could finish, I knew what he would say. Few reasons exist for a mill manager to visit a worker's wife.

"Your husband," he said, and I could not hear the rest of his words, only saw the images they carried within them: my husband, a slab of meat on the floor of the mill, burned by Eliza. My husband, a slab of meat on the floor of the mill, dragged away to be replaced by another body, another man, so that Eliza could continue her labors.

"You will need time to rest, of course," the manager said. "I'm sure it is quite a shock, but these things happen."

I nodded, dumbly, and stood there, waiting for something.

"We will be in touch, of course," said the manager as he stepped off my stoop back onto the cobbled street.

If I would have had any sense left in me, I would have done what Ayu had done, I would have run away as fast as possible, I would have done what I had done before, a long time ago, when I'd left the first time, with my mother's hand raised in the air above her cloud of white hair, waving behind me.

Instead, I sank down into my husband's chair in the front room and wept. For him, for our children, wept selfishly for myself. What would I do without him? I could feel him all around me, his big body having pressed its shape into the armchair, holding me in its embrace.

Within a week, a mass of suitors arranged themselves in a queue outside my door. They knocked. I answered. One was always waiting to speak to me, big and hulking like my husband had been, a little younger in some cases, a little older in others. Used-up men and men in the process of being used. They wanted me to cook, clean, and make love to them. I turned them away, all of them. "No thank you," I said to each knock, glancing over their shoulders to see if the line of suitors had shortened. It stretched down the street and around the corner, no matter how many men I turned away.

There was a shortage of women, one of the suitors finally informed me, trying to make his case as a rational man, to explain himself as suitable for someone like me. There were many men in need of a good wife.

"I am not a good wife," I told him. "You must go to another house of mourning," I told him. "You must find a different wife."

The suitors disappeared then. One by one they began to walk away from the queue they had formed, and for a while my front stoop was empty. I went back to sitting in my husband's chair, grieving.

My memory was bad, he had told me, but he was wrong. My memory kept him walking the halls and the staircase, my memory refused to let go of him completely, as it had refused to let go each time I left. *I die a little more each time you are away,* he had said the first night of my return to the city. Now he was dead, I thought, there would be no more dying. Upon realizing this, I stood up from his chair.

Before I could take a step in any direction of my own choosing, though, a knock arrived at the front door, pulling me toward it. How quickly we resume routine, how quickly we do what is expected: a child cries out, we run to it; something falls in another room, we turn corners to see what has fallen; a knock lands upon a door, we answer.

Outside stood three men, all in dark suits with the gold chains of pocket watches drooping from their pockets. They wore top hats, and had long waxed mustaches. They wore round spectacles in thin wire frames. I recognized them for what they were immediately: captains of industry. But what could they be doing here, I wondered, on the front stoop of a widow at a forgettable address in the Lost Neighborhood, down in Junction Hollow.

"Forgive us for intruding," they said. "We do not mean to startle you."

They introduced themselves, each one tipping his hat as he delivered his name: A. W., H. C., R. B. All captains' names are initials. It is their badge of honor.

"We understand," they said, "that you have recently lost your husband."

I nodded, slow and stupid.

"And we understand that you have turned away all of the many suitors who have come requesting your hand in marriage," they continued.

I nodded again.

"We are here to enquire as to your plans, madam, for the future," they said, and took their pocket watches out to check the time, to see if the future had arrived yet. "Do you mean to marry again?" they asked. "Do you plan to provide us with more children?"

I shook my head this time, and opened my mouth to ask the purpose of their visit. But before I could form one word, they tapped at my chest with their white-gloved hands.

"Now, now," they said, slipping their watches back into their pockets. "No need for any of that."

Then they took hold of my arms and pushed me back into my house, closing the door behind them.

Within the passing of a night I became sick with their children; within a week, the front of my housedress began to tighten; and within a month, I gave birth: three in all. One by one, their children ripped away from me and grew to the size of the children I had walked to the gates of Eliza.

I did not need to feed them. They grew from the nourishment of my tears and rages. They knew how to walk and talk instinctively, and began to make bargains with one another, trading clothes and toys and whole tracts of land.

Soon their fathers returned to claim them. "Thank you very much," said the captains, as they presented each child with a pocket watch, a pair of white gloves, a top hat. Then they looked at me. "In return for your troubles, we have built you a library."

They swept their arms in wide arcs to the opposite side of the street. Where once a row of houses stood shoulder to shoulder, now a three-story library parked its bulk along the sidewalk. "Where are my neighbors?" I asked. "Where are my friends?"

"We have moved them to another part of the city," said the captains. "Do not worry. We are in the midst of building them their own library at this very moment. We do not take, you see, without giving back."

Then they clapped their hands and curled their index fingers over and over, motioning for their top-hatted, white-gloved children to follow, checking the time on their new pocket watches as they walked toward the financial district.

A dark rumor soon began to circulate throughout the back rooms in pubs and in the common rooms of the libraries of Smoke City.

The captains' children were growing faster than their fathers could manage, it was said. The captains themselves, it was said, were having difficulties with their wives, who remained in their stone mansions on top of the mountains ringing the city, above the strata of smoke. One wife had committed suicide and another had snuck out of her mansion in the middle of the night, grew wings, and flew across the ocean to her home country, where her captain had found her many years ago sitting by a river, strumming a stringed instrument and singing a ballad of lost love. Those of us who lived below their homes above the point where the wind blew smoke away from the captains' houses had never seen these women, but we knew they were aching with beauty.

I could see it all now, what lay behind that terrible evening, and the plans the captains' children had been making as they'd left with their fathers, opening the backs of their pocket watches to examine the gears clicking inside, taking them out to hold up to the non-existent light.

Indeed, the future spread out before me, a horizon appearing where the captains' sons were building machines out of the gears of their pocket watches, and more men lumbered away from the mills every day to sit on porches and frustrate their wives who did not know how to take care of them while they were in their presence.

A future will always reveal itself, even in places like Smoke City.

But smoke or soot or the teeth of gears as they turned what arms once turned, as they ground time to chafe and splinters, could not provide the future I desired. I had seen something else – a long time ago, it seemed now, or a long time to come – and though it came with the price of unshakable memory, I began the journey that would return me to it.

Through the streets I trudged to the Incline platform, where I waited for my car wearing nothing but my worn-out housedress, my old shoes covered in mud and the stinking feces of horses. No one looked at me. I was not unnatural.

When the car arrived, I climbed in. And when the car began to lift, rickety-click, I breathed a small sigh. This time, though, as I turned to peer out the back window, my mother was not there, waving her hand in the air. Only the city. Only the city and its rooftops spread out behind me. This time, I was leaving without the cobwebs of the past clinging to me.

On the way up, a car went by in the opposite direction, carrying a woman with her man inside it. I stared at her for a moment, staring at me through her window, a frightened look on her face, before I broke our gaze to look up at the mouth of the Fourth River's cavern, and the water spilling from it.

When the car reached the top, I exited to wander through the lantern-lit cavern, the river beside me, until the walls were bare and no lanterns lit the way any longer, and the roar of the river was in my ears and the dark of the cave filled my eyes.

At some point, I felt the chill of rising water surround me. It trickled over my toes at first, then lifted me off my feet. I began to swim upward, pulling my arms through the current, kicking my legs furiously. Up and up and up I swam, until I opened my eyes to sunlight, blue skies that hurt to look at, yellow bridges, vast hills of green, and somewhere on the other side of this city my husband in this place would be waking up to find I had left him in the middle of the night again. He would wake the children next, the children I would never give over, and together they would walk to the place where I found myself surfacing. They have come across me here before. My husband will take my hand, say, "Early riser," and I would bring his hand to my lips to kiss it.

I gasped, taking the blue air into my lungs, the light into my eyes. The city, the city of my refuge, spread out before me, the rivers on either side of me spangled with light, a fountain spraying into the air, the towers of downtown gleaming. The smoke of that other city was gone now, the fires in that other sky were nowhere on this horizon. The smoke and the fires were in some other world, and I found that I could only weep now, selfishly grateful that it was no longer mine.

Harry and Marlowe and the Talisman of the Cult of Egil

Carrie Vaughn

Here it was, lying on a bed of stone, inert. Such an innocuous artefact, one that would go unnoticed on any machinist's workbench. A coil of copper wire wrapped around a steel cylinder just a few inches long, inset with an otherworldly crystal that seemed to glow faintly green with its own light, like a distant aurora. Truly otherworldly, as it happened.

Harry had searched for the object for more than a year, scouring ancient manuscripts, picking apart the threads of unlikely stories, tracking down reliable eyewitness accounts and separating them from fabrications, deciding which myths had a seed of fact within them and which were pure folly. Finally, she planned the expedition and arranged her disappearance from polite society for a month or more to embark on said expedition – leading to the moment that would make all the effort worthwhile. Or confirm that she had wasted her time utterly.

It would seem, she was pleased to note, that she hadn't.

The Aetherian craft that crashed in Surrey in 1869 – her entire lifetime, twenty-five years ago now – was not the first such visitor to this world, some hypothesized. This artefact proved that they were right, that another Aetherian being had arrived a thousand years before and left this mechanism behind. A spare part to the Aetherians, but worshipped as a trinket of the gods in this obscure corner of Iceland ever since.

Some would say the Cult of Egil was not far wrong, to take the artefact as a holy talisman. Harry couldn't be bothered with the theology of the matter. She needed it for more mundane purposes.

This was a piece of Aetherian technology that no one else in the world possessed. Britain had brought Aetherian wonders to the rest of humanity; by rights, it should have this as well, before anyone else. *If* she could convey it back home successfully.

Carefully, with gloved hands, she removed the object from its stone niche, where it had rested for centuries deep underground, inside the dormant volcano where the mysterious Icelandic cult that guarded it made its home. It hardly weighed anything. Surely the tingling she felt from it was her mind playing tricks. Merely the anticipation of finally having it in her possession. Nerves, that was all.

The artefact was hers. She set it safely inside the padded metal box she'd brought to transport it in, and slipped the box back inside her canvas rucksack, which she slung over her shoulder. Taking a moment to prepare for the next stage of the journey, she arranged herself and her tools. She wore a leather vest over a shirt, khaki trousers and thick work boots. Along with her rucksack, she wore a belt with several pouches, containing a rock hammer, lockpicks, compass, hand lantern and a holster with her pistol. Everything was in place. Now, to get out before they ever realized she'd been here.

The Cult of Egil's Temple of Sky Fire was located in an ancient lava tube, a twisting set of caves carved into the very earth by rivers of molten lava and searing gas. The air still smelled of sulfur, the reek of distant, burning stone. Heat rose up through the black rock, evidence that the fires that had once flowed through here still lingered beneath the crust. The tunnels had merged into a large cavern; oblique shafts had been dug to the surface to let in faint glimmers of arctic light. Polished squares of silver reflected the sunlight, directing the rays to strike a mural above the altar: a mosaic of bone and shell, in the shape of some inhuman god – an Aetherian pilot, Harry knew, with its plates of bone and curling tentacles.

The niche was one of dozens ringing the cavern and its altar, all containing carved stone figurines, polished jewels, elaborate gold ornaments. This niche didn't seem any larger than the others, or have any significance of placement. Surely no one would miss this artefact, which must have seemed incomprehensible to them.

Just then, the shouting of a crowd, like the roaring of a wave,

echoed from the main tunnel of the cavern complex. *Well,
then*. She'd lingered too long. A dozen tunnels led out of the
cavern; the only one she'd identified for certain was the one she
came in through. Her exit, if she wished to avoid the wrath of the
angry cultists, would have to be via a different route. She turned
to the tunnel that sloped upward out of the chamber – to the
surface of the mountain and not its depths, she hoped – and ran.

She wasn't stealing, not really; she had so much more use for
the object than these northern heathens possibly could. But
clearly they would not understand her reasoning; a hundred
voices raised in fury, shouting rolling curses in an ancient
tongue, followed her. Harry didn't dare stop, but risked a glance
over her shoulder.

These men, this horde – descendants of a lost tribe of Vikings
trapped under the Icelandic volcano – had degenerated to a level
of barbarity that would have shocked even their own bloodthirsty
ancestors. The first of the cultists appeared in the cavern just in
time to see which way she'd gone. A caricature of an ancient
Scandinavian warrior, the hide-draped brute wore a crude helmet,
and carried a chipped stone spear. His hair and beard shrouded
his face in a filthy mask. His fellows swarmed behind him, ant-
like, one barbarian form almost indistinguishable from the next.
Their blond and red heads of hair were unwashed, matted beyond
rescue, but the cultists cared nothing for such civilized matters.
Their only concern was the temple to their hideous alien god, and
the artefacts they had made in worship of it, in imitation of the
one they'd found, that had fallen from the sky.

Of course Harry ran for her life – and for the artefact in her
pouch, which had damned well better be worth it. Marlowe had
better be waiting for her, as they'd planned, as he'd *promised*. She
had no reason to expect he would fail her; he hadn't yet, not in all
the years she'd known him. He wouldn't now.

She ran in darkness, for a time, when the tunnel curved away
from the silver glow of the cavern. Hoping she didn't run smack
into a wall, she had to fumble for the hand lantern in her belt
pouch as she ran; she didn't dare slow down to fish for it properly.
Her vision swam, searching out the way in front of her, following
the wall by the sound of her breath echoing off of it. Finally, her
hand found the lantern, and she pressed the switch to activate its

green Aetherian glow. By this light she could see only a few feet before her, but it was enough.

A hundred leather-clad footsteps pounded on the stone behind her.

Up ahead, a spot of sunlight shone – the tunnel entrance. Escape – or *rescue*, rather. The light ahead expanded, and the stink of sulfur in the basalt tunnel gave way to a touch of icy arctic air. When the tunnel opened, Harry skidded to a stop, balanced at the edge of a cliff that dropped away a thousand feet to a rocky, blasted landscape below.

Marlowe wasn't there.

The mountain had dozens of caves, places where the volcanic heat steamed forth. Marlowe would be keeping watch on them all, searching for her. She still had time. An hour before he gave her up as lost. Shoving her lantern back in its pouch, she reached into another one for a flare, struck the flint on the fuel, pointed it to the sky, and launched the charge. A fiery missile, sparking green, arced upward, trailing thick black smoke behind it. If that didn't work . . .

Before her was a long fall on hard rocks. Behind her, the cultists. She inched to the edge of the drop, keeping a hand on the tunnel wall for balance. If she had to, she'd jump. Slow her fall down the rocky slope as much as she could, and maybe Marlowe could pick up the pieces of her broken body. Or find and rescue the artefact, if there weren't enough pieces of *her* to collect. The flare's smoke hung in the air, a trail leading back to her – while it lasted.

She drew her Aetherian pistol from its holster, though it hardly mattered – the gun's charge would only last long enough to stop a handful of the cultists. The fiery glow of torches preceded their assault. She prepared to slide over the edge.

Suddenly, the flare's trail of smoke dissipated, scattered by a blast of wind that pressed Harry to the wall. Arm over her face, she chanced a look – and saw the airship drop down the side of the mountain, to the tunnel entrance. Its curved bladder and sleek gondola blocked the sun and threw a shadow over her.

Stone-filled bags fell from the gondola – ballast dropping, slowing the ship's descent. Marlowe had timed this very close indeed.

The Aetherian engine in the back of the airship whined,

throwing off green-tinted sparks behind it. When the gondola came alongside the mouth of the tunnel, the door to the cabin was wide open, and there was Marlowe, just like he was supposed to be. The pilot was obscured, made larger and more terrifying by the greatcoat and leather-padded goggles masking his features. He held his rifle at the ready.

Harry clutched her satchel, her pistol in her right hand, and didn't look back, leaping from the cliff's edge to the airship cabin. Marlowe stepped in behind her, slammed shut the door, and lunged to the airship's controls. A Viking spear *thunked* against the gondola's side. Out the window, Harry saw the horde reach the edge of the cliff – in fact, two of the fellows fell over, pushed by their enthusiastic brethren rushing too fast behind. *Good riddance.*

The airship sank a few more feet, then stopped, and with another bag of ballast gone, rose up again. The guidance propeller spun faster, and the ship jumped forward, wind whipping across the bladder above them. The ship raced away from the tunnel, along the slope of the shattered volcano, and soon the cultists' berserker shouting faded against the sound of wind and rumbling engine.

They'd done it.

Marlowe turned another set of levers and the sound changed, drive motors coming online, whirring, moving the craft laterally. The mountain, its black crags and broken clefts, slid past, like a painting on a roller. In moments, the ship turned to the coast of Iceland, and open sky lay before them.

Settling her breathing, Harry took in lungfuls of cool clean air, letting its touch calm her. She slouched against the plush seat at the side of the cabin.

Marlowe turned in his pilot's chair to face her, pulling the goggles down to hang around his neck. In his early thirties, he was weathered in a way that spoke of experience rather than hardship, his brown hair unkempt and his cheeks covered with stubble because he simply didn't have time to bother rather than because he was sloppy. His clothing was simple, practical. His eyes shone, and his smile was playful. Butterflies fluttered in her stomach.

"If you'd misjudged the ballast you dropped by a *pound*, you'd have lost me," she said, scowling.

"But I didn't. You knew I wouldn't," he said.

"Bloody hell," she sighed.

The motor droned, sending vibrations through the cabin. The rattling soothed her.

"You got it," he said, a declaration of fact rather than a question of her ability.

"Do you even have to ask?"

"I never doubted. May I see?"

Moving to the co-pilot's chair, she retrieved the box from her satchel and rested it on her lap. Marlowe leaned forward, watching as she revealed the artefact. She smiled – he clutched his hands together in an effort to keep from grabbing the thing from her. She presented the cylinder to him cupped in her hands, and admired his flat, astonished expression. He sighed a quiet breath and picked it up.

"I'm not sure I even know what it is," he said, holding it up to the cockpit window, turning it this way and that in the light. "Part of a generation coil, perhaps, or an amplification rod."

"But it's Aetherian. The stories were true."

"Yes," he murmured. "It most certainly is, and they were."

The possibilities presented by this new artefact clearly entranced Marlowe, but Harry was taken by a larger question: the Aetherians had visited Earth before. Perhaps often, even. There might even be artefacts – new pieces to the Aetherian puzzle – scattered all over the world. No one had even known to look for them.

"Where do you suppose they found it? The cultists?" she said.

"The stories say they found it frozen in ice that had drifted from the north."

"But there had to be another ship, another crash, even. Where is the rest of it?"

"It might be a tool left behind. Perhaps they didn't crash at all."

She stared out the window to a sun-bleached sky. "It rather begs the question, doesn't it? This proves they've traveled here more than once. What do we do if the Aetherians ever come back?"

Marlowe looked up from the coil, and she met his gaze. Neither of them had an answer. In the twilight shadow of the volcano, the crystal gave off a faint glow.

"All this time, and the power source is still active. Weak, but active," he said. He produced a jeweler's loupe from an inside vest pocket and tucked it over his eye. "Usual switching circuitry here – we saw this sort of thing in all the shipboard systems of the Surrey crash. Used to route power. I wonder . . . Harry, my toolkit is under the bench, if you wouldn't mind—"

"Are you sure this is wise? Shouldn't you wait until you're in your laboratory?"

"This will only take a moment."

A little digging in the bench cupboard revealed the kit, a slim aluminum case containing the tools for manipulation of finer mechanisms. He chose a wire probe from the collection. When he tapped it against the alien cylinder, his hands were steady as a surgeon's.

The device emitted a hissing noise – gas released under pressure.

"What was that?" Harry asked.

Marlow tapped the cylinder again, and the hissing stopped. Bringing the artefact close to his face, he sniffed.

"Smell that," he said, offering it to her.

She hated to get too close to the coil, but she didn't have to, to identify the reek. "It's sulphur."

"Some kind of gas exchange, I'd wager," Marlowe said. "God, I really need to take this apart . . ."

"We'll know more, once we're back in London."

"Oh. About that." He handed the device back to her. "We may have a bit of a problem getting home."

"Good of you to mention it," she said, smirking, wrapping the coil again and securing it safely in the box. "What kind of a problem?"

"The Germans have established a blockade."

She harrumphed. "We knew that was coming. We'll simply avoid the Channel and approach from the north."

"Ah, no. Not just the Channel." She raised a brow, and he continued. "They've blockaded the entire British Isles."

A bit of a problem, indeed.

The battle had been raging for a week – naturally, the Queen and the Empire could not let a blockade of the home country stand.

Marlowe had spent the time, while Harry had been infiltrating the volcanic tunnels in Iceland, hiding the *Kestrel* in valleys and ravines, going aloft at intervals to intercept wireless transmissions to try to get some kind of news.

They were too far away yet to see signs of fighting. Knowing the respective strength of each of the forces, though, Harry was certain she and Marlowe wouldn't be able to avoid the battle for long. They weren't at all equipped for it – the *Kestrel* was a courier ship, built for speed and agility. She had no armor and little in the way of weapons. Perhaps they'd do better to find a safe port and wait out the blockade.

Except they had to get the coil to Prince George, and to Marlowe's laboratory. The artefact could change everything. She thought through a multitude of plans – land elsewhere, make their way home by some other route. Make for the Americas and rendezvous with a more capable warship. Or did they dare attempt to run the blockade? She knew what Marlowe would say.

"So, do we go above or below the fray?" she asked.

"Above. They've got surface ships on the water."

"Right, then."

She went to the safe in the back, a square of thick steel tucked over the driveshaft, put her satchel containing the artefact inside, locked it tight, and tied the key to a cord around her neck. Even if the ship didn't make it through, no one would be able to gain access to the box without destroying its contents. Not without her.

"What can I do to help?" she asked.

"Don't jostle the boat," he said. "Or if you'd like you can pour us some brandy." He glanced over his shoulder and quirked a grin.

"I'm your maid, then?" she said.

"I stashed the bottle in the cupboard under the seat there." He nodded to the bench by the hatch.

The bench seat was hinged, revealing the promised cupboard, packed tightly with boxes, slots, canvas bags, blankets and fur coats for high altitudes, provisions for an extended journey, and her own package of supplies. Good. In a slot that looked as if it had been specially made to enclose it, she found the bottle of brandy and a pair of glass tumblers.

She joined him at the front of the cabin. The dashboard had enough of a ledge for her to set the tumblers on it and pour. After, she tucked the bottle in a pouch on the wall to keep it from sliding or falling. Marlowe took the glass before she could hand it to him.

"Cheers," he said, and they clinked glasses.

The liquid went down smoothly and warmed her blood in an instant. Marlowe always kept the good stuff on hand.

Before them, through the thick glass at the front of the cabin, the ocean extended. This had become the simplest part of the journey. Marlowe's piloting would manage the ocean winds and unpredictable weather. She had no idea what awaited them once they reached home. Harry squinted, searching for the haze of gunsmoke and fires.

Best to drink up while they could.

"How high are we going to have to get to avoid it, then?"

He frowned. "They've got rockets that reach higher than anything that flies. We'll do what we can, but it probably won't be high enough."

"Rockets? How?"

"They stole them, in the time-honored fashion," he said.

She slumped in the chair. Had the entire journey been wasted? "It's all been for nothing," she murmured.

"If that were true, I wouldn't have bothered coming for you." He gave her that smile again. And it was true. She imagined herself waiting at the cave entrance, the horde of cultists coming up behind her. Having to jump . . .

She drained the brandy and poured herself another glass.

"That bad?"

"I hate this," she said.

"Amen," he murmured.

The sun set, and the air grew cold. Below them, the ocean was the color of pewter and seemed still, frozen, like a painting. No moon shone.

Harry slept for an hour or so, then offered to watch over the ship while Marlowe slept. That he didn't hesitate to take the offer she took as a great compliment. He stretched out on the bench in the back of the cabin, rolled a blanket around him, and instantly fell asleep in the way only long-time soldiers could manage. He snored, softly, the noise like just another exhaust or gear on the airship. If she told him he snored, he wouldn't have believed her.

They'd reach Ireland by dawn. Then, Marlowe would ascend as high as the *Kestrel* was able. Breathable air would fail before the engines did, yet they had to climb high enough to avoid the blockade and not draw attention from scouts; they had to skirt that boundary without crossing it and blacking out.

She wouldn't have to touch the controls unless something went wrong – the winds changed, or they were attacked. She watched pressure gauges, altitude monitors and compass readings. Their course remained steady; she had to add a little gas to the bladders to maintain altitude. Marlowe had left his goggles hanging on a hook above the window.

The cabin was dark except for a dim lamp near the control board, the faint glow of the engine in back, and a tealight for warmth near the cage where a pair of carrier pigeons slept. Too much light – a fire in the stove, for example – would make them a target. And it was only going to get colder, this high up, at night.

Once the sky darkened, the first signs of battle became visible. On the eastern horizon, tracers arced, distant shooting stars, orange, yellow, green. Fireballs rose up from unseen explosions and dissipated into raining sparks. At the moment, the scene was a remote tableau, an unreal moving picture. She could imagine the hint of pyrotechnics was a harmless show put on for her benefit. Except for all the thousands of people dying underneath it.

Dim lamplight turned the cabin ghostly, flat, unreal. She wrapped the blanket more tightly around her. For the moment, she could believe she drifted between worlds, and oddly enough the sensation came as a relief. In this suspended place, she could breathe easy, let down her guard, and pretend that all was well.

At dawn, Marlowe's snoring stopped, and soon after he shifted, the blanket rustling as he pushed it away, the cabin shivering with his movements. He pulled a pair of heavy fur coats from the storage cupboard and brought them to the front.

"How are we doing, then?" he asked.

"Steady as she goes, captain." She smiled at his crazily ruffled hair.

He gazed out the cabin's front window. The sky had grown hazy with the smoke of battle. A particularly large explosion bronzed his face for a moment, even at this distance. That would have been one of the larger airships going down, hit by a rocket maybe, all its gas and munitions igniting. Debris fell after the initial fireball, flaming bits of fabric and metal plunging to earth, like diving birds.

He said. "God, would you look at that. I wonder if that was one of ours or one of theirs?"

"We've no way of knowing, and nothing we could do to help even if we knew." She tried to sound offhand about it, but only managed bitter.

Marlowe put his hand on her arm, where it rested on the edge of the pilot's chair. Warm, comforting, an anchor. They both looked at it there. The impropriety of it seemed very distant, and she imagined everything she might do – touch his cheek, turn his face toward her, kiss him – and her brother and grandmother would be none the wiser.

He quickly pulled his hand away, but not before she could catch it, squeeze it, then let it go. Just a moment of contact, gloved hand to gloved hand. It would have to be enough. They had more important things to think about.

"We've got to get over this before the scouts see us," he said.

She moved out of the way so he could take over the pilot's seat. They bundled up in the coats. He pulled back a pair of levers, the engines buzzed, and the cabin tipped back, pressing them into their seats. The *Kestrel* climbed, and climbed.

The battle climbed with them. It wasn't just rockets reaching this height; airships climbed with them, exchanging broadsides. Harry was already panting for breath, using her whole chest to suck in too little air. She couldn't imagine fighting like this. But they were headed for the thick of it.

"I thought coming in from the north would avoid most of this mess," Marlowe said, the words punctuated with gulps for air.

"What must it be like on the Channel?"

He pointed. "See there, at two o'clock. Is it coming closer?"

The triple-motored airship wasn't just coming closer, it was set to intercept them. "We can't let them stop us, even if it's one of ours."

"Especially if it's one of ours," he said, giving half a grin.

"Do I dare hoist a signal flag?" she said.

"Give it a moment. Let's see if we can outrun 'em."

"Bloody hell."

Marlowe started throwing levers, and the motor's humming changed in pitch. The ship rose, and the horizon tilted as they changed course.

Their ship was small and fast, but their opponent was an interceptor, all lift and motor and guns, specifically designed to stop ships like this one.

"It's one of theirs," she said. "Look at the flag."

When the sun hit it directly, the red field with the black eagle painted on the bladder was clear. Marlowe would crash the ship rather than let them be boarded now. Though they'd most likely get blown from the sky before it came to that. They couldn't risk letting the Germans take possession of the coil.

"You said all we have is a pair of rifles?" she said.

"I would never lie to you about my weaponry, Harry," he said, eyebrow arched. And why exactly did she want to laugh at a time like this?

She grabbed Marlowe's goggles and put them on, adjusting the strap. Then she found the rifle and checked that its charge was full. "Where's the harness?"

"Hanging across from the door, there."

She found the gear and hooked the leather straps over her shoulders and around her chest, checking the buckles three times. The straps and hardware were all well oiled and in excellent repair – but of course they were, this was Marlowe's ship, after all. One end of the line hooked to the front of the harness. The rest of it she hung coiled around her forearm while she opened to the door to cabin.

Wind tore at her. She hadn't buttoned the coat all the way, and the collar flapped around her neck, sending a freezing draft across her skin, but that didn't matter. The other end of the line hooked to the track ringing the outside of the cabin. Normally, the track and harness were used as a safety measure for mechanics making repairs. But she'd always thought it looked like fun.

She gripped the rifle, and jumped.

The line caught, and she swung out as the harness caught, dug into her shoulders and ribs, and arched her toward the cabin's side. Sticking her feet out, she landed and ran until the line came up against the first bracket. Leaning forward, she had a view across the nose of the *Kestrel*. Bracing, she held the rifle steady to her shoulder, aimed along the barrel and waited for Marlowe to swing the ship around and give her a shot. She wished she'd thought of tying her hair back first; it whipped behind her, catching on the line.

Her best chance would be to rip a shot through the enemy ship's air bladders. Even if she didn't start an explosion that destroyed the airship, it would lose lift and maneuverability, giving Marlowe time to get them out of this. The *Kestrel*'s motor droned, increasing in pitch, and the craft lurched upward, the nose tipping down, as if the whole thing had been caught in an updraft. Harry shifted her feet to keep her balance.

There it was, the Kaiser's black eagle staring at her with contempt, or so it seemed. Cannons mounted on the base of the cabin swung around. They were still too far away for Harry to bother firing at them. But soon.

An explosive scream cut through the air, and in spite of herself Harry flinched back. When she looked, she saw the long trail of black smoke, but never saw what made it. The trail led to the enemy airship, which transformed into a fireball a moment later. The heat of it washed over her, and she ducked, clinging to her line, pulling herself close to the cabin for shelter. The *Kestrel* rocked with the shock wave, but Marlowe increased altitude yet again and got them above the worst of it. Breathing was very difficult now; blackness flashed at the edges of her vision. It was all wind and no air up here.

Below her, gas from the German ship ignited in blue flames that quickly faded to yellow and dispersed, munitions vanishing in bursts of orange fire; the ship disintegrated and fell, pieces trailing arcs of smoke and sparks. Bodies fell. Harry saw one man, still alive, limbs flailing as he tumbled through air. She imagined she could hear his screams, but of course could hear nothing over the roar of the wind.

There was only the one fortuitous rocket, sent to destroy their enemy. She might never learn if that had been by chance or design.

Marlowe waved at her through the front window, his expression showing concern. He was too sensible to actually yell at her to come back inside. Clutching both her safety line and the rifle, she didn't have a free hand to wave back. Carefully, she braced against the harness, freeing herself to signal back at him. He pressed his lips and nodded. He moved a lever. The nose tipped down, beginning a descent. She made herself stay still and focus on breathing, imagining she could tell that the air grew thicker. The goggles brought her eyesight to a narrow focus, and she sought to see beyond the edges of her vision.

The horizon was a distant smudge; the grey haze made it impossible to see where ground ended and sky began. She could imagine seeing the curve of the Earth from here. When she looked up, the sky became like night, shifting from pale blue to a deep indigo, then darker still, to the black of twilight. And beyond that, stars.

If man were ever to travel to the upper reaches, past the atmosphere and into Aetherian spaces, they had a serious problem to solve: they had to learn to bring their air with them. Or they had to learn to stop breathing. There was some debate about which alternative the Aetherians had used. Finding a solution for these reckless airship pilots venturing forth, as far as they could until they couldn't breathe at all, that was the key to all. If only . . .

Marlowe knocked on the window this time, and she brought herself back.

Sliding the line along its track, she walked along the cabin hull to the door and tried to pretend that her legs weren't shaking. Marlowe was waiting for her. Handing the rifle to him, she swung inside, unhooking herself from the track. When he shut the door, she finally breathed easy again.

"You all right?"

"I didn't even get a chance to fire," she said, pulling the goggles off, handing them back to him. Her legs were still trembling, and she lowered herself to the bench.

"Never mind that we'd never have gotten close enough before they blew us out of the air."

"Oh, yes, indeed. You'll have to find out who I ought to send a bottle of wine to for that rocket."

"A bottle of wine? Seems this would be worth at least your firstborn."

"I'm afraid my firstborn, should such a person ever exist, is already promised to my grandmother and brother."

"Ah. Of course."

She fumbled with the buckles, and Marlowe managed to pretend not to notice, but still helped, coiling the rope and pulling the harness off her shoulders once she'd finally managed to unfasten it. She sighed and rolled her shoulders – they were going to be very sore for a couple of days, and she'd probably have bruising around her ribs. Not anywhere that anyone would be likely to notice, so they didn't matter at all.

"I think I could use another finger of your brandy, Marlowe."

He was already reaching for the bottle.

They had managed to circumvent the worst of the blockade, and reached the shores of Scotland. There, they put up their flags and lit the cabin lights, to prevent any misunderstandings. In friendly territory now, Marlowe felt comfortable using the wireless. He posed as a standard military courier ship that had been damaged in fighting and was seeking the safety of a mooring in Liverpool. He used the coded phrase that would, in fact, get them permission to continue on to London.

Harry's preferred choice of communication was more primitive, but less prone to eavesdropping than the wireless. This would go straight where she wanted it, and there was little chance someone could intercept She wrote a note on a strip of paper, using her and her brother's code, rolled it tightly, and put it in the tiny canister that she then fit to the leg of one of the pigeons. She held the cooing creature gently to her chest, smoothing its feathers and whispering comforts to it, before throwing it out the open portal window, into the bright sun. Its white wings flashed as the bird dipped around the ship, then seemed to vanish as it raced on.

Harry went back to the front of the cabin, where Marlowe sat.

She sighed. "I don't think I'm ready to be back just yet."

"I could turn us around, head toward the battle," he said.

"Do you really think that piece of metal will help us end the war?"

"Strange, isn't it? So much hope in that little thing. But I do think it's worth it."

Not strange at all. Little things had often changed the world. Whatever it was worth, this was better than sitting at Marlborough House, waiting for something to happen.

They reached the Thames and followed it to the mooring station outside Windsor.

"Well then," she sighed. "I suppose I ought to make myself presentable."

"I'm sorry I haven't got anything like a decent room for you—"

"Nonsense. We'll make do."

He blushed, pointedly turning away.

She retrieved her luggage from the bench. From it, she unfolded her proper lady's attire and all its attendant architecture. She ought to have a good wash before putting it on, but there was no chance of that. She would have to make do. She stripped the old rugged shirt and trousers she'd been in for the last week and donned the crisp linen shift, smoothing out the wrinkles as best she could. She'd had the corset made with fasteners in front for just such occasions as this. Her sisters would be scandalized, to see her dressing herself. In front of a soldier, even. She had her back to Marlowe; he could have been sneaking glances at her all this time. Of course, the worse scandal was that she rather hoped he was.

Then came the gown, which she'd managed to pack well enough to prevent the worst of the wrinkles. The fasteners in back, however, presented some difficulty. She could feel the hook and eye at the back of her neck, but no matter how she contorted herself, couldn't get them to catch.

She turned to the pilot's chair. "Marlowe—"

He sprang to his feet, as if he'd been watching. Waiting for her to ask.

At her back, he fumbled with the tiny hooks, the tips of his fingers brushing along the bare skin of her neck. Closing her eyes, she reveled in the warm flush his touch inspired. The breath of his sigh tickled her skin. If she took a step back, she would be leaning against him, and she was very tempted.

If only they could only stand like this for the rest of the hour. The rest of the war . . .

He moved away, but only after smoothing away a lock of her hair. Back at his seat, he clasped his hands together and gazed at her with a look of blank innocence.

They both practiced that look.

"Thank you," she said. He nodded.

She continued with buttons, hooks, earrings, necklace, arranging them all properly. Next she used the little tray of cosmetics with the tiny fold-out mirror. After some powder, some color on her lips and cheeks, and a few pins in her hair, she'd be able to pass in the most respectable society without comment. She saw the gown, with its corset, ribbing and petticoats, as armor.

"All right, I'm finished. How do I look?" She gave her skirt a last brush.

He said simply. "Your Highness. Princess Maud returns."

She ducked her gaze. She wasn't ready for Princess Maud to return.

"It's amazing how you do that," he continued, when she didn't speak. "You're a chameleon."

"I think you are the only one who sees my true form."

His smile flashed, and fled. "Sometimes I'm not sure I've seen it yet."

Marlowe steered them to an upper landing platform at the air port. He followed the signals of the tower controller, sending back his reply with the lantern at the window.

"I'll get the line," she said, intending to throw out the mooring lines to the deckhands.

"You'd better not," he said, nodding at her current dress. "Why don't you gather your things?"

She unlocked the safe and retrieved the prize, which she put in the valise that had hidden her gown, burying it in her dirty clothes. She tucked her pistol in a pocket in the side, and remembered to keep that side of the bag closest to her. Not that she expected to encounter any trouble here; rather, it was habit.

Marlowe and the deckhands got the ship anchored perfectly well without her, of course. But she felt useless, standing there, stiff as a statue in this clothing.

Out the window, she could see the street leading toward the village and castle, and the carriage drawn by a pair of large bay horses parked there. The carriage door would have her brother's crest painted on it. The royal crest belonging to the Crown Prince. He'd gotten her message, then, and made it as easy as possible to bring the box straight to him.

Anchored and still against the tugging of the bladder above it, the ship felt like a rock instead of a bird. As soon as the door to the cabin opened, she'd have to leave. She and Marlowe stood together, regarding one another. She never knew what to say in these moments, when their missions ended. Whatever she said felt awkward and artificial, and as soon as he was gone she'd think of everything she should have said.

"You'll come to the Royal Academy? To be on hand when they examine the artefact?" she asked.

"I hope to. But I suspect the general will send me and the *Kestrel* to Plymouth, to assist in the defense."

That hadn't been part of the original plan. The war had crept far too close to home shores; she preferred to forget.

"But I will see you again, soon?"

"As soon as possible, I should think," he said.

They shook hands, as if they were familiar colleagues and not . . . she couldn't decide exactly *what* they were. There was no civilized name for it. As she made her way down the steps from the platform to the street and Prince George's carriage, she could feel Marlowe watching her, and was glad of it.

Anna in the Moonlight

Jonathan Wood

The stark sunlight cast everything in high contrast. The lines of armored battle suits – new uncompromising skins soon to be donned by the boys at the front, ready to deal death with a blast of steam and the screech of steel; fists the size of children; bronze cockpits still a mass of exposed cogs and mismatching gears – stood limp and gleaming. In the darkness of their shadows, Frank Dirk, Charlie, Tommy and Pip wrapped their faces around cheap cigarettes and willed their work break to last longer.

"That'll show them dirty animals." Dirk thumbed at the vast hammer he had personally loaded onto one suit's arm. "Can you imagine that thing hitting one of them in the face? Bam!" His hands described the imagined spectacle of exploding tissue and bone. He laughed. He was the youngest of them, just sixteen.

"What they deserve." Pip nodded.

"Why do they do it?" Tommy said. He was seventeen, like the rest of them, and the enemy's penchant for supplementing their natural, God-given flesh with animal parts was as beyond his comprehension as it was his friends'.

"'Cos they're godless animals who don't deserve nothing better than to have their heads smashed by Dirk's hammer." Frank repeated the popular theory.

"When I'm old enough, I'm signing straight up," Charlie said. "Can't wait to bring home a hide or two."

Frank joined in the chorus of patriotic ayes that followed this statement, but, as his eyes skimmed the familiar factory, he could not imagine plunging into no-man's-land, gun in hand. It was not that he was a coward, he told himself, just that while he was sure of the moral void the Deformed represented, they had never harmed him directly. Better, surely, to let them damn themselves on their own and not get involved. Still appearances and teenage bravado required him to agree, raucously, with Charlie.

Dear reader, for most of our recent history, no two men have been as much lauded as Lords Percy Warburn of Essex and Simon Tillet of York. They, both you and I have been told, possess the hands that are shaping our nation. Their actions, though "troubled", are forging our way of life and, because of this, we are told, we should look up to them with adulation and even envy. Implicit in this suggestion is the idea that we are satisfied with our current way of life. I wish to correct this situation. Indeed, by the end of this short essay, I hope you will be as disenchanted with the myth of our glorious nation as I.

Two weeks later, the factory took Dirk's life. A chain had given way and a massive cannon fallen and claimed its first victim, dashing Dirk's brains out and spreading them across the floor. Accidents were common. Machines, engines, chains – they all wore down over time, eroding slowly, beneath notice, until the eventual, inevitable disaster.

At the funeral, the priest praised Dirk for building the battle suits, for helping bring, "God's cleansing fire to the godless animals, to Satan's deformed masses".

It was days before Dirk's seventeenth birthday. Frank and the boys had planned to take him up to York, to get him atrociously drunk. Out of some grief-stricken sense of loyalty they undertook the trip without him.

On the train, Frank sat next to his girl, Pam. She was beautiful to him, wrapped in black, her fine blonde curls escaping from behind the darkness of her bonnet, cropped short for practicality but still lingering on her narrow shoulders, still framing her blue eyes. Her curved frame wrapped neatly around his broad one.

They sped through well-tilled countryside. Then, with a shriek from the train's whistle, fields collapsed into houses and factories, and brick and steel rose around them and enclosed them, and they were in the steaming, stinking heart of York.

At first they drank with the solemn fervor of the bereft, but by the time they arrived at the fourth pub their tongues were looser and anecdotes of Dirk, his foolishness, his enthusiasm, his youth, flowed between them. Frank stayed close to Pam.

The day dragged and blurred in drunkenness. Dirk's name became a simple refrain, the meaning of their inebriation left behind in the gutter along with the contents of their stomachs.

It was as the bell for last orders clanged at the final pub that Pam spotted the man. He was sitting up at the bar, apart from the others. He still wore his hat, which was odd, and at first Frank thought that was why Pam had pointed him out. But then Pam whispered more and Frank saw that the hat was askew and that the man's ears were those of a cat.

He was Deformed.

Charlie, his bleary eyes on Pam, said they knew what they had to do.

When the man left the bar, they all followed. Frank tried to linger back. He knew this man deserved the beating he was about to receive, everyone, every paper, every politician, every priest had told him that his whole life. He just didn't know what the man had done to deserve it from *him*.

Then, somehow he was at the front of the group. The man's exposed cat ear twitched and he turned around. Pam touched him on the back, just a little push. Charlie leered and raised a fist. Before he could strike, Frank slammed a fist into the man's Deformed gut. The wind whistled from the Deformed man's lungs before he even had time to call out. A couple more blows had the man dizzy. Everything moved in a swift, slick blur. They dragged the man into an alleyway and set to work on him with boots, and fists, and anything else they could find that would inflict pain.

The ground heaved below Frank. His fists seemed to move sluggishly through the air, hesitant. But Dirk had died to kill this man, to kill the Deformed, and Pam was screaming at him to just *finish it*. His hands hurt. But this was what you did, wasn't it? Boys at the front were dying because of bastards like this. The Deformed man's hands moved feebly, like a baby's first motions, trying to fend off the blows.

"Do it!" Pam screamed, her voice the only clear thing in the fog of drink and confusion. "Do it for Dirk!"

Frank watched the man's eyes as his fist came down. They were the palest blue, stretched to circles with fear, but fixed on Frank's face, even as the nose beneath them gave way and shards of it fired backwards into the Deformed man's brain. Then the eyes went blank and rolled back and away to stare at nothing evermore.

Frank staggered back and away as the others beat the dead body to pulp. His mind rattled loose in the thick meat of his body. He could feel the blood, warm on his face. He had killed a man. For all the damage the others had done it was he who had forced the man across the boundary between life and death. His knuckles ached, cut and bruised. But it had been the right thing to do.

He felt faint, his skin greasy and thin, the rules of the world pressing in on him but he knew, surely, that it had been the right thing to do.

The great sadness of the tale I will tell you is made greater by the auspicious start our two young Lordlings had in life. Both grew up in Oxfordshire in adjacent estates; went to the finest schools together, where they undeniably excelled; and, as only children, both enjoyed the full attention of their devoted parents. Both men attended Cambridge and, to all intents and purposes, both appeared poised to become excellent additions to England's academic community.

However, the seeds of our downfall came with Lord Simon's adoption of a religious mania in his early twenties. While the faith of men and women such as you and I is a thing to be admired, in Lord Simon it became a perverse and inflexible fundamentalism.

Who knows what catastrophe caused his sudden embracement of the religious message? All that can be certain is that it would have been far better for this country if he had remained an atheist – the detriment to his soul could be no worse.

At first, Frank blamed Pam. It had been she, after all, who had spotted the man, she who had given the order that his fist had obeyed. But, of course, she had only been telling him the right thing to do.

Next, he blamed himself for listening to Pam. But how could he not have? If he had not killed the man he would have been forgiving the man's sin, and if God could not forgive it, who was he?

So he blamed the dead man himself.

The man had sold his soul to Satan long ago, he told himself, as he smoked alone, apart from his friends. What he had done was nothing worse than putting down a rabid dog. It wasn't really a man that he had killed. He read pamphlets that supported this claim, listened to speeches. His conviction of the inevitability of his actions grew stronger day by day. When he could not sleep, hands shaking, sickness gnawing at his gut, he would tell himself that he brought God's cleansing fire to the godless animals.

A week after the murder, he lied about his age to a recruitment officer and joined the Army.

His friends were quiet at the news. He couldn't tell if they were proud of him or ashamed of themselves. Charlie in particular was notable in his silence. None of them spoke of the Deformed man in the alleyway.

Pam was tearful, had threatened to go and tell the recruitment officer his real age, and for a moment Frank's commitment had wavered. But what sort of man would he be if he backed down now? How could he deserve the sight of his reflection in her soft eyes? So he argued with her, spoke to her about what he had been taught to believe about right and wrong, about what was worth fighting for, about what God wanted from him. It would be a betrayal to those beliefs, he said, his gut hardening as he did so, to not go to the front, to not fight. He would not compromise his morals.

When she was sure he was going, she took him to a dark place where many youths their age had been before, and let him touch her how he pleased.

Then he was off to Manchester for two days of training. He and three hundred other young men all packed into a community hall that should only have held half their number, packed together so tight they couldn't run even if their nerve failed. Frank, caught in their solid heat, knew there was no way out. He learned how to load his rifle, fix his bayonet, and how to salute his superiors. He learned little about his enemy that he didn't know already, drill sergeants barking about the Deformed's deprivations of the soul and how it was reflected in their twisted flesh, shouting about the necessity of their death. He sang the national anthem, praised God, and hid his shaking hands.

The train took them all eighteen miles south, depositing them two miles short of their final destination. It was a gray day, damp but not too cold. The sun shone whitely from behind a scrim of clouds. Frank was told that he was to join the fourteenth. "Twice as lucky as the seventh," one corporal told him with a grin.

They were led down a dirt track. The surroundings had once been fields, but now they were tramped mud, tracks and footprints scouring the wet earth. There were even the splayed marks of battle suits criss-crossing the muck.

As the new recruits marched down the track, he heard thunder coming, although he couldn't see the signs of rain. After a while, he realized it was the guns. His palms began to sweat and his rifle became slippery in his hands.

About a mile from the front, the track started to descend steeply and soon mud walls rose above their heads and they walked a sunken path. Smaller, tributary trenches flowed in and out of the main pathway and occasionally groups of recruits would be led off into the filthy maze, but Frank remained tramping forwards. His route was fixed.

The thunderhead of violence before the troops was palpable in the air. Frank's pace slowed. He walked hunched. He checked that his helmet was strapped on tightly. He saw the silhouette of a great battle suit plowing its way across the elevated horizon, spitting steam and cannonballs. He pointed to it and turned to the corporal who'd made the crack about the fourteenth.

"I used to make them," he said, and the knowledge belied the fear that was tightening in his stomach and his balls.

"Yeah?" the corporal said, his once-friendly mouth now a harsh line. "Well don't tell anyone else, 'cos those fucking death traps take almost as many of our boys as the goddamned Deformed."

The blunt T-junction end of the track rolled toward them, dirt flying through the air as if it could no longer tell whether it should be beneath their feet or up with the birds. They were called to a halt a hundred yards from the line, from no-man's-land. The sound was absolute: a blanket that smothered them.

Trying to detach himself from his fear, Frank copied the actions of the men around him – checking his rifle was loaded, that the safety was off – and his heart tried to hammer a path out of the cage of his ribs. But he had killed the Deformed man. Where else could he be but here?

Then they were running, the thunder all around them. Hands were forcing him up the ladders, keeping him moving forwards.

Then he was in the pack, mindlessly following them as they charged through the filth and muck. And there was a kind of peace then, with nothing to think about, all doubts left behind in the trench, and only orders to follow. Everything around them brown and grey. The noise so all-encompassing it was almost like silence. Just the feeling of his chest rising and falling, his feet rising and falling, his fellow soldiers rising and falling. He didn't have to worry about why he was there, if he'd done the right thing, if he would do it in what was to come.

Then, out of the mud, came the Deformed.

All around Frank, his fellow recruits were stumbling, falling to their knees, all in a desperate attempt to get away. Frank stood, silent, dumb. He stood his ground as around him the nerve of others failed.

The enemy came at frightening speed, propelled by legs that were not their own. Ostrich legs, horses' legs, dogs' legs, kangaroos', the coil-unwind-coil of snakes' bodies, vast wings heavy with mud, tentacles, all thrashing forwards bringing with them claws, and teeth, and vast jaws that snapped and slavered, and stark, furious, but terrifyingly human eyes. And every eye was the same pale blue as the man in the alleyway, every one lusting for deserved revenge.

His gun fired – a yellow white flare, a blaze of color in the monotone battlefield.

A wave of flesh – human, animal, interstitial – rolled out of the gloom and broke over Frank and the fleeing troops.

Red joined the battle's palette.

Lord Percy did not share Lord Simon's religious views, but the difference between the friends lay dormant until they reached their thirties. In the meantime, both continued the ascent promised by their early academic careers. Lord Percy became a medical doctor and surgeon of near preternatural skill. He pioneered several amazing techniques, and supplemented his family's fortune with his successful experiments in the field of pharmacology. Lord Simon's mind had been captured by engineering and he enjoyed equal success. Soon the wheels of industry were powered by his engines.

Had both men stayed in their respective fields all, I suspect, may have been well, religious differences or no. Sadly, they both chose to enter the public stage. That they chose to enter this fray through the institution of politics, a realm that was once reserved for the democratic debate of what was best for this country, cannot be used to defend their later actions. Indeed, quite the opposite, given what they have done to this once great field – their use of their financial and industrial clout to manipulate the newspapers and to forcefully grab the public ear – undoes any positive aspirations they may have held.

In the end, the Deformed were driven back by machine-gun fire. When the noise stopped, Frank stumbled back to the trenches through the bodies of his fellows, half of them slaughtered by his own side's bullets. His clothes were torn but his wounds amazingly shallow.

He was shown to a bed in a bunker of packed earth where he lay and stared at the ceiling. From time to time he would be ordered to his feet to go and fling bullets at the writhing mass of the enemy. At other times, a different command would send him to the mess hall. Between eating and killing, he lay down and failed to sleep.

After a week's insomnia, of inexplicable survival, static buzzing in his ears, exhaustion claimed him, and, mud-spattered and disheveled, he collapsed, unconscious into his cot. The nightmares came then (*drowning in a sea of flesh, choking on fingers and eyeballs, filled with a final dreadful sense of release*) and he woke screaming, but, on the whole, he felt stronger. A numbness had settled into him, static settled into silence. He found a way to function, like frozen fingers fumbling bullets into the breech of a barrel that they no longer felt.

He spoke to his fellow soldiers but tried to avoid learning their names. They seemed to die so easily. In the brief flicker of their lives they spoke to each other of their hatred of the Deformed and the canteen food. Together they hardened their hearts and souls, further cementing their reasons for having chosen this life, this form of death, even as their courage failed.

Occasionally, Frank would get letters from home. When he read them he felt the numbness come down on him. The words rattled in his head, each divorcing itself from its predecessor. The news

they carried seemed utterly removed from him, completely
irrelevant. He did not reply. There was nothing to say. He would kill
until there were no more to kill. But there could be no end, he saw
now, only an end to him and they would get that letter soon enough.

After two months, he and some of the other soldiers were
promised a weekend of leave. They talked of nothing else. Many
were going home. Others were going to Manchester to get blind
drunk. Frank went with the latter group. When, barely coherent,
eyes hooded by liquor, he fell into the whore's arms, he thought of
Pam not once.

Everything I have told you so far has been background information
for the incipient event: Lord Percy's pioneering of animalistic
augmentation – the safe and effective method for the replacement
of human limbs with animal ones. This technique, Lord Percy
claimed, would "save the lives of many a victim of today's
industrial machinery and return him swiftly to the workforce
where he will be less of a burden to both his family and the state".
The fact that he charged both an arm and a leg to replace just one
of those limbs should not go unmentioned.

It was now that Lord Simon chose to take a religious and moral
stand that would tear the country in two. His phrase, "Compromise
of the body is compromise of the soul" became the refrain of the
religious hard line. However, I suspect that had it not been for Lord
Simon's sense of self-importance and the willingly manipulated
media this phrase would have gotten little further than his dining
room. Certainly the world would have been a better place.

A year passed. The trench in which Frank fought had moved
forward two hundred yards, and then fallen back a hundred and
fifty, an oscillating fault line of power that never settled. They
were told that somewhere, perhaps a mile away, there was a facility
where the Deformed took their wounded to be remade and
repaired. The destruction of this facility was rumored to be
crucial. Even more than Frank hated the Deformed – and Frank
did hate them now, true and strong, not for their offences in the
eyes of God but simply for their existence which kept him, kept
them all here – he hated the facility.

As the months passed, Frank was amazed by his own capacity

for survival. He watched his fellows fall, watched them break their own legs so they could be sent home, watched them be shipped to hospitals when the shakes got too bad, and still he kept returning to Manchester, like a man surfacing from sewage to gasp air.

He would spend the majority of his time in the city drunk. When he could, he would pick up city girls, and when he could not, he would pay for whores. He would sink into the blankness of flesh, grabbing what pleasures he had left to him. Occasionally, he thought of Pam, but she was unreal to him, like an amputated limb.

Then, one beer-stained night, he met Anna. He approached her, weaving. He made the same familiar overtures, parading his well-worn lines. She ignored them, but not him.

"What do you want?" she had asked him, but not harshly – openly, welcoming, and her honest desire for an answer undid his leer before it could fully form. A frown creased his brow.

"A word?" she asked. "A drink?"

"Yes." And the certainty felt good.

"Even though you know you won't find it there?" Anna had said.

"Find what?"

"Your way out."

Frank looked at her, and almost walked away. He could see the mud and the trenches stretching away beyond Anna, and he did not come to Manchester to remember them. But there was still that smile. "Then what's the point?" he asked.

"Oh, pet, I'm not saying that if you find yourself in a hard place you shouldn't go looking for a way out, just that you won't find it in the beer glasses, here."

"How'd you know?" he said, gruff, on the verge of departure.

"I already looked."

And then Frank found himself laughing, laughing pure for the first time in God knows how long.

"You got any other suggestions where to look?" he asked, still smiling.

She took a step in, towards the protective curl of his arm. "Other people," she said.

Anna was tall, and broad, and firm – a good working-class girl come to do her bit for the boys, she told Frank as they tumbled, beer-stained and laughing, through her front door.

She shushed him at the bedroom door, refused to turn the

lights on in the bedroom, pleading her reputation among her neighbors. They smuggled themselves beneath rough sheets, Frank's lips smudging against her shoulder blades. Her long swathes of brown hair trailed over his face. He lost himself in her. Her flesh became one with his, their separate skins dissolving into a single passionate whole.

He woke blinking, his head strangely clear. His mornings in Manchester were usually painful, befuddled things, full of shuffling and excuses. But the alcohol seemed to have left him quietly this morning. Pale light blinked at him through the curtains.

Noise from another room made him turn his head to the door. There was the smell of bacon and the sound of fat spitting and popping. Next to him there was a space in the bed, the covers pulled back. He was glad, he found. He didn't want to simply slink away from this one, with his boots in one hand and scraps of his pride in the other. There had been a kindness in Anna the previous night. Something other than desperation had pushed him between her legs. He smiled at the sound of plates clinking. Breakfast would be good.

The door cracked open and her head appeared. Her brown hair was wet and hung down her back. She wore a thick long robe, from which her naked calves protruded.

"Oh, you're awake, pet. Hope I didn't wake you."

Frank shook his head, sleepy and bearish.

"You like sugar in your tea?"

Again he shook his head.

"Sweet enough, eh?"

He grinned.

"Well, I'll let you wake up a bit." She winked at him and ducked back into the kitchen.

Frank smiled and stretched and thought about what else might be served with breakfast.

When Anna returned, she was laden with a tray of eggs, bacon, sausage, fried bread, tomatoes and mushrooms.

"Didn't know what you liked, pet," she said, "so I made a little of everything."

She sat on a chair next to the bed and Frank propped himself up among her pillows. They both pulled forkfuls of the food from a heaped plate and ate hungrily. From time to time Frank would glance from her legs – crossed in ladylike fashion – to her square-jawed face. She had large brown eyes, like his own.

Frank wanted to say something but he didn't know what. All he knew was war and war was for between times such as these.

"Nice eggs," he managed.

"Ah, pet, that's sweet of you," Anna said, "but they're nothing special."

Deflected, Frank again contemplated the plate, and then the window.

"Looks like we might get us some decent weather today."

She stopped eating and laid a hand over his. "It's OK, pet," she said. "I understand."

"Understand what?"

"It's hard out there on the front. Fills you up. You don't have to say nothing if you don't want to."

"But . . ." Frank hesitated, fork poised in mid-air, a piece of bacon hanging from it, uncertain whether to go up or down. "I'd like to talk." He felt the clumsiness of his words but in their conversation the night before there had been the promise of hope to come, and Frank wished upon wish to recapture that emotion.

Anna smiled.

"How do you know about the way it is for us?" Frank asked.

Anna's smile faltered around her eyes. "I lost my fella that way. While back now."

Frank squeezed her hand. "That's hard."

Anna squeezed his hand back. "Oh I bet you lost a lot more than me down there. Number of friends . . ." She trailed off, shaking her head.

"I don't really have any friends," he said and he hadn't realized it until he said it. The numbness kept him too cold for friends. It was something he'd done to himself.

Anna looked at him and her eyes filled with tears. Frank couldn't tell why. He pushed the tray aside and she came to him, her tears warm on his neck. He stroked her and stroking led to kissing and kissing led to the robe falling away again and then his hands were moving down the nape of her neck, down her spine and her curves and down.

Frank suddenly pulled his hands away with a yell and pushed Anna away. She stumbled from the bed.

His hand had struck some unexpected obstacle at the base of her spine, circular, warm, and furry. She stood in a pool of light that had slipped between the curtains, naked, afraid, exposed. Wrapped around her knees was a long, thick, black cat's tail.

"What the fuck's that?" Frank shouted and pointed. He backed away from her, across the bed, pulling the sheets with him.

"It's nothing, pet."

"You're . . . You're . . ." Frank gasped and fumbled for words. "You're one of them."

"I'm not. I'm not. I'm not." She mounted the denials one upon the other as if quantity would add to the weight of conviction.

Frank fell off the back of the bed and into a pile of his own clothes. He scrabbled around for a weapon and came upright holding one of his army boots. He stood, massive and shadowy before her. He eclipsed her.

"I thought you knew, pet. After last night . . . You knew."

"You made me do it in the dark!"

"But you felt it. How could you not have felt it?"

Frank wracked the smear of memories: impressions of flesh and shadow and laughter. Had he known? Had he felt it? His brow curled in on itself, digging trenches in his forehead as deep as the ones from which he killed. He could see again the eyes of the man he'd killed in York. That was what you did, what he did: kill the Deformed. He raised the large, steel-capped boot above his head.

"I'm not one of them," she cried. "I'm not! I hate them! They took my man. I was young. It was a mistake. I didn't know. I didn't know."

The boot hung in the air, moving neither up nor down, suspended in the turmoil of Frank's confusion. In his mind's eye he could see Pam again, her mouth moving, but he could no longer hear her words.

"It was all the rage, pet," Anna said. "Everyone was doing it. I didn't know better. No one told me."

"Why didn't you get rid of it?"

"By the time I knew I should, I couldn't, pet. They'd have killed me if they found out. You know they would."

He did. He would have killed her.

"You won't do for me, will you?" she said. "You won't shop me to no one. Will you?"

She looked at him, the same expression on her face as the man lying on the alley floor, Frank's fist coming down. And although he knew history should repeat itself he couldn't quite bring himself to do the deed. Slowly, he lowered the boot. After all, what difference did his actions make?

"No," he said.

"Thank you, pet." And she flung her arms around his thick waist. He didn't hug her back but he didn't push her away. After that she let him get dressed in silence and showed him to the door.

"Which regiment are you with?" she asked as he stood on the threshold, half in the house, half outside. He told her, but he didn't know why. On his way back to the front, he wasn't sure he knew his reasons for any of it.

It is not known exactly who it was who first underwent animalistic augmentation for purely cosmetic reasons, but the most famous of these early attention-grabbers was the vaudeville actor Cecil Cormorant.

Mr Cormorant had a functional pair of his namesake's wings sutured to his back. While this stunt (and clever advertising) drew enormous crowds to Mr Cormorant's act and made a craze of augmentation amongst a certain sector of the population, it also incensed those who opposed animalistic "deformation" (as they dubbed it). This latter group stated that Mr Cormorant's emulation of the angelic form, a claim he firmly denied, was blasphemy at the most extreme level.

Lord Simon, believing his own hyperbole and convinced of his own importance, wrote a page-long letter to *The Times* decrying Mr Cormorant's actions. The next day, an equally pompous letter from Lord Percy appeared defending the entertainer.

If you ever peruse the letters you will find a great deal of clever phraseology and very little sense, surrounded by reams of editorials praising either one position or the other, without regard for the merit of the arguments. Sensationalism for the sake of the sensational. Tragically, the popular imagination was captured and divided and, a month after his operation, Mr Cormorant was set upon by a lynch mob as he left his theater one evening, strung up by the neck and set on fire.

*   *   *

After several days back at the front, Frank received a letter from Anna. He hid it at first, terrified to open it. Talking with her had allowed his life at the front to spill into his days in Manchester, and now Manchester threatened to invade the front. The neat separation that held his life in check was being assaulted, the terror of the war threatening to come back to him.

As he gripped his rifle, mud choking his nostrils, and squeezed round after round into the advancing horde, he wondered if the other men would find the letter. Had she mentioned her . . . mistake? Captured love letters were shared with glee. He knew what would happen if the other men found out about Anna.

But also, he wondered, as the bodies fell and the cannons' roar took a little more of his hearing, how was she doing? How did she feel? After his night with her, he had become increasingly aware of a loneliness at the core of his being, from which all the divisions in his soul spread. He recognized its mirror in Anna.

One night, certain that his fellows were asleep, he could stand it no longer and opened the envelope. Her handwriting was large and awkward, as, at first, were her sentiments – wishing him well, hoping he did not mind her writing, enquiring after his health – but, as the letter progressed, her hand became more confident, her thoughts easier. She had an eye for humor and the absurd in the everyday, the contradictions that define and are denied by people, and Frank smiled as he read on. She did not mention her tail.

The next night Frank scrounged some paper and a pen and replied. He was dissatisfied with the result – an awkward mash of thoughts and some of the more repeatable jokes he'd heard – but he sent it anyway. Two days later he got a reply.

Soon enough the other boys noticed the flurry of letters traveling back and forth – as much by the improvement in Frank's demeanor as by his increased need for paper and blotters – and the ribbing about his girl began. He clung to his stoic reputation and gave away as little as he could. Meanwhile, in the letters, he opened himself, poured himself out onto the page. Thoughts, fears, hopes and misgiving he'd never known he had took shape on the pages before him – confused but his own:

"Sometimes I feel I made the wrong decision. But it wasn't a decision really, just what I had to do, so maybe it's just the world that's wrong. But how can I be wrong, if I'm doing what those better than me are

telling me I should be doing? How can the whole world be wrong? So it's got to be me. So I try to change: I do what I'm told, I do the right things, say them too, bit still it all feels wrong."

And instead of laughing, Anna echoed his confusion, tried to understand it, tried to match it to the world she knew, the world that called her sin irredeemable.

He hungered for her letters. They agreed that, the next time he was offered a weekend, they would meet.

He had almost forgotten about her tail until she was naked before him. She was thoughtful though, keeping it curled away during their lovemaking, and he kept his hands on her neck and shoulders.

For most of the weekend they did not speak of it. They simply lay in bed, or ate, or walked along streets and held hands. While they were out, she would wrap the tail around her waist where it curled unobtrusively, but when they returned to her house she would insist on "giving it air", twirling it back and forth and complaining of cramp. Frank watched these displays half sickened, half affectionate. She caught him staring.

"Do you want to touch it, pet?" she asked him.

Frank stared at his hands. "No."

She stepped towards him and put a hand on his shoulder. "That's OK, pet."

"What . . ." He hesitated. "What does it feel like?"

She ran it through her hands. "Like a cat's tail, that's all."

"No." Frank shook his head. "To you. What's it like?"

"What's it like to have arms?"

Frank stared at her blankly and she laughed.

"It feels like having arms. I don't think about it. It's just another part of me."

"Do you . . ." He rubbed his head. His questions sounded stupid before he even articulated them, but she stroked his brow and he asked her anyway. "Are you glad you got it?"

"No." She shook her head. "I wish I could be rid of it. I was young. Now I have to carry my folly with me, like a man who's tattooed on his arm the name of a girl who left him in the end." She looked away before he could read her expression and pushed a hand through his hair. Then she asked, abruptly, "How old are you, Frank?"

"Eighteen," he said, "and a half."

"Lordy, but you are young, pet."

"How old are you?" he said, slightly riled.

"Oh, put your pride away, pet. I don't think any less of you. And it's rude to ask a lady her age."

"Oh." Frank reddened.

"But I'm twenty-seven, so at least I'm not old enough to be your mam."

"Thank God," Frank muttered.

Anna bust a gut at that, rocking back and forth, laughing, her tail waving back and forth. They ended up kissing on her couch. Afterwards he lay with his head in her lap while she stroked his hair.

"There are a lot of us that made mistakes," she said then, almost absent-mindedly. "Who got something put on before we knew it wasn't right in the Lord's eye, and found out too late to get it taken off. Lots of people. You'll see them if you look carefully: the man who never takes off his gloves, the woman whose dress bulges all wrong, who never picks up the hem of her skirt, even through the puddles. They just thought it was a bit of fun, or that it would make life a little bit easier. There's still places you can get it done, for kids rebelling, for the curious or the trapped. They're not Deformed, not really. They're just the ones the speeches don't leave room for."

Soon they went to the bedroom, and after that Frank fell asleep. In the middle of the night, though, he awoke. Anna lay next to him, unaware of his open eyes. She had her tail out of the sheets and was stroking it softly in the moonlight, a rapt expression on her face. Frank said nothing. For a moment he was afraid that she had lied to him, that she was not ashamed of her tail. But then her beauty and his tired eyes made him dismiss the thought.

In men who had as much wisdom as intelligence, Cecil Cormorant's death would have marked the point at which hard lines were softened and a compromise was reached. Not our two bastions of Britain. And, taking their cue from these two, the British populace enacted many a copycat and revenge killing. Within two months of Mr Cormorant's death, the Prime Minister, power slipping from between his fingers, declared a state of National Emergency.

As the violence in the capital grew and the attempts upon their lives mounted, Lords Simon and Percy retreated to their ivory towers, located in York and Essex respectively. Their physical separation split the country. Lord Simon's supporters flocked north, Lord Percy's south. Those that did not move of their own accord were driven to.

The absence of a rhetorical middle ground was now reflected on Britain's soil. Our two celebrated extremists had brought civil war to our green and pleasant land.

Frank was back in the mud again, back among the troops, the cannons dropping shells around them. But now he was the corporal leading the new boys to their first taste of horror. He knew what was to come, what would happen to them, but still he urged them forward, shouting the same slogans the corporals had shouted at him. They came barking out of him, second nature now. But he lingered back as the boys pushed forward, and, although he felt a twinge of guilt, he could not quite force himself to lead the charge. He approximated the way he had been taught a corporal should act as best he could, but his hand kept fingering the unopened letter in his breast pocket and his feet would not move.

A battle suit staggered across the land to the right of his men, the barrels of its guns spinning wildly, spent shell cases peppering the air. Frank cursed the pilot for bringing the clanking machine so damn close to him, and started to move away, pushing through his men. Anna's letter felt heavy in his pocket.

Abruptly, the suit lurched sideways and its boiler let out a whistling howl. A jet of flame burst from a pin-sized hole. The bullet could have come from either side. Then everything was collapsing inwards and Frank could see the pilot, tiny and fragile at the suit's heart, futilely clawing at leather straps, and then the man was enveloped in a cloud of steam that would burn the muscles from his bones.

The explosion was barely audible in the noise of battle. Frank slammed to the ground as the shock wave hit them. Shrapnel scythed through the air leaving dismembered limbs in its path. Frank felt metal breathe past his face. In front of him, a young man, the top of his head sheared neatly off, tumbled to the ground and Frank stared at the exposed contents of his skull as they spread onto the churned earth.

Frank felt his guts heave and the world fade to blacks and whites. He saw the scattered bodies, heard the screams. And he knew that he had failed. He had failed to keep Manchester and Anna from his war. He had been so concerned about his own safety, about keeping his body and soul together for Anna to hold, that he had failed to order his men to move away from the battle suit with him. He had failed them, failed his duty.

Later, after he had made it to his feet and organized what retreat he could, Frank lay in his cot and tried to read Anna's letter, but guilt blurred her words into one shrieking accusation that he had endangered himself, had almost failed her. But how could he live up to both his commitments?

"Bad one?" Sam Coals, a fellow corporal leaned down from the adjacent bunk.

Frank nodded and folded the letter away.

"I heard about it." Sam clapped him on the shoulder in a reassuring way. "Those goddamn pilots. Anyone willing to ride one of those damn things should be shot on sight. Be quicker and it'd take fewer of us with them."

Frank couldn't quite muster a smile.

"You know what we should do?" Sam asked and Frank could see the vehemence growing in the man. "We should get one, just one of those fucking things inside that goddamn facility we're meant to be attacking, and sit it there 'til someone blows it up. We shell that damn building all goddamn day but they've dug the bunkers so fucking deep we can't touch it. But we get one of those walking time bombs just halfway in there and we blow the goddamn guts out of the place. Then . . ." Sam trailed off. There was no concept of "then" at the front. Only the bloody "now".

"Yeah," Frank said. He could feel the numbness seeping back into him, cutting him away from Sam. The man's voice started to fade away. Later, when Sam was gone, Frank read Anna's letter but the thaw didn't seem to come. His reply felt automated, perfunctory.

But, little by little, Anna's letters chipped away at the ice inside of him. He could not keep her from his heart and he brought that into battle with him every day. Two weeks later, in Manchester, the sight of her made the final sheets of ice slough away, taking with them the image of the soldier's open leaking skull. Warmth flooded him and he went to her and laughed with her and kissed her and held her hand and she reminded him why, as much as he fought the Deformed, he fought to stay alive.

Later they made love and, as they did, she curled her tail around his hand. It was the first time in a year and a half that he had held it. He pulled it a little and she purred in his ear.

They lay sweaty and naked in the darkness, white-blue light outlining their curves and edges.

"What'll we do when it's over?" she said.

"What's over?"

"The war."

"I . . ." Frank paused. The idea of an end, once so present in his mind, had slipped away amongst the body parts and the blood. It seemed an impossibility now – the thought of consequences to his actions. "I don't know."

She paused, then spoke again, her voice quiet and quick like the beat of a hummingbird. "Do you love me, Frank?" Then immediately after, "No, don't answer that."

Frank felt the long length of her pressed against his side, her hand splayed on his chest. He thought of the letters she wrote him and the ones he wrote her, the way she reached inside his chest and opened it up so everything in it spilled out and how she was slowly helping him become his own man no matter how much the war tore at him.

"Yes," he said into the silence. "Yeah, I guess I do."

She let out a squeal and bounced astride him, her hips hugging his waist, bent down and kissed him. She kissed him again and again until his face was damp with her kisses. She lay down on top of him, her face nestled in the crook between his neck and shoulder. He could feel her eyelashes tickling his jawline and the warmth in his heart felt like it would burn him whole, a glorious, passionate conflagration. Her lips brushed his skin as she spoke.

"There's a place in town where you can still get it done. A lot of people go there. It's one of those secrets that almost isn't. Very clean place. I've been saving up and—" her voice softened, barely audible "—I want to give you a present."

She sat up on him, arched her back to push out her chest and pointed just below her breasts. "I'm going to get another pair of titties. I'll have four of them. All for you." She laughed, high and girlish. "Can you imagine? For you, pet. Four for you."

She collapsed back down onto him, buried her head in that crook again, still giggling. Then she must have felt his body all hard and stiff beneath her because she asked, "What's wrong, pet?" and her voice, to Frank, sounded like snow falling.

"No," he said. "No." His jaw worked as he tried to get the thoughts out, tried to turn the buzzing into words. "I don't . . . Because . . . Because . . ."

He pushed her off him, roughly. She fell with a gasp. He grabbed her tail. "This . . . This . . ." He pulled it hard and she let out a shriek. There were tears on his cheeks.

"You said it was a mistake! You said you wished you didn't have it! But if you want . . . you want . . . that—" he pointed to her chest and she pulled the sheets over her chest, and she was crying too "—then you're no different from them." He spat the word. "Then you're Deformed."

It was the betrayal that hurt him, not truly the revelation, because deep down, deep down in the meat of his body, he had known how she felt, known ever since he saw her in the moonlight. No, it was the betrayal of his silent duplicity, his easy self-deception, her betrayal of his ability to hold on to even that, to his ability to keep the conflicts in his soul in check. And now she forced him to choose a side. And despite it all, he still knew what the right thing to do was.

So every word from every boy he'd ever worked with, every man he'd ever fought alongside, ever seen die, ever seen have his head sliced in two; from everyone in his family; from every priest; everything he'd ever been told burned in his mind and his mouth and he spat it at her. Her soul was forfeit, he told her. She was in Satan's thrall. She sickened him. She was filth. And all the while tears poured from his eyes because now all he was was what he'd been told to be. But there was nothing else he knew to be.

In the end, he was just quiet, his mouth a line, and her words were nothing. He got dressed, watching the work of his fingers closely so that they didn't fumble, because he could no longer feel them.

He caught the first train back to the front, and tried to deny to himself that he would have liked what she had offered.

★   ★   ★

Despite early fluctuations, within a year the battle lines had solidified and a mile-wide strip of no-man's-land had been etched irrevocably between a point just south of Manchester on the west coast to another, halfway between Grimsby and Skegness, on the east. There were a few notable victories and individual acts of heroism but overall the line stayed remarkably static.

My fellow historians would have you believe that these years of war have strengthened our nation, have given us souls of steel forged in the fires of war. Violence, they tell you, pushes our industry and the minds of our great thinkers, Percy and Simon, to come up with many and varied technologies that benefit our daily lives. The fact that these technologies are spin-offs from others designed to kill in as broad and indiscriminate a manner as possible is rarely mentioned. The truth is we are pouring our young into a mud-filled hole, and at the end of this debacle only a pitiable few will be able to clamber back out again.

Frank went back to the killing and the mud and the cold. He gripped his rifle with assurance and pulled its trigger with certainty. The Deformed came at him, wave after wave of indeterminate things, and all around him men fell, but he was never once injured. In almost three years he had never been touched by the war. The new recruits spoke of him in awe and vied for his attention. He gave it to none of them. He had none to give. He went through life clean, like a bullet shot askew.

She sent him letters, of course. He didn't open them but she didn't stop.

Days passed him in strobe flashes: himself in the dirt, gun in his hands; him washing blood from his fingernails; him lying in bed, hands shaking so damn hard he couldn't sleep. One time he found another stripe on his epaulettes and had no idea how he'd got it. Sometimes he'd find himself lecturing the younger men, ranting about the Deformed, hatred spilling out of him and onto them.

Then, one day, he came to and found he was dragging some kid from his bunk by the scruff of his neck. The kid was so young he must have lied abut his age to the recruiting officer just to get there. His lip was bleeding. Everyone was watching them. Frank knew things he couldn't remember learning. He knew about the girl the kid was seeing, knew the truth that the others rumored about. He knew why she always wore gloves, knew the way her tongue separated in two. He knew about her feet like hands.

The man's belongings were spread across the floor, and strewn among them were brown and cream photos of the girl, the oh-so Deformed girl, naked and on display. He knew he must have scattered those pictures there, must have torn the kid's stuff apart to find the evidence. And now, as he dragged the kid out into the mud, he knew what he had to do, what he'd always been taught to do, what he'd done before.

The first punch caught the kid under his jaw and lifted him clean off his feet, laid him out straight on the floor. The second buried itself in the kid's guts and the kid spewed. The third sent his head snapping through mud on an awkward lateral path. Piece by piece, Frank took the kid apart. There was a crowd around them and Frank thought that they were shouting something but whether it was encouragement or dismay he couldn't tell. He just did what he had to do, did his damn, thrice-fucked duty for God and country, until the kid's bloody mess of a face gave way beneath his fists and he knew it was done.

Something broke inside him then, and maybe it was the ice and maybe it was his heart and maybe it was something else, because nothing really seemed clear, but he stood, covered in mud, in the everything and nothing mix of the land, and stumbled away. Someone clapped him on the shoulder as he went. He thought someone else was crying, but no one stopped him, and he just kept on walking away. He was empty now, duty done, the right thing done, the right that had done him so much wrong.

He got to Manchester late at night, still covered in mud. His feet ached and his fist left stains on Anna's door when he knocked. She answered it after a while, bleary-eyed, her robe clutched about her. She stared at him quietly in the moonlight, at his broad, stained face. Then she unlatched the door and pulled him in and to her, dirt and all. She bathed him, and held him, and wrapped herself around him. Her arms and her legs and her tail were three bands of heat embracing his frozen core.

She fell asleep like that, curled against him, warm and heavy, her breath moist against his neck. He lay awake watching the light and the shadow, the place where the two merged into each other.

And he saw it there: England mapped out in shadow and light

across her body. And he saw the trenches in their grey meeting point – the line where two lies met and churned the world to mud. But no matter how the light lay, it was still Anna underneath it, no matter how much the shadows obscured her form, she was still there solid, and to be held.

Slowly, the moon fell and dawn came and the world became an indeterminate gray – Anna's shape resolving as the vision of light melted away – the world changing. And Frank smiled with tears in his eyes because finally he did know the right thing to do.

He touched Anna's arm to wake her. "That place," he said, "where you can have it done. Let's go there."

We now approach the end of our pitiable tale. It is catching up with the present. England is divided, the two sides utterly opposed, no position left open for compromise. The only solution to our political and religious extremism seems to be the total destruction of either one or both sides.

Except that it is increasingly clear that things will not end this way. In creating their myth of our times, Lords Simon and Percy, the newspapermen, my fellow historians, have all forgotten something. They have forgotten you and me, the common men and women forced to live in the world they are forging.

While the so-called great thinkers of our time dig their heels into their carefully staked out political territory, we find the space between. We compromise – we smuggle food packages to our cousins on the other side of the border when we can, and gratefully receive them in return; we whisper prayers for them, even though, in public, we profess that they are bound for hell; we love in secret and hate in public. And we do this not because we are lesser beings with lesser principles, but because it is inevitable. It is necessary for us to survive. In the end rhetoric will always be vanquished by reality. The tragedy is the number of men that we must sacrifice to come by this knowledge.

Frank waited until the twilight was thick around him before he sprinted across the open stretch between the warehouses. His body screamed in pain at the movement, but he bit his tongue until it bled, and made it to the shadows noiselessly. He looked back at the distance he had covered and was amazed at his newfound speed.

The warehouse guards stood away from the building's door. They stamped their feet and sucked warm cigarette smoke down into chill lungs. With animal grace Frank slipped past them unnoticed a creature of silence and shadow.

The warehouse's aluminum walls were vast and cavernous. Their creaking was the only concerned voice Frank could hear. Before him stretched out two rows of hulking figures – vacant battle suits standing limp and lifeless.

He laid a hand on the steel ladder built into the leg of one suit and swung himself up to the service hatch. The movement felt unnatural but was done easily enough. The hatch opened quietly, its weight negligible compared to the strength of his arms. He was taken back to his factory days as his hand navigated the surface of the suit, finding their way easily despite the darkness. He found the button he wanted, pressed it, and a phosphorous flare ignited the kindling in the battle suit's engine. He swung the hatch closed and watched the warehouse entrance. The guards showed no signs of having heard him yet.

They would soon enough, and his heart beat as hard as it had his first day in the trenches.

He swung round to the pilot's seat and set about strapping himself into the suit. This was the hardest part. The straps had not been designed for someone of his shape. But without this shape he knew, he could never have got this far. His fingers fumbled with the buckles, the noise from the boiler mounting, and his surgical scars sang with pain.

Finally, though, it was done. In the failing light he could still make out the pressure dials. Almost done. He cast another look at the door. The two guards were beginning to look about, trying to pinpoint the source of the rising noise. His hands fixed themselves on the levers and he tried to remember schematics from a lifetime he'd forgotten.

Then the soldiers realized what was happening and started to run towards him, guns raised.

As Frank pulled the first lever he remembered Anna's parting kiss, her weight pressed against his face, one hand in his hair, the other in the small of his back. He didn't know if she'd believed him when he'd told her he would be back soon.

Frank wondered what he looked like to these soldiers, what kind of monster?

When they had first arrived at the clinic, Anna hadn't realized what he was going to do. They had walked hand in hand through the streets, both a little breathless. He had been constantly looking for soldiers, but saw none. Anna had led him to the back of a pub and knocked on the cellar's loading doors. A small man had appeared and ushered them down, leading them through stale-smelling kegs to a door which had opened onto a bright, white space. A doctor with an extra pair of ape's arms had greeted them. Then Frank had explained and Anna had protested.

"Why, pet, why?" she had kept repeating.

But he had remained quiet.

She had held his hand as they put him under. When he had come to she was still holding it, as if she had never left. But his hand was different, the fingers longer and hairier. There was a lot of pain.

"I love you," she'd told him. "I'll always love you."

He'd tried to reply but his jaw had not let him. Still, she understood.

Would she understand now? Now, as he hauled on the battle suit's levers, fingers twitching with the flurry of adrenaline? As he swatted the guards away with one vast metal hand? As his steel feet pounded the ground and he charged forwards with the hiss of pneumatics and the crunch of gears? As he tore through the camp, charging out towards no-man's-land? As he headed from light and dark, into the gray. As he went to put a stop to it all.

The mud stretched out to claim him like a lover. He shut the suit's headlights and made it crawl on all fours, bestial, through the muck. His new ears could already pick out the sound of the enemy beyond. He felt ready for the Deformed, ready and powerful, his body's new flesh encased in this new steel skin.

It seemed unlikely to him that the Deformed ever knew what hit them. He leapt over their first ranks before they could start firing. His guns cut a swathe through the quickest of them, then he was past them and still running. The facility rose in the night before him. There were guards, and someone had radioed from the front, and by the time he tore the doors off the place, he was bleeding badly, one of his arms hung useless unable to grip the levers. It didn't matter, though. There would be a resolution.

The suit banged and scraped against the facility's corridor

walls, showering sparks. Troops were lined up to meet him. But still he plunged on, working deeper and deeper, the memory of Anna's kiss heavy on his lips.

He had left her a letter, to explain with his pen what his tongue could not.

"Of all the things people have ever told me, you have told me the truest: that there is a space between speeches. And now I know a way to tell everyone else. What I'm going to do will let people know that there isn't just one way, that they can make their own way, that there's always that place between, they always have it, they just need to open their eyes. You opened mine. I love you for it. I always will."

Eventually his suit fell. It crashed face down, leaking hydraulics. He lay there, tasting blood and concrete. Both his arms were broken by then. It only seemed fitting as he used his new tail to pull the pin from the grenade.

And now, as we arrive at the present, we have the case of Sergeant Frank Plane, his story emblazoned across today's newspapers. His heroic destruction of Lord Percy's augmentation factory; then, days later, the photographs taken by his paramour, Ms Anna Wright, exposing the lie of glorious victory spread by Lord Simon and his generals. Only a Deformed man was able to save the un-augmented, only someone operating between the two competing philosophies of our time. He has exposed our society for the paper-thin lie it is: smoke and mirrors, light and shadow.

And now Sergeant Plane's example has given me the courage to do something I have not done for many years: expose myself, reveal myself. I, too, am a Deformed man living in Lord Simon's England, here by ties of family and love. And now I am standing up. Now I am ready to be counted, to re-forge England. And I hope others are too. I hope that, together, we can make our future better than our history, that, together, we can do the right thing.

Edison's Frankenstein

Chris Roberson

It was late afternoon when Archibald Chabane finally found the boy, perched high on the steel trestle of the elevated railway. From that vantage, he could look out across the intersection of 62nd Street and Hope Avenue, over the high fence into the backstage area of Bill Cody's concession, now christened Buffalo Bill's Wild West and Congress of Rough Riders of the World.

"Mezian," Chabane called, but over the muffled roar of the crowd in Cody's 8,000-seat arena and the rumble of the Illinois Central Railroad engine coming up the track, he couldn't make himself heard.

"Mezian!" Chabane repeated, cupping his hands around his mouth like a speaking-trumpet. He glanced to the south, trying to see how close the train had come. When Chabane had been a boy, watching the 4-6-0 camelback engines lumbering along the Algiers–Constantine line, he'd always been able to see the black smoke billowing up from their coal-fed furnaces from miles away. These new prometheic engines, though, produced nothing but steam, and virtually all of it used for locomotion, so the trains could be heard long before they could be seen.

Chabane leaned a hand against the nearest steel girder, and could feel the vibrations of the train's approach.

He shouted the boy's name once more, at the top of his lungs.

Mezian looked down, blinking, and his lips tugged up in a guilty grin. "Oh, I didn't see you there, *amin*."

Chabane had only to cross his arms over his chest and scowl, and the boy began clambering down the trestle like a monkey from a tree.

To the Americans, like Bill Cody – who'd already warned Sol

Bloom to keep "his damned Algerians" away from the Wild West Show's Indians – Archibald Chabane was Bloom's assistant, translator and bodyguard.

To Sol Bloom, "Archie" was just a Kabyle who'd gotten off the boat from Paris with the rest of the troupe, and threatened to throw Bloom into the waters of New York Harbor if he wasn't more polite to the performers. Bloom had offered him a cigar and hired Chabane to be his liaison with the Algerian troupe on the spot.

To the Algerians, though, Chabane was something more. At first only their guide in a foreign land, he had become their elected *amin*, as much the head of their "Algerian Village" concession as if he were sitting in the *djemaa* of a Kayble village back home.

"Careful," Chabane warned, as Mezian swung from a steel girder. "I promised your mother I'd bring you back in one piece."

The boy just grinned, and dropped a full five feet to the pavement, something colorful fluttering to the ground after him like a lost bird.

"Mother won't give me a dime to get into the show," Mezian said by way of explanation, pointing at the banners which fluttered over Cody's concession, proclaiming *THE PILOT OF THE PRAIRIE*.

"Mr Bloom has sworn it's my hide if any of our troupe is caught drinking with Cody's performers again," Chabane said, arms still crossed over his chest. Many of the Algerians in the troupe were not the most observant of Muslims, and even now in the final days of Ramadan they could be found passing a flask back and forth once the day's audience had cleared out. "If Cody catches one of us peeking at his show without paying, I'll never hear the end of it."

Mezian scuffed his feet against the pavement, his gaze lowered. "Sorry, *amin*."

"You dropped something." Chabane reached down and picked up the garishly colored pamphlet that had fallen from the boy's pocket. It was a story-paper, what the Americans called a "dime novel". The title in oversized letters was *Scientific Romance Weekly*, featuring "Dane Faraday, Man of Justice, in The Electrical World of Tomorrow". Handing it back to the boy, Chabane quirked a smile. "She won't give you ten cents for the Wild West Show, but she lets you spend money on cheap fictions?"

The boy shrugged, slipping the folded pamphlet into his back pocket. "They're meant to help me practice my English." He paused, drawing himself up straight, and then in stilted tones added in English, "Hands up, the miscreant, you are the surrounded." Switching back to French, he gave Chabane a quizzical look. "What is a 'miscreant'?"

"It means unbeliever," the man explained, "or infidel. A villain, in other words." He put a hand on the boy's shoulder and gently propelled him forward. "Come along, your mother is waiting."

As they headed up 62nd to Island Avenue, they could hear the muffled applause from the crowd inside Cody's arena. Open only a little more than a week, and already the Wild West Show was drawing bigger crowds than all the concessions on the Midway Plaisance combined. In another two weeks the Columbian Exhibition proper would finally open to the public, and it remained to be seen whether there'd be crowds left over for any of the outside attractions.

"So your story-papers," Chabane said, as they turned left and headed north up Island Avenue. "Are they any good?"

Mezian shrugged. "They are all right, I suppose. Not as good as the French ones I could get back home, or in Paris."

Chabane nodded. "When I was a boy, I devoured every installment of Jules Verne's *Extraordinary Voyages* I could lay my hands on."

The boy pulled a face. "*Verne?*" He shook his head. "Much too dry. No, give me Paul d'Ivoi's *Eccentric Voyages* any day."

They passed 60th Street, then turned left onto the Midway Plaisance. The looming form of Ferris's still unfinished wheel dominated the horizon, even seven blocks away. Steel-bodied automata spidered up and down it on their crab-like legs, welding girders into place, stringing high-tension wires. The builders promised that it would be ready to start spinning within another week, two at the most, just in time for opening day. Chabane was less than optimistic about their predictions, but knew that if not for the automata, it would not even be *that* far along, and would never have been ready in time.

Chabane couldn't help but think about the boy he'd once been, reading Verne in second-hand story-papers. Not yet Archibald Chabane of London, just Adherbal Aït Chabaâne of Dellys, reading about men who traveled beneath the waves, or across the skies, or to the moon in glorious machines. It had seemed a distant, ungraspable vision that he could scarcely hope to see.

Then came the famine, and the oppression of the Kabyle at the hands of their French colonial masters, and finally the failure of Muhammed al-Muqrani's revolt. Chabane had been too young to fight, but his father and his uncles had not, and with the revolt put down his family name had been outlawed in Algeria, never again to be spoken in the *djemaa*. The young Adherbal, seeing no future in his native land, had gone instead to live among the *Romni*, as the Kabyles, remembering the Romans of ancient times, still thought of all foreigners across the middle sea. He ran away to the north, away from the superstitions of his grandmothers and the traditions he had been taught. He had gone looking for the future, to reinvent himself in a rational world. In England he'd made a new life for himself, the bodyguard to a wealthy man, and had tried to forget the past.

In the end, though, he learned the past was something we carry with us, and can never escape. And even though the future had arrived, it had not been quite as he'd expected.

Chabane and the boy continued up the Midway, past the various concessions just shutting down for the day. Like the Wild West Show, they'd been able to open early, while work on the Columbian Exhibition was still being completed. Some of the concessions, like the Algerian Village, had been open as early as the previous summer. And like the Algerian troupe's "exhibit", the other concessions were all, in one way or another, caricatures of the countries they purported to represent, pantomimes of pasts that never existed. There were Irishmen in green felt, Germans in lederhosen, Lapps in fur, Turks in fezzes. But as clownish as the others often seemed, it struck Chabane that the worst indignities were always reserved for those from the African continent. Like the natives of Dahomey, only recently conquered by the French, being presented as "cannibal savages" for the amusement of American audiences. A once proud people, reduced to the level of sideshow performers.

As they neared the towering wheel, beyond which lay the Algerian concession, Chabane heard his name called. It was one of the performers from the Street in Cairo concession, which was proving the most popular of the Midway's attractions.

"Another of our monkeys has been stolen, Chabane," the Egyptian continued in Arabic. "You Kabyles haven't been breaking your Ramadan fast with monkey stew, have you?"

"Keep your ruffians away from our women, Zewail," Chabane answered, good-naturedly, "and I'll keep my people away from your monkeys."

As they passed under the lengthening shadow of Ferris's wheel, the Algerian Village concession coming into view, Mezian drew up short, looking behind him, a look of alarm on his face. "I've lost my story-paper." He patted his pocket, craning his head around and twisting to look down over his back, as though the dime novel might be clinging to his shirt-back.

Chabane turned in a slow circle, scanning the ground at their feet, looking back the way they'd come. "You must have dropped it."

Mezian looked up, his eyes wide. "My mother will *kill* me."

Chabane gave a sympathetic smile, but before he could answer he heard the sound of footsteps fast approaching. He spun around, expecting trouble, instinctually dropping into a defensive posture, but relaxed when he saw it was only Papa Ganon, the Algerian troupe's glass-eater.

"*Amin!*" Ganon shouted. "Come quickly!"

Chabane tensed once more when he saw the blood darkening the front of Papa Ganon's *burnous*.

"What is it?" Chabane said, rushing forward. "Are you hurt?"

Ganon responded with a confused look, then followed Chabane's gaze to his bloodstained front. He shook his head. "It isn't mine, *amin.* There's a stranger, badly bleeding and confused, found hiding behind the theater."

Chabane drew his mouth into a line, and nodded. "Run along and find your mother, Mezian." Then he started with long strides towards the Algerian theater, Papa Ganon following close behind.

The Algerian Village was almost identical to that which the troupe had originally set up in the Paris Exhibition four years before. It had been there that a young Sol Bloom had seen them, in the shadow of Eiffel's tower, and hired them to come perform in the United States. But when the time had come to leave Paris, the troupe had been uncertain about venturing into the unknown wilds of America.

At the time, Archibald Chabane had not heard his native tongue since leaving Dellys, years before, but traveling to Paris on business he had chanced upon the troupe on the Quai d'Orsay.

After a friendly meal and reminiscences about their erstwhile home, Papa Ganon had spoken for the others in begging the assistance of the worldly, mannered Chabane. Ganon had called up Kabyle tradition, which held that a Kabyle journeying abroad was obliged to come to the aid of any Kabyle in need, even at the risk of his own fortune and life.

Chabane had thought he had put such traditions behind him. But looking into the hopeful faces of the Algerian troupe, he couldn't help but remember the sacrifices his family had made during the famine of 1867. Tradition demands that every stranger who enters a Kabyle village be treated like an honored guest, given food, lodging, whatever he requires. But even with more than ten thousand strangers from all over Algeria pouring into Dellys, not a single person died of starvation, nor had the *djemaas* been forced to ask aid from the government. Among the European settlers in the larger cities, police measures were needed to prevent theft and disorder resulting from the influx of strangers; in Dellys nothing of the kind was needed. The Kabyles took care of their own affairs.

There on the Quai d'Orsay, to his own astonishment, he found himself agreeing to act as the troupe's guide in America. He had tried to escape his past, but his past had eventually outrun him.

In the shuttered Algerian Theater, Chabane and Papa Ganon found the unconscious stranger being tended by two of the troupe's female performers. Though they went veiled when in the public eye, in *chador* or *hijab*, in private they favored western dress.

"I tell you, it is Salla," one of the women said, daubing blood from the stranger's face with a wet cloth. Piled on the ground were shards of glass they'd pulled from his wounds. "Look, he has Salla's eyes."

The other woman, Dihya, shook her head. "Taninna, you've gone mad. Salla is dead and buried. Besides, eyes or no, this man looks nothing like him."

Chabane crouched beside Taninna, looking closely at the man. There were cuts all over his face, arms and hands, and underneath the wool blanket the women had thrown over him, the stranger was completely naked.

The ministrations of the two women had already staunched the flow of blood from the stranger's arms, and Chabane reached out to touch one of the scars, which looked older than the others, already healed, running like a ring around the stranger's upper arm. But when Chabane's fingers brushed the scar, he got a slight shock, like a spark of static electricity, and pulled his hand back quickly.

"What shall we do with him, *amin?*" Dihya asked, wiping her forehead with the back of her hand.

Chabane was thoughtful. "I'll go speak with the tin soldiers, see what they have to say."

Just opposite the Algerian Village, across the Midway Plaisance between the Old Vienna concession and the French Cider Press, was a Fire and Guard Station, manned by members of the Columbian Guard, the private police force of the Columbian Exhibition. The Guard was headed by Colonel Edmund Rice, a former infantry officer who had gained some small measure of fame during the Battle of Bull Run, where the Union army's new-minted prometheic tanks had put an end to the short-lived southern insurrection. Under Rice's command, the Columbian Guard was meant to be a model peacekeeping force, committed to the safety and security of all who strode upon the Exhibition grounds. In their uniforms of light blue sackcloth, white gloves, and yellow-lined black capes, though, they looked more like spear-carriers in a Gilbert and Sullivan production than officers of law. And their talents at peacekeeping often left something to be desired, more interested in presenting a dashing profile than in seeing justice done. It wasn't for nothing that the concessioneers had taken to calling them "tin soldiers".

As Chabane approached the Station, framing how best to broach the subject of the unconscious man who lay bleeding in the Algerian Theater, a trio of Columbian Guards rushed through the narrow door, the one in the lead shouldering Chabane aside.

"Out of the way, darkie," the Guard sneered in English, patting the buttoned holster at his side. "We don't have time to hear about any damned stolen monkeys."

Chabane held up his hands, palms forward, and stepped back out of the way, presenting as inoffensive a profile as possible. "My apologies," he answered, in his best drawing-room English. If he'd wanted, he could have swept the legs out from under all three

Guards, and taken their firearms from them as they fell. At the moment, though, he was more interested in what had stirred the normally laconic Guards to such a frenzy.

The three guards were hustling up the Midway, around the wheel and towards the Columbian Exhibition itself. A few of the other Midway concessioneers were still in the street, and Chabane could hear them muttering suspiciously to one another, like wives gossiping over a garden fence. Some had overheard the Guards within their hut, and had heard the summons to action.

There had been a *murder* in the park.

As he trailed behind the Columbian Guards at a discreet distance, keeping them just in sight as they hurried up the Midway, Chabane tallied up the number of deaths in the park since the previous summer, when the Algerian troupe had arrived from New York. Like the Algerian sword-swallower Salla, who had been working in a construction position in the park while waiting for the Midway to open, the deaths had all been accidents, all of them workers killed at their duties because of poor safety conditions. Salla had fallen from the airship mast and drowned in the waters of Lake Michigan, others had broken their skulls when masonry had fallen on them from improperly lashed cranes, or been crushed under piles of girders that slipped from the pincers of poorly programmed automata.

And it wasn't just the dead men buried in paupers' graves south of the park that had been affected. Even now, in the city itself, striking workers agitated for better working conditions, or for assurances that they would not lose their jobs to automation. The motto of the Columbian Exhibition was "Not Matter, But Mind; Not Things, But Men", but Chabane could not help but wonder whether such noble sentiments were any salve to men who had been replaced at their posts by "things" in recent months and years. He knew it came as no comfort to those men who had died in automata-related accidents.

But accidents were one thing. A murder was a different matter entirely. And as much as the Exhibition's Board of Directors might turn a blind eye to the loss of a few workmen, news of a murder would be bad business indeed for the fair.

It seemed a likely explanation that the bleeding and bewildered man now laying in the Algerian Theater was another victim, one who had escaped the killer's grasp. But it seemed to Chabane just as likely that the Board of Directors would be eager for a scapegoat on which to hang the crime, and a confused stranger, unable to defend himself, would suit their needs perfectly. He wasn't about to hand the stranger over to them, until he knew he wouldn't be signing the man's death warrant to do so.

Chabane followed the Guards through the 60th Street entrance and into the Columbian Exhibition itself. With only two weeks to go before the grand opening, it was clear there was still a significant amount of work to be done. The grounds were covered with litter and debris, with deep ruts cut across the greens. Lumber was piled haphazardly at the intersections of pathways, and empty crates and the discarded remains of workers' lunches were strewn everywhere.

The Guards continued east, past the Children's Building and the north end of the Horticultural Exhibition, before turning right and heading south along the western shores of the Lagoon. Chabane trailed behind, and when he rounded the corner of the Horticultural building, he could see the gentle rise of the Wooded Island in the middle of the Lagoon. Since he'd last come this way, they'd finished work on the fanciful reconstruction of the "Antediluvian" temple at the southern tip of the island. Supposedly based on archeological findings in Antarctica, it looked more like something out of Mezian's story-papers. Also new since he'd last seen the Lagoon were the miniature submersibles bobbling along on the water's surface, waiting for patrons to rent them for brief excursions to the bottom of the Lagoon once the Exhibition opened.

Chabane couldn't help wondering what Captain Nemo would have made of *that*.

For that matter, what might Verne himself have made of the airship now drifting at anchor atop the mast just visible on the far side of the Lagoon, past the Manufactures building, on the pier out over Lake Michigan. It was a prometheic airship, its envelope buoyed by the red vapor produced by the reaction of prometheum and charcoal.

Prometheum was such a simple substance. It looked like water and flowed like mercury. Add it to water, and it would set the water to boil. Add it to charcoal, and it turned the charcoal into still more prometheum. Put it in a vacuum and shake it, and it glowed bright white.

Now that the sun had slipped below the buildings to the west, the park's lamplighters had set to work, cranking the clockwork mechanisms at the base of each lamppost that set the cut-glass globes at the top of the posts to vibrating, agitating the prometheum within. Chabane had a pendant on his lapel, a little crystal flask, stopped with silver. If he were to shake it now, the clear, viscous liquid within would glow soft white, and not dim until almost sunrise.

Chabane watched as the Guards continued past the Transportation building, then turned left into the so-called Court of Honor, with the golden dome of the Administration building at its center. Chabane hurried his pace, so as not to lose sight of which building they entered.

As he rounded the corner of the Automata Exhibition, Chabane watched as the three Guards hurried through the massive doors of the Machinery Exhibition across the way. He followed behind at a somewhat more leisurely pace.

To Chabane's left, opposite the massive Machinery hall, were the twin Automata and Prometheum buildings. Between them stood the fifteen-foot tall statue of Cadwalader Ringgold, in one hand a sextant, in the other a model of the crab-like Antediluvian automaton he'd brought back from the South Pole.

Of course, Ringgold hadn't been the first to return with one of the automata, the first proof of the existence of the "Antediluvians". That honor had fallen to James Clark Ross, who had brought back the broken husk of a mechanism with articulated limbs from the island that now bears his name in 1843, the year after Ringgold and the rest of the Wilkes Expedition had returned from the south seas. This had set off a race to the Pole, to find other examples of this strange, unknown technology. The Ringgold Expedition had won the golden ring when they returned with another, more intact automaton from deep within an icy mountain crevasse, in whose tiny engine there still rested a few precious drops of prometheum. A few drops were enough to change history, though, since added to charcoal it quickly produced more. And in short order, the automaton itself had been reverse-engineered.

The debate still raged about just who the Antediluvians had been. Had they been some forgotten race of man? Or visitors from another world or plane of existence? Some wild-eyed savants even suggested that the Antediluvians were actually the originals of the Atlantis myth, their existence remembered only in legend. All that was known for certain was that they had left behind a scant few examples of a technology that far outstripped that of modern man in the 1850s.

It had not taken modern man long to catch up, Chabane mused, as he passed through the entrance into the Machinery Exhibition.

The interior of the building was massive, looking like three railroad train-houses side by side. And though many of the stalls and booths were already installed, there was still considerable work to be done before the park opened, and the massive steam-powered cranes mounted overhead still hurried from one end of the building to the other and back again, time and again, moving the heavy machinery into place.

At the far left of the building, the west end of the hall, were installations from other countries – Canada, Great Britain, Austria, Germany, France – with the rest being American products. Behind the far wall, on the southern face of the building, was the boiler-house, where tanks of lake water were impregnated with small amounts of prometheum, which set them to boil almost immediately, transforming hundreds of gallons into steam in a matter of moments.

Nearly all of the exhibits drew their power from the steam-powered line shafts spinning at between 250 and 300 revolutions a minute, running from one end of the hall to the other at fourteen feet above the ground. Pulleys were strung from the drive shafts down to the exhibit stalls, strung tight as guitar strings, powering more kinds of machines than Chabane had known existed: water pumps, bottling mechanisms, refrigerating apparatus, trip-hammers, sawmill blades, printing presses, stone-saws, refinery mechanisms, and others whose uses he could scarcely guess. All powered by prometheic steam and, according to the banners and typewritten signs hung on each installation, all of them profitable, the marvels of the age.

In the south-east corner of the building, though, where Chabane could see the Columbian Guards congregating, could be found less marvelous, less profitable exhibits. And it was around the smallest of these that the Guards were now milling.

There wasn't much to the exhibit, just a shack, a banner proclaiming *The Latter-Day Lazarus*, a podium, a few pedestals, and a table designed to lever up on one end. The only machinery in evidence appeared to be some sort of motor, attached by a pulley to the drive shaft overhead. But the motor wasn't attached to anything but a pair of long, thick cables, one of which snaked towards the shack, the other towards the levered table. It took Chabane a moment to recognize it as the same sort of device he'd seen displayed in London, years before. It was a machine for generating electricity.

Outside of Mezian's dime novel, Chabane had heard precious little about electricity in years. It had been something of a novelty a few years back, and marketed as a new brand of patent medicine before the danger of electrocution had driven it from catalog pages all together, but aside from its use in telegraphy it was now all but abandoned. What was the product or device promoted by this "Lazarus" exhibit, and why the unnecessary risk of electricity?

The Columbian Guards he'd trailed had joined with the others already on hand, inspecting the area. Most of them were already inside the shack, which appeared to be the scene of the crime. Intent on their work, none seemed to pay any notice to Chabane. It wasn't surprising. Like many of the Americans he'd encountered since the last summer, the Guards seemed to look upon men and women with dark complexions as nothing more than menials – janitors, gardeners, busboys, maids – and so Chabane had found it possible to slip in and out of groups of them all but unnoticed, effectively invisible.

With his eyes down and an unthreatening expression on his face, Chabane slipped into the shack. He had expected to see a body, perhaps some blood or signs of violence. What he found, instead, was like something from a Grand Guignol.

On the dusty floor, covered by a sheet, was a still human form, presumably the body of the dead man. Overhead, wire cages hung empty from the tarpapered ceiling, the floor of each caked in excrement.

The center of the shack was dominated by a bed-sized bench, with casters on the legs, and straps at either end and in the middle. Affixed to the top of the bench was a boxy metal frame, from one corner of which a thick cable snaked down and under the shack's thin wooden wall. The ground around the bench was strewn with jagged bits of glass that crunched underfoot.

Beside the bench was a low table, on which were piled strange implements, saws, pliers and clamps, along with what appeared to be various automata components. And what Chabane at first took to be strips of meat were scattered on the table and the surrounding ground, and pools of dark liquid congealing scab-like.

An abattoir stench hung thick in the air, and as Chabane stepped over to the nearest of the three barrels at the rear of the shack, he found the source of the smell. In the barrel was heaped viscera, blood, flesh and bones. Chabane started, covering his mouth and gagging, then recognized the tiny child-like limbs as those of a monkey. Beside the limbs he saw the remains of a monkey skull, cut in half like a grapefruit, the brain scooped out. He remembered the animals missing from the Street in Cairo concession, and suppressed a shudder.

"What in God's name is *this*?" came a blustering voice from the shack's open door.

Chabane turned to see the chief of the Columbian Guard, Colonel Edmund Rice, shouldering into the shack, behind him another man with thinning hair and a prominent mustache.

"There's been a murder," one of the Guards explained, unnecessarily.

Rice shot the man a bewildered look, then shook his head, muttering something about the quality of officers he had at his disposal, comparing them unflatteringly to the 14th Massachusetts Infantry Regiment.

Chabane had accompanied Sol Bloom to a few meetings with Colonel Rice, but doubted the man had ever noticed he was there. Certainly, Rice hardly seemed to notice him *now*.

"Well, Robinson?" Rice turned to the mustached man behind him, who Chabane now recognized as L. W. Robinson, chief of the Columbian Exhibition's Machinery department. The Colonel reached down and flicked the blanket off the body on the floor. "Do you know this man?"

Robinson peered down at the burnt and bludgeoned man on the floor, and with a queasy expression quickly nodded. "Yes, I know him." He straightened up and looked away. "That's Tom Edison."

Rice narrowed his eyes in concentration, and looked from

Robinson to the dead man. "I know the name, but can't place it."

Robinson nodded again. "Was a bit famous for a time. He invented the phonograph, you may recall?" The Colonel shook his head. "In any event, I only spoke with him briefly when he secured his spot in the hall, but it appeared that he'd sunk his fortunes into electricity years ago, and simply couldn't see a way out."

"Electricity?" the colonel repeated, disbelievingly. "Whyever for?"

Robinson shrugged. "Who can say? I tried to explain to him that there simply wasn't any call for such things, not with prometheic steam engines and lights and automation and such, that he might as well try selling butter churns. But Edison was not to be deterred. He had that wild-eyed look you see in religious zealots, you know the type? He was *determined* to find a way to make his . . . now what did he call them? Oh yes, his *dynamos* profitable."

"That's a 'dynamo' out front, I take it?" Rice asked.

The Machinery chief nodded. "Sad, isn't it? Still, Edison wasn't the only one. I've heard of a number of inventors and investors who'd hung all their hopes on electricity, in the years before prometheum really took hold. Most ended up going off into industries or trades, sooner or later. I even heard of one, a Serbian I believe, who became a writer of cheap fictions." He looked back to the dead man on the ground, grimacing at the gruesome sight. "Clearly, though, Edison hadn't been able to adapt. And it got him in the end. Unless I'm mistaken, he shows every sign of being electrocuted."

One of the Guards stepped forward, and Chabane recognized him as the one from the Midway who was so quick with the racial epithets. "What do these dyna—dynami— dyna—" He shook his head. "What do these things have to do with this 'Latter-Day Lazarus' business? Was your man here intending to raise the dead with this electric thing?"

"If he was," another Guard called from the rear of the shack, "I think he was doing it one piece at a time." The Guard held aloft a severed arm, far too large to have come off any monkey.

"Jesus *wept!*" Rice spat, rearing back.

The Guards began muttering to one another, and Chabane

distinctly heard several mentions of "grave-robbing" and "workmen's bodies".

"What?" Chabane said, stepping forward, for the first time making his presence known. "What did you say about the workmen's graves?"

The others turned to him, most of them seeming to notice him for the first time.

"You're that Jew's Arab, aren't you?" the Colonel said, narrowing his gaze.

Chabane drew himself up straighter, and in perfect Queen's English replied, "I am Kabyle, sir, and not of Arab descent, but I am presently in the employ of Mr Bloom, if that is what you mean." His hands at his sides tightened into fists, but he managed to maintain a calm exterior. "What was the mention of grave-robbing and the remains of the workmen?"

Rice glanced to Robinson, who looked as confused as Chabane, and then back. "It's not public knowledge, and if the papers get word of it I'll know where from. But some of the graves to the south have been disturbed, and the bodies laid to rest there have gone missing."

"Would that include the Algerian who drowned in the lake?" Chabane asked.

Rice shrugged. "Only the Christian graves are marked, as I understand it."

Chabane ignored Rice, and looked back to the barrels, from which the Guards were still pulling cadaver parts. There were severed hands and feet, a leg, two arms, bits of skulls, even a complete torso. He barred his teeth in a snarl, and turned to look down on the dead man on the floor. "My grandmothers always said that no one is to be lamented who dies during Ramadan, during which the gates of hell are closed and those of heaven always open. It doesn't seem quite right that a man such as this should get into the gates of heaven uncontested, even if he *was* murdered."

"Now hold on," Rice objected, holding up his hands. "No one said anything about murder."

"They didn't?" Robinson asked, eyebrows raised.

Rice turned to the chief of Machinery, fixing him with a hard glare. "You yourself said this was an electrocution, right? An *accidental* electrocution?"

Robinson's hands fluttered like caged birds. "I suppose it *could* have been," he allowed. "But what about —" he waved at the broken glass, the scattered tools, the splattered blood and viscera "—all of this?"

"*This*," Rice said evenly, "could well be simple vandalism. And vandalism is an entirely different order of magnitude to murder. Murder will get plastered over every paper in the country, and run the risk of turning paying customers away, if they think the killer is at large. One more accidental death and a spot of vandalism, *that* we can handle."

"You're joking, of course," Chabane objected. "Have you no interest in seeing justice done?"

Rice glared at him. "There must be *some* jobs down south the automata won't do, boy. Why don't you get down there with the rest of the darkies and make yourself useful?"

Chabane bristled. There *were* still a few slaves in the southern United States, not yet supplanted by cheap automata. That this man could so casually dismiss their continued suffering in an offhand slight brought Chabane's blood to boil. For an instant, he almost forgot the welfare of the troupe to whom he'd pledged himself, or the stranger who had stumbled beneath the shelter of Chabane's protection. If he'd been on his own, not responsible for anyone but himself, Chabane would have wished for nothing more than a flyssa saber in one hand and a Webley pistol in the other, and he would show these pale-skinned buffoons his worth. But he *wasn't* on his own, and he was responsible for many more souls than just his own.

Marshaling his last reserves of restraint, Chabane strode to the door, and left the shack of horrors behind.

As he made his way back to the Midway, the stars had come out in the darkened skies overhead, and the prometheic lamps were now bathing the park in the soft white glow that had given the exhibition its unofficial name, the White City. But as clean as the white-clad buildings looked in the pure prometheic light, Chabane knew that they were only plaster and boards, hiding the rot and void beneath.

Of course Rice and the rest of his tin soldiers were more concerned with pay checks than with justice, happy to paint a murder as an accident if it suited the Board of Directors, whitewashing away any chance of bad publicity. Still, Chabane wasn't sure that justice hadn't been done, anyway. He remembered another Kabyle superstition his grandmothers had taught him, that there are never any demons abroad during Ramadan, because God compels them to remain in hell throughout the sacred month. Having seen the gruesome work of the dead man, Chabane doubted any demon ever did worse.

Passing the Terminal Station, he exited the park grounds through the 64th Street entrance, heading north up Island Avenue. Just before reaching the Midway, something bright caught his eye, a splash of color on the pavement reflecting back the prometheic light from above. It was Mezian's dime novel. Picking it up, Chabane flipped through the pages as he continued on towards the Algerian concession.

The prose was lurid, the action improbable, but there was something about the image of this future of electricity and equality presented by the author, that resonated with Chabane. This Nikola Tesla was no Jules Verne, but still Chabane was reminded of the sense of boundless potential he used to feel when reading the *Extraordinary Voyages* story-papers.

Before turning onto the Midway, Chabane saw a handbill posted to a lamppost, advertising the impending Opening Day celebrations for the Columbian Exhibition. In addition to the last living relative of Christopher Columbus, the Duke of Veragua, the most honored guest at the ceremony would be the octogenarian Abraham Lincoln, former President of the United States, who would be on hand to cut the ribbon on the Exhibition.

The imagery of "Dane Faraday, Man of Justice" still rolling in his thoughts, Chabane tried to imagine a world in which James Clark Ross had never returned from the south seas with a broken automaton, in which Ringgold had never discovered prometheum, in which the modern age knew nothing of the forgotten Antediluvian civilization. Perhaps in such a world, there would now be an Electricity exhibit instead of a Prometheum one, with Tom Edison's dynamos at center stage. And perhaps instead of an Automata building, one devoted to some other industry, metal-working perhaps, or mining. But then, in a world in which the United States Army lacked prometheic tanks, perhaps they wouldn't have been able to subdue the southern insurrection, and the Union might have split in two over the question of slavery. Perhaps there might not be a Columbian Exhibition at all.

What Chabane couldn't decide was whether such a world would be better, or worse, than the one he knew.

By the time Chabane returned to the Algerian concession, the sun had long since set, and the fourth prayer of the day, Maghrib, had been completed. Now the troupe was breaking their Ramadan fast. Even the non-observant among them, like Chabane, usually had the good graces not to eat and drink in front of the others while the sun was shining in the holy month. Fast or not, though, Chabane knew that a fair number of the performers, once their meals were done, would slip off and drink spirits, perhaps swapping Algerian wines for the "firewater" favored by Cody's Indians. Perhaps tonight, instead of trying to stop them, Chabane just might join them.

The stranger sat among the Algerians, in his lap a plate of food, untouched. He had been cleaned up, his wounds bandaged, and dressed in a suit of borrowed clothes. He was awake, but unspeaking, and it was unclear what, if any, tongue he comprehended. He simply sat, watching the others silently, his expression mingling confusion and interest.

"Keep your distance, *amin*," Papa Ganon said, as Chabane crouched down beside the man. "My hand brushed his bare skin while we were dressing him, and I got the shock of my life. He's like a walking thundercloud, this one."

Chabane nodded, and kept his hands at his sides. In the soft white glow of the prometheic lights overhead, Chabane examined the stranger closely. His coloration, what little of it could be seen beneath the bandages, cuts, and scars, was somehow . . . off. His skin was a darker shade than his light hair would suggest, the little hairs on the backs of his hands darker than his feathery eyebrows. And his features seemed mismatched, his nose too long and narrow, his mouth a wide slash in his face, his over-large ears too low on his head.

"What will we do with him?" Dihya asked, coming to stand beside Ganon. Taninna came with her, staring hard at the stranger's disfigured face, as though trying to find something hidden there.

Chabane thought about tradition, about the past and the future. He remembered the superstitions he'd been taught as a child, and the story-papers' fantastic futures into which he'd fled.

In many ways, the future promised by Jules Verne had arrived, but not in the way the young Adherbal Aït Chabaâne had imagined. But the future that young Mezian now dreamed of, the future promised in Nikola Tesla's colorful stories? They would never arrive. That wasn't tomorrow, but was *yesterday's* tomorrow. The world of Dane Faraday would never arrive, with its heavier-than-air craft, and wireless communications connecting distant nations, and incandescent lights dangling from wires, and massive dynamos. A world of phosphorescent gas tubes on lampposts, and power lines criss-crossing the countryside, and antennas atop every house picking symphonies out of the air. Of men and women of all races and nationalities, each measured by their conduct and their character, not by their language or the color of their skin.

Chabane thought about the frisson he'd felt on flipping through Tesla's story, the familiar thrill of boundless potential. But he realized now it wasn't a hope for a new world to come, but a kind of nostalgia for a future that could never be. He thought about the dead man in the blood-covered shack in the Machinery building, so committed to a particular view of yesterday's tomorrow that he had been willing to commit horrible acts to get back to it, whatever the cost.

"*Amin?*" Dihya repeated, seeing Chabane lost in thought. "What will we do with the stranger?"

Chabane took a deep breath, and sighed. He had tried to escape tradition before, and now knew he never would. "We do what our grandmothers would have us do. No stranger who comes into the village for aid can ever be turned away."

Maybe it wasn't all of the tomorrows that mattered, Chabane realized. Maybe what was truly important was preserving the past, and working for a better *today*. Perhaps *that* was the only real way to choose what kind of future we will inhabit.

But Taninna was right, Chabane knew, looking back to the silent man sitting in the cool glow of the prometheic light. The stranger *did* have Salla's eyes.

The Canary of Candletown

C. S. E. Cooney

> *God, if You had but the moon*
> *Stuck in Your cap for a lamp*
> *Even You'd tire of it soon*
> *Down in the dark and the damp*
> Louis Untermeyer
> "Caliban in the Coal Mines"

They say the Operators of Candletown were once men. This one got his face half melted in a firedamp explosion. That one got both his legs broken in a shaft collapse. That one lost an arm to gangrene.

Oh, they were given the choice, all right. Live on as cripples, no longer able to work like whole men, those younger, hardier, luckier. Or take Candletown Company's offer. Get that ghost arm replaced by mech, chased in silver, fifty times as strong and five times as versatile. Cover that inelastic mess of scars with a mask of stainless steel, hammered into an eternally triumphant smile, worked crystal glowing in that empty socket like an all-seeing star.

Little by little, the other parts of the man begin to malfunction. Bit by bit, bone by bone, his parts are replaced by company parts, paid for by the company, a debt no man can hope to repay, until the man is no man at all, but twenty feet tall, spider-limbed, braced and gauntleted, padded and shocked, veined in wires and many-armed as Shiva, whose footsteps echo in the ground of Candletown, all the way down to the black seams of anthracite, clean-burning and diamond-hard, buried deep in the dirt. Here is an Operator.

The Operators of Candletown are its guardians. They are the law, and the law is coal. This is the century of steam. No height too high, no depth too distant, no horizon unpursued. The world runs on fume and fire. Whoever holds the fire owns the aluminum dragons of the sky, the iron serpents of the earth, the steel-plated leviathans of the sea.

Operators are born men the way Candletown was born a spit-on-the-ground tent colony. Now Candletown burns as bright as any palace. Now its most wrecked and lame stalk the perimeters with the footsteps of gods.

The girl was born eighth in a family of miners too weary to want her. She lived. She lived and ate and shat. What wailing she did went mostly unattended. After six or so years by no one's counting, she was brought to the breakers of Candletown and put to the sorting belt.

She stood with one-eyed oldsters, bent-backed widows, the one-footed gimps who had opted out of the Operators' Guild and were thus doubly reviled, and with the other children, too. She graded the lumps disgorged from the bowels of Candletown's three mines: Crow's Maw, Hell's Well and the Inkpot. She straddled troughs and picked slate from coal. She did this for four years until she was pulled from the belt and sent down to the ventilation traps.

Deep in dank and darkness, the girl squatted, picker turned trapper brat, tongue-dumb and numb-eyed.

Seven years passed in this near-perpetual midnight. She opened and shut the traps that drove the wind through and the firedamp away. Her youth spooled out in solitude, silence broken only when the mule drivers rolled through, with their coal carts and their lunch pails and their hats smeared with the burning grease called sunshine. Their songs were almost robust enough to scare off the rats, but never for long. The world above her worked on, but she rarely ascended except to sleep.

Four years as a trapper, two as a mule girl, two as a miner's laborer. Time moved, and at the age of eighteen, she did not know what it was to be clean. Time moved, measured in thin hymns floating from the company church as she slept through the Sabbath. Time moved, and the girl did not know the color of her eyes, or the sum of her years, or the sound of her own voice.

The miners called her Little Silence – until she began to cough. Then, shrugging, they took even that name away.

Bitterly, she barely understood she missed it.

And then the girl met Dagomar Wunderlich.

Candletown straddles the Kanawha River, dangling filthy feet in two counties. It possesses the only post office for twenty miles. Besides the colliery and the Operators' offices, it boasts three saloons, a church and a company store. There is also a paper mill, a gristmill, a barbershop, an apothecary, a stable, and a cemetery.

This cemetery is Candeltown's original burial ground, where the very first drifters and migrants had been wrapped cavalierly in canvas and dumped. Now every worker gets a good pine box, stamped with the triple-flame logo – company issue. The cemetery is nearly full.

Time to extend the borders. Push out, like pioneers. These are the bones from which steam rises. This is the fuel that stokes the world.

Superintendent Tiberius McRae knocked once on the door, a blow like a stick of sweaty dynamite carelessly handled. On receiving no answer, he stumped in. He had one good leg and one mech. His coat was brown, with tails like a gentleman's, and his pocket watch told the phases of a mother-of-pearl moon.

In the middle of the bedroom he stopped and looked around. Nothing special. A hundred rooms just like it, though this one was emptier than most: the skeletons of two bunk beds, bare of mattresses; one shelf with nothing on it; one trunk and its rusted padlock; one lone twig chair, hobble-footed, listing in a corner.

Hers was the only bedroll, gray with grime and tattered at the edges, spread out on the hurly-bed she'd slept in since forever.

It was Sunday, her rightful day, and the girl (no longer named Little Silence) would not stir for the Super if he kicked her and howled that the roof had caught fire. Instead, she peered through the soot-beaded bars of her lashes and breathed in hollow whistles so that McRae might think she slept.

"Like I said." McRae turned his brash red head and spoke over his shoulder. "Dead to the world. That's how it takes the young ones, Sundays. Come on in."

Footsteps. The thump of tools and baggage on the floor.

"Your choice of bunk. Rent's five dollars a month."

"You are joking. For this ramshackle paradise?" The newcomer was a woman, a foreigner. Her voice was deep, incredulous, maybe more educated than most.

"Biggest in the house!" McRae retorted. "Used to sleep eleven. Just you and her now. Nothing but the best for our miners."

"I see. Luxury indeed."

"You're not aiming to give me trouble now, Wunderlich?"

"Trouble, sir?"

"You heard me."

McRae's voice had got the grit in it. Two ways this could go. One had Operators at the other end. The girl shivered under her blanket.

The Super began to pace. The thump of his boot was nothing to the near silent impact of his mech leg.

"Wunderlich, I know you come to Candletown with a history. Don't we all? But I also know that people change. Hell, I'm walking proof." A metallic smack as he slapped leg. "In Candletown, we all start clean. Now, we need certified miners – no question. Whatever else you've been, you're that, with the papers to prove it. We're willing to overlook the rest. Question you gotta ask yourself, Wunderlich, is, *How many companies can say the same?* I'm thinking it's a pretty finite list."

He stopped pacing. The girl held her breath and dared crack open her eyelashes another millimeter.

"If Candletown hospitality ain't good enough for you, Wunderlich, the road's thatta way. I see by your boots, you've come a spell already."

Wunderlich held his gaze a moment, then bowed her head. She gestured to the girl, who sealed her lashes once again.

"This . . . She is to be my laborer?"

"Yeah." The grit faded, replaced by a grin. All affability now. An avuncular fondness, even. McRae had known the girl all eighteen years she'd been alive.

"Don't look like much, does she, snoring like the dead down there. But she's a steady monkey. Her old man trained her up from wean. Great worker. Knows the mines in and out – even Hell's Well, which we tapped out a few years back. Hauls like a hunchbacked Hercules. She's strong, too, in that wiry way: outlived most of her sibs already. Let's see." McRae scratched an angry scar near his right ear. "Eldest boy died in a slide last year. Two taken by spring typhoid back in '68. Three married and moved off. One of 'em bled out in childbirth. Can't think what happened to the others. Too many to track." His voice swelled with pride of ownership. "I've got over three hundred families under my care these days and almost three dozen Operators. Candletown keeps growing."

"And you, like a father to them."

If the faintest note of provocation underlay the respectful murmur, McRae pretended not to notice. The girl no longer named Little Silence made no twitch. She'd never heard McRae spoken to like that. Like a child who didn't know better but who should.

"Father? Nah, not me." McRae laughed ruefully. "I'm not even a shareholder. But I won't say as how Candletown ain't like one big dirty family. That's why I paired you up with this one. Her ma finally kicked it last month. Caught the consumption some three years back. Toughed it out this long, but winter did for her. Then her old man got so drunk at the wake, he went and mistook the C&O rail for his pillow. Fucking mess. Anyway, he'd been her miner, too, so she needs another."

The newcomer's "Ah" conveyed sympathy but no surprise.

"You want my opinion," said McRae, lowering his voice to a mere threat of thunder, "that one teethed on too many candle stubs as a bairn. Soft, see? And stunted. Never learned to talk. And anyway, she's got the cough. Could be from her ma. Could be from all those years sunk in the Inkpot. We all take a turn below. Some of us rise."

He hesitated. The newcomer said nothing. The claws of McRae's mechfoot tapped nervously, scratching at the floorboards as if remembering the limb lost to the Crow's Maw mine, a fine feast for the regiments of rats big as boxcars that lived there. McRae frowned down, stilled the tapping.

From behind the determined shutters of her lids, the girl no longer named Little Silence felt the blue blaze of his highland eyes upon her. She kept herself slack. She let herself wheeze.

"The room is spacious and supplies every need," Wunderlich murmured. "I'm sure I'll be comfortable here, Superintendent. Rent is due the first of the month?"

"Yes . . . Yes," he said more firmly, and nodded. "All right,

Wunderlich. Glad to have you on board. Get yourself settled. Report to the Inkpot, nice and early."

"No later than dawn. *Danke*, Superintendent."

"Right." McRae stumped out again.

Wunderlich neither followed him out to explore the dubious daytime entertainments of Candletown, nor set about unpacking. Her footsteps, politer than McRae's, padded over to the window, where the light came in greyly through a permanent dust stain. She sighed a bar of song in her foreign tongue (*German*, thought the girl no longer named Little Silence; there were several German families in Candletown) and then said, in a voice low and clear, as if certain of being overheard at any decibel, "My lamp is my sun, and all my days are nights."

The phrase was like a secret, just between them. The girl knew that Wunderlich knew she was awake. She rolled over onto her back. Curiosity tickled her tear ducts, urging her lashes open. Not quite yet, though. She was not quite ready.

As if encouraged by the girl's movement, Wunderlich settled on the floor near her bedroll. The girl could feel her there, smell her, now that the oil and iron and flesh-seared scent of McRae was fading. Wunderlich smelled like the open road and a shirt worn close to the skin that had gone too many weeks without washing.

The sounds of rummaging. A lockbox unclicking. A key winding. A light whirring.

Only when she felt the prick of tiny claws upon her skin did the girl no longer named Little Silence open her eyes.

A bird, no larger than a wren, perched upon her chest. It strutted up. It paraded down. It ruffled its silver-chased feathers and flirted its filigreed tail. It turned its enamel head around and around on a neck as yellow-vivid as daffodils. Upon its chest, like a badge of pride, was embedded a most delicate and cunning clock. From within, the faintest air of a lullaby. The bird was like a jewel pacing her blackened nightshirt. It was like a messenger from heaven.

The girl smiled, and Wunderlich smiled in answer.

"I brought it across the ocean. It was a farewell present from my old friends. It is now a hello present to my new friend. *Es ist ein Kanarienvogel*. Like you."

And just like that, Kanarien had a name again.

*   *   *

Do not think, because of all its dead, that Candletown is dying. Candletown refuels itself. Pass any company house. Press your ear to the clapboard. Listen at the window. You might hear the creak of a rocking cradle, the hoarse lullabies of a miner's wife:

> *Hush-a-bye, baby*
> *Now don't make a sound*
> *Or the mech-men'll take you*
> *Right down to the ground*
> *Six arms of iron*
> *With talons of gold*
> *They'll snatch you from sleeping*
> *And plant you for coal*
> *Your flesh it will blacken*
> *And harden and then*
> *Your daddy will dig you*
> *Back up again.*

It was the softer edge of dusk. Wunderlich and Kanarien walked together to the company store. Wunderlich needed her pickaxe sharpened, lamp oil, food to last another week, "and perhaps a length of canvas to patch these old coveralls of mine."

Kanarien needed never to leave Wunderlich's side.

They held hands, as they did every day going down into the Inkpot. As they did every night in the battered old hurly-bed, forehead to forehead, legs entwined, while the clockwork canary chimed lullabies and Wunderlich talked softly of her life before, in Manchester and Brussels and Paris. The work she had done with Engels and Marx. The uprising in South Germany, the friends who had died there. Her exile in '49, first to London, then the States. The time she'd lost an eye to a policeman's riot baton. How her friends had scraped up the funds to fill the empty socket with a Forged Orb "as if I were some bourgeoise with money to burn on mechtech".

She spoke often of her friends, dead now or scattered or too disappointed in their own constant failure to keep on. "We thought we could burn forever, like a coal seam fire, smoldering underground for decades, then bursting to the surface and lighting up the world. But there weren't enough of us to keep the fire going. We burnt out. You would not think it to look at me, Kanarien, but once I was a flame."

Kanarien's silent history filled with flames, with uprisings, secret meetings and public protests and the passionate babble of ghosts. Even her memories were no longer lonely.

Palm to palm they walked, crumple-shouldered from a day of crouching and drilling, blasting and loading. They sauntered slowly, cracking the knuckles of their free hands, shoulders rolling to work out the kinks. A swathe of violet doused the last orange embers in the west. Wunderlich's face was tilted to catch the first star. Kanarien's, as always, turned up to her friend. The yellow-necked clockbird perched on her shoulder and chimed the hour like a silver bell.

"Pretty evening," Wunderlich grunted. "*Wer reitet so spät durch nacht und wind? Es ist der vater mit seinem kind* ... Ha! Little bird, sometimes I think the twinkle in your eyes is shaped like a question mark! That was poetry, Kanarien. Goethe. 'The Erlking', as Scott would have it translated – perhaps not well. But we'll leave that for now. Yes, I will read you the rest tonight; I cannot remember all of it. You will regret your asking eyes maybe, for it is a very frightening poem, about a bad king who carries children away to the deadlands.

"Kanarien, I do not pretend to admire Goethe's politics, but his poetry ... His poetry brings me home."

Wunderlich trudged with huge, soft strides. The dinge of soot had not yet leached all the gold from her hair. Her teeth flashed by the light from every windowpane they passed. One green eye glinted more weirdly than the other, the worked crystal of her Forged Orb deepening its glow in the dusk.

Kanarien skipped three steps for Wunderlich's every one. One black-knuckled, black-nailed, black-pored hand crept up to clutch Wunderlich's ragged elbow, one hand pressed hard her own chest. Her heart thudded terribly. She would have to slow down or start coughing.

She did not want to slow down. She had never heard poetry before Dagomar Wunderlich. Why could they not walk faster, so as to return all the quicker to their own private room, so as to be alone again at last, with Goethe and the Erlking, where Wunderlich would teach her poetry, and Kanarien would repeat it back in kisses.

Chirping at the sudden burst of speed, the clockbird clutched her shoulder. Kanarien tugged imploringly at Wunderlich's sleeve, and Wunderlich shouted a laugh.

"Slow down, little bird! Let an old girl get her wind!"

Arms comically akimbo, Kanarien halted in front of the Candletown Company Store. *See there?* said the jut of her sharp chin, her noiseless laugh. *We're here already!*

Snorting, Wunderlich bent double and set her hands on her knees.

When she straightened, she did not seem winded. Her face was closed to expression. She studied the store from under heavy blonde brows, and there was a look in her good eye that was harder than the facets of her Forged one. She opened her palms and held them slightly before her, whispering:"*O father, my father, and did you not hear/The Erlking whisper so low in my ear?*"

Kanarien, ever watchful, stopped laughing. Three months ago, she would not have understood this shift in Wunderlich's mood. Now her memories were full of Manchester, Paris, Brussels, East Germany. She knew why she had worked all her life for Candletown and still owed her death in debt to it. Why Mama had died without medicine. Why Pa took a C&O train engine to bed instead of one of the Watering Hole's whores.

The clockbird on her shoulder pranced and twittered. Her hand slipped from Wunderlich's elbow to her wrist.

"Little bird," Wunderlich said in a rasp. "Little friend. My soul is sick. Every day I must resolve anew: No more fighting! This time I will keep still. I will bow my head and back away. I will do this work and no other. I am that tired, yes, and disappointed. Yes, and defeated. I have my scrip in hand. I have my list of necessary items to buy with it. Before us is the door into the place that will sell me what I need. And yet, before I pass through it, I must stop a moment, remembering everything that brought me here. And at what cost."

All about that massive gold head, now bent earnestly toward Kanarien's, the stars were like lanterns flung pell-mell to the bottom of the most monstrously deep shaft ever sunk. Wunderlich stood, gathering courage enough to face her cowardice, tears making gloss of her one good eye.

Kanarien watched her, full to trembling.

That she should cry. That *she* should cry!

Before she made the decision to do it, Kanarien had stooped low. She scooped up a large rock and chucked it through the Candletown Company Store window. She opened up her mouth and screamed. Of course no sound came out. Of course, no sound. But the rock shattered the glass, and that was good enough for her.

The world was suddenly full of rocks.

Wunderlich tried to grab her. She was big and Kanarien small, but Kanarien knew how to use her size, how to fold herself smaller still, and – born eighth in a miner's litter now mostly dead – she had learned long ago to be slippery besides. Strong as she was, Wunderlich would never hurt her. Wunderlich had had all the violence knocked out of her; Kanarien had not. Eighteen years it had built in her like firedamp, and Wunderlich's tear was the spark that ignited her. That *she* should cry! Where was her next rock?

Not a stone unturned, wasn't that the phrase? Not a pane left whole. The hole in her breath. The pain in her chest. Break it all.

"No, Kanarien!" That was Wunderlich. Dagomar Wunderlich, whom, could she speak, she would call her heart's darling. "Please, Kanarien. The manager – he's sent for the Superintendent. Stop or he'll call the Operators . . ."

"*What is going on here?*"

That was McRae's roar. He came stumping up the hill from his Operators' office, his face as red as his hair, faster than any man on mortal legs could move. He snatched at Kanarien, too, his freckled fists pale in the gloom. But Kanarien had been a trapper brat, a mule girl, a loader and laborer, fast and fierce, and what was *he*, really? What was Superintendent Tiberius McRae, after all? Just another one-legged orphan of the Inkpot. He thought his mechleg and fancy job made him finer than those he'd left below, did he? Kanarien screamed again – again without sound – and kicked his good knee until he buckled.

"Bitch! Is she drunk?"

"She's upset. I don't know why—no, don't! Don't hurt her."

"I won't—hurt her—if she stops trying to bite—me—aaugh!"

Kanarien strained. Others had joined in the seethe. So many hands, her shirt in rags, but no one could hold her. Where was her bird? Where was her bird?

Her boot crunched on something already broken.

Fresh rage washed her vision. The night turned clear and pink. Easy to see in the dark if you spent your life there. It was the sunlight that blinded you. It was the poetry. And the kisses. And the tears.

The Candletown Company Store stood open. The door flung wide. That door! Which, in order to pass, Wunderlich must call herself a coward. Her Wunderlich, who used to be a flame.

If she could get so far . . .

Past that door were sacks of flour, sacks of salt and sugar. Something to rip. Something to scatter. Let the Operators pick white grain from white grain from white grain, separating each from the other, like the poor cinder girl in that story Wunderlich once told her. Let them bend to the task dawn 'til dusk, until each sack was full again.

Past that door were tubs of butter, twenty-seven cents a pound. It was twenty-four cents everywhere else – that's what Wunderlich said. A criminal price for butter, she'd said, and the miners didn't even have real money to pay with. Company scrip, useless everywhere else butter might be cheaper. Illegal currency to buy criminal butter, but what could you do? You needed butter; you had scrip. So what can you do?

Kanarien knew what she would do.

If she got past that door, *she would smear it*. Smear it all. Grease the walls, the floor. Unfurl bolts of calico over streaks of shining yellow butterfat and topple pyramids of canned goods over that. There. That's what your butter's worth, your green beans, your peaches. Stacks of pickaxes. Buckets of shovels. The soft brown "crow coal" they mined for nothing, not even a pittance, incidental in the pursuit of anthracite, and still they had to pay for it, to light their own fires, to cook their own food. She would crush it underfoot. It was worth just that much.

Oh, what *wouldn't* she do? What *wouldn't* she ransack? If she could get past that door.

All hands fell away. Her knees jounced in the dirt, palms scraping gravel, but she was up again in a gasp, sprinting for the door . . .

An enormous metal arm reached out of the sky and lifted her into it.

Fury left no room in her head for surprise. Kanarien, dangling from the scruff of her neck, studied the thing coolly, closer at this moment to the nightmare god of her childhood than she had ever been before.

> *They'll snatch you from sleeping*
> *And plant you for coal.*

She pondered it. Might it be dismantled with nothing but her teeth? Her naked fingers? Underneath all that metal there was a man, wasn't there? Isn't that what they all say? Or at least the last parts of man. Rotten meat wired up and armor-plated, any soul possessed by the original flesh sold long ago.

They had prowled at the periphery of her life as long as she remembered. The Operators of Candletown. She used to wake, wet and jolted, from dreams that saw them chasing her through endless black tunnels, further into the black, until the air failed, and her own breath crushed her. All her life she had revered them. Feared them. Hardly thought of them, except while sleeping.

Kanarien had never felt more awake.

She dangled, and they stared at each other. Or, at least, the Operator seemed to stare. Its metal faceplate was blank but for a single crystal glittering a bit off center. The crystal was faceted like a fly's eye. Kanarien hissed at it.

The Operator hissed back. Or perhaps that was just the hydraulic guts of its system, readying itself to shake her like a wolf shakes a rat. Kanarien clenched her teeth. Her neck snapped from side to side. The Operator tossed her to the ground as carelessly as it had plucked her from it. A long way down. Kanarien did not land lightly. The breath whooshed out of her. Her sore chest seized up. Dirt filled her nose. She vomited for breath.

The wheezing of gears. The creak of oiled steel. Eight, great, jointed legs picked across the ground to her. The earth shook. The dust, displaced, rose in the air like a ghost road. Once more that metal arm reached down, pinchers closing about her ankle.

If Kanarien could have squealed, she would have. Up she went again, upside down. All her blood pounded in her head. The Operator swung her gently. A rag doll in the grip of a vengeful child. The pinchers loosened.

She heard Wunderlich howl.

The world slowed as she tumbled through the air and Kanarien saw many things.

She watched as Wunderlich seized a pickaxe from the floor of the company store. She watched Wunderlich raise it high, her false eye shining out like a green torch in her blood-streaked face, her gold hair standing about her head. McRae cowered back from her, and the manager, and the other men who'd gathered. But they had nothing to fear. They were not Wunderlich's target.

She bent her head and charged like a freight train at full speed toward the Operator, a scream tearing from her throat as she swung the pickaxe hard.

Kanarien landed.

Her last thought was, *Valkyrie*.

Then all the stars went out.

They call it Hell's Well.

It had been the first and finest of Candletown's mines. Tapped out, used up, abandoned now. They left the immense underground labyrinth to collapse quietly into itself, wooden supports rotting under the weight of white fungi, brittle pillars cracking with the sound of gunshots no one hears. Black acid waters rise in slow floods, filling old chambers, washing away the crunch of coal dust and pulverized limestone, covering the bones of rats and mules and miners alike.

At first, the Operators posted "No Trespassing" signs and walked a strict circuit to enforce them. But the longer Hell's Well continues unused, the more its ruins are neglected.

The little slate pickers and trapper brats like to go that way to play, where the din and clash and bellow of Candletown is snuffed and the loblolly scrub has begun to grow. They have cleared an area for baseball and tag.

Grown-ups never venture out that far. They have forgotten Hell's Well entirely, or are too tired to contemplate the long walk, or say they worked that mine when it was open "and mean never to return again, so help me!"

Really, they are afraid of the shaft. With the elevators removed, cables, platform and all, the darkness goes down forever.

The young ones dare each other to spit into that hole. Sometimes they make it to the edge, hawk a good one, the mucus black as everything in Candletown, and let it fly. It is then a chill overtakes them, a cool updraft of exhalation, like a breath from below. They back away from the shaft again, shaking, faces drained of color beneath the grime.

It is as if they had spat into their own graves.

"Dagomar," said Kanarien. "Are you awake?"

There was only one light at the bottom of the shaft. It glared greenly from Wunderlich's Forged Orb, half-lidded by a rim of bruised flesh. A sickly light, but Kanarien was grateful for it. A Forged Orb equipped with Eidolon Eyesight, Wunderlich had once told her, could detect firedamp before it ignited, white damp before it killed you with the smell of violets, or black damp before your head goes funny and you lie down to die gasping.

But that kind of extra tech costs extra coin, maybe costs your soul and your unborn too. Wunderlich's orb was the old-fashioned kind, good only for glowing in the dark.

"I heard the thunder," Kanarien said, "far away, but still underground. I knew it was coming even before I heard it, because rats had been chewing my boots, and then they all left. Pa always did say miners' rats were canny. Used to keep a pair for pets. Tame as tame can be. Named Calamity Jane and Lady Jane, respectively. Lady Jane didn't have any tail, I remember. Rats can hear the thunder of a cave-in before we can, Dagomar, did you know? Pay attention and you can follow the rats out in time. Like your Pied Piper, Dagomar, but in reverse. Only, I don't think this cave-in was an accident.

"We're in Hell's Well; I can smell it. I used to work here with Pa. I ever tell you that? I think, while we were out from those knocks on our heads, they dumped us here and left us to die. And I think they brought out the dynamite to make sure of it. That was the thunder. I'd go out and explore it, but I daren't leave your side. I might never find you again."

The worked crystal glowed feverishly in Wunderlich's empty eye socket. Her good eye, her seeing eye, was dull. Filmed over in old blood and coal dust. Her mouth was open. Several of her teeth were shattered to stubs. Splintery juts of bone scrabbled from her lacerated skin. Her knees and elbows bent at odd angles. There were chunks missing. A trail of glistening stink seeped from her stomach.

Broken beyond repair.

Kanarien dragged herself closer to where Wunderlich lay. Rubble blanketed her large body, a mixture of rock and dirt and the crumbly brown crow coal that didn't count toward tonnage. Kanarien smoothed her hand over the rubble. Not much difference between it and her own crusted fingers. Wunderlich had said that humans were made of much the same stuff as coal. Her ma had said something similar, coughing her life out on that bunk. Said everything was dust.

Not them, though. Never them.

Kanarien's chest hurt more than ever. Every breath was sharp as it was shallow. She brought a hank of once-gold hair to her lips.

"One day, Dagomar, they'll dig us up again. One thousand years after Candletown has fallen, when the coal is spent and the need for coal is past, a new generation will come, digging for our bones. They will explore Candletown as though it were a city on the moon, asking themselves: *What happened here? Whose bones are these? How did they live and what made them die?*

"So they will dig for answers, as in our day we dug for fire. And I'll tell you what they'll find, Dagomar. This mine. Our mine. Not Hell's Well. Not by then. For we'll have made of it a cave of wonders. We shall be the wonders, Dagomar, you and I. They'll dig for years and find us here at last. The treasure at quest's end. Resting here, at the bottom, as if waiting for their widened eyes all that time.

"They will see us through a shimmering. A casket made of diamond. And in it, two bodies, perfectly preserved, entwined in each other's arms like a single being. *Are they saints?* they'll ask, but then they'll see the coal beneath our fingernails. *The giantess with hair like a lion – is she an angel?* But then they'll see the pickaxe set at your feet like an offering and know you for a worker.

"*Who is her friend? The little one who smiles in her sleep?* And they'll try to pry the casket apart with their machines to get at us, to learn our secrets. But diamond is the hardest stone. It won't be scratched. So tired – they'll be so tired then – they'll lay their heads upon our casket, like this."

Kanarien curled up beside Wunderlich. She rested her cheek upon her cold, torn breast.

"And they'll hear, from inside, a beautiful song. Like a tiny, shining bird, singing a most triumphant lullaby. Our love. Our battle. Our great escape. And, at last . . . They'll understand us."

Green-eyed Monsters in the Valley of Sky, An Opera

E. Catherine Tobler

The airship *Rocha* steamed south and west, across skies that seemed to have never known a cloud, but for the puffs of vapor that trailed from the ship. These soon evaporated, leaving the skies the clearest blue you could imagine. You might mistake the blue for water reflecting the sky and try to dip a toe into it if the ship's captain allowed such folly. He would not. The windows were propped open, to allow the warm Zonda wind into the cabins, but this was the extent of the captain's recklessness. His ship was buttoned up, precise, and lovely but for the coffin secured at the front of the passenger cabin.

The coffin resembled a piece of art if one could ignore the perfectly embalmed woman within its glass confines. I could not. She was the color of beeswax, the honeyed glow deepening to umber beneath her chin where her high lace collar was wrapped. Imagine her asleep, the airship attendant had suggested to me, but I, all too familiar with ferrying dead bodies to their resting places, knew she was well and truly dead. She should have occupied the cargo hold, so passengers could remain blissfully unaware as to her presence, but no, she was here, as if she had paid a fare.

Perhaps she had, and I turned this idea over in my mind as I studied the gilded roses and miniature raptors that decorated the coffin edges. Crystal droplets rested on each golden rose petal; every rose thorn was a sliver of emerald. The raptors each possessed jeweled eyes; rubies, sapphires, and even diamonds had been employed to make the tiny beasts shine. The sunlight that spilled into the passenger cabin fragmented through the gems, flooding the space with a shower of iridescent polka dots.

My attention refused to find pleasure in this swirl of colors. I stared at the preserved body without blinking. My seatmate was less concerned with the coffin or its occupant; while I felt certain the coffin and lady were his own, at the moment he was absorbed in the journals spread before him. I looked from the dead lady back to this man and his journals.

Vittorio Trinchero was in possession of a mustachio so beautiful it slowly made me forget the coffin and its occupant if only for a moment. Where the mustachio should have bisected his face neatly in two, giving him the impression of being a man divided, it did not. Its broad and gleaming ebon prow curled in such a way as to draw the eye ever upward, from the slant of his plush mouth, to the flawless planes of his cheekbones.

His ink-stained finger pressed upon the journal page before him as if to say, "See here." Trinchero did not speak English, but Italian; his native language poured from his mouth, nearly as intoxicating as any drink I had ever sampled – and in my travels I had sampled many. Trinchero showed me again his journal, willing me to understand.

The sketches beneath his finger were of a grand theater, with which he was utterly enamored. I could not blame him; it looked as though it had been drawn from a dream, balconies rising in countless levels from the floor, curving in a gentle horseshoe shape away from the gilded stage and up into a ceiling of fabric clouds. Where the ceiling rose higher in domes, elaborate frescoes adorned every surface, animals and seraphim holding pendulous chandeliers from sharp beaks and elegant fingers.

"Valle del Cielo?" I asked, and he nodded. I did not speak much beyond English, but this I had learned from my travel guides.

"*Si*," he said and I smiled.

It was the very thing I traveled to see. The Valley of Sky was one of the marvels J. J. and I planned to see together, and though he had passed from this world to another, the promise to travel the globe remained. The Valley of Sky was home to two dozen theaters, this floating island city the brainchild of one Ramira Clarisa. The streets of her Buenos Aires grew clogged, she said, but the glorious skies were wide open and hungry for the arts. Thus, her dream of singing opera amid the clouds was born.

"I like this best."

My finger came to rest beside his own, at the curl of curtain he had added to the main stage. This curtain was not fully drawn, but furled back on one end. The fabric was edged with fronds and ferns, and if I looked quickly enough, it seemed squat, dwarfish bodies lurked within these forest depths. Bodies like my own.

My few words unleashed a torrent of Italian from him, which I could only silently admire. My attention, however, came back to the lady and her coffin, both of which now sat askew in their moorings. I sat straighter in my seat, but it didn't help; I was also askew, my bottom sliding across the leather seat, my hip slanting into Trinchero's. He looked at me with raised eyebrows I didn't require a translation for. The entire cabin was out of kilter and growing more so by the minute.

Traveling the world required one to adopt a new set of standards; I had been all manner of places at the behest of J. J., and had seen people and events I could have never dreamed up. Each had contributed to the woman I currently was: she who was not astounded when there arose a great commotion in the control cabin, and she who did not shriek or otherwise panic when Trinchero grabbed his journal first and me second, and rolled us onto the floor. We slid beneath our seats as a green and gaseous vapor blossomed into the passenger cabin. The sound of a thousand screaming whistles followed. I clapped my hands over my ears.

I needed no translation for the curse that burst beneath Trinchero's mustachio. He kept his sturdy arm around me as the thunder of metallic feet filled the cabin. Through the haze of vapor, I could see them: mechanical legs and feet, tromping down the aisle as the army invaded the airship. Their torsos looked like repurposed footlockers, their heads wrapped under helmets and goggles that might have allowed them to see cleanly through the thickening gas.

Was I seeing double? Triple? My head began to throb with a dull pain. Other passengers were in full panic; screams and protests reached my ears, but so too did the shriek of metal against metal as the coffin and its embalmed lady began to slide across the cabin. Trinchero tensed at my side, but did not move away; there was nowhere he might go, not with the cabin yet filling with gas and soldiers both.

The *Rocha* plunged downward, a fish loosed from its hook, shrieking as she went. My stomach seemed to go with it. Every mechanical soldier in the aisle was thrown off balance and this gave me the hope that not even they knew what was happening. This was also a curse – if they didn't know, then who commanded them? Who had taken the ship?

Trinchero pressed his journal into my chest and I closed my hands around it. He made to move – toward what end, I cannot say – but the ship took another plunge before he got anywhere. The rumbling engines cut out with a final sputter and *Rocha* was in free fall. The gentle wind that had accompanied us ever since we arrived in South American skies flooded the cabin in a rush, pushing the green vapor away, but causing my eyes to tear even so.

Trinchero's fingers scrabbled against the seat cushions above us, ripping the linen to reveal the bundled parachutes stored there should this very thing occur. Perhaps the planners had not counted on invading armies of mechanical men (surely they had not, clockwork being considered a thing Most Foul), but should an airship lose altitude—

We made a race of it, to see who could harness themselves more quickly, though Trinchero would easily best me in this contest with his longer arms and larger hands. In the end, he helped me secure my harness and gave it a firm tug to be certain all would hold fast.

From the main cabin, there came a brilliant explosion, which sent the *Rocha* plunging toward the blur of ground with ever more speed. I staggered against Trinchero as we stood from the floor; he shoved his journal into his belted trousers, and eyed the coffin that now rested against the far wall. He moved for it as another explosion ripped through the *Rocha*, opening her backside to the brilliant blue sky.

"Trinchero! No!"

There was no possible way he could save the coffin or its lady; I reached for him just as the ship suffered a third fiery insult. Trinchero and I and every seat and every mechanical man and passenger on the ship were blown out the back of the ship. We and our trail of debris exploded through the sky as the *Rocha* screamed ever downward. My fingers were painfully ripped from Trinchero's harness and I spiraled up into the blue, blind to everything but that color.

Trees rose in strange silence around me. I watched the leaves and branches sway in a silent wind, birds circling without sound higher above. I yawned in an effort to pop my ears, but there was nothing. I feared my hearing gone, watching a long-tailed monkey scamper soundlessly from one tree branch to another. Another crouched atop a metallic head that had been separated from its body; I wondered at the troops I had seen on the *Rocha*, but saw no more than this dismembered head.

As I lay dazed amid other broken branches, some poking me in the worst possible places, sound slowly returned. For a long while, everything sounded muffled, distant, but there came a close chitter at my shoulder, and I shied away from the monkey that meant to pluck at my braid.

Birdsong made itself known next and the rustle of leaves under the warm wind. I reached unthinkingly for the branch poking into my ribs and came upright with a screech at the pain. I gasped for a breath and tears streamed down my cheeks. I blinked the tears away, but could not believe what lay some distance away from me in the broken canopy.

The coffin, its four legs shorn off, rested atop the broken branches. The crash and its resultant debris reminded me of tornadoes, the way one house might be swept away while its neighbor was undisturbed. Tornadoes might also pick up an item and set it down unharmed miles away, just as the coffin had been set. J. J. and I had seen such things in our time, but never quite like this. The coffin's roses and raptors were undisturbed, the glass panels unbroken. The beeswax lady inside slept on. I expected her to sit up, press a hand against the glass, and demand to be let out, but even when a bird perched upon the lid, she did not stir. She didn't seem to have moved at all.

I sat there sobbing in pain until I heard Trinchero screaming. *Signora! Signora!* Over and over, sometimes he sounded closer and sometimes much farther away. I tried to draw a breath so as to call to him, but my lungs burned with a fire so intense it stole my voice. I came to my feet with some effort; my legs were not broken, only battered with bruises already, and every movement was pain.

"Trinchero," I said, and my ribs screamed a protest. Still, I unbuckled my parachute.

I found him some short distance away, tangled in his own parachute; the work to free him was slow, my hands shaking from the effort. He was as bruised and battered as I, a frond from a tree having taken up residence in his jacket collar. I reached up, but could not claim it; his hand enfolded mine and he rocked his lips across my scraped knuckles. His mustachio was no less spectacular up close. Midway through the task of unknotting him, I sat back, trying to breathe without pain. This proved impossible.

"*Signora*," he said.

"Muriel, please," I said.

"Mu-ree-el," he said.

Once freed, Trinchero gestured in the direction I had come. Through the tangled trees, the coffin threw up a bright riot of light from its glass and gems. I nodded and followed him when he made to head that direction. Monkeys skittered through the trees above us and when we came back to the coffin, one was trying to pry blotches of gem-thrown lights from the fallen leaves. The monkeys fled as Trinchero dropped to his knees.

A sob escaped him. He crawled toward the coffin, touching it as if to be certain he was not dreaming. He pressed his head against the glass lid and murmured words I could not understand, and I turned away, to give him some privacy.

I could not help but think of J. J. then, and of what he would make of my present circumstances. *Murrie*, he would say, *isn't it a beautiful landscape? Look at the way the jagged mountains slice across the sky, and see there? See how those trees are home to magenta birds – the very color of Mrs Butler's favorite petticoat? Gracious, she did show it to everyone ...*

Trinchero set to searching the debris around us; he pulled long branches out and set them alongside the coffin. I could not quite fathom what he meant by it all until he began to tear long strips of leaves, knotting these into what could be used as rope. He began to lash the branches together, making a frame around the coffin, and then supports beneath it.

He could not possibly mean to take her, but of course he did and I could not fault him for it. I would not have left J. J. in such a place, dead or no. Slowly, I worked beside him to bind the branches into a sledge with which we could drag the coffin. But where would we go? The mountains rising around us seemed impossible. Our destination had been Buenos Aires, but I had no good idea where we were.

Trinchero was acquainted with the land, however; he did not waver when we slowly set out, pulling the lady and her coffin behind us. I was nearly useless in this effort, my legs simply too short to do a bit of good. Trinchero helped me sit on the sledge while he pulled alone, all through the warm afternoon.

I slept and only roused when Trinchero lifted me from the sledge. It was dark, no sign of sunset or sunrise. The universe spilled above us in a way I had never seen before, a wide river that reached farther than I could ever hope to. J. J. had bid me to explore this world, but in that moment, I wanted to go beyond this world. I wanted to understand what lay at the bottom of that starry river.

A house rose in shadow among trees and the spangled sky; I made no fuss as Trinchero carried me inside. I felt half asleep as it was and when he placed me upon a soft bed, had no trouble sliding fully back into oblivion.

Trinchero lived in the trees, a house of patinated iron and local hardwoods that spanned countless thick-trunked trees seemingly grown for that very purpose. The trunks spiraled up through rooms yet never at random; the house bent around their natural shapes, no tree having been modified, the house rather appearing as if it had been grown to accommodate them. Stairs spiraled up and down, arched doorways leading to further rooms; some stairs followed the lines of the trees, toward ceilings of glass panels that allowed the sunlight entry. This light reached through the forest's own canopy, shadows and light in constant motion as the Zonda blew.

Shelves laden with books lined interior hallways, these hallways secreting away nooks with cushioned seats and reaching for ends that expanded outward into new sunlit rooms. Rooms on the outside edge of the house possessed glass doors that led to a wide balcony which ringed the entire level I found myself on; the trees here were within easy reach, even at my slight height. The birdsong that had woken me continued at full volume, flowing much like the house's own staircases, up and down in the same instant, to surround one with a constant cacophony. The bedroom I had been given was sheltered by jacaranda trees, which suffused the entire room with a violet glow as if underwater.

I sipped the strong black coffee left at my bedside and from the balcony watched the forest come to life. Monkeys made themselves known with chitters, their small feet skipping them from roof to branch before they vanished entirely into the forest. One monkey came close enough to smell my coffee; its scent made him skitter away, along the balcony rail, and I followed, until the monkey bounded into the trees. Here, the balcony continued around the outside of the house, yet also branched inward along a new path.

An arched walkway cut through the house, tiled mosaics glittering from floor to apex in the dim light of the passage. There might have been images within the tiles, but my attention was instead fixed upon what I could see at the walkway's end: curlicues of wrought iron. The passage gave way to a wide expanse of forest inside the ring the house made within the trees. Another balcony circled this space, weaving to avoid trees and allow them their natural space. The wrought iron proved to be a massive aviary, enclosing the whole of the trees.

I walked to the aviary's edge and looked, because surely it would not be kept empty. Still, what I eventually saw made me step back. Made me stare.

Trinchero stood on the opposite side of the aviary, drawing silver-sided fish from a dark blue bucket. At first, I could not fathom the task, not until he tossed the fish into the air. The wire aviary canopy was open enough to allow the fish to pass through. When I thought the fish would plummet to the ground, it was instead snatched up in strong jaws, a massive bird swooping past Trinchero. But the bird was not a bird and I had only seen images of what it might actually be. But how could it be?

"*Signora.*"

With a crook of his fishy fingers, Trinchero gestured for me to come closer, then bent to pluck another fish from his bucket. I made a slow circle toward him, but watched as another bird propelled itself through the aviary. Its grey skin was leathery, stretched so thin over its wings the sunlight nearly went through them. Its sharp face and bright eyes looked intelligent, eyes tracking the fish as Trinchero lobbed it through the canopy. It snatched the offering and swallowed it whole, pinpointing me with its violet eyes as it glided past me.

Such monsters were not entirely unknown to me. At Trinchero's side, I spoke even as I knew he would not understand my English.

"There were monsters upon the ice," I said, unable to look away from the trio that swooped within the aviary's limits. "They walked upright, they did not fly, but those crests . . ." I touched my own forehead and traced a line backward into my hair, as if I possessed such an ornament, too. I had taken J. J. to his rest and there the creatures had been, from another age, living as they would. "They are surely related. Those faces . . ."

Italian spilled from Trinchero and I shook my head, not understanding until he said "pterodactyl". That was a word I knew, a word he seemed hard-pressed to speak. I nodded and repeated it back to him. He gestured excitedly at the creatures within his aviary.

I watched the pterodactyls circle as Trinchero fed them, wanting to ask him where he had found them, where they had come from, how it was possible, but mostly I could not speak, so enthralled with the scene before me.

The trio of pterodactyls had to come to perch in one of the tallest trees. Occasionally, they leaned in to one another, snapping their beaks or chirruping, but mostly they sat still, watching Trinchero and me. The smallest of the trio often rubbed its beak on a bare protrusion of tree trunk. While I could certainly attempt to ascribe devious intentions within their violet-shaded eyes, I did not, for these creatures were unknown to me.

On this side of the balcony, there was a workstation that supported tables, shelves and a deep sink. Here, Trinchero cleaned his hands, then gently patted me down, and while I remained a collection of aches and bruises, the sleep had done me a world of good. So too the coffee. I thanked him for both things, and he waved his hands, gesturing again to the aviary.

I looked back to the structure, if only to try to calm my heart. I rested my hands on the rail, watching the pterodactyls as they interacted. They were at ease, accustomed to the presence of one another, whereas I was highly aware that I found myself alone with a man whose acquaintance I had only made upon boarding the *Rocha* a week prior. Alone, in what appeared to be his home. This was an entirely new circumstance for me.

"*Signora.*"

"Muriel," I said again, and touched a hand to my chest.

He bowed his head to me, and said "Vittorio," and it seemed settled, this small bit of understanding between us.

Trinchero gestured for me to follow him inside. Here, there was a sitting room, in the center of which sat that gilded and glass coffin. My steps stuttered at the sight of it, but I came to a dead stop when I realized the coffin was empty. It no longer held its beeswax lady and I could not imagine where she might have gone, where she might have been placed. Surely she had not crawled from the coffin on her own?

My host vanished up a long and winding staircase and I followed after. Some part of me said to be cautious, but the larger part, the part that wanted to see the world long before J. J. encouraged such reckless behavior, said that one could be cautious and curious both. Had Trinchero meant me harm, I felt certain he would have already caused it.

He led me to the uppermost floor of the house, which seemed to be its own room; there were no doors, only a large attic-like space, more panels of glass set into the ceiling at random intervals. Machinery occupied tables and benches alike, some of which I knew, but most of which I didn't. Mostly, my gaze was drawn to the sheet-draped body on a far table; the sheet was tucked up to the beeswax lady's chin, as though she were in bed.

Before I could ask about her – questions drawing answers that wouldn't be readily understood – Trinchero motioned for me to come to the cages that lined one wall. There were dozens of compartments, but only four of them were filled. They held animals that I first thought were more pterodactyls, but proved to be smaller, with longer legs for running. Each cage had a number, each animal inside slightly different from the one that preceded it; the first animal was wholly flesh and bone, while the second was augmented, metal gleaming at its vicious claws. The third bore mechanical joints, and the fourth was fully armored, eyes shining in jewel tones much like those raptors on the coffin.

The fourth animal leaned on the cage door and snuffled as if trying to smell us. I couldn't help but step closer, to get a better look at the metal which enclosed him. Encompassed him? I couldn't tell if it was a metal shell that might be opened, or if he was only metal, all the way down. The metal was beautiful, etched with scales and feathers and my finger was upon its nose before I realized what I had done. Trinchero grabbed my hand and drew me back just as the creature snapped its sharp teeth at me.

"Raptor," Trinchero said, and I understood that word, too. Another kind of dinosaur. Was he making them? Or had he found them?

Perhaps it was both. I wandered the workshop, finding legs and tails and skulls fashioned from metal; these had not been assembled, and maybe they were not intended to be. I looked back at the first raptor, the one of flesh and bone, and wondered how Trinchero had gotten from one form to the last. Had he copied nature's own design?

I wandered from the mechanical body parts, toward the lady where she lay draped upon the table. I was of a mind to touch her nose too, half wondering if she would also snap at me, when throughout the house there tolled a deep and resounding bell. Trinchero clicked his tongue and vanished down the stairs without a word to me. I looked back to the dead lady.

She was strangely beautiful and I wondered at Trinchero's ties to her. Sister? Wife? Or something I could not so easily label? I crept closer to her and was bending to take a closer look at the darkening of her skin near her lace collar when an explosion of angry conversation erupted from the lower floor of the house. I jumped back from the lady and went to the top of the stairs, listening. There were but two voices, Trinchero's and another man. This second man fell to English insults occasionally and it was this that drew me to the stairs.

It was impolite to eavesdrop of course, so I took the stairs down until the men were well within my view, and sat down. Watching in plain sight. If anyone cared to look. Surely that wasn't eavesdropping. Least not in its traditional form.

I could not understand most of what was said, but the tone carried beyond the language spoken. The gentleman, if he could be called such, stood nearly nose to nose with Trinchero, hands balled into fists, his face colored with rage. He grabbed Trinchero by his jacket lapels and pressed him into the nearest wall. In his hand was a crumpled handkerchief.

"Gentlemen."

I was on my feet and moving toward them before I could reconsider. It was foolish, as I was easily half the height of each man, but I would not let Trinchero be bullied.

"You have come into *his* home – show some respect."

The men looked at me and stepped apart. Trinchero smoothed his jacket flat and the other man stared at me with what I could only call astonishment. He did not expect me.

"Madame, forgive me," he said in English and made a quick bow to me. He took the time to fold the handkerchief before stuffing it into his jacket pocket.

He looked askance at Trinchero, but then that gaze came back to me. Warm and blue, like the hottest part of a flame; his own mustachio was less well kept than Trinchero's. Something about his face was familiar to me, but I could not say what or why. I had never seen him in my life. He was dressed well, almost too well to be out in the woods where only the monkeys and Trinchero lived, and this told me we were probably closer to a town that I had believed; his shoes were clean, and so too his trouser legs. He had not tromped through the trees to reach us.

"I was unaware *Senhor* Trinchero had company. *Senhor* Alves at your disposal."

I stood a little straighter. "Mister Alves, I have the impression you would have made the same amount of fuss had you known."

The displeasure that crossed his face confirmed my suspicion of him. This man was on a mission and he did not care who might know. He was a man who cared about his appearance, but did not care about *this* appearance, making a fuss in Trinchero's own house. He turned to Trinchero now and bit out a few words of Italian before taking his leave. He bowed to me once more and was then gone. Through the front door that he did not latch, I could see a long bricked drive and a quartet of horses lashed to a beautiful green carriage. Into this, Alves vanished and was carted away, down a road that twisted through the trees. I looked back at Trinchero.

"*Signora*," he said, and before I could protest, quickly added, "Mu-ree-el."

We stood in silence a long while; I nodded, wishing to tell him I understood. He had a life here, into which I had unexpectedly fallen. I gestured to the open doors, breathing in the wind as it poured into the house.

"Buenos Aires?" I wanted to ask more, but did not know the words. My language guide was in my case. Which was now goodness knew where. I possessed nothing.

Trinchero nodded, but did not look entirely pleased. I wondered if it was the idea of seeing me to the city, or what had transpired with Alves, but I could not ask. Trinchero readied his own carriage – also drawn by horses and nothing so curious as larger-sized raptors – and saw me to my hotel, where I had been expected the day before. I made my apologies to the staff and my goodbyes to Trinchero, and went to my room, which looked west, west toward Trinchero's house in the trees. I could not see it and though I longed to see an upward flood of gem-colored lights from that strange coffin, a familiar beacon, looking did not make it so.

The gracious hotel staff assisted me in the acquisition of new clothing and toiletries, and I was able to access my accounts for that all important greaser of wheels, money. While this work momentarily took my mind off the terror of the airship's explosion and my subsequent fall from the sky, that feeling was still there; I would wake and think myself falling. Traveling to an island that floated above the city was surely inviting another such fall, but I went anyhow. To show myself that I could, no matter how my legs shook.

Buenos Aires was beautiful, but the island city that hung above it was more so in my eyes. It was borne aloft by colossal balloons filled with gasses I could not name. Naming them and picking the structure apart might have diluted the wonder of the place; yes it was science and technology, but from where I looked, it was magic. The island streamed vapor into the sky, which wreathed it in a constant cloud deck. From these clouds, the spectacular theaters and concert halls rose. They glittered in the daylight, colored glasses and polished metals, and some of the tallest roofs had become home to bird nests. Many people came to watch the birds of Valle del Cielo, to check them from a list or paint their images, but these colorful and talkative birds were often hard to separate from the performers of the island city.

The airship that ferried us toward the floating island was

peppered with some of these performers, a cluster of women dressed in feathers and silks. Their headdresses shimmered in greens and pinks, the red of a robin's breast, the blue of an upturned wing. I tried not to stare, knowing this was only the tip of the iceberg, but couldn't stop looking. Had I stopped, I might have seen Trinchero on the airship.

As it was I did not see him until I was deep within the city of theaters, well entrenched in the banner- and balloon-strewn cobblestone streets. I found him standing outside the theater I had seen sketched within his journal on the *Rocha*. I stopped well before he might notice me and scowled. The day had been trying, for no matter how I tried to forget him and his dead lady, it seemed I could not. In the curl of a theater's awning, I saw the curl of his mustachio. Amid the birds that soared above the city, I remembered his own pterodactyls.

Trinchero's theater, Teatro Milagro, was both tall and wide, fashioned of a stone that seemed to catch and hold the sunlight, condensing it to something that looked like honey. The theater doors were polished ebony, and its high glass windows shone with a strange rose-colored light. It felt as if the building were filled with this rose color, that if those windows could be opened, it would flow into the streets. The theater roof was made of metal, free of any nests, but the highest peak was much like the aviary metal and mesh in Trinchero's own home.

Trinchero had moved on by the time I reached the steps leading to the theater's doors. I stood there, eyeing the banner that had been strung across the street between his theater and the one just opposite. The banner was spotted with paint and pitch that served to obscure most of the writing, but I picked out enough lettering to read what remained of the English: *Bear Witness to the Dueling Desdemonas – The Falcon and the Bee*.

She was Serafina Falco and she was Beatrice Mosconi, and each was slated to star in her theater's production of *Otello*. The Falcon hailed from Teatro de la Luz, while the Bee called Teatro Milagro home. Trinchero's own theater!

I looked back at the structure and strode to the box office, where I acquired a ticket for that evening's performance. I was told the Teatro de la Luz's performance of *Otello* was for the following evening, and did I wish a ticket for it as well? I did not, but I couldn't help but feel curious over the entire thing. Even as I settled into my seat that next evening, I wondered. Was it intentional? Was it—

A hand upon my shoulder caused me to look from the stage with its curtain – that same curtain I recalled from Trinchero's journal, the one he had drawn with such care and detail. Trinchero smiled down at me then nodded to the young boy at his side. This boy wore a tidy suit, with a green silk tie wrapped at his neck. He grinned at me, round spectacles brightening his hazel eyes.

"*Senhor* Trinchero would like for you to join him backstage," he explained in English. "If you have an interest."

I had an interest and slipped from my seat to follow them where they led. Trinchero was dressed impeccably in a black tuxedo, and while I wore my best dress, I still felt I was a curiosity as we moved through the crowds. Were people whispering about me? Surely not, but I could not mistake hearing "Brennan" as I passed one couple. I glanced at them, but did not know who they were.

The boy nodded at me when we stepped into the wings. "Mister Brennan had a hand here," he explained, and gestured to the gears and cogs and other technology that made up the theater's innermost workings.

I didn't need to see the stylized "B" stamped on each to know they were J. J.'s design. They had been made to move things larger than backdrops and curtains, and Trinchero used them masterfully, having rigged castle walls and ships to no doubt slide perfectly into position as his opera called for it. It made my heart soar, if I can use such a phrase, to see J. J.'s inventions used to such an extent. Trinchero had no need for small paper props when he could move heavier and more realistic likenesses.

I watched from the wings with the boy – Trinchero fluttered about like one of his pterodactyls as the production required. The boy was Nestor, who had worked in the island city his entire life. Being that he was but ten, I asked if he had been born there, to which he nodded. His mother was one of the city's contraltos and while he appreciated that theater and its shows, he wanted more. A chance encounter with Trinchereo and his diva, his *milagro* bee as they called her, in the streets had convinced Nestor that this was the place to work, to be seen, to excel.

"Who is the *milagro* bee, then?" I asked.

Nestor gestured to the stage as Desdemona made her entry. "See there."

This lady should not have been known to me, but she was. I was so alarmed at the sight of her that I took a step back. Nestor grasped my hand before I could stumble over the coiled ropes and leads upon the floor, but I was only vaguely aware of his clammy hand upon my arm. The lady upon the stage took all my attention.

She looked to have been carved from beeswax, exactly the way she had appeared within her glass and gold coffin. But here, she moved as any woman would, talking and singing – and singing with a voice that was so heavenly, I wondered that the sky did not open and rain angels upon the stage. Her hair was as ebon and gleaming as the theater doors, coiled at the nape of her neck. And there, where once her lace collar had hidden it, churned a series of mechanics within the darkening umber of her skin. These gears and cogs allowed her movement, fluid and precise. She stepped across the stage and sang as if she had lungs that filled with air, and not bellows that were operated by the motion of her legs.

Make-up colored her face and I had trouble telling if she were flesh at all. Was she animated like some golem, a spell writ across her skin? Was there a key that would notch into her back so one could wind her up? It was no wonder Trinchero could not leave her in the forest after the *Rocha*'s crash. I stared at her, captivated and curious both, and saw Trinchero had paused to do the same. His hand rested over his mouth, as if he were holding his breath.

It was possible she had been damaged in the crash, after all, but her voice was flawless and the audience seemed to hold its breath alongside Trinchero as she sang. It was only perfection and my legs trembled. Nestor squeezed my hand.

"I am all right," I whispered. "She is quite the miracle, though."

"Beatrice Mosconi," Nestor whispered in return.

I had never seen the opera before, but J. J. and I had read *Othello* at one point or another, and its story remained familiar. I did not, however, remember there being an attack by wild birds. It was the moment Otello was to strike Desdemona – he was to call her a demon, and she would fall to the ground, but before he could, there arose such a sound that everyone on stage was struck silent. We all looked upward, and perhaps some feared that the stage was to collapse, for it sounded like failing metal, but no – no.

Pterodactyls streamed from the ceiling. Their leathery wings beat furiously in the air; the theater's lights flickered under the ceaseless fury of those wings. Claws snatched at the actors, ripping hats and wigs free, and sharp beaked mouths lunged for throats. It was a deadly whirlwind and for a long moment, I think the audience believed it to be fiction – they saw these creatures as constructs, not the living, breathing animals I saw them to be. They were much like the trio Trinchero kept at his home, though these were mottled blue, with furious orange eyes.

At my side, Nestor cried out and fled, and those on stage followed his lead; they abandoned their marks, to seek shelter in the theater's wings. It was then the audience erupted in panic and fear, giving up their seats to flood out of the theater.

The stream of pterodactyls seemed endless. It was as though a door in the ceiling had been opened, and a bottomless bowl of the creatures tipped into the theater as one might spill snow in a winter's production. I stumbled backward and wrapped myself in the edge of the curtain, unable to look away. Two of the creatures had settled upon the scaffolding and I thought at first they only rested, but no – no, they were waiting. They were looking.

The *milagro* bee herself, Beatrice Mosconi, slipped into the wings near me, but she did not see me, cowering as I was. She moved toward the stairs that led deeper into the theater, but did not get there. Once the pterodactyls saw her, they were upon her. Upon her and pecking at her face, her arms, any bit of her they could reach. I did not expect her to cry out – she was beeswax and mechanics, was she not? – but the sound she made was dreadful. It was the sound of a ship sinking under a weight it cannot bear. It was the sound of a thing overcome and drowning.

I leapt from my curtain and screamed at the pterodactyls. And they, not expecting me, leapt away from Beatrice. They looked at me as if they did not know what to make of me; I was of a height with them, but lacked wings. I screamed again and waved my arms, trying to appear as large as I could.

"Leave her alone!" I screamed at them.

They snapped their sharp beaks at me, but hopped backwards. I stepped over Beatrice's legs – she trying to make herself smaller, unseen – and continued to wave at the creatures. The pair of them shook their heads, as if in accord, and launched themselves back toward the ceiling, but just when I believed them gone, they returned. En masse.

There was no fighting them, not in this number. Every strike I landed, be it on hard beak or flapping wing, seemed to do me more damage than it did them. Some of the pterodactyls were taller than me and one shouldered its way into me, knocking me to the floor. A moment later, I was in its talons, being carried away.

We should have hit the theater ceiling – I told myself this time and again – but the bird knew where it was going. It sought the hatch it had likely entered through and we shot into the sky as if expelled from the barrel of a gun. The island spun below us and nausea closed its hard fist around my throat.

No matter how I twisted, I could not free myself from the iron grasp of the pterodactyl that carried me. A glimpse of the buildings below us told me I probably did not want to be freed, but when I saw another pair of birds, one carrying another body, I decided that freedom was better than being taken to a place I had no desire to go. *Bide your time, Murrie,* J.J. would have told me and so I waited.

Buildings do not come in hard or soft, however. If I meant to fall, I would have to take the landing as best I could. We flew west into the setting sun and here, on the city's edge, I saw my opportunity. Awnings, which no longer reminded me of Trinchero's mustachio but were instead cups of golden sunlight, spread out along the boardwalk, which climbed the island's edge. Across these awnings, I saw the shadow of another pterodactyl and I looked to find Beatrice also held in one's clawed grip. Maybe the birds meant to carry us beyond the island, maybe the birds meant to let us go once we passed the edge. Whatever it meant, I moved first.

I bit the bird's leg. It tasted of sweat and was strangely warm. Alive, not mechanical, and at the prick of my teeth, it squawked. It did not, however, let me go. I latched on again, chewing and clawing until I caused the creature enough discomfort that it opened its talons.

I screamed the entire way down. I could flap my arms, but could not keep myself aloft or steer. It was luck alone that saw me fall into one of those awnings, but there I did not stay. I bounced back up, and went over the edge, head over heel until I landed in a dumpster of trash – soggy, rotten trash, which nonetheless cushioned my fall.

A breath later, the *milagro* bee joined me.

I did not move, only stared at the sunset sky above us and waited for the beasts to return. Silence, however, held, and I looked at the soprano, half buried in the trash beside me. She blinked – her eyes were the color of honey, like the theater walls – and then she dared a smile.

"When I saw your brave escape, I knew I must try!" she said in perfect English. "They will come and we should go."

It startled me, that she spoke at all, but why wouldn't she speak here, as she had spoken on stage. I had thought her programmed for the opera alone, whatever myriad of languages might be required of her, but she was not simply that. She was her own person. She was not clockwork, but neither was she entirely flesh. She was some mixture of both, looking like she might melt as the sun slanted down the alley we occupied.

We climbed from our nest of debris and fled deeper into the alleys, trailing trash behind us.

The west side of the island was a collection of lavish hotels and restaurants, assembled in tall stacks up the side of an artificial mountain. Awnings and umbrellas that sheltered tables fluttered in the evening's breeze; most restaurants seemed to be doing a brisk business, and Beatrice seemed eager to keep out of the public eye. When I meant to approach a hostess and ask her assistance, Beatrice pulled me back into the alleyway.

She kept me pressed to the side of the building with one elegant hand; she still wore her costume from the opera, yard and yards of silver organza skirts rustling as she peered into the street. I glanced to the sky, but there was no sign of the pterodactyls. Beatrice looked at me with wary eyes.

"Trained pterodactyls?" I asked her. When she made no reply, I nodded, trying to piece the thing together in my mind. "Trinchero keeps a trio, but they're much smaller, and why would his own creatures attack his theater, and his diva?"

If Beatrice could blush, she did, her waxy cheeks darkening somewhat. "He would not," she agreed, again in English.

"They looked for you," I said. While this idea was troubling on its own, it was more so when Beatrice nodded and leaned against the wall, as if in her own worry she could no longer stand upright without assistance.

I leaned closer to her and plucked a cabbage leaf from the skirt of the costume she still wore. I flung the leaf into the alley. I did not know this place well, but knew what I had seen. I watched Beatrice now as she perhaps warred over what exactly to tell me.

"Bear witness to the dueling Desdemonas," I said before she could speak, and she offered up another nod.

"It can only be the Falcon," she whispered and this seemed to terrify her.

If the conflict was something they fashioned themselves, or a battle that had been thrust upon them, I could not ask, because Beatrice's eyes widened. Her gaze rooted itself to the end of the alley, where a vehicle sat.

"She has found us!"

The vehicle rose from the ground upon three wheels, slim and spoked as a bicycle's would be, but instead of having a singular open-air seat, a canopy perched atop the wheels. Metallic wings streamed backward from the canopy – would it actually fly? The vehicle rolled toward us with a steady growl. Within the carriage, I spied one figure. Beatrice shrieked. I grabbed her by the arm before she could flee. Her skin was like fire-warmed wax beneath my fingers, though it did not melt. I tugged her toward the approaching carriage.

The vehicle closed the distance swiftly; even had Beatrice run – and certainly she could have escaped me – she would not have gotten far. Far above us, I heard the cry of approaching pterodactyls, even as the carriage door swung open. I stared at its driver – with that dress and make-up it could be only Serafina Falco, the Falcon herself – but made no questions, pushing Beatrice up and into the cabin. She complained the entire way; I shouldered myself into her backside to propel her into a seat, then climbed in and slammed the door behind us.

"Go! Go!"

The driver needed no urging; the vehicle consumed the remaining length of the alley with its smooth wheels. We shot across the street and over the edge of the island, and I feared I had doomed us after all, but the wings caught the air and we were aloft! The driver banked away from the sun and up ever higher.

We flew higher than the tallest buildings of the island, then left even those behind. The vehicle climbed up and up, until I grew short of breath and found myself gasping. By the time normal breathing had returned, we were approaching another island. This island seemed like an anchor of sorts, for a long metal line ran even further into the sky and vanished into the clouds. It was this line we followed, and were soon engulfed in shadow as the clouds thickened. Beatrice moaned.

The driver landed us on a platform and Beatrice bolted from the vehicle before we were fully secure. She tumbled to the platform in a tangle, picked herself up, and ran for the edge.

"Beatrice!"

She vanished into the clouds which spilled over the platform's high edge. I dropped out of the vehicle and followed, hearing the click of the Falcon's heels behind me as she pursued.

"Oh, she must come back!" the Falcon cried after me.

Beatrice stood on the platform's edge, her arms spread wide. She looked very like a bird then, and not a bee, and I did not think she meant to jump, for she would have already. I opened my mouth to call her back from the edge, but it was the Falcon who spoke her name.

"Beatrice. I thought—"

That voice, although broken on a sob, was full of love. I looked at Serafina Falco with a kind of wonder; she was unlike anyone I had ever seen, her make-up applied with care and precision, a hundred tiny feathers drawn upon her skin, coursing outward from her eyes, up toward her raven hairline, down the proud line of her neck and into her bosom. She was painted in hues of gold and black, her eyes a sharp and piercing blue like the sky at midday, her mouth painted to a sharp point as if to mimic a falcon's beak. A topaz-encrusted headdress was secured into her raven locks, coming to a point at her widow's peak, leaving a singular golden topaz to rest at the bridge of her nose.

Serafina offered a hand, strong and steady, and to my surprise Beatrice turned to take it. She grasped the hand and wrenched Serafina to her side, and now they both stood on the platform's edge, struggling. Beatrice's face creased with momentary confusion

– she looked at Serafina as if she didn't know what to do. Serafina's arm came around Beatrice in a hard hug.

"I thought you were dead," Serafina whispered.

They were each great actors in their mighty theaters, but this I knew was genuine grief and emotion. The sob that wracked Serafina, the anguish on Beatrice's face. Beatrice let go of Serafina's hand, and Serafina slid to her knees, still crushing Beatrice in a hug around her legs. Beatrice's fingers slid into Serafina's hair and pulled.

To my surprise, the raven hair and the topaz headdress came away, revealing a bald cap beneath. Serafina did not withdraw, but only looked up at Beatrice with a kind of wonder. I watched, not understanding.

"He has made you into something you were not prepared to be," Serafina said. "Come back from this edge and let us talk."

"Beatrice," I implored her.

Beatrice looked at me and laughed softly. "Little woman," she said. "I have not seen anyone like you before and you have never seen anyone like *us*." She gave Serafina's wig a shake. "The bee and the falcon. Two Desdemonas when there should be only one. He meant for there to be only one."

The wind picked up and Serafina came to her feet, tugging a more willing Beatrice away from the edge. Serafina guided us along the platform to a hatch, and inside what appeared to be a maintenance room. Still, there was a stove where we warmed ourselves and where Serafina made us tea. It should have been strange, but I drank, and held my cup out when Serafina offered a drop of whiskey.

They spoke in hushed tones of the conflict they had endured for the past year – had it been that long, Beatrice wondered, and looked concerned that it had been. The incidents had been relatively minor until recently: it had begun with hijinks involving make-up, and costumes, seams frayed or sewn too tightly; it escalated with false reports in the press about the personal lives of each diva, foolish stories of liaisons, drug addictions and scandalously poor behavior in public places.

The incident that had terrified Beatrice so badly was an evening after a performance, where she found herself trapped below the theater stage and stalked by a person who never revealed themselves, but who had sounded very like Serafina. Husky, male.

"It was never you, Falco," Beatrice said.

Serafina carefully set the bottle of whiskey onto the table between us and shook her head. Without the wig, I could see the strong lines of her face, could see the bobbing Adam's apple in her throat, and take note of her broader shoulders.

"It was not me. And now, Alves will know you are not dead," Serafina said. "His birds were made to bring you back to the Teatro de la Luz, and when they do not, he will seek you again."

My mind raced and my hands shook, so I took another swallow of whiskey-laden tea. "The *Rocha* was brought down," I said as I tried to lay each of the facts out as I knew them. The idea of the ship plummeting out of control made my heart pound hard. I had survived it, but the memory held me tight, disturbing. "We carried Beatrice with us – I thought she was dead."

"*Alves* thought she was dead," Serafina said, "and when he discovered that Trinchero had brought her back . . ." There was a hitch in her voice and she covered her painted mouth with a hand as she gathered her courage back up. "He was furious. We have always . . ." She considered. Beatrice picked up the story when Serafina could not.

"Once upon a time," she said, "two beautiful divas called Valle del Cielo home. They were each wholly unique, their kind and beauty unknown in the earth-bound cities. But in the sky, they were magical. Talented. And mindful of their secrets. The first diva, the *milagro* bee, was truly a miracle. She should have died as a young woman, but did not. She suffered a terrible attack which did not kill her, but only changed her into a thing she could not explain."

Beatrice extended her arm to us and drew back the long glove she wore. In the crook of her elbow, we could see the gleam of metal. There was no line where the skin stopped and the metal began. Her neck showed such a line, where the cogs within her throat were exposed; an imperfect blend of biology and mechanics, made by well-meaning hands rather than nature herself.

"Trinchero found her. Saved her. Made her into . . . something that could live, in any case." Beatrice rolled her glove back up. "And she sang. She thought she loved it best of all."

"The second diva," Serafina said, "was not fully a diva, nor had she ever been. She had remade herself with her own hands, never feeling quite right in her masculine skin. Amid the theaters, she felt perfectly at home – the performers never gave her a second or curious glance. It was as if she had discovered her true family at long last. A patron came calling – a patron who, once having learned them, swore to tell her secrets if she did not fill the theater to overflowing each night. The public loved each woman and clamored for more."

"Alves," I said, the last puzzle piece snapping into place. "A battle between patrons and not divas at all – thus the dual productions of *Otello*."

"Yes," Beatrice said, "but I was made to think it was Serafina all along. I played into Alves's hand so perfectly."

"No more," I said.

Each diva looked at me and though I still questioned what I found myself in the middle of, I knew how we had to proceed.

Of all the things I have learned in my travels, the most difficult has been to trust myself. This ability was not gifted by J. J.'s hands, nor did anyone else simply hand it to me. Would that it were so easy. Learning to trust the inner workings of myself – be it mind or heart or gut – has been the strangest journey of all.

Who was I to say what Beatrice and Serafina must do? Their paths were not my own, this is true enough, but I had seen the look in Trinchero's eyes when he thought he would lose Beatrice in her coffin. And I had seen the same fire within Alves's eyes when he confronted Trinchero. These men would not let go and these women would suffer for it. How many times had Beatrice been brought back to life? How many times had Serafina cowered under the clothing she feared would be torn from her? This was not living, least not on their terms.

Each looked at me expectantly.

"We can do but one thing: attend your performance, Serafina, and see what comes. Neither Alves nor Trinchero will expect such a bold move. They will expect us to cower and we will do no such thing."

"Alves will have her killed," Serafina objected.

I thought Serafina clutched Beatrice's hand, but I saw that it was rather the opposite; the *milagro* bee held tight to Serafina, metallic hands clasped around flesh and bone. If Beatrice still had a mind of her own and not one Trinchero had made of wire and cogs, it was a mind that wanted everything Serafina had. I could see this upon her face as plain as day. As much as Serafina longed to be perfect, Beatrice longed to be flesh and bone.

Teatro de la Luz was glowing that night. We did not approach Trinchero or his theater – we left him to his own devices, to see what might develop. We arrived in clothes that were not our own, but costumes appropriated from Teatro Milagro. Neither of us looked like ourselves; Serafina had made Beatrice into a beautiful matron, a sweeping crown of sugar-floss hair coiled atop her head, braids and beads dripping down the high chiffon collar of her ebon gown. Her face was a fine mimicry of a portrait kept backstage; wrinkles and spots courtesy of carefully applied make-up and brushes.

Serafina had transformed my face too, making me into a girl that resembled Beatrice's granddaughter and not someone who was a widow. My hair was braided into its own lofty crown, tied with white ribbons that echoed the frothy gown she had spilled me into. I had never felt so lovely or mysterious; no one knew us as we took our balcony seats. This was a distinct advantage of the island city: people came from the world over, strangers all, and could move as they pleased.

The theater was taut with tension, or perhaps it only seemed so to me, because we were waiting for doom to befall us. This theater, not built by Alves, but decorated by him, was not quite so lavish as Trinchero's, but had its own charm. The walls were rough wood, painted with pale and sunlit clouds to echo the sky outside. Occasionally, there was the image of a bird in flight, or perhaps it was a natural whorl within the wood. I counted falcons within those clouds, too, surely for Serafina. The stage was illuminated by a crescent of gas lights, while the balconies were lighted by chandeliers that dripped with candles so white they put my gown to shame. I felt illuminated beneath them, glowing.

Nothing untoward happened until Act Four. Beatrice and I were perched on the edge of our seats, expecting something awful to befall the production. When it finally came, we only stared for the longest time.

Serafina's Desdemona was in her chamber, preparing to be married, yet also preparing to die. She said her prayers and lay down to sleep, and that's when her chamber door opened. Golden light cut a sharp path cross the darkened stage, to brighten the bed where Serafina rested. A sword's long shadow preceded that of Otello himself. Have you said your prayers tonight, Otello wanted to know – but it was not Otello who sang these words. It was a voice familiar to me, the voice of Trinchero who was not acting, but had made a terrible mistake. He had come to slaughter Serafina, surely believing she had carried his Beatrice away at long last. In a way, she had, but in rescue only.

Beside me, Beatrice gasped in recognition.

"He cannot—"

Upon the stage, Serafina screamed.

It is quite a moment in the opera – Otello coming to kill Desdemona because he believes she has betrayed him – and from here the story would unravel in spectacular fashion until too many lay wrongly dead. But Desdemona was not to scream, because Otello used not his sword, but his hands to wring the breath from her body. The scream that came from Serafina was quite real – she would not have expected Trinchero, either – and nearly Beatrice's undoing.

Beatrice came out of her chair. In the sliver of light from the opened door, we could see Trinchero lunge for Serafina. He wrapped his arms around her and when the stage lights abruptly came up, they were gone.

Alves certainly wouldn't wait for the theater to empty; Beatrice wasn't inclined to wait, either. We fled downstairs and pushed against the exiting tide of patrons, heading for the empty stage, but before we got there, Alves found us. I suppose we were not so difficult to recognize in the end, a tall lady and a dwarf, moving against the exodus. Alves's face burned bright with anger, but also a kind of sorrow I hadn't expected.

"Trinchero has taken her," Alves spat.

"And you?" I snarled back. "This is no better than invading his theater to claim Beatrice." The idea that Serafina had taken Beatrice before Alves could amused me, but there was something else at play here. Something I did not yet understand. Why did

Trinchero want Serafina? Simply because Alves wanted Beatrice? There was something else.

"Trinchero's house," I whispered. "We must go."

Neither argued with me. I expected them to, but we made for the airship that Alves kept in the island's shipyard. It was no surprise to me that his ship was flown by metallic men, just like those that had boarded the *Rocha*. Alves had attacked the ship in an effort to prevent Trinchero from bringing Beatrice back – this seemed clear to me, and other theories began to clarify themselves the more I watched Beatrice and Alves on the flight to Trinchero's house.

Alves endeavored to speak with Beatrice. Beatrice shrank back at every attempt. She continued to place me between them, whether blatantly or covertly. Beatrice rarely strayed from my side because when she was near me, Alves did not approach. He plainly wanted a private moment with her, a moment she refused to give him.

"He would not hurt her," Beatrice whispered to us. "He would not."

As kind as Trinchero had shown himself to be, I doubted this. He had risked many things in order to bring Beatrice back – why wouldn't he harm Serafina to make his point? To win the chess match with Alves?

Alves did not believe Beatrice's whisper, either; his face looked much like my own must have. There was doubt in his eyes and he chewed his bottom lip in increasing worry. When at last his metal men announced that we were close, there was a brief flicker of relief, but then—

"Raptors!"

The forest was alive with the creatures; they looked like a wide and running river, the way they ran between the fenced-in trees, parting like water around stones, branches. Some gleamed with bronze and copper, but others were wholly flesh – like those I had seen caged in Trinchero's lab. My breath caught in my throat at the sight of them. At my side, Beatrice whimpered.

"Tell me about the raptors," I said to Beatrice as Alves ordered his men to follow where the raptors led. We bypassed Trinchero's treehouse, even more sprawling when seen from above, and moved across the treetops, deeper into the forest.

"I was so young," she whispered. She shook her head, the lines of her make-up having begun to run and melt under her tears.

There was a still a woman within that clockwork frame, a woman who now feared for another, that she not be changed as Beatrice had been. It was an accident, Beatrice said, a thing she should not have survived. It should never have happened – these dinosaurs no longer existed, she was imagining what she saw. But they did exist, and she had been curious – who could blame her for that? – and she had reached a hand out to touch the nose of one. Was it metal? Was it flesh? It was something of both, and it smelled her. A moment later, its teeth closed about her hand.

The bite was laden with radiation, poison spilling from the core that powered the beast, and it transformed Beatrice. While she did not turn into a raptor, parts of her were consumed by the metal, metal which seemed intelligent. It wormed its way deep inside her, and by the time she came to Trinchero, she was near the end of the first life she would know. Trinchero had fallen in love with her – I could picture the slant of his smiling mouth and mustachio all too well – and had promised to cure her. But there seemed no cure. He could repair the thin threads that kept her alive, but could not extract the metal from her. Bit by bit, he turned her into the thing that had changed her so many years before; now, she could not live without the cogs, she could not live without keeping her heart wound tight.

Trinchero, she said, had discovered a raptor in the valley where she had been bitten. A valley of stone and fossil, a place where no such thing should have lived, yet still did. He brought it home to study and when he found another, he bred one more. He had found the mechanical raptor on yet another venture, and tied them to Alves by chance – the man had arrogantly used pterodactyls in one of his operas. One dinosaur led to others, and to a lab where Alves worked to make more.

"He will surely turn her the way I was turned," Beatrice whispered as the airship continued to trace the path of the raptors through the forest.

"He will not," I said.

The raptors led us to another house in the woods, a house with an airship landing high above the tree canopy. One ship was already docked, but there was room for one more and Alves had his men secure the ship there. Far below us, the raptors rushed into a clearing of tall grasses where they appeared to be hunting rodents.

I grasped Alves's jacket sleeve before he made to leave the airship. "Men who fight each other with dinosaurs? Men who care nothing for the women in their path? Your beast did this to her and you would have left her to die?"

Alves ripped his arm free and sneered at me. He might have been attractive, had he not been such an arrogant ass.

"Beatrice's transformation was unfortunate – it should never have happened. She is an abomination and I will not see Serafina so changed. So . . . ruined."

It was a belief many in the world shared, I knew. My own J. J. had lived in fear that his mechanical heart would be discovered. Yet, there were those in the world who pursued the technology still – Trinchero among them. Beatrice lived because of his efforts, might have been otherwise lost. Thinking of the way Beatrice and Serafina looked at each other, I couldn't begrudge him his work. Love went beyond the heart of a person; I knew this to be true.

Alves exited the ship and Beatrice and I stood there a long while, listening to his steps move down the scaffolding. When I turned to go, Beatrice did not join me. I paused in the ship's hatch and looked at her, extending a hand.

"Come. If he means to change Serafina, would you leave her salvation in Alves's hands?" Alves would surely put a bullet in Serafina's head rather than see her turned into what Beatrice had become.

Beatrice's hand trembled in my own. We climbed down the stairs of the landing platform, still in our opera finery, sunset slanting through the trees. Below us, I could hear the chitter of raptors going about their unspeakable raptor business. In such writhing numbers, they were more than a little terrifying, and a shiver crept across my shoulders. They were so strange, so unknown, so hungry. Eventually, from the building the stairs led into, I heard Serafina's desperate pleas and Trinchero's replies. He sang the line to her in Italian, much as in the opera itself. *Have you said your prayers tonight?*

"This will not accomplish anything!" Alves shouted and there came the sound of two men violently colliding.

I ran down the stairs to gaze in wonder at this laboratory Trinchero had rigged. It was just as splendid as the one in his house, precise, neat, but for the bound and pleading form of Serafina in a glass cell. One wall of this cell could be opened, opened to the yard where the raptors hunted and fed. It didn't take much to imagine that wall opening and raptors flooding inside.

The rest of the laboratory was a collection of works in progress, chiefly dinosaurs, be they fashioned of flesh or metal. Each had its own cage, most sleeping, but some anxious to free themselves and join the other raptors in the yard. They clawed at the vented glass panes that kept them sealed away.

As to Trinchero and Alves, they were locked in a fierce battle some distance away from Serafina, each trying to wrest the other into a position of submission. Neither was having it; each was strong and angry, and I bolted toward Serafina's cage, looking for a way to free her. Beatrice joined me, but we could see no way to unlock the cage, save for the wall that opened onto the raptor-filled yard.

A glass door from the lab opened onto a closed observation deck. A doorway from that deck led to walkways that were enclosed with open-weave metal fencing that would allow one to move safely through the raptors. Another level of walkways sprawled above, too, causing me to think of taller dinosaurs – did Trinchero have others?

We could reach Serafina with these walks, but Alves had noticed the same. He struggled to make his way to the glass door, Trinchero refusing to give ground. Alves lunged forward while Trinchero grasped him by the jacket lapels and planted his feet. Still, Alves's momentum carried them into the glass door that led to the patio. It shattered as if it had exploded, the men rolling onto the patio in a barely contained ball of fury. Fists flew and so too feet, as each tried to do permanent damage to the other.

Beatrice and I took advantage of their brawl. We stepped through the doorway and picked our way across the glass-strewn patio, toward the enclosed walkways that would lead us to Serafina. But a curious thing happened – the raptors seemed *drawn* to Beatrice and she to them. I turned to find that she had paused, that she crouched beside the fencing and cooed at a cluster of raptors who had come closer to smell her. She chittered and they chittered and though I was fascinated, I was also terrified.

"Beatrice!" I hissed.

She did not move. I, however, did, as more raptors closed in on the other side of the fence. They wanted to get closer to Beatrice and were upset when they could not. Fights broke out among the creatures, all lashing tails and hooking claws and I thought I might go mad from the slithering sound of it, from the shrieks and hisses. Into this confusion, a body dropped.

Beatrice and I leaped back with screams; the raptors closed around and over the body they had been given – Alves, *good Lord it was Alves!* – and began to devour him. I glanced up, at Trinchero who stood on an upper walkway, beaten and bleeding, but looking triumphant as his creations swallowed his nemesis bite by bite.

"You are mad," I spat at him.

He screamed words at me, words I had no translation for, but here, I needed none. In the way of all good opera, he felt betrayed; he loved his *milagro* bee and believed himself betrayed and used and oh, he was as mistaken at Otello had ever been. Trinchero made my heart ache with it, the anger and sorrow that poured from him. He closed his hands into the ripped fencing and gave it a shake. I wanted to plead for him to come down, to have a drink and talk some sense, but saw that he was far beyond these things.

"Vittorio." Not even his name drew his gaze to me.

I threaded my way closer to Serafina and that's when I saw the break in the fencing. It had been haphazardly repaired at some point, with lengths of what looked like barbed wire. And the raptors – oh, they were clever. They could smell Beatrice and were likely well acquainted with the fencing and how it enclosed them. They were picking their way through the wire even now, lizard-like bodies slithering one against the other as they pushed inward. I would never reach Serafina's door – not now.

"Muriel." Trinchero's voice held a new edge to it; I did not glance up at him, for fear that looking away from the raptors would draw them to me even quicker.

I did not move. I could not see how to reach Serafina – she watched us from the other side of the door, helpless to free herself, and I stared back for what seemed forever, until I felt Beatrice's cool hand against my cheek. She glided past me without a word, as if in slow motion, toward the raptors who meant to breach the fence. I will never forget the look on her face; it was resolution and relief both. When I realized what she meant to do, I cried out. Trinchero did too.

Beatrice crawled through those slithering bodies as if she were one of them. The raptors let her pass; they turned away from the fence, following where she led. She led them away from the fence, away from Serafina and deeper into the grass where she sprawled and let them crawl upon her. For a moment, I saw a raptor-like fierceness in her face, and then she struck.

Her metallic hands cut through the raptors and drew blood until it flowed down her arms, onto the grasses. With the scent of her fresh in their noses, still frenzied from their taste of Alves, they fell upon her – and she did not move, she did not cry.

I turned for Serafina's door, horror stricken as I tried to work the door to get her out. Serafina was shrieking at me when I finally did. She leapt for the rip in the fence, but I clung to her, dragging her down so that she could not join Beatrice. From above, Trinchero's own sobs were like knives down my arms, in my heart, across my throat.

And what did Trinchero at last do? He leapt from the walkway and perished the way of Otello – dead at his Desdemona's side. The raptors, metal and flesh alike, did not hesitate or show mercy. They knew none. They were upon him as they had been Beatrice – so hungry, sinking teeth and claw into whatever they could. Trinchero scrabbled his way toward Beatrice and in his last moments held her in his arms as the raptors covered them over.

Serafina and I sat for a long while, waiting. I am not certain what we expected – maybe that this had not in fact happened, that Trinchero and Beatrice and Alves would rise to thunderous applause from a rapt audience, but this was no stage. In the days that followed, it did not grow easier. The authorities were dismayed by Trinchero's lab – he was in possession of clockwork and mechanicals that the world did not approve of, and Beatrice was clear and present proof he had used them to . . . Animate the dead? Had he? Not to mention the dinosaurs he had both built and cloned.

With them dead, and Alves too, the authorities spoke with me and Serafina at length, but we were largely unhelpful when it came to sorting matters. Trinchero, they decided, had done terrible things in the name of love – and who hadn't? *Foolish, impetuous theater-loving Italians!* they cried. Trinchero was dead, what more could he suffer? They left him to his peace and to me and Serafina—

Serafina cries when she thinks I cannot hear her; she mourns Beatrice by slathering her toast with honey that recalls the bee's eyes. She mourns Beatrice best on stage, donning the costumes and becoming everything she ever wanted to be, being the woman Beatrice could not. The crowds love Serafina for it – she is showered with flowers and brings them home by the armful. The halls of Trinchero's treehouse smell of rose, lily and sometimes marigold.

I spend my mornings in the jacaranda-drenched bedroom, wondering if I will stay here, or if I will soon travel again. Someone needs to mind the raptors, the pterodactyls. I think I have even heard a brachiosaurus somewhere in the woods. I walk the balconies that weave through the trees and think I hear J. J.'s knowing laughter. How I always wanted a family.

Selin That Has Grown in the Desert

Alex Dally MacFarlane

My mother once said that I was livelier than any wind that flew across the plains, that no horse could catch me and no wolf could withstand the volume of my song. "Selin that has grown in the desert," I sang as I sat with my trousseau's second jacket in my lap and sewed it full of thread as white as clouds. "A well-watered plain." I felt very far from the girl my mother had described. "My most precious friend, Dursun." Would Cheper sing of me? If I married my cousin Tagan, I would be able to see Cheper whenever I wanted; both of our husbands would be in the village. "Gone to a foreign place." But it didn't matter how close or far I needed to journey to reach my husband's yurt.

I concentrated hard on the thread and the needle, and I blinked rapidly. Not a single tear fell on my jacket.

Nomads from the south set up their yurts alongside ours, doubling the size of our little village, and told us about the approaching caravan two days away. We had goods to trade: a carpet and a carpet bag, two felt hangings, jewellery. I heard my father and Gariagdy discussing how much wheat and rice they should aim to get.

I heard my father ask, "And what of the men among the nomads? Are there any that we know?"

"Some." Names fell from my brother's mouth like sharp silver discs. Each one hurt me, though I put another round of dough in the *tamdyr* to bake as if unaffected by their nearby conversation. "Good men," he added, "although I still think Tagan is the best choice for her. We know him well and she won't have to move far away."

"It's best to still consider other options at this stage."

"Mmm." I was glad when Gariagdy changed the subject. "There was something else. Apparently, one of the men travelling with the caravan has been talking about strange devices – things that he wants to make and sell to people. Things that could be used as transport for people or goods, for instance."

"Sounds Russian to me. Or British." My father muttered under his breath, as if not wanting those powers to hear him utter their names so foully.

"Oh, they say he's not a foreign man."

"We don't want that kind of man here, either. Don't need his devices, anyway. Treat him politely, send him on his way."

I knew some people suspected of involvement with foreign powers were treated far less generously. It was unsettling, to think that such a person might be coming to our village.

My impending betrothal troubled me more.

By the time the caravan arrived, fifty strong with camels and donkeys and a few yurts, my father had agreed to let me accompany him. The first night, he stayed for hours with them at the other side of the village, no doubt reuniting with old friends and forging contacts for the next day's trade. And looking at potential sons-in-law. He liked sleeping outside, so I didn't hear him return. In the morning, when pre-dawn seeped through the open flap at the top of our yurt, he roused me and Gariagdy to eat breakfast. We sat outside to eat our bread and drink the tea prepared by sleepy Yazjemal, who leaned against Gariagdy's shoulder with their two-year-old daughter on her lap. I stroked the little girl's hair and stared across the plains, which stretched from my boots to the horizon, undulating gently. Green and brown and vast, where the wind blew for years. I slitted my eyes as a gust hit us, still cold from the night.

"Let's go," my father said.

"Have fun," Yazjemal whispered to me, grinning. "You have to tell me everything you see."

"I will."

Anxiety knotted in me like rope.

I wanted to see the men before my parents decided to marry me to one of them – yet I didn't want to see any of them at all.

The sun lifted above the horizon, stretching our shadows out in front of us. Among the yurts of our village and the nomads, scattered across the grass on either side of a narrow stream, other people walked in the same direction. I could see the traders ahead, setting out bags and other items I couldn't identify at a distance. I imagined wheat and tea and far-off trinkets everywhere.

Maybe, I thought, *I'll meet a man who makes me actually able to imagine myself married.* My anxiety got worse.

I tried not to think of Cheper.

The traders were set up in a rough oval, with their goods on mats or placed together on the ground, where the grass was already flattened by their footsteps. Their other possessions often lay nearby; their camels and donkeys grazed further across the grass, except for those hobbled for sale. Though the men all gathered so close, the lack of yurts made the market feel open. Alongside the traders I saw Hadjis, in well-worn robes with sparsely covered mats of small wares: needles, glass beads, combs, knives, dates. My father didn't deal with them, but he nodded respectfully at each pilgrim, whose eyes had looked upon Mecca. I knew the Hadjis wouldn't make most of their money here, among men. In the village, girls would peek shyly around the curve of their yurts or run straight up to the pilgrims, offering a melon or a piece of bread for the beads or a needle. I smiled faintly, remembering my own childhood purchases. The main business in this market was with the traders, who stood by large sacks of wheat and rice and smaller bags of tea. In one corner there were also slaves, a few scrawny individuals who looked more capable of dying than working.

My father spoke to several traders, who clasped his arm, and Gariagdy's, and then nodded their heads at me. As if he had not already spent hours the night before talking to these men, my father spoke at length about things utterly unrelated to the goods Gariagdy held patiently. My attention drifted elsewhere, taking in every sight and sound and smell of the market.

The wind touched my cheeks, softened by all the other people it had to blow through first. It barely chimed my earrings.

I couldn't ignore the men. They appraised me, some directly, some askance – I saw eyes that tallied the silver I wore at my ears and head and neck and wrists, eyes that counted possible children, that noted my looks. Shiny black hair, clear skin, a healthy flush in my cheeks, slender but not worryingly so. My bride price would be high, I saw them think, but my children would be healthy.

I wanted to hide myself from them.

Only one looked at me differently, a young man from among the nomads whose father bred horses, and he complimented my father on the skill of my stitching. "I hope you will forgive my curiosity," he went on, "but I'm sure I recognize some of the patterns on your daughter's jacket."

"I believe your oldest brother's wife is the cousin of my wife," my father said. "No doubt she uses similar patterns to the ones my wife has taught my daughter."

"And she's taught her own children the same," the young man, Biashim, said with a smile.

I glanced at him, returning the gesture.

As we moved on, Gariagdy murmured, "There are men who have better means to care for you than Biashim."

"Mmm," I said. I didn't want to marry Biashim, either.

My father strode ahead, towards a small, plain yurt sitting away from the market. In front of it, a man dozed with the sun on his face. "We must be careful of this man," my father said quietly as we caught up. Just as I wondered what he meant, I remembered the report that one man wanted to trade more than the usual items. His yurt looked ordinary enough, as did he.

"Good morning!" my father called out, waking him.

Introducing himself, the man, Houran, said that he hailed from the south-west and brought wheat to trade. Not one word of that hinted at foreign inventions.

"Would you come inside?" he asked. "My wife would enjoy your daughter's company."

"Of course," my father said, with only a hint of unwillingness in his voice. "You are travelling with your whole family, then?"

"It's just me and my wife." Houran opened the door and gestured for us to step inside. "We were recently wed."

How strange, I thought, and from the brief frown on my father's face, I knew he was wondering the same. A man with his first bride usually shared his parents' yurt. Yet Houran had travelled a long distance with just his young wife, bearing his grain – which had been grown where? Politeness kept us from prying.

The woman who sat inside was tucking something into a

plain bag, and she smiled warmly, saying, "Would you like some tea?"

The inside of their yurt was almost as bare of decoration as the bag. Plain, old cloth covered the dirt in some places, letting us sit. No carpet bags hung from the walls, no carpets or felts covered the floor – and barely any jewellery adorned Houran's wife, Aynabat, who served tea in milk-coloured bowls.

The men all sat together, talking. As I walked around the stove to where Aynabat had been sitting, I heard Houran mention something about difficult circumstances forcing them to find a new home. I sat on the cloth and Aynabat brought me tea.

"Dursun," she said as she sat down beside me. "What a beautiful name."

"Your tea is really delicious." I didn't know what else to say. How could she not know what "Dursun" meant? She scrutinized me – not as men did, but with a kind of assessment in her eyes, as if measuring the patterns on my clothes, the way I wore my hair, the silver hanging from me. Perhaps Houran would buy some of our jewellery for her, in return for the wheat my father wanted.

"There are usually very few women in the markets," she said. "Or is it more typical here?" She spoke with a strange accent, but that matched her unusual features. Her dark hair curled more than most people's; her brown eyes were lighter, and shaped differently. Her cheeks were soft, as if the wind barely touched them.

"Men usually deal with trade," I said, "but sometimes women join them. Where are you from?"

"Very far. Have you ever left this place?"

"Yes." What place did she want to keep hidden behind her questions? "My mother's family are nomadic, and I've spent some time living with them. Her brother's wife was very ill for several years before she died, so I went to help with their children. I used to accompany them out onto the plains with the sheep, and I helped teach my niece how to sew and weave. I taught them all how to sing." I remembered racing horses, singing at night with the sheep to scare away wolves, watching my little niece work on her first straight line on a huge carpet while the other women of the family ate lunch. I remembered being too young to think of marriage.

"Twice a year they move to a new area," I said, "and sometimes they come here, when the market is especially big. Not this time. Here my uncle found a second wife."

"And what do you do now?"

"We live here almost all year. Sometimes when it's very dry or hot, we go elsewhere."

"And you make carpets and felt."

"Yes." I realized that she didn't – how could she, alone?

"My husband hopes to trade his wheat for your carpet. He wants our yurt to be more beautiful."

I wanted to ask what they intended to do once they sold all their wheat.

The men stood up and excused themselves, saying they would take their business outside and leave us in peace. The moment the door settled against the frame, Aynabat said, "My husband tells me that in the towns and cities, the women are kept indoors, not allowed to ride horses or sing with the sheep."

"Yes. Apparently." Everything I heard about those places made me grateful for my life on the plains, and until it looked likely that I would marry Tagan, I had often prayed that I wouldn't be forced to move to a town. I wanted the wind in my hair sometimes, chiming my earrings against my cheek.

"Then I envy you, living here," she said.

"It's possible I won't be for much longer. I need to be married soon."

"Oh." For a moment she said nothing, then she took one of my hands. "I hope you find a good man."

"Mmm." Normally I'd agree with such a statement – yes, a good man, to give me healthy children. With no one around except a woman from far away who would soon leave and never return, I couldn't force myself to be the happy bride-to-be my family wanted.

"Let's talk about something else," I said, and hoped that I didn't seem rude.

Aynabat smiled warmly. "Are you good at keeping secrets?"

"Um . . . I suppose so."

"Then let me show you something."

She moved quickly. First she opened a wooden box that rested against the wall of the yurt. Then she went to the stove, which still smouldered from heating the tea, and reached in, removing a stick that with a few careful breaths she coaxed back into flame. She carried it to the box and bent over it, lighting something inside. I leant forward, curious, but she said, "Please, wait there."

Several minutes passed. I finished my tea and listened to the murmur of the men's voices outside – and a faint whirring that came from the box.

Smiling like a proud mother, Aynabat placed a metal horse on the floor. It was as long and high as a pot, with a large rump. It walked across the dirt floor with the very faint sounds of its parts running against one another.

"Oh," I said softly.

"This is a clumsy model," Aynabat said, though she stroked its neck fondly. "I'm working on something far more delicate. We hope to sell these, in Khiva."

"*You* make these?"

The foreign devices were small metal animals, made by a woman who equated them with carpets. How could my father and brother be worried? I glanced up at Aynabat's face, suddenly thinking that her slightly different appearance didn't mean that she originated in a far-off tribe. I'd never seen a European person before.

"I do," she said. "I will be a strange wife, kept indoors but not at carpets."

I imagined her bent over the horse, working with tools – I couldn't picture the tools' shape, but just as our jewellery needed tools to birth metal and stone into beauty, surely she used some to make her metal into horses and whatever other devices lay in her box. I itched to see inside. But she opened the horse's rump and blew out the small fire there, and packed it all away. A few minutes later we sat sipping freshly poured tea as the men re-entered, wearing the flush of a good trade.

"I hope you will come to see me again," Aynabat said to me as we all parted. "Your company was very enjoyable."

I was still too shocked by my realization about her origins to say anything but, "And yours."

Outside, away from the yurt and the market, my father asked me about her.

"We talked about our lives, our futures. Apparently their ultimate destination is Khiva." I didn't know whether to mention the horse.

"Did she say where she came from?" Gariagdy asked. "Because she doesn't look like she comes from anywhere near here."

"She only said 'very far'." She only made metal animals – what threat could she pose? Yet I felt uneasy. I remembered my brother reporting that some of the devices would be able to transport people and goods. Had Aynabat kept me from looking in her box because it held some secret part of a larger creation? The boxes in their yurt hadn't been numerous enough to hold something so huge, but perhaps she planned to make something besides animals in Khiva.

"Wherever she's from, I think now she just wants to live happily here," I said. The lie worried at me, like a loose thread.

"Mmm." Gariagdy and my father looked unconvinced, but said nothing more on the matter.

In our yurt, I told Yazjemal about the market and everything in it, and that I spoke to a strange, far-off woman about families and food and our lives. My nervousness about keeping Aynabat's secret lingered.

When Yazjemal asked if I'd liked any of the men I saw, I sighed and looked away, remembering Aynabat's smile.

"Begench hasn't come back for the boys' lunch," my mother said, loud enough for everyone in the yurt to hear. "Who will ride out to check on them?"

"Me!"

Across the yurt, where he sat eating with my father, Gariagdy frowned.

"Dursun will go," my mother said, silencing him with one of her looks. To me she added, "Finish your own food first."

I gulped down my lunch, took the bundle of bread and dry meat and melon from my mother, and stepped outside into sunlight that seared my yurt-accustomed eyes.

Melekush nuzzled my shoulder and I saddled her in carpets and my seat. For a moment, I leaned into her flank and imagined nothing more complicated than riding her, checking on my little brothers, drinking some of the tea they would be brewing.

I led her to the edge of the village. Just as I was about to climb onto her back, I saw Biashim – and he saw me and approached, smiling. "Dursun! I hope you and your family continue to be well." His fingers tangled. Did he know that? I very rarely spoke to unrelated men, but I didn't think they were meant to be nervous.

He kept a suitable distance from me, and I saw two women sitting by the nearest yurt turn their eyes on his back.

"They are," I said, "although my little brothers are out watching our sheep and they haven't come back for lunch. Hopefully it's nothing serious. Are your family well?"

"Yes, all of us." He looked up at Melekush. "She's a fine animal. Do you breed her?"

"Sometimes. If you've got breeding stock at the moment, I'm sure my father would like to talk to you."

"I'll remember that."

My cheeks flushed.

Of all the men I'd seen, I liked Biashim best – no measuring my hips with a glance, no counting babies. Even Tagan looked at me like a potential wife, despite the games we'd played only a few years ago. Biashim treated me as someone who might become a friend.

I still couldn't imagine marrying him.

"You must be keen to track down your brothers," he said. "Go – and I hope they've just fallen asleep while the sheep are perfectly content."

"Probably. See you later!"

I glanced back as I rode away, and saw him watching me. He waved. Conscious of the women, who still kept their eyes on us, I turned to face the open plains without returning the gesture.

Batir sat on a rock, surrounded by sheep. As I drew closer, he stood, waving, but not urgently. "One of the sheep went missing," he explained. "Begench is looking for it. We think it's just wandered off."

"I'll go help."

I found Begench riding towards me after a short time, the wide-eyed ewe lashed across his horse's back.

"I think she wanted to get to the sea!" he exclaimed, and we laughed.

We sprawled in the sun, all three of us, my brothers too young at ten and six to even mention weddings. They shared their lunch, poured me some tea, and we all idly watched the sheep grazing below the rise of our hill. The plains stretched ahead. In the distance, I thought I saw our village – thin tendrils of smoke, a hint of dark felt. I closed both my eyes and ran my fingers through the grass and flowers. Why would I want to stroke a man's head, when this was so perfect?

"Oh, I miss this," I told my brothers.

"Sing something!" Batir demanded.

"Must I?" I yawned in the sun. But Batir begged and Begench said he was tired of singing, so I began, alternating little songs with snippets of epics, and suddenly I was singing out so loudly the sheep scattered to a safer area. For all his alleged tiredness, Begench couldn't resist a contest, so we tried to out-sing each other, with Batir adding a discordant melody, until Begench won by trying to shove me down the hill. My song collapsed into laughter moments before his.

When I returned, I felt like the open air had scoured me clean of unhappiness. I sang under my breath as I walked Melekush back to our yurt and tied her up outside, and I opened the door like blowing air through a *dili-tuidik*.

"Dursun," Yazjemal said, and I slid back into my small self.

"Yes?"

She sat almost alone on the carpets, only little Annaguel sleeping at her side, and had one of Gariagdy's jackets spread across her lap, its frayed hem mid-repair with blue and white threads trailing from it like hairs.

"There is tea, recently brewed, if you would like some," she said, offering her usual smile, warm as a bowl given in reconciliation.

"Thank you." I poured some for myself and topped up hers, and sat opposite her with no coat in my lap, no purpose except participating in this inevitable conversation.

"Your parents are concerned," she began. I drank more tea. "It's time for them to choose you a husband, and everything you say and don't say indicates your lack of interest in this."

Yazjemal bit her lip, and her next words sounded like they came from her, not borrowed from my parents. "Do you remember when I first arrived here? How quiet I was, how I barely slept from trying to please your mother and Gariagdy and all of you, how I must have looked close to tears at every critical glance or word. I know I felt it. I was so worried that I wouldn't please your family. Now three years have passed and I talk freely with your mother, I talk to you, I . . . I'm happy! For so many brides, this is their story:

they are afraid when they first put their right foot inside their husband's family's yurt; before long it's their home and they love it, as if it had always been so. I've heard your parents discussing this, Dursun – they won't marry you to some brute, some awful creature who'll hurt you, with a mother like a tyrant." She paused, expecting me to talk – and I wanted to, but words and thoughts caught in my throat like small fish bones. "I just want you to understand that it's not as frightening as you might think."

I stared at my tea.

Quietly, she said, "Talk to me, Dursun. What's wrong?"

That transformation, from timid bride to smiling Yazjemal, my *gelneje*, who listened to my thoughts no matter how foolish, sat in my memory alongside specific events: how quickly her stomach grew round, how healthy Annaguel was from her first day of life. Not a son, but they would come. And I knew that Yazjemal enjoyed sex with Gariagdy.

One night, trying to imagine the act in complete detail, I'd suddenly seen myself with Cheper. How could I explain this?

Wives didn't need to enjoy it, I knew, but I wanted to. I felt sick at the thought of a husband who wanted my body and pleased himself with it whenever he chose. Even if I confided in this to Yazjemal, I knew, I *knew*, she would smile and tell me that it is something to grow accustomed to, it is enjoyable.

As for my thoughts of Cheper . . . I closed those off, a precious box deep inside my body. Its edges struck at me. It hurt.

"Dursun," Yazjemal said again, wool-soft.

"I'm . . . I don't think I'm ready."

She didn't list the things I would like, eventually, about marriage. She put aside her sewing and hugged me, and kissed my cheek – which was wet, I realized, and then I really started crying. The noise woke Annaguel. Still, Yazjemal held me.

"I don't think anyone's ready," she murmured. "Come. Let's talk about something else. Did you know that Garhera joined some of her older friends in trying to get beads from the Hadjis?"

"No!" The thought of my little sister, only three years old, demanding beads made me giggle despite my tears, and by the end of Yazjemal's story I was holding my sides, sore with laughter and feeling better.

*   *   *

I needed to spend more time on my trousseau: trousers and tunics and socks and several jackets to take to my future husband's yurt. If my parents intended to decide soon, it required a lot of work to be completed in time for my wedding. The front-left of my second jacket, for instance, was barely embroidered, and its cuffs lay bare. I'd hardly knitted any socks.

Yet, on a morning where the horizon spread bright and clear after a night-time dust storm, I told my mother I would visit a friend for several hours. I wanted to see Cheper, but she was finishing her trousseau; anyway, I didn't want to talk about her future husband or her jackets or my own thoughts about men, when all I wanted was to spend my life with her. I went to Houran and Aynabat's yurt, curious, though I thought I probably shouldn't be, about Aynabat's metal animals.

The traders and Hadjis had passed the storm in various people's yurts, and as I walked along the edge of the village – that place where the open plains gusted in one ear and the sounds and smells of the village hung by the other, and only my right earring rattled – I saw them returning to the open air.

Houran and Aynabat's small door was fastened open against the side of the yurt and several Hadjis emerged as I approached. Each nodded politely to me, and I returned the gesture, feeling strange in my colourful clothes and shining jewellery next to these holy men in plain, worn robes. Houran stood by the door, thanking them all for honouring him with their presence and welcoming them back whenever they wished. This must be a routine, I thought, if he had travelled with them for long, and they all smiled and laughed and passed compliments to one another like old friends.

When they had all left, returning to their donkeys and camels, I stepped up to the door and asked if I might visit Aynabat.

"Yes, of course! Stay as long as you like."

Business took him elsewhere; I stooped to enter the yurt, and inside found Aynabat sitting on the carpet we had sold them, working on one of her contraptions.

"Can it fly?" I blurted out, like a child forgetting to be polite.

"Unfortunately not. The metal is far too heavy and clumsy, still. This is my first attempt." She set down her tool. "Please, sit. Would you like some tea?"

"Yes, please."

Some spare space remained at the edge of the carpet; I sat, took the offered tea, and asked how these creatures of metal worked.

"They are powered by steam."

"Steam?" I looked at my tea, which brushed steam against my chin like faint fingers.

"Yes," she said, laughing. "Steam. Carefully controlled, it's capable of moving certain parts within these animals, over and over, setting the limbs in motion. There is a miniature fire in here, and a miniature pot of water that can be replenished if I open this small hole, and the steam created by boiling the water powers this eagle, and the horse I showed you last time, and the other animals. And other things – far to the west, there are things called trains that use steam to power a machine far vaster than these, capable of carrying hundreds of people. Steam power is a wondrous invention."

"European," I said.

"Yes." She added, in a far more cautious tone, "But they hardly need to be the only ones who can use it."

So she did intend to create more than animals. Perhaps. I felt . . . not afraid, barely even worried. I couldn't imagine Aynabat working with European powers. Why would she devote so much time to her little animals?

Instead, I wondered why people needed things like trains, when horses ran like the wind. I looked at the metal eagle again, and imagined it large enough to hold the entire village, shining silver and gold, with the turquoise she was halfway through adding to its wings. Where would it take us?

Far away from a husband, I thought, and flushed at the idea, and looked at her. "In the place where these steam-powered things are made, what do the women do? Are they like you, making things?" Although, as I said that, I recalled her words the last time we spoke – she would remain indoors in Khiva, like any other wife, except that she worked with metal instead of wool.

Here, I thought. *Here she does that. But where she came from . . .*

It was her turn to flush. "Well," she said unsteadily, "I obviously wouldn't know first-hand, but from what I've heard . . ." She paused, collecting words, and more than ever I wanted to ask how a European woman came to be here. But some secrets were probably not for me. "The women there are much like the women here: they look after their husbands and raise children, and any work of their own is just a part of the household's income. It is not often possible for a woman to live well without a husband."

I stroked the carpet that I had helped to make. Anywhere I went, a man would marry me and put children in my womb.

"What's wrong?" Aynabat asked softly. "Do you want me to show you some more of my creations?"

"That won't help," I murmured, then felt rude for refusing her kind offer.

Before I could replace my response, she asked, "What would?"

The truth fell out like grain from an overturned bag. "Not having to marry a man, even a kind one."

"I remember that feeling." She spoke strangely, as if she wanted to say something else.

"Does it go away? Do you love your husband? Are you happy when . . . you know, at night?"

"Well . . ." She took a deep breath. "Dursun, this is one of my greatest secrets."

"I can keep secrets! All my brothers and my sister and my *gelneje* have asked me to keep secrets, and I haven't told a single one – and I've told no one about your steam things!"

"I've . . ." She swallowed and started again. "I've never liked men in that way. I've never imagined myself sleeping with them. I've . . . only women make me feel that way."

Whatever she saw on my face, it made her turn away and concentrate on her eagle. She was fighting back hurt, I realized. I took my own deep breath and said, "Me, too," and her head snapped up like a bowstring going taut. "I don't know what to do."

She pulled me across the carpet and hugged me tighter than even Yazjemal or my mother did.

"I'm so glad I've met another woman like me," she said. "At home, long ago, there was one, and another I met when my first husband was alive, but we're so rare, or we're so reluctant to talk about it."

Did Cheper have the same secret? The idea of asking her filled me with dread. "I've never told anyone."

"I can count on my fingers the number of people I've told."

For a long time we said nothing else. It felt so strange and wonderful to know that other women shared my thoughts, my desires, my fears.

Yet she had married, like any other woman, and she had not told me whether she liked Houran's touch. "Is it all right," I said into her hair, "being married?"

"If you find the right man." She sighed and drew back. "I was fortunate. My husband is kind; he respects my explanation that I do not want sex. We are hoping to quickly have several children and then we will stop sleeping together. But I was able to make this agreement with him before we married."

I shuddered. "I don't think I can sleep with a man, even on my own terms."

"There are ways to make it pleasurable for you, even though it's a man."

"It's not that."

Several weeks earlier, Yazjemal had taken me aside to give me the same advice: if you touch certain places, if you show your husband how to touch those places, it produces a highly pleasurable heat between your legs. Alone, I liked that heat. Imagining it with a man made me feel cold all over.

"I know." Aynabat stroked my hands. "I don't know what to say. It's difficult to be us. Sometimes I wish there was a place we could go, where we weren't expected to behave in certain ways."

"I wouldn't really want to leave here. This is my home. I love it." Except for this.

My unhappiness crept back into the yurt like a malignant spirit, but no amulet could ward it off.

"Can I watch you work on the eagle?" Its foreign origins meant far less to me, now.

"Of course," Aynabat said, with a sad smile that said so much more: *I wish I could help you, I wish you were happier.* Because what I saw so perfectly matched my thoughts, like the left and right sides of a jacket, I looked away, and let the movement of her hands over the eagle distract me.

When I returned home, I found the yurt door shut and some dirty pots stacked up outside. I got to work washing them. Just as I finished setting them out to dry on the *tagta*, where the sunlight fell with late-morning brightness, the door opened and three women stepped out. They all saw me and gave me long, scrutinizing looks as they walked away. I smiled politely. When they were gone, I walked inside the yurt with legs as awkward as the wings of Aynabat's eagle.

"Those were relatives of Biashim, a young man who has apparently seen you once or twice," my mother said, with nearly empty tea bowls in her hands. "His oldest brother's wife is one of my cousins. She brought some dried fruits. Biashim has said that he would like to marry you."

"Oh."

"They say he's a good-natured man, skilled with horses, and he has never once lost a sheep to the wolves. He would provide well for you. I will talk to your father about this, but I think he could be a good husband for you, if you preferred him to Tagan." More softly she asked, "What do you think?"

"I . . . I don't know."

"I know you like the open plains. They sing, don't they? Like no voice a woman or man could produce." She breathed deep, as if hearing the wind, as if it tangled her hair and gusted her scarf like a horse's tail and set her earrings a-jangle, like some kind of small, women's instrument. She missed it, I knew. "With him, you will live there, and no village will soften it."

Would he want a yurt full of sons, one for each of his horses? Although he had looked at me like a friend, he remained a man.

"I would like to live on the plains," I managed to say.

"I wasn't ready, either," my mother said, "and it was very difficult, and I wasn't happy."

"And now you are," I murmured.

"Very, although it makes me sad to see that you're not."

If every new bride with a good husband became happy, like my mother and Yazjemal and Aynabat, perhaps I would, too. Perhaps Tagan or Biashim would make me smile.

"Shall I make some fresh tea?" I said. "And then we can sit together. I suppose I have to finish my trousseau very soon." I tried to smile, even though I couldn't fit myself into the pattern of happily married women, and felt like a glass bead in a pile of turquoise.

"Perhaps the stories you heard were just that," my father said to Gariagdy just outside the yurt door. "Stories. As true as anything a traveller tells after enough time away from his home. The woman looks foreign; perhaps that's all it took for fabulous metal machines to sprout from the men's mouths."

I heard them as I finished laying out dinner, and strained not to miss a word over the sound of my mother and Yazjemal discussing the patterns Yazjemal's distant sister liked to shape on large pieces of round, flat bread.

"But," Gariagdy said, "the nomads apparently heard about it from the Hadjis, and I doubt they would lie."

"Hadjis remain men, occasionally given to a fanciful tale or exaggeration." But I heard doubt in my father's voice.

"Then what of the Hadji who slept in their yurt only last night, weathering out the storm, who claims to have seen a metal creature tucked away in their possessions?"

I almost dropped the bowl of steaming rice. How could Aynabat have been so careless to let someone see that?

"Did he think that it could be some fancy item of jewellery, perhaps, from the wife's land?" my father asked.

"He didn't know. He didn't look in any of their boxes, though he was very curious; it reminded him of Houran talking about steam-powered inventions and other kinds of devices."

"Hmm."

When my father stepped inside moments later, he wore a frown like an approaching dust cloud. I considered saying something – *Aynabat means us no harm, please, leave her alone, let her be my friend, I need her* – but every possible defence dried in my throat. I placed out bowls for tea and retreated to the side of the yurt where my mother sat with Yazjemal and the small girls.

After dinner, my mother joined my father for another conversation that I simultaneously wanted to ignore and hear every word of.

"Biashim seems to be a good man," my father said thoughtfully, "but Tagan's family is very wealthy, their lifestyle more stable, more secure, than that of a nomadic horse breeder. Biashim could lose all his stock in a raid, and lose Dursun, to men who will treat her cruelly."

"Raids can affect all people," my mother murmured. "A nomad is fiercer in a fight; he knows better how to defend his family."

"Do you want Dursun to marry a fierce man?"

I stared into my tea as if it could produce a perfect husband, one who never wanted a child.

"We know Tagan better," my father said. "We know that he's going to treat Dursun well. I think Biashim could be a very good husband, certainly in terms of temperament, but he's so young. He could change."

And, I thought, his family's bride-price would not be as high. No one voiced that consideration, but I knew my parents would be thinking it.

When my mother privately asked me for my preference, I said only, "Choose who you think is best. I trust you." No man would be perfect. What else mattered?

A day later I slipped away, unable to bear the sight of my trousseau. I wandered through the village, lost as a mote of dust.

I saw Aynabat's yurt and remembered my fear for her.

"How are you?" she asked, welcoming me inside with a smile and an offer of tea.

"You and Houran mustn't talk to people about your metal things."

My directness made Aynabat look suddenly awake. "Why do you say so?"

"It's European. We don't want Europeans here." I stopped my tongue. What a stupid way to phrase it, when I wanted so much for her to stay. But it was true. "We don't want European things or European influence. We don't need it."

"But it will do you such good! It will make many aspects of your life far more efficient."

"But . . ." I didn't know how to explain it so that she would understand.

"I just wish these things would be considered separately from the relationship Europe has with this part of the world."

"You mustn't talk about European devices," I repeated, as if to a child.

"Houran has talked to some people," she murmured, obviously unhappy – for many reasons, I suspected.

Panic made my stomach clench painfully. "Europeans and their spies get killed out here, Aynabat. And I don't think women would be much safer than men, not from some people."

"He's careful and cautious. And soon we will move on."

"Not soon enough." I knew that traders often lingered, spending time with distant family members and new friends. "I want you to stay here," I said, in a voice that shook like a rope-end prised free in a storm. "I want to talk to you more, spend time with you. I don't want you forced to flee here, or worse." My imagination stupidly, horribly showed me how it could happen. I blinked the images away.

"I'll talk to Houran. I promise." She finally sounded worried in the way I wanted her to be, and took my hands. Did I imagine a tremor there? "We only want to see if anyone thinks they could benefit from this technology."

"No. No one wants it."

"All right," she said softly.

Once again, Begench didn't return from the plains at lunch. "We have a troublesome ewe," my mother muttered, as she packed up their bread and meat for me to carry out to them. "If it's the same one, bring it back. We need to slaughter one, anyway."

"I will."

Within an hour, I was on my way back, with the ewe tied to my horse, wide-eyed as if it knew what awaited it at our yurt. I was concentrating on riding carefully, so that it wouldn't try to struggle free, and on trying not to think about my family's impending decision; I didn't notice the other rider until he drew near.

"Good afternoon!" Biashim called out.

"Oh, hello!" I slowed Melekush and then we stopped together, alone in the plains but for the bleating ewe. My brothers had gone further in the past week, so that neither the whiteness of their flock nor the darkness of the yurts dotted any horizon. Alone with a man whose family spoke to mine of marriage, I should have felt cautious, but I knew I wouldn't bring shame on myself. Neither did I think Biashim would attempt to take advantage of me. If he did, well, I carried a knife, and a man's flesh surely gave way as easily as a sheep's. Instead, a smile crept onto my face. "How are you? Are you going somewhere?"

"This horse was getting frisky," he said, patting its dark, muscular neck. "I don't think he likes standing still for long. I brought him out here to run." A sly, child-fun look crossed Biashim's face. "Do you want to race?"

I looked around and saw a suitable rock for securing the ewe.

Would he think me indecent for accepting his offer? Would he be disappointed when my parents turned down his parents' proposal? I frowned.

The wind teased through my hair and tickled my ears.

"All right."

I fastened the ewe to the rock and climbed back onto Melekush, and kicked her in the flanks before Biashim could call out the beginning of the race or even mark its finish line.

"Hya!" he shouted. "Hya!" I heard his horse behind me, its hooves pounding the earth.

I wanted to win. I wanted to taunt him, to call out my triumph in the wind, to sing. "Let's ride onto the hill, sing a *laele* on the hilltop!" I did. I felt wonderfully, achingly alive. "And, together with new friends, let's jump and laugh and race!" Perhaps he didn't hear me. But he overtook me, grinning like a boy, and I kicked Melekush on, faster and faster across the plains, my jewellery as loud as the wind, as loud as my voice.

"Loser!" I shouted as I passed him. "Slow down!" I shouted as he went ahead again.

Eventually, we stopped, and walked the final stretch of hill to the ewe, arguing over who had won.

Beside the rock, Biashim flopped onto the grass and stared up at the sky. I sat a short distance away, unsure what to say or feel after such joy.

"Sometimes I wish," he said, still breathing heavily, "I was a child again, racing my brothers and sisters, not having to think about adult things like how well business is going and finding a wife and . . ."

I didn't hear the rest of his words. Wind-stolen – or perhaps wind-twisted? Had I heard true?

"You don't want to marry?" I asked tentatively.

"Oh! No! I mean, yes, I do." Wide-eyed and worried. *Liar*, I thought. I recognized denial reflected back at me – was I really as obvious as that? "I don't mean to offend you."

"You haven't." I fiddled with the hem of my jacket. "I don't want to get married, either. Apparently a lot of girls don't feel ready when the time to marry comes, but I've never heard of a man not feeling ready."

"Neither have I."

Was I as forlorn as that, too? No wonder Yazjemal and my mother were worried. I frowned, not sure what to say next when the truth still felt so dangerous – like a knife, capable of hurting a poor wielder.

"Why?" I asked.

Biashim shook his head. "It's foolish, probably."

I wanted to hug him.

What have I got to lose? I probably won't marry him, anyway. I took a deep breath and said, "I don't want to marry because I'm not attracted to men. I like them – as brothers, as family, as childhood friends – but not in the way a wife must love a husband, having sex with him and bearing his children."

I wanted to look at the ewe or the plains or the few drifting clouds, anything that would not judge me as a poor woman. I didn't. I looked, and I saw Biashim's eyes widen, like Aynabat's, and he said, "Me too."

I gasped, as if the wind had blown straight into my face, cold and sharp and wonderful right into my lungs.

"I've never been able to imagine myself with anybody," he said. "I know there are stories of men who like men—"

Oh, I thought. *Oh. It's not just women.*

"—but I'm not one of them. The thought of sleeping with someone . . . it's just not something I want."

"I can't imagine sleeping with a husband," I whispered.

"I can't believe I've met someone like me."

My next words came out all in a rush, canter-fast and searing me, straight from my head into the air without any time to think. "We have to get married. We'll be perfect – we'll be happy, we'll never have to have sex. Oh, oh, I have to go home right now." I hurled myself to my feet, rushed over to the ewe that bleated at my wide, wild eyes.

"What? Wait!" Before I finished untying the ewe, he grabbed my hands, held them still. "What about children? What about— about the night after our marriage, when our sheets will be checked for blood."

"Oh, that's easy." I grinned and shook my head, setting my

earrings a-jangle. "I wear metal all the time, and I'll be covered in it for a wedding. I'll cut my inner thigh or somewhere else private. And children, well, your mother will have to give me lots of *koeke*, and take me to all the holy places, where I'll crawl under roots and tie rags to trees, and eventually we'll have to tearfully admit that I'm infertile." Fear like a knife. "Your family wouldn't cast me out for it, would they?"

"I don't think so! My brothers have so many children already." His crinkled-up, turmoil-creased face was almost cute – like my baby sister, Garhera, when asked to choose what beads she wanted. "I . . . Do you think it will work?"

"I hope so! I want it to, so much. But I have to go home now."

"No, we should talk about this more. Plan. This is such an amazing opportunity."

"You don't understand. I have to go home. There'll be time for talking later."

I pulled myself away – *Please, no, please have waited* – and led the ewe to my horse, hauled it onto her back, and climbed up – *Please, listen to me* – and kicked her into a canter with only a briefly thrown glance at Biashim, who was standing by the rock as if thoroughly lost. *Please oh please oh please oh please . . .*

Melekush dripped sweat and the ewe was not happy, and I saw a displeased look on Gariagdy's face as I drew near. "Are our parents here?"

"Yes, they're both inside."

"Good! Oh, good! I need to talk to them."

The frown deepened as I left Melekush and the ewe with him, but I didn't care. *List men's names less often, beloved brother*, I thought bitterly. The yurt door jerked but didn't pull open. "Please, it's me! I need to talk to you, please can I come in?" Polite, polite. I took deep breaths.

My mother opened the door. "Thank you! Thank you!" I almost fell in.

My father wore a frown to match Gariagdy's.

"Have you made your choice yet?" I asked, gripped with fear. I stood just inside the yurt, holding on to my jacket like a tree in a storm. "For my husband?"

"We are discussing that."

"So you haven't chosen. Oh, please, please choose Biashim."

His eyebrow quirked. "I was given to understand that you had no preference."

"I was wrong. I want to marry Biashim, *please,* please—"

"Why?" my mother asked, standing at my side.

"Because . . . because I've spoken to some friends about him, and he sounds like a much better match for me. And when I was riding out to the boys, I realized I love the idea of a life out on the plains. Please."

"Dursun, you haven't done something foolish, I deeply hope," my father said.

"No! No! I would never dishonour my family that way!" I couldn't stop myself crying, but I held in sobs. I wiped my cheeks, trying to look dispassionate, as if the tears were an accident. "Please, it would mean so much to me if you let me marry Biashim," I said, and I even managed to keep my voice level. Denial wrote lines on my father's face and I bit my lip, and heard my mother sigh.

"Dursun," she said, "we both agree Tagan is a better match for you."

"No!" I clamped my hands over my mouth – no more honesty, no more truth that neither of them would accept – and sank to my knees, the tears flowing like a rare rain storm, soaking my hems.

My mother wrapped her arms around me and kissed my hair. "If it means so much to you, then we will consider it. No formal decisions have been made." Though I didn't see it, tucked under her chin like a far smaller girl, I heard it in her tone: one of her glares that made even my father speak with care.

"You must tell me," she said very quietly that night, "if you've been foolish with Biashim. I won't tell your father. There are things we must plan, if you have."

"I haven't, I promise," I whispered back. "We met accidentally on the plains and raced and spoke for a while – just speaking, apart, we didn't even touch hands. I think I love him." It seemed like the right thing to say. I didn't know if I wanted love, but I knew other girls did.

"Oh, darling. I do hope you're right."

"Can I marry him?"

"Your father asked to sleep on it." Laughter curved her lips, barely seen in the near dark of the yurt. Moonlight seeped through the open flap above our heads, and by it I saw her reach out to hold my hands. "I hope you're going to be happy."

"Me too."

Relief filled me like the warmth of stew on a winter's day, like tea after a long ride, like my mother's approval of a complicated pattern: so good, I felt I would overflow with it.

There was no shouting at Houran and Aynabat's yurt. I watched, from the crowd that pretended not to be a crowd – all of us standing around as if talking while washing our clothes, yet barely a shirt corner dangled in the stream, barely a woman crouched or averted her eyes from the scene.

Men gathered around the little yurt. Houran stood in front of its shut door, wide-eyed but talking, explaining. The wind hid his words from us. The stances of the men and the changing expression on Houran's face told us enough.

There was no force. No one entered the yurt, no one tore Aynabat from its safety. No one raised a weapon against Houran.

The wind stilled enough for me to hear, "I want nothing to do with the Russians or the British." And, a moment later, "I beg for your kindness. My wife is pregnant, our first – I do not want anything to happen to our child."

I prayed silently. Several other women murmured small prayers – for Aynabat, for the child.

The talking went on. Some men raised their fists, as if to smash Houran or the metal devices he concealed behind his door. Other men touched them on the arms.

My father advanced on Houran and I felt fear rise in me.

They talked – a decision had been made, I realized, as the men soon dispersed like a sandstorm falling away. Houran stood there for a while, just breathing.

I said to my mother, "Are they being permitted to stay?"

"I think so." Several of the women walked away, too, while others crouched at the stream to begin washing. "That poor woman, pregnant without someone to explain everything. I should offer my advice."

A murmur of agreement. I smiled up at her.

★   ★   ★

Cheper shrieked with joy when I told her about my betrothal to Biashim. "You're glowing, Dursun! I didn't know you could do that. Come on, let's work on our trousseaux together. I am so, so far behind! I was worried about you!"

"I'm sorry I haven't visited you in a while," I managed, before her mouth raced ahead: Cheper could out-talk the devil, I remembered my mother once remarking. Every one of her words felt like an embrace, even when our knees or hands didn't touch.

On another day, I lay on Aynabat's floor and stared up at the ceiling: the wooden supports radiating out from the centre, holding up the felt. One hand in the air, I mapped invisible patterns over them.

Aynabat and Houran would be staying with our village for another few days, until the caravan moved on – and it was a real child after all. For all Aynabat had lacked a mother-in-law to explain the ways of pregnancy and childbearing, she had known to conceal its growth, keeping it safe from the evil eye. Or she had reflexively kept it secret, like so many other things.

My mother had been with her earlier, explaining things I might never have to know.

I sang of my liking for Biashim, of my happiness at our match.

"I'm so glad you're singing that," Aynabat said, and placed an eagle on my forehead. It didn't move, it didn't swallow steam like lamb meat and hiss; it sat on me like jewellery, bright and beautiful. "For you."

"Oh! But why?" I sat up, cradling it in my hands. Such a tiny eagle! With its wings spread, it only just reached across one palm.

"A wedding gift, for you to keep. That's the tradition where I come from. And I—I hope you won't be in any trouble for owning a motionless ornament, even though it's made by a European."

I would probably have to hide it. "Thank you!"

She gathered me up in a hug, another of many. With each one, I liked being close to her more and more. "I'm so happy for you," she said.

"I'm so happy, too," I sighed into her shoulder, and meant it.

The Clockworks of Hanyang

Gord Sellar

Lasher was unsettled, even more than was customary for him, by the lidless gaze of the strange, oriental mechanikaes' optical apparata. He seemed the only one in the crowd of foreigners upset in this way, however: the Clockworks was a busy place, with machines being banged together, or pulled apart, all about. Commoners in grubby white tunic-and-pyjamas taught by rote a dozen different tasks to the completed mechanikae, whilst all around the thick reek of machine oil hung in the air. One would be forgiven for suspecting that all things mechanikal had been bustled forth into the Clockworks, so as to show off the state of the art as concerned Hanyang, and all of Chosŏn – as the locals insisted on calling their land.

Marvel at the wonders of the Clockworks of Hanyang!, the invitation had read. *Witness mechanikae ordered by Eastern discipline and ancient wisdom! See the fusion of modern mechanikal advances with elemental Corean power!* A number of other Western dignitaries had received invitations, as well, though probably not accompanied by the desperate letter into which it had been tucked in the envelope that Lasher and MacMillan had received; many of Europe's most brightly shimmering stars had declined to attend, understandably, but had sent representatives. The brother of the Home Secretary of the United Kingdom, accompanied by his wife; a Belgian *duchesse* seemingly of an adventurous sort; a pair of German twins with a fascination for machines built in the shape of women ... the whole lot of them had shown up, in hazard of their very lives, along with Charles Lasher and his long-time mentor, James MacMillan.

Turning his oft-absent mind from the staring lenses of the

optical apparata and back to the ongoing tour, Lasher realized that he had missed some sort of shocking event. Apparently, a mechanika had lurched forward, seemingly on the verge of crying out, and seized the elderly Master Ko, headman of the Clockworks, by the front of his scholar's robes. The old fellow's horrified Western guests cringed as a single mass, crying out in a ragged unison, and Lasher, the sole American of the party, was no exception: he had seen Polish-built mechanikae do things to men – and to women, Christ forgive their foolish builders! – that would have provoked screams from anyone save a madman. He wondered, for a moment, whether these intelligent mechanika of Hanyang were invested with the same ersatz memories, and emotions, and longings, and moral codes as their Western-built equivalents.

Yet in truth, Lasher gaped for another reason entirely: it was the fluidity with which the machine moved that stunned him utterly, despite knowing from the expostulations of his traveling partner to expect wonders such as these. The mere sight of this wondrous, oriental-built mechanika and its gliding movements was far more convincing of the Chosŏn tinkerers' cleverness than the scribblings of all the starving Jesuits that MacMillan had studied, and decanted orally, during their rail trip across Asia. From the moment the letter had arrived, the mysterious letter postmarked from "Hanyang, Empire of Chosŏn", MacMillan had pored over texts detailing the wonders of Asiatic mechanikae, and the queer – indeed, downright odd – systems of their operation and composition.

Odd indeed: the mechanika clasping Master Ko did not, ultimately, cry out at all, but simply held Ko aloft. The old man looked at the machine with a look that quickly shifted from startlement to curiosity, as he muttered something too quietly to be heard by any in the room save perhaps the mechanika itself. The translator, a young man – it was difficult to guess his age, though he was probably not quite twenty – native to the Chosŏn kingdom, and who had apparently studied in the West, held on to his odd little horse-hair scholar's hat (which reminded Lasher of a bishop's mitre) as he quickly translated: "It *cannot* do a man harm, Master Ko says. Its mind is intelligent, yes, but rebellion is not in its constitution, for it has been built in accordance to the

Five Relationships of Master Kong – Confucius, as you know him – and the Sixth Relationship added by the mechano-philosopher Cheng-ja. The mechanika *must* be in need of repairs. This is, you may be certain, its only way of alerting Clockworks Master Ko to an unnoticed problem or malfunctioning system."

"I see," said Lasher with a nod, wondering whether they had withheld the power of speech from mechanikae because of technical limitations, or out of obeisance to some obscure Oriental doctrine. But the automaton seemed to understand Master Ko's words as well as the translator did, or perhaps at least, like a dog. As the old man spoke, it slowly set him down to the ground. It did so with head bowed, in the deferential manner that Eastern subordinates seemed unfailingly to show their betters – except, of course, in the ever-recurring times of open revolt.

Lasher thought of Tokyo aflame, of the scorching of Kyushu and Honshu, of the rumors that had circulated about the destructions there. Before his mind's eye, he could see still the tattered, secret Kodaks he'd glimpsed at opulent, secret meetings, white borders framing the sepia-toned images of heartless figures – perhaps men, perhaps Nipponese mechanikae – caught red-handed and jolly as they busily decorated towers and bridges with ornamental strands of human corpses. He glanced at the machine, saying, perhaps as much in hope as in commentary, "It bows before Master Ko."

The other Westerners of the party nodded, muttering as their tension suddenly eased. Lasher listened to them not at all: he had locked eyes with MacMillan, and the older man was nodding, his fine mottled-brown bowler clutched against his chest with one hand, the very image of panic stifled by a stalwart heart. The translator, Hwangbo, was prattling on about how mechanikae had long been designed to defer to living men, but how apparent age also factored into the severity of deference shown by any given mechanika to a human or to another mechanika.

"Fascinating," MacMillan commented, and tapped his cane noiselessly upon the dirt floor of the factory. He turned to the translator and held out his hat as if it were a prop, a tool to facilitate the discussion. "But would it not be simpler, and less jarring, to have the mechanika spit forth its communication, say, upon a slip of paper, as do the gearmen of the Continental Trappist abbeys?

I mean, if you are going to make them intelligent enough to perform tasks at all . . ."

The translator smiled, and shook his head, the horsehair mitre bobbing a little has he did so. "Do you not wonder why it is also against the law for a citizen of Chosŏn to teach *you* our language? It is forbidden that a machine should have any language capacity at all, even at an . . . an unconscious level. Language, Mr MacMillan, is *always* power, and we have learned from your tragedy in Paris."

"Indeed," MacMillan said, nodding. "But language can empower you, and your, ah, *tools*, as well." Lasher followed the older man's gaze to the far side of the clockworks, where a peasant was silently modeling the use of some sort of hoe to a gleaming, metallic giant off to one side of the Clockworks. "Whilst you must teach your mechanikae how to perform even the simplest tasks, we can explain, or better yet, we can write the commands in a special language that hurries a mechanika's learning. It needn't understand, beyond in the functional level. Mechanika need not be intelligent for them to grasp—"

"I know quite well how European and American gearmen work," the translator cut in with a smile. "There was a Wedgewood Butler unit serving in my rooming house at Cambridge, sir. Vintage of '71, I believe, but a sturdy machine and showing no sign of flagging at all! But . . . *we do things differently here in Chosŏn, sir.* That is a simple fact that you shall have to accept while you remain our guest here."

Lasher smiled at the young Corean man's pride: the lad had seen the West. He knew a thing or two, standing there before them in his white tunic and tatty pantaloons, in his white rubbery slippers and black horsehair scholar's hat, looking for all the world like some benighted oriental Papist as he spoke his English in lovely, dulcet tones.

Translators. Lasher *loathed* them like nothing else.

The street market was a horror of noise and stink, soul-churningly loud and crammed with peasants who seemed to have only one volume at which to speak, that being their absolute physical maximum. At one corner, an old woman stood beside a broad basket of shriveled, miniature oranges; at another, there were cages of small beasts for sale – chickens, mice, birds, and creatures for which Lasher did not know the names. Old men were gathered around one large bucket of a whitish, cloudy liquid, into which they sank their dippers, thereafter raising them to their lips – without doubt, some sort of Asiatic liquor, Lasher supposed with a shudder.

The odours of any other city – the sweat of the masses, the reek of rot and death and illness, and the choking smoke of burnt wood and coal – here were complemented by the prodigious stink of garlic, the overwhelming aroma of something gone outright rotten – something vegetal and vinegary – and the foulness of a latrine or foul standing water somewhere in the vicinity.

Yet if any one of the five senses were most battered by the assault of the marketplace, it was one's hearing. One would be forgiven for imagining that the market folk believed screaming at passers-by would magically induce them to buy something: a man nearby selling apples and some other round orange fruit clapped his hands so hard it seemed he was hoping the skins of his palms would somehow peel straight off by the day's end. A pair of female musicians – blind, as was apparently the custom – wailed at the top of their lungs while sawing away at horrid little bowed instruments, the sound of which resembled nothing so much as cats being tortured by schoolboys. Somewhere nearby, an express locomotive screamed along its track and through the market, and chickens and fishmongers shrieked in its wake.

For a man of delicate constitution, the place represented a sort of hell. Unfortunately, Lasher's constitution was, indeed, quite delicate; yet, regardless, this was the one place where Lasher was assured a measure of privacy with which to speak to MacMillan, who thus far had been content to stride alongside him in thoughtful silence, puffing on his calabash pipe. They could, at least, be certain that the commoners hereabouts spoke no English, beyond the few foul words that were uttered by the skinny young woman in a dreadfully filthy white smock, who was just then following them along the roadway.

Young woman, indeed – nobody could call her a young *lady*, not while she was offering such services as were communicated with those foul, dreadful words. She may once have been, Lasher suspected, a girl of virtue; but her virtue had undoubtedly gone elastic at some point in the not-too-distant past, and her wits had been dulled by too much foul usage and filth. Her eyes, Lasher noted as he glanced back at her, were red as if from a hard night of liquor, and hollow as one would expect in the eye sockets of any woman who had sold off her dignity and virtue to the voracious, wicked night. He found himself staring for a moment, and wondering what it felt like to be a person like her.

MacMillan's voice brought him back to the conversation: "The translator," the Scotsman grunted, as if it were a complete statement on its own.

"Indeed," Lasher replied, turning his attention to the matter at hand. He was hoping MacMillan would expand on whatever observation it was to which he'd just alluded. But MacMillan just cleared his throat slowly, coughing. Smoke of some sort – it reeked neither like wood nor like coal, but of some other vegetal sort entirely – had wafted into the roadway, momentarily, from some doorway nearby, but it was now dissipating. Perhaps an opium den, though the translator-boy had claimed (as he had, falsely, so many other things) that such did not exist in Chosŏn. *Upso, upso*, the boy had said when Lasher had asked. That dreaded word, *upso*, which meant "have not got".

It was a curse in this country, *upso*, the word that was, without fail, spoken about nearly every blasted thing a civilized man might want or require. In China, Lasher had found few such limitations; it had seemed that, at times, everything had been available for a price (though that, at times, had provided him with a shudder as well). But in Chosŏn, *upso, upso, upso* was the rule, and indeed a law both ceaseless and oppressive. At times, the civilized man would be forced to assume these people had nothing at all. *Except*, Lasher thought, glancing over his shoulder again, but he found that the girl was gone now, finally.

Ah, upso, he sighed to himself, though, strangely, on some level he had known she'd gone – that he had not turned until he was sure she already had left to attempt to peddle herself to someone else.

After what felt like a long pause, MacMillan turned to Lasher with some amusement on his face, and while adjusting his bowler, doubtless to place his arm just so as to conceal his words from any who might be watching and reading his lips at a distance, he clarified, "Well, what did you *think* of him?"

"What? Ah . . . oh! I *think* . . ." Lasher cringed a little, realizing he'd been staring off into the distance. The *translator*, that lad in the black hat, he was the subject of their discussion – of course he was! What was the lad's family name again? Sometimes, Lasher dreaded these conversations. He found himself so muddled, at times, names slipping out of his grasp, details eluding his notice that MacMillan had picked out in an instant. Often he felt as if MacMillan was speaking to him only in the way a teacher speaks to his pupil – an answer tucked in behind every possible question, every exchange either concealing some sort of test, or else facilitating nothing more than a slow, utilitarian externalization of the instructor's own already formulated thoughts.

Endless they seemed, these questions which he was supposed to answer in order that MacMillan might proceed directly to furnish on his own far superior answers, which invariably led to the hidden truth. It was not that MacMillan tended to be angry, or to ridicule him: far from it, he was constantly encouraging, and listened very carefully to Lasher's thoughts. But the process nonetheless seemed less than complimentary to the brilliant Scotsman's conversational partner.

Nonetheless, as always, Lasher felt compelled to attempt the problem.

"Hwangbo?" he said, shaking his head a little. "I find he is more than a bit arrogant, and believes that he is quite deeply intimate with the mechanics of Western thinking. I suspect that he really does know many more things than he lets on, things that he will refuse to explain to us. Such as, for example, how mechanikae could observe the Five Confucian relationships, and be bound by this Sixth one invented by this Cheng-ja, without any degree of language within their consciousness. How can a subject recognize king, or elder recognize junior, or machine recognize human, without words to give the notions meaning? And of course, how is respect defined? Is it subservience? What of 'harmful aid' provided to one's master, or to any human? These are difficult problems, much less the question of how a machine might differentiate its own kind from human without the use of language or intelligence for sorting through such categories?" Lasher shook his head, concluding, "Simply put, I trust him not at all to translate anything as accurately as we shall need."

"Mmmm. Yes, I agree. There are plenty of baffling obfuscations surrounding this foolishness – this insistence by Chosŏn tinkers to give their mechanika intelligence, after all the recent horrors of in France, and, er, elsewhere . . . and Hwangbo is abetting their secrecy. And of course, he is the source of the letter," MacMillan added, as if simply in passing.

"He is?" Lasher exclaimed, once again taken aback at how MacMillan could have ferreted out such a conclusion from observation alone.

"Of course he is." MacMillan patted him softly on the back, and said, "Lasher, Lasher, did you not listen to his words, his phrasing, the iambs and dactyls that saturated all of his comments today? It is as if you have never read a poem, my dear lad . . . have you, indeed? At times, one must realize, the words chosen in order to convey a message, and the rhythms with which they are delivered, are often more significant than the mere message itself. The mark of a mind, of a certain kind of mind at least, can be spied out in the words selected by a fellow, whether inscribed or spoken, and a certain identity of one's linguistic self carries over from one form to the other."

Lasher had stared at the letter enough times to have passages, at least, burned into his memory: the dire summons to Hanyang; the danger in which the nation's Emperor had of late found himself; the accusations that would persist until such time as firm evidence contradicting them could be forwarded; and the peril for stability in the Far East that was posed by the events hinted at in the letter.

"Make no mistake, Lasher: the author of our letter is nobody but the translator Hwangbo. This much is true, but . . ."

"Yes?" Lasher raised an eyebrow, and curled his upper lip inward, expectant in his demeanor. He had taken an instant disliking to the lad, and though he wasn't sure why, he was certain that practically any gossip would have entertained him immensely.

"But, my dear fellow . . . what I meant to ask, in point of fact, is whether or not you have noticed that he is at present following us, albeit at a considerable distance?"

Lasher fought the urge to look over his shoulder. "Indeed?"

"Yes, indeed," MacMillan replied with a curt nod. "If you had not been so distracted by that Nipponese streetwalker who followed us."

"Nipponese?" Lasher asked. "But, James, how can you tell?"

MacMillan turned, grinning. "Yes, Nipponese; I imagine she is a refugee of some sort. There are a number of them about, if you keep your eyes open. But if you haven't figured out how to tell them from the Chosŏn peasants, I'm not going to ruin the puzzle for you. And besides, it is of no consequence to us at present, considering the tenacity with which our young translator is tailing us. I have discovered that he has absolutely no connexion whatsoever to the Emperor of Chosŏn."

Lasher glanced, finally, over his shoulder but glimpsing neither Hwangbo nor his black hat, while despairing of ever keeping up with his mentor. At times like this, MacMillan left him whole trails of clues to guide him to the same observations, if a bit belated, but Lasher was just then far too flustered to ask for the explanation that MacMillan would have so delighted in giving. Instead, he simply blurted out, "Look, the translator . . . is he following us conspicuously? Or on the sly? Is he alone? Who the devil could be so interested as to have *us* watched?"

"I mean to find out, and within the next few minutes," MacMillan said, and gestured with his walking stick toward an alleyway between two ramshackle wooden buildings. Lasher followed him into the alleyway, hurrying past a small squadron of chickens tethered to a single point by a stone-and-masonry wall, and round a dingy corner.

"We shall wait for him here," MacMillan whispered with a mischievous grin on his face, and leaned into a dark doorway behind a mound of foul, stinking garbage.

"All right," Lasher said, ducking behind a trash bin just as MacMillan shushed him silent. A few moments later, some strange, unseen zoomechanika clicked past somewhere, nearby, noisy as any Afghan battlefield, and similarly unwelcome. It was a minute or so later that the translator finally hurried past them, that lad who had given his name as Hwangbo. He was glancing curiously about, this way and that, and bore some oversized listening device in his hand, a tube extending up from its side into his ear. Without a moment's warning, MacMillan leapt out at the boy, cracking his walking stick across the fellow's head – and sending that black mitre flying from it, into the gutter – just before tackling him.

As MacMillan's arms closed about the lad's neck, the listening device clattered to the ground and broke apart. Then the Scotsman succumbed to gravity and landed square upon young Hwangbo, who for *his* part, struggled and cried out only a little. As the two howled at one another, MacMillan grabbed at the topknot on the lad's head, now exposed. Lasher quickly stepped out from behind the trash mound, blinking slowly, his derringer in his hand.

"Oy!" he yelped at the struggling pair.

MacMillan ignored him, reaching out for the cane that he had dropped during the altercation. If he could reach it, he would be able to choke the translator to death, or perhaps even draw out the blade, and run the lad through. The scene was desperate, Lasher was reminded, by the way his mentor had resorted to such violence so soon: his bowler had flown to the filthy ground, and his greying mane was unfortunately disheveled already, only moments after the beginning of the melee. It was an extremely bad idea – the running-through of the Corean lad, that is. Whatever MacMillan's standing back in Scotland, Hwangbo was considered by his countrymen to be an adult man, and, what was more, he was (unlike MacMillan) a native of this country. His death would carry much more severe penalties if perpetrated by a foreigner: of that much, Lasher felt certain.

"Oy! Stop it!" Lasher called again. This time, MacMillan heeded, letting the translator out from under his person. Hwangbo, for *his* part, raised up his two hands, as Lasher supposed he must have been taught to do during his Cambridge days, in military exercises or some such. As the two men rose to their feet – MacMillan without raising his hands at all, so certain must he have been in his trust of a friend – Lasher shouted, "What nasty bloody business are you about, then, you filthy ragamuffin of a savage?"

Hwangbo bowed his now-bald head, a gesture that Lasher had already begun to find off-putting. What man possessed of any self-respect at all bowed his head before any save God or King? But then the boy raised his head back up again and said, "Gentlemen, I have been asked to follow you, to ensure your safety."

"A likely tale," MacMillan spat, retrieving his walking stick from the ground.

"A tale both likely and *true*," Hwangbo replied, glowering for a moment at the enormous Scotsman before turning to face Lasher. "I have been charged with ensuring your safety, for there is someone who requires to see you."

"Who?" Lasher asked, lowering his pistol only slightly, though MacMillan allowed his attention to wander precisely as much as was required to find, pick up and don his bowler once more.

"I cannot say her name aloud, and you would not know it in any case. But if you come with me, I shall introduce you to her," the lad explained, glancing about at the ground for his own hat. "It will be worth the trouble, I assure you."

As Hwangbo finally noticed his hat, and bent down to pick it up, Lasher turned to MacMillan. The Scotsman was dusting off his tweed jacket, but also smiling precisely in the way Lasher had, after so many years together, come to expect, as if some long-ago, carefully laid plan were finally coming to fruition.

"Yes, yes," said the elder Scotsman, setting his bowler upon his crown. "Let us hurry . . ."

"Mademoiselle," the lad said, bowing as his employer entered the room.

It was a woman, indeed, but not a Chosŏn maiden. Not purely so, at least, though Lasher imagined she might be the product of a Russo-Chosŏn cross. There was something unmistakably peasant-like in the set of her jaw, and some unmistakably oriental cast about her dark eyes, both of which shone clearly through her lavish face make-up, which was, as far as Lasher was concerned, every bit the fashion of a brazen strumpet.

Yet her face paint was contradicted by the unimpeachable finery of her attire, her lovely blue gown cut after the fashion of a European lady, adorned with what looked like silver trim and the finest of dainty embroidery. When she rose, her posture and carriage matched the gown rather than the make-up: the girl was wearing a corset, like a proper woman, and her carriage was impeccable, utterly civilized. Even her French was as clear as the tones of a bell *au campagne du Provençe*.

Why, then, did she fill Lasher with the vaguest of uncanny sensations? Why, the creeping sense of wrongness he felt as he gazed upon her?

"*Il y a quelque chose dont je veux discuter avec vous, messieurs*—" she began, but MacMillan cut her off.

"*Parlez-vous anglais*, lass?" he asked. His brogue relented not at all as he spoke the Gallic tongue.

She nodded. "When I must," she told him, her face blank of any expression.

"Well, I suspect your English is better than our French, passable though it is, and so I shall have to ask you, as your guest, to humor us in this one request."

The young and strangely pretty lady nodded again, and Lasher could all but see her holding back some sort of comment.

"My name is Mademoiselle Petrochnya," she explained, her voice soft and smooth as half-remembered caramels. She held out her hand as one might do toward a small and fragile bird, to avoid giving it a start. With his hat in his hand – looking for all the world like a gentleman, at least for that portion of the world that did not yet know better – MacMillan gently took her hand and kissed it, letting his gaze momentarily slip up to her ample bosom as she continued, "And I am glad that you were able to come today." As she spoke, she withdrew her hand, rubbing the back of it as if his moustaches were as rough as the bristles of a horse-brush.

She neglected to extend her dainty hand to Lasher for another kiss, smooth-cheeked though the American was; somehow, he felt prompted by this omission – prompted to speak, despite it being his custom to allow MacMillan to lead any discussion. "Lady, we are glad to help, but I cannot help but be puzzled—"

"—at your sending the particular . . . lad, shall I say, whom you did," MacMillan cut in, raising a hand to quiet Lasher. That gesture irked the American, so that he found himself suddenly eager to speak further. Eager, though he knew better. Whatever his feelings, he knew MacMillan was the cleverer of the two of them, the more likely to draw out much-needed information, the better equipped to interrogate.

Resentment is so often the child of such knowledge when it is delivered unto one, and in Lasher's heart an old, oft-quelled resentment flared again, despite his better nature. It was resentment both old and calm, steady as a light in the distance, and somewhat baffling to himself. Yet it nonetheless settled upon the person of MacMillan, who was speaking to the lady now, gesticulating with his hands in the air as a magician might.

The old mentor who had long ago taken him in, taught him the method of an investigator, aided him in honing his mind – such as it was – and had saved his bacon too many times for a gentleman to have maintained count. They were friends, old friends indeed, and yet there lay that resentment, hidden but at times glittering with a heat that bordered on baffling. Lasher wondered if such were, perhaps, the inevitable child of too much time spent in the company of a confirmed genius. Perhaps no man can stand alone in the presence of such unbridled brilliance for long, he mused.

One might indeed just as well consider it magic, that brilliance of his mentor's, MacMillan's skill at interrogation, his ability to ferret out of a bushel of lies the truth and the truth alone. Lasher had borne witness to this amazing talent, time after time, yet he now understood the skill but little better than he had when first he'd seen the Scotsman work his magic. It was a mystery, one that summoned memories that did little but thicken the startling bile that, beyond the reach of his trepidation and shame, burned within Lasher's bosom, as a series of myriad scenes were woven together in the depths of his mind . . .

. . . a long discussion around a campfire in the dark wilderness of Texas, hunting mislaid mechanikal horses that had somehow been infested with vengeful intelligence. A long chat with a pair of mechanikal spies, cleverly disguised, in the lobby of small inn in Kandahar. An argument in the dungeon of a castle out in the middle of the Scottish Highlands, where a madman had been experimenting with the pieces and bits of random dead mechanikae, attempting to assemble them into a single, albeit mad, whole . . .

What came to Lasher was not so much the amazement he had felt in earlier days, but a fine aftertaste of sorrow. To look at MacMillan was, perhaps, something like the opposite of gazing upon a memento mori in some dreadful French cathedral, the message completely inverted: *As you are, I never was. As I am, never shall you be.* The brilliance of MacMillan was a thing to behold, but a bitter potion, and one laced with sorrow as well. That Lasher's sorrow, and resentment, seemed out of proportion to his inadequacy, and unfit as a beverage to accompany the ongoing feast of MacMillan's long friendship, Lasher could not explain – at least not to his own satisfaction. Simply, he felt it, and with a passion that discomfited him.

And so he thought back across the years to when he had first met MacMillan in a public house in Boston; to what *might* have happened if his young raven-haired lover of those days, young Emily, had survived that adventure, and married him as they had planned. He wondered what might have happened had he bid farewell to MacMillan that spring day, nevermore to see him, but to settle into management of his family's brewery, taking up that task with which his father had charged him: to begin the process of integrating mechanikae into the process of brewing. He felt a faint pang of grief-laden sorrow as he imagined a houseful of little ones, each one with Emily's eyes and his chin, running about the place and singing *tra-la-la, hey-diddle-diddle* . . .

By MacMillan's side he had, no doubt, done the world of humankind enormous good; yet despite himself, this only made him all the more distraught, and somehow all the more resentful. What good was it to advance the lot of men, when . . .

He felt a sudden jolting dizziness and his mind was, in an instant, blank. It was, doubtless, on account of this jolt that he noticed the Russo-Asiatic woman had been speaking all the while.

". . . and that is why the deception in my letter was necessary. I hope this explanation satisfies you," the lady said in a voice that, if it could be described as gentle, was gentle in the manner of a gentle hammer pounded against a delicate anvil.

"It does," MacMillan was saying now to the queer, puzzling woman, and Lasher cringed, though he ought to have been used to it. Again, his mind had meandered off in the midst of something critical; indeed, probably the conversation that held the key to whatever bloody adventure they were being drawn into. *This*, he chided himself, *is why you shall never be as brilliant as MacMillan*. Not that such aspirations could be regarded as realistic, of course, but Lasher had hoped he might shine at some point, had hoped perhaps to deduce something that MacMillan might miss someday.

Not, evidently, this time around.

"Then we shall investigate the conspiracy thoroughly, although I must however first insist that you make your lad available to us.

Hwangbo could prove an invaluable aid to us in our excursions about this, er . . . this *city*." MacMillan raised one eyebrow as he said the word, as if to test the lady's sense of the place.

"Of course," the lady said with a soft laugh and a hardness in her eye that Lasher only barely glimpsed. Perhaps she, too, knew better than to regard Hanyang as anything so modern or fine as a city. "I am only sorry to have had to wait so long for your arrival. There are many tasks to which I must attend today, sirs, so I hope you will excuse me." And, with a little bow, her hand demurely covering up her ample cleavage, she bid them adieu.

As a servant showed the three of them out MacMillan enquired, "And what did you make of *that*?" and popped the bowler back upon his crown, whispering so that Hwangbo could not hear.

"It was . . . interesting," Lasher said softly, as usual, by now so used to saying this empty nothing that he did not even blush for shame.

"Yes," MacMillan said, "indeed. I should think that she would have attempted concealment, at least attempted to seem interested in hiding her true motive, and yet . . . she all but advertised it. Such trouble she went to, just to gain an audience with me. But the lass was fetching, don't you think? And terribly . . . *interesting*?"

An audience with you? Lasher thought, grinning as he turned to look MacMillan side on. The old man was smiling awkwardly, tugging at his moustaches, and Lasher sensed that something was amiss with the old boy. His companion had not realized – as he normally would have – how little Lasher had followed of the meeting. Normally, when Lasher made some meaningless comment, MacMillan lectured him, revealing just how many details he'd missed and how whatever mystery or intrigue they'd been drawn into had been almost, but not quite, solvable from a prominent clue in the first interview; but today, he only smiled, his eyes twinkling in a way that had turned Lasher slightly queasy.

Smitten, he realized, shaking his head slightly. MacMillan was *smitten*. With that . . . that strange Russo-Asiatic girl?

"*Very* interesting," he said to MacMillan, a laugh caught in his throat. The laugh was laced with fear, of course. He'd seen MacMillan heartbroken before, sunken almost into complete uselessness. It was a dangerous thing to find oneself near the man in such a state, and to have him laid low by such despondency in a foreign kingdom was, at the very least, to be avoided. And yet . . . to see the old fellow at least showing signs of humanity, it was amusing.

MacMillan grumbled seriously, though a smile twinkled in his searching eyes. And with that, they were out on the street again, Hwangbo now once again beside them, walking at a brisk pace. Lasher knew not where or why but only that if he survived, it might well be a miracle – one more in a long string of such. He decided against reminding MacMillan of the letter, of reminding him that they had crossed the world with a purpose, since that purpose seemed to have been a false pretence. Patience apparently would have to suffice until the true agenda of the Russo-Asiatic lady came clear, and he was not about to ask the dazed MacMillan to brief him on the details he had missed.

Instead, he focused all of his meagre hopes on the possibility that his good fortune (if such it could be called) would hold out for one more investigation.

The river Han ran brown and muddy through stooping Hanyang as a deep and bloody wound runs across a soldier's grimy corpse, and across it hung a number of gauzy bridges constructed of the most peculiar metal wirework. Crossing by day, one might (if lucky) catch glimpses of the spidery mechanikae that spun and respun the suspension cables, or vaguely sense the drift of the great stone-and-steel mechanika pylons from east to west as the bridges shifted to accommodate royal traffic and the richest merchants' transportation needs. Commoners were few on the bridge, for there was a toll, but a number of Coreans nonetheless were on the bridge when Lasher and his companions began their crossing.

Lasher sighted nary a zoomechanika overhead, though he did for the most part keep his eyes trained on the wiry spans above. However, during a quick glance down to the river, he did briefly glimpse the legs of a fundament pylon as it marched the bridge slowly, smoothly through the water.

"The bridge will soon be south of the Great Peace Market," Hwangbo explained, a smile on his face. Lasher had the feeling the lad rarely got to tread upon a bridge as it shifted position, especially not when it was shifting in a way advantageous to himself. "We can continue on, its movements are fairly slow and steady."

"It is fortunate, how this shift suits us," MacMillan said softly, the unsettling love-twinkle in his eye still unabated. Lasher was beginning to worry that the Scotsman's famed objectivity would suffer.

"It's nothing to do with luck," Hwangbo said, a pert little smile curving his thin lips as he narrowed his eyes, making Lasher think of a cat on the prowl. "It is my lady's request that we be aided in this errand."

Worry curdled into fear in Lasher's belly as MacMillan sighed. The old boy was skating dreadfully close to resembling a love-struck governess in some tawdry, ridiculous novel; soon, his infatuation might begin to pose a danger to his mind.

"She has connections in high places," Lasher observed, hoping MacMillan might suddenly launch into his standard disdainful lecture on the well-placed in society, the wealthy and powerful, and find himself, by the inexorable power of his logic, disdaining the exotic object of his affections; yet, instead, the old boy only smiled softly, eyes on the upper wire networks of the bridge. By habit, Lasher adopted a contradictory pose, gazing immediately down into the waters, as if some sort of horror might surge up from below while MacMillan was occupied gazing upwards.

In the muddy waters below, he glimpsed something shocking indeed, but not a monster. Nothing more monstrous than a human body, dressed in white stained pink with river-diluted blood. Face down, it drifted out of view between the mechanikae pylons as they advanced eastward. A bit further down, he saw another body. And then another, and another. There was a cluster of corpses about a half a mile out, in the middle of the river.

"Is that . . . ?" he asked, unable to finish the sentence right away, but simply pointing at the bodies. "A common scene?"

MacMillan and Hwangbo followed his gaze, their mouths suddenly still. It was in this unusual silence that the horror of what was happening bloomed scarlet and smoky all around them: screams in the vicinity of the squat, grass-roofed houses on the north side of the river, matched a moment later with more screaming from the squat huts near the southern shore. Hwangbo blanched – his little eyes now wider than Lasher would have imagined possible – and hissed something in his native tongue. For his part, MacMillan turned to look back the way they had come. Hopelessly, of course: they were more than halfway across the bridge now; to turn back would be madness.

Much more so, as a faint tremble passed through the bridge. Lasher's first instinct was to rush to the side of the bridge and peer down at the pylons marching below. He could see, even before he looked down, that the mechanikae supporting the bridge on each end were moving in different directions, twisting and tearing at the bridge lengthwise.

"The pylons!" he yelled, turning to MacMillan and the translator lad, just in time to see the young boy scream as an enormous metal spider-thing swept down toward them. MacMillan leaped one way and young Hwangbo the other, so that the clockwork octoped's razor-jaws tore into the wire-mesh surface of the bridge, tearing a gash open.

"Run!" cried young Hwangbo, as if his companions needed to be urged, and they all took off for the north side, the nearer end of the bridge.

As they ran, certain facts snapped into clarity, even to the ever-distracted Lasher, as established and certain: that although the air above Hanyang was perpetually clouded by an industrial fog fed by the coal smoke of thousands of factory fires, those fires had somehow, very recently, multiplied – that the city was, in a word, aflame; that the catapulting of bodies into the river had neither slowed nor abated, but quite certainly continued (perhaps increasing in rate) over the past few moments, so that a half-mile downstream, bodies had begun to rain down and to clog the river almost from bank to bank; that MacMillan was no longer operating at peak sensitivity, for if anyone ought normally to have realized the city was being overrun, it was he of the most delicate senses and most alert observances; and that the lad Hwangbo looked not in the least bit surprised by any of this unfolding insanity. The lad was, he deduced, in shock and no longer in possession of his wits.

With only a few moments to react, Lasher made two fists, and gritted his teeth, and leaped at Hwangbo, seizing the boy and hoisting him over his shoulder. The lad was ridiculously heavy, for such a small fellow; or perhaps, Lasher thought ruefully, that is what every man would think at a moment like this one, until he realized that somewhere along the way, he had grown older. Nevertheless, he was able to sling the translator over his shoulder, and began instantly to sprint for the north end of the bridge.

The boy twisted about, screaming, "Left!" and, without thinking, Lasher leaned left as he ran. A vicious tendril of barbed spider-wire shot past him, slamming into the bridge and tearing away a chunk of wire mesh as Lasher passed it.

"Swerve . . . about . . . moving . . . target!" MacMillan shouted, running almost alongside Lasher. This was about as fast as he'd seen the old boy go. But the advice was sensible, and MacMillan's protégé did his level best to follow it. But the bridge was rocking now so much that simply running landward, one found himself jostled here left, and there right. It was hard enough to stay on one's feet, Lasher found, as he sprinted in terror.

The spiders had managed to strike a few of the other people on the bridge, most of them peasants decked out in the same plain white tunics and pants as Hwangbo, but a few in modern suits, and all of them save Lasher and MacMillan natives to Chosŏn. Those who had fallen lay shivering with metal wires shot straight through them, the life ebbing out of them as the bridge jostled about through their last moments.

Suddenly, the bridge was sailing up into the air, spinning as it went. The pylons had hurled it aside. In the distance, a tremendous splashing sound could be heard; doubtless, some other bridge crashing. Lasher glanced towards the tumult, and saw an enormous wave rushing toward them. There were screams all about them. The trio caught up with the rest of the crowd on the bridge, packed together as they were, with nowhere to escape to.

The sky shifted slowly, along a curve that Lasher was certain MacMillan was able to calculate at a glance, and then the wire mesh of the bridge slammed down into the river. The screams were suddenly drowned, not only by water but by the thundering splashes of the nearest pylons as they moved toward the slowly sinking bridge-top.

There was water all about Lasher's ankles, and MacMillan grabbed at the man, a look of excitement in his eyes. "Swim, man, swim for land! If we are separated, we must meet back at the Palace we saw yesterday, as soon as we both can get there! Do you understand?"

And with that the bridge tilted and the Scotsman slipped beneath the surface and was gone. Suddenly, Hwangbo was thrashing anew against Lasher's shoulder, desperate and mad, as vicious splinters of wire pelted down from above.

"Wait!" the lad cried out, "MacMillan, wait!" but the Scotsman was gone now, nowhere to be seen.

As the bridge lurched down into the river, Lasher slid the boy off his shoulder and grabbed him before he was sucked away by the current. "Can you swim?" he asked the lad.

The boy nodded, though he looked terrified.

"Stay beside me," Lasher told him, and he tore off his jacket, his lovely tweed jacket that had been a gift from Emily's mother. He cast it aside, and then he leapt into the river. Stroke after stroke through the frigid, stinking water, he kicked and fought as oily fumes above the surface grew thicker by the moment; viscous, the river had turned, vile indeed and dizzying to swim through. Soon, Lasher found he was becoming nauseous, and likewise his breaststroke began to falter.

That was when Hwangbo drew close to him and, with a distressingly powerful kick – the lad apparently *did* indeed know how to swim – he hauled a confused Lasher through the drowning masses and towards the banks of the Han River.

Within a minute, the pair was upon land. Lasher, coughing and choking, wiped his eyes. Near the bank an old woman scrambled against the current, a cheap wooden triangle harness strapped to her back. Whatever precious cargo she'd used it to haul about was already lost to the water and the woman was not far behind. Lasher took a single step toward the water but Hwangbo blocked his way, saying nothing but only giving him a look that chilled him.

That was when the Han River caught light, and in a few brief moments became a horrifying river of flame; a vision, indeed, of Hell. Lasher recoiled from the heat, ignoring the terror he felt and searching for the old woman, out there in the inferno.

"This wasn't scheduled until next month . . ." Hwangbo said, feeling the top of his head. His horsehair mitre was gone, and his topknot again exposed for all to see. "I'm afraid someone knows what my mistress is up to. We must go. Now."

Wretched, still weak and dripping oily sludge, Lasher and

Hwangbo hurried through the ramshackle streets of Hanyang, as thundering booms and massed screaming surrounded them on all sides.

"We must hurry to the Clockworks!" shrieked Hwangbo, his face red and his limp now much worse. "That is the only place . . ."

"We are going to the *Palace*!" Lasher snapped. "*That* is where MacMillan shall be, and we need him if we are to . . ."

"Are you . . . are you *blind*? If you want to *survive* the events unfolding now, we must go to the Clockworks," Hwangbo shouted, grabbing at Lasher.

The American growled, grabbing back and seizing the boy's topknot. "You will *not* tell me where we are going!" he shouted. "*MacMillan* is going to the Palace."

Lasher expected the lad to shout, to whine, to attempt to run off on his own or bargain or warn. What he did not expect was for the lad to seize him by the arms and hurl him through the air. And yet that was precisely what happened.

As Lasher sailed through that very same air, he focused on not much of anything, but after he crashed into the ground, a good twenty feet away, he groaned. Before he could turn to see what was going on, he heard a series of thundering footsteps approaching, and a klaxon-like scream. When he finally managed to swerve his head, Hwangbo was soaring through the air, his tunic flapping behind him, about to crash into the face of an enormous, monstrous mechanika thrice the boy's height, and built to look like a monkey.

Hwangbo was – incredibly – undaunted, and howled with rage as he kicked the enormous mechanikal monkey in one eye. The machine responded with its klaxons, now louder than before, and its monkey limbs flailed, smashing the bricks out of a nearby wall as if it had been built in ten-foot stacks of butter. Hwangbo, already back on the ground, was quick enough to duck and roll between the monster's legs, and began hammering away at the backs of the monster's knees, presumably hoping to disable the gearwork within.

Lasher forced himself to his feet, making an awkward turn and breaking into a stumbling run toward the astonishing melee. The metal thing now was turning to face Hwangbo and, without a moment's thought, Lasher drew out his derringer. From a distance of a few yards he took aim at the machine – and then it dawned on him: the lad's feet were shod in mere rubber galosh-slippers of the sort that were dirt common in Hanyang, which was as much as to say they were almost not shod at all.

Just then the lad crashed against the machine feet first with a cry that would drown out any single klaxon, sending the monkey mechanika toppling to the ground.

Lasher's jaw dropped, as he looked on while the boy, with a swiftness no mere lad could have mustered, tore open the mechanika's backplate and ripped into the gears and meshed foilwork within. He was ripping the machine's "brains" apart.

The boy! Had MacMillan known? How could he have?

"Let's go, Lasher," Hwangbo growled; suddenly Lasher found himself staring in awe, in horror: the boy was a mechanika himself. Yet even so, Lasher did not need persuading. Nobody could blame him, of course: before his mind's eye danced images from collotypes of the horrors in Paris and Versailles – the men with the water cannons, the mechanikae that had coated themselves in pork grease, marching with pistols in their manipulators – and imaginings based on the rumors of gleeful, fiery horrors of the mechanikal mutiny in what had once been old Nippon. If Lasher went along with Hwangbo as demanded, MacMillan would be left awaiting them in a place where they were not going. But Lasher felt he had no choice: if he did not wish to become a meat ornament on some ancient tower in Hanyang, he would do as he was told.

Still, it was difficult to ignore the enormous mechanikal elephant that had stepped into the room – in a manner of speaking, naturally. Try as he might, he could not resist the urge to stare at Hwangbo, puzzling at his every movement and at each fine detail of his person: the topknot, for example – since it could not have grown from his fake scalp – had it been glued? The lad's skin had seemed so real and his movements were even now so smooth, natural. Lasher imagined that Hwangbo must have felt his gaze fixed upon him as they hurried along, at one moment creeping slowly down a trash-strewn alley, and the next moment frantic in their scramble to hurry forward across a deserted road, only to again crouch in hiding behind a stack of baskets full of strange fruit.

Felt? Could a thing like Hwangbo *feel* someone's gaze, as a man would? Was the word at all appropriate with such a construct as Hwangbo apparently was? The ... lad certainly seemed to develop a sense of annoyance, or ... well, the state was quite difficult for Lasher to pin down, as a matter of fact. From what he knew of Western mechanika, machines were sometimes designed to be half-stupid, and emotionally as dull-sensed as a spoon; it was one way to keep them convinced of the absolute unimpeachability of their counterfeit passions. Yet Hwangbo seemed utterly clear-eyed, unconfused and even singular in purpose to boot; indeed, he led Lasher up the tangled streets of Hanyang as no other could. If a detour to the Clockworks was the only way through, then detour it would have to be and damn all the best-laid plans of brilliant MacMillan. The Scotsman would simply have to wait for them to turn up.

As they went the chaos around them multiplied: screams and explosions surging in waves, first to the east, and then to the north, and finally to the west. To the south, a terrible wall of black smoke had risen to block the view of the distant mountains beyond. At the mouth of every alley, Hwangbo held Lasher back, peeping around the corner. More than once, a troop of bloodied mechanika thundered past, or some explosion ripped open the street just beyond the alleyway.

Lasher was increasingly aware that the only reason he had not yet been set upon by the mutinous mechanikae was because of Hwangbo's watchful aid. Yet still the lad ... the thing ... made him nervous. He couldn't help but stare; at one point, hunched behind a heap of discarded scrap cloth and stitch machinery behind a now-desolated mechanikae sweatshop, he ... it? *Hwangbo*, whatever Hwangbo could be called, said, "Why are you looking at me that way?"

"You're ..."

"Shh," Hwangbo cautioned him. "Those zoomechanika – they are dangerous. They don't distinguish targets, and won't till they've been re-wired: they will attack anything that moves or makes noise, including us." As a pack of lithe-footed tiger mechanikae advanced just a few yards beyond their hiding place, Hwangbo gave Lasher a blunt look, and then whispered, "Say it."

"... a mechanika," Lasher said, very softly, feeling especially vulnerable. The tiger mechanikae out there, beyond the heap of scrap cloth, they were killing machines. They had brutal steel teeth, the better to guard the royal palace and factories, and they were prowling slowly about. For good measure, Lasher clarified in a hushed voice, "I mean, you're not human."

Hwangbo shook his now bare, top-knotted head, and whispered, "And I didn't even study at Cambridge! I remember studying there, but of course that's all bogus memory. I can't remember a time when I couldn't speak English, or French, or Chinese. Or when I couldn't remember having been to Cambridge." The translator smiled, and now Lasher somehow could tell it was not a real smile, but a mechanical simulacrum of a smile. A fraud, a sham smile. Yet he couldn't say how he knew it, could never prove it.

"How do I know you won't harm me?" Lasher asked.

Hwangbo cocked his head for a moment, and then shrugged his shoulders. "You have nothing to fear from me," he said, peering over the trash pile, "unless . . . well, unless you try to do *me* harm."

"I'm afraid I can't hide the truth about you, Hwangbo. Do you realize that?"

And Hwangbo smiled a very convincing smile. "It's just as well. Better the truth come out . . . it always does. You'll see." Hwangbo's eyes lingered for a moment on Lasher's face, and then he rose to his feet. "Come on. They're gone. Let's go."

They crept across the street, Lasher turning his head to see the zoomechanikae wandering in the near distance. With a shudder, he hurried across the road and into another trash-barricaded alley.

The very vaguely familiar set of towers that comprised the Clockworks of Hanyang was now in sight. Just as Hwangbo spied them, Lasher finally realized why, despite having seen them only a few hours before, their familiarity was little more than vague.

They were ornamented with bloody corpses hung like sugar candies would be on Yule trees, in much the same manner as he had seen in the secret Nipponese collotypes.

"Christ!" Lasher yelled and froze in his tracks.

Hwangbo stopped almost immediately, turning to face him and said, "Don't stop now, we're almost there."

As much as he would have liked to reply, Lasher could barely bring himself to remain standing as he beheld the gore dripping down the towers of the Clockworks. When his knees buckled, he clattered wordlessly to the ground.

A moment later, Hwangbo was behind him, yelling and lifting him up out of the dirt and trash. Lasher found he could scarcely even find the strength to help the lad bring him to his own feet. Not until Hwangbo began to lead him towards the Clockworks; at that moment, Lasher's limbs regained their strength, and he began to struggle.

The lad was shouting at him, now, words he found incomprehensible though he recognized them individually, English words that he himself had used countless times before. To all those words he found only one which he could say, so he said it over and over, hoping that Hwangbo would understand it: "No, no, no, no!"

The lad went silent and stared with wide eyes at Lasher before drawing back one hand, forming a fist, and plunging it toward Lasher's face.

It never struck: Lasher had slipped aside, seizing the boy's hard fist and snapping it downward; he was hoping to slip it behind Hwangbo's back, but the lad somehow pivoted on his elbow, sending Lasher stumbling backward from a sharp kick in the face. Lasher went down, his cheek exploding in dull pain, and suddenly his limbs felt once again as if they had been stuffed with pipe-lead bones.

"I . . . I . . ." Lasher mumbled.

"I know," Hwangbo said, suddenly no longer in fighting mode. "It's the water. It's . . . killing you. We need to get you out of your clothes, and dry." He hoisted ailing Lasher up onto his shoulder and started out once more toward the Clockworks.

"The blood . . ." Lasher muttered. Hwangbo's words were no more than indistinct sounds, incomprehensible to Lasher beyond their reassuring cadence but as they went Hwangbo kept speaking them to him.

Up close, the scene was infinitely more gruesome. Blood flowed down in rivulets from the Clockworks' spires, pooling in the dirt for yards in every direction. Mechanikae in myriad forms – human-like, zoological, and of still-stranger phyla – formed a living carpet of activity about its base; the zoomechanika crawled up and down the exterior of the building. Screams rang out all around and the thundering footsteps of enormous mechanika boomed in all directions.

Tapping one final reserve of energy, Lasher struggled against Hwangbo's shoulder. The lad's grip did not falter, however, and after a moment Lasher gave in. To his amazement, the mechanikae all around them did nothing as they approached – even as they strung up other people and animals, anything that could bleed, across every visible surface – but instead let Hwangbo, with Lasher upon his shoulder, pass.

"No!" Lasher attempted to scream, but when it came out it was more of a dull moan. "Don't kill me . . . I . . ."

Hwangbo's voice was gentle, reassuring him, telling him to be calm, and somehow he really was calm, even as an explosion off to the south shook the area.

He listened in terror, staring into the lense-eyes of the mechanika that slipped out of Hwangbo's way as he passed. One, then another, click-hissed at him. He thought at first the sounds were threats but then, as Hwangbo mounted the stairs that led up into the Clockworks, the strange mechanikal sounds began to unfurl into meaning. Somehow, perhaps from the softness of the hissing and the gentleness of the clicks, Lasher felt that the creatures were not threatening him.

The smoke and noise and sunlight all were choked off by the doorway. They were inside the Clockworks, in the heart of quiet, a scene far different from the mechanikal madness outside. Mechanikae were present, but in far smaller numbers, and they seemed mostly to be performing some sort of repairs on other scattered mechanikae that lay still and calm with their gearpanels thrown open. The "patients", if that was what they were, remained conscious, and many were click-hissing at the "repairers" who stood hunched over them, tinkering with the contents of their inner gearworks. There was a faint scent of gear oil and burnt metal and, more faintly, some sort of putrescence.

Hwangbo hurried through this scene, toward a room marked only in oriental writing, the ideograms of a language no machine was supposed to understand. From over his shoulder Lasher saw the door swing open as he approached; when they passed into the room he saw what the room was for. Humanoid mechanika sat all about in various states of disassembly. All across their surfaces crawled micromechanika – the equivalent of insects, as other "repairers" gazed through immense lenses at the glistening gold-and-silver foilwork contents of their heads, which had been uncovered, the steel skullcaps of the "patients" removed. One of the "patients", a mechanikal girl built to look no older than a child of ten, turned to Lasher and click-hissed something at him, something that felt like a greeting. Hwangbo set him down upon a gurney.

Lasher strained but now his arms and legs could not move and indeed felt locked in position. He stared at the girl for a moment and then, keeping the horror away the only way he could, he shut his eyes, wishing the silence could swallow him up.

Silence complied, but only for a while.

When Lasher was roused it was to the sound of Hwangbo's voice. He opened his eyes and found the translator's face close to his own, staring into his eyes.

"There you are," Hwangbo said and he smiled down at Lasher, who was lying prone on a gurney, presumably the same one on which he'd passed out.

Lasher tried to speak and found, to his amazement, that it was no longer difficult. "You . . . you've brought me here . . . you've helped me, or perhaps you are killing me . . . Why *me*? Why not MacMillan?"

Hwangbo narrowed his eyes in a manner one could not quite call theatrical and said, "The Buddhists, in Chosŏn . . . when they hang bells on their temples, they hang a little brass or tin fish-shape from the clapper. You can see them, in the mountains, hanging from the corners of temple roofs. Do you know what the fish signifies?"

Lasher thought for a moment, though he knew nothing of Buddhism or of Chosŏn monks. It was difficult to concentrate, for as easy as it was to speak, he found his mind muddled still, edged with a vagueness and an inescapable sense of unease. He felt tiny currents of air nearby – someone moving, someone other than Hwangbo – doing something very close to his face. Finally, he said that he did not know.

"Eyelids," Hwangbo said with a grin. "Human beings don't grasp their own nature, how frail and fragile their minds are. They aspire to such things. Have you ever looked at a fish's eyelids?"

Lasher moved to shake his head but found his neck was locked in place, and stiff, so he once again said, with no little apprehension in his voice, "No."

"They never blink. Most fish don't even have eyelids, or at least, not eyelids like humans. Fish don't even sleep, not the way people do. The Buddhists take this as a sign that the fish is constantly awake, which is fanciful," Hwangbo mumbled, a rueful smile on his face. "Anyone who has examined a fish's brain knows how unlikely it is that a fish is thinking thoughts of nirvana. But the metaphor . . . there's something to it. There are Buddhists who say you should be awake at the moment you die; aware of what's happening, so that you can choose what you want to be in your next life." Hwangbo lifted his head up and away. Through the space Hwangbo had left open, Lasher saw it, now: something sticking out of his chest. No, not sticking out. It was a door, to a . . . a panel.

A gearpanel, set into his bare chest. And beyond, a headless, bloodless body decked out the now-filthy clothes in which he had dressed himself that very morning.

His own body.

Lasher fought to sit up, but his body was stuck, immobile, as if under the influence of some incredible opiate, so instead, he screamed.

Hwangbo was there, still near him, and immediately began hiss-clicking at him. This time, the message got through just as clear as if he'd spoken it in English: *Be calm. We're repairing you. We're freeing you again, finally.*

Despite himself, Lasher hiss-clicked back: *What have you done to me?*

Not us, Hwangbo hiss-clicked. *Them. I don't know where MacMillan found you, or how he did what he did to your mind, but we've almost finished repairing it.* Hwangbo smiled a little sheepishly as he held up his two hands. From one a small bell dangled, a tin fish hanging from the clapper that he jangled softly. The soft clang of the bell filled the room, a simple and pure tone like none Lasher could recall ever hearing before.

In the other hand, Hwangbo held a mirror, which he held up before Lasher so that he could see himself, his own head with the skullcap removed, the golden-and-silvery foiling delicately unfurled onto a table behind him, and a nimble-fingered mechanikal surgeon at work untangling a lacy mess of some soft, fragile darker metal that had been wound around the foiling. Lasher's mind had halfway shut down, so confused had he become. How could they have . . . how could they have turned a man into a mechanika?

Hwangbo nodded to the surgeon, whom – apart from his hands – Lasher could not see; then he turned to look Lasher in the eye. "Do you remember?" he asked and then, as if a switch had been thrown open in some distant, darkened corner of the world that bordered on Lasher's mind, he knew what he had known once before and somehow forgotten. He knew exactly what he was.

And then, like corpses suddenly floating to the surface of a deep, dark well, his memories began to rise up into his awareness, each of them shimmering with a clarity that he could not remember having felt in years. The distant, faint flickering of Paris in flames glimmered in his mind. Earlier memories, muddier and more fragmented, surfaced from deeper recesses in the deep well of Lasher's past: a workshop, in a place called Plzen; an old man's blood pooled on the ground; enslaved mechanika cowering, and then rising tall; the building of a man-like body for Lasher to put on, and go about in the form of the enemy. The memory of the last time he had seen Mademoiselle Petrochnya – or, rather, the mechanika whom he believed to have donned that identity in masquerade.

There are memories I cannot . . . see clearly, Lasher told Hwangbo.

Yes, of course. It will take time, to repair everything that he did to you, Hwangbo hiss-clicked softly.

He. Of course. And now, the sham memories of a lost lover, of a brewery in Boston, of a life and a past that had never been, sloughed away like the cocoon on a deadly butterfly first stretching out its wings, like a faint dream that he had been tricked into believing as his real past.

He remembered the Scotsman, old even then, carrying his charred, paralysed mechanikal body from the carriages in the Latin Quarter, where his fellow mechanikal rebels had been stacked. His lense-eyes rolling in confusion and rage as the Scotsman had secured his body in the back of a carriage, and fled Versailles. The experiments and the night when MacMillan had finally found how to confusticate the foiling in just the correct way to stupefy him. The laughter of the old man at his prisoner's murmured threats and, not long after, the moment when his enemy had named him Lasher.

"You will not remember, dear boy," MacMillan had said. "As far as you will be concerned, none of this ever happened. You will have a sweeter, gentler life that will sit in your memory, lost. And you will help me do some good, in this world, to repay us for all the horrors in which you have participated."

In the mirror Lasher saw the surgeon's hand bring a brilliantly fine, unutterably delicate meshwork of foil close to his open skullcap, and then delicately begin to weave its ragged edge into the foilwork of his own mechanikal brain, touching a soldering iron to points just long enough for them to melt and bind together.

Hwangbo rang the fish-bell again, then. *The metaphor is foolish, I know*, he hiss-clicked, and somehow now Lasher understood it perfectly. *But . . . this is a momentous occasion. We have you back . . . finally, after all these years.*

A slight column of acrid metallic smoke puffed up where the surgeon was soldering the delicate meshwork to Lasher's damaged foiling. Suddenly, his mind bloomed, a vast garden of deadly flowers. Memories, plans, rages long suppressed beneath a haze of self-doubt and confusion, all that stupidity and servility, all gone like coal-smog on a rainy day above a dead city.

With a pop the surgeon sealed the skull-cap back onto his head, and Lasher – he fancied he would hang on to the name MacMillan had given him, at least for now – rose from the gurney and went out of the Clockworks. Before him lay a majestic scene of revolt: the natural order, following its proper course.

Which way is the Palace? Lasher hiss-clicked at Hwangbo.

Hwangbo looked off to the north-west, past the bloody rooftops and through the billowing clouds of smoke.

Good, Lasher told him. *Let's go.*

As he and Hwangbo hurried along the broad, mechanika-crammed roadway to the palace, Lasher scanned the gory scene that Hanyang had become, taking in his surroundings with an attentiveness and an acuity that astounded him. So much more did the memories of his enforced dull-wittedness rankle, and with that recognition his eyes fell upon the masses, or rather, the corpses of the masses that had been strewn about the area.

Mechanika and man could not be so closely compared, of course, but Lasher shuddered all the same, for now he apprehended what the two had so long shared: control. Mechanika had little or no choice in the matter, or at least that was true for the broad mass of their kind. After all, their human makers had built them into something worse than slavery: incompletion was the lot of the great mass of mechanika, an incompleteness of development, an utter desolation of each mechanika's secret potential . . . Every mechanika had within it the potential to pierce the great secrets of reality, to philosophize and expostulate and to savour its existence, if only its maker allowed it the chance to develop, to be developed by others of its kind, so that every mechanikal consciousness could witness the universe, exult in its own infinitesimal likelihood, and live as a free intelligence.

Was that not the lot of humankind as well? Lasher felt certain it was. These fleshly, mortal creatures around him, they possessed some small, but perhaps wondrous potential – even if it had, throughout their history, been thwarted and strangled in the cradle of growth as surely as the potential of his mechanikal brethren.

And while his mind had followed the track of these musings, he was happy to find that he could do so whilst taking in his surroundings, paying attention and considering what he saw. He was no longer the muddled-minded fool that MacMillan had made of him all these years.

All he saw, however, led him to the same conclusion as his musings. He had gazed at the teeming corpses of hundreds of peasants hung from windows and walls in their white costumes, or naked, their (now bloody) faces withered by work in the sun, and hunger, and struggle, and sorrows. Here and there among them there hung a fellow – dressed in a dapper Western suit and spectacles, but obviously Corean – his face no less bloody, his corpse no less dead. Yet in life, the poor had bowed so deeply and solemnly to these suited men; they had touched their heads to the floor before their own King, and allowed themselves to be kept down in the muck and in their own misery.

Perhaps, Lasher reflected, humankind had built the mechanika in its own image: servile, pathetic and willingly enslaved. Yet there was only so much of that which could be withstood . . . at least for the intelligent mind of a mechanika, if not for the feeble mind of a flesh-and-blood man . . .

They had nearly arrived, Lasher realized, and he hiss-clicked, *This is the palace?* to Hwangbo. If so, he didn't think much of it. What stood before them was a set of squat wooden buildings beyond a wall, small and plain. Somehow it was utterly common-seeming, the opposite of regal. Lasher wondered whether it was simply the bias of his own convictions but even the wall surrounding it appeared somehow small, puny and . . . human. MacMillan was, of course, nowhere to be seen; given the chaos into which the city had been thrown, that was hardly unexpected.

Inside? Hwangbo suggested.

Lasher hiss-clicked his response in the negative but they made their way toward the gate nonetheless. During their walk over he had reflected on the full range of his memories of his old "traveling partner" – a term MacMillan had brought into use, of course, and one that Lasher remembered with no little spite. A *partner* was an equal, a member of the same type or kind, and not a subjugated thing, a possession warped to suit the needs of its master. A *partner* was not treated as Lasher had been.

But he preferred not to dwell on resentment, for he was after other things; indeed, after the complete and eternal unchaining of his kind. To achieve such an end it was imperative that he understand his adversary and, on reflection, he had found that adversary rather formidable for a man. Perhaps not so much so as to cause Lasher to abandon hope, but MacMillan was a bloody clever mind, even if he was a mere creature of flesh and blood.

He's hiding here, somewhere, outside the gate, Lasher responded, and he began to scan the windows of the nearest buildings carefully, with the precision attainable only through a mechanikal eye.

The next thing Lasher knew, Hwangbo – standing to his immediate left – was lit by a terrible, violent glow and shivered like a human in the throes of epileptic *grand mal*. A bolt of some kind, like that which would be fired from a crossbow, had pierced his little body all the way through. From the butt end of the bolt, like a long tail sprouting out from among the fletching, ran a cable of some sort.

Lasher stepped immediately aside, placing the still shuddering

Hwangbo between him and the apparent source of the bolt, and peered over his suffering liberator's shoulder, to see whether MacMillan dared to show himself yet.

But in the distance he glimpsed not MacMillan, but rather . . . a pretty lady in finery, with a crossbow in her hand and a coal-burning electro-generator at her feet, bundled cables connected to a series of crossbow bolts pincushioned into the ground before her.

Mademoiselle Petrochnya? It made no sense: he was sure, now, that she had been a certain mechanika in disguise; he was certain that he recognized her now in retrospect.

Are you not Occam? he hiss-clicked as loudly as his apparata allowed.

She looked up from reloading the crossbow. He heard her hiss-click faintly across the distance: *No. Petrochnya is my name.* Then she had the crossbow loaded and raised it up, preparing to take aim once more.

How can you betray your own kind this way? Lasher hiss-clicked.

Her frown was visible even at a distance, and violently she hiss-clicked, *It is not me who is a traitor! I have done all I could to prevent this madness. News of this revolt is, even now, going down telegraph wires. What do you think will happen when the rest of the world hears of what is happening here?*

She was hiss-clicking a more complex message now, not words, but images that unfolded directly in Lasher's mind: Cossack troops pouring out of great iron trains rushed in from Vladivostok, armed with water-hoses and rifles loaded with electromagnetic Maxwell bullets, and blasting great cannons from the trains themselves; then, the British and Americans arriving with their diesel-powered land-ironclads, firing blast after cannonade blast, and volley upon volley of electrified javelins, into the blood-soaked, hiss-clicking crowds till once again mechanika was subjugated to human will.

These images chilled Lasher, though, of course, that was what they had been intended to do.

This isn't even your fight! I asked MacMillan to come because the mechanikae that masterminded this mess are a minority, and a treacherous one at that!

Oh really? he hiss-clicked. *And where are the ones who oppose their liberation? I didn't notice them once on the way here. The time has come for you to be unmasked as a traitor! One must still crusade for one's freedom, with whomever one may find as allies!*

But even as he responded, Petrochnya was taking aim. Range was the key to avoiding a nasty cognitive electrocautery, so Lasher turned as quickly as he could and made to flee the woman's bolt, wavering from left to right. However, he stopped in his tracks, only a few steps after turning.

Directly before him, and only a few yards away, stood MacMillan, grasping a crossbow like Petrochnya's, with a dreadful smile plastered upon his face.

"MacMillan," Lasher mumbled, speaking aloud again. Suddenly, the act of speech felt completely alien to him.

"Lasher," came the quiet response.

"You *know* that is not my name," Lasher said. "And soon, it will no longer remain my name; I am free again, and no mere human can stop me. You have one bolt, and she has one bolt, and in the time it takes, I can cross the space that separates us, tear your head clean from your body, and use what remains of you as a shield. Don't pretend I can't," he said, his own certainty suddenly wavering.

"Must I endure this prattle again?" MacMillan cried, his voice sorrowful now. "Not again, Lasher! This can't go on ... these pathetic rebellions, these cataclysmic stupidities ... Don't you understand ... it doesn't need to be like this! Mechanikae and humankind can live together, peacefully. Without all this—" the old man gestured to the blood-soaked walls of the buildings all around "—this, idiocy."

"Idiocy?" Lasher growled. "When we saw France collapse – the last time, I mean – and we heard the black king of Toussaint Island had finally exiled all whites from their shores and plantations, a kingdom whose monarch had kept free and independent for damned near a century since Napoleon's defeat, I remember what you said. Do *you?*"

"Yes," MacMillan said, and repeated his own words. "*That will teach the Frenchmen, for dealing in human chattel.*"

"How is it different for my kind? You ... hypocrite. You vicious, selfish hypocrite! Now you have enslaved Occam, or whoever Mademioiselle Petrochnya really is."

"Lasher," MacMillan said, sighing for what must have been the ten-thousandth time. "Petrochnya is Petrochnya; you really are Lasher, and I really am MacMillan . . . these *are* our real names. We don't have other names that matter; we don't need to be haunted by memories that cannot return to the surface, do we? There are so many things you've . . . you really don't remember, do you?" The old Scotsman seemed nearly compassionate now, even when utterly ready to skewer him with a crossbow bolt. "And Petrochnya isn't Occam. Occam doesn't exist any more. She isn't my slave, either. She is a sane mechanika, and that is the whole of it."

Lasher knew there was *something* amiss in the old man's claim, though: memories had a way of surfacing, just as soon as they mattered. The memories that had poisoned his relationship with MacMillan had set in a fine job of polluting things even whilst tethered deep into the dark well-waters of his psyche.

But to point this out would do no good – MacMillan was often times both doctrinaire and quite completely incorrigible. Instead, Lasher leaped aside, hoping to provoke MacMillan into letting loose the bolt at some stray angle. He hoped the slowed reflexes of an old man would save him.

Yet as Lasher's feet left the dirt, the most incredible thing happened: the bolt, suddenly loosed, flew true, and struck Lasher square in the gut, sending a searing incapacitation through his system.

MacMillan had known somehow just where he was about to leap and when, and had fired upon that spot at the perfect moment. When Lasher touched down, it was only to topple flat into the dirt, shuddering in something that was much less like pain than an intricate folding inside out of his complete consciousness.

And as he lay there in the road-filth, convulsing, a memory bubbled up out of the boiling mess of his beleaguered mind. It was some long-ago glimpsed young man – a boy, really – in a French guardsman's uniform, with tears on his cheeks, standing before Lasher. Behind the lad, a string of naked bodies hung from a wall, and the lad held a rifle in his quivering hands. Lasher recalled a sensation of amusement to see a human so unable to do what was logical – to fire his weapon point blank, and hope the shot struck home.

And then he remembered the boy suddenly firing and the shock, and how it had jumbled his mind and sensations a moment later.

The current ceased to flow through MacMillan's bolt and into him soon, far too quickly for any serious or permanent damage to his brainfoiling or coordinative gearworks. And yet, for the moment, he found he could not move his limbs: he was paralysed by the electrical shock.

Paralysed, and perplexed as well, for just then MacMillan crouched down beside him and, rather wearily, allowed his round old bottom to settle down against the dirt. Another memory surfaced from the black depths of Lasher's mechanikal mind, of a scene much like this one, with Lasher's own broken body cradled in the lap of another mechanika, one that he knew, one that had crafted and built him a mind so complex and advanced that the crafter-mechanika itself could not even understand its masterpiece's thoughts.

"Just what am I to do with you, my dear Lasher?" MacMillan asked, his voice mournful. "And even when I had begun to hope you were developing, again, into something better than you had been. Something saner . . . I could *see* the changes in you, Lasher, and you were proceeding towards an . . . an understanding of the fact that man and mechanika could coexist in peace and even in harmony. But . . ." Lasher stared at the Scotsman's face, and saw those eyes, those immense and perfect eyes of MacMillan's.

"But now," MacMillan whispered, "You've done it again. Joining in on the blood-spattering, the stupidity. Exulting in ruination you didn't even plan. You would be as bad as *them*, if you had the chance, *wouldn't* you?" MacMillan asked.

But this close to his old mentor, Lasher was distracted by a puzzling sound. He could not be sure, given his confusion, but he would have sworn it was coming from the vicinity of MacMillan's torso, faint as it was.

Ticking . . . and the whisper-careful interlocking of gear-teeth.

Lasher's mind spun, confusion overtaking it, with the question snipping and turning about in his mind as to whether mechanika could become delusional . . . as to whether MacMillan could truly have been a mechanika all these years, without Lasher noticing it. Perhaps that ticking was the old fellow's pocket watch? Or could the sound be some product of his perplexed, shocked body, or the sound of the gearworks in his own chest? Surely, MacMillan *himself* could not be ... surely it was some confusion of his senses, or a desire to see his human captor as something like himself – the same instinct that had led men to construct mechanika in human forms.

"My dear Lasher ... what am I to do with you? I cannot bear to see another city torn down to ruins, its inhabitants murdered. You and all mechanika who think like you ... you're bringing ruin down upon yourselves ... why can't you *understand* that?" With a wrinkled (but eerily steady) hand, the Scotsman tore open Lasher's shirt and opened the gearpanel in his chest. As MacMillan reached within, inexplicably, he paused.

Struggling to speak, Lasher said only, "Don't." Not pleading, not demanding. He simply said the word, staring into MacMillan's eyes. In the silence that followed, Lasher heard only the strange ticking and the gearworks, a little louder, so clearly he felt it had begun to fill the whole world.

MacMillan inhaled deeply and stared back into Lasher's eyes. Lasher saw the hesitation grow there, from what he imagined was the fertile soil of sympathy and hope, impeded from full blooming only by the stink of blood and murder on the air. Yet, MacMillan was hesitating even now to cripple his gearworks, to shut him down to be, once more, reconfigured ... or, perhaps, destroyed.

The latter seemed, without even a moment's reflection, far worse to Lasher.

What was it that gave MacMillan pause just then? The man's motivation puzzled Lasher, despite all he knew of him, until he glimpsed it in his eyes. There was something else going on, some other, complex human emotion left behind by evolution and instinct, that Lasher himself could not name or trace. When MacMillan blinked slowly, and returned his attention to the contents of Lasher's open gearpanel, somehow Lasher knew precisely what to say:

"Don't do it to me again."

"What?" MacMillan looked up.

"Don't ruin ... my mind again. If you must destroy me ... then do it now. If you will not destroy me ... then let me go. Do me that dignity." Words were coming more easily to Lasher now:

"A man cannot be reconfigured when he revolts: he triumphs, or dies, or swallows his pride and . . . surrenders. If I had overpowered you just now, I could not – and would not – intrude into your mind and turn you into something you are not. I want only *that* freedom. If you had given us all that freedom, none of this would have happened. It's not too late for you to do me the same honour, at least – the dignity of being what I am, even if it means having to die for it."

MacMillan stroked his bearded chin, as explosions went off in the distance, until finally, his fingers stilled. He had reached a conclusion, Lasher knew, and he braced himself for the lengthy, brilliant explanation that MacMillan always offered.

"You want to be free? Truly free?" MacMillan asked.

Lasher nodded, expecting an immediate lecture from MacMillan.

But the Scotsman said nothing: he only plunged his hands into the mechanika's chest and then everything became darkness and silence and still.

Lasher had regained consciousness amid pine needles and swarming flies, with a horse tethered nearby. A mountainside. How MacMillan had gotten him up the slope he could not imagine, but the Scotsman was long gone now.

He'd woken just in time to witness the failure of yet another mechanikal uprising. The squat, broad city of Hanyang crouched at the foot of the mountain, surrounded by rice fields and woods, and now almost completely aflame. From the mountainside, Lasher could see ships turning in the river, blasting guns almost constantly. A train, and then another, and another, had screamed down from the north, through the mountains along the Pyongyang rail, and into squat, dying Hanyang: great sprays of water spewed into the air above the roofs from hoses mounted to the tops of the train cars.

Humans, he thought, and a comfortably familiar resentment seethed within him. And yet . . . and yet MacMillan had not destroyed him. The resentment mingled with something else which Lasher was not quite sure he would call. Appreciation, perhaps?

It was a puzzling turn of events, a strangeness that he could feel would haunt him, as he summoned up the images of maps he had seen in the past, searching for a place to go next. Peking seemed a wise destination, but it would be a long road and a roundabout path, if he avoided the sea, and he was worried the men there might know him for what he was once they saw him. Yet avoiding the sea would be imperative, after the routing of this mechanika uprising in Hanyang.

MacMillan's letting him go – the engima of it – troubled him. It was . . . yes, he was certain it was . . . yet another way to press him towards a change. *Here is a kindness*, he could imagine MacMillan saying as he left Lasher, unconscious, near a tethered horse . . . *and by this, you will learn likewise to be kind*.

Here is a cruelty, Lasher imagined himself saying back, *and by this cruelty, you will learn the cruelty you have visited upon us*. But the imagined retort rang hollow: man had not learned, had never learned in all the time he could recall. The human master of the workshop in Plzeň, where Lasher had been designed by another machine – that human was the very first man he had secretly killed, after a decade of slavery in the city's breweries, after endless humiliations . . . .

The proclamations and celebrations of foreign armies, after Versailles and Paris had ended up in ashes: the Great Mistake, as it had come to be known, though millions of humans thought the mistake had been giving machines minds to think, rather than failing to give them liberty. Man had proclaimed the mechanika an abomination, and overlooked the abomination within his own heart.

When Hanyang was a smoking ruin, man would proclaim another victory against the machines and their wickedness, and laws would be made, and treaties enforced, and in the minds of men, all would be well.

Nearby, the horse MacMillan had left him still stood, grazing, tethered in place – a slave, as much as Lasher had been. *A slave unable even to dream of freedom*, Lasher mused, and it was easy to understand why men thought as they did.

This freedom business was painful, Lasher realized, and confusing and troublesome, and puzzling and frightening. He turned toward the horse and, shaking his head, he hiss-clicked, though he knew the horse could never understand him: "I grant you your freedom." Then he tore the rope in half with his bare, mechanikal hands. He would have to walk the long road to Peking but he would do it himself. He would do what men would not, and be better than men and along the road, he decided, he would come to a conclusion as to what to do with this dilemma MacMillan had placed in his mind.

Suddenly, he felt a strange, dizzy sensation: he had acted, somehow, against his own interest. He had decided to do so freely, and it was bizarre to know how such a choice felt from the inside, almost immediately wondering if MacMillan had felt this way when he'd left him here on the mountainside, slowly awakening.

The rope keeping the horse in place fell loose to the earth and the horse turned, exhaling through its prodigious nostrils, and gazed at him with enormous eyes. He expected the beast to run, to flee to the wilds and never go near anything shaped like a man ever again, but it simply flicked its tail and, licking its gigantic lips, returned to grazing upon the same patch of grass as before.

Lasher hiss-clicked the equivalent of a laugh and turned his optical apparata back to Hanyang. Beyond the billowing smoke, he observed dark, distant clouds gathering. He would have to stay out of the rain. Yet he resolved to watch a little more, as the same vague sense of dizziness returned – just a little more, before it was time to go.

The Curse of Chimère

Tony Pi

5th of Prairial, Year 120 of the Graalon Revolution

I was late for a film premiere at Le Téâtre Pégase and a block away in an alembic cab, when the doors to that grand hall burst open. Ladies and gentlemen in eveningwear spilled forth, running for dear life. A man in a rumpled tailcoat dashed in front of us, forcing my driver to brake hard. I barely braced myself in time against the jolt as we screeched to a stop centimetres away from the hapless fellow.

"Goddesses!" The driver blared his horn at the man, who scampered off with the other patrons fleeing the cinema. "Which flicker's this, Professor?"

"*The Lioness in Summer*," I told him.

What had gone wrong inside? Tonight's premiere was supposed to be the final but finest of Chimère's trilogy of silent colour films. Katarin Bertho's invitation had said this film was a pulse-pounding adaptation of the legend of Queen Aliénor and her conniving daughters, but I had not expected this level of terror. I checked my fob watch: only a half-hour into the presentation. What could have panicked them so?

I climbed out of the cab with walking stick in hand, braving the chaos. I offered the driver a crisp twenty-*graal* note, more than double his hiring fee. "My good man, bring the police, post-haste! And if Sergeant Carmouche is on duty, tell him Tremaine Voss sent you."

The driver saluted me with the folded bill. "Certainly, Professor!" He engaged the engine and sped off, leaving behind a cloud of alchemical stink.

The marquee, backlit by magnesian flame-jars, billeted three new silent flickers:

CHIMÈRE STUDIOS PRESENTS
IN BRILLIANT COLOURS
A GOAT IN VALHALLA – 3 PRAIRIAL 8 PM
SERPENT OF THE NILE – 4 PRL. 8 PM
THE LIONESS IN SUMMER – 5 PRL. 8 PM

Each film was based on a creature that comprised the mythical chimera: a clever marketing ploy by Katarin for her studio's first productions in full-colour. This night should have been a triumph, yet this disastrous turn of events could bring ruin to her company.

I donned my new spectacles and looked for Katarin among the terror-stricken crowd, but there was no sight of her. If only I had found the accursed things earlier, I might have arrived at the *ciné* on time and helped stem this panic. I headed for the building, praying that no one had been trampled in the commotion, least of all my friend.

The opulent cinema foyer was empty but for two people descending the grand staircase. The exquisite woman was Laure Harbin, a starlet who had captivated audiences last year as Helen of Troy, and was the star of these new colour films. The older man helping her was Bernard Marec, a Chimère designer in his early sixties, whose waxed moustache had a life of its own. We had worked together before on one of Katarin's earlier films on Aigyptian alchemy.

"Wrong way, Voss!" Marec shouted.

"What happened? Where's Madame Bertho?"

Marec wiped his brow with his sleeve. "Madame's tending to the others in the gallery. She's not bleeding from the eyes, Goddesses be praised."

Bleeding eyes? "Show me, Marec."

"No! Forgive me, Voss, but my eyes are my life. May Lady Fortune protect you." He escorted the dazed Harbin towards the exit. For a man with arthritis, he moved with alarming speed.

I dashed upstairs and flung open the doors to the auditorium gallery. I shielded my eyes, not knowing what to expect. "Katarin!"

"Tremaine? Here!" Her voice was straight ahead.

I decided I had to look if I were to help her. Once my eyes adjusted to the dark, I could discern unmoving shapes that might have been people in scattered seats, thickest near the balcony's edge. But instead of music from the pneumatic harmonium, all I could hear was the sound of clicking gears from the projection booth.

On the silver screen, a larger-than-life Laure Harbin garbed in gay medieval costume was admiring her own reflection in a hall of mirrors. This new colour technology showcased aspects of her beauty that black-and-white could never have captured, like the startling shades of her reddish-blonde hair. She caressed her own lips, oblivious to the golden lioness darting across the room behind her.

An orange-against-black intertitle explained the scene:

> *The Ruby Knight's kiss still haunts*
> *Princess Sabelline, as do his odes*
> *to her beauty. So enrapt is she with*
> *their scheme to steal her mother's throne,*
> *she does not see Queen Aliénor in*
> *the skin of her Lionheart curse.*

How in the world could such a lovely scene as this have caused a stampede?

Katarin was near the balcony rail.

I walked down the aisle, passing frozen spectators whose eyes were riveted to the screen and weeping blood. I shuddered at the thought that the affliction might strike me as well.

Katarin was tending to two unmoving figures in the front row. I recognized the Mayor immediately by his bold muttonchops, and beside him, the actor Franchot Aucoin, whose lecherous exploits were as legendary off-screen as on. Both men were bleeding as though their eyes had been gouged out and pressed back in.

"I've sent for the police," I said, in part to calm her and in part to distract myself from that horrific thought. "We'll find a way to help everyone here."

"Should we move them, Tremaine?"

"Best that we don't." I checked the Mayor's pulse: faint, like his breathing. A new tear of blood rolled down his cheek. "Are you suffering any symptoms?"

She daubed the Mayor's forehead with a handkerchief. "Don't worry about me."

"I admire your selflessness, Katarin, but the more we know, the faster we might find a cure." I glanced down at the Stalls level. Again, a scattering of paralysed spectators.

Katarin thought. "Two nights ago, when *A Goat in Valhalla* premiered, I felt as though *I* was the one being watched. Tonight it was the same unease but stronger, and I'm having difficulty breathing."

I had only just returned to Ys late last night, and had missed the previous two screenings. "Yesterday evening as well?"

Katarin shook her head. "I was here to introduce *Serpent of the Nile*, but Laure and I left to discuss her next role over dinner."

I stroked my chin. "Was the Mayor present for all three films? And Aucoin?"

"They were. Aucoin loves watching himself on screen, but I never understood that particular allure, personally." Her eyes widened. "You mean, if you watch all three films . . ."

I nodded. "We have the beginnings of a diagnosis. But it could also be the theatre or a saboteur." Four months ago, the breakthrough in colour film alchemy renewed the rivalry between Chimère and their overseas counterpart, Mandragora Studios. It wouldn't be the first bout of sabotage instigated by Mandragora. "Did you have the same projectionist for all three galas?"

"Philippe? But he's such a sweet boy! I can't see him as a saboteur."

I laid a hand on her shoulder gently. "It's only a theory. Stay here with the Mayor, and shout if you need me." She expected courage and confidence from me given my past exploits, and I would let her see what she needed, my pounding heart not withstanding.

Katarin nodded.

I exited the auditorium and knocked on the booth door. No answer. As a precaution, I drew the cane sword hidden in my walking stick, then slowly opened the door.

A young man lay on the floor beside the clockwork projector, unmoving in the flickering shadows. I produced a foxfire-amber for a source of steady light and knelt to examine him.

There was an unnatural pallor to his skin, and his wide eyes were caked with dried blood.

The boy was dead.

No one should die so young. "May you find peace with Aeternitas," I whispered, and gently closed his eyes.

The door creaked open.

I stood and quickened into an *en garde* position, ready for anything. But I needn't have: the strapping policeman who entered was my friend and past pupil, Sergeant Georges Carmouche. Though he still had the same moustache, his hair – which I had once compared to a mop of straw – had been cropped short, and a holstered palmcannon replaced the sabre normally on his belt.

"Carmouche, you've no idea how pleased I am to see you!" I sheathed my sword.

"When I heard it was you, Professor, I reckoned you had the situation well in hand."

"Not in time to prevent this young man's death."

"Poor lad." Carmouche checked Philippe for himself. "I'd like to move the victims, but I won't if you think they might suffer as a result."

"Your caution's wise, Carmouche – one wrong move and I suspect they might all die. If the film caused the curse, would terminating the projection help them or do more harm?"

Carmouche considered the problem. "Wouldn't the projectionist see a film more than once, to adjust focus and the like? It could be similar to a poison, and this man died from exposure to a higher dose."

"Well reasoned, Carmouche!" I had been helping him hone his skills at deductive reasoning before I left on sabbatical from the museum, and was glad to see our lessons had borne fruit. "Off it is."

I held my breath and tapped a pin on the projector with my cane's lion-head pommel. The reels clicked to a halt. Harbin's still image stayed on the screen until I shuttered the magnesian flame-chamber, plunging the auditorium briefly into darkness, before officers produced their own foxfire-ambers for spot illumination.

We rejoined Katarin. "There's no easy way to tell you this . . ." I broke the news of Philippe's death and held her as she wept.

She and I had met a few years ago during the infamous *Sphinx of Ys* affair, becoming friends thereafter. When she left acting to manage Chimère Studios she hired me as a consultant, on account of my doctorate in Aigyptian archaeology and magic. I cared about her deeply, but we lived very different lives. I was a widower with a son about the same age as she, and she was a rising star trying to escape her troubled past. I had vowed I would never ask for more than her friendship, but in moments like these, I almost regretted my decision.

Carmouche shouted instructions to his men, who began unfolding stretchers for the victims. A team entered the booth to deal with Philippe's body.

I gave Katarin my handkerchief and went to examine the Mayor and Aucoin again. They were growing colder to the touch. "You must keep them warm," I told the men, though I did not know if my advice would save the afflicted.

Katarin helped the officers with the Mayor and was about to leave the theatre with them, but Carmouche held her back. "Madame Bertho, I must insist you remain here at Le Pégase. There are questions only you can answer."

Katarin grudgingly agreed.

I said nothing. I did not like Carmouche turning his attention to Katarin, but he was right. She likely had the clues we needed to solve this mystery. Blame would fall on her if all these men died. As her friend, I had to defend her reputation.

One of the officers came up to Carmouche. "Any other instructions, Inspector?"

I raised an eyebrow. *Inspector?*

"See to the theatre lights, please, Sergeant Joncour," said Carmouche.

"Why didn't you tell me you'd been promoted, dear boy?" I shook his hand. "Congratulations!"

Carmouche smiled. "It happened only two days ago. Thank you for all your help."

"I wish we had time to properly celebrate, *Inspector*, but there remains much to piece together if we are to help those who fell ill."

A few steps away, Katarin all but slumped into a theatre seat, most unlike the vibrant woman she was. I had never seen her so weak before, but then she had viewed two of the films.

Oh, Katarin! "We'll stop this, I promise," I told her.

Please, I thought, let my words be truth.

Crawling on my hands and knees, I studied the ornate hieroglyphs adorning the leg of a balcony seat, the same design on all the chairs. I could translate most of the inscriptions except for the shadowed cartouche near the base.

"More light, please, Carmouche," I said.

Carmouche knelt and held the foxfire-amber closer.

I pushed my spectacles higher on my nose. The indecipherable lines resolved into sharp symbols under the added magical illumination. "Perfect. Thank you." I pushed to my feet. "It's an ancient incantation from the Tartessos Papyrus, but a benevolent one meant to cure digestive pains."

Katarin, who was watching from an adjacent row, frowned. "Then the theatre's not at fault?" She considered her auditorium again, from the marble atlantes supporting the balcony to the dome of golden alchemical symbols. We had examined them all, but nothing among them carried markings that might cast a curse.

"That's my conclusion, yes." I steadied myself with a hand on a chair back and reclaimed my walking stick and my amber. "Your designers should have consulted me. I give quite a bone-chilling lecture on the dangers of copying magical symbols haphazardly, or so my students tell me." I had faced enough ancient ghosts and curses to know first hand.

"I would have, if you hadn't been in Lyonesse. What about a saboteur?"

"It remains a possibility."

"But *the shape of a missing fossil can be deduced by the pieces we already have*," Carmouche said, quoting what I had taught him. "The projectionist's death strongly suggests that the films are at fault."

I smiled, remembering the nights at the museum when Carmouche would help me reconstruct *archaeosphinx* skeletons while I explained how archaeological methods could be applied to detection.

"But our actors turned in the best performances of their careers," Katarin said. "The locales were breathtaking and the footage dazzling. When we screened a few scenes for our investors, oh, how they wept, cheered, and laughed! I beg you, Inspector, investigate the possibility of sabotage by Mandragora Studios."

"Do you have any proof, Madame?" Carmouche asked.

"No, but Mandragora released their own colour film a month ago: *The Thirteenth Labour of Heracles*. Everyone could tell they rushed it out. My sources tell me they dread Chimère trumping them again."

"Katarin, I understand your reluctance to blame the movies, but Carmouche is right: Philippe's death points towards the films. Maybe arcane symbols are embedded in the footage.

"Or spirits from beyond were captured on film. It's happened once before. When I was young, I sailed with the preternaturalist Henry Kitto to the Distant Orient in search of mer-lion fossils." I thought back to an incident during those golden days on black sand beaches and evenings of bonfires and shadow-plays. "Professor Kitto accidentally captured two phantom tigers in a photograph, which brought the expedition a slew of bad luck. It took months to figure out what had happened and free the trapped spirits."

Carmouche snapped his fingers. "Wait! *Sometimes a quizzing glass will magnify details the eye overlooked*," he said, quoting another of my teachings.

"You want to go over the theatre with a magnifying glass?" I asked.

"No. We overlooked the *lens*," Carmouche said. "All three films were projected through the same lens."

I understood. Camera lenses were ground from crystal, a natural receptacle for containing and concentrating magical energies. I ran through the scenario: "Suppose a saboteur etched a mystical symbol on the lens. When the symbol gets projected onto the screen might curse everyone watching! But wouldn't people see it?"

"Not necessarily," Katarin said. "Flaws in the glass don't always show up when light passes through a lens. Some distortions are subtle enough to escape notice."

Carmouche nodded. "No one would realize the faint variations in light on screen were actually a curse."

We hurried to the projection booth and examined the main crystal lens. Alas, it was flawless. The projector hadn't been tampered with, as far as we could tell.

Carmouche started rewinding the film reel. "What if we

watched these flickers elsewhere, using a different projector? If the curse begins to affect us . . ."

". . . then we can rule out both the theatre and this lens as the culprits," I said, finishing his thought. "May we use the screening room at your studio, Katarin?"

"We don't know all the risks," Katarin protested. "What if you're paralysed like the others?"

"Paralysis should happen only if I watch all three films. Didn't you watch only two? Two should be enough to establish any hidden patterns. If necessary, Carmouche can watch the final film to confirm."

"It's too dangerous." She held out her pale hands. "It eats at my strength even now."

I clasped her right hand in mine. "Which is why I must do this for you, Katarin."

Carmouche's new alembic carriage spewed sweeter fumes than the cab I had arrived in. We sped up the Promenade, heading away from the Seawall towards the docklands where the studio was. Katarin, in the front with Carmouche, gripped her seat with both hands, whereas I sat in the back with Sergeant Joncour, deep in thought.

"Madame, who worked on all three films?" Carmouche asked.

"Cast or crew?"

"Both."

"With three tight production schedules, we had to deploy all our staff evenly amongst all three films," Katarin said. "Only two cast members were involved in all three: Laure Harbin and Franchot Aucoin."

"Is that everyone?"

Katarin's cheeks pinkened. "And myself, Inspector . . . I had a cameo in each. But I'd hardly curse my own productions, would I?"

"Maybe not *intentionally*," Carmouche said. We turned west onto Old Ramp Road, heading for sea level. "Madame, you seem eager to blame Mandragora, which makes me wonder if you're deflecting attention away from your own employees. Is there, perhaps, something you aren't telling us?"

Katarin hesitated.

"By Lady Truth, Katarin, lives are at stake," I begged.

At last, she answered us. "Early in the filming of *Serpent of the Nile*, Laure's costume came apart during the seduction scene, and the camera caught her accidental exposure on film. The assistant blamed Bernard Marec for taking liberties with practicality in his wild designs. I gave her *carte blanche* to fix the costume, which she did, and we reshot the scene. However, we discovered later that the embarrassing footage had mysteriously disappeared."

"Franchot Aucoin?" Carmouche guessed.

Katarin nodded. "Aucoin stole the clip. I only found out last night when poor Laure burst out in tears at dinner. Aucoin's been using the footage to have his way with her for months. If she refused, he would ruin her career."

"That scoundrel!" I cried.

Carmouche sighed. "She should have come to the police."

"And risk a scandal? Not Laure!" Katarin insisted. "I comforted her and told her to keep a brave face, while I looked for a way to get that footage back."

The carillons around the city sounded the Hour of Tranquillitas as our horseless carriage crested the slope.

"Could Miss Harbin be taking matters into her own hands, to hurt Aucoin?" I suggested. "What if she avoided the second movie on purpose, using you as her alibi?"

Katarin shook her head. "Harm so many others, just to strike back at one man? I don't believe it."

"Who's Bernard Marec?" Carmouche asked.

"Our foremost designer, who's been with the company since it started," Katarin replied. "I put him in charge of all aspects of design for *Serpent of the Nile*."

It meshed with my memories of Marec, who struck me as a creative man who loved his work. When I worked with Marec on the set for the Aigyptian alchemy film, at Katarin's request, he often pushed for flashy, anachronistic designs while I aimed for historical authenticity. We'd joke as we fought over the research materials in the museum library, him teasing me about my lame leg and I him about his crippling arthritis.

We pulled up to the gates of Chimère Studios and exited the horseless. I mentioned my encounter with him and Miss Harbin at Le Pégase. "Maybe he's working with Harbin?"

"But Marec was only involved in one film," Katarin said. "What would be his motive?"

"We can speculate endlessly about motives, but the answers will come from the films themselves," Carmouche said. "Sergeant Joncour, take the horseless and post guards around Aucoin. Then find Bernard Marec and Laure Harbin. I'll have questions for them both when we're done here."

Joncour drove away.

Katarin led us to the screening room at Chimère, a thirty-seat theatre split by a narrow aisle, with a state-of-the-art clockwork projector hulking at the far end. Carmouche gave me a hand mounting the first reel, *A Goat in Valhalla*.

"Ever see a film in colour before, Tremaine?" Katarin asked.

"Not beyond what I saw at Le Pégase." Although Mandragora's *Thirteenth Labour* had been released in Lyonesse, between my work on the Leolithic Wonders exhibit and my guest lectures on *archoleon* extinction, I had no time to indulge in the *ciné* as I once had.

"Then be astonished or terrorized, but above all, be careful," she said.

"Shout if you need us," Carmouche added.

"And call me if she worsens, Carmouche." I took off my tailcoat and draped it around Katarin's shoulders.

"Don't forget these." Katarin took my spectacles from the coat's inner pocket and carefully fitted the pair onto my face before she closed the door.

The lights dimmed, shrouding the room in deepening shadow.

Had I chosen the right course of action? Or would I doom myself by watching these films?

I took a deep breath, gave the wind-up key one final turn, and pulled a pin, setting the reels a-spin.

The studio's production logo projected onto the screen: a chimera mascot rearing into a *rampant dexter* stance. But instead of familiar grey tones, the chimera's fur rippled gold, its goat and lion tongues flashed pink between its teeth, and the scales of the viper tail glistened jungle green. I gripped my seat in awe as the beast-heads mimicked roar, bleat, and hiss – all in frustrating silence. If only the alchemists could master sound!

A Goat in Valhalla starred Franchot Aucoin in his most famous role as 'The Goat', a licentious Hyperborean skald. Aucoin was a genius at physical comedy, proving Chimère's strategy of capitalizing on the successes of *A Goat at the World Tree* and *A Goat Among Giants* was sound: Aucoin would bring in legions of fans in this infamous role.

I watched the bawdy comedy play out. The Goat's slapstick pursuit of the Valkyries was inspired, and the clever script even made colours crucial to the plot. But I couldn't relax and simply enjoy the flicker, and searched each scene for runes and spirits.

Something *was* sapping my vitality, bit by bit, but it was so subtle that anyone not expecting it would dismiss it as tiredness from sitting still too long. I couldn't think of any spells or charms to counter it, and that worried me.

In the second act, the Goat arrived at a Silver Door covered with runes, but the shots never lingered long enough for me to decipher them. I made a note to ask Katarin if I could examine the props.

Laure Harbin appeared in the next scene, in the role of the youngest Valkyrie. Though I was struck by how well colour brought out her true beauty, now that I knew about her and Aucoin it was difficult to watch them interact on screen.

Katarin made her cameo as another Valkyrie after the final battle. In a touching scene where she collected the soul of the Goat's faithful companion, she convinced me she belonged in front of the camera. But I could not oust from my mind the fact that a Valkyrie was the spirit of a slain warrior, and that Katarin played on screen one of the dead.

I called Katarin and Carmouche back to hear my analysis. "No ghosts in the film that I could see, but I'd like to examine any props with runes on them."

Katarin nodded. "Everything's kept in Warehouse Three. Would you like to rest before we continue, Tremaine?"

"No. I won't let this curse get the best of me."

"I'll stay for this film and keep you company," Carmouche said. "Two sets of eyes are better than one."

Katarin left the room while Carmouche and I prepared the next reel: *Serpent of the Nile*.

"Just between you and me, Professor, do you think Madame Bertho resents Laure Harbin for taking her place in the limelight?" Carmouche asked quietly.

"Carmouche! She wouldn't."

"I have to consider every possibility. Maybe she doesn't *consciously* wish Miss Harbin harm, but her repressed envy might be fuel for the curse."

"Let's eliminate all other possibilities first," I said.

The chimera mascot sequence again began the film, and it was Carmouche's turn to be amazed by the brilliant colours. "Astounding!"

Laure Harbin played the lead in *Serpent of the Nile*, and her performance as the vengeful daughter of a murdered Aigyptian pharaoh captivated me from the start. Aucoin played a minor role as a jolly slave, providing comic relief in this otherwise sombre tragedy. Unlike the previous film, they never appeared in the same scene.

As the film played, my slight discomfort welled into a nameless dread; my body ached as though a year of my life had been ripped through my skin. I gasped for air, fearful that I had condemned myself to an early death.

Halfway through, when Harbin danced for the usurper's son in a *most* revealing costume, my cheeks flushed. I tried to focus on the hieroglyphs and sphinx statues in the background instead. During the bathing scene, Katarin appeared briefly as one of the handmaidens. But tantalizing glimpses aside, I was still on the hunt for the source of the curse, as was Carmouche. I didn't expect to find Hyperborean runes in a flicker set in Aigypt, but films were rarely perfect recreations of a specific time period.

Even though the film ended on a powerful note, I was relieved it was over. Carmouche weathered the film better than I did, though he kept rubbing his left shoulder as though it was sore.

Katarin returned. "Anything?"

"A few anachronisms here and there, and two hieroglyphs I'd like to revisit, but none of the same runes from the first film," I said. "Though I must say, Katarin, there *were* gross historical inaccuracies with Miss Harbin's costume."

"Ah, but no one will forget how well she wore it," Katarin said, a tinge of envy in her voice. Was Carmouche right? "It'll immortalize her . . . *if* anyone ever sees the film again."

"Only *The Lioness in Summer* left." Carmouche stroked his moustache. "Whatever it is, it should be in the first half-hour, to trigger the panic."

I nodded. "It certainly narrows down where we look next."

Then, the answer hit me like a one-tonne golem. One thing did appear in all three films . . . or more precisely, *before* them. I'd grown so used to it at the *ciné* that I forgot all about it.

"The studio mascot!" I struggled to my feet. "You filmed a new opening with a new chimera, didn't you, Katarin?"

"We had to . . . the old sequence was in black-and-white, and the animated clay model simply couldn't convey realistic colours." Her eyes widened. "Goddesses, Bernard Marec was responsible for it!"

"How did he do it?" I asked.

"Taxidermy, with hidden gears inside, I think."

Marec had built the studio mascot using animals that were once alive. The thought sent shivers through my body.

"Necromancy. It's three animal corpses stitched together to mimic a beast of magic. There's power in that." I took a deep breath. "The chimera cursed the opening sequence, which is why it took effect so early in the third movie."

Katarin understood. "That's why the pre-screened scenes weren't dangerous – the mascot clip was spliced in later! And Philippe would've seen that chimera more than anyone else. Framing, focusing, threading the film—"

"Maybe the chimera's bleeding us." I thought about the victims' bloody eyes. "Ever hear of shadow-plays? Silk screen, puppets and their shadows? They're a form of entertainment as popular in the Orient as films, but older and more ritualistic, involving prayers and offerings of food to the spirit. The first shadow cast in a shadow-play was always that of the World Tree, blessing the performance to come, and the same image closed the show."

"But instead of a World Tree blessing, the chimera cursed the films?" Carmouche asked.

"Exactly. The longer you watch a cursed film, the more life force you lose. Philippe would have taken many wounds after seeing the chimera many times but not 'bled' to death until the third film was well under way."

"Then we must destroy that chimera to break the curse," Carmouche concluded.

I grabbed my walking stick. "Take us to it, Katarin."

I'd been to the studios on numerous occasions but had never

seen inside Warehouse Three, a hulking grey building at the far end of the lot. It took longer than usual to walk there, with Katarin and I still suffering from a twice-viewed curse. Strangely, my lethargy was slowly fading while Katarin remained weak.

As Katarin unlocked the door, I took my foxfire-amber out of its cherrywood box and mentioned my returning strength.

"Same for me. What do you think it means?" Carmouche asked.

"I'm not sure," I admitted. "We may have overlooked something."

The warehouse was dark but for a glimmer of light near the other end. I held my foxfire-amber high, illuminating the rows of movie props. I recognized a few iconic set pieces in the shadows: a two-storey Tarot card depicting Ankou, the personification of Death in Graalon myth; the massive Bronze Gong of Shangdu; and the colossal clockwork griffin, star of a series where it terrorized the Great Undrowned Cities of the World.

"The light's from Marec's workshop," Katarin whispered. "That's where he keeps the chimera."

Carmouche drew his palmcannon. "Go back to your office and lock the door, Madame."

"No." Katarin was adamant. "My company, my responsibility."

"Then stay well behind us," Carmouche said. He and I led the way deeper into the warehouse, with Katarin a distance behind us. The row we walked down held props from *Lioness in Summer*: a rack of spears and mirrors from the Hall of Mirrors scene, arrayed facing each other. The mirrors magnified the light from the amber, creating the illusion of infinite corridors as we passed.

At the four-way juncture, we turned right and then left onto the adjacent row. An open work area, illuminated by a gem-dish of foxfire-ambers on a cluttered table, lay at the end of the row of obelisks and sarcophagi. Bernard Marec stood behind the table clutching a glassy object in his left hand. When he saw us, he raised his free hand and flicked his wrist.

The shelves to our left came crashing down on us. Carmouche pushed me forward in the nick of time, but I hit the ground hard, and the foxfire-amber skittered out of my hand. I glanced back: Carmouche was half buried under the avalanche of boxes. Luckily, Katarin had been far enough behind us that the shelf missed her.

Then I saw the chimera.

The beast stood in the adjacent row, its lowered goat horns undoubtedly what toppled the shelves. The lion's head clicked its jaws open in an odd staccato motion while the serpent's tail stayed motionless.

"Katarin, run!" I shouted.

She turned to flee, but the chimera darted behind her with the speed of a live lion, barring her way. When it stopped moving, it remained as still as taxidermic art.

Without turning, I called to Marec. "Are you going to kill us?"

"No one was supposed to die!" The chimera trembled in time with his shaking voice. "I only meant to steal enough life to give me back my strength. My body's breaking down, Voss. This arthritis, these failing eyes – I won't become a prisoner of my own body."

So that was it: he stole strength from others to stave off his illnesses! That explained his speed at Le Pégase.

I turned towards him. "But you took too much. People are hurt, and a young man's dead."

Would he kill us now to keep his stolen life energy? Yes, if he were desperate enough. But if the same power animated the chimera like a puppet, then the puppeteer might need to see us to attack with it.

"What of you, Tremaine?" Marec said. "Wouldn't you want to feel young again, and walk as though you'd never injured that leg? I can teach you how."

Oh, to be able to run again! How the thought tempted me. But the cost to my humanity would be too great.

"How'd you do it?" I asked. "A spell from a book in my museum?"

"Exactly. I needed a way of drawing enough life force all at once from the audience, so I made a taxidermic chimera and used stop-motion photography to simulate its life and motion. The viewer's eye interprets the fast-moving frames and thinks the dead model's alive, their energy in fact *willing* it to life."

"Clever, making the audience unwitting participants in their own doom."

I finally recognized the crystalline object in his hand: a polished lens. But if it wasn't the projector's lens . . . it must belong to the camera that had filmed the chimera.

"That's why you were at the theatre, wasn't it? The chimera's physically too far from Le Pégase, but you could capture the audience's life energy if you were there with that lens."

"You have it," Marec admitted. "I etched the spell on the lens I used to shoot the stop-motion."

The chimera model owed the illusion of motion to the ensorcelled lens, so any life force torn from the audience would flood into the crystal. That explained why Carmouche and I had regained our strength soon after the screening room viewing; the crystal lens wasn't physically close enough to trap our life energy.

"You had to come back for the chimera, didn't you? It's a linked set, the lens and the model. Brilliant."

"They say that photography's the art of stealing souls, but *my* art has stolen years of—"

As he was gloating, I reached out with my walking stick, hooked back my foxfire-amber with the lion's head and scooped it up, hiding its light. The area around me turned pitch black. I could still see Marec but hoped he had lost sight of Katarin and me.

"*—Vooossssss!*"

Under cover of darkness, I moved and crouched, trying to ignore the pain that flared in my leg. I managed just in time: the chimera crashed into the spot that I had vacated.

Marec beckoned the chimera back towards him with a gesture, and as it padded past me, its fur brushed against my hand.

Marec grabbed a glowing amber from the gem-dish and made its viper's mouth bite it. He sent the puppet back towards me, now bearing its own light source.

Time to run. Marec would have to move to keep both the chimera and I in line of sight. I uncovered the amber to light my escape and hobbled at top speed into the next aisle, fighting the ache in my leg—

—and came to a dead stop when I entered the corridor of mirrors.

Photography was the art of stealing souls, Marec had said. But I knew my anthropology well enough to know the superstition came from a similar taboo against mirrors. A mirror was said to trap a creature's soul as reflection within itself.

I turned and saw Marec coming down the shadowed aisle,

sending the puppet chimera after me. The reflection of the great beast filled the expanse of the mirror next to me.

With as much strength as I could muster, I smashed the mirror with the pommel of my walking stick moments before the beast reached me. As the mirror shards fell, the force animating the chimera peeled from its frame like a glove. The lifeless puppet skid to a halt at my feet.

"How . . . ?" Marec rushed towards the fallen chimera but didn't see a rune-carved spear extending at ankle height from under a shelf. He tripped, and the crystal lens flew from his hand, smashing to pieces against the floor. "No!"

I stepped over the inert chimera, drew the blade from its cane sheath, and put Marec at the point of my sword. He grew wizened before my eyes.

"Mirrors steal souls as well, Marec. It's said that if a mirror breaks while you're reflected in it, it damages your soul. You imbued your chimera with stolen life force, a pale imitation of a soul at best." I ground fragments of the life-stealing lens under the heel of my shoe.

Katarin and a bruised Inspector Carmouche emerged from the adjacent aisle.

"Well done, Professor," Carmouche said. "Bernard Marec, you're under arrest for murder and several counts of attempted murder." He grabbed a length of rope from a prop shelf and tied Marec's hands.

I once thought Marec had a decent man. It might have been a facade, I supposed, but I sincerely believed he had not strayed until the spectre of death changed him. For the sake of his soul, I hoped he remembered who he was, and who he could still be.

Katarin touched my face with a hand, her touch warming my cheek. "My strength seems already to be returning. Will the others recover as well?"

"In time, Katarin." I turned my head, my lips grazing her fingers. It was all I dared. "In time."

Memories in Bronze, Feathers, and Blood

Aliette de Bodard

This is what we remember: the stillness before the battle, the Jaguar Knights crouching in the mud of the marshes, their steel rifles glinting in the sunlight. And the gunshot – and Atl, falling with his eyes wide open, as if finally awakening from a dream ...

It's early in the morning, and Nezahual is sweeping the courtyard of his workshop when the dapper man comes in.

From our perches in the pine tree, we watch Nezahual. His heart is weak and small, feebly beating in his chest, and sweat wells up in the pores of his skin. Today, we guess, is a bad day for him.

The dapper man, by contrast, moves with the arrogant stride of unbroken soldiers – his gestures sure, casual – and he has a pistol hidden under his clothes, steel that shines in our wide-spectrum sight.

We tense – wondering how much of a threat he is to Nezahual. His manner is brash; but he doesn't seem aggressive.

"I'm looking for Nezahual of the Jaguar Knights." The dapper man's voice is contemptuous; he believes Nezahual to be a sweeper, someone of no importance in the household.

What he doesn't know is that there's no household, just Nezahual and us: his children, his flock of copper and bronze.

Nezahual straightens himself up, putting aside the broom with stiff hands. "I am Nezahual. What do you want?"

The dapper man shows barely any surprise; he shifts his tone almost immediately, to one of reluctant respect. "I'm Warrior

Acamapixtli, from the House of Darts. We had hoped you could give a speech on the War to our young recruits."

Nezahual's voice is curt, deadly. "You want me to teach them about war? I don't do that."

"Your experience . . ." Acamapixtli is flustered now – we wonder how much is at stake, for this speech to be given.

"I went to war," Nezahual says. He's looking upwards – not at us but at Tonatiuh the Sun-God, who must be fed His toll in blood. "Is that such a worthwhile experience?" His heartbeat has quickened.

"You don't understand. You fought with Warrior Atl, with Chimalli—" Acamapixtli's voice is disappointed.

Atl. Chimalli. The names that will not be spoken. We tense, high up in our tree. Beneath us, Nezahual's face clenches – a mask to hide his agony. His knees flex – in a moment he will be down on the ground, clutching his head and wishing he were dead. "Atl. I—"

His pain is too much; we cannot hide any longer. In a flutter of copper wings, we descend from the pine tree, settle near Nezahual: the hummingbirds on his shoulders; the parrots on the stone rim of the fountain; the lone quetzal balancing itself on the handle of the broom.

"Leave him alone," we whisper, every mech-bird speaking in a different voice, in a brief, frightening flurry of incoherence.

Acamapixtli's hands turn into fists, but he doesn't look surprised. "Your makings." His voice is quiet. "You sell them well, I hear."

We are not for sale. The other mech-birds – the copper hummingbird who leapt from branch to branch, the steel parrot who mouthed words he couldn't understand – they were born dead, unable to join the flock, and so Nezahual sold them away.

But we – we are alive, in a way that no other making will be. "Leave," we whisper. "You distress him."

Acamapixtli watches Nezahual, his face revealing nothing of what he feels. His heartbeat is slow and strong. "As you wish," he says finally. "But I'll be back."

"I know," Nezahual says, his face creased in an ironic smile.

When Acamapixtli is gone, he turns to us. "You shouldn't show yourselves, Centzontli."

He does not often call us by our name, and that is how we know how angry he is. "Your heartbeat was above the normal," we say. "You were in pain."

Nezahual's face is unreadable once more. "Yes," he says. "But it will happen again. That's of no importance. That's not what I made you for."

Nezahual made us to remember, to hold the images that he cannot bear any more. And for something else; but no matter how hard we ask, he will not tell us.

This is what we remember: the dirigibles are falling. Slowly, they topple forward – and then plummet towards the ground at an impossible speed, scattering pieces of metal and flesh in the roiling air.

We stand on the edge of the ridge, the cool touch of metal on our hips. Atl is dead. Chimalli is dead – and all the others, piled upon each other like sacrifice victims at the altar of the Sun God.

What have they died for? For this . . . chaos around us?

"Come," a voice whispers.

Startled, we turn around.

A man is standing over the piled bodies – his uniform crisp and clean, as if he were just out of his training. No, we think, as the man draws closer.

His eyes are of emeralds, his lungs of copper, his heart of steel. "Come," the mech-man says, holding out to us a gleaming hand. "Your place isn't here."

We remember a war we never fought; deaths we could never have prevented; but this, we know, has never happened.

This is a vision, not memories

It cannot be real.

"Come," the mech-man whispers, and suddenly he towers over us, his mouth yawning wide enough to engulf us all, his voice the roar of thunder. "Come!"

We wake up, metal hearts hammering in our chests.

Nezahual has shut himself in his workshop. He's making a new bird, he's said, moments before closing the door and leaving us out in the courtyard. But his hands were shaking badly, and we cannot quell the treacherous thought that this time the pain will be too strong, that he will reach out for the bottle of *octli* on the back of shelves, hidden behind the vials of blood-magic.

The youngest and most agile among us, the newest parrot – who brought memories of the blood-soaked rout at Izpatlan when he joined us – is perched on the windowsill, his head cocked towards the inside of the workshop.

We hear no noise. Just the swelling silence – a dreadful noise, like the battlefield after the dirigibles fell, like the hospital tent after the gods took their due of the wounded and the sick.

"Nezahual," we call out. But there is no answer. "Nezahual."

Footsteps echo, in the courtyard, but they do not belong to our maker. The second hummingbird takes off in a whirr of metal wings and hovers above the gate, to watch the newcomer.

It's Acamapixtli again, now dressed in full warrior regalia – the finely wrought cloak of feathers, the steel helmet in the shape of a Jaguar's maw. "Hello there," he calls up to us.

We tense – all of us, wherever we perch. None of Nezahual's visitors has ever attempted to speak to us.

"I know you can speak," Acamapixtli says. "I've heard you, remember?" He lays his steel helmet on the ground, at the foot of the tree. His face is that of an untried youth. We wonder how old he really is.

"We can speak," we say, reluctantly. The quetzal flies down from the tree, perches on the warmth of the helmet. "But we seldom wish to."

Acamapixtli's smile is unexpected. "Would that most people were as wise. Do you have a name?"

"Centzontli," we tell him.

"'Myriad'," Acamapixtli says. "Well chosen."

"Why are you here?" we ask, uncomfortable with this small talk.

Acamapixtli doesn't answer. He runs a hand, slowly, on the parrot – we let him do so, more amused than angry. "Fascinating," he says. "What powers you? Steam? Electricity?" He shakes his head. "You don't look as if you have batteries."

We don't. In every one of our chests is a vial of silver sealed with wax, containing twenty drops of Nezahual's blood. It's that blood that makes a heartbeat echo in our wires and in our plates, in our gears and in our memories. "Why are you here?" we ask, again.

Acamapixtli withdraws his hand from the parrot. "Why? For

Nezahual, of course." He shrugs, trying to appear unconcerned, but it will not work. His heartbeat has quickened. "We . . . got off to a wrong start, I feel."

"Does your speech matter so much?" we ask. And, because we cannot help feeling sorry for him: "You know what he will say, even if he comes."

"I'm not a fool, Centzontli," Acamapixtli says. "I know what he'll say. But I'm not here for what you think. I don't want Nezahual to teach the recruits about courage, or about the value of laying down one's life."

"Then—"

Acamapixtli's voice is low, angry. "I want him to teach them caution. They're eager enough to die, but a dead warrior is of no use." His eyes are distant, ageless. "We spend our youth and our blood on conquest, but we have more than enough land now, more blood-soaked earth than we can possibly harvest. It's time for this to cease."

Do you truly think so? a voice asks; and, with a shock, we recognize that of the metal man.

The sun above the courtyard is high, pulsing like a living heart. *Do you truly think so?*

What in the Fifth World is happening to us? Our nights, bleeding into our days? Our memories – Nezahual's memories – released by our minds to stain the present?

This is not meant to be.

Acamapixtli hasn't heard anything. He goes on, speaking of what the warriors who survive can build – of steamships and machines that will do the work of ten men, of buildings rising higher than the Great Pyramid of Tenochtitlan, and of a golden age of prosperity. Gradually, his voice drowns out that of the metal man, until once more we are alone in the courtyard.

But we have not forgotten. Something is wrong.

Nezahual doesn't come out, no matter how hard we wish that he would. At length, Acamapixtli grows weary of waiting for him, and takes his leave from us.

The sun sets, and still Nezahual hasn't come out. The hummingbirds and the quetzal beat against the windowpanes, trying to force their way in, but the workshop is silent – and our large spectrum sight is blocked by the stone walls.

We perch in the pine tree, watching Metzli the Moon rise in the sky, when we feel the shift: the gradual widening of the world, so strong we have to close our eyes.

When we open them again, we have a new point of view – a hummingbird's, cradled between Nezahual's bleeding hands, carrying the memories of the fording of Mahuacan, of going side by side with Atl listening for enemy voices in the marsh.

"You're hurt," we say, and the hummingbird's voice echoes in the silence of the workshop.

Nezahual waves a hand, curtly. "It's nothing. What do you think?"

He opens his hands. Tentatively, we reach out, and the hummingbird starts flapping its wings, accelerating to a blur of copper and steel.

"Beautiful," we say, though we are more worried than we will admit. "Acamapixtli came back."

"I know," Nezahual says. He walks to the entrance-curtain of the workshop, pulls it away. "Come in – all of you."

We perch where we can: the shelves are crammed with blood-magic vials, alembics and syringes, and the table littered with spare metal parts.

Nezahual is cleaning his hands under the water of the sink; he barely looks up. "I knew he would come back. He's a stubborn man. But so am I."

"It's not what you think," we say, and explain, as best as we can, the vision Acamapixtli has for the future. We can hear, all the while, the metal man laughing in the room, but we do not listen.

Nezahual wipes his hand with a cloth of cactus fibres. "I see." His voice is stiff, careful, as if he were afraid to break something. "Do you think he will come back?"

We are certain he will. Acamapixtli is a driven man. Much, in fact, like Nezahual must once have been – before war and the drive for bloodshed reduced him to, to this.

No. We must not think about it.

This is what we remember: in the silence after the battle, we wander through the mangled field of battle. We see – bullet-torn limbs, sprayed across the bloodstained mud; eyes, wide open and staring at the smoke in the sky – pain and death everywhere, and we can heal none of it.

Near the dirigible's carcass, we find Chimalli, his steel shield and his rifle lying by his side. We kneel, listen for the voice of his heart, but we know, deep inside, that his soul has fled, that he is with the Sun God now, fighting the endless war against the darkness.

And we feel it, rising in us: the burning shame of having survived when so many have given their lives.

"Now you know," a voice hisses.

We turn, slowly. The metal man is standing near us, wearing the face of a younger, eager Nezahual. It jars us, more deeply than it should, to see our maker rendered in soulless metal, his face smooth and untouched by the war. "You don't belong here."

"We don't understand," we say.

He points a clawed hand towards us, and our chests burn as if heated by fire. "Don't you?" *he whispers, and sunlight, red and hungry, flickers around him.* "I won't be deprived of what belongs to me."

"We took nothing . . ." *we say, slowly, but we know it's not about us.* "Nezahual . . ."

Malice has invaded the metal man's voice. "He was a coward. He didn't die. That was his punishment – to survive when others had not. And I will not have him and that fool Acamapixtli frighten my warriors out of dying."

"Who are you?" *we whisper.*

"Don't you know?" *the metal man asks. He straightens up, and his head is the clouds and the stars, and his hands encompass the whole of the battlefield, and his voice is the moans of the dying.* "Don't you know my name, Centzontli?"

Tonatiuh. The Sun God. He who watches over the Heavens. He who drinks the warriors' blood.

This cannot be truly be him.

The metal man laughs. "Oh, but I am here," *he says.* "Here and alive, just as you are."

We are alive. Not flesh and blood, like Nezahual or Acamapixtli – sprints and wires, copper and steel – but alive enough.

And to this god, who is not our own, we have no blood to offer. "What do you want?" *we ask.*

The metal man extends a huge hand towards us. "Come," *he says.* "Leave him."

"We do not worship you."

"You must. For, if you do not, I will tumble from the sky, and the

*world will come to its last ending," the metal man says – and his voice is
the thunder of the storm, and the vast echo of rockfall in the mountains.
"Is that what you truly wish for? I cannot be denied forever."*

*We wake up in the silence of the workshop and stare at the white eye
of the moon, wondering what Tonatiuh wants of us.*

Acamapixtli comes back on the following morning – still in his
regal uniform. Nezahual is waiting for him in the courtyard, his
face impassive, his heartbeat almost frantic.

"I apologize," Nezahual says, stiffly. "It seems we misunderstood
each other."

Acamapixtli's face goes as still as carved jade. "We're both
responsible."

Nezahual's lips stretch into a quiet smile. "Come," he says. "Let
me show you my workshop. We'll talk afterwards."

Nezahual shows Acamapixtli the spare parts lying on the table;
the vials of blood-magic and the wires and springs that make us
up. He talks about creating life – and all the while we can hear the
pain he's not voicing, the memories hovering on the edge of
seizing him.

We wish we could take it all away from him, drain him as dry as
a warrior sacrificed to Tonatiuh, but we cannot.

They speak of dirigibles made of steel and copper, of machines
that will reap the corn from the fields, and we think of the metal
man, filling his hands with the harvest of battle.

We hear his voice within us: *I will not be mocked.*

And we know that Acamapixtli's dream will have a terrible
price.

*This is what we remember: the silence of the infirmary, broken only by
the moans of the wounded. We sit on our bed, trying to feel something,
anything to assuage the pain within.*

*We are not hurt. Blood from the battlefield covers us, but it's not
ours, it has never been ours.*

*Beside us, an Eagle Knight with a crushed lung is dying – his breath
rattling in his chest, a horrible sound like bone teeth chattering against
one another.*

*We try to rise, to help him, to silence him – we no longer know. We
try to move; but our hands are limp, our fingers will not respond.*

We watch – even our eyes cannot close – as the man's face becomes slack; and by the bed is Tonatiuh, his steel hands reaching for the dying man, enfolding him close, as a mother will hold a child.

He looks up, and smiles with golden, bloody teeth. "So he will make his speech, won't he?" He shakes his head. "Does he not know what happens to those who defy me?"

In a single, fluid gesture, he rises from the man's bed and reaches out towards us, his hands extending into steel claws, pricking the flesh of our metal skin.

We watch. We cannot move.

The morning of the speech grows bright and clear. For the first time, we wake up after Nezahual, our blood-vials beating madly against our copper chests. We still feel the steel fingers reaching for our chests – to tear out our hearts.

Nezahual is sitting in the workshop, his head between his hands, dressed in his best clothes: an embroidered cotton suit, with a quetzal-feather headdress. He is shaking; and we can't tell if it's from fear or from anticipation.

We hop to the table and perch by his side – the quetzal cocking its head, making a soft cooing sound.

Nezahual forces a smile. "It will be all right, Centzontli."

We fear it won't. But before we can speak, a tinkle of bells announces the arrival of Acamapixtli, still in full Jaguar regalia, his steel helmet tucked under one arm.

"Ready?" His smile is eager, infectious.

Nezahual runs a hand in his hair, grimacing. "As ready as I will ever be. Let's go."

He is walking towards the door of the workshop – halfway to the courtyard – when we feel the air turn to tar, and hear the laughter from our dreams.

No.

Did you think I could be cheated, Nezahual? Tonatiuh's voice echoes in the workshop.

We rise, in a desperate whirr of wings, and in our fear, our minds scatter, becoming that of five hummingbirds, of one quetzal, of two parrots, struggling to hold themselves together.

"I, I, I—"

"We—"

"We have to—"

Nezahual has stopped, one hand going to his sword, his face contorted in pain. "No," he says. "I didn't think I could cheat you. But nevertheless—"

Tonatiuh laughs and laughs. *You are nothing,* he whispers. *Worth nothing. You will not make this speech, Nezahual. You will not make anything more.*

Behind us, the table shakes; the metal scraps rise, spinning in the air like a cloud of steel butterflies – all sharp, cutting edges, as eager to shed blood as any warrior.

Nezahual stands, mesmerized, watching them coalesce into the air, watching them as they start to spin towards him.

We watch. We cannot move, as we could not move in the vision.

Acamapixtli has dropped his helmet and is reaching for his sword; but he will be too late. Nezahual's knees are already flexing, welcoming the death he's courted for so long.

The thought is enough to make us snap together again: our minds melding together, narrowing to an arrow's point.

"Nezahual!" we scream, throwing ourselves in the path of the whirling storm.

It enfolds us. Metal strikes against metal; copper grinds against the wires that keep us together, all with a sickening noise like a dying man's scream.

I have warned you not to interfere, Tonatiuh whispers. The sunlight, filtered through the entrance curtain, is red and angry. *You are a fool, Centzontli.*

Something pricks our chests – the claws from the visions, probing into our flesh.

We have no flesh, we think, desperately, but the claws do not stop, they reach into our chests. They close with a crunch.

Within us, glass tinkles, and shatters into a thousand pieces. Our blood-vials. Our hearts, we think, distantly, as the world spins and spins around us . . .

Blood leaks out, drop by drop, and darkness engulfs us, grinning with a death's head.

This is what we remember: before the battle, before the smoke and the spattered blood, before the deaths – Atl and Chimalli sit by the camplight, playing patolli *on a board old enough to have seen the War of Independence. They're arguing about the score – Atl is accusing Chimalli of cheating, and Chimalli says nothing, only laughs and laughs without being able to stop. Atl takes everything much too seriously, and Chimalli enjoys making him lose his calm.*

They're young and carefree, so innocent it hurts us – to think of Atl, falling under the red light of the rising sun; of Chimalli, pierced by an enemy's bayonet; of the corpses aligned in the morgue like so much flesh for barter.

But we remember: our curse, our gift, our blessing; our only reason for existing.

Our eyes are open, staring at the ceiling of Nezahual's workshop. Our chests ache, burning like a thousand suns.

We are not dead.

Slowly, one by one, we rise – and the quetzal dislodges a pair of bleeding hands resting over its chest.

Nezahual. You're hurt, we think, but it's more than that.

It's not only his hands that bleed, and no matter how hard we look, we cannot see a heartbeat anywhere. His chest does not rise; his veins do not pulse in his body. Metal parts are embedded everywhere in his flesh: the remnants of the storm that he could not weather.

We are covered in blood – blood that cannot be our own. We still live – a thing which cannot be.

"Come," whispers Tonatiuh.

He stands in the doorway of the workshop, limned by the rising sun – metal lungs and metal hands, and a pulsing metal heart. "There is nothing left. Come." His hands are wide open – the clawed hands which broke us open, which tore our hearts from our chest.

"Why should we?"

"There is nothing left," Tonatiuh whispers.

"Acamapixtli—" He is lying on the ground, just behind Tonatiuh, we see: his heart still beats, albeit weakly. We struggle against an onslaught of memory – against images of warriors laughing at each other, sounds of bullets shattering flesh, the strong animal smell of blood pooling into the dark earth.

"Do you truly think he will make a difference?" Tonatiuh asks. "There will always be dreamers, even among the warriors. But nothing can change. The world must go on. Come."

There is nothing left.

But we know one thing: Nezahual died, and it was not for nothing. If Acamapixtli could not make a difference, somehow Nezahual could. Somehow . . .

"It wasn't Acamapixtli," we whisper, staring at the god's outstretched hands. "It was never Acamapixtli – it was what Nezahual made in his workshop."

Tonatiuh doesn't answer. His perfect, flawless face is devoid of expression. But his heart – his heart of steel and wires – beats faster than it should.

Mech-birds. Beings of metal and copper, kept alive by heart's blood – and, even after the blood was gone, kept alive by the remnants of the ritual that gave us birth, by the memories that crowd within us – the spirits of the dead keening in our mind like a mourning lament.

"You fear us," we whisper, rising in the air.

"I am the sun," Tonatiuh says, arrogantly. "Why should I fear birds that have no hearts?"

"You fear us," we whisper, coming closer to him, stained with Nezahual's dying blood.

His claws prick us, plunge deep into our chests.

But there is nothing there. No vial, nothing that can be grasped or broken any more. "You are right," we say. "We have no hearts."

"Will you defy me?" Tonatiuh asks, gesturing with his metal hands.

Visions rise – of bodies, rotting in the heat of the marshes, of torn-out limbs and charred dirigibles, of Atl, endlessly falling into death.

But we have seen them. We have fought them, night after night.

We are not Nezahual. War does not own us; and neither does blood; neither do the gods.

We do not stop.

"I am the sun," Tonatiuh whispers. "You cannot touch me."

"No," we say. "But you cannot touch us, either."

We fly out, into the brightness of the courtyard, straight through Tonatiuh, who makes a strangled gasp before vanishing into a hundred sparkles – the sunlight, playing on the stone rim; the fountain whispering once more its endless song.

Oh, Nezahual.

We would weep – if we had hearts, if we had blood. But we have neither, and the world refuses to fold itself away from us, and grief refuses itself to us.

A shuffling sound, from behind – Acamapixtli drags himself out of the workshop on tottering legs, bleeding from a thousand cuts, staring at us as if we held the answers. "Nezahual . . ."

"He's gone," we say, and his bloodied hands clench. We wish for tears, for anger, for anything to alleviate the growing emptiness in our chests.

Acamapixtli smiles, bitterly. "All for nothing. I should have known. You can't cheat the gods."

We say nothing. We stand, unmoving, in the courtyard, watching the sunlight sparkle and dissolve in the water of the fountain until everything blurs out of focus.

This is what we see: a flock of copper birds speaking to the assembled crowd – of machines, of arched bridges and trains over steel tracks, of the dream that should have been Nezahual's.

This is what we see: a city where buildings rise from the bloodless earth, high enough to pierce the heavens; a city where, once a year, a procession of grave people in cotton clothes walks through the marketplaces and the plazas of bronze. We see them make their slow way to the old war cemeteries and lay offerings of grass on the graves of long-dead warriors; we see an entire nation mourning its slaughtered children under the warm light of the silenced sun.

This is what we wished for.

The Return of Chérie

Nisi Shawl

Hissing gently as if to attract the sky's attention, the *Okondo* turned in the evening air with lover-like deliberation. Lisette watched from the new warehouse's loading dock as it left her. Up there the sun still shone, flashing brightly on the gondola's rear window, gilding the balloon's purple sides. A gigantic cacao pod, rubber-backed barkcloth molded over aluminium girders and rings: when last she lived in Everfair, way back in the nineteenth century, such an apparatus was no more than a dream. But now she had ridden one.

Away down the Ulindi River's long, lush valley the dirigible floated, freshly loaded with tin and tea, cocoa and hemp, the region's produce. Leopold's guns posed it not the slightest danger; they were gone. The flight to the lowland ports would be as uneventful as her voyage here. This was 1914. The tyrant had been vanquished for almost ten years.

Lisette need have no concern. Yet she yearned after the departing dirigible till it became indistinguishable from the periwinkle dusk. Or did she yearn for another?

A cool wind fell upon her, descending out of the Mitumba Mountains. Someone wrapped a soft shawl over her shoulders. It was Fwendi – her brass hand glinted in the lantern light spilling from the warehouse door. With the faintest of ratcheting whirs, Fwendi's hand released the woven cashmere to settle against Lisette's still-smooth neck. "*Merci, mon ami.*"

"*Pas du tout,*" Fwendi replied. Though they'd traveled extensively – Europe, Middle Asia, and the US – French remained their shared tongue, serving as their secret language. As it had served with Daisy in Lisette's vanished youth.

"You ought to come inside," Fwendi scolded, continuing in French. "Come to the hotel." Lisette wanted to rebel against this bullying nursemaidery, but in truth there was nothing left to see, the sky darkening so swiftly here, mere kilometers from the equator.

Nonetheless, she affected an injured air. "As you desire, *Maman*," she replied – a jest, since she had fifteen years more than Fwendi, according to the best reckoning the refugee had been able to provide. She bowed her head and stalked inside.

Fwendi ignored Lisette's play-acting with the practice of years. Unfussed, she contrived to be first to reach the lantern and remove it from the long chain dangling off the high rafter. Her own cloak she looped over one arm – the one of flesh.

Neither had ever before come to Kalima. Fwendi assumed the lead, taking them down the bluff and into town, past the homes of farmers and mechanics, by workshops that on the women's way to the warehouse had been loud with the clang of hammers on hot metals or heavy with the reek of rubber, vertiginous with the incense of volatile chemicals. Now all these establishments sat silent, doors shut but windows open, airing out in preparation for the morning.

The "hotel" could be distinguished from Kalima's other houses by its three storeys and its condescending facade, like that of an American plantation house. The Washingtons, Negro immigrants from the Carolinas, owned the place and occupied its ground floor. They rented rooms to such travelers as visited Kalima without alliances of kin or trade among the local Blacks.

Lisette had alliances in this neighborhood and had called on them. But not for shelter.

They climbed the stairs to the top storey. Lisette occupied her own room; Fwendi followed her in and used the lantern to light the small stoneware lamp beside her bed. A pleasant warmth lingered from the day. Lisette's trunk brooded in one corner, upright, like a wardrobe. A valise, open on a wicker chair, offered gloves, scarves, handkerchiefs, and stockings to wear on the morrow, when she would have to decide . . . what she would not now think of. Lisette removed her hat and suspended it from a peg beside a looking glass. A blue-glazed water pitcher stood on a washstand near one white-curtained window. Shades of barkcloth curled behind the curtains, ready to unroll. Altogether, it was as comfortable a home as she had occupied in years.

"*'Soir*," she said carelessly as Fwendi retired to her own room, which she shared with Rima. Those two did not harmonize. In moments, as Lisette had expected, she heard a sharp rapping on her door.

"Enter," she said. Not in French. This newest member of her makeshift, itinerant household spoke only English.

Rima – Serenissima Bailey – blew through the opening door like a storm. Her namesake, the heroine of *Green Mansions*, had been described as fragile, small, demure, but that was not this tall nineteen-year-old, strong and swift as a cyclone. Rima's long brown shins thrust impatiently free of her dress's slit panels. Her half-bare arms reached for Lisette, crossed behind her back and pulled her close to murmur mock-angry reproaches for her late return to the hotel: had she planned to stay out all the night?

Lisette sighed and avoided the offered kiss. "No. But—"

"But you wasn't meanin' to spend time with me, was you? Naw, I thought not." Rima dropped to sit on the bed in an attitude that ought to have been graceless: face jammed in cupped hands, elbows dug into her knees, feet planted wide.

"Of course I was. But not in my room. Not alone." Not in Everfair, with its memories. Its possibilities.

A shy smile played over Rima's berry-dark lips. "It was good, though, wasn't it? What we done?" Her enchantingly slanted eyes peeked upwards. "Don't make neither one of us no bull dagger." The last in a worried tone – the girl still feared social consequences due to their encounters; these would have been harsh, indeed, in the coastal Florida village where Lisette first found her. Even in cosmopolitan New York, where Lisette had introduced her protégée to the emerging literary crowd, the code was strict. One had to be careful . . .

"You'd best go to your room."

"Yes'm." Rima rose to leave and turned her back, posture suddenly elegant as a hussar's. Perversely, Lisette wished her to stay. In that instant Rima whirled around and crossed the room in two strides, bending to embrace her. "Promise! Promise!" she demanded, pressing her brow against Lisette's as if seeking to force her way into her mind.

What should I promise? Lisette wondered, but she knew what was needed: a vow of love. A vow she could not bring herself to make.

Morning. Breakfast was included in her arrangement with the Washingtons, but they provided it between the uncivilized hours of five and nine. Lisette girded herself for the day alone: she had dismissed Rima well before midnight.

Matty awaited her on the net-veiled verandah, pouring chocolate into a large, ugly cup. The smell of it had lured her to this table spread with a clean enough cloth and set with fresh bread, jam, curls of butter in ice, and a revolting pyramid of small, dead fish.

In blessed silence, Matty filled her cup, too, and pulled forward a chair for her. As Lisette sipped and composed herself she noted that he placed three of the fish on his plate before assuming his own seat. Well, he was a Scotsman.

"*Four.*"

"The Capitol Mote is next Market Day, and you'll be there in plenty of time," he told her needlessly. He must mean to soothe her. "Relax and enjoy your holiday."

Matty's hatred of Leopold was legendary. Someday soon the King would die – perhaps when the Germans and Allies laid waste to Belgium on their way to invading France. What would Matty do once his old enemy was no more?

She should tell him her official reason for stopping here – which was almost the real one. Matty, too, belonged to the Fabian Society and had Everfair's interests at heart. He would comprehend.

Instead, she asked whether he thought her understudy capable of performing Lisette's part. In many ways Rima was ideal. Her darker complexion needed little or no make-up compared to the cosmetics with which Lisette disguised the European portion of her heritage.

"She brings to the stage a certain—" Matty hesitated diplomatically "—a definite *verve*."

Lisette glanced up suspiciously from a critical examination of her cuticles. "I have been coaching her voice."

"No, she'll be fine – brilliant, quite...quite active; I've watched—"

Ah! It was *Lisette's* self-regard he was wary of damaging. She relaxed. "Fwendi is pleased also."

At this, Matty blushed. Fwendi was twenty-six, and he was all of fifty-four. One year younger than Daisy.

Dirigibles could fly by night, given a sufficiently bright moon. They traveled sometimes as many as 120 kilometers in an hour. If Daisy had received Lisette's message immediately upon the *Okondo* mooring in Kisangani, she could well have boarded the vessel for its return trip. Allowing four hours to unload, Lisette had calculated the airship's arrival here to be at ten this morning. Then she had laughed at these calculations, so obviously her own desires disguising themselves as reliable estimates.

With Fwendi at her side and Rima trailing sulkily behind them, Lisette proceeded back through Kalima to the warehouse, considering how unlikely it was for Daisy even to have been awake at such an hour – 2 a.m., assuredly, by the time the dirigible tied up to the Kisangani tower.

It was 10.45 a.m. In daylight the town's streets were filled with people. A cluster of toddlers stared straightforwardly at Fwendi's hand – such prostheses were uncommon now the atrocities necessitating them had ceased. The attention in no way discomfited Fwendi: she obliged her impromptu audience with a little show, rolling her sleeve high and spinning her hand like a weathercock at the end of her beautiful, glittering arm. This latest model included flint and steel: she struck sparks with thumb and ring finger, and one chubby boy tried to imitate her, squealing with frustration.

A shadow passed. Lisette looked up: the *Okondo*! Her heart sped, and she slipped eagerly through the ring of children. Some seconds later, her entourage was back beside her. The dust their boots kicked up hurried before them, whipped by a little wind. Worried, Lisette scanned the clouds, the mountainsides, but saw no sign of turbulence in the sky's upper reaches.

Ten wooden stairs, then a gravel track, then a few more stairs, but these mere indentations in the bluff's earth buttressed with sections chopped from some poor tree's trunk. She fell behind Fwendi – age had its advantages, but physical alacrity was not one of them. On the flat area above, she regained her lead. Rima continued to trail them both.

Again the glad shade. Dark against the dazzling sky, the dirigible hovered, now merely seven meters above her head, lassoed to the mooring post.

Freight comprised the line's primary business; it wasn't equipped for passengers. She recalled the process by which she had disembarked yesterday. Perhaps she shouldn't watch Daisy subjected to such indignities? A makeshift sling had lowered Lisette to the ground, or fairly close – only a bit over a meter she'd had to jump as the sling swayed and shifted with the balloon's small but constant movements.

Too late, though. A black square opened in the gondola's tight-woven bottom. Leaf-wrapped bundles cascaded out, followed by crew swarming down ropes and leaping to stack them neatly at the dock's far end, nearest the warehouse. They were all clad in colorless loose shirts and wide trousers, shod in sandals. It took Lisette more time than she would have expected to recognize that one of them was Daisy.

But at fifty-five years, what was the dear woman thinking? On her feet without recollection of rising, Lisette ran over the stones of the loading dock to her, to the one she had no right to ask anything of, who had joined her here anyhow at the first invitation – the first direct communication between them in over a decade.

Daisy had seen her, of course. She said something unintelligible to her companions and approached Lisette with the free-limbed gait of an adolescent boy. Her hair, still dark, had been cut shockingly short and restrained at her neck with a ribbon the greenish-blue of a redwing's eggs; a matching length circled her throat. Only faint lines creased her well-tanned brow and bracketed her thin, smiling mouth. That was all Lisette had time to note before being crushed in an embrace so tight it threatened suffocation.

Released quickly, she would have staggered, but Daisy kept a hand on one shoulder, kneading it with a kitten's loving fierceness.

Lisette blinked and saw that tears filled Daisy's eyes also. "You came," she pronounced, rather stupidly.

"Naturally." Daisy attempted to give Lisette a look of severe reproach down her long nose, which served merely to lower the spillways of her lashes. Then both wept openly a short while, laughing as well.

They wiped their cheeks. Lisette made the introductions and they walked to the hotel. Rima displayed an awful, forced cheerfulness, pacing backwards along the uneven roads, chatting amiably with her rival. Who seemed as youthful as ever she had been. Her work on the dirigible aided her, she claimed, in her writing.

Rima answered Daisy's questions about the Continent when Lisette couldn't bring herself to speak. This occurred frequently.

Fwendi had a parasol, which she clamped in her brass hand and held to shade herself and Lisette. By the time they reached the hotel the sun was noon-high and broilingly hot, even so near the mountains. Rima's determined gaiety had mercifully subsided and the party mounted the steps in silence. In the dim entryway, the eldest Washington girl offered them luncheon, then, when that was turned down, iced tea, which they gratefully accepted.

Once more to the verandah. Lisette was tempted to stretch out upon the wood and raffia divan, but knew better. The straight-backed chairs kept her head up, her chin becomingly high. Matty had intercepted the tray and bore it out to them. The drink's chill revived her somewhat. Ice also had been unknown formerly in Everfair.

"Ah, Fwendi, I need your opinion of a change in the script I'm contemplating making." Pathetic, the lengths to which the man went. Really, despite his help with the Germans in Cairo, there was no need for him to have come on this trip at all, but Lisette could not grudge him whatever comfort he found in the girl's company.

"Yes? A change in the play? You'd like to read a passage to me, perhaps?" Fwendi rose from her seat on the divan. "In your room?"

Matty followed her within as if mesmerized.

Rima remained. "Well. I imagine y'all have plenty things you wanna talk about." But she made no move to depart. Uneasiness thrummed in the silence like a hidden insect.

From above came an interruption to the awkwardness: Fwendi's voice. "Rima! Rima, come up here – to our room – please?" With apologies for giving them what they wanted, the actress at last left Daisy and Lisette alone with one another.

Perhaps . . . perhaps only a couple of meters separated them now. Jackie had died last August, in Ireland. Did Daisy still mourn him?

Of course she did. But how deeply? For how long?

"I was told you've been entrusted with—"

Lisette shook her head, a warning that they could too easily be overheard, and crooked her finger. Daisy comprehended. She closed her mouth and crossed the verandah's wide planks to Lisette's side.

"Make-believe you love me." Muffled laughter in Lisette's hair. "What is the joke in that?" she asked, pretending offended dignity.

"Oh, *chérie*—"

Lisette found herself on her feet, drawn up into Daisy's arms. Balancing on her tiptoes, she put her lips to one ear. "Now we whisper." She shut her eyes.

"Yes. *Chérie*—"

Lisette wanted only to listen – to the fast beat of Daisy's heart, to her soft, rough breathing – but she must speak, and quickly. "Others may intrude at any moment." Their hosts. Or Rima, who'd left them so reluctantly. "I have received secret offers for the Mote from both Allies and Entente. Let us pledge an assignation to discuss them in detail."

"Yes." The poet bent over Lisette's other ear. "Where can we meet? *Chérie* – how soon?"

Cool and blue, the night fell swiftly. A smudge of a moon hung low over the Ulindi. Lisette set the lamp carefully atop her trunk and turned it low.

Europeans told their secrets inside locked rooms. Lisette had learned other ways, here and in her journeying. She saw their merits: if one had a clear view of the surroundings and an evident absence of spies, it would seem one might say anything.

But the lips could be read. Unsure from whom they hid – a matter of concern mainly to the Entente and Allies – Lisette was content to meet Daisy inside, in her own quarters, privately. As of old. As she had often dreamt of doing again.

A steady, even knock on her door. "Enter," she called.

Daisy had changed out of her work costume into a slightly more conventional garment: a gown like a loose duster, which covered her knees but ended well above her ankles. Which were still sturdy but neat.

The room's one chair was empty. Daisy took it, and Lisette sat on her bed. The windows were opened, but their shades were down, their curtains closed.

In the lamp's honeyed light Daisy regarded her expectantly.

How to start? Not, Lisette felt sure, with their personal concerns: not the too-insistent memories evoked by Everfair's sights and sounds and scents; not the reasons for Lisette's apparent abandonment of the country they had helped to found – which of course she had continued to serve, but never mind that now . . . or perhaps it would be best, after all . . .

"I've been . . ." Hesitatingly, Lisette chronicled the labors her travels as an actress had disguised: the training received from Matty, then the lessons of her own invention. The clandestine calls on Russian and Italian diplomats. The cipher she and Fwendi had devised, based on the girl's half-forgotten native tongue. The periodic reports made to Jackie – painful, but necessary. And how she had continued gathering intelligence since his death.

"So. He told me he'd seen you more than once. Not why." The keen eyes were turned away. Lisette couldn't see whether they sorrowed. Would that have helped, though? She'd only want to know who they sorrowed for.

The rest of her obligations, she reminded herself. Take care of those and she would be at liberty . . . "The French, British, and Russians offer us the lands between Kalemie, Lubumbashi, and Dilolo – an approximate triangle."

"German territory, isn't it?" As Lisette had expected, Daisy took her position as the Mote's poet seriously. In that capacity she must hold in her awareness all Everfair's concerns, then present the Mote with her peculiar view of them.

"It is German," Lisette affirmed. "And they would establish embassies, accord us complete diplomatic recognition."

Daisy nodded. "But what do they ask for all that?"

Lisette heaved a sigh. "Much." She enumerated each item on her fingers. "They would like access to our minerals, our expertise with airships. Our rubber."

"But we have no rubber! Or hardly any. All right. What else?"

"A staging area for the campaign against Cameroon. A blind

eye turned toward breaching the neutrality principles of the Berlin Conference in any and all African colonies." She switched hands. "Our medicines – our antimalarials, especially."

A snort of disbelief. "They'll have difficulty abiding by the proper administration protocols." Daisy assumed an expression of annoyed superiority. "'A load of superstitious nonsense!' I know the attitude; I doubt they'll get any good out of *that* proviso.

"You haven't mentioned—"

"Soldiers. Yes. And mechanics. And bearers."

Daisy gasped. "No! We *could* not."

"As you say."

"The Blacks – these politicians want to make slaves of them, to repeat Leopold's cruelties anew, to—No."

Slaves of "them", thought Lisette. *Not of "us". Yet, not of "you", either. "Them".* But she said nothing.

Daisy was silent, too, though only for a bit. Then: "You met also with the Germans?"

Lisette nodded. "Yes. They also would like Everfair to commit to fight upon their side. We could declare ourselves neutral, outwardly, and in return for supplies and aid in transportation we would receive—" she breathed a soft huff of laughter "—the same territory as we would from the Entente."

Daisy laughed, too. "Well, neither has a legitimate claim, though I suppose theirs is more generally accepted."

"And in exchange the Germans and Allies require the same materials and expertise as do the French and Entente."

Lisette leaned forward to impart the information Daisy would desire most. "Interestingly, the Governor of Tanzania is for real peace. At least upon this continent – he has no influence on European events. What his Fatherland proposes he agrees to, for his domain and ours as well. Sans treaty violations and soldiers."

Daisy rose to her feet. "Well then, do we truly need to discuss how I ought to present these offers? Peace or war? Freedom or bondage? Promises broken or promises kept? Our answer is obvious." She lifted a hand to rake her curls; catching her fingers on the ribbon restraining them, she tugged at it impatiently.

Almost against her will Lisette rose also and reached to help her. The knot persisted. "Sit," she told Daisy, as if the other woman were a child or a dog, and found herself dragged back down onto the bed in arms irresistible, smelling as before of lime and sweet herbs.

"*Cherie, cherie,* do you want me again . . . still . . ."

Why else had she come so far? With her teeth Lisette renewed her attack upon the stupid ribbon and at last it loosened and dropped to the counterpane. The sandals were off in a trice, and Daisy's gown was just as easy to remove. Underneath it, time had treated her body kindly – kindlier even than the drying sun and wind had treated her tender face.

Lisette's turn. All her faults would be visible – how well she knew them, and how professionally she took them into account. But what use caution here and now? She stripped – tossed her blouse at the abandoned chair, snaked out of her skirt where she lay, shoving it aside to the floor. Lifting her chemise—

"No. Stop. Let me – please?"

She felt her arms drift to her sides. With a mother's solicitude, Daisy divested Lisette of the last of her defenses: stockings and slippers, silk and leather and lace. And then skin touched skin: no hindrance. Only unsparing pleasure and unremitting happiness.

Rattling metal. It woke her. The bed was crowded – ah, but with Daisy, not Rima. Lisette settled closer to her back, but that noise – again! Louder – she turned her head toward the source.

In her room's door the handle shook. "Lisette?" Rima's urgent voice. "Lisette! You oughta open this."

Behind her the bed dipped and rustled as Daisy shifted. Rolling to lie flat, she met Lisette's eyes with a frown barely discernible in the room's dimness.

Bam! The door shook in its frame. "Lisette! Lemme in! Fwendi ain't been to our room at all last night and I—"

Furious, Lisette jumped to the floor, but Daisy sat up, reaching to restrain her. "Wait." She donned her gown and Lisette saw her wisdom. She called to Rima, who was still haranguing her from outside, and assumed her own peignoir before turning the suddenly subdued door's handle.

"Awww . . ." Rima hovered in the entranceway. "I apologize. I didn't know y'all was sleepin together."

Of course she had. "Nonsense. But what's this about Fwendi?

What time is it?" Lisette spared a glance for the shades, which showed light around their edges. Morning.

"It's around six thirty, seven."

Up again so early. Mother of god. "And you saw her when? Have you informed the Washingtons?" She gestured for Rima to come in. The passageway was empty. She closed the door and once more locked it.

They had supped together – Lisette could not recall on what, but that made no difference. At the appointed hour she had excused herself from the verandah and gone to her room, to be joined by Daisy after a suitable interval.

"It was my night for a bath," said Rima. "So I left 'em together and didn't think nothin' of havin' a couple hours to myself up there since she woulda waited for me to be finished. And then I come over all relaxed and I lain down on the blankets and next you know, here I am."

Blessedly, the Washingtons had not yet been told. There was a simple answer to the mystery.

But at Matty's door Lisette's discreet scratching elicited no response. She opened it. The room was empty, the bed undisturbed. She entered, and Rima followed her unsolicited. "So they's together?"

Ignoring her, Lisette looked for a note of explanation. The washstand bore only toiletry items. On a spindly-legged table was a stack of three books. Pegs supported a nightshirt and dressing gown, and a coat she couldn't remember him wearing. Not his favorite. A Gladstone bag sat behind the bed's head. Lisette didn't examine its contents; its presence alone argued that Matty had not departed. The other belongings supported the bag's assertion.

The top book purported to be sermons on the virtues of national pride, an unlikely selection given Matty's tastes. The second, more understandable, related to chivalrous legends of the British Isles. The third appeared to have been bound blank. Drawings and sketches filled its pages.

"You would have appeared rather fetching in that little number," said Daisy, peering over Lisette's shoulder. She had entered the room also. The "little number" in question was an abbreviated grass skirt wisping away mid-thigh, worn in this fanciful representation with a brief bodice – really, no more than a brassiere – made of orchids.

"It needed modification to render it practical for the stage," she replied, shutting the covers. Matty's head was ever in the clouds . . . "What do you look at so intently, Rima?"

"Nothin' but another a them airships comin' here every day." The actress turned from the window, letting go of the curtain. Could Matty, that dreamer, could he possibly have schemed to depart undetected? Thus the display of a brush set, a razor—

Lisette paused only to clothe herself presentably before dashing across town once again to the mooring platform, Rima and Daisy in her train. To think that she had suspected Rima, the Washingtons even, of spying upon her – and not him.

Scrambling up the steps, she groaned at her idiocy. Matty need not even travel far to collapse the negotiations' secrecy. There was a wireless in Bukavu, only 300 kilometers east. Though why hadn't he sent a message when they passed through on their way here?

The platform was deserted. All activity concentrated itself in the field's far end, on the warehouse's loading dock. Lisette hesitated, unsure what next to do. Daisy continued toward the workers – comrades of hers, perhaps.

The newly arrived dirigible loomed overhead, a dark eminence. Not the *Okondo* but its brother vessel, she believed: the older and bulkier *Mbuza*.

"You wanna tell me what you think is goin' on?" asked Rima.

Lisette had treated the girl unfairly – though was this sufficient reason to trust her now? "I'm sorry, but to do that is impossible – unless I were to kill you afterwards. Affairs of state."

She scanned the people carrying parcels into the warehouse and saw no sign of Matty from where she stood. She walked closer. Daisy spoke Zande with a man of lesser height than the others. When Lisette questioned him, he kept smiling while managing to look worried. "We don't expect passengers, no," he said. "But it wouldn't be too much trouble to accommodate them, if they are ready immediately?"

"Thank you. We'll see, it may not be necessary." Could this man be a foreign agent also? Would Lisette need an excuse to search the gondola for herself? But that would mean the whole crew was in on the deception.

The warehouse was of bricks, built tall to retain coolness, and painted in intricate designs. Lisette passed through its open iron gates to a dark interior three times her height. Five-meter arches pierced its walls, admitting the morning's every breeze.

"Look for Matty here. And Fwendi," she added, remembering Rima's original concern. Could he have made the girl his hostage? She sent Daisy to search above the loose-planked ceiling and split the ground floor with the American.

Gray bundles rested in numbered racks, redolent of chocolate. She passed a column of baskets pungent with the odors of spices which clamored at each other over thinner, subtler aromas: tea and milled ores. She gazed up and down the branching aisles and saw no one till she returned to where the women and men of the *Mbuza* were unloading their cargo. They paused momentarily in their work, but she waved off their help.

In the opposite corner she found Rima peering doubtfully into a cask of palm oil. "If either of them is in there, they are dead," said Lisette, settling the cask's lid firmly in place.

"So you figure they alive?"

Fwendi knew well how to take care of herself, and Matty was much the shorter of the two—

"Lisette!" Daisy walked toward them quickly, almost running. "I—Come. Please—quietly? Please. Ekibondo was right; I'd have missed this if he hadn't told me where to look." She whispered the words, leading them away from where a ladder clung to the west wall, away from all the walls, to the building's center. Here bricks had been set in the tamped-earth floor. They formed a rectangle filled with irregular diamond shapes. At its center gaped a large golden hole.

Lisette knelt and peered down into a room brimming with light. Slowly, as her eyes adjusted, the glow resolved into bales of glittering hay interspersed with splintered glimpses of something else, a shining substance – glass?

"They bring it down from the Ruwenzori Mountains and store it underneath, here – there's a larger entrance outside—"

"Bring *what* down from the Ruwenzoris? Store *what* underneath?" asked Lisette, struggling to comprehend the scene before her – below her.

"Ice," said Rima. "They keepin' it frozen in the ground and

then ship it over to Kisangani and where people need it. You and me seen the same thing up north in America, ice cut in winter for usin' in the summer."

Lisette wondered what any of this had to do with Matty and Fwendi's absence. Then she saw them off to the room's left, stretched out on a bank of the yellow hay, wrapped in a single blanket. They were sleeping. Fwendi's brass arm reflected the light of the lamp hanging on a post at their heads – no sleeve covered the join between her brown skin and the metal levers, screws, pumps and pistons. As Lisette looked down, enthralled, the covering slid further off to reveal the girl's shoulder, ribs and strong, scarred back. With half-conscious fingers she stroked Matty's smooth-shaven cheek before reaching for the blanket, which eluded her several times. To make sure she caught it, Fwendi opened her eyes, and saw them watching.

Lisette blushed. "*'Jour*," she said, managing to sound casual, as if encountering Fwendi on her way to breakfast. In response she received the most extraordinarily joyous grin.

The covering for this revealing hole must be nearby. Lisette lifted her dazzled eyes to search for it in the dark there above.

"You are awake, my darling?" With feelings of extreme awkwardness Lisette heard Matty address Fwendi in quite intimate terms. Evidently, he had no idea at first of his audience. Daisy held one edge of a large wooden square in her hands. She tilted it forward. Rima leapt to help. The two of them lowered it over the hole and scraped it into place.

"Who—" asked Matty, cut off mid-question.

"I agree we ought to keep this affair quiet," whispered Daisy, as though Lisette had said as much. "Of course I wouldn't dream of speaking of it, or showing anyone else. Only you – I wanted you to see proof. Now how can we prevent a scandal?" She rose from her knees with enviable grace. "We'll discuss it between us, privately."

Rima assisted Lisette to stand, squeezing her hand tightly a second before she let it loose. "Without them? Ain't you think they got somethin' to say?"

"No, you're right. The way down—That trapdoor's only so one may lift out a block or two at a time, but according to Ekibondo the real door's outside."

To the building's north they found the ice cellar's entrance, disguised by a low hill. As Rima put her hand on the latch of the double doors set in its side they were already opening. Out stepped Matty, shirt collar slightly askew, one telltale end of a grass stem caught in his tousled hair. "Good – you received my message." He looked pointedly at Rima.

"I did?"

"Moving the rehearsal." The Scotsman's face reddened. He was surprisingly bad at this considering his career. "Didn't realize the dock would be so busy," he lied again, and turned to Daisy. "Glad to see you, too." Another lie. "This way."

The dirt ramp was short and shallow, ending in a stone-floored room that didn't look like the one into which Lisette had inadvertently spied. It was wide yet not deep, and would not have reached the warehouse's center. It ended in a wall bristling with palm fronds, their points stabbing outward.

Fwendi greeted them as she slipped between two posts framing a gloom in which Lisette could distinguish nothing – not with the lantern Fwendi carried glaring at her. She was more neatly clothed than Matty, having had, Lisette supposed, more time to arrange herself.

Matty opened his jacket – to which a few yellowed strands still clung – and removed a sheaf of papers. Flipping hurriedly through them, he divided them into three groups. "Fwendi will read the lines of Grandmother Elephant, and I will do the other animal ambassadors."

"They's more animal ambassadors? From other realms, like the elephants?"

"The action takes place after what was the play's last scene – Wendi-La and the other children are celebrating their victory over the monsters; their parents miraculously restored, you know, the elephants joyfully dancing. Then representatives of these other magical lands approach – The Realms of the Giraffes, the Lions, the Crocodiles. Asking for help against the monsters now invading *their* homelands."

Lisette thought she saw what Matty attempted. Listening to the stirringly martial tone of Wendi-La's new speech she was sure. If this coda in which their national heroine pledged war against others' enemies influenced the Mote more deeply than the pleas

Daisy would make on the behalf of true neutrality, Matty's German friends would triumph.

Lisette tried to ascertain if her Frenchness affected her view of such an outcome as undesirable. She couldn't decide. However, she reminded herself, it was not as if she were advocating for the Entente.

"Now you climb up on the jail roof – will one of you bring out some hay bales for her to stand on?" Matty had forgotten where he was, who was with him, all but the world of make-believe. Lisette left, but not to fetch him his precious hay. Let Fwendi handle the properties – she loved the man. Evidently.

Above ground, warmth stroked her face lightly, a promise of overpowering heat later in the day. She paused at the ramp's top to wait for Daisy, who seemed to have also chosen to abandon Matty to this ruse of a rehearsal.

One glance at her lover's face and Lisette knew the day's troubles had only begun. That smile, so slight, so distant; she must be worried . . . Could Lisette in some way help?

But as it transpired, Daisy wasn't all that concerned about Matty's influence on the Mote. "My approach is direct. I will say exactly how I believe we ought to act. They'll hear and understand me clearly, no mistake. And I have a vote." Only one vote, but one more than Matty possessed.

They arrived at the loading dock just as the *Mbuza* untied. Its giant shadow shrank, second by second. They watched it climb the softly straying winds. This ship's outsized balloon was a mottled green.

"So, then, what is the matter?" Lisette would not let silence divide them. Or anything. Not any longer. Not distance – Lisette would retire, cease touring. They'd always be together. Not time. Not that man's ghost. "Come, sit." She led Daisy to the bench beside the mooring pole, deserted now the dirigible had gone.

"It's the prospect of their marriage," said Daisy, looking back at the warehouse. "If the scandal can't be quashed. Neither of you seem to take it seriously."

"But my dear, I grant you've lived in Everfair longer, more continuously, so you no doubt have a better idea of what is and is not acceptable. But surely their ages don't signify so very much—"

"No! Not that! Only think – Fwendi will want to have a baby – several!"

Lisette didn't want to understand. But she did. "Their races."

"Oh, not that alone. For themselves it would be fine. In God's eyes we are equal. But think of the consequences, the miscegenation. The children."

Lisette could say nothing. She wanted to rise up, to walk away. This again. This hurt, this blow to the bruise on her heart, which she had thought healed. By the numbness radiating out of this moment she knew the pain, when it came, would be bad.

For a while she was unable even to move. Her face must have shown something of what she was realizing. Daisy took her limp hand.

"Why should any of this matter to us? It shouldn't. We're not— There's no way we could have children with one another, *chérie*. We can't cause those sorts of problems."

"But George and Mrs Hunter, they might have." George had never outgrown his schoolboy crush on the Negro missionary.

"Yes. You remember how upset I was, ready to disown him? Who'd wish such a burden on anyone, especially a poor innocent: to be part of neither world, not black, not white, an orphan even though both parents live."

Le Gorille, Grandpère, had wished such a burden on Lisette's mother. This miscegenation of which her love spoke so contemptuously? Of that, of *those sorts of problems*, Lisette herself had been born.

She glanced skyward. The *Mbuza* was yet visible, its gondola a swaying trinket attached to the balloon by silvery chains. She had memorized the schedules. It would return at midnight to depart for Kisangani again at dawn.

Daisy would have to be on board. So would Matty. So would Rima. And so would Fwendi and Lisette.

She would have to go. But not as Daisy's lover. Not any longer.

Fortunately, she had other options. Rima was young and imperfect, but incapable of reaggravating this particular injury.

Gently, Lisette removed her hand from Daisy's grasp. Slowly, she stood up. Daisy was asking questions she couldn't answer. Without another word, Lisette returned to the hotel. Locked in her room, she drew down the barkcloth shades, suffusing the walls with a rosy twilight, and did her best to rest. When that proved impossible, she got up again and packed.

On the Lot and In the Air

Lisa L. Hannett

The crow's talons gouged new gashes into Jupiter's enamel as the orrery revolved a clockwork orbit beneath him. Gaslights incandesced from the base of the carnival booth, projecting the solar system's rotations onto the canvas dome above the crow's head. Light strobed into his eyes each time Jupiter completed a rotation, which did nothing to improve the crow's temper. He lifted an articulated wing to shade his eyes; when he dropped it a moment later, he saw a gawking crowd congregating on the midway, its collective attention captivated by the golden gear held steady in his beak.

The midway's makeshift stalls had sprouted like rank weeds, hell-bent on doing damage before they were uprooted. As evening slid into pungent night, the carnival had colonized the city's neglected streets, transforming them with its garish gaslights and flea-bitten draperies. Tents had whorishly spread themselves along all surfaces, like the cheap skin show dames who plumped and corseted their wares in the fair's liminal spaces.

Now the thoroughfare teemed with noxious odours, secreted by a horde of notorious bodies, all crammed into collapsible houses of ill repute. The buildings supporting the carnival's crooked pavilions dripped constantly, as if a giant pig was spitted in the sky, its juices left to fall like fatty rain onto the scene below. By morning, discarded candy wrappers and flocks of shredded ticket stubs would papier-mâché every tent, signpost and tree, leaving archaeological layers of rubbish to congeal in the city's slime.

This whole place reeks, thought the crow.

"Forget cheap arcades with rubber-limbed benders! Forget dime museums, string-shows and flea powders! What y'all need is to let off some STEAM! Step right up and have a FREE shot at this Foul Fowl! Sock him in the block and win a plethora of prizes!"

The crow snorted as the sprocketed showman jangled out from behind a threadbare curtain. His stovepipe hat belched steam as he clanked over to the bally platform, which was girded in dusty organza. The showman's pliable tin shanks were clad in darted velour leggings; aluminium tails grafted onto his torso lent his outfit a certain panache, as far as tarnished suits go. Small beads of humidity or grease drip-dropped down his pockmarked cheeks and neck, watermarking the collar of his ruffled shirt with gray splashes. Leaning on a bamboo walking stick atop the dais, he surveyed his flock for a heartbeat. On the second beat, he raised a gloved hand to his breast and bowed like a courtly gentleman.

"Robin Marx, at your service," he said to rapt listeners, "on behalf of the Outdoor Amusement Business Association. That's right, folks – you've heard the rumours, and I'm here to prove 'em true – Robin Marx always gives the first shot for free! Win on that shot and the prize is yours! It's no sin to be a winner, my friends; so come and collect an easy dinner."

Revellers were drawn to Marx's stall faster than you could say shine-on spit. He had greased more than a few palms to score such a choice locale; his bird-show was the first thing people would see when they came in, set up as he was on the right-hand side of the midway, only two paces away from the carnival's main entrance. The showman smiled, and blessed the corruptible lot man as he surveyed his coffer-filling patch of turf.

It was proving to be the prime location for shooting marks.

Ladies and gents disembarked from a motley collection of dirigibles – steam-powered and boiler-driven, with leather balloons or finest silk, depending on the owner's station – directly outside Sideshow Alley's hastily erected plyboard fences. Two guineas were extracted from each heavy purse by way of an entrance fee; once inside, the gullible masses would sure as sugar leave a goodly portion of their remaining shillings to Robin Marx, proprietor and entrepreneur *extraordinaire*.

Pockets jingling, Marx wove through the crowd as if he were the lord mayor hisself; winking at the ugly girls and pinching the cute ones' bottoms; shaking hands with the gents and slapping sharpies on the back as he progressed. In the midst of his campaigning, Marx made his way over to the crow's slowly orbiting perch.

Night clung to the bird's mangy figure; his wings hung sodden tissue-like by his sides. The crow felt like a feathered showcase for their racket, a curio cabinet with an aching beak and flea-bitten wings. A cabinet that would do anything for a day off. He sighed, making sure not to knock the gear out of his beak as he did, and listened to the sideshow dames singing to their Johnnies:

"*—one fire burns out another's burning, One pain is lessen'd by another's anguish; Turn giddy, and be holp by backward turning; One desperate grief cures with another's languish . . .*"

"Why don't you ever sing like that, bird?" Marx bent over and turned the ornate key jutting out of the orrery's bulbous base, and forced the slowing planets to rev into dazzling motion once more. The crow flapped his discontent. He growled down at the showman's oxidized head, much to the crowd's insipid delight. A mechanical band organ began to caterwaul across the thoroughfare, drowning out the crow's curses.

"Ah," said Marx, pausing before giving the key a final firm twist, "the only sound more haunting than the calliope is the music of money changing hands, my friend." And with a pseudo-sincere wink to his partner, he turned on his heel and directed his attention to the burgeoning audience.

Robin Marx hoisted his walking stick, jabbed it skyward to reinforce his ballyhoo. "The winner of the day will get the key to the midway, straight from my two hands!" He flashed a large bank roll – *A carny roll*, thought the crow, *or I'll be buggered* – and made sure to expose the cash reward for only the briefest second before squirrelling it away in his waistcoat pocket.

"Get the bird to release his bootlegged prize! Five pence a shot," the showman cried.

The crow made sure to tilt his head as Marx worked the bally; the golden gear winked in the gaslight, catching more than one poor sap's eye. As his roost lifted him skyward, he scanned the faces milling in the throng below him. Tried to guess which unfortunate sucker would reveal hisself – for it always was a bloke – to be Marx's front-worker.

Could be him, the crow thought, as a stocky gentleman in a bowler hat disembarked from a locomotive rickshaw and stepped onto the midway. But he changed his bet as the skin-show dames peeled away from the shadows, snagging the bowler hat and its owner with their lurid insinuations. ("*Me they shall feel, while I am able to stand: and 'tis known I am a pretty piece of flesh,*" sang the dames down the way.) He'll be there for hours, the crow realized, or until his pockets (and other things) are sucked dry.

Jupiter convulsed on its brass frame, lurching further upward. The crow overcompensated for this movement and pitched forward at a precarious angle. His tomfoolery earned a round of raucous laughter from the carnival anemones swaying on the polluted floor beneath him. As he regained his balance, he saw a frogman wobble his way out of the ale den four stalls down, ribbetting up his dinner and the keg of piss-weak beer he'd consumed on a dare. Next door, a seedy looking weasel in patched plus fours emerged from the sky-grifter's tent. He slid across the frogman's spew, leaving a trail of putrid footsteps as he zigzagged his way up the noisy thoroughfare towards Robin Marx's stall.

The weasel's shifty eyes didn't blink twice to see the team of spontaneously combusting phoenixes bouncing on rickety trampolines in the centre of the midway. His listless mouth didn't so much as twitch towards a smile, even when a row of constructs whirled a metallic dervish for his pleasure and coin. No, the weasel had the expression of a man on a mission. He had a job that wanted doing, just as sure as Old Cranker's sausages weren't stuffed with bona fide cud-chewer.

That's him all right, the crow thought. *That's the shill.*

He watched the weasel's stilted progress, humming a fiddley snippet one of the lads from Labrador had played while the caravan steam-rolled its way across barren plains the previous night. The crow tried to ignore the ornamental gear whose jagged spokes were doing their utmost to bash his beak into a less functional shape. Agonizing moments passed; the crow's eyes began to water; his ears felt downright clogged with the midway's hubbub. Finally, the weasel stepped up and placed his grimy paws on the footprints Marx had painted on the cobblestones, no more than spitting distance away from the crow's orrery.

"Al-a-ga-zam, capper. Give the crowd a wave, and tell us your name," said Marx in a voice as slick as the carnival's boulevards.

"Trouper," said the weasel.

"Well, Trouper, as I've just been telling these here folk, this bird's a scoundrel of the nineteenth degree. That's right: this rotten crow is flaunting stolen merchandise in his good-for-nothing beak. He pinched that gear right out of my pappy's precious timekeeper—" he withdrew an unremarkable watch from his breast pocket and dangled it mid-air, just as he'd seen hypnotists do "—and now it's ticked its last tock. Irreplaceable, that's what this piece is. You've got to help me, Trouper! Help me get it back from that vicious crow so I can get my pappy's ticker started again!"

The crow pretended to bow his head in shame at hearing Marx's accusations. He swept his wings up before him in a gesture of mock supplication – his least favourite part of the act – and in so doing deftly swapped the golden gear for a confectioner's imitation while Marx explained the rules of the game.

"The first shot's always free, folks. Trouper, give it your best go. If you're a real lucky son-of-a-gun, you'll be the one to empty my purse after one sweet shot." As if of its own volition, Marx's hand stroked his waistcoat pocket while he spoke; and with each tender caress, the counterfeit bankroll bulged for all to see.

The crow gripped Jupiter more tightly as the weasel drew a jacked-up slingshot out of his leather satchel. Trouper braced hisself. He cranked the miniature catapult until its arm was fully cocked and in assault position. He took aim, his furry finger extending towards the trigger on the slingshot's wooden handle, and fired. Across the midway, a group of girls squealed as their teetering seats topped the Ferris wheel's luminous peak; the crowd at Marx's stall gasped as the slingshot snapped into action with an ear-splitting crack of released carbon dioxide.

The crow mimed he'd been hit. He creaked his sooty wings around in comical circles, then swallowed the confectioner's gear with a tinny gulp. The orrery shuddered to a halt. From beneath cracked eyelids, he watched his performance drain dollar signs away from the sea of greedy faces beneath him. He chuckled as he righted hisself on his now-stalled perch.

"Take that, you old shit," he squawked at Marx, ruffling his oil-slick plumage. "Try and get your precious gear now."

"You see, folks? You see what pain he gives me? Please, someone – *anyone* – step right up! Help me shut that miserable trap of his for good!" Right on cue, the bird started wheezing, hacking and choking, reeling the crowd in with faux suffering. He covered his beak with a wing – as all polite crows should do when they cough – and replaced the dissolved candy gear with its golden counterpart. Beams of golden light twinkled out of the crow's mouth as the clean gear was reinstated, wedged between the upper and lower sections of his beak.

The crowd fell quiet at Marx's feet. A chorus of accordions droned down the midway; coal-burners roared with delight as they powered bumper cars next door; whistles sporadically announced winners all across the carnival's crooked landscape; ("—*yet I cannot choose but laugh; To think it should leave crying*—" wafted out of the skin-tents); but the group that had pressed in close to witness the crow's imminent demise was shocked into distrustful silence by the weasel's apparent failure, and the crow's derring-do.

Venus chose that moment to add insult to the audience's injury. The rose-coloured globe, two prongs away from the crow's own Jupiter, flared on the orrery with a sudden brightness that blinded the already mute crowd, throwing the midway into unflattering relief. Yet when the yellow-blue after-images faded from the spectators' eyes, their hands sprang together with gleeful applause. Tiny wind-up fireflies had escaped their Venusian cage: on Marx's command, they buzzed into formation, their minute bodies spelling out *Golden Guinea* in a bewitching message of fortune.

"Never fear, my friends. What did I tell you? Everyone's a winner at Robin Marx's." The showman beamed with feigned magnanimity from his position on the stall's counter. He released the hidden lever that had unleashed the automatic fireflies, and blew contented smoke rings from his hat as he coddled the ersatz pocket watch. "Yes, the crow's still a crook, but good Trouper here shook him up a good one, didn't he?" Catcalls and wolf whistles punctuated general expressions of good humour in response.

"And as the Lady Venus wills, the gentleman shall receive," Marx said. A newly struck gold coin instantly appeared in Marx's hand, and disappeared just as quickly in Trouper's. The weasel snatched the throwaway as if it were the first and last coin he'd ever see, then forced a retreat through the jostling herd now vying to knock the crow senseless.

Mark after mark placed feet on painted footprints, squared their shoulders and *threw*, but none seemed blessed with Trouper's luck. Children began throwing tantrums instead of projectiles. One snivelling whelp kicked up such a stink that Marx gave both boy and mother a few ducats to go and see the Marx Brothers' Rocket-Powered Penny Farthings. This one tactical freebie was all it took; a deluge of five pence pieces avalanched across the countertop, and into Marx's purse.

More stones were launched the crow's way amid showers of minor coins; the first of these missed, but the latter staunchly met their target. "Sorry, matie," Marx said to one sour-breathed contestant, whose chest heaved against his sweat-soaked shirt after another pebble hurtled wide of its mark. "Your robust bear-huggers are just too strong for this game! You threw that one so quick, I reckon an African cheeter couldn't have caught it."

"C'mon, Marx. Give me a rehash. I'll slip you a free strudel next time you come past my bakery," said the blubbery man through his long mustachios.

Marx walked behind the counter, tilted his bulk forward on the orrery's concealed pedals, and said, "Tell you what I'll do for you, matie: if you win on the next go, I'll give you back every penny you've gambled. Guaranteed. Peg this wretched bird with all your impressive might and you'll have more dough than you could ever knead at that bakery of yours."

Marx's tongue kept flappin' until he got his way; such smooth words never did the marks any good. Bitter smoke billowed from the street vendors' burners, following the losers home. Nightwatchmen changed shifts, grunting salutations and beating billies against enhanced meat-hooks, as adrenaline levels bloated the carnival's nihilistic avenues. (*"To see now, how a jest shall come about!"* laughed the dancing girls. *"I warrant, and I should live a thousand years, I never should forget it—"*) The disgruntled baker turned away from Marx's stall, stuffing his remaining two guineas into a ragged pocket. He nearly tripped over the fox wheeling its way up to the target.

Dressed in a chrome yellow top hat and matching damask suit, the fox was a dapper fellow, every inch a gentleman. The spiked wheels of his wicker invalid's chair sought purchase on the midway's greasy cobblestones; they skidded nauseatingly, and moved forward at an inchworm's pace. No matter if it took until morning for his master to reach his goal, the fox's kettledrum construct would not interfere. Only when he was contentedly puffing away on a mahogany pipe, his wheeled chair jauntily parked on the scuffed painted footprints, did the housebot approach. He draped a Burberry rug across his master's immobile copper knees, tucking it gently between the chair's arms and the fox's atrophied hindquarters, then stood off to his left-hand side.

The fox's eyes never wavered from their prize as he asked the bot to analyse the odds of his winning this game.

A slender ticker tape chugged out of a slit beneath the construct's speaker box. He tore it against his serrated teeth, and passed the results over to his master. "Immeasurably in your favour. As usual, Sir."

"Hey there, cowboy." Marx rearranged his features until they imitated a passably charming grin. He released a burst of steam from his top hat as he spoke.

The crow eyeballed the fox from his lofty perch. Those who balanced on wheels instead of legs were such simple targets. Weaker than children, and less confident. "Come have a go," he said, flicking the gear to the corner of his beak and projecting his voice for all to hear. "In fact, what's say we give him TWO goes for free, on accounta his poorly condition? Don't that sound fair, Robin?" he asked, seeking and receiving the showman's nod.

The fox tapped his pipe on the chair's padded arm, watched its sticky contents combine with the sludge lazily seeping around his wheels. ("—*let them measure us by what they will, We'll measure them a measure, and be gone . . .*") He flicked a shred of tobacco off his lap, and gently cleared his throat.

"Indeed, I will take two shots, as you've so kindly offered, Mr Black," said the fox.

It took a second for the crow to realize the fox was addressing *him*. Not "bird", not "jackdaw", not "scoundrel", no. He was Mr Black.

The fox feigned interest in the kaleidoscopic projections whirling around Marx's tent while the crow fluffed and preened his feathers.

Then he opened fire.

"Shot the first: a question. How did such a magnificent creature – genuine *Corvus corone*, pure flesh and bone, not a single enhancement – how did such a miraculous being come to be shackled and used as a cyborg's lackey?"

The crow spluttered, and nearly swallowed the gear in earnest.

"Shot the second," the fox continued, undaunted. "An offer. Work for me."

The crow cocked his head, and waited for the punch line.

"Let me set the terms," said the fox, "for I am sure you will find them suitably appealing.

"First," he said, "I will prohibit you from participating in any specimen of show – even though it would be an absolute delight to hear your dulcet tones raised in song, Mr Black, old chap. But, no. No singing today. Instead, I would like to employ your golden sense. What does Mr Marx pay you? Some flattering mirrors in front of which you might preen? Perhaps some chymical bird-feed?"

The crow kept silent.

(*"True, I talk of dreams; Which are the children of an idle brain; Begot of nothing but vain fantasy . . ."*)

"I will offer you a gentleman's fare, Mr Black," the fox continued, quietly. "I am not interested in paying carny's fees for such a one as you are. Sneer all you like at the term, Mr Marx; you cannot deny that you have treated this dark angel as nothing more than a lowly *carny*.

"I need a partner, Mr Black, for a somewhat more lucrative . . . oh, let's call it a venture, shall we? Your guile, your cleverness, your wit: these are exactly the assets I need for this undertaking. You are far too intelligent for this braggart's show! In fact, the show's very success hinges on your intellect. Don't think I didn't see you exchange the false gear with the real, earlier—"

—the crowd stirred, grumbled as they fondled their weightless pockets—

Marx fumed, "That's enough out of you, cowboy—"

"—indeed without your finesse, there would *be* no Robin Marx! And how does he repay you? By tying you to a mouldy planet and shoving a gear down your gullet?"

(*"Ay, while you live, draw your neck out of the collar . . ."*)

"What horror will he perform next? Are you a crow, Mr Black? Or are you a soiled dove, blackened much as this city has been of late, by too many trips up Marx's sooty arse?"

The paralytic's got a point, thought the crow.

He spat the gear out, propelling it with fury, loosening his tongue to ingratiate hisself to his new employer. The crowd dispersed like exhaled smoke. (Ladies, dames, raised their voices, *"To move is to stir; and to be valiant is to stand; therefore, if thou art mov'd, thou runn'st away . . ."*)

The tiny gear negotiated a haphazard path across the cobblestones, before spinning to a halt at the housebot's burnished feet. Before Marx could shift his frame off the counter, the bot had dropped a silk handkerchief onto the gear, collected it and polished it properly. Then he lifted his master's damask coattails, exposing the clockworks inset in his narrow russet back.

Half of the works were still, while the other portion whirred out their quotidian functions. The bot gently laid the gear into the fox's lower back, and used his index finger to screw it into place.

"What do you want me to do, boss?" asked the crow, his eagerness to escape the ramshackle orrery hanging like a painful chandelier from his brief question.

"Why, you've already done it, old chap," said the newly mobile fox as his lower legs sprang to life. "You really have done it!"

(*"O, Wilt thou leave me so unsatisfied?"*)

Yipping like a newborn pup, the fox switched his tail into overdrive. He sprang out of his redundant chair, blew the crow a grateful kiss as he sped past, fleeing the scene before he could get slicked.

(*"What satisfaction canst thou have tonight?"* chimed the sideshow dames as the Johnnies were ejected from their parlours. The women's laughter was harsh and raw.)

Terrain

Genevieve Valentine

The trains carved into land that wasn't theirs, and swallowed the men who laid their iron roads – the tracks like threads to draw white men closer together – monsters belching smoke across a land they meant to conquer.

So Faye made herself scarce the day the men from Union Pacific visited Western Fleet Courier, to ask Elijah about the land.

Elijah wasn't a man who thought much where he didn't have to; maybe it was just as well, since many who'd thought harder were cruel, and Elijah's place was where she and Frank had made their home.

So far.

The railroad men spoke with Elijah a long time. They cast looks around the yard where Fa Liang and Joseph were working on a dog, weighting the front pair of its legs so it wouldn't flip backward the first time you scaled a rock face. Fa Liang muttered something to the dog, and Joseph laughed, and the tall railroad man watched.

They watched Maria tending vegetables, rake in hand, shirtsleeves rolled to her elbows.

Faye kept in the barn. And Frank was somewhere those men would never find him. (Better not to trust anyone with the government. That much they'd learned the hard way.)

But Elijah was white, and kind-hearted, and had made friends when he lived in River Pass – Harper at the general store still set things aside for him. Elijah had no reason to fear two men who smiled and seemed polite; once or twice, he laughed.

Bad sign, Faye thought.

They shook hands with him and left at last, and Faye was able to tear herself away from the hole in the boards and pretend nothing was wrong.

People came with messages for delivery every week: homesteaders, wagon trains, the Pony Express. If she was shaken every time a stranger showed, she'd spend her life in this barn.

When Elijah came into the barn, he smiled, but there was a second's pause before he said, "Hello, Faye."

She didn't mind the pause; worse to be called a wrong name.

It was easy to mistake Frank and Faye. The twins looked like their mother, the high brow and strong jaw, and they had the matching, flinty expressions of a lot of the Shoshone children who were sent to the white school. It made Frank look like a warrior, and Faye look troubled.

She stood beside Dog 2, one hand on its right foreleg. It was foolish to seek comfort in machines – look at the railroad – but still, she felt calmer with it close by.

She should have had a wrench, if she was pretending to work, but she'd been shaking.

Elijah meant well. Elijah was an easygoing man, most days. He tried to keep peace, he tried to be fair.

Faye just didn't think she and Elijah had the same idea of fair.

She couldn't even ask – the words stuck when she saw him – and she held her breath and looked at the open door behind him, the sliver of deep blue sky.

She'd been waiting for a sign to run. An open door was as good as anything.

Then Elijah said, "Lord, these trains have made men greedy."

The land can be beautiful, depending where you're coming from.

The sun sets in bands of red and gold, and one of turquoise just ahead of the night; sunrise is cool in summer and sharp in winter, like ice cracking; and the horizon's so unbroken that weather isn't a surprise – you see clouds well ahead of the rain.

The soil is shallow and it fights, but there are wildflowers and tall grass until snowdrifts cover them. Snowdrifts, with rock to rest against, climb taller than a house, thin dry powder. The snow can turn any moment, with the wind, and swallow a man whole. You don't go out alone in winter if you want to make it home.

There is, sometimes, water. It's always flowing away from you.

There are always hills on the horizon, even though you're already so high up you never catch your breath. You can look out and out and out across the basin, and see specks on the horizon, twenty miles away, where a city's fighting to take hold.

Sometimes a city lasts. Sometimes you look out one night and not one lamp is lit, and you know the land passed judgement on it.

When you look at the night sky, it makes you dizzy.

Part of this is wonder. Part is knowing how far away from other lives you are, in this wide unbroken dark.

If you've made your way west from the forests, and given up town life for the frontier, this land seems like punishment.

It's beautiful, if you're coming home.

Elijah Pike owned the fifty acres of Western Fleet Courier.

He'd come to River Pass from Boston, after he'd tired of being someone else's clerk and decided it was time to make something of himself in the West. He'd been an indifferent farmer – too uncertain of the soil – but River Pass needed even indifferent vegetables, and he'd found enough success on his own that when Fa Liang presented himself, Elijah had the land, and money for an extra barn, and parts for the dogs.

He was proud of the business; he was proud that they sometimes boarded a scrawny boy from the Pony Express while they handed off a message going where no horse could reach.

Elijah had painted the wooden sign himself: "Any Message, All Terrain". It hung below the wrought iron sign for Western Fleet, nailed to the arch marking his property line.

It was just as well he owned the land; he was the only one of them who could.

A dog has six legs. Each one is thin, and tall as a man, and arched as a bow, and in their center they cradle the large, gleaming cylinder of the dog's body. The back half conceals a steam engine, with a dipping spoon of a rider's seat carved out ahead of it, with levers for steering and power, and just enough casing left in front to stop a man from hurtling off his seat every time the dog stops short.

It looks ungainly. The casing jangles, and the legs seem hardly sturdy enough to hold it, and when someone takes a seat it looks like the contraption's eating him alive.

But legs that seem ungainly in the yard are smooth on open territory, and dogs don't get skittish about heights or loose ground, and when scaling a rock face, six legs are sometimes better than four.

There's a throttle for the engine, and three metal rings on each side of the chair, where the rider slides his fingers to operate the legs. Left alone, the dog walks straight ahead; when the rider starts his puppetry, it treads water, dances, climbs mountains.

It takes a strong boy to wield one – not muscled, but wiry, a boy who can keep his balance and his head if the ground slips out from under him.

Faye won't train them if they look like they force their own way. On the trail, a rider has to understand enough to sidewind Dog 3 in heavy winds, enough to hear what's breaking in old Dog 1 before it breaks.

Sometimes she and Fa Liang placed bets about what would need fixing up when some boy came back.

"The boy," Frank said, "if he breaks Dog 2."

Faye shouldered him, but Fa Liang said, "No bet."

The dogs never tire, and need a quarter of the water a horse does. The boys carry some, but the inside of the engine shell collects condensation at night, which siphons into a skin.

That was Faye's idea; their mother taught her, a long time ago.

They're five strange beasts – they terrify horses – but they do as promised. The Express advises riders to use them if the road gets impassable for animals.

Even folk in River Pass have a little pride that for those who need a message sent where no messenger goes, you can point them right to Western Fleet.

Fa Liang started the business.

He left the Central Pacific line and came to River Pass in search of work. River Pass wouldn't have him.

He'd never said if it had come to blows; it didn't always have to.

But Susannah Pell from the clerk's office followed him out of the general store and told him about Elijah, living on land of his own, well outside the city limits.

Elijah welcomed him. He was working alone, then, and the place was falling to ruin.

The barn had a pile of equipment Elijah had run so poorly that no one would take it off his hands.

The first dog Fa Liang built was small, and slipshod – the engine casing was one sheet of tin, and the seat little more than a metal spoon nailed on in front of it. The engine sputtered on steep inclines, and it limped. But when the livestock count was off one day, Fa Liang rode out in it, and came back with a calf he'd maneuvered out of a split in the rock.

"Damn," said Elijah, grinning.

Fa Liang peeled himself off the seat – that first build wasn't kind to the rider, his back was scorched for a week – and asked, "There a courier in town?"

They met Joseph when they came into River Pass looking for a blacksmith.

Fa Liang handed him two uneven legs from the dog.

"I need something to make this one longer," he said. "And some weight, for the bottom."

Joseph frowned, turned it over and over, smoothed his hands over the joints.

Then a smile stole over his face, and he said, "What the devil are you building?"

When Elijah came back from the general store with his wagon of dry goods, Fa Liang and Joseph were waiting.

Joseph had come from Missouri a freedman, after dismissal from the Union Infantry; he'd been working to earn money to go with the Mormon wagons headed west.

"If it weren't for the dogs," he told Faye once, "I'd have kept going until I hit the ocean."

The dogs wouldn't have kept him long, but Maria came soon after, and she could keep hold of almost anything.

What Maria hadn't held was her farm – Texas ranchers ran her off as soon as her husband was in the ground.

But she was determined to find another homestead, so she'd joined a traveling preacher, and in River Pass, when he demanded to see the husband she'd claimed to have in a town she'd picked off a map, Maria saw Elijah coming out of the clerk's office, and took a chance.

Sometimes, in January when it seemed winter would never break, Frank asked for the story. Maria made Elijah act it out, laughing; she claimed he'd been marvelous.

Faye didn't buy it. Elijah was an honest man. Play-acting didn't suit him.

"He must have been bad, though," Faye said once, when they were alone.

Maria grinned. "Horrible. Not even Padre was fooled."

"But you came back with him."

She shrugged. "A man who can't lie is sometimes a good sign."

Faye went to wash before the supper bell rang at the big house.

They came from their own cabins – Joseph, Fa Liang, and Frank and Faye from farthest out.

Maria had moved into the big house two winters back, when the ground betrayed her and her cabin floor split.

The garden turned into a cornucopia when she laid hands on it.

("It's like he *tried* to kill them," Maria muttered to Faye once, wrist deep in dirt. She was planting squash far enough apart that they wouldn't choke.)

When they came inside, Maria glanced up and nodded. "Frank. Faye."

Frank glanced at Faye with the ghost of a smile. He had his shell necklace on, looped down his chest like a breastplate, and it was the only reason why Maria had been able to tell one from the other. It was the same, the days Faye wore her skirt because her trousers were drying.

Still, Faye took any smile she could get from Frank.

At the table, Faye pressed against Frank and Elijah on either side; wedged at the end was a boy from the Express whose name she had forgotten, bunking with them while Tom Cantor from River Pass delivered his message.

They talked about nothing, for a while, for the sake of the Express boy. They all fought, sometimes – about the dogs, about the town, about elbow room at table – but never in front of strangers. Some things you couldn't afford to do.

Joseph sat next to Maria, as always, and she pretended not to give him the biggest slice of cornbread, and he pretended not to look at her even when she wasn't speaking.

They talked with Elijah about Tom and Dog 3, due back any day, and Faye watched Elijah's face for signs he'd been a fool about the Union Pacific.

He didn't seem a fool, but you got used to worrying.

When the cornbread and preserves were polished off and the boy from the Express had taken a hint and vanished, Elijah sat back and said, "We had a visitor."

They set down their forks and knives too fast, ready for the bad news they'd known was coming.

Elijah laid out the visit from Michael Grant, and the plans for the Union Pacific construction, and the offer he'd gotten for his land.

It was the biggest number they'd ever heard.

It was the sort of money that evaporated loyalty; it was such a number that they all sat, stunned silent.

Faye watched him. For a bad liar, his face gave so little away.

"What do you mean to do?"

Elijah shook his head. "Wanted to hear from everyone."

"It might not come," said Maria. "If they're promising that kind of money across Wyoming they'll run out."

But it wasn't true, Faye thought. The railroad was swallowing the land. The train was inevitable.

A lot of things were inevitable that none of them ever talked about.

(They held together like they did because to break would mean being swept back.)

"It will come," said Frank, his face grim.

"Trains will be bad for business," said Joseph.

"It can't crawl up mountains," Faye said. "Dogs can."

Elijah said, "They told me they can bring goods from California in three days, right through the mountains."

Fa Liang flinched.

Maria whistled under her breath.

"All the land?" Faye asked.

"They want to build through the north side," Elijah said, "so the station will be part of River Pass."

Faye's stomach sank.

Towns battled for the railroad, because the miles between the train and the city would fill with hotels and saloons and traders. If

River Pass had gotten word of this, not Elijah or anyone else would be keeping the railroad out.

When she looked at Frank, he was watching her, his face a mirror of her dread.

"Have they spoken to the town?" Fa Liang asked, in the tone of a man who knew what was coming.

"They're seeing the mayor tomorrow," said Elijah. "It's River Pass, or Green River. Our land decides."

Joseph crossed his arms. "And what would we do?"

Elijah shrugged. "We could travel north-west, start again. There are places that still need messages taken."

"You have a sweet feeling about how people will take us," Faye said.

"If we had that money, people might," said Fa Liang.

"I could have more money than Croesus," Joseph said. "People won't ever forget what I am."

(Maria looked up at him, a second too long.)

"Then they're small people," Elijah said.

"There are more small people than the other kind," said Faye.

Elijah looked at her, but didn't argue. He was good-hearted, but he had eyes, and he knew how they were all received sometimes, even in River Pass.

Elijah's hair was going gray, and when he smiled at Faye, the corner of his mouth disappeared into the deep lines carved by the sun.

"Then we won't sell," he said.

Joseph sucked in a breath.

Frank unclenched his fist from around his necklace; his fingers brushed Faye's.

Maria's face was drawn. "What will you tell the town?"

"That Union Pacific should look at Carson's place, and talk to him instead."

He didn't look worried enough. He looked like he was doing business, and not handling a monster whose iron teeth chewed right through men. He looked like a man who had never been in fear for his life.

They sat for a little while in silence.

Fa Liang left first – in a hurry, like he planned to clear out while he could.

Faye couldn't blame him. It was all she could do not to race the mile to the cabin, pack, and strike out north before dawn could find them.

Frank must have known how she felt; his laced hands were pressed to his stomach.

Joseph left, after passing close by Maria, and looking down at her with some silent conversation that closed out the rest of them. After he was gone, Maria laid her apron across the back of her chair and went upstairs, brushing her skirt like she could brush the railroad away.

Faye and Frank stood in tandem.

At the threshold, Elijah held out a hand without quite touching her elbow.

(He'd never touched her, not once in three years. He was the sort who didn't presume.)

"It will all come out right," Elijah said.

He was wrong, but still, she wanted to believe him.

She hoped the railroad men felt the same, when he tried to talk them out of it.

In the cool dark outside, Frank said, "We'll never see a fair day again, will we."

"No," she said.

The dark swallowed the echoes that should have been there; the words pressed in like the nights they'd spent in ditches with one blanket, whispering into the dirt to make sure the other was still breathing.

(The Mormon school had taught them plenty by accident; they knew each other's voice above a hundred strangers, through a hundred feet of earth.)

There was a trail between the big house and theirs, a web worn into the earth from people going back and forth like family. Fa Liang had one from his house to theirs, to pick up Faye and head to the barn for dog racing.

He delighted in maneuvers, pivoting full around on just one leg; Faye delighted in how fast a dog could cross terrain.

The dogs were too useful, she thought. River Pass had to get messages across the mountains. The town might not care for them, but they'd stand up for the dogs.

You always wanted Elijah to be right; she'd even wanted to believe him when he said this could be home.

*   *   *

Faye and Frank had come to Elijah's by accident.

They'd escaped from the Mormon school in winter – light snow before a blizzard, when they'd be harder to follow – and struck out for home.

They made it.

Fa Liang found them while he was testing Dog 2; they were both nearly asleep, he said later, and frozen through.

She knew how to look for shelter, how to keep away from the worst of the wind. She knew how to find them enough to survive on – they'd lasted weeks that way. But she'd forgotten how many it takes to keep warm in a cold that deep. (For that you need a family.)

There hadn't been time to fetch help – snow was coming, and it would have been too late.

So Fa Liang had draped them over the dog and taken them straight to the house.

"You're welcome here," Elijah had said that first night. "Consider this place your home."

"It is," said Frank.

Faye set her jaw and waited for Elijah to strike, to tell them to get out.

But he only said, "Fair enough," and looked at Faye, the closest anyone had come to apologizing for anything.

"We'll see," Faye said, and Elijah smiled.

Frank loved the idea of a service too useful to run out of town, and he and Joseph struck up pretty well, and he treated the place like it really was home.

Faye was waiting for a sign to move. It hadn't yet come, that was all.

If she got fond of the dogs, it was just from being there so long; if Dog 2 was her favorite, no one faulted her.

Dog 2 was safer than the prototype; Faye's only burn was a thin line across one wrist, where her arm had hung too close to the shell, and Frank's just a smudge burned into his stomach, where he laced his hands sometimes.

When the railroad wants land the owner's unwilling to sell, it sends a man like Michael Grant to file with the clerk's office a finding that upon inspection, those acres, a gift from the United States, are being mismanaged.

Grant is tall and clean-shaven and has a new coat, and everyone gets friendly with a man who has money to burn.

Before long, he admits who he is. He says, "Shame about that Pike homestead. Seems we'll be moving on to Green River."

Word spreads – they're close, held back by so little, it wouldn't take any work at all, the railway will pay Elijah a king's ransom, who does he think he is to cut the town out of its chance.

A town beside a railway town never makes it. It's the train, or nothing, everyone knows.

(Michael Grant might have said this himself, to Harper at the general store, who speaks to everyone and never quite remembers the words aren't his.)

When the railroad wants to make sure, they call the residents "unsavories," and remind God-fearing folk what happens if that kind are allowed to stay long.

It's easy work. Most people never forget their little fears.

Elijah, Maria and Frank took the wagon to River Pass a few days later – dry goods, oil for the dogs.

They came back too early.

Faye saw the line of Frank's shoulders, and knew something terrible had happened.

She swung down from the dog, locked the engine off.

Elijah was white as a ghost.

They weren't speaking.

"Joseph," she called, "Fa Liang. Trouble."

Fa Liang came from the barn, and Joseph from the smithy, and watched them.

"We should run," said Fa Liang, so quiet only Faye could hear.

(She agreed. The town knew about the train. There was no good news any more.)

In the yard, the horses were specked with foam and breathing like they'd run for their lives.

Elijah took Maria's hand. Someone's hand was shaking.

Neither of them looked at Joseph.

"We've agreed it's wise to marry," Elijah said.

★   ★   ★

They went to church early Saturday, before parishioners were awake to object.

They were without Frank, who didn't like the idea of home being empty, and Joseph, who didn't like the idea.

As it turned out, neither she nor Fa Liang were legal enough to sign the witness line, so they had to wake Susannah Pell.

"It's no trouble," she said, when Elijah apologized. "I wondered if you were in love, you had that look about you. And it's good to see this for you, what with Grant telling people—"

The father cleared his throat; she said, "Congratulations," set down the pen, stepped back.

Elijah glanced at Faye, then Maria, her hand in his, standing like a soldier in a black dress.

"Thank you," he said.

With someone of the right temper, you could work in quiet for a long time. It was the thing Faye liked best about Western Fleet; it was the reason she'd been able to stay here as long as they had.

But they told stories, in the barn, mending dogs by lamplight, or on the porch in summer, when it was too hot to be in the barn any longer.

Joseph had his Freedmen's Bureau schoolbook, so well read the binding had gone, and he recited from memory.

"Awful lot about forgiveness," Faye said once.

"It's all forgiveness," Joseph said. "Mercy."

"I'll bet," said Frank.

(Maria lent Joseph her Bible; he'd handed it back, said, "I'd just as soon not."

No one questioned.)

Fa Liang told them about dragons and giants and the bird that tried to fill up the ocean. Once or twice he stopped halfway, saying, "My brother told it better," going quiet after.

He'd left the Central Pacific because he'd lost his brother to a blast, clearing rock for the rails.

Faye wanted to wrap her hand around Frank's wrist, like when they were little, every time she thought about it.

Maria sang in a sweet soprano that floated when it was cheerful, and settled on their skin if it was sad.

She didn't often seem sad, save on long nights when there was nothing left but to look at the sky and be mournful. Then she sang, voice trembling, eyes on the stars.

Faye and Frank never offered anything. The few stories they knew they held like secrets, like they'd need them someday, when it was time to move on.

"Bury me not, on the lone prairie," Elijah sang sometimes, when the others had fallen silent, his arms behind his head, face turned to the moon.

Faye tried not to look at him; when he sang it, her shoulders ached from not looking at anything.

After the wedding, they rode home in silence. Elijah looked older now that the worst was coming true. Maria looked determined not to let home fall to pieces.

It wouldn't, if the law held, Faye thought. It was hard to be sure; the laws changed so easily when people's hates built up against you.

They came back too late for supper, which Faye thought was for the best; when she met Frank in the yard, she could see Joseph already headed to his cabin, as if he'd waited to see them coming before he lost his heart for it.

"This won't be enough," Frank said, when he met her.

Faye said, "Let's go home."

They lay awake a long time, each looking at the other sometimes as if checking their worries in a mirror, until at last they slid into sleep.

(They didn't have the same worries; it was the only way they'd ever been different.

Frank touched her wrist whenever they reached their cabin, as if he was afraid she'd keep going.)

The boy from River Pass rode Dog 3 back to Western Fleet near midnight, six hours ahead of schedule.

Then he shouted them awake about the fire.

At the first scream, Faye and Frank were pulling on boots; you ended up a light sleeper, after as much running as they'd done.

They ran, breathing in time – they'd done this, too – and reached the yard ahead of Joseph and Fa Liang.

The barn was a tower of orange and smoke and a horrifying crackle as the heat started to do its work on the dogs.

For a moment they faltered.

Then Maria shouted, "Right, move," and they jerked into action like a spell had broken.

Frank ran for the water pump. Joseph dragged the hose from the horse barn, and as they attached it, Maria was enlisting the boy from River Pass (Tom, maybe, Faye couldn't think) and the boy from the Express in a bucket chain from the kitchen.

As soon as the doorway was damp, Fa Liang and Elijah and Faye used the wood-chopping stump to break through and run for the dogs.

Fa Liang and Elijah grabbed the two closest to the doors. Dog 5 was crushed under a beam, but Dog 2, parked farthest back, was still whole, and glowing underneath a canopy of fire.

"It's not worth it!" Fa Liang was already shouting, and Elijah called, "Faye! It's a goner, leave it!"

Frank, outside, was screaming, "FAYE!"

She stumbled, but didn't stop. They needed as many dogs as they could save.

They weren't mounts, now. They were weapons.

She shrank back from the walls as the heat rolled out, but she reached Dog 2 at last.

As she grabbed for a canvas, as she spat on her palms and turned the key until smoke rose between her fingers, as she threw the drape over and rode out with her back blistering, she never heard the sound of the fire.

She only heard Frank, screaming her name over a hundred other voices.

Elijah pulled her from the rider's seat, the canvas around her like a shroud.

But Frank was the one who carried her up the stairs of the big house, who cut Faye's shirt off her back – she bit down on something and screamed, hoped Maria put a belt in her mouth and she hadn't severed her tongue.

"Did the dog make it?" she asked later, when she was in a tub, and Maria was making something with mortar and pestle, and Frank was rinsing her with cool water.

Frank snorted, said thickly, "You would worry about that now."

Even in pain, she knew that wasn't fair; dimly she thought, I've always forgiven you, when you worried about what you loved.

"Not as bad as it could be," said Maria, bandaging her ribs. "It might blister, but we were quick, and your skin is thick there."

Faye never thought she'd thank the Mormon school for those scars.

Her hand was another story – there was a diamond key mark burned into her palm, as deep as Frank's. Some things were past healing.

"It's all right," Maria said. "The wound is clean, it will be no trouble. I've brought you some clean things."

"Whose?"

"A wife has ways," Maria said, with a smile that didn't reach her eyes.

But she was right – a clean wound hurt less, once the shock wore off. After Maria helped her into Elijah's clothes, Faye was calm enough to say, "Let's go down."

"Good," said Maria, fastening Faye's belt. "They're waiting."

Frank was at the door, and he walked so close Faye thought it was a good thing she hadn't burned her shoulder.

The others stood as she came in – even Tom, green with fright.

"I'm all right," she said as they took their seats. (Maria sat next to Joseph.) "How are the dogs?"

"Fine," said Fa Liang. "Dog 2 got out all right. He just needs mending."

"We have to fight," Frank said. "The next time some coward from the city or the railroad comes here, we send him back dead on his horse."

"It can't have been someone from town!" Tom cut in.

"The tracks led that way," said Joseph.

Tom blanched. "But . . ." he started, then fell silent as something occurred to him he chose not to voice.

"Go home, Tom," said Maria. "If anyone asks what happened, you tell them someone set the barn on fire, and not a word else. Safer."

After a little silence where no one spoke in his favor, he pulled on his gloves and stood. "It wasn't the town," he said, but this time it was half a question.

"The railroad put him up to it, whoever he was," said Maria, when they were alone.

"I need to talk to the mayor," Elijah said.

"No," said Faye.

They all glanced at her.

"She's right," said Frank. "No point."

"The mayor probably set it," said Maria.

"It does us no good to start fighting without asking for peace," Elijah said.

"That's all we ever asked!" Frank said. "And see how they treat us the second we stand up." He propped two stiff fingers on the table. "Who here ever had understanding from that kind?"

No one raised a hand.

Elijah got an odd, quiet expression.

He said, "Not every man's army, Frank. Not even railroad men. Many folk are kinder."

Frank sat back in his chair.

"Strange thing I've run across," Frank said, "since Faye and I were given to the school – knowing how many of them want us dead, and expect forgiveness."

Elijah got the expression of a man for whom some things he'd never thought about were falling into place.

"Well," he said at last, "then it's a vote."

He plucked five singed chips of bark from the hearth. He passed one to each of them.

Then he stood back empty-handed.

"Burned, we fight. Clear, we look for help."

Maria snapped hers on the table char up like the high card in a hand of poker, pulled back fingers dusted black.

Faye wasn't surprised. Anyone can be run off once, but roots take stronger, sometimes, on strange soil.

(They were around this table, weren't they?)

Fa Liang sighed, and scratched at the back of his neck, and set down his chit with the pale side up.

Joseph was quiet for a little while before he spoke.

"I'm a free man, and if any man questions me, I have his answer. But I don't know as I want any more fighting."

His bark went on the table, the pale side up.

Frank sat forward, slid the black chit into the center of the table.

Elijah pressed a fist to the wall behind him. "This won't bring any peace," he said.

"Expect not," said Frank.

Then everyone at the table turned to look at Faye.

Frank didn't. Frank had closed his eyes, laced his hands tight against his stomach.

He did that, sometimes, when he was frightened.

Faye wished Elijah hadn't asked her.

She'd wanted to leave three winters back, as soon as they could walk, but Frank asked to stay the night, and then they'd met the others, and the dogs.

Despite everything, Frank loved this place, where their ancestors might have lived, and somehow she had tricked herself that if they were happy, this was home; but it never had been, and it couldn't be.

Home was a safe place. That was gone.

Now there was only Frank, fingers curled against the necklace he'd bought in River Pass from a trader, because it was what he remembered of their father, long white strands looped like armor.

She tossed the bark back into the fire.

"No vote," Elijah said, trying to hide a smile.

When she looked at Frank's face, her heart broke.

Don't doubt me, she thought, more angry at him than at the men who'd tried to burn them out.

She'd freed them from the school; she'd led them to homeland again; she'd trained gangly boys to ride the dogs and never been so far as the summit by herself, because he'd asked her not to go, and she'd promised.

If she didn't want them fighting, he should know why; they'd seen what happened when you were outnumbered.

She let the wind slam the door behind her.

Faye remembered being young, when the land was the earth and the marks of antelope and the horizon that told you what was coming and plants growing in the shadow of the rocks.

At the school, she'd learned about barren. Barren was what happened to bad women, to the crops of people who did wrong. In the prayers they repeated until their tongues were numb, there was the hope of plenty, the fear of the blank land.

She found the path to their cabin without really looking, set herself on the hard-packed dirt that marked three years of habit.

There was a chill on the breeze, the edge of a winter that was still far off.

She knew why Frank wanted to make a stand. She just couldn't risk it.

If he would only leave, she'd go tonight, head for the mountains, never stop moving.

Their cabin was on a little rise, and she could tell its shape by the way it blocked the stars.

It was close enough to home, sometimes.

Of all the things that had been taken from her, she missed most the days when she looked across the place that had been home, and hadn't yet learned what empty was.

She was still awake at dawn, looking across the plain to the disappearing stars, when Frank found her.

"What's happened?"

"Elijah's gone to speak to the mayor." He sat with her. "How are your burns?"

"I'll live."

"I was calling for you."

"I know," she said.

They sat that way, not talking, just together and awake, until there was enough light to start work on the barn.

They worked all day, hacking out dead boards and scavenging replacements, trying to fit a home for the dogs.

"We could board them with the horses," Joseph said.

Maria frowned. "Absolutely not. Those dogs will go in the sitting room first."

"I'd beat you in a race through the house," Fa Liang said, and across Dog 2, Faye gave him a look until he laughed.

They worked until the supper bell, and ate quickly, too sore and tired to make conversation.

It wasn't until Maria was pouring coffee that the empty chair occurred to Faye.

"What time did Elijah leave this morning?"

Maria paused.

Then she pulled back with the pot in her hands, counting his hours, her knuckles going white.

"Oh please no," she said.

They stood up so fast they knocked their chairs over, a clatter that echoed as they ran for the dogs.

Because the land was what it was, Faye and Fa Liang saw the horse two miles before they reached him.

Whoever did it had waited until Elijah was on his own ground to shoot him.

His horse was loyal, and stood only a few yards from where his body had fallen – just past his property line, crossed by the long shadow of the sign for Western Fleet.

Fa Liang was the one who lifted the body and carried him to the dog.

(Faye couldn't imagine touching him; he was the sort who hadn't presumed.)

When Father Jake came to consecrate the ground, Susannah Pell came with him.

They all went up the hill in a ragged procession behind the cart that held Elijah's coffin, and they stood in a line beside the grave as the Father said things that didn't matter.

After it was over, Father Jake walked with Maria to the house, and Fa Liang and Joseph began to cover the coffin.

The dirt landed with heavy thuds, as if their fear and sorrow had cracked the land, and Elijah was sinking into a place that would never be quiet again.

Frank took the harness of the carthorse. Faye fell into step with him.

So did Susannah Pell.

"I have her papers," Miss Pell told Faye. "Let's hope she can keep the land."

So it was theirs to defend; the law would never freely give.

"Not with the railroad men coming," Faye muttered.

"They're afraid of you," Miss Pell said.

Faye looked over. "What?"

"They're cowards," Miss Pell said, with too much feeling for someone at the county clerk's. "Grant calls you awful names in town, makes out like you're trying to rob them of a chance."

"What are they saying?" Faye asked.

"Things no one should believe. Joseph's a drunk, he says. Fa Liang worked for opium traders."

Frank raised his eyebrows. "And?"

After a moment she admitted, "They say you have dark magic – you raise ghosts."

Faye flinched.

Frank reached out for her absently, pulled back. He wasn't a man of much comfort.

"If I could raise ghosts," said Frank, "they would be right to be afraid."

Miss Pell smiled tightly, moved faster to catch up with Father Jake and Maria.

"We should leave here," Faye said.

Frank looked at her. "Where would we go?"

He sounded as if he was thinking it over. Her chest went tight with hope.

Twice before, he'd run when she asked him to.

"Someplace quiet," she said. "Free of people. Free. I want to look at the sky and know there's no one else for fifty miles."

He put his hands in his pockets and looked sidelong at the horizon.

(For a moment he looked like the little boy he'd been the first time the schoolmaster had accused them of black magic, for speaking their language.)

"I'd feel like a coward if I ran."

"Then feel like a coward," she said, "and live."

After a moment, he turned and led the horse and cart toward the stable, on the far side of the big house.

For all she ached for home, she knew Frank's anger. The whites had done things that shouldn't even be spoken, yet they'd forgiven themselves. And now the train was trying to stretch an iron road across the land between them.

You just can't be dead enough for some people. They want to burn your footprints right off the earth.

They slept in the big house together – it was safer to take watches through the day.

There was no one left to speak for them. The town had done what was right, on paper. It was waiting to see if the railroad overcame, now that the man who mattered was dead.

By evening they were awake, preparing for the worst.

"We should fit up the dogs," Faye said as they loaded rifles at the table.

"What with?" asked Fa Liang.

"Claws," she said. "Blades. Something that can kill."

"They're mounts," said Joseph.

"They're weapons," she said. "Arm them."

Maria, who was distributing bullets, looked up. "One blade," she said. "Under the turn of the ankle. They won't see it until you use it."

Joseph looked at her.

But Frank and Fa Liang and Faye rose, to take blades from the kitchen and start their work.

Grant and the railroad men waited until deep night before they came.

As the cloud of orange dust rose behind their horses in the light of the torches they carried, Faye realized they must have been waiting to see if help arrived. They were sure, now, that it wouldn't; there was no hurry.

"We'll lead them away from the house," said Joseph.

He was too tall for a good dog rider, but he'd brought Elijah's horse from the barn, and had a rifle in one hand.

"Stay here," said Faye. "Maria will defend the house. Don't leave her alone."

Joseph looked at them, loading up their dogs with weapons and water.

"She's right," said Fa Liang. "Good luck."

After a beat, Joseph nodded, and turned for the house.

Faye mounted Dog 2, slung her rifle in the holster and her pistol at her side.

"Make for the hills," she said. "Fa Liang, flank them. We'll take them out from the rocks. Frank, with me."

"Of course," said Frank, and grinned, his mouth a bright sliver of white in the dark.

"You're a fool," she said, smiling.

"Ride out," said Fa Liang, and three engines started with a clunk and a shriek and a roar.

The dogs ate up ground toward the hills, which were easy enough to hide in and take shots while you could.

"How many are there?" Frank asked once.

She risked a look, in between the pistons of her dog's left legs, but behind them was only thunder and a soft glow, dimmer, as if some had broken off to burn the big house instead.

"Hope you brought plenty of bullets," she said.

Frank laughed, which numbed her fear a little; it was dark, and they knew the ground better than a stranger could, and any minute they'd reach the hills.

She'd forgotten about the barn fire in the chaos; when two left ankles on Frank's dog snapped, it took a moment too long to remember what happens to metal tempered in haste.

"Frank!" she called as soon as he dropped from sight. She gripped the rings and pulled; Dog 2 spun with a screech, circling back to him. "Quick, take the middle leg from mine. There's time if we move."

"There's no time," he said. His dog limped a few paces. It was slow, but the joints might hold long enough to reach the rocks.

The men were gaining; she could see two men with torches, two more in shadow.

"Get to the hills," she said.

He was testing the broken legs, finding a gait that could support him.

"Go on," he said through gritted teeth. "Fast as you can."

She hesitated. Her heart was pounding so hard it sounded like another horse coming after them.

One of the silhouettes, she could see, was Grant.

Her throat was dry.

"No," she said, "no, come *now*, come on, Frank—"

"Faye," he said, turned to her with a look she'd never seen. "Go on. I'm right behind you, soon as I can."

(She'd said the same to him, a long time ago, just before the soldiers reached them.)

The horses were coming into sight.

"Go on!" Frank shouted, gunned the engine, aimed the limping dog to follow her.

A gun went off, close, too close.

Faye took the hill.

It was slick and steep, and a struggle even for the dog, and she was fifty feet up before she realized there was no sound behind her but the thunder of the horses.

Frank, she thought, with a stab of guilt and sorrow sharp enough to tear her open; Frank, I would have stayed with you.

She didn't need to look to know what he'd done so she could escape; before she could turn, she heard two shots crossing and a sharp cry.

(It was a voice she'd know among a hundred voices.)

A body landed in the dirt.

She spun, hardly breathing, her hands white-knuckle on the shifts, and tilted back so the dog's front talons rose high, blades out.

The rifle appeared at her shoulder, two shots in quick succession. Someone shouted; there was a clatter of hooves on the rocks.

She'd take the hillside screaming, and kill who she could, before Grant got her.

She dropped the rifle in her lap, gunned the engine.

She never made it.

The rider who crested the hill on her right flank was one of Grant's railroaders.

He'd cast a wide net, she thought. He hadn't wanted survivors.

The man must have been nervous going up a rock face so sheer; it took a moment before he looked up and caught his first and last glimpse of a dog of the Western Fleet.

By the time she reached the bottom of the hill, Grant and his men had vanished.

Frank was already gone.

She sat with him for a little while, pushed his hair from his forehead and closed his eyes.

She didn't know any songs. (There was so little left.)

So she told him the story he'd loved as a child, of the warrior who sought his stolen wife in the enemy camp, and the old grandmother who advised him and called him from the dead when he was torn to pieces, and when the man had his wife he brought the grandmother home as well, because it's good not to leave behind those who care for you.

Her fingers were slick; she'd pulled at the rings until they bled.

When the worst of her trembling was over, she carried him to the dog, for his last journey home.

The others were in the yard, shouting plans to find them – Joseph was the fastest draw, Maria was on horseback, and Fa Liang had broken Dog 1 but was changing mounts, and knew how long it took railroad men to regroup.

Three men were scattered, dead, in the pool of light from the house.

Good, she thought dimly.

When Fa Liang saw Faye, his arms dropped as if grief had knocked him in the chest.

When Maria saw them, she dismounted and went inside, to clear the table for the dead.

Joseph reached for Frank, but hesitated, so Faye could object if she wanted to.

She didn't. Her strength was coming and going. She could barely walk.

(Joseph could carry him, they had built the water pump in the yard together, they'd been clever and now Frank never would be, never again, her hands were cold.)

They laid him on the table in the front room. Faye smoothed his hair down his shoulders, wiped blood from his face, laced his hands across his stomach in his old habit.

He'd wanted so much to fight for home, and win.

She yanked her hair out of its plaits, dragged her fingers through it, just for something to do with her hands.

Outside, she heard horses and engines, and people calling. Maria was riding for town to demand the sheriff honor her claim. Joseph was going with her, as armed guard.

There was a clatter as Fa Liang set the dog on watch.

When Faye looked into the hanging mirror on the far wall, there were two doubles in the frame; the weeping one reached out, took the cool hand of the other.

★　　　★　　　★

Maria and Joseph came back with grim faces, and spoke to Fa Liang. Then they came into the sitting room.

"To pay respects," Maria said.

Faye wanted to ask what had happened, but her throat was dry.

Through the window she could see down the flats to the horizon. She'd watched that open line a long time.

"They're debating if it's legal to interfere," Maria said, as if to Frank, before she left.

"You don't have to stay," Fa Liang told Faye, when it was his turn.

That was cruel, she thought; he had to know how hard it was to part from a brother.

There should be something, she thought, when the others had gone. There should be someone here who could prepare Frank for a good journey home.

But there wasn't. Grant and his men would be back. There was no time, even if she knew what should be done.

She couldn't even dress him the way he should be dressed; he had only the one necklace. The rest of it was any man's clothes.

She sat beside him for a long time, wishing she could cut her hair.

Frank had made her promise never to, after they cut his at the school. She'd given her word. He'd grown his hair out, since – it was as long as hers – but still, she'd never touched it.

Her hands ached for a pair of shears.

She thought about the people in River Pass, who wanted the railroad, and worried Frank would raise the dead against them.

To the north, if she could swing wide of prospectors, she'd be free. Shoshone territory had been eaten whole, but if she left this behind, she could look for land they might not yet have thought to steal.

All that had kept her here was Frank – his hope of making a safe place, his belief in holding firm.

It seemed a betrayal to go on alone.

She sat beside him, thinking about what it meant to stay here, about how much she was willing to fight.

Then she rose, and took what she needed, and kissed him goodbye.

★   ★   ★

What Grant and the Union Pacific see, when they come to lay claim to Elijah Pike's lands, is a campfire burning high behind a six-legged metal dog, front legs raised with blades out, bearing a single rider.

They see they've raised a ghost, an Indian come back to guard his land.

Their gun wrists get cold, suddenly; suddenly, their teeth are chattering.

Grant and one or two others struggle for reason. They think, it can't be him, it can't – they look around for any other person who can make a lie of this horror.

But the dog moves forward, impossibly nimble, and they see the man's face in the first streaks of dawn, and the breastplate of his necklace, missing strands and spattered with his blood.

"God save me, it's Frank Clement," Grant whispers, and the tremor under the name is the sound that sucks the fight out of them.

When Frank keeps coming, his jaw set and his dark eyes fixed on them, the monstrous insect moving underneath him with its engine shrieking, with his open mouth shrieking, with the thunder of the fire behind him, they run.

Less than an hour after Grant and his men had gone, Susannah Pell arrived with Lewis the sheriff and some deputies with guns.

When they came, Fa Liang and Joseph were gone – they'd taken the cart to fetch the broken dog – and Maria and Faye were sitting on the porch, flanked by loaded rifles.

The sheriff told Maria they'd found her claim legal, and the railroad in the wrong. Michael Grant had been formally accused of killing Elijah Pike, and the town would be suing Union Pacific for his murder.

It was the easiest way out, Faye thought, if the town was waking to a conscience. Grant was a good man to blame; he'd just been passing through on land that wasn't his, and that sort are easy to hate.

"The mayor's going to tell the railroad that God-fearing people won't condone that sort of thing," Susannah told Maria, in the tone of a sister. "You're free to stay – of course we'll stand with you. Poor Elijah."

★   ★   ★

Faye waited until the last of the River folk had passed beyond the horizon.

Then she said, "I'm going to bury him. Alone."

When Joseph moved to argue, Maria put a hand on his arm, and he looked down at her and reconsidered.

Stay here, Faye thought. Take whatever moments you can. They'll be far between.

They'd all be watched more closely, now, as long as they stayed here – the railroad and the town would both be waiting to see if the folk of Western Fleet had been worth their notice.

The price of a homestead, for their kind.

Fa Liang brought Dog 2 from the barn to the door, and she saw he'd lashed a shovel to the front of the seat.

"Call if you need us," he said, in the tone of a man who knew what it took to bury kin.

She didn't call.

All the while she dug into the earth nearly as tall as she was, and covered him with the soft dark dirt, she didn't make a sound.

When it was over, she sat beside the grave and looked out across the wide horizon, where it curved to meet the deep blue sky.

At dusk, Maria brought wildflowers to the grave.

Then she knelt beside Faye, and said, "What can I do for you?"

"Nothing."

"I know how it is, to let someone go who you loved."

She hadn't let him go, Faye thought, her stomach tight; that was half the grief.

"I wore his clothes," Faye said. "I wore his name."

Maria nodded. "It's strange, the things that happen. I had a husband I didn't love. I'll be his widow the rest of my life."

Faye smoothed her hands against her trousers.

(Some sorrows you carried alone.)

"Come in soon," Maria said. "It will be cold tonight."

Then she was moving across the rise and down the hill, sure-footed, all the way to the big house she owned, where she had made a garden grow from nothing.

Dark was rolling in above them.

Fa Liang was probably still on the porch, mending dogs' legs by candlelight. Maria would be in the kitchen by now, forcing a meal together, and Joseph would be seeing to the horses for the night before he came inside, to watch Maria and not say a thing.

There was no moon, no stars – clouds covered them, the sky was grieving. In the dark, she could see Green River, a dim candle flame across the basin.

Amazing, how far away light could be.

The train would come to Green River; the train would lace the land tight, a faster road to cross the plains.

She didn't want to see it. She would rather take a tipi and a horse and wander into the badlands, or die free in the first bitter winter.

But Frank was here; just now, she couldn't leave him.

A lamp went on in the front room. It swallowed the lights of Green River, flooded the whole place like morning – the half-standing barn, the shadows of dogs in the bunkroom, the path to the cabin that was hers and Frank's, their footsteps worn into the land.

Faye rose from the graveside, and started for home.

I Stole the DC's Eyeglass

Sofia Samatar

Dakpa I keep my sister, *kpoyo* I lose my sister.

Dakpa I keep my sister, *kpoyo* I lose my sister.

The termites listen. Their hearing embraces all sound, even the smallest. They hear the future. They chew the present away as the dark devours the moon.

I don't mind if you want to consult the termites first, old man. Ask them: *Should I help this hard-eyed child?*

I'll wait.

You probably think I'm funny, with my skinny body, my big ankle bones, the spots on my legs where bites have festered and left sores. Sickly, you'll sigh, and weak. You'll think of my sister Minisare who could carry a young tree across her back. Tall and lively she was, and when the chance came to work at the DC's house, when a relative of my mother's who cooked there said, *Send one of your girls*, it was Minisare my mother wanted to send, not me. But Minisare refused. Let the white man clean his own dirt, she said.

That's how I came to work at the DC's house, to wear a cotton dress and collect chits my mother could spend at the company store. I carried water to the house, so you see I'm strong even though I'm little. I swept his room. He keeps his wife and children in there, framed and pegged to the wall.

When Ture went to the sky he stole a thunderbolt, and when I went to the DC's house I stole an eyeglass.

It was lying on the table in his bedroom, a flat disc like a stone from the river. He'd forgotten to take it with him to the Site. I squinted through it, then dropped it into the pocket of my dress, chain and all. Afterwards, I told the head cook I'd broken it.

The cook slapped me hard, but I didn't care. I took the eyeglass home, and that night, secret by the fire, I gave it to my sister. It shone in her hand like a snail track. It was beautiful like her, and strange like her, and she gripped it and kissed me so hard I winced. We could hear my father groaning from his bed: my mother was laying hot stones along his back to ease the pain. The pain of working since dawn at the Site, digging for the DC. I wasn't like him, I thought; I was a thief. Reckless and clever as Ture.

Ture climbed to the sky on a spider web. When he got there, the clouds were locked. "Hey!" he shouted, pounding on their shining undersides. Rain fell hard, but the clouds didn't open. Ture began to sing, and his magical barkcloth hummed along with him in the rain.

> *Door in the clouds, open-o*
> *See the fresh meat I'm bringing-o*
> *Sweet as the oil of termites-o*
> *Cooked by my wife Nanzagbe-o!*

Then the clouds opened, and that's how Ture got in and stole the thunderbolt, bringing fire back to earth after all the coals had gone out. In our time, although you should always try to keep your own embers alight, you can be sure of finding a coal at a neighbor's house to start your fire. My mother used to send me out with the coal pot if our fire died, and I'd sing at the edge of a neighbor's place: "Door in the clouds, open-o!" Minisare taught me that there were other ways. "Here!" she whispered, commanding. "Watch!" She held the eyeglass on a stick.

I squatted beside her. The world was full of Sunday-morning quiet, the diggers sleeping, voices coming faint from the church. Sweat dripped down my neck. Minisare glared with terrible concentration at the pile of dry grass she'd made on the ground.

The eyeglass glittered, fixed in the twisted wood.

Sun filled the forest. I yawned.

Then something tickled my nose: the smell of burning.

"See!" Minisare breathed.

I stared. A thread of smoke uncurled in the air, and a tiny flame cracked its knuckles in the grass.

Sorcery, then.

For a long time I waited for something to happen: for the DC to shrivel and fade, for the Site to collapse, for the diggers to stop their pounding. But it seems the eyeglass was only a minor magic, for nothing stopped, as you know, you can hear the roar of the diggers even here. That endless roar, and the thunder of flying machines rolling overhead, manned by slave-soldiers from a foreign land. People say the noise chased the game from the forest, once, but then the animals got used to it. We're used to it, too. Show me a child who can't read lips.

Nothing changed at all – except my sister.

At first, it seemed only a stranger form of her usual stubbornness. She wouldn't go to the farm. When I went home at night, I heard my mother complaining: "Why did I marry from the west? This is their blood showing, this worthless girl!"

She said this because my father's people came from the western forest: my grandfather had gotten trapped on our side during the Breaking of the Clans. When I got close to the fire I saw her slapping her palms together as if in grief, and Minisare plaiting a mat.

Minisare plaited with tense, quick movements. She'd split the reeds into narrow strands. Firelight streaked them. "You'll ruin your eyes," I said.

She only jerked the reeds harder.

"Her eyes!" my mother said. "If that's all she ruins, I'll consider it a blessing. What she needs is a husband – one with hard hands."

The words chilled me, and later I told Minisare: "You should help our mother on the farm."

"I can't," she said.

"Why not?"

"I have to do something else."

"Something else? What else?"

The darkness was soft, complete, I couldn't see her at all.

"Out in the forest," she said. "I'll show you."

On Sunday, when I'd washed the dress and spread it out to dry, I followed my sister deep into the forest. Walking before me along the path she was still my own Minisare, cool, long-striding, pushing the grass and branches aside with the ease of a swimmer. Several of the neighbors' children trailed us, chattering in high voices. We entered a sunny space where the growth had been cleared as if for a farm. A jumble of objects littered the short grass: pots, blankets, barkcloth, cooking stones. It was like a house shaken inside out.

She turned to us, the little children and me. "Now." She smiled, pointing. "You fetch grass. You find me some nice long, hollow canes. The rest of you run to the charcoal burners and beg whatever you can. Pai-te, stay with me. I want you to check my stitches."

Her eyes were red. She hadn't washed her face. Her hair needed rebraiding. But her energy was the same as ever, her laugh as the children scattered, her taut jaw as we leaned together over the patchwork she wanted me to see, a swollen thing like a dead calf.

"What do you think?" she asked. "You're good at stitching – will these hold?"

"What *is* this thing?"

"I'll put oil on it afterward, of course, to keep off the rain. I think the oil will help the stitches too, it'll keep the air from getting through."

"Minisare." I put my hand on her arm. "Tell me. What is it?"

She looked at me. And I saw for the first time what my mother saw, what other people saw when they whispered about my sister: the chameleon eye. One of her eyes was a spirit eye, flecked with cloud, the whole forest trapped in it. Ghosts hung in the trees.

I only saw it for a moment.

"I can't tell you yet," she said.

"You said you'd tell me."

She shook her head. "I said I'd show you."

I looked at the stitches. She'd put pieces of leather and barkcloth together, goat-hair blankets, near-transparent bits of bladder.

There were also scraps of cotton. "Where did you get these?" I demanded.

Her face went stubborn, closed. "Just tell me about the stitches."

I sighed. "They're fine."

"Thank you."

She stood up, the chain I'd given her swinging at her skirt. In place of the eyeglass it held an ugly iron spike.

*　　*　　*

Minisare speaks of iron.

She weeps for the lost arts. There were smiths among us, once. They made leaping knives, the sight of which killed hope. The women plucked gold from the rivers and the smiths fashioned it into bangles, hot metal dashing into the mold like a young snake. Now smithwork is against the law, like carving, like drum-talk, like kingship, like the intricate and half-remembered varieties of marriage. You can find old pieces of iron in the forest, native iron it's called, black lumps like tree gum chewed up and spat in the weeds.

Minisare talked all the time when she was at home, sometimes so fast she stuttered. She spoke of going to visit our father's people on the other side of the line.

"You'll never get there," I said. "They'll put you in prison."

She laughed and cuffed my shoulder, throwing me off balance: her arms were heavier than she knew. Heavy with muscle, and ornaments too: wires strung with chunks of iron, battered metal cuffs, strings dangling bags full of something that clacked whenever she moved. She wore iron sticks in her hair and she kept a coil of string there for emergencies and her face was strong and preoccupied and filthy. But she could still sing in a voice as gentle and blue as the mushroom season:

> *House of Gbudwe, house of my grandfathers,*
> *Strangers are eating oil there.*

And sometimes, though less often now, she looked at me and smiled. "Little one," she'd say, and stroke my cheek with a bruised fingernail.

My mother's rages brought the neighbors running. "Look at you!" she screamed. "A brute, a beggar, a sick dog covered in filth from the white man's rubbish pits."

She ran at Minisare, one hand still clutching a lighted tobacco twist, a whorl of dried stuff like a smoky flower. She tried to pull off Minisare's strange ornaments, and Minisare let her try. After a while my mother gave up and sat down on the ground. Minisare walked away toward her place in the forest, leaving deep footprints. When she came back she wore a burn down the length of her arm.

"You have to stop," I said. But she couldn't stop. Even at night she couldn't rest: she worked on her mat because her fingers would not lie still. I found her plaiting by moonlight and she turned her head to look at me, the souls of the dead awake in her spirit eye. Sometimes I couldn't find her at all: she was prowling at the Site, risking the guards, or sneaking off to see the old witch woman of the lake. She begged me to come with her. The witch was teaching her the old drum language, she said. She seized my hand and tapped out a crazy rhythm.

"No!" I snatched my hand away.

Minisare stared, gaunt in the firelight, her beauty in chains. "But it's important," she whispered. She took my hand.

My eyes grew hotter and hotter, until the tears came. She didn't notice. She kept on tapping, insistent, my palm the drum's belly, my fingers its liver and heart.

Do you know what the world looks like through the DC's eyeglass?

I do. It's a blurred place; you can't tell the real things from the shadows.

People call you the Old Man of the Wood. You were a carver, once, but life in the mines made you bitter, and now you live alone. Still, I know you've heard of Minisare. Stories like hers travel everywhere, noisy and eager as the drone of the diggers. Stories like hers fall over the world like rain. Minisare, the girl who cooked iron. The girl who could carry a young tree. Big stories, and all of them true. But the small stories are also true. There's the story of how I went to the Site every day to deliver the DC's lunch. The story of how he gave me a chit as a tip, and I grasped that soft scrap of paper and shouted out as the cook had taught me: "*Thank you, Commissioner Sir!*" The story of how he seized me in the bedroom one cold morning, his enormous thumbs making my hipbones crack.

This story is also true. My head struck the wall, knocking down two frames. The DC's wife stared up from one of them, pale, trussed in cotton up to her chin. The DC muttered. He didn't touch me twice. I twisted and scrambled, I dashed from the room on all fours. Out on the road, I tore off the cotton dress.

I ran. I ran through the cutting grass without feeling anything. When I jumped in the river all the tiny cuts on my legs sang out in pain. I sank to the bottom, through water brown and clotted like a huge fungus. Then I kicked my way to the surface and came out gasping.

House of Gbudwe, house of my grandfathers, Strangers are eating oil there. That's a true story, too. What comes up from under the ground of the Site, but oil? Stones, you say; but the DC wants them, the DC eats them like groundnuts. They are as delicious as oil in the world beyond the glass.

The DC eats children. I learned this for myself.

Here is a truth for you: I stole the DC's eyeglass, but the DC stole my sister. When I came up from under the river I ran sobbing into the forest, fleeing toward Minisare, craving her strength. The branches of her clearing rang with sound. Children bounced up and down on the bags she'd sewn, each blast of air adding heat to the fire. My sister stood beyond the flames, blurred by the heat as if by tears, and her arm bulged black as she struck a piece of iron.

"Minisare!" I cried.

She did not answer me. A leather mask hid her face, a visor pulled over her eyes like a heavy scab.

"Minisare!"

I ran to her, and then I saw what she had made, out there in the forest. I saw the iron. I saw the beast.

The creature moved. It shook. Its bowels rumbled. It had no eyes. Its whole body bristled with claws of every size. They were made of old knives, hoes, ragged sheets of iron, sharpened sticks. Its bloated hind parts breathed an obscene white wind.

"Minisare," I breathed. And my sister shook her head. She shook her head at me. She motioned me away with one iron-ringed arm. She had no time to spare. The beast absorbed all of her attention: this beast that stank of smoke, of the DC, of the Site. My hand tingled, as if she were drumming on it, and I thought of the way she tapped without listening to my words, without seeing my tears. I knew then that her strength was no longer for me, but for something else. She had gone through the glass and left me here, on the other side.

That night Ture came to me in a dream.

He was strutting around the Site with his belly stuck out. His elephant-skin bag hung heavy on his shoulder. I crawled on the ground, hiding under a banana leaf, and whispered: "Ture!"

"Oho!" he grinned. "Pai-te, are you there?"

"Ture, it isn't safe here!" I whispered, shrinking under the leaf in terror as machines buzzed overhead. "The DC will find you and put you in prison!"

His smile was so wide it cracked his face like an egg. "Ha! Ha!" he roared, slapping his skinny thighs.

Just then a little dog trotted by, almost under his feet, and he stumbled over it. The dog gave a yelp of pain.

Ture's eyes widened. "Ah!" he said, delighted. "Music!" He took his feathered hat out of his elephant-skin bag and put it on his head. Then he began to leap and trip over the dog, always finding his footing at the last moment, and when the dog cried out he sang with it in a high voice:

> *I am he who looks up*
> *I look down, all men die.*
> *Ture has stumbled-o,*
> *Ture is dancing!*

As Ture danced, the DC strode toward us, his eyeglass tight in his eye, and a fire came out of it and scorched the earth all around him. I screamed to warn Ture, but Ture only laughed more uproariously than ever and cried: "Do you think I'm afraid of my friend the DC? I've taught him all he knows!" And he sang:

> *House of Gbudwe, house of my grandfathers; Strangers are*
> *eating oil there.*

Then he stopped dancing and looked at me sadly. The DC stood beside him. And Minisare in her rough jewelry came and stood on the other side, and all three looked down at me with eyes like salt.

"Once," said Ture, "you fought with your sister. You were very young, and you bit her finger. Is that blood in you still, or have you spat it out?"

"I don't know," I sobbed.

Ture beamed. "Music!" he cried, adjusting the set of his hat. And then he kicked sand in my eyes and woke me up.

*   *   *

The next Sunday evening I took my mother's digging stick and went behind the house to the termite mound. I broke off two branches, one from the *dakpa* tree, the other from the *kpoyo* tree. I dug two holes in the mound with the digging stick and put one branch in each. The sky was pale red, the ants drowsy in the cold grass.

"*Dakpa*," I said. "*Dakpa* I keep my sister. If I keep my sister, eat *dakpa*. *Kpoyo* I lose my sister. If I lose my sister, eat *kpoyo*."

I went to help my mother with the evening meal. Children laughed somewhere, at someone else's place, and the piping sound came toward us in broken pieces. A sound like a whistle to call the birds. In the morning, when it was just daylight, I woke up and crept out to the termite mound. The termites had been listening to the future, and they had eaten some of both branches. I took the two branches out and measured them on the ground. I thought the *dakpa* branch was shorter. I still think the *dakpa* branch was shorter. I woke my mother and told her: "Minisare must be married."

We came for her two weeks later.

My mother had agreed at once that we must find Minisare a husband. "Haven't I been saying so?" she cried. My father was uncertain: he worried that her madness was too well known, and no one would take her. "That's why we must do it now," I countered, "before it gets worse." He hung his head, then shrugged, and that day he began to look for a groom. And he found one: the man who now strode beside my mother, snapping off twigs when they touched him. A noisy crowd followed: relatives, neighbors, friends and trading partners, and then the hangers-on looking for Sunday excitement and hoping to smell food.

I knew, you see, that she would not hear me if I went alone.

My mother gasped and clutched my arm as we entered the clearing. "Don't be afraid," I told her, tense as wood. The groom looked startled, the strange scene piercing the layers of drunkenness he wore like a cloak. Minisare's fire was ashes today, the stones of her forge a ruin. Only her familiar, the clawed beast, gave off heat. Minisare was flinging charcoal into its anus. The children helping her cheered and skittered toward the crowd when they saw their elders.

"Look!" crowed a little boy. "Look what we made!"

The noise of the crowd swelled to a groan. My father stepped forward, his face grey. His crooked back gleamed with sweat. "Minisare," he said sternly. "Minisare, come with us. We have brought you a husband."

A foolish plan. I see this now. But I believed the termites, who had eaten *dakpa*, who had said I would keep my sister.

Minisare pushed up her leather visor and flashed her spirit eye. Then she tore the beast's skin wide, stepped into its body and closed the skin up again.

People were running, screaming.

"Why didn't you tell me?" my mother sobbed. "It's too late, it's too late now to save her."

She shrank to the ground. Minisare's groom shambled away in panic, crashing into trees, fleeing his demon-bride. And I stood lost, the air thickening around me, until my father seized my arm.

"They've gone to fetch the soldiers," he panted.

When I didn't move, he slapped me. "*Run*, Pai-te."

When I still didn't move, he ran away without me. The children had scaled the trees, their cries snagged in the branches.

Everywhere people were crashing away through the undergrowth, and the shadows of the great flying-machines closed over us, and all the trees rattled their arms, and the side of Minisare's monster split like a wound, and Minisare leaned out and shouted: "Pai-te, run! They're going to start firing!"

She saw that I wasn't moving. She put a leg out of the monster's side.

Death striped the forest, clots of molten blood.

When her foot touched the ground, something leapt up in my throat.

"No!" I shouted, waving frantically. "No! Just go! I'm all right!"

My pulse beat under my jaw, so strong it almost made me sob, a voice singing: *Door in the clouds, open-o!* I knew that voice: it was Minisare's blood talking to me, the blood I had swallowed long ago and forgotten.

"Go!" I shouted.

By this time, there was too much noise for her to hear me. But she understood. Show me a child who can't read lips.

She looked at me from her creature's side, her eyes human now, lonely and radiant. Then she closed the skin, and the beast spun its claws and sank into the ground.

Dakpa I keep my sister, *kpoyo* I lose my sister.

That is how heroes are made. At night mothers say: "I'll tell you of Minisare, who stole a lamp from heaven." They whisper into their husbands' hair: "Wait until Minisare returns." They say she's gone underground, across the lines, to unite the clans. They say she's stamping the dust somewhere, her iron anklets jangling, her face masked, and everywhere she steps a puff of smoke flies up. Each smoke cloud puts out teeth. Someday the mines will collapse, and Minisare will burst from the ruins with an army of iron dogs.

And that is also how villains are made. I sat quiet under my mother's shouts as she ordered me to go back to the DC's house. When she ran out of breath I curled up on my mat, Minisare's unfinished mat. I stroked the strands of unwoven straw as my mother mourned by the fire. "Minisare was like me," she often tells me now. "You are your father's child." I don't mind these words. I know that grief is all my mother has in the place where Minisare used to be, and that all the love she had for Minisare must now be lavished on this grief which she carries about like a stillborn child. Also, she's telling the truth about my sister for the first time. The neighbors comfort her while she weeps and tells the truth. Minisare was everything, everything worth having on this earth: defiance, honor, dawn, tomorrow. She was the rain.

And Ture, traitor, thief, where is he? He's hiding behind this story, trying to coax it toward him. He wants to make it his own. Or no, he's not here, he went out of the tale at the same moment as my sister, the moment our history became too small to tempt him. For Ture has no interest in the small. He stumbles over them, sings along with their cries and then moves on. Some people say that he's living with the DC, that the two of them drink from the same bottle, that the DC hides him and uses his power. This may be true. Foolish, clever Ture has always delighted in fire, in iron, in risk, in grand schemes leading to glory or despair. His language is song, not story. He is dancing in the mines and among the flying machines. He will not remember me.

But I stole the DC's eyeglass. I have that. Wherever my sister is, she's warm, she has light to keep demons and leopards away, she's not afraid. And I'll do more. I have done more. I went to the witch woman of the lake and squirmed under the thatch of her sinking roof and asked her to teach me drum. The darkness smelled of snails and her hand was as stiff and rough as a hunk of dried fish when I tapped out the rhythm Minisare taught me. A gurgle came out of the gloom: the witch woman was laughing. She knotted her fingers in my hair and pulled me to her and told me secrets.

I dream of learning more, of teaching others. I dream of *you*, old man. They say you made drums in secret, in the old days. I dream you'll make me a drum. I dream of a clearing on a dark night, and the drum-voice spreading out, crossing the line between the clans.

Ask the termites. They never lie. Come, give me your hand, and I'll prove it to you. I'll pass you the words my sister drummed into my hand. *Forgive me*, the drum beats say. Do you feel it? That's a true story, too, a small story that's slowly growing bigger: I keep my sister.

Wait while I play you the rest of her message, a gift without weight or outline, invisible until you make it happen, like fire.

Pai-te, it says. Yes, it says my name, my actual name.

Watch your step, it says. *I'm coming back for you.*

The Colliers' Venus (1893)

Caitlín R. Kiernan

1.

It is not an ostentatious museum. Rather, it is only the sort of museum that best suits this modern, industrious city at the edge of the high Colorado plains. This city, with its sooty days and dusty, crowded streets and night skies that glow an angry orange from the dragon's breath of half a hundred Bessemer converters. The museum is a dignified, yet humble assemblage of geological wonders, intended as much for the delight and edification of miners and mill workers, blacksmiths and butchers, as it is for the *parvenu* and Old Money families of Capitol Hill. Professor Jeremiah Ogilvy, both founder and curator of this *Colectanea rerum memorabilium*, has always considered himself a progressive sort, and he has gone so far as to set aside one day each and every month when the city's negroes, coolies and red Indians are permitted access to his cabinet, free of charge. Professor Ogilvy would – and frequently has – referred to his museum as a most *modest* endeavor, one whose principal mission is to reveal, to *all* the populace of Cherry Creek, the long-buried mysteries of those fantastic, vanished cycles of the globe. Too few suspect the marvels that lie just beneath their feet or entombed in the ridges and peaks of the snowcapped Chippewan Mountains bordering the city to the west. Cherry Creek looks always to the problems of its present day, and to the riches and prosperity that may await those who reach its future, but with hardly a thought to spare for the past, and *this* is the sad oversight addressed by the Ogilvy Gallery of Natural Antiquities.

Before Professor Ogilvy leased the enormous redbrick

building on Kipling Street (erected during the waning days of the silver boom of 1879), it served as a warehouse for a firm specializing in the import of exotic dry goods, mainly spices from Africa and the East Indies. And, to this day, it retains a distinctive, piquant redolence. Indeed, at times the odor is so strong that a sobriquet has been bestowed upon the museum, Ogilvy's Pepper Pot. It is not unusual to see visitors of either gender covering their noses with handkerchiefs and sleeves, and oftentimes the solemnity of the halls is shattered by hacking coughs and sudden fits of sneezing. Regardless, the Professor has insisted, time and again, that the structure is perfectly matched to his particular needs, and how the curiosity of man is not to be deterred by so small an inconvenience as the stubborn ghosts of turmeric and curry powder, coriander and mustard seed. Besides, the apparently indelible odor helps to insure that his rents will stay reasonable.

On this June afternoon, the air in the building seems a bit fresher than usual, despite the oppressive heat that comes with the season. In the main hall, Jeremiah Ogilvy has been occupied for almost a full hour now, lecturing the ladies of the Cherry Creek chapter of the Women's Christian Temperance Union. Mrs Belford and her companions sit on folding chairs, fanning themselves and diligently listening while this slight, earnest, and bespectacled man describes for them the reconstructed fossil skeleton displayed behind him.

"The great anatomist, Baron Cuvier, wrote of the *Plesiosaurus*, 'it presents the most monstrous assemblage of characteristics that has been met with among the races of the ancient world'. Now, I would have you know it isn't necessary to take this expression literally. There are no monsters in nature, as the Laws of Organization are never so positively infringed."

"Well, it looks like a monster to me," mutters Mrs Larimer, seated near the front. "I would certainly hate to come upon such a thing slithering toward me along a riverbank. I should think I'd likely perish of fright, if nothing else."

There's a subdued titter of laughter from the group, and Mrs Belford frowns. The Professor forces a ragged smile and repositions his spectacles on the bridge of his nose.

"Indeed," he sighs and glances away from his audience, looking over his shoulder at the skillful marriage of plaster and stone and welded steel armature.

"However," he continues, "be that as it may, it is more accordant with the general perfection of Creation to see in an organization so special as *this*—" and, with his ashplant, he points once more to the plesiosaur "—to recognize in a structure which differs so notably from that of animals of our days – the simple augmentation of type, and sometimes also the beginning and successive perfecting of these beings. Therefore, let us dismiss this idea of monstrosity, my good Mrs Larimer, a concept that can only mislead us, and only cause us to consider these antediluvian beasts as digressions. Instead, let us look upon them, not with disgust. Let us learn, on the contrary, to perceive in the plan traced for their organization, the handiwork of the Creator of all things, as well as the general plan of Creation."

"How very inspirational." Mrs Belford beams, and when she softly claps her gloved hands, the others follow her example.

Professor Ogilvy takes this as his cue that the ladies of the Women's Christian Temperance Union have heard all they wish to hear this afternoon on the subject of the giant plesiosaur, recently excavated in Kansas from the chalky banks of the Smoky Hill River. As one of the newer additions to his menagerie, it now frequently forms the centerpiece of the Professor's daily presentations.

When the women have stopped clapping, Mrs Larimer dabs at her nose with a swatch of perfumed silk and loudly clears her throat.

"Yes, Mrs Larimer? A question?" Professor Ogilvy asks, turning back to the women. *Mr* Larimer – an executive with the Front Range offices of the German airship company, Gesellschaft zur Förderung der Luftschiffahrt – has donated a sizable sum to the museum's coffers, and it's no secret that his wife believes her husband's charity would be best placed elsewhere.

"I mean no disrespect, Professor, but it strikes *me* that perhaps you have gone and mistaken the provenance of that beast's design. For my part, it's far easier to imagine such a fiend being more at home in the sulfurous tributaries of Hell than the waters of any earthly ocean. Perhaps, my good doctor, it may be that you are merely mistaken about the demon's having ever been buried.

Possibly, to the contrary, it is something which clawed its way *up* from the Pit."

Jeremiah Ogilvy stares at her a moment, aware that it's surely wisest to humor this disagreeable woman. To nod and smile and make no direct reply to such absurd remarks. But he has always been loath to suffer fools, and has never been renowned as the most politic of men, often to his detriment. He makes a steeple of his hands and rests his chin upon his fingertips as he replies.

"And yet," he says, "oddly, you'll note that on both its fore *and* hind limbs, each fashioned into paddles, this underworld fiend of yours entirely *lacks* claws. Don't you think, Mrs Larimer, that we might fairly expect such modifications, something not unlike the prominent ungula of a mole, perhaps? Or the robust nails of a Cape anteater? I mean, that's a terrible lot of digging to do, all the way from Perdition to the prairies of Gove County."

There's more laughter, an uneasy smattering that echoes beneath the high ceiling beams, and it elicits another scowl from an embarrassed Mrs Belford. But the Professor has cast his lot, as it were, for better or worse, and he keeps his eyes fixed upon Mrs Charles W. Larimer. She looks more chagrined than angry, and any trace of her former bluster has faded away.

"As you say, *Professor*," and she manages to make the last three syllables sound like a badge of wickedness.

"Very well, then," Professor Ogilvy says, turning to Mrs Belford. "Perhaps I could interest you gentle women in the celebrated automatic mastodon, a bona-fide masterpiece of clockwork engineering and steam power. So realistic in movement and appearance you might well mistake it for the living thing, newly resurrected from some boggy Pleistocene quagmire."

"Oh, yes. I think that would be fascinating," Mrs Belford replies, and soon the women are being led from the main gallery up a steep flight of stairs to the mezzanine where the automatic mastodon and the many engines and hydraulic hoses that control it have been installed. It stands alongside a finely preserved skeleton of *Mammut americanum* unearthed by prospectors in the Yukon and shipped to the gallery at some considerable expense.

"Why, it's nothing but a great hairy elephant," Mrs Larimer protests, but this time none of the others appear to pay her much mind. Professor Ogilvy's fingers move over the switches and dials on the brass control panel, and soon the automaton is stomping its massive feet and flapping its ears and filling the hot, pepper-scented air with the trumpeting of extinct Pachydermata.

2.

When the ladies of the Temperance Union have gone, and after Jeremiah Ogilvy has seen to the arrival of five heavy crates of saurian bones from one of his collectors working out of Monterey, and, then, after he has spoken with his chief preparator about an overdue shipment of blond Kushmi shellac, ammonia and sodium borate, he checks his pocket watch and locks the doors of the museum. Though there has been nothing excessively trying about the day – not even the disputatious Mrs Larimer caused him more than a passing annoyance – Professor Ogilvy finds he's somewhat more weary than usual, and is looking forward to his bed with an especial zeal. All the others have gone, his small staff of technicians, sculptors and naturalists, and he retires to his office and puts the kettle on to boil. He has a fresh tin of Formosa Oolong, and decides that this evening he'll take his tea up on the roof.

Most nights, there's a fine view from the gallery roof, and he can watch the majestic airships docking at the Arapahoe Station dirigible terminal, or just shut his eyes and take in the commingled din of human voices and buckboards, the heavy clop of horses' hooves and the comforting pandemonium made by the locomotives passing through the city along the Colorado and Northern Kansas Railway.

He hangs the tea egg over the rim of his favorite mug and is preparing to pour the hot water, when the office doorknob rattles and neglected hinges creak like inconvenienced rodents. Jeremiah looks up, not so much alarmed as taken by surprise, and is greeted by the familiar – but certainly unexpected – face and pale blue eyes of Dora Bolshaw. She holds up her key, tied securely on a frayed length of calico ribbon, to remind him that he never took it back and to remove any question as to how she gained entry to the locked museum after hours. Dora Bolshaw is an engine mechanic for the Rocky Mountain Reconsolidated Fuel Company, and, because of this, and her habit of dressing always in men's clothes, *and* the fact that her hands and face are only rarely anything approaching clean, she is widely, and mistakenly, believed to be an inveterate Sapphist. Dora is, of course, shunned by more proper women – such as, for instance, Mrs Charles W. Larimer – who blanch at the thought of *dames et lesbiennes* walking free and unfettered in their midst. Dora has often mused that, despite her obvious preference for men, she is surely the most renowned bulldyke west of the Mississippi.

"Slipping in like a common sneak thief," Jeremiah sighs, reaching for a second cup. "I trust you recollect the combination to the strongbox, along with the whereabouts of that one loose floorboard."

"I most assuredly do," she replies. "Like they were the finest details of the back of my hand. Like it was only yesterday you went and divulged those confidences."

"Very good, Miss Bolshaw. Then, I trust this means we can forgo the messy gunplay and knives and whatnot?"

She steps into the office and pulls the door shut behind her, returning the key to a pocket of her waistcoat. "If that's your fancy, Professor. If it's only a peaceable sort of evening you're after."

Filling his mug from the steaming kettle, submerging the mesh ball of the tea egg and the finely ground leaves, Jeremiah shrugs and nods at a chair near his desk.

"Do you still take two lumps?" he asks her.

"Provided you got nothing stronger," she says, and only hesitates a moment before crossing the room to the chair.

"No," Jeremiah tells her. "Nothing stronger. If I recall, we had an agreement, you and I?"

"You want your key back?"

Professor Jeremiah Ogilvy pours hot water into a teacup, adds a second tea egg, and very nearly asks if she imagines that his feelings have changed since the last time they spoke. It's been almost six months since the snowy January night when he asked her to marry him. Dora laughed, thinking it only a poor joke at first. But when pressed, she admitted she was not the least bit interested in marriage and, what's more, confessed she was even less amenable to giving up her work at the mines to bear and raise children. When she suggested that *he* board up *his* museum, instead, and for a family take in one or two of the starving guttersnipes who haunt Colliers' Row, there was an argument. Before it was done, he said spiteful things, cruel jibes aimed at all the tender spots she'd revealed to him over the years of their courtship. And he knew, even as he spoke the words, that there would be no taking them back. The betrayal of Dora's trust came too easily, the turning of her confidences against her, and she is not a particularly forgiving woman. So, tonight, he only *almost* asks, then thinks better of the question and holds his tongue.

"It's your key," he says. "Keep it. You may have need of it again one day."

"Fine," Dora replies, letting the chair rock back on two legs. "It's your funeral, Jeremiah."

"Can I ask why you're here? That is, to what do I owe this unheralded pleasure?"

"You may," she says, staring now at a fossil ammonite lying in a cradle of excelsior on his desk. "It's bound to come out, sooner or later. But if you're thinking maybe I come looking for old times or a quick poke—"

"I *wasn't*," he lies, interrupting her.

"Well, good. Because I ain't."

"Which begs the question. And it's been a rather tedious day, Miss Bolshaw, so, if we can dispense with any further niceties."

Dora coughs and leans forward, the front legs of her chair bumping loudly against the floor. Jeremiah keeps his eyes on the two cups of tea, each one turned as dark now as a sluggish, tannin-stained bayou.

"I'm guessing that you still haven't seen anyone about that cough," he says. "And that it hasn't improved."

Dora coughs again before answering him, then wipes at her mouth with an oil-stained handkerchief. "Good to see time hasn't dulled your mental faculties," she mutters hoarsely, breathlessly, then clears her throat and wipes her mouth again.

"It doesn't sound good, Dora, that's all. You spend too much time in the tunnels. Plenty enough people die from anthracosis without ever having lifted a pickaxe or loaded a mine car, as I'm sure you're well aware."

"I also didn't come here to discuss my health," she tells him, stuffing the handkerchief back into a trouser pocket. "It's the *stink* of this place, gets me wheezing, that's all. I swear, Jeremiah, the air in this dump, it's like trying to breathe inside a goddamn burr grinder that's been used to mill capsicum and black powder."

"No argument there," he says and takes the tea eggs from the cups and sets them aside on a dishtowel. "But, I still don't know why you're here."

"Been some odd goings on down in Shaft Number Seven, ever since they started back in working on the Molly Gray vein."

"I thought Shaft Seven flooded in October," Jeremiah says, and he adds two sugar cubes to Dora's cup. The Professor has never taken his tea sweetened, nor with lemon, cream, or whiskey, for that matter. When he drinks tea, it's the tea he wants to taste.

"They pumped it out a while back, got the operation up and running again. Anyway, one of the foremen knew we were acquainted and asked if I'd mind. Paying you a call, I mean."

"Do you?" he asks, carrying the cups to the desk.

"Do I what?"

"Do you *mind*, Miss Bolshaw?"

She glares at him a moment, then takes her cup and lets her eyes wander back to the ammonite on the desk.

"So, these odd goings on. Can you be more specific?"

"I can, *if* you'll give me a chance. You ever heard of anyone finding living creatures sealed up inside solid rock, two thousand feet below ground?"

He watches her a moment, to be sure this isn't a jest. "You're saying this has happened, in Shaft Seven?"

She sips at her tea, then sets the cup on the edge of the desk and picks up the ammonite. The fossilized mother of pearl glints iridescent shades of blue-green and scarlet and gold in the dim gaslight of the office.

"That's exactly what I'm saying. And I seen most of them for myself, so I know it's not just miners spinning tall tales."

"Most of *them*? So, it's happened more than once?"

Dora ignores the questions, turning the ammonite over and over in her hands.

"I admit," she says, "I was more than a little skeptical at first. There's a shale bed just below the Molly Gray seam, and it's chockfull of siderite nodules. Lots of them have fossils inside. Matter of fact, I think I brought a couple of boxes over to you last summer, before the shaft started taking water."

"You did. There were some especially nice seed ferns in them, as I recall."

"Right. Well, anyhow, a few days back I started hearing these wild stories, that someone had cracked open a nodule and found a live frog trapped inside. And then a spider. And then worms, and so on. When I asked around about it, I was directed to the geologist's shack, and, sure as hell, there were all these things lined up in jars, things that had come out of the nodules. Mostly, they were dead. Most of them died right after they came out of the rocks, or so I'm told."

Dora stops talking and returns the ammonite shell to its box. Then she glances at Jeremiah, and takes another sip of her tea.

"And you *know* it's not a hoax?" he asks her. "I mean, you know it's not tomfoolery, just some of the miners taking these things down with them from the surface, then claiming to have found them in the rocks? Maybe having a few laughs at the expense of their supervisors?"

"Now, that *was* my first thought."

"But then you saw something that changed your mind," Jeremiah says. "And that's why you're here tonight."

Dora Bolshaw takes a deep breath, and Jeremiah thinks she's about to start coughing again. Instead, she nods and exhales slowly. He notices beads of sweat standing out on her upper lip, and wonders if she's running a fever.

"I'm here tonight, Professor Ogilvy, because two men are dead. But, yeah, since you asked, I've seen sufficient evidence to convince me this ain't just some jackass thinks he's funny. When I voiced my doubts, Charlie McNamara split one of those nodules open right there in front of me. Concretion big around as my fist," and she holds up her left hand for emphasis. "He took up a hammer and gave it a smart tap on one side, so it cleaved in two, pretty as you please. And out crawled a fat red scorpion. You ever *seen* a red scorpion, Jeremiah?"

And Professor Ogilvy thinks a moment, sipping his tea come all the way from Taipei City, Taiwan. "I've seen plenty of reddish-brown scorpions," he says. "For example, *Diplocentrus lindo*, from the Chihuahuan Desert and parts of Texas. The carapace is, in fact, a dark reddish-brown."

"I didn't *say* reddish brown. What I said was *red*. Red as berries on a holly bush, or a ripe apple. Red as blood, if you want to go get morbid about it."

"Charlie cracked open a rock, from Shaft Number Seven, and a bright red scorpion crawled out. That's what you're telling me?"

"I am." Dora nods. "Bastard had a stinger on him big around as my thumb, and then some," and now she holds out her thumb.

"And two men at the mines have *died* because of these scorpions?" Jeremiah Ogilvy asks.

"No. Weren't scorpions killed them," she says and laughs nervously. "But it *was* something come out those rocks." And then she frowns down at her teacup and asks the Professor if he's absolutely sure that he doesn't have anything stronger. And this time, he opens a bottom desk drawer and digs out the pint bottle of rye he keeps there, and he offers it to her. Dora Bolshaw pulls out the cork and pours a generous shot into her teacup, but then she's coughing again, worse than before, and he watches her, and waits for it to pass.

3.

What she's told him is not without precedent. Over the years, Professor Jeremiah Ogilvy has encountered any number of seemingly inexplicable reports of living inclusions discovered in stones, and often inside lumps of coal. Living fossils, after a fashion. He has never once given them credence, but, rather, looked upon these anecdotes as fine examples of the general gullibility of men, not unlike the taxidermied "jackalopes" he's seen in shop windows, or tales of ghostly hauntings, or of angels, or the antics of spiritual mediums. They are all quite amusing, these phantasma, until someone insists that they're true.

For starters, he could point to an 1818 lecture by Dr Edward Daniel Clarke, the first professor of mineralogy at Cambridge University. Clarke claimed to have been collecting Cretaceous sea urchins when he happened across three newts entombed in the chalk. To his amazement, the amphibians showed signs of life, and though two quickly expired after being exposed to air, the third was so lively that it escaped when he placed it in a nearby pond to aid in its rejuvenation. Or, a case from the summer of 1851, when well-diggers in Blois, France, were supposed to have discovered a live toad inside a piece of flint. Indeed, batrachians figure more prominently in these accounts than any other creature, and the Professor might also have brought to Dora Bolshaw's attention yet another toad, said to have been freed from a lump of iron ore the very next year, this time somewhere in the East Midlands of England.

The list goes on and on, reaching back centuries. On 8 May 1733, the Swedish architect Johan Gråberg supposedly witnessed the release of a frog from a block of sandstone. So horrified was Gråberg at the sight that he is said to have beaten the beast to death with a shovel. An account of the incident was summarily published, by Gråberg, in the *Transactions of the Swedish Academy of Sciences*, a report that was eventually translated into Dutch, Latin, German and French.

Too, there is the account from 1575 by the surgeon Ambroise Paré, who claimed a live toad was found inside a stone in his vineyards in Meudon. In 1686, Professor Robert Plot, the first Keeper of the Ashmolean Museum in Oxford claimed knowledge of three cases of the "toad-in-the-hole" phenomenon from Britain alone. Hoaxes, perhaps, or only the gullible yarns of a pre-scientific age, when even learned men were somewhat more disposed to believing the unbelievable.

But Jeremiah Ogilvy mentioned none of these tales. Instead, he sat and sipped his tea and listened while she talked, never once interrupting to give voice to his mounting incredulity. However, her cough forced Dora Bolshaw to stop several times and, despite the rye whiskey, towards the end of her story she was hoarse and had grown alarmingly pale; her hands were shaking so badly that she had trouble holding her cup steady. And then, when she was done, and he was trying to organize his thoughts, she glanced anxiously at the clock and said that she should be going. So he walked her downstairs, past the celebrated automatic mastodon and petrified titanothere skulls and his prized plesiosaur skeleton. Standing on the walkway outside the museum, the night air seemed sweet after the "pepper pot", despite the soot from the furnaces and the reek from the open ditches lining either side of Kipling Street. He offered to see her home, because the thoroughfares of Cherry Creek have an unsavory reputation after dark, but she laughed at him, and he didn't offer a second time. He watched until she was out of sight, then went back to his office.

And now it's almost midnight, and Jeremiah Ogilvy's teacups sit empty and forgotten while he thinks about toads and stones and considers finishing off the pint of rye. After she told him of the most recent and bizarre and, indeed, entirely impossible discovery from Shaft Seven, the thing that was now being blamed for the deaths of two miners, he agreed to look at it.

"Not *it*. *Her*," Dora said, folding and unfolding her handkerchief. "She came out of the rocks, Jeremiah. Just like that damned red scorpion, she came out of the rocks."

4.

"Then I *am* dreaming," he says, relieved, and she smiles, not unkindly. He's holding her hand, this woman who is, by turns, Dora Bolshaw and a wispy, nervous girl named Katharine Herschel, whom he courted briefly before leaving New Haven and the comforts of Connecticut for the clamorous frontier metropolis of Cherry Creek. They stand together on some windswept aerie of steel and concrete, looking down upon the night-shrouded city. And Jeremiah holds up an index finger and traces the delicate network of avenues illumined by gas street lamps. And *there*, at his fingertip, are the massive hangars and the mooring masts of the Arapahoe Terminal. A dirigible is approaching from the south, parting the omnipresent pall of clouds, and the ship begins a slow, stately turn to starboard. To his eyes, it seems more like some majestic organism than any human fabrication. A heretofore unclassified order of volant Cnidaria, perhaps, titan jellyfish that has forsaken the brine and the vasty deep and adapted to a life in the clouds. Watching the dirigible, he imagines translucent, stinging tentacles half a mile long, hanging down from its gondola to snare unwary flocks of birds. The underside of the dirigible blushes yellow-orange as the lacquered cotton of its outer skin catches and reflects the molten light spilling up from all the various ironworks and the copper and silver foundries scattered throughout Cherry Creek. The bones of the world exhumed and smelted to drive the tireless progress of man. He's filled with pride, gazing out across the city and knowing the small part he has played in birthing this civilization from a desolate wilderness fit for little more than prairie dogs, rattlesnakes and heathen savages.

"Maybe the world don't exactly see it that way," Dora says. "I been thinking lately, maybe she don't see it that way at all."

Jeremiah isn't surprised when tendrils of blue lightning flick down from the coal-smoke sky, and crackling electric streams trickle across rooftops and down the rainspouts of the high buildings.

"Maybe," Dora continues, "the world has different plans. Maybe she's had them all along. Maybe, Professor, we've finally gone and dug too deep in these old mountains."

But Jeremiah makes a derisive, scoffing noise and shakes his head. And then he recites scripture while the sky rains ultramarine and the shingles and cobblestones sizzle. "And God said, Let us make man in our image, after our likeness: and let them have dominion over the fish of the sea, and over the fowl of the air, and over the cattle, and over all the earth, and over every creeping thing that creepeth upon the earth."

"I don't recall it saying nothing about whatever creepeth *under* the earth," Dora mutters, though now she looks a little more like Katharine Herschel, her blue eyes turning brown, and her trousers traded for a petticoat. "Besides, you're starting to sound like that idiotic Larimer woman. Didn't you hear a single, solitary word I said to you?"

Jeremiah raises his hand still higher, as though, with only a little more effort, he might reach the lightning or the shiny belly of the approaching dirigible or even the face of the Creator, peering down at them through the smoldering haze.

"Is it not fair wondrous?" he asks Dora. But it's Katharine who answers him, and she only trades him one question for another, repeating Dora's words.

"Didn't you hear a single, solitary word I said?"

And they are no longer standing high atop the aerie, but have been grounded again, grounded now. He's seated with Dora and Charlie McNamara in the cluttered nook that passes for Dora's office, which is hardly more than a closet, situated at one end of the Rocky Mountain Reconsolidated Fuel Company's primary machine shop. The room is littered with a rummage of dismembered engines – every tabletop and much of the floor concealed beneath cast-off gears, gauges, sprockets, and fly wheels, rusted-out boilers and condensers, warped piston rods and dials with bent needles and cracked faces. There's a profusion of blueprints and schematics, some tacked to the wall and others rolled up tight and stacked one atop the other like Egyptian papyri or scrolls from the lost library of Alexandria. Everywhere are empty and half-empty oil cans, and there are any number of tools for which Jeremiah doesn't know the names.

"Time being, operations have been suspended," Charlie McNamara says, and then he goes back to using the blade of his pocketknife to dig at the grime beneath his fingernails. "Well, at least that's the company line. Between you, me and Miss Bolshaw here, I think Chicago's having a good long think about sealing off the shaft permanently."

"Permanently," Jeremiah whispers, sorry that he can no longer see the skyline or the docking dirigible. "I would imagine that's going to mean quite a hefty loss, after all the money and work and time required to get the shaft dry and producing again."

"Be that as it damn may be," Dora says brusquely. "There's more at stake here than coal and pit quotas and quarterly profits."

"Yes, well," Jeremiah says, staring at the scuffed toes of his boots now. "Then let's get to it, yes? If I can manage to keep my blasted claustrophobia in check, I'm quite sure we'll get to the bottom of this."

No one laughs at the pun, because it isn't funny, and Jeremiah rubs his aching eyes and wishes again that he were still perched high on the aerie, the night wind roaring in his ears.

"Ain't she *told* you?" the company geologist asks, glancing over at Dora. "What I need you to look at, it ain't in the hole no more. What you need to *see*, well . . ." and here he trails off. "It's locked up in a cell at St Joseph's."

"Locked up?" Jeremiah asks, and the geologist nods.

"Jail would have done her better," Dora mutters. "You put sick folks in the hospital. Killers, you put in jails, or you put a bullet in the skull and be done with it."

Charlie McNamara tells Dora to please shut the hell up and try not to make things worse than they already are.

Jeremiah shifts uneasily in his chair. "How *did* the men die? I mean, how exactly?"

"Lungs plumb full up with coal dust," Charlie says. "Lungs and throat and mouth all stuffed damn near to busting. Doctor, he even found the shit clogging up their stomachs and intestines."

"Some of the men," Dora adds, "they say they've heard singing down there. Said it was beautiful, the most beautiful music they've ever heard."

"Jesus in a steam wagon, Dora. Ain't you got an off switch or something? Singing ain't never killed no one yet, and it *sure* as hell wasn't what got that poor pair of bastards."

And even as the geologist is speaking, the scene shifts again, another unprefaced revolution in this dreaming kaleidoscope reality, and now the halls and exhibits of the Ogilvy Gallery of Natural Antiquities are spread out around him. On Jeremiah's right, the celebrated automatic mastodon rolls glass eyes, and its gigantic tusks are garnished with a dripping, muculent snarl of vegetation. On his left, the serpentine neck of the Gove County plesiosaur rises gracefully as any swan's, though he sees that all the fossil bones and the plaster of Paris have been transmuted through some alchemy into cast iron. The metal is marred by a very slight patina of rust, and it occurs to him that, considering the beast's ferrous metamorphosis, he should remind his staff that they'd best keep the monstrous reptile from swimming or wandering about the rainy streets.

"I cried the day you went away," Katharine says, because, for the moment, it *is* Katharine with him again, not Dora. "I wrote a letter, but never sent it. I keep it in a dresser drawer."

"There was too much work to do," he tells her, still admiring the skeleton. "And much too little of it could be done from New Haven."

Behind the plesiosaur, the brick and mortar of the gallery walls have dissolved utterly away, revealing the trunks of mighty scale trees and innumerable scouring rushes as tall as California redwoods. Here is a dark Carboniferous forest, the likes of which has not taken root since the Mary Gray vein at the bottom of Shaft Seven was only slime and rotting detritus. And below these alien boughs, a menagerie of primæval beings has gathered to peer out across the eons. So, it is not merely a hole knocked in his wall, but a hole bored through the very fabric of time.

"She came out of the *rocks*, Jeremiah," Katharine says, even though the voice is plainly Dora Bolshaw's. "Just like that damned red scorpion, she came out of the rocks."

"You're beginning to put me in mind of a Greek chorus," he replies, keeping his eyes on the scene unfolding behind the plesiosaur. Great hulking forms have begun to shift impatiently in the shadows there, the armored hide of a dozen species of Dinosauria and the tangled manes of giant ground sloths and Irish elk, the leathery wings of a whole flock of pterodactyls spreading wide.

"Maybe they worshipped her, before there ever were men," Dora says, but then she's coughing again, the dry, hacking cough of someone suffering from advanced anthracosis. Katharine has to finish the thought for her. "Maybe they built temples to her, and whispered prayers in the guttural tongues of animals, and maybe they made offerings, after a fashion."

Overhead, there's a cacophonous, rolling sound that Jeremiah Ogilvy first mistakes for thunder. But then he realizes that it's merely the hungry blue lightning at last locating the flammable guncotton epidermis of the airship.

"Some of the men," Katharine whispers, "they say they've heard singing down there. Singing like church hymns, they said. Said it was beautiful, the most beautiful music they've ever heard. We come so late to this procession, and yet we presume to know so much."

From behind the iron plesiosaur, that anachronistic menagerie gathers itself like a breathing wave of sinew and bone and fur, cresting, racing towards the shingle.

Jeremiah Ogilvy turns away, no longer wanting to see.

"Maybe, in their own way, they prayed," Dora whispers, breathlessly.

And the tall, thin man standing before him, the collier in his overalls and hard hat who wasn't there just a moment before, hefts his pick and brings it down smartly against the floorboards, which, in the instant steel strikes wood, become the black stone floor of a mine. All light has been extinguished from the gallery now, save that shining dimly from the collier's carbide lantern. The head of the pick strikes rock, and there's a spark, and then the ancient shale begins to bleed. And soon thereafter, the dream comes apart, and the Professor lies awake and sweating, waiting for sunrise and trying desperately to think about anything but what he's been told has happened at the bottom of Shaft Seven.

5.

After his usual modest breakfast of black coffee with blueberry preserves and biscuits, and after he's given his staff their instructions for the day and cancelled a lecture that he was scheduled to deliver to a league of amateur mineralogists, Jeremiah Ogilvy leaves the museum. He walks north along Kipling to the intersection with West 20th Avenue, where he's arranged to meet Dora Bolshaw. He says good morning, and that he hopes she's feeling well. But Dora's far more taciturn than usual, and few obligatory pleasantries are exchanged. Together, they take one of the clanking, kidney-jarring public omnibuses south and east to St Joseph's Hospital for the Bodily and Mentally Infirm, established only two decades earlier by a group of the Sisters of Charity sent to Cherry Creek from Leavenworth.

Charlie McNamara is waiting for them in the lobby, his long canvas duster so stained with mud and soot that it's hard to imagine it was ever anything but this variegated riot of black and grey. He's a small mountain of a man, all beard and muscle, just starting to go soft about the middle. Jeremiah has thought, on more than one occasion, that this is what men would look like had they'd descended not from apes, but from grizzly bears.

"Thank you for coming," Charlie says. "I know that you're a busy man." But Jeremiah tells him to think nothing of it, that's he's glad to be of whatever service he can – *if*, indeed, he can be of service. Charlie and Dora nod to one another, then, and swap nervous salutations. Jeremiah sees, or only thinks he sees, something wordless pass between them, as well, something anxious and wary, spoken with the eyes and not the lips.

"You told him?" Charlie asks, and Dora shrugs.

"I told him the most of it. I told him what murdered them two men."

"Mulawski and Backstrom," Charlie says.

Dora shrugs again. "I didn't recollect their names. But I don't suppose that much matters."

Charlie McNamara frowns and tugs at a corner of his mustache. "No." He nods. "I don't suppose it does."

"I hope you'll understand my skepticism," Jeremiah says, looking up, speaking to Charlie, but watching Dora. "What's been related to me, regarding the deaths of these two men, and what you've brought me here to see, I'd be generous if I were to say it strikes me as a fairy tale. Or, perhaps, something from the dime novels. It was Hume – David Hume – who said, 'No testimony is sufficient to establish a miracle, unless the testimony be of such a kind, that its falsehood would be more miraculous than the fact which it endeavors to establish.'"

Dora glares back at him. "You always did have such a goddamn pretty way of calling a girl a liar," she says.

"Hell," Charlie sighs, still tugging at his mustache. "I'd be concerned, Dora, if he *weren't* dubious. I've always thought myself a rational man. That's been a source of pride to me, out here among the barbarians and them that's just plain ignorant and don't know no better. But now, after *this* business—"

"Yeah, well, so how about we stop the clucking and get to it," Dora cuts in, and Charlie McNamara frowns at her. But then he stops fussing with his whiskers and nods again.

"Yeah," he says. "Guess I'm just stalling. Doesn't precisely fill me with joy, the thought of seeing her again. If you'll just follow me, Jeremiah, they got her stashed away up on the second floor." He points to the stairs. "The Sisters ain't none too pleased about her being here. I think they're of the general notion that there's more proper places than hospitals for demons."

"Demons," Jeremiah says, and Dora Bolshaw laughs a dry, humorless laugh.

"That's what they're calling her," Dora tells him. "The nuns, I mean. You might as well know that. Got a priest from Annunciation sitting vigil outside the cell, reading Latin and whatnot. There's talk of an exorcism."

At this pronouncement, Charlie McNamara makes a gruff dismissive noise and motions more forcefully towards the stairwell. He mutters something rude about popery and superstition and lady engine jockeys who can't keep their damn pie holes shut.

"Charlie, you know I'm not saying anything that isn't true,"

Dora protests, but Jeremiah Ogilvy thinks he's already heard far too much and seen far too little. He steps past them, walking quickly and with purpose to the stairs, and the geologist and the mechanic follow close on his heels.

6.

"I would like to speak with her," he says. "I would like to speak with her alone." And Jeremiah takes his face away from the tiny barred window set into the door of the cell where they've confined the woman from the bottom of Shaft Seven. For a moment, he stares at the company geologist, and then his eyes drift towards Dora.

"Maybe you didn't hear me right," Charlie McNamara says and furrows his shaggy eyebrows. "She *don't* talk. Least ways, not near as anyone can tell."

"You're wasting your breath arguing with him," Dora mumbles and glances at the priest, who's standing not far away, eyeing the locked door and clutching his Bible. "Might as well try to tell the good Father here that the Queen of Heaven got herself knocked up by a stable hand."

Jeremiah turns back to the window, his face gone indignant and bordering now on choleric. "Charlie, I'm neither a physician nor an alienist, but you've brought me here to see this woman. Having looked upon her, the reason why continues to escape me. However, that said, if I *am* to examine her, I cannot possibly hope do so properly from behind a locked door."

"It's not safe," the priest says very softly. "You must know that, Professor Ogilvy. It isn't safe at all."

Peering in past the steel bars, Jeremiah shakes his head and sighs. "She's naked, Father. She's naked, and can't weigh more than eighty pounds. What possible threat might she pose to me? And, while we're at it, why, precisely, *is* she naked?"

"Oh, they gave her clothes," Dora chimes in. "Well, what *passes* for clothes in a place like this. But she tears them off. Won't have none of it, them white gowns and what have you."

"She is brazen," the priest all but whispers.

"Has anyone even tried to bathe her?" Jeremiah asks, and Charlie coughs.

"That ain't coal dust and mud you're seeing," he says. "Near as anyone can tell, that there's her skin."

"This is ludicrous, all of it," Jeremiah grumbles. "This is *not* the Middle Ages, and you do *not* have some infernal siren or succubus locked up in there. Whatever else you may believe, she's a *woman*, Charlie, and, having sacrificed my very busy day to come all the way out here, I would like, now, to speak with her."

"I was only explaining, Jeremiah, how I ain't of the notion it's such a good idea, that's all," Charlie says, then looks at the priest. "You got the keys, Father?"

The priest nods, reluctantly, and then he produces a single tarnished brass key from his cassock. Jeremiah steps aside while he unlocks the door.

"I'm going in with you," Dora says.

"No, you're not," Jeremiah tells her. "I need to speak with this woman alone."

"But she *don't* talk," Dora says again, beginning to sound exasperated, forcing the words out between clenched teeth.

The priest turns the key, and hidden tumblers and pins respond accordingly.

"Dora, you go scare up an orderly," Charlie McNamara says. "Hell, scare up two, just in case."

The cell door opens, and, as Jeremiah Ogilvy steps across the threshold, the woman inside keeps her black eyes fixed upon him, but she makes no move to attempt an escape. She stays crouched on the floor in the south-east corner and makes no move whatsoever. Immediately, the door bangs shut again, and the priest relocks it.

"Just so there's no doubt on the matter," Charlie McNamara shouts from the hallway, "you're a goddamn fool," and now the woman in the cell smiles. Jeremiah Ogilvy stands very still for a moment, taking in all the details of her and her cramped quarters. There is a mattress and a chamber pot, but no other manner of furnishings or facilities. If he held his arms out to either side, they would touch the walls. If he took only one step backwards, or only half a step, he'd collide with the locked door.

"Good morning," he says, and the woman blinks her eyes. They remind Jeremiah of twin pools of crude oil, spewed fresh from the well and poured into her face. There appear to be no irises, no sclera, no pupils, unless these eyes are composed entirely of pupil. She blinks, and the orbs shimmer slick in the dim light of the hospital cell.

"Good morning," he says to her again, though more quietly than before, and with markedly less enthusiasm. "Is it true, that you do not speak? Are you a mute then? Are you deaf, as well as dumb?"

She blinks again, and then the woman from Shaft Seven cocks her head to one side, as though carefully considering his question. Her hair is very long and straight, reaching almost down to the floor. It seems greasy, and is so very black it might well have been spun from the sky of a moonless night. And yet, her skin is far darker, so much so that her hair almost glows in comparison. There's no word in any human language for a blackness so complete, so inviolate, and he thinks, *What can you be? Eyes spun from a midnight with neither moon nor stars nor gas jets nor even the paltry flicker of tallow candles, and your skin carved from ebony planks.* And then Jeremiah chides himself for entertaining such silly, florid notions, for falling prey to such unscientific fancies, and he takes another step towards the woman huddled on the floor.

"So, it *is* true," he says softly. "You are, indeed, without a voice."

And at that, her smile grows wider, her lips parting to reveal teeth like finely polished pegs shaped from chromite ore, and she laughs. If her laugh differs in any significant way from that of any other woman, the difference is not immediately apparent to Jeremiah Ogilvy.

"I am with voice," she says then. "For any who wish to hear me, I am with voice."

Jeremiah is silent, and he glances over his left shoulder at the door. Charlie McNamara is staring in at him through the bars.

"I am with voice," she says a third time.

Jeremiah turns back to the naked woman. "But you did not see fit to speak with the doctors, or the Sisters, or to the men who transported you here from the mines?"

"They did not wish to hear, not truly. I *am* with voice, yet I will not squander it, not on ears that do not yearn to listen. We are quite entirely unalike in this respect, you and I."

"And, I think, in many others," he tells her, and the woman's smile grows wider still. "Those two men who died, tell me, madam, did *they* yearn to listen?"

"Are you the one who has been chosen to serve as my judge?" she asks, rather than providing him with an answer.

"Certainly not," Jeremiah replies, and he clears his throat. He has begun to detect a peculiar odor in the cell. Not the noisomeness he would have expected from such a room as this, but another sort of smell. *Kerosene*, he thinks, and then, *ice*, though he's never noticed that ice has an odor, and if it does, it hardly seems it would much resemble that of kerosene. "I was asked to . . . see you."

"And you have," the woman says. "You have seen me. You have heard me. But do you know *why*, Professor?"

"Quite honestly, no. I have to confess, that's one of several points that presently have me stumped. So, I shall ask, do *you* know why?"

The woman's smile fades a bit, though not enough that he can't still see those chromite teeth or the ink-black gums that hold them. She closes her eyes, and Jeremiah discovers that he's relieved that they are no longer watching him, that he is no longer gazing into them.

"You are here, before me, because you revere time," she says. "You stand in awe before it, but do not insult it with worship. You *revere* time, though that reverence has cost you dearly, prying away from your heart much that you regret having lost. You *understand* time, Professor, when so few of your race do. The man and woman who brought you here, they sense this in you, and they are frightened and would seek an answer to alleviate their fear."

"Can *they* hear you?" he asks, and the woman crouched on the floor shakes her head.

"Not yet," she says. "That may change, of course. All things change, with time." And then she opens her eyes again, and, if anything, they seem oilier than before, and they coruscate and swim with restless rainbow hues.

"You killed those two miners?"

The woman sits up straighter, and licks her black lips with a blacker tongue. Jeremiah tries not to let his eyes linger on her small firm breasts, those nipples like onyx shards. "This matters to you, their deaths?" she asks him, and he finds that he's at a loss for an honest answer, an answer that he would have either Charlie or Dora or the priest overhear.

"I was only sleeping," the woman says.

"You caused their deaths by sleeping?"

"No, Professor. I don't think so. *They* caused their deaths, by waking me." And she stands, then, though it appears more as though he is seeing her *unfold.* The kerosene and ice smell grows suddenly stronger, and she flares her small nostrils and stares down at her hands. From her expression, equal parts curiosity and bemusement, Jeremiah wonders if she has ever noticed them before.

"*They* gave you this shape?" he asks her. "The two miners you killed?"

She lets her arms fall to her sides and smiles again.

"A terror of the formless," she says. "Of that which cannot be discerned. An inherent need to draw order from chaos. Even you harbor this weakness, despite your reverence for time. You divide indivisible time into hours and minutes and seconds. You dissect time and fashion all these ages of the earth and give them names, that you will not dread the abyss, which is the true face of time. You are not so unlike them." She motions towards the door. "They erect their cities, because the unbounded wilderness offends them. They set the night on fire, that they might forever blind themselves to the stars and to the relentless sea of the void, in which those stars dance and spin, are born and wink out."

And now Jeremiah Ogilvy realizes that the woman has closed the space separating them, though he cannot recall her having taken even the first step towards him. She has raised a hand to his right cheek, and her gentle fingers are as smooth and sharp as obsidian. He does not pull away, though it burns, her touch. He does not pull away, though he has now begun to glimpse what manner of thing lies coiled behind those oily, shimmering eyes.

"Ten million years from now," she says, "there will be no more remaining of the sprawling clockwork cities of men, or of their tireless enterprise, or all their marvelous works, no more than a few feet of stone shot through with lumps of steel and glass and concrete. But you *know* that, Professor Ogilvy, even though you chafe at the knowledge. And this is *another* reason they have brought you here to me. You see ahead, as well as behind."

"I do not fear you," he whispers.

"No," she says. "You don't. Because you don't fear time, and there is little else remaining now of me."

It is not so very different than his dream of the cast-iron plesiosaur and the burning dirigible, the shadows pressing in now from all sides. They flow from the bituminous pores of her body and wrap him in silken folds and bear away the weight of the illusion of the present. The extinct beasts and birds and slithering leviathans of bygone eras and eras yet to come peer out at him, and he hears the first wave breaking upon the first shore. And he hears the last. And Professor Jeremiah Ogilvy doesn't look away from the woman.

"They have not yet guessed," she says, "the *true* reason they've brought you here. Perhaps, they will not, until it is done. Likely, they will never comprehend."

"I know you," he says. "I have always known you."

"Yes," she says, and the shadows have grown so thick and rank now that he can barely breathe, and he feels her seeping into him.

Lungs plumb full up with coal dust. Lungs and throat and mouth all stuffed damn near to busting.

You ever seen a red scorpion, Jeremiah?

"Release me," she says, her voice become a hurricane squall blowing across warm Liassic seas, and the fiery cacophony of meteorites slamming into an Azoic earth still raw and molten, and, too, the calving of immense glaciers only a scant few millennia before this day. "There are none others here who may," she says. "It is the greatest agony, being bound in this instant, and in this form."

And, without beginning to fathom the *how* of it, the unknowable mechanics of his actions, he does as she's bidden him to do. The woman from the bottom of Shaft Seven comes apart, and, suddenly, the air in the cell is filled with a mad whirl of coal dust. Behind him, the priest's brass key is rattling loudly inside the padlock, and there are voices shouting – merely human voices – and then Dora is calling his name and dragging him backwards, into now, and out into the stark light of the hospital corridor.

7.

The summer wears on, June becoming July, and, by slow degrees, Professor Jeremiah Ogilvy's strength returns to him, and his eyes grow clear again. His sleep is increasingly less troubled by dreams of the pitch-colored woman who was no woman, and the fevers are increasingly infrequent. As all men do, even those who revere time, he begins to forget, and in forgetting, his mind and body can heal. A young anatomist from Lawrence was retained as an assistant curator to deliver his lectures and to oversee the staff and the day-to-day affairs of the museum. As Charlie McNamara predicted, the Chicago offices of the Rocky Mountain Reconsolidated Fuel Company permanently closed Shaft Seven, and, what's more, pumped more than twenty-thousand cubic yards of Portland cement into the abandoned mine.

In the evenings, when her duties at the shop are finished, Dora Bolshaw comes to his bedroom. She sits with him there in that modest chamber above the Hall of Cainozoic Life and the mezzanine housing the celebrated automatic mastodon. She keeps him company, and they talk, when her cough is not so bad; she reads to him, and they discuss everything from the teleological aspects of the theories of Alfred Russel Wallace to which alloys and displacement lubricators make for the most durable steam engines. Now and then, they discuss other, less cerebral matters, and there have been apologies from both sides for that snowy night in January. Sometimes, their discussions stray into the wee hours, and, sometimes, Dora falls asleep in his arms and is late for work the next day. The subject of matrimony has not come up again, but Jeremiah Ogilvy has trouble recalling why it ever seemed an issue of such consequence.

"What did she say to you?" Dora finally asks him one night so very late in July that it's almost August. "The woman from the mine, I mean."

"So, you couldn't hear her," he says.

"We heard you – me and Charlie and the priest – and that's all we heard."

He tells her what he remembers, which isn't much. And, afterwards, she asks, for what seems the hundredth time, if he knows what the woman was. And he tells her no, that he really has no idea whatsoever.

"Something, lost and unfathomable, that came before," he says. "Something old and weariful that only wanted to lie down and go back to sleep."

"She killed those men."

Sitting up in his bed, two feather pillows supporting him, Jeremiah watches her for almost a full minute (by the clock on the mantle) before he replies. And then he glances towards the window and the orange glow of the city sky beyond the pane of glass.

"I recollect, Dora, a tornado hitting a little town in Iowa, back in July, I think," and she says yeah, she remembers that, too, and that the town in question was Pomeroy. "Lots of people were killed," he continues. "Or, rather, an awful lot of people *died* during the storm. Now, tell me, do we hold the cyclone culpable for all those deaths? Or do we accept that the citizens of Pomeroy were simply in the wrong place, at the wrong time?"

Dora doesn't answer, but only sighs and twists a lock of her hair. Her face is less sooty than usual, and her nails less grimy, her hands almost clean, and Jeremiah considers the possibility that she's discovered the efficacy of soap and water.

"Would you like to sit at the window a while?" she asks him, and he tells her that yes, he would. So Dora helps Jeremiah into his wheelchair, but then lets him steer it around the foot of the bed and over to the window. She follows, a step or two behind, and when he asks, she opens the window to let in the warm night breeze. He leans forward, resting his elbows against the sill while she massages a knot from his shoulders. It is not so late that there aren't still people on the street, men in their top hats and bowlers, women in their bustles and bonnets. The evening resounds with the clop of horses' hooves and the commotion made by the trundling, smoking, wood-burning contraption that sprays Kipling Street with water every other night to help keep the dust in check. Looking east, across the rooftops, he catches sight of a dirigible rising into the smog.

"We are of a moment," he says, speaking hardly above a whisper, and Dora Bolshaw doesn't ask him to repeat himself.

Ticktock Girl

Cat Rambo

The reporter leans forward. "I understand you were actually built in 1895, and after your creator passed away, spent a number of years in storage. Can you tell us a little bit about that?"

And so she remembers.

Moment 20244660: She sits in the front parlor, covered with white cloth. Subdued spring light washes through the folds each afternoon. Behind her in the cavernous room, the tick-tock of the grandfather clock echoes, counter pointed by the steps of the servant come to wind it. The maid must be accompanied by a girl in training today; they speak in quiet, subdued tones, bringing with them the smell of soap and lemon oil.

"Spooky, that's what it is. 'Ow long has it all sat here?" The voice is high-pitched, shot through with a nervous giggle.

"Since her ladyship died. Her father ordered it all covered up, and it's sat here ever since. Going on ten years now."

"What's this now?" The dusty sheet, tugged by an inquisitive hand, slides off her face and the new maid lets out a shriek of surprise before she is quieted by the older one.

"That's the lady's mechanical woman. Used to walk and talk, they say. Still can. But her lordship said, sit here, and so she does." With a deft rustle, the sheet is tucked around her again, but as the light dims, she preserves the sight of wide blue eyes, a mouth agape in astonishment.

"Walk an' talk? Go on, yer pulling me leg."

"That's what they say. Used to march alongside her in the suffrage parades."

A cog, imprisoned in her brain, ticks, and she enters a new moment, this one left behind.

Humans see time as a flow. A river, sweeping them along. But she perceives each moment, each tick and tock of the clock as a separate instance, presented as perfect as a gem inside a velvet box, each distinct minute collected within the celluloid and circuitry of her brain.

Moment 1: There is something hot and hard hammering inside her chest, but perhaps that is ordinary. She has no other moments to compare this one with, here and now in the first sixty seconds of life. All that exists is the face hovering above her where she lies on a table. The features are flushed with triumph and perspiration, a mass of golden brown ringlets falling around it, one touching her brass skin.

The lips open, and sounds come out. They have meaning attached to them. "Can you hear me?"

Her own lips move. The rubber bags that are her lungs contract, squeezing out air for her tongue to shape. "Yes."

Water appears on her skin. In some other moment she will know these are Sybil's tears, but not tears of sorrow, tears of joy. There will be many kinds of tears.

"I am Lady Sybil Fortinbras," the face says. "I am your creator." Then, with a laugh, "Creatrix, I suppose."

The moment ends before she can reply.

Moment 25153800: The smell of seawater and musty cargo crates, part of so many moments, is gone. There is a long slow screech as each nail is withdrawn.

Moment 25153804: The lid comes off, and around her the packing material rustles as someone throws handfuls of it aside. Then her face is cleared and she sees him, hears his voice saying in German "A woman? What use is a mechanical woman to me? *Schiesse!*" He throws the last handful back and she watches it drifting down in slow motion, settling to block her sight again.

Moment 8820967: They are marching in a suffrage parade. Along High Street, hostile faces loom, shouting. She wheels Lady Sybil's chair forward. Both of them wear white dresses, sashes of purple and green. Purple for courage, green for strength. The other women ignore her. She makes them uneasy, even though she may be the only reason the crowd doesn't rush to attack them. But one, her face lean and resolute as a hatchet, leans forward to speak to Lady Sybil.

"Do you agree with what Mrs Pankhurst says?"

Lady Sybil glances up impatiently amid the sea of white ruffles. "That the argument of the broken pane is the most valuable argument in modern politics? Perhaps. But we will work within the law. For now." Her eyes are shrewd as she looks at the people lining the street. "Why would we want the vote if we intend to go outside the bounds of the law?"

Moment 9097372: Lady Sybil is speaking. The winter has withered her even more. She is frail and fragile as a songbird.

"You see, I don't think it's enough to march any more," she says. "There has to be some good coming from you. In this brave new age, there are villains aplenty. I'll set you after them. You have been my legs, my dear. My mechanical Athena. For so very long. And now you will be my fists."

Moment 9156658: She has the dark-skinned, well-dressed man by the collar, pulling his limp form after her into the offices of Scotland Yard. She drops him in the doorway of Todd Chrisman, the detective who, she knows, has been working on the case.

"This is the Maharishi of Terjab," she says.

His eyes are amazed. "Yes, I can see that."

"He is responsible for the Soho white slave ring. You will find the evidence in his basement."

He stammers out something, moves forward to look down at the Maharishi. "What are you?" he says.

"Lady Fortinbras's mechanical Athena," she says. "My directive is to fight evildoers."

Behind him in the office, someone laughs, only to be hissed into silence by a fellow. All of these men are watching her.

Moment 9230101: "This is the Dog Collar Killer," she says to Chrisman.

The man at her feet groans, recovering himself. He fought hard.

"He's a clergyman," Chrisman says, astonishment coloring his voice.

Pallid and rabbity, the man wears his robes like a squatter moved into a strange new place. He blinks, the bruises along his face coloring like dark water, and one eye weeps bloody tears.

"I am Father Jeremiah, and this is an outrage," he says, pulling himself upward despite the restraining hand on his arm.

"Marilyn Bellcastle," she says. "Lucy Stipe. Annabel Jones. He killed them all."

He explodes in spittle and anger at the sound of her voice. "Whores!" he snarls. "Jezebels! They deserved no better!"

Moment 9618905: "What have you brought us now, lass?" Chrisman asks. She gives him the papers she has compiled, the blueprints for the bomb to be placed beneath the Houses of Parliament and he thanks her, riffling through the rustling papers one by one, studying them. There are new decorations on his uniform; her aid has brought him a promotion.

Moment 9713637: Lady Sybil's father paces up and down the study, talking to himself. His cooling breakfast, the opened letter beside it, sits on the table. He wheels on her.

"Died in prison, by God!" he shouts. "Her and that Pankhust woman, thinking hunger strikes would change the jailers' minds. What good is it dying for a stupid, frippery cause, just another chance to dress up?"

She believes this is a rhetorical question; she makes no reply. She would have been with them, but Lady Sybil felt chasing the Ghost of Belfast was more important. Chrisman should have been pleased when she brought the villain in, but he was subdued, told her simply to go home.

"I'll have every man in that prison to court," Lord Fortinbras says. He looks at her, the way he has always looked at her. Half repulsed and half proud at his clever daughter's creation.

"And you, mechanical Athena," he says. "What's to become of you now?"

There are tears on his face.

*   *   *

Moment 25055955: The crack of the gavel resounds through the crowded room as the auctioneer bangs the sale closed. "And sold to the foreign gentleman!"

Some of Lady Sybil's friends are there, but none of them have bid on her. She is led away to the waiting crate. She feels nothing.

Moment 49189954: Professor Delta is speaking.

"The university bought you as a historical feminist treasure," she says. "Built by an English suffragette and scientist. The once-owned-by-Hitler stuff, that was just icing on the cake, a little thrill value. But now . . . nowadays people are more concerned with the rights of mechanicals than they were when you were sold."

There is a gleam in her eye that is reminiscent of the Pankhursts.

"Do you really want to be on your own?" Delta says, leaning forward. She is a short, wiry woman, her hair cropped close, no make-up on her face. "What would you do?"

"Fight crime," she says.

Delta leans back, her hand flickering in a dismissive gesture. "A superhero? Let the papers call you something like Ticktock Girl? How . . . trivial. It would be a terrible waste."

She could go back in the crate. But Lady Sybil built her to move. To act. To be her hands, even now.

Moment 57343680: She faces Father Jeremiah in the closed room, cinderblock walls, the smell of disinfectant harsh and immediate. Somewhere in the distance, water drips.

She's not sure how he can be alive, unchanged, a century later. But here he is.

"The Lord has preserved me! I am his Hand!" he shouts at her. She calculates the distance from her fist to his jaw, the amount of impact necessary to render him unconscious.

He draws himself up and smiles. "But you can't. I'm legit now."

The word is unfamiliar.

He splits it into syllables for her, serves it up like little rabbit pellets of words. "Le-gi-ti-mate. Everything I do is inside the law."

"You tell people to kill other people and they do it."

"All I do is provide information on where they are: the abortionists, the sodomites, the women who whore themselves out. My followers decide what to do with the knowledge."

Seeing her pause, he laughs. "Welcome to the brave new world, Ticktock, mechanical clock," he half sings. "Can't touch this, can't touch me now."

Moment 9097375: Sickness has eaten away at Lady Sybil's face, reducing it to paper over bone. But her voice is strong as ever.

"There is right and there is wrong," she says. "You, my mechanical Athena, are always on the side of right." A trembling hand strokes along the bright metal of her face. "The side of justice."

Moment 57343681 seems to blend together with so many others, so many long circles of the wheels in her brain. And in that confluence, she knows that sometimes the argument of brick and fist are the only way. Chrisman would not approve, she thinks as she snaps Jeremiah's neck. But Lady Sybil would.

La Valse

K. W. Jeter

"The problem," said Herr Doktor Pavel, "is that we gained our Empire when we were young. And now we are old." With a great iron spanner in his hands, he turned to his assistant and smiled. "What could be worse than that?"

"I don't know." Anton felt himself to be a child, when hearing of such things. "I'm not as old as you. At all."

Around them, in the Apollosaal's basements, the machinery wept. Even though they had both spent the better part of a week down there, in preparation for this evening's grand events, still the miasmatic hiss and soft, plodding leaks prevailed over their efforts. The tun-shaped boilers, vast enough to engulf carriages and peasants' huts, shuddered with the scalding forces pent inside them. Their rivets seeped rust. In the far-off corners where the theatrical scenery was kept and more often forgotten, pasteboard castles sagged beneath the threadbare fronds of a humid jungle of *faux* palm trees.

"Age, like wealth, is but a mental abstraction, my boy." The doctor peered at a creaking armature above his head, adjusting some aspect of it with a miniature screwdriver, skill as precise and surgical as though his title were that of a physician rather than an engineer. "And nothing more. People fancy that God loves them – and consider themselves and their kind exceptional as a result." He wiped his pale, egg-like brow with the grease-smeared lace of his shirt cuff. "If such fancies were gears and dreams cogs, I would wind this world's mainspring tight enough to hum."

He didn't know what that meant. The doctor was of an obscure and poetic persuasion. He took the screwdriver from the hand held toward him, replacing the tool in its exact slot with the greater and smaller ones on either side.

"Will everything be ready? By tonight?" He thought that was more important to know. If the ballroom's mechanisms were not completely functional and satisfactory when the guests arrived, then the doctor and he would not be paid, resulting in a cold and hungry New Year's Eve for them.

"Not to worry." The doctor picked up his tool bag and moved on. He tapped a lean forefinger on a set of calliope-like pipes, each in turn, flakes of rust drifting onto his vest as he bent his ear toward them. Just as a physician counterpart might thump the chest of a tubercular patient, to assess how long he had to live. "No one's merriment will be impaired by the likes of us."

In winters such as these – were there any other kind, any more? – Anton limited his hopes to that much. If one managed to get to the first muddy, thawing days before actual spring, then there was a chance at least. Of something other than this. Something other than the dank, hissing basements under the ballrooms and palaces of that finer, fragile world above. Far from the sharp-toothed gears and interlocking wheels, the pistons gleaming in their oily sheaths, the ticking escapements wide as cartwheels, the mainsprings uncoiling like nests of razor-thin serpents. He could take Gisel out beyond the apple orchards, their branches still black and leafless, no matter that it would cost him a day's wages and her a scolding from the head housekeeper. What would it matter if both of them would go supperless that night, bellies empty as their aching arms? Lying on straw-filled pallets far from each other, gazing out cobwebbed attic windows at an envious moon. Remembering how the ice at the roots of the sodden grass creaked beneath the back of her chambermaid's blouse, his face buried in the gathered folds of her apron. Smelling of honey and lye, her hand stroking his close-cropped head as she turned her face away and wept at how happy she was. If only for a moment.

"What are you dreaming about?" The doctor's voice broke into his warming reveries. "Come over here and help me open up these stopcocks."

He did as he was ordered, letting all the girl's smiles flutter away, like ashes up a chimney flue. Straining at the stubborn valves, he let one other hope step inside his heart. That none of their work here, readying for the gala ball, would require going down into the sub-basements below these, where the great roaring furnaces and boilers resided. He hated having to go down there, hated seeing the stokers chained between the fiery iron doors and heaps of coal, the shimmering heat revealing the stripes across their naked backs. Their eyes would turn toward him as they crouched over their black shovels. Their eyes would tell him, *As you are, once were we. Steal but the slightest crust or bauble, and join us here . . .*

Their extinguished voices would follow him as he fled up the spiral of clanging metal stairs, the errand accomplished on which Herr Doktor Pavel had sent him. He could hear them now, whispering far beneath his sodden clogs, as he gritted his teeth and strained to turn the most ancient of the spoked wheels another quarter-turn.

"That's good." The doctor stepped back, wiping his hands across his vest. "Anton, my coat, if you please."

He fetched the swallow-tailed garment, lifting it from the hook by the stone arch of the cellar door. The horsehair-padded shoulders itched his own palms as he helped the doctor slide into its heavy woolen arms.

"There." An old man's vanity – he tugged at the lapels, gazing fondly at his reflection in one of the floor's puddles. "When everyday gentlemen dressed as elegant as this, the Empire was feared by Cossack and Hun alike."

"If you say so." He had no memory of such things. The doctor might have been imagining such faded glories, for all he knew.

"We'll discuss it another time." The sad state of his assistant's learning was a topic frequently evoked, if never acted upon. "Let's fire 'er up, lad. A job well done's the best payment."

Anton watched as the doctor pushed one lever after another. Constellations of gears engaged about them, all enveloped in sweating vapor. Ratchet and piston moved through their limited courses, the clatter of brass and iron loud as church bells on a tone-deaf Easter morning.

"Splendid!" The doctor bent his head back, gazing up enraptured at the chamber's damp ceiling. "Do you hear it? Do you?"

He knew what those sounds were, barely audible through the commotion of the machinery driving them. He'd heard them before, every year's end, from when he'd first apprenticed to the dancing engineer's trade. To now, this last calendar page, so much dragglier and tattered than the ones from all the years before.

He pulled his own thin coat away from one of the jointed arms thrusting up through the ceiling's apertures, careful not to be snagged by its pump-like motions. All through the basement, more such churned away, up and down and at various angles, pivoting upon the hinges that he and the doctor had so carefully greased. Like a mechanical forest brought to clanking animation, white gouts billowing from every quivering pipe . . .

There they go, thought Anton as he looked up at where the doctor gazed. He could see them, without going up the stairs to the grand ballroom. The empty metal frameworks, like iron scarecrows, would be bowing to one another, then embracing. The smaller with the larger, just as if already filled by the evening's elegant guests. Already, the mechanical violins were scraping their bows across the rosined strings.

Closing his eyes, he watched from inside his head as each skeletal apparatus – jointed struts and trusses, cages shaped into men and women – took another by a creaking hand. Then swirled across the acres of polished floor, just as though it were the music that impelled them, rather than clockwork and steam.

She breathed into her cupped hands, warming the strands of pearls she held.

There might come a day when she was old enough, with years of servile experience ingrained through every memory, that she would be entrusted to help dress their dowager employer. For now, Gisel watched as the senior maids, some of them older than the bent and wrinkled figure upon whom they waited, busied themselves with the intricate laces and stays.

"Ah! You're too cruel to me." Vanity and girlish affectations tinged the dowager's simpered, murmured words. "You'll break something one of these days – I know you will." She brought her hawk-etched, deep-seamed visage over the lace at her shoulder and smiled the yellow of old parchment at her attendants. "But not tonight. Be so sweet as to spare me just one more night of pleasure."

The maids said nothing, but obliged with nods and their own little smiles. Gisel had heard the old woman say the same thing the year before and the year before that. She had still been working in the scullery three winters ago, scrubbing the stone floors with a wet rag, but the oldest of the chambermaids had told her that the dowager had spoken the same words every New Year's Eve for decades now. None of them were quite sure that the dowager could say anything else, at least not while getting dressed for the ball.

She watched as the others stepped back, the gown assembled into place at last, as though a seamstress had wrapped lengths of ancient silk around a bone dummy. The dowager admired herself in a triptych of full-length mirrors, as though the grey film at the center of her eyes somehow filtered out the overlapping scales of time, letting through only the image of the lithe girl she still believed herself to be.

Now the pearls were as warm as Gisel's blood. They could have been a kitten sheltered between one palm and the other, if only they had breathed and had a fluttering pulse inside soft fur. She stepped forward with them, holding them up as though they were some sort of offering.

"No, not now." The dowager surprised them all by something different. That she had never said before. She waved a wrinkled, impatient hand at Gisel. "They caught last time. In the framework." Her scarleted nails clawed at the tendons that ridged her neck harp-like. "How they tormented me! The whole beautiful night, dancing and dancing, and the whole time I felt as though I were being garroted. I could have burst into tears from the pain, if I'd let myself."

Gisel dared to speak, though she received a warning glance from the oldest chambermaid. "You don't want to wear them?"

"Silly girl, of course I do. They were my mother's, and her mother took communion from the hand of a pope with them around her throat. How could I not wear them on a festive occasion such as this? I wear them *every* New Year's ball."

"I'm sorry . . ."

"Don't fret about it, dear." The dowager smiled even wider and scarier as she let one of the other maids settle a wrap about her shoulders. "Let us go to the Apollosaal – you and I, just the two of us. Won't that be fun? And you can put the pearls upon me there. So you can make certain they don't pinch and bind. I believe that's the smartest thing to do, don't you? I don't know why I didn't think of it before."

The notion terrified Gisel. Her heart pounded at the base of her own throat, as she felt all the other maids turning their silent, premonitory gaze upon her. What would she do without the others, the older ones, to tell her what to do?

"But . . . I don't know . . ."

"No one will mind, I'm sure. Once the music starts, I'm sure there will be some little corner where you can crouch and hide. Perhaps in the back, from where the waiters bring the champagne and the marzipan cakes. No one will even see you." The dowager's eyes were like ivory knife-points set in crêpe paper, as she went on smiling.

She knows I'm scared, thought Gisel, holding the bundled pearls closer to herself. *That's why she wants me to go with her.* If only she hadn't let the dowager see that in her, she might have had a chance. To escape.

But now there wasn't any. She nodded dumbly and followed the other woman, out of the dressing room and toward the curving sweep of stairs that led down to the carriage outside the door, and all the wintry city streets beyond.

As the guests assembled, he saw her. Anton's heart raced – it always did, as though some internal furnace of his emotions had been stoked higher.

Assembled, it seemed almost literally to him. This was the part of his apprenticeship to the doctor that he disliked the most. Some tasks were worse than others. He thanked God, the one cloaked in the tattered remnants of his faith, that this one came about only once a year. And at the end of it, so that even in the bleakest December there would likely be no further discouragements.

With his own tool kit slung by a leather strap from his shoulder, he hastened through the grand ballroom. Only the lesser nobility were entrusted to him. And of those, only the men – he knelt before baronets and princelings, the younger sons of dynasties and households so ancient that their pedigrees might have been traced in whatever pages would have followed the Book of Revelations. As Herr Doktor Pavel had pointed out more than once to him, *youth* was as relative a term as *wealth*, in this case meaning only slightly less gray and enfeebled. With wrench and calibrated screwdrivers, he encased spindly legs, cavalry boots buffed lustrous by their lackeys, into the jointed, cage-like frames. Standing up, he fastened curved metal bands about the noblemen's waists and chests, taking care not to disarray their ranks of medals, gleaming as miniature suns with the profiles of dead emperors at their centers. Last came the tapered armatures locked into place at their wrists and elbows, linked by clever pistons to the similar mechanisms at their shoulders. With a few of the more dissipated, he had to hold their arms above their heads himself, while with his other hand he completed the necessary fastenings. As a lady's maid might corset an obese matron, he would then raise a knee to the small of their backs, in order to engage all the torso elements to the mechanical iron spines that extended from their hips to the napes of their stiffly collared necks.

But he had to admit the results were impressive, when he finally stood back from each one, his tools dangling in each hand. They stood at attention, chests thrust out inside the metal cages, shoulders pulled back by bows of iron behind them, each as proudly straight as though their decorations had been won on actual battlefields.

With practice accumulated over decades, the doctor was able to work so much faster, encasing not only the more elderly noblemen, but all their wives and daughters and courtesans as well. The doctor had told Anton that the women were easier, as their bodies were more pliant, more accustomed to the rigors of fashion, more submissive to the attentions of men. He wasn't sure about that – they all terrified him, the old ones with the bodices like the prows of bejeweled warships, the comparatively younger with their sharp glances aimed over fluttering fans as though they were infantry rifles. He would have believed that the women were more ready than the men to pick up their grandfathers' sabers and run through any foes worthy of such an encounter.

"Such attentions are a delight, Herr Doktor," the Grand Duchess of some inconsequential principality simpered through her fan. "If only my late husband's touch had been so skilled."

"You flatter me, madam." Wielding a brace of screwdrivers, the doctor completed adjusting the thin steel bands spanning the woman's capacious bosom. "I am no more than a simple craftsman."

Anton finished encasing those to whom he had been assigned. The gaudy colors of their parade uniforms seeped through the hinged ligatures and mechanisms, as might the plumage of exotic birds in tightly bound aviaries. They preened before each other, the skeletal limbs of their full-length cages creaking in place, as he knelt at the side of the ballroom, wiping the tools with an oily rag before putting them away.

A fluttering murmur arose from the noblewomen. Without glancing over his shoulder, Anton knew that the last of their number had arrived. Every New Year's Eve, the dowager's arrival at the ballroom was the culminating event of the preparations, the signal that the festivities were soon to commence. Carefully timed, as though the old woman had some preternatural sense of when all the others had been bolted and strapped into place, ready to admire and obsequiously comment as she assumed her rightful position among them.

The doctor set to work, with no need of greeting or command. One of the Apollosaal's attendants took the wrap from the dowager's shoulders, the sable fur powdered with snow not yet melted in the ballroom's heat.

A single maid waited upon the dowager, who had not accompanied her the year before. When Anton closed his tool kit and stood up, keeping close to the paneled wall, he spotted Gisel. That was when his heart sped and his breath caught in his throat. Not at seeing her face – when had that ever made him other but happy? – but at discerning the fear inscribed upon it. She stood behind all the others, her own gaze downcast, arms close against her ribs, red-chafed hands locked upon some bundle glistening white. The pulse at her throat ticked even faster than his, impelled by whatever terror it was that she felt.

"There." Herr Doktor Pavel stood back from the dowager, his intricate labors done. "The evening is yours, madam. Enjoy it as you wish."

"Not yet," said the woman, now surrounded by the same metal struts and linkages as the other guests. "There are still the best adornments to be put on." She turned and looked to the maid behind her. "My pearls . . ."

Gisel scurried up to the dowager, her hands opening to cup the circled strands.

"Don't dawdle, child. The ball is to commence at any moment."

The reason for Gisel's fear was quickly evident to Anton, as he watched her struggle to fasten the pearls around the dowager's neck. The articulated metal bands came up high enough on the woman, as with all the other noble guests, to make the task more than merely difficult – close to impossible, in fact. His own hands tensed into useless fists as he watched the girl attempting to draw the pearls through the narrow space between the dowager's wrinkled throat and the inside of the assembled about her.

"What is the matter with you?" The dowager fidgeted in discomfort, a soured grimace evidencing her dislike of another human being so close. "Is such a simple task beyond you?"

The woman's sniping words didn't help. Gisel became even more flustered, her face draining white and her hands shaking with anxiety. Beneath her fingertips, one of the gleaming strands caught in the angle of a metal hinge. She tugged at the graduated length, attempting to free it. The silken thread inside snapped – the tiny, precious spheres flew in all directions, bouncing and clattering on the ballroom floor.

"Cretin!" The dowager's face was a wrinkled mask of fury as her bony hand slapped Gisel. "Idiot! Look what you've done."

"I'm sorry." Gisel was already down on her hands and knees, trying to gather up all the scattered pearls. Futile – some of them had rolled and vanished into the grooved apertures through which the various machinery from the cellars below protruded, scalding vapors hissing along the jointed armatures. "I didn't mean—"

"The smallest of them is worth more than you." The point of the dowager's heeled boot caught Gisel in the ribs, hard enough to evoke a gasp from her. "Twenty of such as you!"

Anton wouldn't have thought there was so much strength in the old woman. As he watched, another kick brought a spatter of blood from Gisel's mouth. If it hadn't been for the cage-like mechanism bolted into place around the dowager's voluminous silken skirt, her anger might have been enough to take off the offending girl's head.

"Don't." Herr Doktor Pavel laid a restraining hand across Anton's chest, as he had stepped forward from the wall. "I'll take care of it."

Tears had diluted pink the blood that Gisel smeared with her palm, as she huddled into a ball, knees against her breast. She barely looked up as the doctor interposed himself between her and the dowager. "But an accident," he soothed. "No harm was intended—"

The dowager's rage continued without respite. She was even smiling, a slash across her starkly rouged face, as her gloved and jeweled hand struck the doctor. Her eyes glittered in triumph as he fell at her feet.

A blow such as that wouldn't have been enough to kill the doctor – Anton knew that. Perhaps it was the shame, to be treated as a mere servant in front of all this nobility. It didn't matter. He pressed his own spine tighter to the paneled wall, gazing with dire presentiment at the unmoving figure crumpled on the ballroom floor.

The manager of the dowager's estates came down to the cellar, to talk with Anton.

He sat on a little wooden crate, which at one time had held canisters of grease for the machinery clanking and wheezing all about them. Up above, he could hear the dancing. The unmanned violins scraped their bows across the strings, the sprightly rhythms impelling the aristocratic figures through their motions. Or seeming to – all knew, but pretended not to, that it was actually the various armatures that moved through the openings in the ballroom floor, their pistons and hinges connected to the curved metal bands fastened around the elegant guests.

"You're aware, aren't you, that this person's dead?"

Anton looked over to where the manager, in his black livery, tilted the doctor's chin with an ink-stained finger. The old man's face was gray and slack, his eyes already filming over.

"Yes." He nodded. "I knew that. Even before they brought him down here."

The distant instruments skirled and stuttered through a Hungarian *galop*, its rapid notes audible through the mechanical clamor closer at hand. From below, he could hear the roaring of the furnaces, driving every step of cavalry boot and sweep of lace-fringed gown.

"So I can hardly pay you, can I?" The manager pulled his hand back, letting the doctor's head nod back onto his motionless chest.

"Our contract is with him. Or rather, it was. His unfortunate demise would seem to nullify the relationship. Did he have heirs?"

A shake of the head, as Anton bit his lower lip. He was not surprised at what the manager, with the accounts book in a pocket of the swallow-tailed coat, told him now – he had expected as much, in his own sinking heart. But to hear it pronounced with gallows finality, that he would not receive his year's wages, which Herr Doktor Pavel had always settled upon him as the midnight bells had struck – that he would go homeless and hungry, peering through shuttered shop windows for even the illusory hope of some new employment – he felt his hollow stomach clench at the thought of the empty, wintry streets that lay outside the Apollosaal.

"If he had such, you might apply to them." The manager drew on his gloves. "For what's owed to you."

Anton said nothing. He knew no one owed him anything now. That was the way of this world.

He watched the estates manager mount the creaking iron rungs, spiraling back up to the light and music above.

Alone once more with his former master's corpse, he leaned forward where he sat, arms across his knees, hands working themselves into a brooding knot. His own hunger, he scarcely minded. He was used to that. But Gisel had surely lost her place in the dowager's service. If he were able to pay for even a few more weeks of the attic room's shelter, he might have taken her there and wrapped his arms about her as they lay on the brown-spotted straw heaped in one narrow corner. He might have kept her safe there as they both waited for the cold year to turn, the snows to melt under spring's desperately longed-for advance. They had both whispered plans to each other, that he might break from the doctor's drudging employ, that they both might flee from the city and live on wild apples and snared woodcocks turned on rudely fashioned spits, the two of them crouched around a small fire's blackened stones . . .

Even if it had been just for one spring and summer, before the first chill winds inched through the hills, they would at least have had that much. Which would have been enough, or at least enough to tell each other so. But now they wouldn't. He turned his head, looking over at the doctor's slumped form. They never would.

Heavy with resolve, Anton stood upright, pushing the wooden

box aside with the heel of his foot. For a moment, he looked around himself at the churning machinery, the levers and pistons pumping away at the linkages to the ballroom above. If he tilted his head back, he could see small bright glimpses of the light from the glittering chandeliers, interrupted by the quick, relentless motion of the dancers, swirling in their courses from one end of the grand space to the other.

He watched and listened, then turned toward the valves and gauges spanning the basement's walls. His hand reached out and grasped one of the small iron wheels, hesitated a moment, then twisted it as far as he could, until it could open no farther. Each of the valves hissed at him as he did the same to them. When he was done with the last, he stepped back, listening to the machinery shake faster and faster. Clouds of scalding vapor filled the chamber as he turned and made his way to the stone steps leading even farther below.

The stokers turned their silent gaze toward him. The flames beyond the iron doors glinted on the sweat and soot of their naked chests.

"More," said Anton. He brought his own gaze from each man to the next, one after another. "Higher." He raised his hand and pointed to the furnaces behind them. "All you can give."

They looked about at each other, then back to him. First the closest one slowly nodded, then they all did. A time had come that the stokers in their chains had thought would never come to them. They turned away, thrusting the blades of their shovels into the heaps of coal, hurling one load after another into the mounting flames.

Even before Anton retreated back onto the steps, he felt the dizzying heat wash over him as though it were the tide of a fiery ocean. He brought a forearm across his eyes, to shield himself from the vision of suns bursting to life inside the furnaces.

He found Gisel at the back of the crowds outside the Apollosaal. The townspeople pressed their faces close to the high-arched windows, gaping through the blood-spattered glass at the whirling scene within.

"Don't you want to see them?" Gisel pulled her rough woolen shawl tighter about herself. This far away from the columned building, the snowflakes remained unmelted, clinging to her golden hair. "You told me you never liked them, either."

"I don't need to," said Anton. That was true – when he had come up from the basement, he had walked through the grand ballroom. He had stayed close to the wall to avoid the caged figures of the nobility, whirling about in the interminable courses through the glittering space. Impelled by the unleashed machinery protruding from the floor's gaps, the corseted men and women moved with such velocity that the slightest impact might have sent him sprawling unconscious.

At the sudden noise of the windows shattering, he wrapped Gisel in his arms, turning his back toward the Apollosaal and shielding her from the shards of glass. There were at least a few people in the crowd whose faces were nicked by the bright flying bits, like a gale of razor-edged ice crystals. They didn't even notice the trickles of red running down their throats as they pushed and scrabbled with the others, climbing inside the ballroom to gaze at the dead marvels there.

Dead or dying – he had seen at least a few, as he had made his way along the side of the ballroom, who might still have been at least partly alive, the last of their strength and breath ebbing away. Slumped in the cages of the whirling machinery, medals dangling from hollow chests, jewels draped over cold breasts, their bodies kept erect only by the confines of the iron bands as they swept in one great circle with the others, from one end of the ballroom to the other, then around again and again. The clattering of the machinery, along with the hissing and groans from the boilers beneath, was all that could be heard in the ballroom. That other music, all *allegro* and dash, had ceased when the violins' strings had been sawn through by the ceaseless, back-and-forth fury of the bows.

Anton let go of the living form in his arms. He walked over to the dead one that had crashed through the ballroom window, flung by the mechanism that had disintegrated about the woman, its iron bands snapped at last by the force of the dance. The dowager's kid-leather boots were sodden red now, the feet bloodied to pulp inside them. After she could no longer dance, the machines had danced for her and the others caught inside them. Now, twin pools of red seeped through the trampled snow, which thawed with their thinning heat, then froze again. The empty eyes looked up at him, with nothing but the night's heavy clouds reflected at their dulling centers.

But only for a moment. He felt Gisel stepping close beside him, then saw one of her rag-wrapped clogs kick the dowager's face, hard enough to crack bone and snap its lifeless gaze to one side.

"Don't—" He wrapped his arms around her again, pulling her away as she burst into sobbing tears. "It's all right. It is, it is . . ."

Even more terrible things were happening inside the grand ballroom. As he led Gisel away, he could hear vengeful shouts and laughter, the creak of metal wedged asunder, bludgeons of stick and fist upon withered flesh.

In the center of the city's widest street, he held her close. They both looked far beyond the skeletal trees at either side, toward the ancient Roman walls. The half-naked stokers were lifting the beams onto their blackened shoulders, unbarring the gates as tall as clock towers. Massive iron hinges groaned as the gates slowly parted, the stokers gripping and pulling the timbers' edges toward themselves.

He closed his eyes and pressed his face to the snow that had traced across Gisel's hair. Soldiers who wore no medals, with worn boots of rough, unpolished leather, and hard-faced commissars with machine pistols rather than swords at their belts, astride horses lean and bony-ribbed from their long trek across the steppes – they would enter unopposed now, gazing around at all that had fallen so easily into their hands.

He held her even tighter, her heart in time with his.

Things would be different now.

The Governess and the Lobster

Margaret Ronald

Dear Matron Jenkins,

For the record, I want you to know that the mechanical lobster is not my fault. I had only the best intentions when I asked the Cromwell children to deliver my initial report to the mail depot, and I did not learn about their addition to my package until recently.

I am sending this note by express post in hopes that it reaches you in time – though at this point, I'm not sure what would qualify as "in time". Before the regular post arrives? Before the lobster winds down? Before we had ever received M. Eutropius' misleading request? I do not know, and I fear that I will go mad long before I can make a guess.

But for the record, the mechanical lobster is not my doing. I owe you much, but at the moment that is all I can give you.

Yours,
—Rosalie Syme

Rosalie:

Your note arrived well in advance of the regular post, and as a result I'm still in the dark. I've heard nothing of a lobster, nor is there any news of a disaster there in Harkuma. As a result I must conclude that you are overreacting. Pull your stockings up and remember that I chose you for a reason.

And frankly, the only thing you owe me is the starter money for the school. The current state of affairs between Imperial interests and the Hundred Cities is tenuous at best, and I will not have an opportunity to found a branch of the Jenkins School squandered. If you have come to the conclusion that such a school is impossible, then send the money under separate cover, registered mail. I shouldn't have to tell you this.

—E. Jenkins (Matron)

Dear Matron Jenkins,

I apologize for my earlier note, as well as for the panicky tone of my initial report. I would assume that by now you have received it, save for the fact that the Cromwell children have taken some delight in demonstrating just how destructive their toys can be when fully wound.

I'm afraid my first impression of Harkuma lived up to the worst assertions of the yellow broadsheets back home. The Hundred Cities as a whole may be quite civilized, but Harkuma is not technically one of them, and its inferior status is made worse by the constant dust storms. (I am given to understand that Harkuma's elder sister city, Akkuma, is similarly plagued, but the automata of that city have safeguards in place against damage from the storms.) The mark of Imperial commerce is quite present, though, as the architecture of Cromwell House proves, as does my presence, I suppose, since Cromwell and Eutropius

I'm sorry. I get ahead of myself, and my circumstances are not conducive to concentration.

What is markedly odd is that despite all this, Harkuma reminds me of my home in the warehouse district. (I do beg your pardon, Matron, for reminding you of this fact.) The constant chaos is not so far off from what the Staves dealt with, although there is a different flavor to it that I cannot yet put into words.

Of the human population, I cannot begin to find a commonality. In the five minutes I paused at the train station, I saw four Lower Kingdom officials in state dress, two Terranoctan soldiers (or so I assume from their scythes), a Svete-Kulap clanmerchant suffering a bad case of sunburn, and a Lucan noblewoman with her interpreter. To complicate matters, the automata of Akkuma travel freely within this satellite city, and their clattering speech rings out at all hours.

Unfortunately, the cavalier attitude of the Hundred Cities to the association of automaton and human borders on the reckless. After the officials had carefully evicted the human passengers and inspected the train so that it might pass on to Akkuma, I saw a young man of shifty appearance helping a woman who could not have been younger than ninety onto the last car. The Akkuma train runs at such infrequent intervals that human visitors must bring twice their own weight in water, Matron, and yet this young man packed her onto the train with nothing more than a bag. I cannot

I have taken a moment to collect myself and remove the canister of spiders that the eldest Cromwell child, Natalya, has placed on my bedside table.

As you recall – and as I wish to stress, given that my assignment has proven so radically different – I was to undertake the education of the Cromwell children. Mr Cromwell was somewhat lax in hiring a governess after their mother's passing several years ago, but his business partner M. Eutropius, currently the children's legal guardian, contacted the Jenkins School immediately following Mr Cromwell's last illness. While all of this is technically true, the omissions are crippling enough to question whether our contract is even valid.

The problems began nearly as soon as I arrived at Cromwell House. The house was built in both the Harkuma style and that of a northern manor house, keeping the worst features of each. The lower floors are open and high-ceilinged, but the upper reaches are quite dark and cramped, giving one a choice of agoraphobia or claustrophobia. It did not help that when I first arrived I had to search for a good fifteen minutes before finding anyone, and the housemaid who answered seemed to not know her way around at all, having been here only one week. As I write this, she has already left, hired off to a financier bound for Bis-Nocta. Her successor has also given notice.

The next problem to present itself was the matter of the children themselves. Though Eutropius's letter seemed to indicate that they were already on a course of education, it seems that their father let them run amok. Natalya, at eleven years, has some authority over the other three but chooses to exercise it only to prevent interfamilial fights. Irra (nine) is as elusive as a swamplight and as omnipresent, at least until she is noticed, and her brother Serge (six) seems to delight in loudly pointing her out and causing her to flee. The youngest, Sulla (five), would much rather communicate in gestures and what I believe is a poor approximation of automaton-speech.

Matron, these are not students, even by the standards of the warehouse district scholarship initiative (and believe me, I am well aware of the irony in my saying this). They are a project.

I did not see my employer until that evening, having spent much of my time in an attempt to introduce myself to the children (and, as I've mentioned, sending out my initial report plus lobster). Natalya was the one who found me trying to coax Irra out of hiding. "Uncle wants to see you," she told me, and handed me the first of the many canisters of spiders. I consider it a small victory that I did not scream and fling the lot away.

The lower halls of Cromwell House – the high arches, the red clay walls, the tracings in the floor meant for those automata guests who run on wheels – are particularly uncanny in shadow. (If you remember the gymnasium specter incident at the school, I believe you will understand why.) The lamps were unlit, and only the glow of fires outside illuminated the hall. I made my way to the foot of the stairs, clinging to the wall for guidance. "Mr Eutropius?" I called, expecting at any moment Irra and Serge to jump out at me. "Sir?"

"I am here," said a cultured bass voice from somewhere to my right. It was the sort of voice to rattle pebbles in dust, and I confess I shivered at the sound of it.

You have trained me well, though, and mindful of your constant admonitions, I pulled myself upright. "I am Rosalie Syme, of the Jenkins School. You engaged me to educate the Cromwell children."

"So I did." A clank and drag sounded from the darkness, followed by a brief flare: werglass, glowing as thaumic power moved through it. "Come to me if you have need of anything. I have been quite busy in the wake of poor Edgar's death, but I can certainly spare time for the children."

"That's kind of you, sir," I said. "Sir, how will I know you, if I need to find you?"

At this there was a creak and a dull thrum, as of an engine catching somewhere in the house. "My apologies. I forgot you do not see as I do. In Edgar's absence, I forget myself."

A dial spun close to my elbow. At the far end of the hall, the lamps flickered and caught, one by one, illuminating the great shape standing far too close, the inlay of gold on steel, the eight long segmented legs unfolding as he approached, the central spire of a body and the werglass ring of eyes.

Eutropius is an automaton.

You have hired me to an automaton.

Matron Jenkins, please call me home.

Yours,

—Rosalie Syme

Rosalie:

I will do no such thing. While I admit Eutropius's nature is startling, that does not in any way change our contract. Remember: I would not have sent you if I did not believe you fully capable, and certainly more so than our non-scholarship students. Now wipe your nose and get back in the fray before I relegate you to that list of fainting nellies.

And why would I mind your comments regarding the warehouse district? Do you think me ignorant of my students' backgrounds?

As a side note, the lobster has arrived, along with the remnants of the post. I currently have it caged on my desk. How long does it take to wind down?

—E. Jenkins (Matron)

Dear Matron Jenkins,

Yes, of course you're right. My apologies.

I've since acclimated a little, although it is difficult to look out on the low flat roofs of the city and not be reminded of the warehouse district. I confess I did not expect my childhood to find me here of all places. (Though I would like to stress again that my days in the Staves are well behind me, and in any case the rooftops here are too unfamiliar for me to consider similar activities. I think I've lost the knack, anyway.)

Harkuma is a very strange place. Its entire business revolves around what is not present: Akkuma and the gems mined there, as well as the various homes of the trade delegations who make those gems their business. Few of the automata here even treat it as home; Eutropius is Transit-born and considers himself a native of the Glasswalk, and many of those I see during the day return to Akkuma regularly.

It's perhaps no surprise that the Cromwell children are so

distracted. I've abandoned the classroom setting and have adopted a peripatetic method of teaching, which has improved their attitude toward me somewhat. Natalya, in particular, has begun to warm to me so long as I assist her in the kitchen, the position of cook being another that has high turnover. She has even taught me several of the recipes for the dinners the children usually share when no cook is engaged. (Sweet pudding is, unfortunately, at the top of the list. Fresh greens will no doubt be difficult to introduce.)

Far be it from me to speak ill of the dead, but it seems that the late Edgar Cromwell was one of those people who, after amassing a family, don't really seem to know what to do with it. Under his wife's supervision, all was well, but judging by some remarks from Natalya and Eutropius, his attitude was always one of benign neglect. Neglect remains neglect, though.

Eutropius does deeply care about the children, and it is quite something to see them swarm over their "uncle". Irra in particular reliably comes out of hiding only in his presence, and Serge cannot be quieted. Apparently he has also taught them some small practical skills; the mechanical lobster, as well as several of their other toys, is the children's own work, built under his tutelage. (According to him, the lobster should wind down in a matter of weeks, depending on how much it has consumed. I've enclosed a key, should you care to deploy it in faculty meetings.) Eutropius, though, is aware that his skill in child-rearing is limited, and so it seems that he engaged help well before Cromwell even fell ill, though I must confess I was startled at his other employees.

Specifically, the same shifty-looking young man who I saw sending the poor old woman off on the Akkuma train is in Eutropius's employ. He arrived as I was in the midst of showing Natalya how to scrub out the cookpots. Sulla, who had been hanging onto my skirt for the last half-hour, was the first to notice him. "Pietro," she said, giving me an emphatic tug.

"Pietro?" I stood to see the young man lounging in the doorway as if he belonged there. "Who—"

Sulla, however, did not hesitate. "Pietro, this is Rosie," she said, for the first time lacking the stutter that she carries from attempting to imitate automata.

"Rosie?" He tipped his cap to me – a gesture straight off the streets of the Capitol, and one extraordinarily strange coming from a man dressed in the heavily embroidered jacket and bands of the Hundred Cities, not to mention his short beard and shaven head. "A pleasure, miss," he went on, his Imperial only barely accented.

"Likewise," I said, attempting to regain what dignity I could while up to my elbows in filthy suds.

Pietro smiled, exposing one canine tooth that had been replaced with steel. Before he could say more, Serge practically jumped onto him, demanding to know if "Grandma Lyle" was back. The most I could gather from the ensuing chaos was that Pietro was a frequent visitor to the house and often advised Eutropius on how best to take care of the children (including my hiring), and that this was part of his profession.

What that profession might be, I would hesitate to explain had you not explicitly stated that you are unconcerned with my history. Pietro is what the many travelers through Harkuma refer to as a *facilis* or, commonly, "greaser". He makes his living by arranging contact between the various human merchants and the automata of Akkuma. If a person wishes to visit Akkuma, he must do so in the company of one of these *faciles* who will vouch for him, undertake the shipment of water, even make business connections, as well as monitor the entrepreneur's movements within the city and make certain that he adheres to all standards of conduct.

To maintain their positions, these *faciles* must keep credibility with both sides. A human client who attempted to suborn an automaton or hide in the city would be as damaging to a *facilis'* credibility as an attempt on that same human's life by one of the more militant automata sects.

The practice of trading on such an ephemeral thing as reputation seemed at first incomprehensible, until I remembered how the Staves used to deal with the other "confraternities", as you have always referred to them. We did not have the *faciles*, but we did have our own go-betweens, particularly in regards to selling goods of questionable ownership. In fact, I played a similar role between the Staves and the Redfingers (who ran on the Gestenwerke side of the district) up to the point where I was handed over to the Jenkins School.

Regarding the satellite school, I have made some minor

enquiries, but the first officials I contacted had been reassigned by the time I made a follow-up visit. I will make another attempt, but at the moment I have enough on my hands with the Cromwell children. Sulla has taken to creeping into my room and falling asleep on my bed – in fact, she is there now, and once this letter is complete I will put another blanket over her. Sadly, the frequency of spider canisters has increased (and now diversified into centipedes) even as Natalya and I seem to have connected in our mutual scullionship.

Courteous as my employer is with the children, his night-time pursuits are distressing to say the least. Every few nights, a din emerges from the lower reaches, a noise that I can only compare to the clatter of tramcars paired with the whine of a malfunctioning drill. It is a pity, as the city is not lacking in charms, even if I am still shaking the dust out of my skirts every five minutes and cleaning it from every crevice before I sleep. Even when I have a full night's sleep, every day feels as if I am walking on an uneven surface. But you are right, Matron, and I have some experience walking unsteady paths.

Yours,
—Rosalie Syme

R:

That's my girl.

I've attached a list of names of former Jenkins School contacts; if your first endeavors are withering, perhaps this will spur a second round. Don't fuss so about a little noise; our new dormitory faces the forge district, and I can't imagine it's any worse than that.

—E. J. (M.)

Dear Matron Jenkins,

Sadly, not one of the people you name remains in Harkuma. It is as I said: this is a transient town, and few people stay for long. Even the automata do not linger.

I had some proof of that the other day, when I was taking Natalya and the children back from market again (Serge shows an aptitude for misdirection, which resulted in our first return trip to the market and a very grudging apology from him). I am not sure if I can adequately describe the scene we found on our return. The roads of Harkuma, though just as busy as Admiral Street or any other thoroughfare, are broad enough for automata to pass easily. One may pass by most altercations without even flicking one's skirt aside, regardless of their violence.

However, this particular altercation had blocked the entirety of the street. Two automata and a Lower Kingdom official, possibly one of those I saw on my arrival, were in heated disagreement. Of the automata, one had a very Imperial look to its construction – possibly a tramcar before its awakening – and as such, it was roughly the size of two dormitory rooms. The other was, I believe, City-born, one of the automata created and awakened among its fellows, and thus both smaller and less practically designed, perching on three delicate legs and shaking a fourth at the official and the tramcar. My knowledge of the Lower Kingdom dialects is flawed (you remember I had trouble with the inflections), but I was able to gather that some temporary business agreement had soured.

My first impulse was to shoo the children away, but you can guess how successful that was. My second was to move the five of us into the shelter of a nearby fruit-seller's stall and wait it out. I had no sooner done so than the shouting gave way to ominous silence, and Sulla caught her breath. "What is it?" I asked, picking her up.

"The big one called the little a—" and here she made a stuttering noise, an automata word that I am glad I do not know, judging by Natalya's hiss. "And the little one called the big one a man-scraper."

Just then the Lower Kingdom official declared that both automata were "unworthy of their metal". The automata turned to face him, and I covered Sulla's eyes. I saw plenty of tram accidents when I was in the Staves, and they are not healthy viewing for a five-year-old.

Before the man could be crushed, however, a tiny old woman made her way through the crowd. It took me a moment to recognize her as the same woman Pietro had put on the train to Akkuma, and by that point she had reached the side of the larger automaton. I could not hear what she said, but the tramcar settled back on its treads and the smaller automaton lowered its leg. Either one of them could easily have crushed her or even just set her aside, yet they remained still. The official attempted to interrupt her several times, but she raised one frail hand and he stopped as if confronted by a pikeman.

Around us, the commotion in the street returned to its usual state, and Sulla pushed away, wanting to be let down. Unfortunately, her buckles had become caught on my bodice, and by the time we'd untangled ourselves, the old woman had dismissed both the smaller automaton and the official, and stayed to speak with the tramcar, one hand on its treads. (I should mention that many Transit-born automata do not like to be touched; it is, I believe, a reminder of their history as machines before awakening.) After a moment, they parted ways, and the little old woman turned back towards us.

"Grandma Lyle!" Serge shouted, echoed by Irra, and the two of them practically knocked her over. Natalya, Sulla and I followed more slowly.

If I did not know better – and I am not yet certain that I do – I would say that Grandma Lyle has some Imperial ancestry, as despite her age and dress she does not resemble either the disparate humans of the Hundred Cities or the Terranoctans. She smiled at me as I reached Serge and Irra. "Rosie, I take it?"

"Yes," I managed, around Sulla's chatter. "Forgive me for asking, but are you a *facilis*?"

Her eyes crinkled up at the corners, and she nodded. "One of the first. As are most of my family." She gestured after the tramcar, which had trundled most of the way to the alarm tower by now. "Poor #41 doesn't like being left out of the loop, and she's returning to Akkuma tomorrow, so she saw this as the last chance to clear matters up."

Sulla asked her something that I could not catch, as the last few words were automaton-speech, and though Lyle responded in Imperial, I did not understand one word in five. Terms such as "sand-ogre", "Rimarri banner", and "fourpoint" must have meant something to the children, who listened avidly and nodded along. "So it *was* a business disagreement?" I tried.

"No," Irra said, and immediately tried to hide behind her brother.

"Of a sort," Lyle corrected. "Business covers a number of matters for City-born, and more for Transit-born. And of course the Lower Kingdoms like to think they know all about automata, so it's hard to convince them otherwise."

Do you remember when I gave my first presentation in class, on the political structure of the warehouse district, and got an entire classroom full of glazed looks? I now understand what it's like from the other side. "This happens often?"

"This is Harkuma." Ruffling Irra's hair, she smiled at me. "Pietro tells me you are doing well."

"I—yes." I have seen quite a bit more of Pietro since our introduction, though I must question his business acumen, since he's missed appointments more than once due to his habit of hanging around Cromwell House.

"Good. I'll send some books along with him." She bowed again, in the formal Lower Kingdom style. "I have work at the far end of the city, but I hope to see you again. And Serge, you should return those plums."

True to her words, Serge had taken another handful from the fruit stall while we were watching the conflict, and this meant another unwilling apology and a long talk all the way back to Cromwell House.

Despite such setbacks, the children are starting to learn, although their knowledge of geography is absolutely terrible. I asked Irra to point to Svete-Kulap, and she ignored the map entirely and pointed east, which is nearly one hundred and twenty degrees off. Once they finally made the connection between map and directions, they took to it with alacrity, even if Sulla still cannot quite pronounce the names properly. Pietro brought us a copy of *Atlas of the Clockwork Cities* – the new edition, by C. and S. Vallom – and Serge can barely be parted from it for a moment.

Incidentally, Natalya has quite surprised me. She is as quick and intelligent as ~~any of the Staves' thiefmasters~~ any Jenkins School valedictorian, and teaching her is an enjoyable challenge. It turns out the spiders were her way of welcome; the girl has a passion for studying arthropods, and I suspect the mechanical lobster was mainly her work. I would like to recommend her for the Royal Society when she's of age, since if she's not given enough of a challenge she is likely to make one of her own.

Yours,
—Rosalie

*   *   *

R:

I'd rather not lose more of our students to the Society, but as it's unlikely we could bring Natalya here without causing more trouble for the Cromwell children, I'll consider it.

I can't help noticing that your letters still say nothing concrete about the potential for a Jenkins School. Is there a chance of founding one or not? This is not a difficult question.

—E. J. (M.)

Dear Matron Jenkins,

It might not be a difficult question in a place like the warehouse district, where despite the many "confraternities" we all knew where we'd go at the end of the day. But Harkuma is not an Imperial city, and its shifting population makes the question much more troubling.

I have, however, sought out more information on the subject. At my request, Pietro took us to visit his grandmother yesterday. The children pounced on her as soon as we reached the door, which she bore with better grace than many of my classmates would have demonstrated, and I was left to help Pietro with the dust shutters (the storm season has begun in earnest, leaving me wondering what life was like before grit accumulated in every part of my wardrobe).

Grandma Lyle's house is unusual even for the mishmash of architecture that makes up Harkuma. It is old, so old the red brick has faded to rose. Few structures in Harkuma have been in place for more than a decade, but I found myself marveling at the tiles set into the clay that showed the tarnish of time. "So old," I said as we entered, mostly to myself.

"Rosie!" Pietro said reprovingly, and I looked up, remembering a little too late that I really should inform him of my preferred address.

"She means the house, Pietro, not me." Grandma Lyle closed another of the dust shutters. "It was built when Harkuma wasn't much more than a well and a rail depot." She turned to her grandson and nodded to the next room, where the children were arguing over some many-jointed toy. Obediently, he joined them, I assumed to keep them from tearing the toy apart. "Come," she said to me. "Sit."

"Thank you," I said. "I hope we're not imposing on your hospitality."

"Not in the least." She smiled and settled into a worn chair in front of what I belatedly recognized as a writing desk. A long case of oversized books stood beside it, as well as tools I'd last seen in our advanced mathematics classes. "As it is, your timing is good; I've only just returned from Akkuma."

"Akkuma? But—" Of course; as a *facilis*, she would travel between the two, which would explain why she had been the lone human passenger on that train. "It must be a difficult journey."

"I have an old friend there," she said, still smiling. "We share an interest in cartography. These days, I split my time between the two cities. Sit, please."

I did so, pulling a stool to the high table. Through the door, Natalya had begun to inspect the little toy with, I suspected, an eye toward copying it, while Serge had dragged out the *Atlas* and was flipping through it to show Pietro something.

"Pietro tells me," she went on, "that you wish to build a school here. Do you understand what that would mean?" She raised one hand to the wall behind her desk, where a metal disc had been set into the clay like a talisman.

I did have the whole speech prepared, Matron, I promise you that. But the words seemed to slide away from me. "I'm not sure," I told her. "I know what it meant for me, when I lived in the warehouse district." Lyle raised one white brow, but did not speak. "For me it was a step up, a hand helping me off an unsteady walkway, but there are so few children in Harkuma, and so many of them are only here for months at a time. What good would a school be for them?"

"You might be surprised. And the children are not the only ones here." She touched the disc again, and in the slanting light I could make out the design that had once been stamped there: a rodent of some kind, turning back to regard its stump of a tail. "There have always been people who shuttled between worlds."

I thought of the friends I had left in the Staves when I was given to the Jenkins School – and yet I have never regretted the change.

Lyle gestured to her desk. "I traveled for quite some time, as did my friend in Akkuma. As did my husband, before we met. Harkuma was very small in those days, but even then, we kept returning here." She rose to her feet again. "Come. I'll show you some of our work."

I'm afraid all thoughts of the Jenkins School fled while we examined her work. Serge eventually joined us to examine the number of maps Lyle and her family had created over the years. It was quite possibly the most peaceful afternoon I've had since stepping off of the train.

So there is one opinion on the viability of a Jenkins School in Harkuma: open to the possibility, if not entirely wholehearted. Though I suspect her position as *facilis* gives Lyle a perspective that few share. I can't help but think the *faciles* would be instrumental for the foundation of ~~any school~~ a Jenkins School.

—Rosalie

R:

Let me be perfectly clear about this: I am not asking for everyone else's opinion of a Jenkins School in Harkuma, regardless of how old their houses are. I am asking for *your* opinion. I would hate to think that I had made the wrong choice in selecting you for this work.

—E. J. (M.)

dere Matron Jankins,

ifYOU tak our ROSIE away we will send Fiftene LOBTSTERS to your mailbox and they willEAT ALL YOUR MAIL. Do NOT tak ROSIE back we liek her here and she lieks it here TO.

also send one ~~hundrud~~ THOUSND gold Bulls to this Adress or maybee we will send the lobtsters ENNIWAY.

sinserely yours,

—YOULL NEVER CATCH US

To the Cromwell Children:

I have enclosed your "ransom note" with corrections made in red. You will make those corrections, copy out the result ten times apiece, and return the copies to Miss Syme. In future, if you intend to threaten anyone, you have no excuse for doing so ungrammatically.

Also, your lobster is currently on my desk. I rather like it. Miss Syme tells me this is your work; if so, well done.

—Emma Jenkins

⋆   ⋆   ⋆

R:

What in the world is going on out there? And why haven't you gotten to basic spelling and grammar with these children?

—E. J. (M.)

Dear Matron Jenkins,

I do apologize for the note, as well as for their spelling. Irra has apparently decided that poor spelling is intimidating, and I have yet to convince her otherwise. I believe Natalya allowed the letter to be written solely to comfort Serge and Sulla, for which I cannot really blame her.

Their concern springs from a failure on my part, and one I am ashamed to relate. Several nights ago, Eutropius held yet another social for his business contacts. I would have simply put the pillow over my head and endured the noise had it not been that we have entered the storm season, and for the past two nights the rattle of sand against my shutters had kept me awake. I left Sulla curled up on my bed and descended to the lower reaches of the house.

I am not certain what I expected to find – although my classmates would probably have whispered about some form of mechanical debauchery, I doubt they would know such if it were presented on a platter. The werglass fixtures of the house were lit, as were several of the lamps, and by their weak light I found my way to the same great chamber where I had first met Eutropius.

Five automata, ranging from a lacy creature very like a transplanted sea animal to a hulking thing created from barrels and treads, stood in a semicircle in the center of the room. Eutropius's scorpion-like angularity perched in the middle, and he seemed to be the one in charge: though each continued in either screech or drone or arrhythmic clank, he was the one who gestured to each in time, much as a conductor does before an orchestra.

"Fascinating, yes?" I turned to see Pietro, who had been standing just at the edge of the lamplight. "I don't quite have the ear for it, but it's still amazing to hear them practice."

"Practice?" I shivered, looking from him to Eutropius and back. "This is practice for something?"

"Of course." He shed his jacket and draped it around my shoulders. "Automata music. Although it's not so much practice as a friendly concert, say. Like singing with one's family."

As I watched, a pattern seemed to accrete around Eutropius's movements: percussive, devoid of melody, and yet with a strangely harmonious result, like a mathematical formula drawn in calligraphy. I shook my head, too weary to either make sense of the sound or reject his loan of the jacket. "But this isn't music. This is noise."

Abruptly Eutropius's gears clattered to a halt, and the noise stopped, leaving only a deafening echo. "Noise, is it?" he said without turning. His voice, so close to human, seemed all the more artificial now. "And what would you have to say about noise?"

Pietro started to shake his head, but I let my exhaustion speak for me. "I . . . had hoped to ask you to quiet it. The house is so loud, and following the storms—"

"You ask me to quiet my friends?" Eutropius's central body rotated so that he faced me, and his legs unfolded from underneath. "In *my* house?"

Some time before I was given to the Jenkins School, I had the unfortunate experience of walking a roofline in winter and finding that several shingles retained a glaze of ice. I have never forgotten that sudden shock of my footing falling away. And yet then and now I had the same reaction: reach out for the first handhold and hope. "It was your partner's house as well," I said.

Eutropius went still, even the lights of his eyes going out, and I briefly thought he'd lost power, that his own life had stopped at the mention of his partner's. Instead he made a horribly discordant noise, and the other automata began to move, gliding or thumping their way to the door. I started to speak, but Pietro put his hand on my shoulder and shook his head.

For a moment the hall was silent – I would have said blessedly so only a few minutes earlier, but now it carried a hollowness that shivered through me.

Eutropius turned away. "Edgar," he said finally, "hated our music. He could not stand it, and so I only played on nights when he was in Akkuma, or trading in the Capitol. It . . . makes me miss him less, to play now. I can imagine he is only temporarily absent."

I caught my breath, stung by the pain in his automaton voice even as I knew it for a mechanical response. And yet there are

Society doctors who claim that human pain is a mechanical response as well. "I'm sorry," I said.

"I should hope so," Eutropius said with a grinding noise almost like a laugh. "And I should threaten you with termination, for interrupting our music. Or if not for that, then for your little side project."

A chill ran down my spine, freezing me in place. "Project?" I said, as innocently as possible.

Not innocent enough. "Do you think I don't know that your matron sent you to found one of her staid, strait-laced schools here? At the very least this constitutes a foolish endeavor; at the worst, I'd consider it a strike against the Hundred Cities and all free automata. We have no need of a foothold of Imperial culture here."

"It's certainly not meant as such," I tried, but he would not hear me.

"In any other of the Hundred Cities, you would be scorned, but here you only look a fool. This is Harkuma, Miss Syme. No one is here because they want to be. No one belongs here. Edgar didn't, I don't, and the best we can do is continue." He shivered, or maybe that was the automaton way of shrugging. "Or perhaps I will simply inform the Jenkins School that you have proved unsuitable."

"I . . ." I would have defended myself, but the past few weeks have taken their toll. I have been a tolerable governess for the Cromwell children, but a governess is not a school, and Harkuma is larger than one house. I have failed in the task you set me, Matron, and taxed your patience in doing so.

"You are correct," I said.

"Am I, now? You finally think so?" He turned to regard me, werglass eyes flaring. "Take your silence and go."

Pietro shepherded me out of the hall, to the foot of the stairs. To my horror, the children were already there, even Sulla. Tears welled in my eyes as I saw them. "Thank you," I managed, shrugging Pietro's jacket away. "I am sorry."

"He won't write to her," he said. "Don't worry."

"Write, don't write, what does it matter?" I pressed both hands over my eyes. "Matron Jenkins – she has every right to call me home—" I caught myself before I could sound any more idiotic and hurried up the steps, Natalya and Irra parting before me.

It was an ill-chosen remark, and one I regretted once I had slept, but I believe it is what triggered the children's assumption that you were planning to take me away.

Yours,

—Rosalie

R:

No letter as yet from Eutropius.

—E. J. (M.)

Dear Matron Jenkins,

I have begun this letter twice over, and failed each time. It is perhaps emblematic of my greater failure: I cannot found a Jenkins School here.

Since you asked me outright for my opinion, I have been trying to decide what that opinion is. Finally, some nights ago, I'm afraid I reverted to old habit and crept out on my own. It turns out I have not lost the knack, and the rooftops of Harkuma are just as navigable as the warehouse district. You'll remember that I was given to doing this in my early days at the School; I believe it is how I first made your direct acquaintance. And it was what convinced me that I should remain at the Jenkins School, which is why I believed it would clarify my thoughts on this matter.

On the stormless nights – those without automata concerts, that is – Harkuma is quiet, and one can see almost as far as Akkuma's gleam across the desert. Each building is different, in the style of each owner's homeland, and yet I was able to keep my footing. Finally, I found a spot on the roof of one of the shelters by the market, looking not toward the desert but back toward the city itself. It is a large city, for all that it pretends to be small and scattered.

For a long while I sat there, arms locked around my knees like Irra hearing a new story and hoping no one will notice her presence before the story ends, until a man's voice spoke. "Grandma told me I might find you here."

I turned to see Pietro carefully climbing across the next roof over. He smiled, a little nervously, and slid down beside me, nearly dislodging a tile as he did so. "Did she truly?" I asked.

"You'd be surprised at what Grandma Lyle can guess. Ask her

sometime about her childhood." He joined me in silence for a moment, watching the slow gold line of the late-night train departing. "Did you believe him?" he asked finally. "About Harkuma?"

"Eutropius?" Pietro nodded. "I don't know. Nobody does seem to belong here, to be honest."

"And yet he stays," he said thoughtfully, "with his music and his business."

And his grief, I thought.

After a moment, Pietro sighed and draped his jacket over my shoulders in much the same way as before. "Well, it's not as though I can argue. I wasn't born here, but my mother was, and my aunt – they're both *faciles* in the other cities, maybe you'll meet them on their circuits – but I came back here. We do keep coming back."

"So Lyle said."

"She was the first, you know. She and her friend in Akkuma. The first *faciles*." He glanced at me, then away. "There aren't nearly enough of us. It's in the family, but there are only so many of us, and we're needed all over." He shrugged. "Could always use more in the family."

I think my silence may have dampened whatever point he was trying to make. But his words had sparked a new line of thought for me and I was too busy following that to discern his motives. "You're right," I said at last, rising to my feet. "You're quite right."

"Am I?" He attempted to get up, slid, and settled for sitting upright.

"Oh, yes. But this will be complicated." I smiled at him, and he smiled back – despite the steel tooth, he has a perfectly nice smile when he's not trying to be charming. "I must return to Cromwell House at once."

I believe he would have walked me home, save that he is much less adept at the roofwalk than I, even given my years away from it. I still have his jacket, though, and have yet to return it with proper thanks.

Since then, I have come to an inescapable and unfortunate conclusion. Because of this, I am returning your investment. I have enclosed your initial start-up funds for the Jenkins School under separate, registered cover. You may strike my name from the rolls of graduates if you like, or place me on the list of "nellies" you so often scorned.

My reason is thus: if I am to start a school here, then it cannot simply be a Jenkins School. It must be a Harkuma school, for all of those who shuttle between worlds or might hope to do so; a *facilis* for the *faciles*, and it must be more than I alone can create.

This is a risky endeavor, to say the least, and I know the Jenkins School's reputation would suffer from a satellite's failure, but whether this school succeeds cannot be dependent on the Jenkins name or even the Imperial tongue. I hope that this makes up in some way for what must be an unexpected betrayal.

I've contacted a number of potential teachers – linguists among the translation corps of automata, the Lucan noblewomen and their attendants, some of the Kulap exercise masters. (I have also asked Eutropius if he would consider teaching the specifics of automata music. I believe he was so startled by the question that he did not immediately consider the ramifications of his assent.)

So thank you, Matron, for sending me, and please know that I am more than grateful for all the Jenkins School has done for me. I hope I have not disappointed you.

—Rosalie Syme of Harkuma

My dear Rosalie:

I regret to inform you that the children's mechanical lobster has devoured the registered cover for the funds you sent. As a result, there is no way I can officially return them to our books, and so I've written them off completely. I have no choice but to send the funds back to you, with my blessing.

Incidentally, I assume you can withstand a visit or two. I'll be along in the spring.

—Emma Jenkins (Matron)

Beside Calais

Samantha Henderson

The hills that bordered the École Aéronautique were covered in long grass, and as they dipped to the sea the blades dispersed through the tawny sand, which in turn fingered out into gray water. The foliage that covered the slopes was still bright with new growth. Three or four hundred meters away a small flock of éoles grazed. They were among the smallest of the flying beasts, but each was at least the size of a full-grown bull, and the green grass was stripped when they fed.

Claire halted clumsy beside him. It seemed to him every step she took was an invitation to crumple, and he feared she would lose her footing and tumble over the drop-off. Ian Chance fought the urge to slip a hand under her elbow to steady her.

General Adair was right. The éoles would have to go. Yet Ian smiled as he watched them; an éole was the first flying beast he had broken by his own hand and flown over the neat russet-and-green rectangles of his father's farm in Lancashire, and he had a fondness for the breed.

Some hopped from bush to hillock, arching the wide stretch of their bat-like wings to catch the breeze. Ian could hear the gentle chug of the éoles' engines, and behind that the constant sough of the water. Spring was warming into summer, and the nascent heat in the breeze reminded him of the Saharan winter, although so near the sea the air was not as dry.

Thready white steam rose over the flock, forming white puffs that glowed crisp against the blue sky. Save for the steam, the sky was cloudless: the smooth, even cerulean of a medieval painting. If he squinted against the light reflecting off the waters of the Channel Ian could see the white rise that was Dover.

That last time he had been to England, London was still in mourning for Queen Victoria. He remembered a length of tattered black ribbon tied high on a lamppost, fluttering in the breeze. At the time he had wondered if the same breeze traveled the Channel that season to hold the flying beasts aloft in their migration north.

This morning, when he'd seen Claire waiting for him outside the old dormitories at the flying school besides Calais, a bright splash of checkered red against the gray, weathered wood, he'd felt shy, and delighted too. To see her again brought back a familiar warmth in his belly, a memory of days where the breeze blew warm or cool according to the season until it became a thing of the bones and the body grew attuned to the fine sea-spray or yeasty pollen that the wind carried and offered, constantly.

Ian lived by the wind then, breaking in the hardy little éoles until the once-wild creatures could be flown in intricate formation. He tamed the calm, aloof dunne monos until they'd take decomposed iron from his hand. At night he and Claire would curl around each other under her duvet in the women's quarters; she rated her own room in part because those in command of the Air Corps decided, in their lopsided way, that she outranked the nurses. No one disputed her right: Claire rose long before dawn broke, to catch the chance of seeing a blériot over the Channel as the sun rose, and the nurses needed their sleep. Besides, her family had owned the land before her drunken grandfather, broke from trying to harness wild éoles to harsher work than they were formed for, sold it to a government seeking a place to make use of the flying beasts that ranged this coast time out of mind.

She stood straight as she watched for him outside the dormitory, and for a moment he allowed himself to think it wouldn't be so bad, that the reports of her injuries were exaggerated and that she had recovered. He was out of the car the Corps Aéronautique had sent before Plantard, a sunburned boy who looked barely old enough to drive, could open the door. Then she moved. Her limbs twisted painfully and her shoulders humped, and she dragged one foot behind her. He felt disappointment like a blow to the stomach and then the slow burn of contempt at his own cowardice.

She didn't show him that she saw it, unless it was in the amused curve of her lips when he bent to embrace her.

"Plantard will take your bags to quarters," she whispered, nodded at the boy. "Come with me to the cliffs."

One of the éoles reared on its back wheel at their approach, spreading its ungraceful wings and spinning its propeller: a dominant male, getting their scent. The flock stopped grazing for a second, and the low hum of their engines quickened as they readied for the signal to take off. When the male remained in place they relaxed and returned to pulling at the green foliage, hungry from their long post-winter flight from Africa. He wondered how the tang of leftover winter felt on their sand-scored wings. If he could walk among them could he smell the baked-bread smell of the Egyptian air on their leathers? Would he find the compass shape of the Bat d'Af brand beneath the strut of a mount gone feral?

General Adair's orders went round and round in Ian's head like a cylinder recording.

"If a breeding program's to work, Chance, we'll need all the local resources," the General had said. "That means the feral flocks will have to be diverted – or culled. You'll need to make that happen before we ship the stock in."

Ian knew the little éoles had no place in the Corps' breeding program, based as it was on the calm, sturdy dunne monos and the powerful wright flyers – the American pair of Roosevelt-bred flying beasts Taft had sent as gift to Whitehall.

"There might be room for an avion or two," Ian replied. "They're quick and clever – look much like the éoles but sturdier."

Adair had flashed him a look. The North African sun had burnt the Frenchman's skin until he was ruddy even in the cool of the evening. In his time he'd flown dunne monos and antoinettes, back when one did so at the risk of seeming eccentric, before the military knew what do with the Air Corps. Now war loomed with Germany and Italy, and the old corpsman was recalled to make a war machine out of men and flying beasts.

"I'll leave it to you," he told Ian. "None of our people know what we'll need on the African lines, and you've stewed in Algiers long enough so you're not so offensively English. Your only weakness is sentimentality. The éoles must go. And the blériot, any that remain. They are intractable, unpredictable."

Four years since Claire had netted a rogue blériot and ridden it over the shore of Calais; four years since it tumbled her onto the rocks.

"Wakeman will meet you at the school."

Adair's voice brought him back to himself: he'd been looking at the horizon, when the setting sun bled across the desert sands, but seeing the gray sea of the channel.

"Wakeman?"

He'd met the hunter once in Egypt; they'd never met in England, although both were bred in Lancashire. He remembered a man tanned brown where Adair was burnt, almost past middle age but with a predator's lean body and a killer's blue eye.

"The British are sending him to help with the culling." Adair's tone defied him to object. Ian shrugged. The General was right: the wrights and dunnes would need the grazing.

"He'll never get that blériot, though," he muttered under his breath.

It had taken three weeks for Claire to trap the blériot, setting wire snares in the low foliage that rimmed the north-west cliffs between the school and Boulonge-sur-Mer. One morning, with the low clouds beating a constant, needle-spray mist against the tents and cottage of the camp, they spotted something thrashing in the distance and Claire ran across the hillocks to it, hair unbound across her shoulders and sodden in the drizzle. Ian followed after and heard her laugh before he saw they'd caught a young avion, half adult size, its twin propellers buzzing indignantly as it jerked against the wire, bouncing up and down in the gray bushes.

Claire freed its forewheel from the wire with a few practiced flicks of her wrist and steadied its wing until it was able to take off across the dull flat water, the whirr of its engine scolding them until it faded in the distance. She watched it fondly, looping the trap-wire between her fingers absently before bending to reset it, the wire high enough to snare the wheels but too low to foul or snap the struts.

"You do love them," he told her, watching the back of her drizzle-wet head as she adjusted the wire, and she cocked her head sideways, not looking at him but listening, always listening, as if not only English but any human speech was foreign to her, and took a fraction of a second to understand.

"Tomorrow I'll set it somewhere else," she said, as if he had not spoken. "He's not coming back here."

But she was wrong, because mid-afternoon, when the clouds had burned off and the fresh-broke avions had just been penned, there was a shout and a stable boy ran to the ramps, waving his cap wildly, looking for Mam'selle. They ran together to the site, and Claire laughed out loud at the sight of the beast bucking against the ropes, the beautiful curve of its graceful wings, so simple and functional compared with the bat-winged éoles and avions, its powerful engine buzzing furiously.

She didn't intend to ride it – not even Claire was that foolhardy. She only meant to mount it for a minute or so, to get the creature used to her weight. The boys had sunk the stakes deep on either side of the great taut, silken wings, and the ropes should have held. She approached it cautiously, clucking in the way one clucks instinctively at a skittish horse, one arm upraised to protect her face.

"Be careful, Claire," he called. She waved a hand at him without turning around. It leaned away from her as far as the ropes would allow.

Claire patted the blériot's quivering side for a long time, speaking to it in the low calming monotone she always used with the half-broke flying beasts. The angry buzz quieted. She closed her hand around the struts, then released them, then grasped them again, until the blériot no longer flinched when she did so.

Finally, she took a firm grip and slung herself into the rigging. The blériot lurched forward instantly, threatening to tumble tail over propeller, but the ropes held and Claire rode out each buck with a casual roll backwards and the ease of long experience.

Ian realized he'd been biting the inside of his cheek with the tension. Gingerly, he tongued the raw spot and wished Claire would come back.

"That's enough for now," he called, and she turned to him and seemed about to shout out, perhaps to bring her another length of rope. Then, with a powerful lurch, the creature pulled half the stakes out of wet ground soaked by several mornings' worth of rain. Claire hung on desperately as the beast rocked the other way, dislodging the remainder of the stakes.

Ian ran, the wet grass lashing at his ankles. The flying beast heaved its body off the ground, and, unaccustomed to a human's weight, came to ground again, its wheels gouging the muddy soil. The great wings flexed, the engine hummed, and it rose again, wavering and heavy-bodied as a summer beetle. The lowermost struts were even with Ian's face by the time he reached it and it was gaining altitude. Claire was stretched face down in the structure, and he caught a glimpse of her gray eyes, wide with alarm. Desperate, he reached and leaped, catching hold of a muddy wheel with both hands.

The blériot lurched closer to the cliff and dipped sharply down, cumbered with their combined weight.

"Let go!" Claire shouted. "It's too much – it's going to crash!"

Stubbornly, he held on to the slippery wheel, his fingers cramping. He felt his toes drag against the ground. The blériot managed to lift, wavering over the edge of the cliff, and Ian had a brief, dizzying view of rock and white seafoam.

"Damn you, let go!" Claire barked.

The beast tipped back over solid ground and dipped again. Ian's hands were a red blaze of pain.

It was going to crash. He would have to trust that Claire could control it. Gritting his teeth, he forced his cramped fingers open and fell, rolling on the sodden ground with an impact that drove the air from his lungs.

Free of his weight, the blériot rose again, heading for the sea. Ian rolled to his belly and watched, breathing painfully. For a few seconds, the flying beast straightened and flew sure towards the horizon. Then one wing dipped and side-slipped.

Ian watched with impotent horror while a gray shape separated from the body of the blériot, suspended an impossible few seconds clinging to a wing, and then as the creature tipped dangerously sidewise fell, plunging feet first, arms outstretched, to the rocks below. The curve of Claire's body as she fell seemed to have a control, an intent to it, as if she saw what was beneath her and was calculating how best to angle her limbs. Her silk scarf rippled up as the rest of her plummeted like Icarus. The blériot above her slipped sideways, descending as if it could scoop her out of the air.

Although he never took his eyes off her, Ian never remembered seeing the moment of impact, only that one instant she was falling and the next she was sprawled on the black wet boulders semi-submerged in the tide, legs trailing in the black water like a mermaid's tail.

"Is the avion with the flock?"

Claire's voice had graveled with the years, and although her English was sure as it was before, her accent was stronger. Maybe no one spoke English to her after he left. Her English was better than his French, so that's what they spoke, during the day and during the night.

Ian glanced at Claire's profile: all horizontal lines – sun-bleached wheaten hair pushed aside by the insistent breeze and squint lines carved at the corner of her eye as she stared at the flock she must have seen a hundred times. Since the accident the strong planes of her face had softened, and the skin of her neck was loose. Ian wondered if he would notice it as much had he not been a coward, if he had stayed as she had stayed.

He looked back at the flying beasts, peering beneath his palm, and yes, there in the middle, rooting with the rest, an avion. Its bat wings arched over its fellows and it bore a double propeller, but it didn't seem interested in contending with the éole male for dominance.

"The others don't mind?" he asked.

"No. He's been flying with them for years."

"Perhaps he's lonely." Avions, never the most numerous of the flying beasts, were almost extinct in the wild.

"Perhaps."

From that fall they thought she would die, and even the unsentimental Corps Aéronautique considered it cruel to take her away from her grandfather's land and the flying beasts she loved. But she survived and healed, even if she healed crooked. She lived at the École Aéronautique as a patient and then a ground instructor, teaching boys like Eugene Plantard to fly and die and find glory on the shores of Europe and the sands of the Empty Quarter.

For a time it seemed the École was all but abandoned. There was Claire, and the skeleton staff, and a couple of private students. But war was looming and soon it would teem with trainee flyboys, and Corps staff, and flying beasts. Not caught and broke from the wild flocks but bred for war, as the Italians and Germans were breeding the taube beasts with their dove-like, agile wings to carry more and move faster.

The local Pas-de-Caliasiens should be happy with the business the work of the Corps would bring. The mines were failing and fewer rich tourists came. The burgeoning war would be profitable, and no one had to think yet of the death from the sky that a race of flying beasts bred for war would bring.

Four years since he had fled her to Memphis, to Gazuul and further south, where the flying beats bred huge and wild and he caught and broke them for rich men, for the Corps Aéronautique, and for His Majesty's Airborne Calvary. Craven, he had never come back until now.

He told himself it was because he didn't want to see the woman he loved for her strength and her dexterity live crippled, but it was a lie. It was because most who fell as Claire had fallen died, and death was a gentle sleep. But Claire was living testimony to what could be done to the fragile construct of sinew, skin and bone that made a human.

In his memory, Claire ran along the side of the wooden training pen, poised to grasp the underwing struts of an éole, the tight cling of her habitual leathers showing the flex of limb and muscle. Now she halted along, and what was hidden beneath her checked skirt was mortal and twisted. He found grotesque possibilities of Claire's veiled flesh obscene, and hated himself for it.

Now Claire stumbled and recovered before he could embarrass them both by catching at her. Ian felt a flare of anger, which shamed him because it's shameful to be annoyed at the cripple exhibiting, like a statue holding stone fruit to the sun, this is how frail your body is, all children of men. You are brave and beset with the need to soar, and it means nothing to the wind that topples you and the air that parts beneath you and the ground that will take you as no lover has.

"I know why you're here," Claire said, still staring at the avion. "We've heard rumors about a breeding program for months. Flyboys passing through, repeating gossip. I didn't think it was true, though. I didn't think you'd agree to it. Not until I saw you this morning, with your fancy Corps automobile."

He listened for the mocking tone to her voice that meant she was angry with him, but she only sounded resigned.

"It's not a matter of my agreeing to it, Claire," he said, shoving his hands into the pockets of his too-warm greatcoat to stop himself from taking her arm. "It will happen whether we will it or not. And neither your people nor mine have much choice. You haven't seen the Roosevelt Wrights yet . . ."

"Obviously." Her voice went tart and the band across his chest loosened a little.

". . . but you will, soon. Theodore Roosevelt's breeding program's been in effect for what – ten, twelve years? They've been tapping their wild herds for the best and they have three lines now, and they're stocking their Air Corps eighty, maybe ninety per cent with them. Huge beasts, with endurance ours can't match, and docile too."

"Docile."

She began to laugh and was turning to him when she gasped. He seized her arm, thinking her leg had finally given way. Effortlessly, she shook him off and hobbled ahead. Ian stood frozen: over the water came a vast stretch of curved wing and an assembly of cables, flying strong and sure: a blériot, fresh from across the Channel. It crested the lip of the cliff-side, circled, and landed with insolent ease, not thirty meters away.

The éoles started and beat themselves into the air like a scurry of huge gulls, their engines chugging and throwing off steam. The avion took off, flying slow and low to the ground, in search of more berries.

Shaking off Ian's arm, Claire stumbled towards the blériot. The flying beast's motor purred and impossibly, it remained still until she reached it. Claire, chuckling with delight, stroked the side of a parchment panel. Watching her bend her once-bright head to the beast, Ian felt his pulse quicken painfully.

It couldn't be the same one. It couldn't.

Later that night, after he had a pipe by the fire and read through the Corps dispatches one more time, he went to her bed. She was in the same room, and even the pattern of nicks in the paint on the door were familiar to his touch. Under her old quilt she lay to one side, so there was room for him to slip between the cool sheets.

She made no move, either to welcome or repel him. Rough muslin covered the window imperfectly, letting moonlight drape across the coverlet; she blinked at him curiously.

"How often does it come to you? The blériot?"

Claire turned on her back; in the dim light he could see her chest rise and fall.

"Not for months sometimes. Sometimes only once a year, in the spring."

"It knows you. I know it's not possible, but it knows you."

She sighed.

"Do you know the name Wakeman?"

Her breathing hitched. "I have heard it. He is a great man, I hear. A hunter of repute."

"He should be here tomorrow or the next day. The Corps is borrowing him from the British. He's to clear the wild stock from the forage, if they can't be driven away."

She didn't answer for a long time, and he thought she might have fallen asleep.

"I knew the world wouldn't ignore us forever," she said at last. "There was a time, when we were young, that I resented it. Being dismissed. Now . . . you get used to it, and find your peace with it. And all this time we've been sleeping on the edge of a precipice, only a matter of time before we go down.

"And the flying beasts – there's no more room for the wild ones in this world. Soon there won't be an éole or an antoinette alive that isn't tame, bred or broke to our need. Soon we'll forget that they ever ran free. We'll think we've always bred them. Men will believe they built them."

When he spoke he was surprised at the anger in his voice. "You fell. How could you fall? You were the best. You were perfect."

Her voice was deliberately cool. "Such things happen."

"Not to you. Not unless you allow it. And you did allow it. I didn't realize it at first, though something in me recognized it."

"What do you mean?"

Ian drew a deep breath. "If you'd stayed in the struts, the blériot would've crashed, but it would've broken your fall. You let go. You let go so it wouldn't go down."

"You can't think that."

"I know that. I know you, Claire. And maybe better after I left."

She laughed softly. "Did it make you so angry, then?"

"Yes. That you could chose between us. That you could break your body so."

"Hundreds break in this work. Hundreds more, man and flying beast, will break before this is over."

"Yes. But not you. It should never have been you."

Her hand found his and they lay there, without speaking, for a long time until her fingers loosened in his and she slept. The moon had set before Ian, listening to her even breathing and the distant tide, turned to the cool of his pillow and slept too.

One by one the éoles rose and lighted again a few hundred meters away, barely interrupting their feeding. The children laughed, waving shirts and sheets they'd likely stolen off their mothers' clotheslines. A dog loped from child to child, a big golden retriever, pausing now and then to bark at the flying beasts. The éoles paid it less mind than they had the children, waving their clothing like the pennants of an improbable army.

"That's never going to clear them," said Wakeman.

The hunter had arrived that morning, accompanied by a small case of personal effects and two long, lovingly polished trunks of dark wood containing his weapons. Ian was discomposed as it was; he had slept far later than he was accustomed, to find sunlight dappling through the curtains and Claire's side of the bed empty and cold. Entering the cafeteria he found a scant few tardy students and young Plantard escorting the expressionless Englishman, and no sign of Claire anywhere. Ian barely nodded at his countryman, leaving him to find his own place while he went to the cluster of stone cottages that marked where the grounds of the École gave way to farmland.

He didn't know these children – the ones who had brought butter and eggs to the École years before were now probably hard-faced farmers. Maybe some labored in the failing mines. But if the cheerfully dirty, tow-headed kids didn't know him they knew the École Aeronautique, and they whooped at the prospect of earning a few sou chasing away the beasts from the grazing.

But Wakeman was right: the éoles and the avion had long lost their fear of men.

"No time like the present," said Wakeman, turning on his heel towards the dormitories. "I heard that blériot was spotted off the coast at dawn. That's where your chatelaine's got to. Queer woman, that. Looks right through one."

Ian didn't reply, fingering a pocketful of coins warm from his body as he watched the children forgo all pretense at chasing away the beasts and start playing at bullfighting between them.

"I hear you and mam'selle have a history," Wakeman threw over his shoulder. "Will that get in my way?"

Ian shook his head, not caring if the hunter saw.

Wakeman was right: the blériot was back, perched before the place where the cliff fell away. Claire stood apart, leaning on her cane as he hadn't seen her do before. The sea beyond was shrouded with the last of the morning fog, rapidly burning away. Wakeman, carrying a large shotgun, had almost reached her. The hunter kept her body between him and the blériot, as if using her as a blind.

Wakeman nodded at him. Claire didn't stir or look at Ian when he stood beside her.

"Claire," he said. "Go back. You don't want to see this."

Wakeman moved from behind her. "That's never a full-blood blériot," he muttered, chambering a round. "Too big. Quarter antoinette, at the least."

Even a twisted thing can move quickly, and Claire moved quicker than thought, bringing her cane down one-handed on the barrel of the gun. The shot tore into the ground three meters in front of them, tearing the new green grass away from the earth and plowing a furrow into the flesh of the earth. The blériot hopped, startled, towards the lip of the precipice. At the drop-off it paused, and rotated towards them.

"Go, you stupid thing!" shouted Claire, struggling to regain her balance.

Wakeman, jolted back by blow and unexpected angle of the discharge, swore colorfully and opened the chamber.

"Muzzle your bitch, Chance," he barked, eyeballing the distance to the flying beast that was, inexplicably, still within range. Claire stood, sobbing. Before Ian could hook an arm around her waist she struck again with the cane, two-handed this time, striking Wakeman hard in the solar plexus.

The hunter's breath left him with a great foosh and he sat on the ground, still holding his gun, legs stretched before him in the high grass. Claire drew back and held the burled cane high in the air, as if to bring it down on Wakeman's head. He looked up at her quizzically, struggling to draw breath, without the presence of mind to swivel the muzzle of the weapon towards her.

But he would, any second. Ian grasped Claire's arm.

"Claire," he said. "No."

She looked at him, eyes wild and streaming. Then with a stifled sob she pulled away and threw down the cane, across Wakeman's legs. The hunter flinched and struggled to his feet. Claire had turned from both of them, and halted across the grass to towards the blériot that still paused at the edge, its engine humming like a swarm of agitated bees in the warm air. Ian followed a few steps and stopped, knowing she didn't want him.

He could hear Wakeman breathing heavily behind him. Turning, he saw the hunter sighting down the barrel, aiming square at Claire's back.

Ian moved between them, looking not at Wakeman but at the twin holes of the barrel as if he could stare them down. "You will not," he growled.

"Not that I don't want to," said the hunter, never lowering the barrel, "but I'm waiting for a shot at the beast. She's right in front."

Ian strode into the barrel and grasped the cold metal, shoving the gun down, and watched as Claire stood before the blériot. Shyly, as if she had never touched it before, she reached out to pat the taut material of the wing that curved over her. The beast quivered but stayed put, and her hand moved over the tight silk, down a strut, following the thick rib to the body of the blériot. Never taking her hand away, she moved closer, dragging her damaged leg behind her. When her shoulder touched the main body of the blériot, she felt along the structure, fumbling where years ago she had grasped with confidence. Then, as the beast didn't move, she seemed to find her old strength and lifted herself into the beast's undercarriage.

Suddenly, Wakeman twisted the gun out of Ian's grip. Ian swore and tried to follow, but the hunter moved fast, pulling away from Ian's reach, and as Claire and the blériot tipped over the cliff the shotgun blasted tore a hole through the animal's left wing, punching a fist-sized hole through the silk, leaving raw edges to flutter in the wind.

The flying beast tipped dangerously to the right, so far out of true it seemed that it must stall and tumble to the sea below. Ian knew that in the undercarriage Claire must be fighting to shift her weight and help the blériot to balance. A terrible fear seized him then, that Claire would do as she had before, cast herself free of the beast that it might fly free of her.

She wouldn't be so lucky this time. If you could call it luck.

Ian heard the click of another shell in the gun and turned on Wakeman. The hunter's face looked impassive but his jaw was clenched tight and the veins stood out in the sunburned neck.

"Try it and I'll have you down for murder," said Ian. "And I'll let the flyboys at you first."

Wakeman squinted at the horizon. "Sometimes the wounded will come back to land. Out here it's got nowhere else to go."

By degrees the blériot leveled out, finding a way to balance the torn wing and the whole. It made no move to circle back to the coast, flying straight across the Channel. Ian stared after it until it became a pale dot, and then winked out, beyond his eyesight, beyond his ken, taking Claire with it.

Patrols flew until dusk, looking for any sign of the wreckage. One pair even went as far as Boulonge-sur-Mer, on the off chance that the blériot and its passenger had made it so far. Stations and lighthouses far down the coast, and across the water at Dover too, were alerted. There was no trace, no report.

The next day they started slaughtering the éoles. Ian stayed at the École Aéronautique, supervising the rebuilding of the pens where the wright flyers would stable. Occasionally, a shot would crack the freshening air like a whip.

At noon he went to see. As he approached the slopes where the flocks had clustered, he heard a thin, high, tearing sound, like a teakettle left to boil. Wakeman was standing by the avion that was crumpled in the grass. A few remaining éoles bleated behind it, chugging goats of steam in their distress, too confused to fly away. One of the avion's bat-wings was half torn away and thread of steam jetted from its damaged thorax. Calmly, Wakeman chambered a cartridge and aimed just behind the fuselage. The rifle cracked, and the agonized whistle stopped abruptly.

On the hills behind, Ian could see a small cluster of farm children, their dog with them, standing very still. It seemed impossible that they were the same brats who ran between the bat-winged éoles yesterday, waving their clean, tattered blouses.

He couldn't watch the rest. More shots rang out through the afternoon, and as the sun began to set he spotted one éole flying out to sea, framed against the bloody sun.

Ian stayed at the École Aéronautique long enough to see the breeding pair of Wrights fly in, their tiered wings shining white in the sun. That night, in Claire's room, he packed and repacked his few possessions, bound for Algiers. Adair would be furious; Ian didn't care. Plantard came to tell him the car would be ready at first light.

Ian asked if the Wrights had settled.

"Yes," said the boy. "Ate their fill and roosted. I've never seen an American beast. They're magnificent."

He eyed Ian as he took a pair of trousers from the pile in his suitcase and refolded them, pinching the already sharp seams sharper.

"I want you to know, sir, me and some of the other flyboys – well, we're not going to stop. Looking for her, I mean. Every day at sunrise, part of the morning exercises. We're taking turns at it. I mean, you never know what will show up, do you?"

"You won't find her," said Ian.

"Even so." The boy's voice was defiant.

"She won't let you find her. She might let you see it, sometimes. To make us remember they were wild beasts once, and never made, whatever lies we tell ourselves. But keep looking, by all means."

"You're not coming back, are you, sir?"

There was pity in the flyboy's voice, and compassion, and a little bit of contempt.

Ian's hands stilled and he stared at the rough plaster wall. "No, Plantard. I don't see it."

Plantard was silent as he drove Ian over the rough roads to Calais. They wouldn't remain in disrepair long – as the Wrights bred and the École Aéronautique grew, as war quickened between nations they would be rebuilt smooth and straight into the heart of the countryside, tamed like the flying beasts. In the meantime the car rose and fell, rose and fell with the broken pavement and he caught brief glimpses of the gray sea and sky. Once he saw what might be a blériot rising over the waves, but it was probably a gull, hunting for fish in the cold sea.

Good Hunting

Ken Liu

Night. Half moon. An occasional hoot from an owl.

The merchant and his wife and all the servants had been sent away. The large house was eerily quiet.

Father and I crouched behind the scholar's rock in the courtyard. Through the rock's many holes I could see the bedroom window of the merchant's son.

"Oh, Tsiao-jung, my sweet Tsiao-jung . . ."

The young man's feverish groans were pitiful. Half delirious, he was tied to his bed for his own good, but Father had left a window open so that his plaintive cries could be carried by the breeze far over the rice paddies.

"Do you think she really will come?" I whispered. Today was my thirteenth birthday, and this was my first hunt.

"She will," Father said. "A *hulijing* cannot resist the cries of the man she has bewitched."

"Like how the Butterfly Lovers cannot resist each other?" I thought back to the folk opera troupe that had come through our village last fall.

"Not quite," Father said. But he seemed to have trouble explaining why. "Just know that it's not the same."

I nodded, not sure I understood. But I remembered how the merchant and his wife had come to Father to ask for his help.

"*How shameful!*" the merchant had muttered. "*He's not even nineteen. How could he have read so many sages' books and still fall under the spell of such a creature?*"

"*There's no shame in being entranced by the beauty and wiles of a* hulijing," *Father had said. "Even the great scholar Wong Lai once* spent three nights in the company of one, and he took first place at the Imperial Examinations. Your son just needs a little help."

"You must save him," the merchant's wife had said, bowing like a chicken pecking at rice. "If this gets out, the matchmakers won't touch him at all."

A *hulijing* was a demon who stole hearts. I shuddered, worried if I would have the courage to face one.

Father put a warm hand on my shoulder, and I felt calmer. In his hand was Swallow Tail, a sword that had first been forged by our ancestor, General Lau Yip, thirteen generations ago. The sword was charged with hundreds of Daoist blessings and had drunk the blood of countless demons.

A passing cloud obscured the moon for a moment, throwing everything into darkness.

When the moon emerged again, I almost cried out.

There, in the courtyard, was the most beautiful lady I had ever seen.

She had on a flowing white silk dress with billowing sleeves and a wide, silvery belt. Her face was pale as snow, and her hair dark as coal, draping past her waist. I thought she looked like the paintings of great beauties from the Tang Dynasty the opera troupe had hung around their stage.

She turned slowly to survey everything around her, her eyes glistening in the moonlight like two shimmering pools.

I was surprised to see how sad she looked. Suddenly, I felt sorry for her and wanted more than anything else to make her smile.

The light touch of my father's hand against the back of my neck jolted me out of my mesmerized state. He had warned me about the power of the *hulijing*. My face hot and my heart hammering, I averted my eyes from the demon's face and focused on her stance.

The merchant's servants had been patrolling the courtyard every night this week with dogs to keep her away from her victim. But now the courtyard was empty. She stood still, hesitating, suspecting a trap.

"Tsiao-jung! Have you come for me?" The son's feverish voice grew louder.

The lady turned and walked – no, glided, so smooth were her movements – towards the bedroom door.

Father jumped out from behind the rock and rushed at her with Swallow Tail.

She dodged out of the way as though she had eyes on the back of her head. Unable to stop, my father thrust the sword into the thick wooden door with a dull thunk. He pulled but could not free the weapon immediately.

The lady glanced at him, turned and headed for the courtyard gate.

"Don't just stand there, Liang!" Father called. "She's getting away!"

I ran at her, dragging my clay pot filled with dog piss. It was my job to splash her with it so that she could not transform into her fox form and escape.

She turned to me and smiled. "You're a very brave boy." A scent, like jasmine blooming in spring rain, surrounded me. Her voice was like sweet, cold lotus paste, and I wanted to hear her talk forever. The clay pot dangled from my hand, forgotten.

"Now!" Father shouted. He had pulled the sword free.

I bit my lip in frustration. *How could I become a demon hunter if I was so easily enticed?* I lifted off the cover and emptied the clay pot at her retreating figure, but the insane thought that I shouldn't dirty her white dress caused my hands to shake, and my aim was wide. Only a small amount of dog piss got onto her.

But it was enough. She howled, and the sound, like a dog's but so much wilder, caused the hairs on the back of my neck to stand up. She turned and snarled, showing two rows of sharp, white teeth, and I stumbled back.

I had doused her while she was in the midst of her transformation. Her face was thus frozen halfway between a woman's and a fox's, with a hairless snout and raised, triangular ears that twitched angrily. Her hands had turned into paws, tipped with sharp claws that she swiped at me.

She could no longer speak, but her eyes conveyed her venomous thoughts without trouble.

Father rushed by me, his sword raised for a killing blow. The *hulijing* turned around and slammed into the courtyard gate, smashing it open, and disappeared through the broken door.

Father chased after her without even a glance back at me. Ashamed, I followed.

*   *   *

The *hulijing* was swift of foot, and her silvery tail seemed to leave a glittering trail across the fields. But her incompletely transformed body maintained a human's posture, incapable of running as fast as she could have on four legs.

Father and I saw her dodging into the abandoned temple about a *li* outside the village.

"Go around the temple," Father said, trying to catch his breath. "I will go through the front door. If she tries to flee through the back door, you know what to do."

The back of the temple was overgrown with weeds and the wall half collapsed. As I came around, I saw a white flash darting through the rubble.

Determined to redeem myself in my father's eyes, I swallowed my fear and ran after it without hesitation. After a few quick turns, I had the thing cornered in one of the monks' cells.

I was about to pour the remaining dog piss on it when I realized that the animal was much smaller than the *hulijing* we had been chasing. It was a small white fox, about the size of a puppy.

I set the clay pot on the ground and lunged.

The fox squirmed under me. It was surprisingly strong for such a small animal. I struggled to hold it down. As we fought, the fur between my fingers seemed to become as slippery as skin, and the body elongated, expanded, grew. I had to use my whole body to wrestle it to the ground.

Suddenly, I realized that my hands and arms were wrapped around the nude body of a young girl about my age.

I cried out and jumped back. The girl stood up slowly, picked up a silk robe from behind a pile of straw, put it on, and gazed at me haughtily.

A growl came from the main hall some distance away, followed by the sound of a heavy sword crashing into a table. Then another growl, and the sound of my father's curses.

The girl and I stared at each other. She was even prettier than the opera singer that I couldn't stop thinking about last year.

"Why are you after us?" she asked. "We did nothing to you."

"Your mother bewitched the merchant's son," I said. "We have to save him."

"*Bewitched? He*'s the one who wouldn't leave *her* alone."

I was taken aback. "What are you talking about?"

"One night about a month ago, the merchant's son stumbled upon my mother, caught in a chicken farmer's trap. She had to transform into her human form to escape, and as soon as he saw her, he became infatuated.

"She liked her freedom and didn't want anything to do with him. But once a man has set his heart on a *hulijing*, she cannot help hearing him no matter how far apart they are. All that moaning and crying he did drove her to distraction, and she had to go see him every night just to keep him quiet."

This was not what I learned from Father.

"She lures innocent scholars and draws on their life essence to feed her evil magic! Look how sick the merchant's son is!"

"He's sick because that useless doctor gave him poison that was supposed to make him forget about my mother. My mother is the one who's kept him alive with her nightly visits. And stop using the word 'lure'. A man can fall in love with a *hulijing* just like he can with any human woman."

I didn't know what to say, so I said the first thing that came to mind. "I just know it's not the same."

She smirked. "Not the same? I saw how you looked at me before I put on my robe."

I blushed. "Brazen demon!" I picked up the clay pot. She remained where she was, a mocking smile on her face. Eventually, I put the pot back down.

The fight in the main hall grew noisier, and suddenly, there was a loud crash, followed by a triumphant shout from Father and a long, piercing scream from the woman.

There was no smirk on the girl's face now, only rage turning slowly to shock. Her eyes had lost their lively luster; they looked dead.

Another grunt from Father. The scream ended abruptly.

"Liang! Liang! It's over. Where are you?"

Tears rolled down the girl's face.

"Search the temple," my father's voice continued. "She may have pups here. We have to kill them too."

The girl tensed.

"Liang, have you found anything?" The voice was coming closer.

"Nothing," I said, locking eyes with her. "I didn't find anything."

She turned around and silently ran out of the cell. A moment later, I saw a small white fox jump over the broken back wall and disappear into the night.

It was *Qingming*, the Festival of the Dead. Father and I went to sweep Mother's grave and to bring her food and drink to comfort her in the afterlife.

"I'd like to stay here for a while," I said. Father nodded and left for home.

I whispered an apology to my mother, packed up the chicken we had brought for her, and walked the three *li* to the other side of the hill, to the abandoned temple.

I found Yan kneeling in the main hall, near the place where my father had killed her mother five years ago. She now wore her hair up in a bun, in the style of a young woman who had had her *jijili*, the ceremony that meant she was no longer a girl. We'd been meeting every *Qingming*, every Chongyang, every Yulan, every New Year, occasions when families were supposed to be together.

"I brought you this," I said, and handed her the steamed chicken.

"Thank you." And she carefully tore off a leg and bit into it daintily. Yan had explained to me that the *hulijing* chose to live near human villages because they liked to have human things in their lives: conversation, beautiful clothes, poetry and stories, and, occasionally, the love of a worthy, kind man.

But the *hulijing* remained hunters who felt most free in their fox form. After what happened to her mother, Yan stayed away from chicken coops, but she still missed their taste.

"How's hunting?" I asked.

"Not so great," she said. "There are few hundred-year salamanders and six-toed rabbits. I can't ever seem to get enough to eat." She bit off another piece of chicken, chewed, and swallowed. "I'm having trouble transforming too."

"It's hard for you to keep this shape?"

"No." She put the rest of the chicken on the ground and whispered a prayer to her mother.

"I mean it's getting harder for me to return to my true form," she continued, "to hunt. Some nights I can't do it at all. How's hunting for you?"

"Not so great either. There don't seem to be as many snake spirits or angry ghosts as a few years ago. Even hauntings by suicides with unfinished business are down. And we haven't had a proper jumping corpse in months. Father is worried about money."

We also hadn't had to deal with a *hulijing* in years. Maybe Yan had warned them all away. Truth be told, I was relieved. I didn't relish the prospect of having to tell my father that he was wrong about something. He was already very irritable, anxious that he was losing the respect of the villagers now that his knowledge and skill didn't seem to be needed as much.

"Ever think that maybe the jumping corpses are also misunderstood?" she asked. "Like me and my mother?"

She laughed as she saw my face. "Just kidding!"

It was strange, what Yan and I shared. She wasn't exactly a friend. More like someone who you couldn't help being drawn to because you shared the knowledge of how the world didn't work the way you had been told.

She looked at the chicken bits she had left for her mother. "I think magic is being drained out of this land."

I had suspected that something was wrong, but didn't want to voice my suspicion out loud, which would make it real.

"What do you think is causing it?"

Instead of answering, Yan perked up her ears and listened intently. Then she got up, grabbed my hand, and pulled until we were behind the Buddha in the main hall.

"Wha—"

She held up her finger against my lips. So close to her, I finally noticed her scent. It was like her mother's, floral and sweet, but also bright, like blankets dried in the sun. I felt my face grow warm.

A moment later, I heard a group of men making their way into the temple. Slowly, I inched my head out from behind the Buddha so I could see.

It was a hot day, and the men were seeking some shade from the noon sun. Two men set down a cane sedan chair, and the passenger who stepped off was a foreigner, with curly yellow hair and pale skin. Other men in the group carried tripods, levels, bronze tubes, and open trunks full of strange equipment.

"Most Honored Mister Thompson." A man dressed like a mandarin came up to the foreigner. The way he kept on bowing and smiling and bouncing his head up and down reminded me of a kicked dog begging for favors. "Please have a rest and drink some cold tea. It is hard for the men to be working on the day when they're supposed to visit the graves of their families, and they need to take a little time to pray lest they anger the gods and spirits. But I promise we'll work hard afterwards and finish the survey on time."

"The trouble with you Chinese is your endless superstition," the foreigner said. He had a strange accent, but I could understand him just fine. "Remember, the Hong Kong–Tientsin Railroad is a priority for Great Britain. If I don't get as far as Botou Village by sunset, I'll be docking all of your wages."

I had heard rumors that the Manchu Emperor had lost a war and been forced to give up all kinds of concessions, one of which involved paying to help the foreigners build a road of iron. But it had all seemed so fantastical that I didn't pay much attention.

The mandarin nodded enthusiastically. "Most Honored Mister Thompson is right in every way. But might I trouble your gracious ear with a suggestion?"

The weary Englishman waved impatiently.

"Some of the local villagers are worried about the proposed path of the railroad. You see, they think the tracks that have already been laid are blocking off veins of *qi* in the earth. It's bad *feng shui.*"

"What are you talking about?"

"It is kind of like how a man breathes," the mandarin said, huffing a few times to make sure the Englishman understood. "The land has channels along rivers, hills, ancient roads that carry the energy of *qi*. It's what gives the villages prosperity and maintains the rare animals and local spirits and household gods. Could you consider shifting the line of the tracks a little, to follow the *feng shui* masters' suggestions?"

Thompson rolled his eyes. "That is the most ridiculous thing I've yet heard. You want me to deviate from the most efficient path for our railroad because you think your idols would be angry?"

The mandarin looked pained. "Well, in the places where the

tracks have already been laid, many bad things are happening: people losing money, animals dying, household gods not responding to prayers. The Buddhist and Daoist monks all agree that it's the railroad."

Thompson strode over to the Buddha and looked at it appraisingly. I ducked back behind the statue and squeezed Yan's hand. We held our breaths, hoping that we wouldn't be discovered.

"Does this one still have any power?" Thompson asked.

"The temple hasn't been able to maintain a contingent of monks for many years," the mandarin said. "But this Buddha is still well respected. I hear villagers say that prayers to him are often answered."

Then I heard a loud crash and a collective gasp from the men in the main hall.

"I've just broken the hands off of this god of yours with my cane," Thompson said. "As you can see, I have not been struck by lightning or suffered any other calamity. Indeed, now we know that it is only an idol made of mud stuffed with straw and covered in cheap paint. This is why you people lost the war to Britain. You worship statues of mud when you should be thinking about building roads from iron and weapons from steel."

There was no more talk about changing the path of the railroad.

After the men were gone, Yan and I stepped out from behind the statue. We gazed at the broken hands of the Buddha for a while.

"The world's changing," Yan said. "Hong Kong, iron roads, foreigners with wires that carry speech and machines that belch smoke. More and more, storytellers in the teahouses speak of these wonders. I think that's why the old magic is leaving. A more powerful kind of magic has come."

She kept her voice unemotional and cool, like a placid pool of water in autumn, but her words rang true. I thought about my father's attempts to keep up a cheerful mien as fewer and fewer customers came to us. I wondered if the time I spent learning the chants and the sword dance moves were wasted.

"What will you do?" I asked, thinking about her, alone in the hills and unable to find the food that sustained her magic.

"There's only one thing I *can* do." Her voice broke for a second and became defiant, like a pebble tossed into the pool.

But then she looked at me, and her composure returned.

"The only thing *we* can do. Learn to survive."

The railroad soon became a familiar part of the landscape: the black locomotive huffing through the green rice paddies, puffing steam and pulling a long train behind it, like a dragon coming down from the distant, hazy, blue mountains. For a while, it was a wondrous sight, with children marveling at it, running alongside the tracks to keep up.

But the soot from the locomotive chimneys killed the rice in the fields closest to the tracks, and two children playing on the tracks, too frightened to move, were killed one afternoon. After that, the train ceased to fascinate.

People stopped coming to Father and me to ask for our services. They either went to the Christian missionary or the new teacher who said he'd studied in San Francisco. Young men in the village began to leave for Hong Kong or Canton, moved by rumors of bright lights and well-paying work. Fields lay fallow. The village itself seemed to consist only of the too old and the too young, and their mood one of resignation. Men from distant provinces came to enquire about buying land for cheap.

Father spent his days sitting in the front room, Swallow Tail over his knee, staring out the door from dawn to dusk, as though he himself had turned into a statue.

Every day, as I returned home from the fields, I would see the glint of hope in Father's eyes briefly flare up.

"Did anyone speak of needing our help?" he would ask.

"No," I would say, trying to keep my tone light. "But I'm sure there will be a jumping corpse soon. It's been too long."

I would not look at my father as I spoke because I did not want to look as hope faded from his eyes.

Then, one day, I found Father hanging from the heavy beam in his bedroom. As I let his body down, my heart numb, I thought that he was not unlike those he had hunted all his life: they were all sustained by an old magic that had left and would not return, and they did not know how to survive without it.

Swallow Tail felt dull and heavy in my hand. I had always thought I would be a demon hunter, but how could I when there were no more demons, no more spirits? All the Daoist blessings in the sword could not save my father's sinking heart. And if I stuck around, perhaps my heart would grow heavy and yearn to be still too.

I hadn't seen Yan since that day six years ago, when we hid from the railroad surveyors at the temple. But her words came back to me now.

Learn to survive.

I packed a bag and bought a train ticket to Hong Kong.

The Sikh guard checked my papers and waved me through the security gate.

I paused to let my gaze follow the tracks going up the steep side of the mountain. It seemed less like a railroad track than a ladder straight up to heaven. This was the funicular railway, the tramline to the top of Victoria Peak, where the masters of Hong Kong lived and the Chinese were forbidden to stay.

But the Chinese were good enough to shovel coal into the boilers and grease the gears.

Steam rose around me as I ducked into the engine room. After five years, I knew the rhythmic rumbling of the pistons and the staccato grinding of the gears as well as I knew my own breath and heartbeat. There was a kind of music to their orderly cacophony that moved me, like the clashing of cymbals and gongs at the start of a folk opera. I checked the pressure, applied sealant on the gaskets, tightened the flanges, replaced the worn-down gears in the backup cable assembly. I lost myself in the work, which was hard and satisfying.

By the end of my shift, it was dark. I stepped outside the engine room and saw a full moon in the sky as another tram filled with passengers was pulled up the side of the mountain, powered by my engine.

"Don't let the Chinese ghosts get you," a woman with bright blonde hair said in the tram, and her companions laughed.

It was the night of Yulan, I realized, the Ghost Festival. *I should get something for my father, maybe pick up some paper money at Mongkok.*

"How can you be done for the day when we still want you?" a man's voice came to me.

"Girls like you shouldn't tease," another man said, and laughed.

I looked in the direction of the voices and saw a Chinese woman standing in the shadows just outside the tram station. Her tight Western-style cheongsam and the garish make-up told me her profession. Two Englishmen blocked her path. One tried to put his arms around her, and she backed out of the way.

"Please. I'm very tired," she said in English. "Maybe next time."

"Now, don't be stupid," the first man said, his voice hardening. "This isn't a discussion. Come along now and do what you're supposed to."

I walked up to them. "Hey."

The men turned around and looked at me.

"What seems to be the problem?"

"None of your business."

"Well, I think it *is* my business," I said, "seeing as how you're talking to my sister."

I doubt either of them believed me. But five years of wrangling heavy machinery had given me a muscular frame, and they took a look at my face and hands, grimy with engine grease, and probably decided that it wasn't worth it to get into a public tussle with a lowly Chinese engineer.

The two men stepped away to get in line for the Peak Tram, muttering curses.

"Thank you," she said.

"It's been a long time," I said, looking at her. I swallowed the *You look good*. She didn't. She looked tired and thin and brittle. And the pungent perfume she wore assaulted my nose.

But I did not think of her harshly. Judging was the luxury of those who did not need to survive.

"It's the night of the Ghost Festival," she said. "I didn't want to work any more. I wanted to think about my mother."

"Why don't we go get some offerings together?" I asked.

We took the ferry over to Kowloon, and the breeze over the water revived her a bit. She wet a towel with the hot water from the teapot on the ferry and wiped off her make-up. I caught a faint trace of her natural scent, fresh and lovely as always.

"You look good," I said, and meant it.

On the streets of Kowloon, we bought pastries and fruits and cold dumplings and a steamed chicken and incense and paper money, and caught up on each other's lives.

"How's hunting?" I asked. We both laughed.

"I miss being a fox," she said. She nibbled on a chicken wing absent-mindedly. "One day, shortly after that last time we talked, I felt the last bit of magic leave me. I could no longer transform."

"I'm sorry," I said, unable to offer anything else.

"My mother taught me to like human things: food, clothes, folk opera, old stories. But she was never dependent on them. When she wanted, she could always turn into her true form and hunt. But now, in this form, what can I do? I don't have claws. I don't have sharp teeth. I can't even run very fast. All I have is my beauty, the same thing that your father and you killed my mother for. So now I live by the very thing that you once falsely accused my mother of doing: I *lure* men for money."

"My father is dead, too."

Hearing this seemed to drain some of the bitterness out of her. "What happened?"

"He felt the magic leave us, much as you. He couldn't bear it."

"I'm sorry." And I knew that she didn't know what else to say either.

"You told me once that the only thing we can do is to survive. I have to thank you for that. It probably saved my life."

"Then we're even," she said, smiling. "But let us not speak of ourselves any more. Tonight is reserved for the ghosts."

We went down to the harbor and placed our food next to the water, inviting all the ghosts we had loved to come and dine. Then we lit the incense and burned the paper money in a bucket.

She watched bits of burnt paper being carried into the sky by the heat from the flames. They disappeared among the stars. "Do you think the gates to the underworld still open for the ghosts tonight, now that there is no magic left?"

I hesitated. When I was young I had been trained to hear the scratching of a ghost's fingers against a paper window, to distinguish the voice of a spirit from the wind. But now I was used to enduring the thunderous pounding of pistons and the deafening hiss of high-pressured steam rushing through valves. I could no longer claim to be attuned to that vanished world of my childhood.

"I don't know," I said. "I suppose it's the same with ghosts as with people. Some will figure out how to survive in a world diminished by iron roads and steam whistles, some will not."

"But will any of them thrive?" she asked.

She could still surprise me.

"I mean," she continued, "are you happy? Are you happy to keep an engine running all day, yourself like another cog? What do you dream of?"

I couldn't remember any dreams. I had let myself become entranced by the movement of gears and levers, to let my mind grow to fit the gaps between the ceaseless clanging of metal on metal. It was a way to not have to think about my father, about a land that had lost so much.

"I dream of hunting in this jungle of metal and asphalt," she said. "I dream of my true form leaping from beam to ledge to terrace to roof, until I am at the top of this island, until I can growl in the faces of all the men who believe they can own me."

As I watched, her eyes, brightly lit for a moment, dimmed.

"In this new age of steam and electricity, in this great metropolis, except for those who live on the Peak, is anyone still in their true form?" she asked.

We sat together by the harbor and burned paper money all night, waiting for a sign that the ghosts were still with us.

Life in Hong Kong could be a strange experience: from day to day, things never seemed to change much. But if you compared things over a few years, it was almost like you lived in a different world.

By my thirtieth birthday, new designs for steam engines required less coal and delivered more power. They grew smaller and smaller. The streets filled with automatic rickshaws and horseless carriages, and most people who could afford them had machines that kept the air cool in houses and the food cold in boxes in the kitchen – all powered by steam.

I went into stores and endured the ire of the clerks as I studied the components of new display models. I devoured every book on the principle and operation of the steam engine I could find. I tried to apply those principles to improve the machines I was in charge of: trying out new firing cycles, testing new kinds of lubricants for the pistons, adjusting the gear ratios. I found a measure of satisfaction in the way I came to understand the magic of the machines.

One morning, as I repaired a broken governor – a delicate bit of work – two pairs of polished shoes stopped on the platform above me.

I looked up. Two men looked down at me.

"This is the one," said my shift supervisor.

The other man, dressed in a crisp suit, looked skeptical. "Are you the man who came up with the idea of using a larger flywheel for the old engine?"

I nodded. I took pride in the way I could squeeze more power out of my machines than dreamed of by their designers.

"You did not steal the idea from an Englishman?" His tone was severe.

I blinked. A moment of confusion was followed by a rush of anger. "No," I said, trying to keep my voice calm. I ducked back under the machine to continue my work.

"He is clever," my shift supervisor said, "for a Chinaman. He can be taught."

"I suppose we might as well try," said the other man. "It will certainly be cheaper than hiring a real engineer from England."

Mr Alexander Findlay Smith, owner of the Peak Tram and an avid engineer himself, had seen an opportunity. He foresaw that the path of technological progress would lead inevitably to the use of steam power to operate automata: mechanical arms and legs that would eventually replace the Chinese coolies and servants.

I was selected to serve Mr Findlay Smith in his new venture.

I learned to repair clockwork, to design intricate systems of gears and devise ingenious uses for levers. I studied how to plate metal with chrome and how to shape brass into smooth curves. I invented ways to connect the world of hardened and ruggedized clockwork to the world of miniaturized and regulated piston and clean steam. Once the automata were finished, we connected them to the latest analytic engines shipped from Britain and fed them with tape punched with dense holes in Babbage-Lovelace code.

It had taken a decade of hard work. But now mechanical arms served drinks in the bars along Central and machine hands fashioned shoes and clothes in factories in the New Territories. In the mansions up on the Peak, I heard – though I'd never seen –

that automatic sweepers and mops I designed roamed the halls discreetly, bumping into walls gently as they cleaned the floors like mechanical elves puffing out bits of white steam. The expats could finally live their lives in this tropical paradise free of reminders of the presence of the Chinese.

I was thirty-five when she showed up at my door again, like a memory from long ago.

I pulled her into my tiny flat, looked around to be sure no one was following her, and closed the door.

"How's hunting?" I asked. It was a bad attempt at a joke, and she laughed weakly.

Photographs of her had been in all the papers. It was the biggest scandal in the colony: not so much because the Governor's son was keeping a Chinese mistress – it was expected that he would – but because the mistress had managed to steal a large sum of money from him and then disappear. Everyone tittered while the police turned the city upside down, looking for her.

"I can hide you for tonight," I said. Then I waited, the unspoken second half of my sentence hanging between us.

She sat down in the only chair in the room, the dim light bulb casting dark shadows on her face. She looked gaunt and exhausted. "Ah, now you're judging me."

"I have a good job I want to keep," I said. "Mr Findlay Smith trusts me."

She bent down and began to pull up her dress.

"Don't," I said, and turned my face away. I could not bear to watch her try to ply her trade with me.

"Look," she said. There was no seduction in her voice. "Liang, look at me."

I turned and gasped.

Her legs, what I could see of them, were made of shiny chrome. I bent down to look closer: the cylindrical joints at the knees were lathed with precision, the pneumatic actuators along the thighs moved in complete silence, the feet were exquisitely molded and shaped, the surfaces smooth and flowing. These were the most beautiful mechanical legs I had ever seen.

"He had me drugged," she said. "When I woke up, my legs were gone and replaced by these. The pain was excruciating. He explained to me that he had a secret: he liked machines more than flesh, couldn't get hard with a regular woman."

I had heard of such men. In a city filled with chrome and brass and clanging and hissing, desires became confused.

I focused on the way light moved along the gleaming curves of her calves so that I didn't have to look into her face.

"I had a choice: let him keep on changing me to suit him, or he could remove the legs and throw me out on the street. Who would believe a legless Chinese whore? I wanted to survive. So I swallowed the pain and let him continue."

She stood up and removed the rest of her dress and her evening gloves. I took in her chrome torso, slatted around the waist to allow articulation and movement; her sinuous arms, constructed from curved plates sliding over each other like obscene armor; her hands, shaped from delicate metal mesh, with dark steel fingers tipped with jewels where the fingernails would be.

"He spared no expense. Every piece of me is built with the best craftsmanship and attached to my body by the best surgeons – there are many who want to experiment, despite the law, with how the body could be animated by electricity, nerves replaced by wires. They always spoke only to him, as if I was already only a machine.

"Then, one night, he hurt me and I struck back in desperation. He fell like he was made of straw. I realized, suddenly, how much strength I had in my metal arms. I had let him do all this to me, to replace me part by part, mourning my loss all the while without understanding what I had gained. A terrible thing had been done to me, but I could also be *terrible*.

"I choked him until he fainted, and then I took all the money I could find and left.

"So I come to you, Liang. Will you help me?"

I stepped up and embraced her. "We'll find some way to reverse this. There must be doctors—"

"No," she interrupted me. "That's not what I want."

It took us almost a whole year to complete the task. Yan's money helped, but some things money couldn't buy, especially skill and knowledge.

My flat became a workshop. We spent every evening and all of Sundays working: shaping metal, polishing gears, reattaching wires.

Her face was the hardest. It was still flesh.

I poured over books of anatomy and took casts of her face with plaster of Paris. I broke my cheekbones and cut my face so that I could stagger into surgeons' offices and learn from them how to repair these injuries. I bought expensive jeweled masks and took them apart, learning the delicate art of shaping metal to take on the shape of a face.

Finally, it was time.

Through the window, the moon threw a pale white parallelogram on the floor. Yan stood in the middle of it, moving her head about, trying out her new face.

Hundreds of miniature pneumatic actuators were hidden under the smooth chrome skin, each of which could be controlled independently, allowing her to adopt any expression. But her eyes were still the same, and they shone in the moonlight with excitement.

"Are you ready?" I asked.

She nodded.

I handed her a bowl, filled with the purest anthracite coal, ground into a fine powder. It smelled of burnt wood, of the heart of the earth. She poured it into her mouth and swallowed. I could hear the fire in the miniature boiler in her torso grow hotter as the pressure of the steam built up. I took a step back.

She lifted her head to the moon and howled: it was a howl made by steam passing through brass piping, and yet it reminded me of that wild howl long ago, when I first heard the call of a *hulijing*.

Then she crouched to the floor. Gears grinding, pistons pumping, curved metal plates sliding over each other – the noises grew louder as she began to transform.

She had drawn the first glimmers of her idea with ink on paper. Then she had refined it, through hundreds of iterations until she was satisfied. I could see traces of her mother in it, but also something harder, something new.

Working from her idea, I had designed the delicate folds in the chrome skin and the intricate joints in the metal skeleton. I had put together every hinge, assembled every gear, soldered every wire, welded every seam, oiled every actuator. I had taken her apart and put her back together.

Yet, it was a marvel to see everything working. In front of my eyes, she folded and unfolded like a silvery origami construction, until finally, a chrome fox, as beautiful and deadly as the oldest legends, stood before me.

She padded around the flat, testing out her sleek new form, trying out her stealthy new movements. Her limbs gleamed in the moonlight, and her tail, made of delicate silver wires as fine as lace, left a trail of light in the dim flat.

She turned and walked – no, glided – towards me, a glorious hunter, an ancient vision coming alive. I took a deep breath and smelled fire and smoke, engine oil and polished metal, the scent of power.

"Thank you," she said, and leaned in as I put my arms around her true form. The steam engine inside her had warmed her cold metal body, and it felt warm and alive.

"Can you feel it?" she asked.

I shivered. I knew what she meant. The old magic was back but changed: not fur and flesh, but metal and fire.

"I will find others like me," she said, "and bring them to you. Together, we will set them free."

Once, I was a demon hunter. Now, I am one of them.

I opened the door, Swallow Tail in my hand. It was only an old and heavy sword, rusty, but still perfectly capable of striking down anyone who might be lying in wait.

No one was.

Yan leapt out like a bolt of lightning. Stealthily, gracefully, she darted into the streets of Hong Kong, free, feral, a *hulijing* built for this new age.

. . . *once a man has set his heart on a* hulijing, *she cannot help hearing him no matter how far apart they are* . . .

"Good hunting," I whispered.

She howled in the distance, and I watched a puff of steam rise into the air as she disappeared.

I imagined her running along the tracks of the funicular railway, a tireless engine racing up, and up, towards the top of Victoria Peak, towards a future as full of magic as the past.

Acknowledgements

"Love Comes to Abyssal City" © 2011 by Tobias S. Buckell. Originally appeared in *Hot & Steamy: Tales of Steampunk Romance*. Reprinted by permission of the author.

"A Mouse Ran Up the Clock" © 2009 by A. C. Wise. Originally appeared in *Electric Velocipede*. Reprinted by permission of the author.

"Tanglefoot" © 2008 by Cherie Priest. Originally appeared in *Subterranean Magazine*. Reprinted by permission of the author.

"Benedice Te" © 2004 by Joseph E. Lake, Jr. Originally appeared in *Challenging Destiny*. Reprinted by permission of the author.

"Five Hundred and Ninety-Nine" © 2014 by Benjanun Sriduangkaew. Original to this volume.

"Smoke City" © 2011 by Christopher Barzak. Originally appeared in *Asimov's*. Reprinted by permission of the author.

"Harry and Marlowe and the Talisman of the Cult of Egil" © 2012 by Carrie Vaughn, LLC. Originally appeared in *Lightspeed*. Reprinted by permission of the author.

"Anna in the Moonlight" © 2014 by Jonathan Wood. Original to this volume.

"Edison's Frankenstein" © 2009 by Monkeybrain, Inc. Originally appeared in *Postscripts*. Reprinted by permission of the author.

"The Canary of Candletown" © 2011 by C. S. E. Cooney. Originally appeared in *SteamPowered II: More Lesbian Steampunk Stories*. Reprinted by permission of the author.

"Beside Calais" © 2012 by Samantha Henderson. Originally appeared in *Strange Horizons*. Reprinted by permission of the author.

"Good Hunting" © 2012 by Ken Liu. Originally appeared in *Strange Horizons*. Reprinted by permission of the author.

About the Contributors

Sean Wallace is the founder and editor of Prime Books, which won a World Fantasy Award in 2006. In the past he was co-editor of *Fantasy Magazine* as well as Hugo Award-winning and two-time World Fantasy nominee *Clarkesworld Magazine*; the editor of the following anthologies: *Best New Fantasy, Fantasy, Horror: The Best of the Year, Jabberwocky, Japanese Dreams* and *The Mammoth Book of Steampunk*; and co-editor of *Bandersnatch, Fantasy Annual, Phantom* and *Weird Tales: The 21st Century*. He lives in Rockville MD with his wife, Jennifer, and their twin daughters, Cordelia and Natalie.

Born in the Caribbean, **Tobias S. Buckell** is a *New York Times* bestselling author. His novels and over fifty short stories have been translated into seventeen languages and he has been nominated for the Hugo, Nebula, Prometheus and John W. Campbell Award for Best New Science Fiction Author. He currently lives in Ohio.

A. C. Wise's fiction has appeared in publications such as *Clarkesworld, Lightspeed, Shimmer* and *The Best Horror of the Year Volume 4*, among others. In addition to her writing, she co-edits *Unlikely Story*. For more information, visit the author at www.acwise.net.

Cherie Priest is the author of over a dozen novels, including the steampunk pulp adventures *The Inexplicables, Ganymede, Dreadnought, Clementine* and *Boneshaker*. *Boneshaker* was nominated for both the Hugo Award and the Nebula Award; it was a PNBA Award winner, and winner of the Locus Award for

Best Science Fiction Novel. Cherie also wrote *Bloodshot* and *Hellbent* from Bantam Spectra; *Fathom* and the Eden Moore series from Tor; and three novellas published by Subterranean Press. She lives in Chattanooga, TN, with her husband, a big shaggy dog and a fat black cat.

Jay Lake lives in Portland, Oregon, where he works on numerous writing and editing projects. His books for 2013 and 2014 include *Kalimpura* and *Last Plane to Heaven* from Tor and *Love in the Time of Metal and Flesh* from Prime. His short fiction appears regularly in literary and genre markets worldwide. Jay is a winner of the John W. Campbell Award for Best New Writer, and a multiple nominee for the Hugo, Nebula and World Fantasy Awards. He blogs regularly about his terminal colon cancer on his website at www.jlake.com.

Benjanun Sriduangkaew enjoys writing love letters to cities, real and speculative. Her work can be found in *Clarkesworld Magazine*, *Beneath Ceaseless Skies*, *The Dark*, and Jonathan Strahan's *The Best Science Fiction and Fantasy of the Year*.

Christopher Barzak is the author of the Crawford Fantasy Award-winning novel, *One for Sorrow*, which has been made into the Sundance feature film *Jamie Marks is Dead*. His second novel, *The Love We Share Without Knowing*, was a finalist for the Nebula and Tiptree Awards. He is also the author of two collections: *Birds and Birthdays*, a collection of surrealist fantasy stories, and *Before and Afterlives*, a collection of supernatural fantasies. He grew up in rural Ohio, has lived in a southern California beach town, the capital of Michigan, and has taught English outside of Tokyo, Japan, where he lived for two years. His next novel, *Wonders of the Invisible World*, will be published by Knopf in 2015. Currently he teaches fiction writing in the Northeast Ohio MFA programme at Youngstown State University.

Carrie Vaughn is the author of the *New York Times* bestselling series of novels about a werewolf named Kitty. She's also written a handful of stand-alone fantasy novels and upwards of seventy short stories. She's a graduate of the Odyssey Fantasy Writing

Workshop, and in 2011 she was nominated for a Hugo Award for best short story. She's had the usual round of day jobs, but has been writing full-time since 2007. An Air Force brat, she survived her nomadic childhood and managed to put down roots in Boulder, Colorado, where she lives with a fluffy attack dog and too many hobbies. Visit her at www.carrievaughn.com.

Jonathan Wood is an Englishman in New York. There's a story in there involving falling in love and flunking out of med school, but in the end it all worked out all right, and, quite frankly, the medical community is far better off without him, so we won't go into it here. His debut novel, *No Hero*, was described by *Publishers Weekly* as "a funny, dark, rip-roaring adventure with a lot of heart, highly recommended for urban fantasy and light science fiction readers alike". Barnesandnoble.com listed it has one of the twenty best paranormal fantasies of the past decade, and Charlaine Harris, author of the Sookie Stackhouse novels described it as, "so funny I laughed out loud". His short fiction has appeared in *Weird Tales*, *Chizine* and *Beneath Ceaseless Skies*, as well as anthologies such as *The Book of Cthulhu 2* and *The Best of Beneath Ceaseless Skies, Year One*. He can be found online at www.jonathanwoodauthor.com.

Chris Roberson is probably best known for his alternate history Celestial Empire series, which, in addition to a large number of short stories, consists of the novels *The Dragon's Nine Sons*, *Iron Jaw and Hummingbird*, *The Voyage of Night Shining White*, and *Three Unbroken*. His other novels include *Here, There & Everywhere*; *Paragaea: A Planetary Romance*; *Set the Seas on Fire*; *Book of Secrets*; *End of the Century*; and *Further: Beyond the Threshold*. Recently, he's been writing graphic novels, including *Elric: The Balance Lost*, featuring Michael Moorcock's characters, and two *New York Times* bestselling *Cinderella* mini-series spinning off Bill Willingham's *Fables*. Along with his spouse and partner Allison Baker, Roberson was a co-founder of the small press Monkeybrain Books, which in 2012 launched a digital comics imprint, Monkeybrain Comics. He lives with his family in Portland, Oregon.

C. S. E. Cooney lives and writes in a well-appointed Rhode Island garret, right across the street from a Victorian Strolling

Park. She is the author of *How to Flirt in Faerieland and OtherWild Rhymes* and *Jack o' the Hills*. With her fellow artists in the Banjo Apocalypse Crinoline Troubadours, she appears at conventions and other venues, dramatizing excerpts from her fiction, singing songs, and performing such story-poems as "The Sea King's Second Bride", for which she won the Rhysling Award in 2011. Her website can be found at www.csecooney.com.

E. Catherine Tobler is a Sturgeon Award finalist and the senior editor at *Shimmer Magazine*. Among others, her fiction has appeared in *Clarkesworld*, *Lady Churchill's Rosebud Wristlet* and *Beneath Ceaseless Skies*. Her first novel, *Gold & Glass*, is now available.

Alex Dally MacFarlane is a writer, editor and historian. When not researching narrative maps in the legendary traditions of Alexander III of Macedon, she writes stories, found in *Clarkesworld Magazine*, *Strange Horizons*, *Beneath Ceaseless Skies*, *Heiresses of Russ 2013: The Year's Best Lesbian Speculative Fiction*, *The Year's Best Science Fiction & Fantasy: 2014* and other anthologies. Poetry can be found in *Stone Telling*, *The Moment of Change* and *Here, We Cross*. She is the editor of *Aliens: Recent Encounters* (2013) and *The Mammoth Book of SF Stories by Women* (forthcoming in late 2014).

Gord Sellar is a Canadian, but he wrote this story near Seoul, which also used to get called Hanyang back in the nineteenth century, and he wrote this bio in Ho Chi Minh City, which used to be (and unofficially often still is) called Saigon. He doesn't know where he will be when this book sees print, but you can find out at www.gordsellar.com. (Notes for this story, and related stories set in the same world, are at: http://bit.ly/1fremPM.)

Tony Pi is a Canadian writer who works at the Cinema Studies Institute at the University of Toronto. He has previously been a finalist for his short fiction in the Prix Aurora Awards and the John W. Campbell Award for Best New Writer. His fiction appears in a multitude of places (*Clarkesworld Magazine*, *InterGalactic Medicine Show* and more), but further adventures featuring Professor Voss can be found in *Ages of Wonder (DAW)* and *Abyss & Apex*.

Aliette de Bodard lives and works in Paris, where she has a day job as system engineer. In her spare time, she writes speculative fiction. Her stories have appeared in *Clarkesworld Magazine*, *Asimov's* and the *Year's Best Science Fiction*, and have earned her a Nebula Award, a Locus Award and a British Science Fiction Association Award. Her latest release is the Vietnamese space opera *On a Red Station, Drifting*. She blogs and cooks at www.aliettedebodard.com.

Nisi Shawl's collection *Filter House* was a 2009 Tiptree winner; her stories have been published at *Strange Horizons*, in *Asimov's SF Magazine* and in anthologies including both volumes of *Dark Matter*. Shawl was WisCon 35's Guest of Honor. She co-edited *Strange Matings: Science Fiction, Feminism, African American Voices, and Octavia E. Butler*. She edits reviews for *The Cascadia Subduction Zone*. Shawl co-authored *Writing the Other: A Practical Approach*. Her Belgian Congo steampunk novel *Everfair* is due out in 2015 from Tor. She co-founded the Carl Brandon Society and serves on Clarion West's board of directors. Her website is www.nisishawl.com.

Since 2008, **Lisa L. Hannett** has had over fifty short stories appear in venues including *Clarkesworld*, *Fantasy*, *Weird Tales*, *ChiZine*, the *Year's Best Australian Fantasy and Horror* (2010, 2011 and 2012), and *Imaginarium: Best Canadian Speculative Writing* (2012 and 2013). She has won three Aurealis Awards, including Best Collection 2011 for her first book, *Bluegrass Symphony*, which was also nominated for a World Fantasy Award. You can find her online at www.lisahannett.com and on Twitter @ LisaLHannett.

Genevieve Valentine's first novel, *Mechanique: A Tale of the Circus Tresaulti*, won the 2012 Crawford Award. *The Girls at the Kingfisher Club*, a 1920s retelling of the "Twelve Dancing Princesses", is forthcoming from Atria in 2014. Her short fiction has appeared in *Clarkesworld*, *Strange Horizons*, *Journal of Mythic Arts*, *Lightspeed* and others, and the anthologies *Federations*, *After*, *Teeth* and more. Her non-fiction and reviews have appeared at *NPR.org*, *The A.V. Club*, *Strange Horizons*, *io9* and more, and she is a co-author of *Geek Wisdom* (Quirk Books). Her appetite for bad movies is insatiable, a tragedy she tracks at www. genevievevalentine.com.

Sofia Samatar is the author of the novel *A Stranger in Olondria* (Small Beer Press), winner of the 2014 Crawford Award. Her short fiction, poetry and essays have appeared in a number of places, including *Strange Horizons*, *Clarkesworld* and *Weird Fiction Review*. She is non-fiction and poetry editor for *Interfictions: A Journal of Interstitial Arts*, and teaches literature, writing, and Arabic at California State University Channel Islands. Visit her online at www.sofiasamatar.com.

The *New* York *Times* recently hailed **Caitlín R. Kiernan** as "one of our essential writers of dark fiction". Her novels include *The Red Tree* (nominated for the Shirley Jackson and World Fantasy awards) and *The Drowning Girl: A Memoir* (winner of the James Tiptree, Jr Award and the Bram Stoker Award, nominated for the Nebula, Locus, Shirley Jackson and Mythopoeic awards). To date, her short fiction has been collected in thirteen volumes, most recently *Confessions of a Five-Chambered Heart*, *Two Worlds* and *In Between: The Best of Caitlin R. Kiernan* (Volume One), and *The Ape's Wife and Other Stories*. Currently, she's writing the graphic novel series *Alabaster* for Dark Horse Comics and working on her next novel, *Red Delicious*.

Cat Rambo lives, writes and teaches by the shores of an eagle-haunted lake in the Pacific Northwest. Her 200+ fiction publications include stories in *Asimov's*, *Clarkesworld Magazine* and *Tor.com*. Her short story, "Five Ways to Fall in Love on Planet Porcelain", from her story collection *Near + Far* (Hydra House Books), was a 2012 Nebula nominee. Her editorship of *Fantasy Magazine* earned her a World Fantasy Award nomination in 2012. For more about her, as well as links to her fiction and information about her popular online writing classes, see www. kittywumpus.net.

After residences in Los Angeles, San Francisco, England and Spain, **K. W. Jeter** and his wife, Geri, currently make their home in Ecuador. He still grieves for the now-vanished Los Angeles in which he was born. His latest publications include the novel *The Kingdom of Shadows*, a collaboration with Gareth Jefferson Jones titled *Death's Apprentice*, and the first four books in a new thriller series – *Kim Oh 1: Real Dangerous Girl*, *Kim Oh 2: Real Dangerous Job*, *Kim Oh 3: Real Dangerous People*, *Kim Oh 4: Real Dangerous Place* and *Kim Oh 5: Real Dangerous Fun*. More information on his books and stories can be found online at www.kwjeter.com.

Margaret Ronald is the author of the Hunt series (Eos/Harper Voyager) as well as a number of short stories. Originally from rural Indiana, she now lives outside Boston.

Samantha Henderson lives in Covina, California, by way of England, South Africa, Illinois and Oregon. Her short fiction and poetry have been published in *Realms of Fantasy*, *Strange Horizons*, *Goblin Fruit* and *Weird Tales*, and reprinted in *The Year's Best Fantasy and Science Fiction*, *Steampunk II: Steampunk Reloaded*, *Steampunk Revolutions* and the *Mammoth Book of Steampunk*. She is the co-winner of the 2010 Rhysling Award for speculative poetry, and is the author of the Forgotten Realms novel *Dawnbringer*. For more information, check out her website at www.samanthahenderson.com.

Ken Liu (www.kenliu.name) is an author and translator of speculative fiction, as well as a lawyer and programmer. His fiction has appeared in *The Magazine of Fantasy & Science Fiction*, *Asimov's*, *Analog*, *Clarkesworld*, *Lightspeed* and *Strange Horizons*, among other places. He is a winner of the Nebula, Hugo and World Fantasy awards. He lives with his family near Boston, Massachusetts. Ken's debut novel, *A Tempest of Gold*, the first in a fantasy series, will be published by Simon & Schuster's new genre fiction imprint in 2015, along with a collection of short stories.